The Injun Project

D. Thomas Gochenour

Good River Print And Media

Copyright 2025 by D. Thomas Gochenour

ISBN: 978-1-966615-35-4 (Paperback)
ISBN: 978-1-966615-36-1 (Hardback)
ISBN: 978-1-966615-37-8 (Ebook)

Good River Print And Media

CONTENTS

Chapter I

Eastern Shore Maryland, high summer, 1914

Standing on a hardpack dirt road, engulfed in a cacophonous cloud of cicada voices, crickets and the clapping of corn stalks and leaves, there was a small white clapboard store with a single gasoline pump standing out front. Late one morning, after the delivery of the weekly issue of the Baltimore Sun—with its headlines screaming about war in Europe—a young black man stepped into this small store. He was dressed like any farmhand, in overalls and barefoot. But that was not what was most noticeable about this man who carefully closed the screen door behind him and began to shuffle across the wood plank floor toward the cashier's counter in the back of the main room. What made the swarthy, black-haired, middle aged woman tending the store look up and focus on him immediately was that this man totted a shotgun in his right arm and he had a nervous expression of malign intent on his face. He pulled the gun up parallel to the floor and aimed it at her as he slowly approached the counter. "Wuman, gimme the money yous have in your register. All of it. Quick." The woman did not say anything. She cautiously moved to behind the NCR cash register and lifted her hand up to the keys and rang up a no sale so the cash drawer opened with a clinking sound and a bright bell. With both hands she scooped together all the bills and coins in the drawer. "I'm afraid that this is all there is." she said in a bare whisper. "Seventeen dollars and thirty-six cents. Not much business this morning." She reached out with the money toward the young man. He was evidently quite nervous and sweating heavily. He grabbed at the money. And then there was a sudden scramble. The woman moved quickly to the right side of the register while at the same time the door to the back room opened and in rushed a teenaged girl, also with dark hair and swarthy skin, shouting, "Momma, I got it ...." before she noticed the black man. This startled the young man and he thought that the woman was going for a gun beneath the counter. His finger twitched and his gun exploded with a loud kaboom. The bird shot hit the woman square in the chest. She had not been going for any gun but only trying to hide behind the register. The slug of bird shot knocked her back against the wall and she slumped down onto the floor with her back against the rear wall. "Momma!" the girl shrieked, horrified. In the same instant the mulatto shouted out at her. "Doan move. Stand still. Hush up." He was swinging the shotgun wildly between the dying woman on the floor and the young girl, who now looked at him with eyes wide open in a look of mortal terror. The girl's mother was rolling her eyes, trying it seemed to look at her daughter, and she was making indistinct gurgling noises. One hand was exploring the bloody hole in her chest. The black man too was wild-eyed. With his left hand he stuffed the money in his overalls pocket. Then he turned his focus on the girl. "Doan you do say nothin, you girl. Be quiet." He approached a little closer, pointing the barrel of his gun straight at her chest. For several long moments nothing moved in the store, no one said anything. Then the man smiled and softly said. "You, girl. Take your clothes off. All ov fem." The girl did not react at once, so he shouted at her. "Take em off. Your trousers first." And the girl slowly began peeling off her brown trousers. She was barefoot. "Now yoa shirt too." The woman sitting in a growing pool of blood on the floor not two yards away from them was trying to look at her daughter, but it was too difficult for her. Her lips were quivering as if she wanted to say something, but she couldn't. "Now your unnerpants too, and that unnershirt also." he said as he pointed the gun barrel at the girl's camisole. And then still without saying a word, the girl was completely naked. She tried to shield her private parts with both hands. "Now down on the floor." the mulatto barked at her as he began to unbutton the shoulder buttons of his overalls.

And quickly as he let them fall to the floor, he put aside his gun and jumped on top of the girl. He began awkwardly fumbling with his shorts and with pushing her hands away from her pudendum.

No one heard when the second man entered the store. No one saw him coming. But he was suddenly there, with catlike stealth he raised his hand and crushed a full bottle of Coke down on the mulatto's head with a force that knocked the man off top of the girl and unconscious and lifeless onto the floor to one side. The bottle exploded with a frothy mess of caramel foam all around, splashing on the black man and the girl. The girl was crying and whimpering in short bursts and she crawled up to her mother. "Momma, momma." But now the woman's eyes were lifeless and clouded. Her hands had fallen limply to her side. The second man, the young white man was the store owner's twenty six year old son, leaned down and checked the mulatto, then he rushed into the back room and just moments later came back with a blanket and roll of cable. He threw the blanket over the naked girl who was crying, curled up against the body of her mother. Then quickly and expertly with cable he hogtied the mulatto who left two little puddles of blood and ejaculant on the wooden floor. He was still unconscious but not dead. The young man, Will Eames, stood upright and turned to the girl who was now uncontrollably sobbing. "You get yourself dressed, miss. And then get back home to the settlement. I'll lock up the store and go to Bristol to get the sheriff out here. Should take about an hour and a half. Remind me, what is your name, again?" "Mena. Willamena Driggers." the girl managed to blubber out. "What about my mother?" "I'm afraid there's nothing anybody can do for her now. Don't worry, Pa and I will take care of you and your family." After Mena had dressed and left, Will closed up the back, then taking some rope he tied the mulatto down to the counter so he could not move off or knock over anything in trying to free himself. Then he took the shotgun and closed and locked the front door and ran off to Bristol to inform the sheriff.

Four months later, the unnamed black man was hanged for murder, rape and robbery at the Eastern Shore prison about twenty eight miles away from the place of his crime. No one took any notice.

Across the peninsula in Bristol only a day or two earlier William Eames married Willamena Driggers in a church ceremony that scandalized the town and the local press. In the following five and half years of their marriage, before he died in the Spanish flu epidemic, Mena bore Will four children. Three survived to adulthood.

Will Eames

Bristol, Maryland Eastern Shore
Mid-Summer, 1997

Will Eames sat in his office waiting for the phone to ring, or for anything at all to happen. He had passed the morning fiddling around reviewing the printouts of the latest postings of properties put on the market. There weren't many. He had looked over the postings for the entire county because there had been recently so few within the town of Bristol. He even looked into Wicomico and Somerset Counties, where there were some recent offers, although he usually did not represent any sellers in those counties. The office was quiet, the low steady humming of the AC was the only noise. His assistant, Lucy, had the day off so the office would stay empty all day. At least he didn't expect anyone to call in. The phone remained quiet. He looked out his window over the Choptank River. There were a few boaters out, but none of the usual traffic. The sun and heat made sure of that. He momentarily thought about calling Karen. But she was at work, and anyway they hadn't gotten together or spoken for more than two weeks. He looked in his computer. Maybe there was an Orioles baseball game that afternoon. Or maybe he would drive over to the beach at Assateague. But he felt too lazy for that, besides he didn't feel like spending the afternoon by himself in the wind, sun and sand. Karen also had long since stopped going with him to the beach. She was bored of that, and also didn't like the sun.

He confirmed there was a double header starting in Camden Yards at two o'clock; that left him enough time to drive over to Baltimore and get a ticket, at least for the first game. He would get a seat in the shady side of the stands, and could have a couple beers and some hot dogs.

That would tie him over for several hours. He jumped up from his desk, turned off his computer, and turned on the answering machine of the office phone. He picked up his keys and sunglasses and grabbed a baseball cap—not an Orioles cap but an old Washington Senators cap he had inherited from his father—and left. The drive up Highway 50 was easy, although south bound traffic was very heavy. He was at the Yards just before one o'clock, but just as he got to the head of the line at the ticket window to buy his single ticket for the Orioles-Tigers game he realized that sitting in the stands for three hours would not help him get rid of this oppressive feeling of boredom. He went into a bar across from the stadium and sat in the cool dimness while he ordered a cold beer and a burger lunch. Just before the game started, he went over and claimed his seat in the stadium, and nearly fell asleep before the first live pitch was thrown. The game was also listless and boring. The Tigers won 2-1 in a game that bore witness to overpaid, overweight men, wearing ridiculous costumes pretending to play a boy's game through a season that lasted most of seven months and throughout which any single game made almost no difference. The only player who ever made any difference to the lackluster Orioles was the old man Cal Ripken Jr. and he wasn't playing that afternoon. By the fourth inning he had had a second beer—but it was lukewarm and tasted diluted. The beers combined with the late afternoon stuffiness sent him to sleep through most of the rest of the game. He awoke at the end of the seventh inning stretch. But still the game did not engage his attention. And before the last pitch was thrown, he, like many of the other fans, stood up to leave. His attending this game did not cure him of his ennui or the general pointlessness he was feeling. On the drive back, his mind continued to run back over the emptiness he was feeling. He was only distracted by the sluggish pace of the traffic. Friday afternoon congestion for those office workers from D.C. and Baltimore heading to Ocean City for the weekend made the one hour drive a two and half hour drive. On the road, instead of cursing the slow congestion, he used his cell phone to call his answering machine. There was one message from Karen, who sounded vexed and bored. "Why don't you give me a call when you have some time?" And one other message from a potential client inquiring about title insurance. That could wait till Monday. And there was one call where no message was left and the call cut off abruptly. That would be his father. His father, Bob, was technically backwards; he did not like to call cell phones, always preferring to call Will on his land line at either his office or his home, and he never left messages on Will's answering machines. So Will called him on his home phone.

"Hey Dad, Will here. You called at my office a couple of hours ago? Need to buy a house?"

"No. Always joking, aren't you? I did call. I wanted to ask if you would like to join me crabbing tomorrow?"

"Sounds like a plan. Is this heat going to continue?"

"Yeah, the forecasters say so. Maybe thunderstorms in the afternoon."

"So when is low tide tomorrow?"

"I checked and it is at 7:30. So we should push off around ten. How's that sound to you?"

"Count me in. Shall we meet at the boat dock around ten, then? I'll bring the ice in the chest. We can have steamed crabs at your place afterwards?"

"Well that's the usual routine, isn't it? I'll bring the stinky chicken bait. Will you invite Karen to join us for the eating?"

"I could. I hadn't thought about it. I'll call her and ask. Let you know. Do you need some beer?"

"Yeah, that would be good."

"Where were you thinking of hauling crabs?"

"I was thinking with the turning of the tide, just around Howell's Point would be a good place."

"Yeah, I think we'll be there for less than an hour. In that time we'll have enough crabs for four crab boils. And we'll be really scorched too."

"Bring your sun block. So agreed; see you tomorrow?"

Will stopped in at his office when he finally reached Bristol. There were some mail flyers, but no other mail and no further messages. He turned on his computer, just to check if there were any new listings since the morning, remaining standing. And right away he noticed an intriguing new listing. The county probate court appointed administrator announced the sale of a 31 acre plot of land on the Nanticoke River, not far from Exeter. Now this is interesting, he thought and he sat down and read the announcement in full. He thought all of the riverbank property on the Nanticoke was either closely held as farms or was locked up in bird sanctuary or wildlife reserves. He took out a plats book to see if he could find this plot. And sure enough, there it was, a small plot that ran along the river bank, nearly half the area in salt marsh or creeks unsuitable for any permanent buildings. But his plat map did not show any houses on the plot so he wondered whether the deceased owner had ever lived on the plot or if it was completely undeveloped. He decided at once that he would go to the courthouse on Monday and check out what more he could learn about this offering. Then he turned off his computer and shut down the office for the weekend and went home.

Only after he got home did he remember he needed to call Karen back. He called her home phone, but there was no answer. He left a message on the answering machine and then called her cell number. When she answered it, he could hear jukebox music being played in the background. She was probably at the Cedar Island Bar and Restaurant, where she often went on the weekend for dinner.

"Yeah, Will. I called you earlier this afternoon. Where were you?"

"I drove up to Baltimore to catch an Orioles game. Just got back and saw your message."

"Well? Are you free? Maybe you could join me for dinner and a few cool drinks. I'm at the Cedar Island."

"'Fraid I can't tonight. Busy with some new deals. But I wanted to invite you for a crab boil tomorrow afternoon. At my Dad's place. Would you like that?"

"Yeah. I would. But I'd rather come over to your place a bit later and give you a massage. It's been a while since I could snuggle with you."

"Yeah. Sure. Do that. I'll go out and get something to drink. Say, after ten?"

"Okay. See you then."

The next day at around noon with the sun blazing high in the sky, Bob, cut the motor and moved to the front of the boat to toss the anchor in the water. The tide turned the boat bow to the Chesapeake as the water was running up the river beyond Howell's Point. The waters were murky, the color of greenish clay. Bob and his son Will then began setting up the lines, the scoop nets, and the bait, which in the heat of the day stank like a foul outhouse. "Crabs will like this." Bob said as he picked up a piece of chicken and tied it onto his line. "Wuwee, it sure smells bad." And he tossed his line into the waters where it sank away. Almost at once there were tugs at the end of his line. "They are swarming." He started at once pulling the line in slowly. Only close to the surface could Will make out two large blue crabs engaged in trying to dice up the bait. He quickly put his net under the crabs and scooped them both dripping into the boat, where they finally let go of the bait and tried to scamper out and back into the water. Will's father gingerly snatched one up and threw it into the large barrel in the middle of the boat. Will got the other one with a little more effort. He got the first of the day's pinches on one finger. And then Bob threw his baited line back into the murky waters. The two crabs made a scuttering sound inside the plastic barrel, but they could not get out. Bob left the line this time longer in the water, about four minutes and then again lifted it slowly. Once more a crab was hacking at the bait, and again Will scooped it out with an experienced flick of the hand, and dumped the crab straight into the barrel. It was humid as well as intensely hoy injd Will was already soaked through with sweat. In this manner, in less than twenty minutes they had already caught seven good sized blue crabs. "Hungry critters today. Don't you think?" Bob asked. "Put some ice on them to keep them safe for eating." Will hadn't said anything at all since they had boarded at the dock more than an hour earlier. "So how was the ballgame, yesterday?" Bob asked trying to elicit some chatter. Will shrugged and quietly mumbled, "It was awful, to tell the truth. Would you like a drink?" Bob nodded yes, and Will pulled out of the ice bucket two cans of beer. He handed one to his father and cracked open the other.

"Thanks for that. Really refreshing in this heat. You know, you've been rather morose the last few weeks. Is something bothering you?"

"Nothing is what is bothering me. That's just it. I'm doing nothing these days. Business is slow, but that's not what's bothering me. I've made plenty of sales so far this year, and have earned enough. But I can't help but think that nothing is happening in my life just now and there's nothing I am looking forward to either. There's no structure to my life, and no direction. I live like I'm floating aimlessly in a boat with no oars."

"So, you're bored, eh? Is that it? Real estate business doesn't enamor you any more?"

"No, not really. It's not as if I am helping people buy a new house and begin new lives. In fact, the opposite. Most of my customers are people grandpa's age who are selling out their family farms because they are too old to continue and their children don't want to farm any more. That's all rather sad, seeing the end of a style of life. Soon there won't be any more farmers left in the county, or in the neighboring counties either. And the buyers I find, have no intention to keep the farms as going concerns either. Most are thinking of a commercial windfall." Will fell silent and put some of the chicken bait on his line and threw it into the water with a plop. He felt that a structured routine was what he most lacked. It was what was most attractive for young men in military service; having your daily waking hours ordered and filled with regular routines that you didn't need to question.

"But maybe boredom has a part in it. What I do is rather mindless work. Followed by long periods of waiting and emptiness, doing nothing. Like a shopkeeper on a long dusty unused road, waiting long hours for the next customer. I don't know how to say it. But there seems that I have nothing to live for."

His father, whistled softly. "Sounds for sure like a serious existential problem you got." He readied his net and slid it quickly under the emerging crab and bait line as they appeared near the surface. "That makes for nine crabs now. We need at least eighteen. We'll need to catch a lot more in the next hour. Maybe we should move the boat?"

Will finished off his beer and put the baited line back in the water. "It is important to have something to live for, of course." his father continued. "I suppose you'll begin telling me that the flavor has gone out of eating, and the colors of flowers seem less vivid."

"You're making fun of me."

"Yes, and no. I gathered that Karen is not the love of your life? That you won't be making a family with her anytime soon. Is she coming to our crab boil later?"

"I don't know, actually. Last night she was out drinking again and called me to ask if she could come over later. She was drunk when she called. But she didn't come. She's bored out of her wits too. Small town girl, unmarried. Gets all the sex she wants—which isn't all that much anymore from me anyway—and then drinks too much—which is more and more. I think after six years we are pretty much finished. She's actually pretty dull and doesn't think about her future at all, or about what she wants to do with her life either. In fact she's not very good about thinking about anything."

"Sounds like you do have a problem. No prospects even for finding love and making a family?"

"Oh quit ribbing me, dad. Bristol is not a lively bustling culturally active metropolis. Not many girls here at all—and then those that are, are probably a lot like Karen. I don't know. I don't spend much time anymore in any of our four bars. Any girl with half a brain and any ideas or ambition leaves town for good after high school—they follow the boys who do the same. The same reasons that farming is dying all around us." Will then pulled up his line and four crabs were tangled with each other around the bait which was hacked to bits. Bob skillfully snared them in his net and went to throw them into the barrel. One crab managed to jump out and fell back into the water and quickly disappeared. "The harvest of the land. Or in this case the seas. Seems good today. You need a new piece of bait. Here I will throw the next line and you man the net."

After they pulled in a few more crabs, Will was ready for another beer. He threw some more ice onto the crabs in the barrel—it kept them alive and quiet—and he took a can from the bucket at the same time.

"You do need to look at starting a family. Don't scoff. It's an important part of what we are all about in life."

"Can't very well start a family without a woman. And I don't see any women on the horizon, certainly not in Bristol, or in Dorset County either. Even though there are thousands of women –most of them unmarried and looking to party--passing through town every weekend on their way to Ocean City. But they are unreachable. It's like they are on an elite train and we are the peasants standing in the dust that they zoom by and hardly see us when they deign to look down on us."

"You might join them there. In Ocean City, I mean. Go looking for fish where the fish are. Just like crabbing. Well, if you aren't out hunting, then you are not likely to snag anything. Girls are not going to come hunting for you. Not in backwater Bristol as you put it. And you won't find any girlfriends on the internet. They will all be in Warshinton or Bawlmere. I think it would be hard to have a relationship with a woman who lives in those cities. Too far away. The only place where girls go out on the hunt for men is Napolis, but you don't want to be a navy man. Do you?"

They fell silent for another thirty minutes or so as they pulled in the last of their need for crabs.

"So you're not going to be trolling at Ocean City any time soon? The summer is almost over and the season will end then."

"No I don't think so."

"Well, I can't think that crabbing in the sun and drinking flat, lukewarm beer, has done much to cheer you up or to look at prospects differently. But as a parent, I still have to try. Doing this is something that creates something to look forward to. Steamed crab and corn, and maybe some fresh fried crab cakes. And some icy cold ice tea. That should cheer you up. And maybe Karen will come again dressed in her sexy halter top. She's got a nice figure, that's for sure."

"I grant you that. She does. I especially appreciate it in the shower, close up. But I think for not much longer. She's bored of me too. See if you don't notice later this afternoon. If she even comes over."

A short while later Bob pulled up the anchor and started the motor with the ripping of the cord. By two thirty they were back in Bristol at Bob's house. The barrel had twenty one pacified crabs in it. Will's mother, Susan although Bob always called her Mar-Sue, had already shucked the white corn and made a large batch of crab cakes from an earlier catch of crabs whose meat she had frozen. Karen had not arrived yet, and Will's younger sister, Kate, with her husband and two young children had arrived earlier, and she had already started the huge crab pot and steamer on a fire out in the back yard. Will had stopped off at his house on his way there, to take a shower and change into fresher clothes. He had a cold beer at home and straight away upon arriving at his parents' house he took a glass of chilled white wine from his mother. The alcohol made him feel light headed and happy at first. He had a second glass of wine before the eating began, and by the time Karen arrived, he was drunk. She was late, and came dressed in a thin halter top which enhanced her bust, along with a pair of very brief yellow hot shorts and summer strap sandals with heels. Will was annoyed by her preening appearance. She looked to him like a hooker on the make, too carnal and openly flaunting her sex. Will's sister, Kate, was thinking the same thing. Karen made flip apologies for being late, but addressed these to Will's family and not to Will. She did not apologize or mention anything about the previous evening. His annoyance grew as they all began eating the crabs, and her cutesy voice--she was giggling gaily, shouting out nothings to the others and voraciously eating crab cakes—grated on him. He felt especially put off by her trying to attract all the attention—a dribble of butter from the corn she was eating was seeping down from the corner of her mouth toward her chin he noticed-- and as she slammed the mallet down hard on the crabs' carapace he felt she was hitting him. But she took no notice of him. When his brother-in-law offered to refill his wine glass he took it and gulped down his third wine. It made him only quieter and more withdrawn. By the time the dinner was finished his mind was very muddled but feelings of anger were spinning around inside. Will continued to sink at the table. Finally he felt he could not restrain himself any more. He was looking at the erect tits of Karen's breasts, which were pushing up under her knit haltertop so slightly. Listening to her laugh like a small, barking dog, he finally snapped; he jumped up and shouted at her. "So, why don't you just tell everyone here? You had sex last night with the latest guy you met at the Cedar Island. And you were still fucking him this afternoon. 'S why you were so late." Karen's mouth dropped open and she looked at him in surprise. All the others were horrified. His father got up and started for him. "What are you raving about, Will?" Karen asked in a normal voice. "You whore! You know we're finished, but you still show up here, parading your sex here like a…" Will shouted as Bob grabbed him by the shoulders and shook him hard, as if trying to shake him awake. "Shut up, son. You're drunk." "I should say so." shouted Karen as she stood up. "Like a what? What were you going to say? Like a what?" she shouted and threw a half chewed corn cob at him. Bob was pushing Will toward the house. Will could barely keep his feet, his head was spinning but the explosion was over. "That does it. It's too much. We're finished, Will." "A cheap prostitute." Will slurred as his father pushed him into the house. By now everyone was standing. The other members of Will's family were looking sheepishly at each other and then at Karen. "That's too much." she shrieked and then she walked off furiously, stumbling a little over her too high high-heeled sandals, until she took them off and carried them in her hands. No one moved to stop her as she stormed around the house and got into her small red car and drove off. Meanwhile, Will's father steered him over to the large sofa in the main room and pushed him down. "You've messed up lots of things today, son. You're too drunk." He now pushed his shoulders down, and Will collapsed and then passed out.

Will spent the next day at his house under the dull throbbing of a heavy hangover, shuffling occasionally from one room to the next, never focusing. He did not know how he had gotten there. He was aware that he had exploded at Karen, he remembered her sexy outfit and lots of bare skin, he remembered pounding on the crabs with especial vehemence, but he could not remember anything that had been said. Or what happened after his father pushed him from the table. He continuously visualized the two of them sitting in the boat waiting for crabs to rise with the bait. And the sun. The sun was pounding down on his head. He felt too hot all day, as if the sun were still burning him. Late in the evening he opened his fridge and took out some frankfurters to eat, washed down with a coke. And after that he passed out again.

On Monday, when he awoke he was feeling very dehydrated and his mouth was caked dry. He noticed in the mirror that he was badly sunburned on the top of his head and on his neck and ears. Someone had left three large crab cakes in his fridge. And he ate one, cold, with some bottled iced tea. He had two more iced teas before he felt restored enough to think what to do next. He took a shower, dressed for work, and was on his way to his office, which was only a five minute drive away, when he realized that he had wanted to look into the plot that had been put up for sale by the probate administrator. It was still early so he turned his car and drove over to the county courthouse instead of to his office.

At the probate court he found the announcement about the sale of the parcel of land. He read it carefully. The plot comprised three hundred and thirty two acres of land on the Nanticoke River just a few miles north of the little town of Exeter. There did not appear to be a hardened road extending into the plot. The announcement described the plot as almost two thirds intertidal salt marsh. That would mean mudflats and large stretches of cordgrass, sedges, and salt rushes. Unusable land that was submerged for half of every day by the tidal flood. But the description excited Will for some reason. There hadn't been any riverside parcels offered for sale in a number of years, and those few that had been offered had already been drained of the salt marsh. And in those cases the land was very expensive. The stated price for this parcel, by contrast, was very low. Almost as if it were impaired land. The announcement said the previous owner had died intestate, and he had no immediate heirs, which was why the probate administrator was disposing of it. He could afford the $26,000 recommended price. Will then went to the land registry office to check the exact borders on the official land plats, and to look at the title history. That was his usual business, checking title histories. The people in the registry office knew him well and helped him get the records he was looking for. The plot had a very long and stable ownership history. Its last owner was a man named Randall. And it seemed that the Randall family had ownership of this same plot going back to the 1820s. Only in the 1920s had the Randall family sold a strip of six acres to the neighboring landowner. And other than that sale, the land had been held and passed down from one generation of the Randall family to the next. This was rare in Will's experience, at least in Dorset County, Maryland. The clerk at the registry suggested that the title could be older, but that no records existed for that tract for earlier dates for some reason. And only shortly before that Dorset County had been cut out of a larger county which occupied most of Maryland's eastern shore.

By the time he got to his office, Will realized that he was thinking only about this Nanticoke River plot of land. It really excited him. Maybe he would buy it. The idea kept rolling over in his mind as noon moved on to afternoon. He could develop the dry land segment and sell it on. Or he could build a camp with a long pier to have his own private crabbing and fishing club. He could afford the price. He had more than that in savings and they were doing nothing but turning over every month. By the time it was closing up time, he had resolved that he would put in an offer to buy for himself this parcel. Now he was really excited. The probate was already closed so he would have to make his offer on Tuesday morning. All evening and into the night, all he could think of was buying this plot of mudflats and mosquitos, across the county on the Nanticoke.

The next morning, as soon as the probate court was open, Will was standing outside the probate clerk's office ready to make an offer. He had his check book to hand. When the clerk was ready, Will explained to him what he wanted and that he was ready to put down the full amount of $26,000 to buy the Randall parcel. The clerk acted outwardly surprised. "I didn't think we'd be able to sell it, at all." he muttered as he took out the documents he needed. "I think, you'll win this contract. Because I don't see any distant relatives coming forward to make claims on this land. You'll have to wait, you understand, three months before we can complete the sale." Will did understand, he had handled probate sales before as a broker. "Tell me," asked Will. "where did this Randall fellow live? I can't see any evidence of a house on this plot." "It's a bit of a mystery, actually. Because he didn't seem to own any house, not on that plot, not in Exeter, or any other place. He didn't have any close family, either, no will. All we could find after we were notified of his death was this property and a small sum in a savings account in Exeter. He didn't own anything else, not a car, house, or any other property, no fixed permanent address. A strange case, as I said."

Will left the probate's office in a high mood. He hadn't felt so elated in a long time. He had accomplished something, for himself; not even his most recent brokered sale had made him feel so good about himself. And he had made $16,000 on that sale. He went to his office, his head spinning with ideas and plans for using this plot of land. Nothing was happening at his office. The caller on Friday had not reappeared. But if he was going to buy a property his broker would come to Will to buy the title insurance. So he didn't need to do anything. Lucy had not come in yet, and his assistant, Marilyn who he had working the title insurance business in the next room told him everything was quiet. Premium payments were rolling in on schedule, as expected. "Just rolling in money," she joked. "But no new business so far this week." He checked his computer for any new listings in the county or in Queen Anne's County or Wicomico County. The only mail was a bill for his agency's advertising for the coming six months. He had been thinking about using the internet to advertise his brokerage services, but he didn't know how to do that so he continued with his conventional advertisements in the newspapers, on billboards, at the restaurants and bars of Bristol and Exeter. But this little bit of business could not distract him much. He left the office to get lunch at the Blue Crab restaurant but he had already decided to drive cross county to see the plot of land first hand.

It wasn't far. He brought with him a detailed topographic map of the county that he had. He had already outlined the coordinates of the land parcel onto this map. He took Highway 50 to Exeter and in twenty minutes he turned north on the old Eastern Shore road which had been the old route connecting East Albany and Exeter before the first draw bridge had been built across the Choptank River at Bristol. That bridge and the newly built Highway 50 after the war diverted all the Eastern Shore traffic through Bristol and made the hardened Eastern Shore highway a lonely back route, scarcely used. His grandfather had told him about this history when Will was still young. One time when they were driving around the county, old man Will Junior, who people still called just Junior in spite of his advanced years, had told him the story of this highway and its relationship to his family. There had once been a family owned store and filling station on this road, but it was long gone. And the first family farm had been situated only a few miles up the road, away from Exeter. Will, the grandson of Junior, had always found those long rambling family histories to be rather boring while they were driving around the seemingly endless fields of corn and soybeans. But after Granpa Junior had died, Will had come to regret that he hadn't paid more attention to those tales, as he now found himself driving into that old family territory.

About three miles north of Exeter, Will slowed down looking for County Farm road 566. He saw it marked by a single small badge on a pole. There were a number of bullet strike indentations which pocked the sign. It was supposed to be a hardened road but it seemed more like a dirt road without the deep ruts. As he turned into it, hardly noticeable was a street sign which said Chicopee Road. It was the right way. He drove down Chicopee Road, cross the Broad Creek directly toward the Nanticoke, but then the road veered sharply to the north and ran parallel to the river. After almost two miles he came to Farm Road 569, Red Marsh Landing Road where he turned again. He had passed only a few isolated farm houses along this route. And on Red Marsh Landing there were fewer, in much poorer condition. The fields looked poorly tended as well. He was looking for any track or path that would turn off toward his newly acquired tract. He knew he was getting close as a large wooded area rose up between him and the river. After a while he passed a small badge sign which said that the land was part of the Maryland state wildlife reserve. No hunting allowed. He thought that strange that the sales announcement didn't identify the land as being in a wildlife reserve. That would certainly be an important easement and curtailment on any use that he might put on the land. The land on the left side of the road was fenced in by a barbed wire fence that was also in a state of neglect. Finally he saw next to an unfenced small field that there was a dirt track leading off toward the river. It looked as if it had been recently used. He turned into it and slowly rolled down toward the woods. He drove on through a low woods of scrub oaks, short stocky pines, and hickory trees. After another three hundred yards this track turned north again and the soil underneath was clearly soft and maybe even moist. Then he emerged from the woods in a cleared, uncultivated area. And then he saw something that surprised him immensely. The track ended at what looked like a settlement of squatters living in camper trailers. Stretched over maybe forty or fifty yards there were maybe twelve or fifteen small campers arranged closely together along the back of the clearing along with one or two mobile homes propped up on cinder blocks, and even one half sized yellow school bus sunk into the ground up to its axles. In front of these obviously occupied hovels, there were some cars, some pick-up trucks, and a few disused rusted cars sunk in the earth. Many of the houses had awnings stretching out in front of them where there were lawn chairs made of plastic webbing, discarded toys, maybe a wooden bench and picnic table, but overall the view was of a littered, run-down, and shabby collection of residences. The entire settlement looked like what he imagined a gypsy settlement would look like, if he had ever seen one. Derelict, dirty, and cluttered with junk and litter, lots crumpled beer cans. Chickens running loose between the houses, and a few roosters crowing and making a fuss over the chickens. A few mangey dogs idling in the shade of some campers. As soon as he stopped his car and stepped out, people began to emerge from the camper-homes. Mostly women and children, there were also a few old men and a few teenaged boys that crept out to have a look at the visitor. After a few moments of silently staring at each other Will took a step forward and his step was matched by an approaching step of a lean, dark skinned older man wearing a tattered blue tee shirt and a Phillies baseball cap over his graying long hair. The old man approached faster, as if to head Will off and keep him from approaching too close. Little younger children now were clinging to or hiding behind their mothers, staring and pointing. As he looked closer he realized that he had seen just such poor villages before, when he was serving in the Marines in Central America.

"Are you lost, stranger?" the old man asked as he drew closer to Will. He stopped about two yards from Will.

"No. I think this is the place that the late Mr. Pellmell Randall owned."

"Oh, he's dead. Died almost three months ago. Really old man, old Pell."

"I know. That's why I'm here. Did he live here?"

"Really old man, Pell was. Maybe ninety-three, ninety-four. Knew everything about the county, and the past century. Saw everything. He was named after a cigarette, you know." the man continued speaking to himself as if in a trance. Then he turned his gaze on Will, "Yes, of course he did. He lived over there." He pointed to the yellow half school bus. The windows of the bus were all boarded up from the inside. "But he did not have any family. So I understand that the state wants to take our land away from us for this reason."

"I'm not talking about the state. But I am interested in buying this land. How many people live here?"

"I'm not sure. Maybe forty. But people come and go, depending on work. All the men are away now at work. In recent years, the young have moved away."

"Does this place have a name? I don't see it on any of the maps of the riverside."

"We call it Wicomico. It means 'place to live'."

"You mean, like Wicomico County across the river?"

"Yes. Like that. The same word."

"What are you all doing here on Randall's land?"

The old man, looked around as if he was afraid someone behind him might have heard Will.

"We're living here. We've always lived here. And all our ancestors before us lived here. We're what you call Indians. Or now locally, Injuns. In the past, savages, redskins. And now Native Americans. Old man Pell was an Indian too, as was his father, and his grandfather before him. The Randalls have been in Wicomico for as long as anyone can remember. But now they are no more. So now I ask you what are you doing here at Wicomico?"

"As I said I mean to buy this land from the county."

"It's Indian land. Nantiquak Indian land. Has been for at least four hundred years. It's not the county's to sell."

"But the county doesn't know yo'awl are living here. There're no records of any of you being here. Your houses or residences are not registered."

"They are our homes."

"Do you get mail delivered here?"

"No."

"Do you pay taxes on your homes?"

"No. Why should we? Did old man Pell pay taxes?"

"Not that I can tell."

"There you go. I suppose you will say that you want to evict us."

"No, I am not saying anything like that. How long have you lived here?"

"I was born here, mister. In that wigwam over there." he pointed to a very beaten up looking camper which had faded awnings stretched from both side walls and from the front. The tires were flat and half buried in the soil. "I can't remember when of course. But my mother told me it was fifty six years ago. We all lived here because old man Pell wanted us to live here. He was older than my father."

"So what is your name, if I can ask?" said Will, now getting a little annoyed.

"Armand Driggers. Everybody here is either a Randall or Driggers. Those were the names that the English settlers gave us. Along with the Duffs and Jacksons. What is your name?"

"Will Eames. William Eames from Bristol. How do you make a living here?"

"We work odd jobs, on the farms, driving buses, fishing, crabbing, or collecting mussels, oystering, some hunting, as cleaners, as cooks, as construction workers, as day laborers over in Salisbury, some of our young men are in the military. They send remittances. We get by. You don't need to worry about us. We're not on welfare. Although if the govment recognized our tribe we'd get all kinds of welfare aid."

"So why aren't you working today?"

"It's a hot day. The harvests are in, until the apples and pumpkins are ready. Nothing to do. And what are you doing today? No work for you too?"

"No I'm a realtor. I'm taking the afternoon off to see this tract of land."

"Well, let me show you around. Not too much to see. Lots of mud if you want to see that."

Armand turned and with a sweep of his arm directed Will to walk to the far side of the grassy field where a scruffy low woods started. Will followed his lead. As soon as they stepped into the deeper grasses and brown knee-high weeds next to the woods, a cloud of mosquitoes swarmed over them. "I hope they don't bother you too much. The mosquitoes, that is. Used to be malaria here. But I don't think there is any more." Will was slapping at mosquitoes as they attacked his arms, and the back of his neck and ears. Some were even biting him through his shirt. "They don't seem to bother us anymore." said Armand as Will was trying to brush the biters off his face and around his eyes. The cloud of mosquitoes tapered off as soon as they stepped into the shadow of the woods. The trees were not tall. The leaf litter was very heavy, and acorns and acorn shells were strewn all about. The ground was very soft and spongey. The undergrowth leapt up from the floor of the forest included butternut, iron weed and poison ivy and Virginia creepers, so Will had to watch his step very closely. He was still snagged a couple times by the iron weed. They walked about thirty yards when the ground began to get squishy. Then, Will saw a narrow channel of brown still water about three yards in front of them. Beyond it he could see the trees clearing out and through the gaps he could see out to the mudflats and stretches of cordgrass and rushes. "Most people call this Black Creek. We don't need to go any closer." Then Armand walked parallel to the creek. There seemed to be a path here. They walked on—Will noisily—for about two hundred and fifty yards until they emerged again from the woods and the Black Creek slithered over into a larger creek, maybe twenty five yards wide. All around them now were the intertidal mudbeds rattling with the rushes and salt grasses. There was a huge noise of birds and peepers surrounding them. The path led on another forty yards until it came to a cleared area on the larger creek. There five or six aluminum boats —none with motors--were beached, keels up, like dead pilot whales, next to a wooden dock which extended into the water. There were oyster tongs, fish line, and fish traps strewn about. Around the boats were muddy tracks, some of which led out onto the dock, which was blistering in the sunlight. "Red Marsh Landing is over there, on Broad Creek." said Armand pointing about 60 yards up the creek. Will could see a concrete dock jutting out into the water. "It sometimes gives us a little competition for going out on the water. For crabs, or fish, or mussels or ducks. But in recent years less and less white people use it these days. These are most of our boats. Let's see. Maybe three are out on the water now, crabbing." Armand continued strolling, this time away from the river and the Broad Creek, up a well-trod path that came in at the far north end of the grassy field, about 70 yards from the Wicomico settlement. He slowly walked by the campers and waved at some of the children and some of the young women with babies. But he did not say anything to anyone until they were back at Will's car.

"Well, Will, you've had the full tour. There's even less to see in the other directions. Most of the land around us is mudflats as you understood. You couldn't go there at high tide even in hip boots. The mud would suck you in. Must be 12 feet deep, at least. And then the grasses and rushes would cut you to shreds. So we mostly get about by boat from that landing you saw, or by car. We can even sometimes go down to Exeter by boat. Doesn't take even an hour. We might sell a catch of crabs or mussels. And catch the incoming tide to get back in about an hour and a half. And, could I ask, you're interested in owning this place?"

"Well yeah. I guess you could say, I already do. But that doesn't mean I will be seeking to exploit this place. Not like you do."

"So you don't need to evict us, then?"

Will did not answer. Instead he asked, "Are you the chief of this group of Indians?"

"Oh no. Old man Pell was. But now we haven't chosen our next chief. It's a hereditary kind of thing. There is a main chief for the Nantiquaks. But he lives in Delaware. We never hear from him. And there is another band of our tribe up the River on the Wicomico County side. We don't much interact with them either. But everyone here is related in one way or another to old man Pell, nephews, nieces, grand nephews, cousins. You get the picture. One big interrelated family. So what is it, Will, that you aim to do with this land, if I may ask?"

"I'm not sure, just yet. But if I plan anything, I'll let you all know in advance."

"If you want to come tell us your plans, it's best to come in the evening when more of the folks are here, back from work."

"Okay, Armand. Fine, But I can't call you any way, can I?"

"Fraid not. There's no microwave coverage over this part of the river. No public phones until you get to Exeter. Lots of our guys have cell phones, but they can only use them when they leave and get back to the main roads, rather nearer Exeter. But we're usually all here before it gets dark in these days."

"Well bye then, Armand." Will got into his car and backed around and turned back to the track. Armand stood silently watching him until he disappeared back into the woods. The little settlement of Wicomico sunk out of sight almost at once. When Will got back on the Eastern Shore Highway and turned towards Bristol he almost at once began to curse. 'Injuns,' he thought, 'who would have believed that there were still any Indian villages around here in this day and age.' He was furious. 'I thought they had all been cleared out of here a long time ago.' He was partially right. But then, he had stumbled across the last vestiges, carefully hidden on land which no one else could think a use for. He couldn't help noticing on the drive back how neat, prosperous, and well-kept the farms were along the road. Unlike the disorder, poverty, and slovenliness of Wicomico. This made him feel even worse. But his temper had cooled down by the time he pulled into the drive of his neatly painted white little frame house.

Through the remainder of the week Will lamely searched for new business. He would call people whom he had spoken to earlier, farmers out in the county, and leads he had gotten from different sources. He even tried calling the owners of stores and strip malls along Highway 50, asking if they could use his realtor services. Nothing turned up.

But he didn't expect anything either. Some of the managers admitted that the stores in their strip malls were not doing well--business was slow-- but they were still paying their leases so there was no thought of selling. On two late afternoons he went out into the county to make unsolicited calls on some of the older farmers. He met five of them, all men in their sixties or seventies. Three turned him away on the porch in front of their doors. But only two were willing to speak with him, and neither of those had thought about selling their farms. And neither were they interested in buying adjacent farms. In each place he left his business card and a printed information package about his realtor services. It was always like that. He had been trawling for business like that in Dorset County and in the neighboring Talbot County over the previous two years. It had not yielded much business. One sale, and two purchases of small farms, but it put his name out across the landscape, over much of Eastern Shore Maryland. He got a better response he thought from the billboard advertisements he had put up along Highway 50. Through those he had gotten several dozen inquiries from interested buyers, most from outside the Eastern Shore. Those people from D.C. or Baltimore who drove through on weekends on their way to Ocean City. Those who occasionally dared to look out of their cars at the surroundings as they drove through. But that same traffic, while reputed to be buyers of holiday real estate in Ocean CItys' booming economy, was not really much interested in what Dorset County had to offer. Most of the county comprised farmsteads after all. And it was located too far from either of those metropolises to be suitable for commuting life.

But while trolling for new work, he also tried to find any information on the Indians of Wicomico. The Bristol public library didn't have any, although the library pointed him to a historian who lived in Salisbury who had written a book on the Indians of the Eastern Shore. She offered to order the book for him on inter-library loan. He agreed to order it on loan. The historian's name was Sylvester Alvey. He made a mental note to go over to Salisbury and introduce himself to this Alvey sometime soon. The internet did not have any information on these particular Nantiquaks. Frustrated he gave up looking any further that week. On Friday, faced again with a long empty weekend, Will decided that maybe he should, as his father had said "go fishing where the fish are", namely go to Ocean City and see if he could meet any young women.

On Saturday morning he packed an overnight bag and another bag with beach supplies and threw them all into the trunk of his car. The weekenders' traffic rush from Friday was already over, and the Saturday visitors had not come yet, so he was able to drive over on a clear road in only an hour. It had been years since he had gone to Ocean City. Usually, if he wanted to go to the beach, he would turn off Highway 50 at Berlin and go to the state park on Accomack Island. That was pure beaching experience, sun, surf, cool breezes. None of the commercialized busy-ness of Ocean City's beach by the boardwalk. But on this Saturday morning he drove into Ocean City and drove slowly up the main road that divided the narrow island into two sides, oceanside and bayside. He pulled into the parking lot of an oceanside hotel. Sand and green weeds collected around the edges of the paved parking lot and at places where the asphalt was cracked. It was still midmorning and too early to get a room, but he went to the desk to reserve a room for the night and to change into his swim shorts. He was lucky, the young blond receptionist told him, there was still a single room available and it was already cleaned, so she let him have the room and gave him the key. As he changed into his swim trunks, he noticed the burn marks left on him from the previous weekend, especially around his head and neck. His skin in those areas was beginning to peel and blister off. So he applied some extra sunscreen and put on a long sleeve sunproof shirt. He remembered to put sunscreen on the tops of his feet and his knees. Thus armed he grabbed his towel and headed out onto the beach.

He had never actually tried to pick up girls on a beach. The whole idea seemed to him awkward and strange. It was hard enough trying to approach an unknown single woman in a bar or night club and getting to know anything about her, except for her willingness to drink and maybe dance. But on a beach where the young women were dressed only in swim suits, it proved to be much harder. There was a good crowd on the beach, not too many families he noticed, mostly young adults in groups of men and women, or groups of just women or just men. He set up his towel and an umbrella and a beach chair he hired in a spot where he thought he noticed some single woman lying about. But it turned out, the single women around him were all accompanied by men, who had stepped away either for a swim in the surf or to buy some drinks. He jumped into the roaring surf and immediately was cooled off by the chill waters and stiff breeze. Refreshed he walked the beach a bit looking for unaccompanied women. Shortly after noon, he noticed one woman in a tight fitting black one-piece swim suit who was sunning herself on her towel. She seemed to be alone. He walked by her a few times, and felt certain she took no notice of him. So he sat some distance away and he began to watch her. She looked nice, good figure, dark hair, long legs. Not too young, in fact she did not look young at all. After thirty minutes of looking at her, he decided she was alone and did not expect anyone. She sat up and began to read a thick library book, which she perched on her folded up legs. Now, he thought to himself, the hardest part is how to introduce himself and deliver that all important opening first line, the one that nearly all comedians made fun of for being always stupid, inane, disingenuous, self-evident, awkward and unnatural. He walked up to her from the side. Only when he approached within four yards of her did she react and turn her gaze at him. Through her big sunglasses he could not tell if she appeared welcoming, surprised, terrified, or upset. His first thought was that she was sending out signals that he was trespassing. He tried to smile, weakly. "Don't worry. I won't bite you. I just wanted to introduce myself. Maybe we can talk and swim and roast in the sun together. My name's Will." Her face took on a hard, unfriendly expression. "And so what, Will? I'm perfectly content by myself." "I mean no harm. Can I join you?" The woman made subtle moves to cover parts of herself, with the book, with one hand, with the edge of the towel. "Are you a salesman? What do you want?" There was a slight tone of disdain in her voice. Will still didn't move closer. "Well, in fact I am a salesman. I'm a real estate broker from near here. But I don't have anything to sell you. Other than to introduce myself and get to know you." "Well, fine, in that case. Then just go away and leave me alone. I am comfortable just as I am." "As you like." said Will thinking that she would be a very hard sale for anything. He noticed now, being closer to her, that she appeared to be middle aged and that her figure was not all that slender, and her tan was far too deep brown. He decided not to push any further. He turned and walked away, back to his spot on the sand. He took off his shirt and went back into the surf. And soon he had forgotten about this rebuff. After a further hour not seeing any other single women on the beach, he left to find some lunch in one of the eateries along the boardwalk. He found a brewery pub, an innovation on the boardwalk. The burger was the same greasy sort, thick and heavy. But the beer was unusual. Served really cold like it should be, he thought it was the first time he had drunk a beer and noticed its flavor. He had drunk a beer like this once when he had been stationed in Germany about eight years earlier. He had a second and then went out to the beach again.

The woman in the black one piece swim suit was still there. This time lying on her stomach catching sun on her already very browned back. He sat not far from her, and put up his umbrella to keep out of the sun and re-applied more sunblock. The sun was sharp, but the air was not too warm. Maybe it was 15 to 18 degrees cooler than back in Bristol. But he still did not want to get anymore sunburn. He did not want to go into the surf straightaway, but as soon as he tried to read a book he dozed off. He woke about half an hour later. The wind had picked up and the clouds were stacking up in the skies to the south of them. Then he noticed the woman had sat up and was putting on a loose shirt. She then stood, pulled on a pair of red shorts and put on a hat, and then collected her things to make to leave. She noticed him and as she started off, with her arms full of gear and bags, she leaned over and shouted in his direction, "Still trolling, Will? Good luck." And she walked off. He waved, but she probably did not see it. She had quite an attractive shake of the hips, he thought. He went into the water and swam a while. Now he felt refreshed and relaxed, and after he got out of the water it didn't bother him when walking up and down the surf line that he saw no single women he could approach. There were a few good looking young mothers with little children. But he wouldn't approach or proposition them under any circumstances. There were also plenty of young women, in bikinis and one piece suits. But almost all of them were accompanied by young men, whether playing ball games on the sand or splashing in the waves, or by coveys of other women. By four o'clock it was clear he had failed, so he picked up and went to his room.

By seven, he was ready to see what the bar activity was like. He went out clean and in light summer wear. He could feel the sun shining off his body—he had gotten burned in spite of the measures he had taken to keep the sun off. His face was bright red. As he walked along the boardwalk, he recalled the pick-up scenes in Boblingen during his brief time stationed in Germany. The bars were raucous, well-lit, and usually overcrowded with both Marines and army soldiers out trolling for girls to pick up. He was young but many of the soldiers were still teenagers. There were often fights, and he preferred to keep out of fights. The young women who came to these bars usually came in groups of two to four and they were looking for some cheap thrills. They always liked it when the men fought over them. It had always seemed to Will that these young German women were also looking at the men and ranking them by their looks alone. He never had much success in these pick -up nights. Only two girls in six months told him their names—probably not their real names-- and at most he would dance with a few who were open to the suggestion. A few drunken girls got sloppy with him, but he never got to first base, as the saying went, never got a follow up date. Those four months were the last time that he went out on pick-up nights. Boblingen was a city, a fairly big suburb of Stuttgart. Bristol was not and did not have a bar scene, even on weekends. It had only one bar, the Cedar Island Bar and Restaurant. Ocean City was different. It was a party town on weekends. But the parties came fully arranged by the visitors who drove in in groups from D.C. or Baltimore; all the party members knew each other, worked together, or were friends of college days who ended up in D.C. Lots of these weekend parties went by pre-arrangement to houses that had been rented just for the season or for private weekends of fun, so these people did not come to the bars or restaurants. This was summer time and the university kids did not come for the weekends. They would appear on September weekends. Most of the restaurants with bars were already fairly full. He stopped in one that was brightly lit and had a long bar. The beer was not as good as it had been at lunch. He looked around and saw that all the women in the place were with men. It was dinner time and waiters were busy running around between the tables like so many confused geese. The white noise of some pop music was piped in, but it didn't disguise the bustle and shouting. The other men in the place, and there were mostly men and only one or two women at the bar-- were watching a baseball game on the TV mounted behind and above the barkeeper. He was not up to trolling at this place, the false gaiety of the people seated at the bar and the groups of young people seated at the larger tables depressed him. He spent only half an hour here, not even finishing his beer which seemed flat and insipid, he paid and went off to find another place. He did not go back to the brewery pub, it was too small and he felt like eating something other than a heavy greasy cheeseburger. Finally about a mile up the boardwalk he came upon an attractive-looking spacious terrace restaurant with a bar at the back. He entered and decided to stay when he saw that there were lots of tables with groups of young women, unescorted by men. He went to the bar, ordered a small beer, and then looked to see which table to join. He spied one table with four young women. They looked like co-eds, sitting eating salads and laughing at something. He decided to be bold: he walked over to their table with his beer in hand and hailed them warmly; "Hi girls. My name is Will. Can I join you?" The girls— who had just raised their wine glasses in a toast-- all looked up, surprised but still laughing. They looked at him and then at each other, giggling, then one said, "And my name's Jenny. Have a seat Will. There's room there." The others laughed again and drank the wine, hardly paying any attention to Will. The one closest to him, a chubby blond girl, had to move to one side to let him have room on the bench. Putting the wine down, she squealed, "And I'm Betty Lou." "How are you Betty Lou?" She squealed a little again and then after a quick consultation with the faces of the other three girls, she said, more soberly, "I'm fine thank you. And how about you?" "Me too. Just a little sunburned and dry after such a scorcher." "Would you like some wine?" asked Jenny picking up the bottle of chardonnay. "Yes, that would be nice. Better than this awful beer." As Jenny poured, Will looked at each of the girls. They were in their early twenties it seemed to him, and all were sunburned. Three were very slender, and Betty Lou was not really so chubby, but she had a round heavy face. They were dressed in light summer tops and light colored slacks. "I'm kind of a local here. From the Eastern Shore—but I'm not a farmer. Where are ya'wl from?" "Silver Spring." said Jenny. "Bethesda," said another. Betty Lou said she was from D.C., and the fourth said she was from College Park. "Oh, you know I went to the University of Maryland at College Park. Centuries ago. I really liked it. We'd go into D.C. for weekend bar hopping. They weren't so strict on carding people then, so we could always get drinks." "My name's Beth." "And I'm Brittany, none of us are actually from Maryland, you know. We all moved there after college. We all went to Michigan State." Then in unison, they gave a cheer, something like, "MSU, whu whu whoo." A waitress came by and interrupted them to ask if Will would like to order some dinner. "Have ya'wl ordered dinner?" he asked. "Yes." they answered in chorus, and began to giggle again. "Well then I'll order some fish. What's the catch of the day?" "Red snapper, but it's from frozen. We also have fresh sea bass." "Good, I'll have that. I like catching sea bass, although I didn't think they were running now in high summer." The waitress looked at him as if he were looney and she screwed up her eyes. She had no idea about anything to do with fish, and could not tell the dishes apart if the cook did not tell her which was which. She retreated. "We all work in D.C. and come out here for the sea air and the parties. Catch some sun." "And to meet some guys," said Jenny, who was clearly the most assertive of the group. "Especially to meet the guys. But today, on the beach, we only met really childish boys. You know the ones who wear their baseball caps on backwards, and all the time are playing with frisbees, and small boogie boards. Really creeps. Today on the beach was a washout." Shortly after, the waitress brought the girls their dinners. She mixed up which plate went to whom, but eventually everyone got their order. "Uuu, look at these shrimp scampi!" cooed Beth. "And I have these scallops St. Jacques. Really special." Will understood that these girls were inexperienced in eating seafood. "Have you tried the local oysters? In season of course." he asked. They all replied with a look of disgust, saying Ugh, or something like that. "Or the mussels or crabs? All the local seafood. The shrimp here probably comes from Viet Nam." "No, maybe next time. You say the crabs are good?" ask Betty Lou. And the girls dived into their plates, they did not even acknowledge his 'Bon Appetite' as they started munching. They completely switched off to Will. Through the rest of their meal, they paid no attention to him, making small comments about their food to each other and acting as if Will was just part of the wait staff. His fish came, just as they were finishing. They paid him no regard, as he began eating. The waitress began clearing their plates even before he took his first bite. While he was eating the four began gossiping about other girls they knew in common. It was not friendly gossip, but they continued to ignore Will and were no longer interested in his presence. He looked at them as they gossiped and giggled, as if he were looking at fish through one side of an aquarium glass wall, both sides unaware of the other. He decided that Jenny was by far the most attractive, pretty face, naturally tan colored hair, nicely shaped breasts. She also seemed to be the smartest of the group, and was the natural leader. While he was still eating and the girls continued gossiping and ignoring him, his cell phone rang in his shirt pocket. He took it out and flipped it open. An unidentified caller, who had already dropped the line. This brief motion caught the girls' attention. "What an interesting cell phone you've got." said Jenny. "What make is it?" "It's the new Motorola." "Wow, that's cool." cooed Beth. The others agreed. "Let me see it." said Jenny. Will handed it to her, and the girls took turns opening and closing the clam lid or pulling out or pushing back the retractable antenna. "Like something from the Star Wars movies. Really cool." He realized that this reference dated him. He had thought it reminded him of Star Trek, the TV series that was some years earlier. They gave it back to Will and again turned their attentions to the gossip, again studiously ignoring Will. He returned his attention to his meal of sea bass. It was a well prepared dish. Just the right amount of lemon. He wondered if the sea bass was also from frozen Chilean bass, but no matter. He slowly finished off his dinner. Outside the terrace windows it was now dark, meaning it was after eight thirty. Before he had even finished eating, the girls were already making moves to leave. They asked for the bill from the waitress, and after they paid they slipped on identical pale blue cashmere sweaters—as if they were team uniforms. "Well, sorry we have to dash Will. We're invited to a party by the pier." said Jenny very matter-of-factly. "It's a private party." Meaning they were not inviting him to join them further. "Nice meeting you. Have a good evening." And with that the four rushed off, waddling through the guest tables like so many blue-backed ducks. Will watched them go. He noticed only then that Jenny had big buttocks already, as if she had been a secretary for twenty five years. What a shame he thought. And then he thought that this pick-up business was still impossibly difficult. And humiliating. Yes, sure, he thought, there were more fish here in Ocean City to troll for, but these fish were not biting, neither baited hooks, nor nets. This exercise had all been a waste of time. And money too, as when the waitress brought his bill, the girls apparently had left to him to pay the $28 for the bottle of wine. He had gotten only half a glass of the wine to drink. "Are you sure of this?" he asked the waitress. "Yeah, that's what they told me. They said that you'd buy the wine." He could just imagine them snickering at him over their little sleight- of-hand. Swindled as well by these youngsters, he thought.

He went back to his room and kicked on the TV. He would watch the evening ball game, and go to sleep early. This junket had been a sorrowful waste of time; he didn't want to think about it. In the morning first thing, he checked out and drove back to Bristol. As he was driving west, he saw thunderheads heading east. So this day on the beach will be rained out, he thought. This whole trip was a washout as well. But he wasn't surprised. When he got home, he went straight to his training machine and worked out hard for fifty minutes to try and clear his mind of his humiliation and thoughts of the wasted effort. There was a hard rain a couple hours later.

The next week started much like the previous two. Except that the afternoons were visited by thunderstorms, a sign that the big dry heat of the summer was over and the Labor Day weekend was nearly upon them. Lucy took off the last week of August as part of her annual leave. That left only Marilyn in the office, sitting in the next room. During the week she had a buyer of a property just across the Choptico River take out one new insurance policy. Pretty limited business. He had to admit it had been a slow summer. Wednesday, a day that started with brilliant blue skies but which turned into a chalky summer sky of heat haze and humidity, Will, as he often did, went to the Poseidon's Palace restaurant for lunch. He was very consistent. He would have crab cakes with fries, read the Baltimore Sun weekly business section and, when he was there, he'd chat with his friend, Tony, the owner's son whom Will had known all his life. On this Wednesday, Tony was in, and that meant that the waitresses were especially prompt and careful with their service for Will.

"You know Will, we're seasonal here. Not just the local catch, but also all the beach traffic—the weekenders from Bawlimore and DC--tapers off by November and doesn't come back until April. That's why we close. Business from the locals is not enough through the winter to keep us open. But my pa and I have been thinking that we should open a beer brewery here on the premises, a microbrewery as they call it. Then we could have a seafood pub. Not a bar, like the Cedar Island place. But a restaurant with locally made, tasty beer. What do you think of that idea?"

"Sounds good Tony. I would support it. I was in Ocean City this past weekend and I discovered there is just such a microbrewery there now. A new place. Serves mainly burgers. But their beer is worth travelling out of your way for. Could work here too."

Will then noticed the main article in the paper. It was about the heavy increase in the traffic from Philadelphia to Atlantic City, New Jersey, and how it jammed the road and increased business all along the road between the two cities all the week long, and not just on weekends. He read on. This traffic had especially exploded after the casinos were built in Atlantic City. It was no longer just weekenders going for the beaches and boardwalk of Atlantic City. The main visitors pouring out of Philadelphia were people going for the casinos. And that was the eureka moment, on the newsprint page; the obvious staring him in the face. Will suddenly realized that his parcel of land, less than six miles from Highway 50, was an ideal setting for a casino. Maybe not as ideal as Ocean City itself would be, but still a destination that could siphon off a large portion of the weekender traffic bound for Ocean City.

"I need to build a casino, Tony. That's it! Build it and they will come."

Tony did not understand what Will was bantering about.

"You see I bought a riverside property near Exeter, cross the county. It's an ideal location to put a casino and capture some of that traffic that flows across here every summer weekend."

"You bought some riverside land? I didn't think there was any riverside property left to be bought on either the Choptico or the Nanticoke."

"Neither did I. But I found some. More than 30 acres. And I would say more than ten acres are suitable for development. And a casino is just the thing."

"You know the Bay Holiday Spa Resort which opened outside town here last year, their developers also wanted to build a casino facility. But the state wouldn't permit it. Casino gambling is banned in 'Merlyn' it seems."

"Oh yeah? Really? I didn't know they wanted a casino also."

"That's what I understood was the case. But they couldn't 'cuz it's against Merlyn law."

"I haven't been out there in quite a while. I wonder if they get enough through traffic."

"Especially considering the absurd prices they charge for everything. I suppose those who like golf go there anyway."

"Yeah, I know. I looked at membership in their fitness club, but as you say, they wanted absurd amounts of money for annual membership. I suppose they have to re-coup some of the money they spend on the advertising flyers they send me by mail all the time."

Will was so excited by this idea, and by his talk with Tony, that his lunch remained uneaten on the platter, and was now cold. He couldn't think of anything now but of developing a casino.

"You should go talk to Jackson Parker. You remember him, from high school, right? Well, after he got his law degree he ran for delegate in the General Assembly. Jack's usually up in Nnapolis, but the Assembly's not sitting now in the summer. So you might find him at his local law office here in Bristol. But then when he's in town here, he often comes by. And I haven't seen him this summer."

"Thanks Tony. I'll give him a call." He took out his cell phone and flipped open the top. "Let me have the number, now." said Will. "Hey that's sure a nifty looking cell phone. Never seen one like it. What make is it?" "It's a Motorola. Their new model. Looks like something out of *Star Trek,* doesn't it?" "I'll say. I think I'll get one like that." Then Tony gave him the number for Jackson's local law office, which Will recorded directly into his phone. "That's really neat. Amazing this new technology." "Yeah, amazing, isn't it. Things change so fast."

Once back at his office, Will right away rang up Jack's phone number. But when he called a secretary told him that Jackson was out, and probably at his Annapolis office. She asked who was calling for him, and when Will told her, she replied, "Oh Will Eames? The same Will Eames on the billboard ads around the county? I remember you from high school. But you probably don't remember me. I was a sophomore when you were a senior. You were my hero, quarterback on the football team. That sort of thing. You know, so big and strong."

"And so tell me your name. I might remember it."

"Becky Armstrong."

"Sorry to say, Becky. I don't remember if I ever knew you by name. Maybe I'd recognize your face if I saw you."

"Oh, I doubt that. That was more than twelve years ago. I've grown up. And I'm married now. Now I'm Becky Cartwright. I'm sure you wouldn't recognize me. But I remember you. Well, I hope you get hold of Jack. I haven't heard from him in a week or two. Bye now."

"Bye, Mrs. Cartwright."

He at once called the number she had given him. A woman's voice answered, very officially, "The office of Maryland Delegate Jackson Parker. How can I help you?"

"I'd like to speak to Jack, or make an appointment to speak with him. Is he in?"

"What is your name?"

"William Eames from Bristol. I'm a constituent of his, and an old friend."

"Mr. Eames, Jackson has not yet come back from lunch. I'll ask him to call you back when he gets in. You'd like an appointment to meet with him, that's right?"

"Yes, that's it."

"Okay, I'll let him know. And he'll call you back if you leave me your number."

Will gave her his cell phone number and then hung up. He was now feeling excited. He began looking in the internet for information on casinos, their history, construction costs, their business. Most of the afternoon he spent reading up on this subject. But there was not a lot of detail available. Shortly after five, his cell phone rang. It was Jackson's Annapolis office. It was the same secretary on the line whom he had spoken to earlier. "Mr. Eames, Jackson told me to tell you that he would like to meet with you, if it's possible for you, at the Golden Bull restaurant for lunch on Friday. He suggests 12:30. Is that alright with you?" "Sure, that's possible. How can I find the Golden Bull?"

"It's at the top of Cornhill Street, just off the State Circle. Park your car first in the municipal lot and walk over." "Fine, I'll be there."

When he hung up, Will thought that Mr. Jackson Parker had become mighty self-important since his high school days. He wondered if he introduced himself to strangers as the Honorable Mr. Jackson Parker. He had only been a delegate for three or four years. When the day came, he left at eleven o'clock to allow himself enough time to drive up to Annapolis and to find his way around in the town and to find the municipal parking lot closest to the statehouse. It was still too early for the weekend traffic to Ocean City coming down Highway 50, and there was none heading west, so he got to the middle of Annapolis in about an hour. At the appointed time, he was already seated in the restaurant at the table that Jackson Parker's office had reserved in advance. But Jackson himself did not show up for another fifteen minutes. A chunky man in an expensive suit bustled through the front door. He wore a power tie—bright red with some black patterns on it. Will assumed it was Jackson. His face looked familiar. The man rushed over to the table, followed by the receptionist bearing menus. Must be his usual table as he knows just where it is, thought Will.

"Will, it's been so long. How are you doing, old man?" said the man as he came up, his arm up to pat him on the back. "I'm so glad you called. So glad to see you. It's been a long, long time. You remember? On the football team? And then when we went off to college together?" He pulled up a chair and sat down abruptly and took the menus from the receptionist and dismissed her imperiously. He settled into his chair with a lot of exaggerated movements. "So, what have you been up to, Will? Catch me up with what you've been doing in Bristol, or since we last saw each other."

"I guess, the last time we met was at College Park, after our sophomore year. When I signed up with the Marines. I suppose that was almost ten years ago. I thought at the time that the experience would toughen me up, and maybe I would also get to see some of the world. As you know, things turned out rather different for me in my two and a half years of service. What started out as the usual peacetime routine-- training in the swamps of Virginia and in Honduras, stationed in Germany-doing body building and equipment training--suddenly Saddam Hussein decided to invade Kuwait and Saudi Arabia. And then I went to war. Not in the tropics, but in the sandy desert around Kuwait. Awful place. The whole Middle East. I was one of the really lucky ones. Saw plenty of action, moved miles and miles through desert that all looked the same. But came out after four months of maneuver and fire fights without a scratch. And was able to come home with a scholarship and a completely different perspective of the world. Finished university at College Park—I guess by that time you had already graduated and gone off to law school. Where did you go to law school?"

"UVA in Charlottesville. The law school for the Eastern Shore."

"Yeah. I guess I didn't know that. So then when I finished I went back home and set up my real estate brokerage business. And also I set up a title insurance agency. But Bristol and Dorset County are as you know well, together a small market. So I also work Tilghman County and parts of Wicomico County. I've done alright."

"Alright? I hear you're the number one man for buying or selling property on the Eastern Shore."

"Maybe. But the real market is in Ocean City, and I don't work there. And there are lots of times when business is slow, like the past four months or so."

They ordered their lunches from an attractive dyed-blond waitress who spoke with a heavy foreign accent. She brought them beers in iced mugs and walked away shaking her hips provocatively.

"I wonder where she comes from." said Will.

"I think she's Russian, or Ukrainian. The State Department has a special visa program to bring young people from the former Soviet Union or East Bloc to work in tourist areas. She told me her name is Natasha. Really good looking, no?"

"I should say so. So she's here only for the summer and then has to go back?"

"That's the deal. The program even finds them the summer jobs. This is the second summer she's done this job here. I don't know how it works. But, I have to say she's better at her job than most of the locals they used the have in this restaurant."

"So I would imagine that they are working in big numbers in Ocean City."

"You're right there. They have a huge labor shortage there in the summer. I mean, the permanent population is not even ten thousand, and yet every weekend in summer up to ninety thousand visitors descend on the place. Every business in town has two or three of these foreign temporary workers, and all the college students they can recruit. There must be hundreds, if not thousands of these Natashas working in Ocean City."

"That many! Well that brings us to the point I wanted to talk to you about, Jack. I bought a parcel of riverside land on the Nanticoke River, not far from Exeter. And I was thinking that maybe I would like to build a casino on that land to try and capture some of that huge flow of visitors to the beach. Would that be possible? Wouldn't that be a good project for Maryland? We could even hire some of those foreign worker visa holders."

"No way, Will. It's not possible to build a casino in Maryland. You're not the first to think of building a casino, or even two or three casinos, for the Ocean City crowds. But it's forbidden by Maryland law. Casino gambling, and public gambling is forbidden and has long been. And all the big players in the gambling business have been here to challenge the law or to lobby to get exemptions or waivers so they could develop their casino resorts in Ocean City, just like in Atlantic City. Even the mafia have lobbied to get the laws to open up, or permit their casinos. And they come at this issue with real force, threats, and I understand huge bribes. But the law is pretty clear and it has stood up for more than sixty years already. But there is huge pressure from really big money interests to throw out that law and permit casinos. So far, most of the delegates, myself included, are against any repeal of the ban, and a legalization of casinos. It's really a dirty business, exploits the poorest, and it only redistributes money, does not actually spur economic growth."

"I don't understand. There's this law that bans gambling and casinos specifically. But isn't there betting on the horse races in Maryland. At the Bawlimore racetrack, what's its name?"

"Pimlico."

"Right Pimlico. That's been around for years."

"Yeah, and look at the punters who hang around there. The corruption around the track, and the doping of the horses. Everything to get a fix. The horses and the races are completely rigged by criminal rackets. No, legalized gambling is just another way of saying licensed crime."

"And there is a lottery here in Maryland. Isn't that also gambling?"

"Yes, of course it is. But we're not going to change lottery betting. That monster is already in the barn and 'rules the roost' as the old saying goes. It's big money interests."

"I can't think of anything that exploits the poor more than state run lotteries with giant pots." said Will.

"I agree with you. All those poor sods who don't have money pouring their cash into lottery tickets. They don't even get any information on the odds against their winning. Long, unfavorable odds."

Natasha brought them their food. After she laid out the plates, she asked, "Will zere be anysing else for you gentlemen?" Jack quickly quipped, "You mean other than that kiss you promised me last month?" She smiled.

"Tell me, Natasha. Where do you come from? asked Will."

"I am from Kharkiv in Ukraine."

"And do you study at university when you're not here?"

"Yes. I'm studying engineering. But zair's no work in Ukraine, just now. The money ere is much better than any job I could get at home."

"Thanks Natasha. Carry on with the good work."

Natasha smiled again and walked off again shaking her hips in an exaggerated fashion.

"She really is a looker." said Jack. "But I don't think she's a natural blond. And I don't think she's studying to be an engineer, either." Jack savored the sight of her until she turned around a corner. Then he turned back to Will. "So you see Will, you should give up on this idea of yours to develop a casino on your riverside plot. It will never happen. The laws have to change, radically. And they won't anytime soon. And besides you are a little man, excuse me for saying the obvious, and only the biggest players in the industry—and they're all from out of state—will get the chance to develop casinos. They have the muscle and money and they will go first and take all the business. And if you try and get some of it, they will crush you. Literally grind you into the ground. So just forget about it. You'll get nowhere with that idea of yours."

"I hear you, Jack."

They attacked their food. Will had a steak with pepper sauce, and Jack had the crab cakes.

"Are you married Will?"

"No. Not yet. And you?"

"No, but I am engaged to a girl who really sends me off the tracks. Met her here. She was trolling for dates with the cadets. Caught me instead. We're going to get married in September. We'll have the wedding party at the Chesapeake Bay Resort and Spa there in Bristol. I'll invite you."

"Thad be nice. My calendar is free in September. And even freer now that I am no longer pursuing a casino development project."

"Cheer up, Will. Are you free now? How about we take in a double header O's game up at the Yard this afternoon? They are in a serious race for the League title and they're playing the Yankees, their only contenders."

Will agreed. And after finishing lunch, they both left for Baltimore for the baseball games. This time the games were livelier and more interesting. Sixteen runs were scored in the two games. Jack only wanted to talk about corruption, especially the corruption in Baltimore. It was a subject that seemed to really upset him. Everywhere he looked in Maryland there was corruption in government. "And you know, Will, that one of the biggest activities of casinos is money laundering for the drug mafias. But crooked politicians can also launder their money in casinos." Will realized how much he enjoyed the companionship and the games were entertaining. He got back to Bristol near 11:30.

When he woke up the next morning Will was at once aware that his idea to build a casino was a non-starter. It depressed him all day. Add to that he had a headache from the beers he had drunk at the games the night before. It was Saturday on the Labor Day weekend and there was still heavy beach traffic coming over the bridge and cutting through town on Highway 50 to Ocean City. The August heat had already abated, but it was still sunny and very warm. He spent the day sitting outside on his rear deck, reading newspapers and professional journals. In midafternoon he decided he would light the grill and grill himself a hamburger. He checked his fridge to see if he had any hamburger meat. He did. Two patties were in the freezer. So he grilled these along with a cob of corn. But before he could start eating he heard his house telephone ringing inside. Not many people called him anymore on his land line. He threw his food down on the table and rushed into his house, catching the receiver on its ninth ring. "Is this Will Eames?" said a weak man's voice on the other end of the line. "Yes, you're speaking to him." "Will, this is Hampton Eames, your great uncle. Remember me?" "Of course, how could I forget my one and only great uncle? How are you on this fine Labor Day weekend?" "Not so well, actually. I'm feeling my age, you might say." "I don't remember exactly, Hampton. It's been a long time since we last met. How old are you exactly?" "Exactly? I cannot remember, but I'm told I am eighty two years old. Too old to carry on with my farm at any rate. I've been too old for farming for a long time already. Only just now admitting my age, and that I won't be living forever. So I've been thinking I need to do something with this place. And that's why I want to talk to you. Do you think you could come out to the farm after Labor Day and we could talk about it?" "Yes, of course. No need to ask even. On Tuesday then?" "Yes, thad be fine. I look forward to seeing you again after sixteen years since our last get together. We've both changed a lot, I should think." Will thought. It was when he had just started high school that Hampton and his wife had come into Bristol and stayed a few nights with his father Robert on some business that Will did not understand at the time. "Do you remember how to get out to the farm, Will?" "I'm not sure I do, Hampton can you remind me?" "We're on Roseland Road, just a half mile beyond Roseland junction itself. The house sits on the south side of the road about three hundred yards off the road surrounded by mature trees. Shouldn't take you more than forty minutes to drive out here. Let's say you come for lunch, then. At 12:00? Is that agreeable to you?" "Yes, I'll be there. Look forward to it. A reunion after sixteen years." "Fine, then I'll see you then. Good bye." Will was elated. A sale and a big one at that. His burgers were now cold, so he put them back on the grill. But after warming them, in his excitement thinking about this prospect, he scarcely noticed their flavor as he scoffed them down. As best he could remember, Hampton's farm was more than two hundred acres, growing soybeans and corn. But he did not know how he knew that. He could still visualize the farm's vast greenness from the last time he visited it with his parents when he was just twelve years old. The rest of the day was preoccupied with thoughts of selling the old family farm. He could not do or read anything. In the early evening, his father called on the land line phone. He asked if Will would join him again in some crabbing on Sunday. Will accepted without a second thought.

The next day, out on the water, after the first crabs had been lured aboard, and the first beers drunk, Bob asked the first question. I don't suppose you've heard any more from Karen, right?"

"No, of course not." said Will. "But last weekend I did follow your advice, and on a lark, I went to try to troll for girls in Ocean City. It was a disaster. Humiliating and uncomfortable, and of course unsuccessful. So I won't try that again. If I want to go to the beach by myself, I'll go to Accomack."

"It was just a suggestion. I have no idea how those party weekends in Ocean City work. Obviously they go there like schools of fish. Hard for outside predators to make a dent or even make contact."

Will then told him that Hampton Eames had called him and wanted to talk about selling his farm, and that Will would go visit him on Tuesday.

"Well, I'm not surprised he called you. It's been a long time since I saw him. He came to visit us, maybe you remember it, you were still living at home, in high school I think, maybe fifteen, maybe sixteen years ago. Wanted to talk about the inheritance of the farm and farmhouse, in the event he died. How old is he now? Let's see, he was born in 1915,1916. That would make him about 82 years old. A real survivor. But after his son died in the Korean War, without children, he didn't know what to do with it. I told him I didn't want it. Didn't want to be a farmer, living there in complete isolation. At that time I had a good-paying job, two kids I wanted to finish school, no debts. Why would I take the farm—as a business it only runs on huge amounts of labor and huge amounts of debt. And it's all a gamble. From one year to the next, you never know how much your harvest will be nor what the market will be for selling the harvest. At the time he came to talk about, I wasn't willing to take risks and gamble on farming."

"Yeah, well I'll see what he's thinking when I get there, I suppose. What's his wife's name?"

"Oh, I don't rightly know. But I don't think he has a wife now. Never knew his second wife. He has housekeeper attending him. Named Phyllis I think.

But I may be wrong. I saw her once or twice when they came to town about six or seven years ago. Hey, get that crab there. Quick your net!"

Will caught the crab just as it fell off the bait. He tossed it into the barrel with the other four crabs where it made a racket of scratching.

"We're doing alright, I reckon. We don't need so many crabs today. No party this afternoon. Just your mother and I and you eating crabs. And we have clams as well."

"I also went out to the parcel I bought on the Nanticoke. To check it out. You know. So what do you think happened when I got out there? I ran into a bunch of black faced Indians who are squatting on the land. Nobody knows anything about their presence. A whole tribe, maybe forty of them. It's really annoying. I thought all the local Indians had long since left Maryland. But then I find the place I bought is crawling with them. Worse than unemployed niggers."

"Careful, what you say."

"What? Political correctness? I could give a damn. They need to get off my land."

"I'm pretty sure that they all feel the same about us. We should get off their land. But they're in no position to evict us. But, I reckon you are, huh?"

"Damn right. But I don't have to right away. The land there has lain unused it seems forever and they carry on collecting and gathering food from the waters around them."

"Like we're doing now. Like all our ancestors did from the time of the first colonization here. Except, we were smart. We started to cultivate the land. Grew Injun tobacco as a big commercial business. Drew boundaries, applied laws, and landownership rights, surveyed, and excluded them from the land so we could collect, and gather, grow and cultivate. Now they are mostly no more, and we hold everything. But mister smarty-pants: Gone to university, gone to war, buys and sells properties, you know those poor black-faced people down there on your property are probably your close relatives."

"What do you mean, my close relatives?"

"Well, you see—aren't you going to put some bait on your line?— my grandmother, her name was Mena short for Willemena, your great-grandmother, who married your namesake Will Eames during the first World War, she was a pure-bred Injun. From that tribe that lives along the Nanticoke River from what I understand. Those people you saw there are probably related to her. We've both got Injun blood in our veins. And there's nothing you can do about it."

"Who told you this?"

"Why my grandma Mena, before she died told me. She was dark skinned. Not like a black woman, but dark. Like a Hindu woman. Nice looking features. She had straight black hair, not kinky like black people from Africa. When I was a little boy growing up, I never knew she was an Injun woman. But she was. Quiet but strong willed. She was illiterate you know. But she could tell stories. To my brother, sister and me she would tell the most remarkable stories. About her family, and their ancestors, going back more than four hundred years. About the places around here where they went to fish for maidenhen, although they called it something different. Or mucking through the mud to catch clams. Or crabbing. She knew the names for everything and everywhere around here. And you know they're all still here—except maybe the oyster beds are a little fished out. She was a good woman. She raised us without a man. Only the help of Robert Eames, my namesake, your great grandfather's father, made it possible for them to survive. Now bring up that line, you're feeding the crabs for nothing."

"When did she die?"

"She died in, let's see, it must've been in 1958. She was sixty two and I was thirty, just starting our family. She died of a heart attack in the second house here in Bristol. She lived all alone there. But she told me not long before that, that she would go away back to her home Injun village to see her other relatives. To take them food and clothes. She'd be gone for two or three weeks at a time. She'd take a bus over to Exeter and walk the six or so miles from there on foot."

"What's the second house?"

"My great grandfather owned that original farm out near Roseland. But around the turn of the century he built two town houses here in Bristol. I'm living in one—with the gingerbread trim—the one you grew up in. And my cousin and his family are living in the other one over on East Center Street, with all the pink crepe myrtle out front. Both passed down, father to son, since the time of Robert and Will Sr."

"This is all confusing. Why haven't you told me about this part of my family ancestry up to now? Have you written it all down somewhere?"

"Yes, it's all written down. And well documented. But I didn't show you, because you didn't show any interest earlier. And besides the effects of segregation are clearly etched on you. You racially stigmatize those people who you don't know, and who you're kept separate from. You know the blacks had segregated lives and schools and churches from us. When I was growing up, and when you were also very young, there were no blacks allowed in our schools. But the Injuns, they were further segregated from even the blacks. They weren't allowed in white man's schools, or black man's schools. They were almost not allowed to come into town here. So I didn't tell you. But enough, I think we have enough crabs, and enough talking about this."

Bob pulled up his line, without a crab chasing it, and stowed his net and line and closed the barrel. "That makes nine crabs for today." And he started the motor with the sharp tug on the starter line. He steered the boat back to Bristol.

"If you want to know a whole lot more, you need to ask your great uncle, Hampton. He was Mena's first son. That's why he inherited the farm. He'll be able to tell you a lot more than I can. About our Injun ancestry, about Mena. He has put together newsclips that he collected from archives. As well as lots of materials he put together from his mother. I haven't seen them, but he's told me about them."

Back at the dock, they quickly put up the boat, threw out the excess ice, and loaded Bob's pick-up truck with the barrel of crabs, the crabbing gear, and the ice box with the undrunk cans of beer and water. They threw out the remaining bait that they hadn't used. "That stinks to high heaven." said Bob as he closed the cover on trash bin at the dockside. When they got to Bob's house, Will looked differently at the house, like he had never looked at it before. The spindlework trim on the porch which wrapped around three sides. The porch itself with it wide floorboards where he had liked to play when he was a little boy. The whitewashed clapboard siding with its now many layers of paint on it. The wide overhanging eaves and the steep pitch of the roof. The sharp pointed gables on the sides of the house. This house which he had always taken for granted, was really a marvel of style. He wondered if this style, so distinctive and comfortable looking on the outside, with its cedar paneling on the inside walls, had a specific name. He had brokered one or two of these types of houses in Bristol in the past few years but he had never given them an architectural name. There were maybe two dozen of similar type houses in the whole town, including that second house. His great-great-grandfather must have been quite prosperous to have had these built. He wondered when exactly they had been built because he realized he never knew. "Do you know when this house was built, pa?" "No, haven't the foggiest idea. I reckon around the turn of this century. But that is just a guess. It's a wonder it is still standing in this condition. The front stairs to the porch, I think have been replaced two or three times. And as you know, I constantly have to treat it against termites."

When they sat down for a crab steamed dinner at the back yard table, Bob suddenly said, "You know, Will, that when your mother and I pass away, this house will be your inheritance. Continue in the family. I hope you realize that." Will said he had not realized that. "And besides you're not going to pass away anytime soon. Look at your uncle Hampton. He's eighty something and still going strong. So you'll carry on a long time now." Bob looked at him with a knowing almost sarcastic expression but did not say anything.

On Tuesday morning Will checked into his office before driving out to his great-uncle's farm. As Hampton had said, it took only twenty five minutes to drive there, and when he drove up to the area half a mile from Roseland Junction he immediately spotted the house sitting a ways off the road. It looked just as he remembered it from nearly twenty years earlier. Maybe the trees were a little bigger, but he couldn't tell. The fields all around the house were harvested and only stubble broke up the dust colored earth. Will turned slowly into the gravel lane which led up to the front of the house, the tires making a distinctive crunching sound the whole way. Parked in front of the house inside the walls made by the maple trees was an old model four-wheel drive Chevy truck, maybe ten years old. It looked in good condition. Will looked at the house, and quickly saw that it was similar in design to the houses in Bristol, only larger and with less ornate trim and simple porch balustrading. And it was painted gray: dark gray on the first level, and paler gray on the second level. The farm buildings and outbuildings were built around the back off to one side. Will could see one red tractor parked in front of one of the outbuildings. Before he got to the steps, the screen door was pushed open by a small, white-haired man with a distinct stoop. He expected Hampton, but this little old man did not look anything like the Hampton of his memory.

"So you must be William. Welcome. Are you William or Will? I don't rightly remember."

"Will." he said as he came up on to the porch to the old man who was still holding the door. "Yes, it's been a long time." As he got closer, he noticed that the face looked familiar, as he remembered it, but that Hampton had clouded watery eyes, as if he had cataracts. "I'm glad though that you called me, and that we can get together after so many years."

"One of my favorite TV shows in years past, was This Old House. I think it is most appropriate to my house here. All the repairs it needs, almost constantly. So welcome to 'this old house' of mine. Maybe you'll remember some of it. Come on in. Would you like some ice tea?"

They stepped inside, Hampton holding the door open for Will and guiding him in with a gentle arm motion. He was maybe three inches shorter than Will, but with his stoop it was hard to tell. Will seemed to remember a robust man who stood as tall as he and maybe two inches taller than his father, Bob. But it was a long time ago. As if he could read his thoughts Hampton said, "And you were a little boy when you last came out here. But now you are a big strapping adult. Looks like you're a professional sportsman or bodybuilder. And so tall. Completely unlike the little Will I first met." He called out a woman's name, "Phyllis, could you bring us both some ice tea?" A white haired, stout woman came from the back of the house. She was wearing a white apron and wiping her hands on it. "Yes, Hamp. Will that be all for the moment?" and she disappeared back down a corridor in the middle of the house. Inside the house had similar pale orange cedar paneling on all the walls, just as in the Bristol house. And large windows that looked out to the porches, windows you could walk through standing up.

"I'm six foot tall, uncle. And I do work-out, lift weights, and I did play football in high school. Maybe you knew that. But I was no professional. Not even good enough to be considered to play for the U of Merilyn football team."

"Oh I know nothing about football. I'm just a simple farmer. All my life, even from by childhood. I cannot understand the game they show on TV. Completely unfathomable to me. Baseball, that's a different matter. I watch the Orioles' games when they show them. Now you might be asking yourself, who is this Phyllis?' Don't be confused. My late second wife was also named Phyllis. But after she died, I quickly needed someone to look after me, and to live here and keep me company in my dotage. This woman approached me at church one day and asked if I had any work she might do. I hired her on the spot when I learned that her name was also Phyllis. That was seven years ago. She's not so old as you might think. But she's a great gal. And she can drive the Chevy and she also does my food shopping for me. In Bristol."

Phyllis brought the ice tea in in tall glasses. She brought a sugar bowl as well and set everything down on a large dining table which sat in the middle of a large room in the front of the house. "Dinna will be ready in about twenty minutes Hamp." Hampton was already sitting down and he steered Will to sit opposite him.

"Well as you can see, Will—great-nephew Will I guess I should call you—I'm not very strong any more. Even managing the farm takes too much out of me. Each year it seems as if the earth around me here is taking something out of me in compensation for all the abundance I've taken out of it over the years. Soon there won't be anything left of me, above the ground. And there'll be a damn-sight little left of me to bury in the ground. But I'm not being morbid. It is true. I'm shrinking away every year, not long left to me."

Will remained silent.

"You may not know but my only son, Benjamin, was killed in the Korean War. He was not even nineteen years old, the same age as my first wife, Lydia when she bore him. She died four years later, in child birth, along with the child. Couldn't get a doctor out here fast enough. Anyway, Ben was so eager to be a soldier. And that damned war started even before people had healed from the great World War. He had finished high school and was feeling all patriotic and the like. He signed up, and was off in no time. I didn't want him to go. Next thing I know the Army comes calling at this very door—and I was still young enough I could have served in that war—to tell me that Benjamin would not be coming back, and that he served his country honorably, and that he would be honored by a medal for his bravery, and all that shit that they always try and serve you. You know, he did not have a family. He did not wed and have children early as I had. And after Lydia died, I had Ben to care for and my mother Mena came to this house from the Bristol house to look after him. It was just like she was his own mother, although Lydia never liked Mena. She was an Injun girl you see. That was a time, when white folks were taught to despise Injuns, just because they was Injuns. I always had Injuns working here on the farm. Good farm hands. Especially good with the animals. I still hire them when they come around to bring in the harvest. Do all the heavy lifting. They come over from the reservation down by Exeter, or the one up by Shapestown on the opposite bank of the river. Did you know, by the way that your great grandmother, was an Injun princess?"

"Yes, my pa just told me the other day. First I had heard about it."

"Well, I loved my mother very much. And so did Ben when he was growing up. My second wife, I married her in 1946 when Ben was twelve, who was named Phyllis, she was only a little older than Ben when we married, being as she was eighteen. She learned to love Mena, although at first she was also an Injun hater. But that is all beside the point. So since 1953—Mena died in 1958—I have been living in this house without an heir. Neither a son, nor a grandson do I have. And after Phyllis died twelve years ago, well I have no living close relatives who could inherit this place when I pass away. By the way, Phyllis is preparing smothered chicken for dinna. You like that?"

"Oh yes sure. I love smothered chicken and I don't have anyone to prepare such food for me."

"Ordinarily we would eat that for Sunday dinna. Smothered chicken and oysters, with mashed potatoes and chicken pan gravy. But we can't hardly get oysters out here anymore. Especially out of season. So it will just have to do: chicken and gravy on mashed potatoes. If you're not married you should get yourself a housekeeper and cook to take care of you. A negress, she would know how to fix you smothered chicken. I think there are plenty of negro women in Bristol who need the work."

"Yeah, but we don't call them negroes anymore. We call them black women."

"Yeah, maybe, but I'm from another generation and another time. Still those negresses should know how to cook for you real good."

"I'll look into it."

"So as I was saying with no heir, I went to your father, Bob. He's my nephew, son of my younger brother Will Junior. Maybe you knew him?"

"Yeah, Grandpa Will. I knew him. He lived in the second house. I think I was fifteen or sixteen when he died."

"Yep, that was the same time as when I went into Bristol with my second wife, Phyllis. I went to attend my brother's funeral. I think he died prematurely you know. And I stayed at your house with Bob. You remember that?"

"Yes, I clearly remember that. I even remember the funeral. I'm now sorry I did not know my grandfather very well, that I was never very close to him."

"I can understand. Junior went to the World War and he came back with something wrong with him. He never really recovered, he was never himself again. He was always spooked; he was suffering something none of us could fathom. He was never quite right after he came back. And he would withdraw into himself. He heard ringing in his ears all the time apparently, and he said he had frequent repeating nightmares. I think your father, uncle and aunt suffered because of it when they was kids."

"So anyway. I offered to make Bob, your father, my heir, to take this house and farm as his, when I was ready to retire or when I passed away. As he is my closest relative. Well maybe not closest, cepting by distance. Ernie had moved away from the Eastern Shore when he was young, and only later moved back to Yarmouth. So I didn't know my oldest nephew at all. Anyway I always liked Bob. Square guy, solid as a rock. But he turned down my offer. Said he did not want to be a farmer. That with a young family it was too big a risk to take over and run a farm for his primary livelihood. I understood. Still do. Now of course, he's too old to want this farm. It's too much work and worry for someone who is retirement age. So I did not give him the farm, and I did not write him into my will to inherit it when I pass away."

"So have you decided to sell the place, now?" asked Will. "Is that what we're going to talk about today?"

"You're jumping ahead of me, young man. I know you're a real estate broker and that you've sold some of the farms that have been put up for sale around the county in recent years. People, I should say, the younger generation and offspring of farmers, don't want to be farmers anymore. They don't want to work so hard, at least not at something that is so open to risk and circumstances beyond anyone's control. But farming here on the Eastern Shore is still quite profitable. We still produce a lot and export it from the region. Even in bad years, we clear a profit. And you know ever since I switched over to growing soybeans, almost forty years ago, all I've seen is growth and more growth. The chicken farms in this county and Wicomico have grown five-fold and demand for feed just continues growing. And the profits have grown year on year steadily. Even in years with bad harvests or weather events. And even while costs have continued to rise."

"Will, I asked you out here not to get your brokerage services or advice, but to ask if you would consider being my inheritor of this farm. I want to leave it to you, if you are willing to carry on farming it. I know this is unexpected and that you have not prepared yourself to go into agriculture as a career. But I think this is the correct decision for the farm and for you as well."

Will had stopped listening. He was completely floored by Hampton's offer, and was left speechless. It was so totally unexpected. His mind was spinning. This farm he understood was a big business, and one that could be developed even further. He had no idea how to react. He had never ever given a moment's thought to farming as something for him.

"So Will I can see you that you're surprised. I don't need your answer straight away. At least not before dessert. That's a joke, Will. I know you'll have to think it over and you'll need to ask many questions. And that everything about my proposition probably seems very foreign to you."

"You're right, Uncle Hampt, I don't know what to say."

"But you're not saying 'no' straight out. That's a good sign. I find it encouraging. I would much rather leave the farm, as a going concern, to one of my kin, than to sell it to someone who won't farm it. That's what's happened to so many of the farms around here that have been sold in recent years. But maybe those farms were too small, or unprofitable because they were poorly run."

"Since you called me, Hampt, and on my way out here, I was trying to figure out how much this farm could sell for in today's market. I was thinking, it should fetch two, two and a half million. But I could only imagine that other farmers would be buyers. You're too far off the main road for property developers to be interested."

"Yeah, well. It could be that other farmers here in the county would want to buy it. But I think they would need to pay more than that. I myself have enough money to buy this farm at such a price. In the past ten years, revenues have been around a million dollars each year. So I think it is worth more than what you said. Of course profits would be lower if the farm was run by an outside farm management team. But it would still be quite profitable. I expect you might even want to run this farm using an outsider manager and his team. If you were to take it as yours, that is. And by the way, I have already put it in my will that my savings will go to your father, your uncle Ernest, and your Aunt May. That will make them very comfortable for the rest of their lives."

Will was wondering how much money Hampton was talking about, but he did not want to ask. It seemed that Hampton had at least two and a half million dollars in savings and investments, because he had said so in so many words. Will would not have that kind of savings, at the rate he was earning and saving, even if he carried on at the same rate as he had been the past six years until he was eighty-two. Not even close.

"But I have not designated you as my heir for the farm yet, because I thought it was important to consult with you first. Do you have any questions you'd like to ask me right away, so you can go home and sleep on the idea?"

"I don't even know where to start. I mean, I assume that this is a pretty complicated business isn't it? This place works only on pretty big yearly lines of credit, am I right?"

"Yes, you're right. But then again I have simplified the business. I grow only two crops, corn and soybeans. I don't do any marketing. What I raise and harvest on this farm pretty much sells itself. The processors come to me. Demand is growing. As for financing, that's not difficult either. The banks seek my business. They practically are throwing money my way. Since I stopped the heavy lifting of farming about eight years ago. I've been managing the farm and rely on a few hired farmers to do 'most all of the work. And I hire laborers to bring in the harvest. I don't raise livestock—I mean I have some chickens and I could if I wanted to raise rabbits. But no vegetable gardening. I have my own silos and loading equipment, but I don't do contract storage. Not my business. The workers I hire are the local Injuns. I don't mess with temporary migrant laborers from Mexico or El Salvador. Too much bureaucratic hassle. Taxes are simple and straightforward and insurance is not complicated either. I don't play in futures for corn or soybeans—that's not really insurance. It's gambling. betting against the future, which you can't really know even two days in advance."

"Where do these local Indians come from that you hire?"

"Oh, some come from the same village my mother, Mena, came from and others come from a reservation across the river near Shapp's Landing. But I never need more than twenty laborers in a season. Rarely more than four at any given moment."

"Do you happen to know the name of Mena's village?"

"Yes, sure. It's called Wicomico. Just like the county next door. My mother grew up there as a girl and lived there until she married my dad."

"Wicomico? I ran into Wicomico, the village I mean, just a week or so ago. Do you mind if I ask you some things about your mother, my great grandmother?"

"No, not at all. I interviewed her several times before she died and I've collected everything I could find out about her and her life. I didn't know my dad because he died of the Spanish flu when I was only four so I hardly had any memories of him. Everything I know about him I had to ask my mother. It was surprising, though how little she knew about him, even though they were married. But they hadn't been married even six years, when the Spanish flu came through and took away dad. I understood from her that she miscarried their fourth child, because she had the flu as well. She herself very nearly died from it."

Phyllis came in, cleared away the dishes. And asked if anyone wanted dessert. Hampton said, "I recommend it. Lemon meringue pie. Phyllis makes a good lemon pie for sure." She brought two pieces and set down a small piece for Hampton and a very big piece for Will. "Now anyone for coffee too?" she asked.

"So Mena was really an Indian?"

"Yeah, of course. Dark skinned, copper colored skin, kind of like the color of a reddish brown mulatto,--but not at all looking like a negro-- beautiful long straight black hair. Deep dark greenish eyes, high cheek bones, a little almost oriental looking. And her voice was magic, so limpid. You know, they met, my dad and her, during an attempted robbery on one of the stores my grandpa owned. The mulatto who committed this also murdered her mother, my grandmother in front of the eyes of ma. Both of them, ma and grandma, were purebred Injuns, Nanticokes. I have newspaper clipping about the robbery and murder. Seems my dad saved Mena, who was eighteen at the time, also from being murdered. He was the gallant knight who rescued my ma. I have the newspaper clipping about the mulatto's hanging. That was his sentence. He was a twisted person, no doubt. And another thing about my dad's—he was named William Senior—marriage. Seems the people at that time were scandalized that Will married an Injun woman, a darkie as they called her. They were married in Bristol and first lived in one of the houses my grandfather built there. I can show you these clippings. They're upstairs in my office. I have some photos too. But they are very few."

"My dad told me only the other day that Mena was illiterate. Is that right?"

"He told you right. She could not read or write her whole life. But then she didn't get any schooling in her day. Injuns didn't get to go to school back then. But she was real good in calculating, and figuring numbers. She had a natural head for business. And she really liked Bob when he was small."

"How then did Will Senior end up marrying her?"

"Will, I don't honestly know. I could never figure it out. The mysteries of love, I suppose. She was young and very pretty. You know, all she told me is that he rescued her from that murderer. So he was her hero. And as she grew older she grew more and more fond of him.

In her memory of him he became like a god to her. But that doesn't explain why he would have wanted to marry her. Against the social ostracism and disapproval. As I said, my dad is a complete mystery to me. After his death, my brother and sister and I with mother left Bristol and came to live with my grandfather, old man Robert, or Bob Senior, in this very house. He took care of us and looked after us for fourteen years, until he died. I was almost 18 when grandfather died. My mother really loved him too. But I can't say that Grandpa loved her. He felt obliged to take care of her, but he resented her. He always said that it was good that none of us kids looked like Injuns. Everything would turn out alright, because we didn't look like Injuns. And you know he was right, of course. Our lives would have been ruined if we looked like we's Injuns. We certainly weren't raised like Injuns."

"So you say that Mena and great grandpa had four kids together?"

"No. Me, your grandfather--Will Junior-- and your great aunt Anne, only three. Born-- bang bang bang-- each 16 months apart. I was born nine months after Mena and my grandpa married. So they were bumptious in bed from the git go. And then she had the miscarriage. So yes, that was four pregnancies in little more than five years."

"When did great grandpa die?"

"My father died of the Spanish flu. And the date was early in 1920, just after New Years. I have the exact date upstairs. Everything indicates that. There were a large number of cases on the Eastern Shore around that time for some reason. Later than the flu elsewhere. But the doctor said the cause of death was pneumonia. That was like lots of the victims. A lot of the Injuns died from the same disease at that time. Their death rate was much higher than white folks who got the flu. They seemed to have no immunity at all. So Will Senior's grave is out back in the family burial plot, next to that of his father's who of course lived another 14 years. You want to see it?"

"Sure, after the big meal, it would be good to take a stroll."

"And I can show you some more of the farm at the same time."

Hampton got up slowly from the table and started for the door. He picked up a walking stick next to the door and directed Will out to the porch.

"Now if you can give me a hand down the stairs that would help." Will took hold of him under his shoulders and supported him slowly down the five steps. "Thanks. The stairs in this house are my biggest headache." And then Hamp quickly moved off to the left of the house, using his stick more to point things out than to support his step. "In that barn you see the tractor. It's only eight years old. And the harvester. You see over there the silos. This barn was the stables, but I haven't kept horses for almost sixty years. Too expensive and time consuming. Now come this way." He shuffled on behind the barns and moved about fifty yards further to a stand of two horse chestnut trees. And there they came upon a number of grave stones. The stones were standing vertically and were uniformly gray polished granite, with gradations of aging and discoloration. Hampton stopped in front of one standing off to the right. Will could barely make it out, but it was the gravestone of Lydia. He noted the dates, and saw that the gilding that had been painted in the incised lettering was mostly missing. He looked at Hampton and saw that he was crying. Next to Lydia's to the right was the stone of Benjamin, and to the left was a large stone with the names of William and Willamena Driggers Eames inscribed on it. Will walked along the line of gravestones, noting the dates of birth and death of each commemorated person. There was the stone of Robert Celestine, Will Senior's father, the most deteriorated, inscribed with only the year of death, 1934. It was inscribed also with the name of his wife, Harriet. Will was surprised to notice that Harriet lived for 103 years, dying only in 1968. There were also the stones for Phyllis, William Junior, Hampton's younger brother and Will's grandfather, and another for Anna Eames Bungins, Hampton's younger sister, who had died a widow in 1970. Will saw that all the stones were coated in a light layer of dust, and he could not help thinking about the ritual phrase, 'from dust to dust' which was so visibly demonstrated before his eyes there.

"This is the family collection." said Hampton, wiping away a last tear from his cheek. "I had every one of these stones carved, incised and the letters gilded, and put in place, from my grandfather's to Phyllis's. I have even had my own incised. Although I am not so prescient as to put my death date on it yet. That is my grave site." He pointed to an empty spot next to the large stone of his parents. "It would be a shame to let this farm leave family ownership. We'd lose this private graveyard."

Will agreed with his uncle with a nod of his head. He had never before given much thought to family heritage and ancestral graves. He had never actually attended a funeral of any of his relatives.

"Well, come on. This is I suppose all rather morbid for you." They walked slowly back to the house. After getting only half way, Hampton stopped and pondered out loud. "You know, you get to a certain age, and you realize that death is your next destination and last remaining accomplishment. And suddenly you find yourself thinking about that all the time. And when the doctor tells you that you have a terminal case of cancer you at once become very aware that time's up. The clock is ticking its final notes for you. You have to make all your final arrangements, and you have a deadline. You see, my doctor told me that I have a very advanced prostate cancer and might not live out this year. Certainly will not survive the next. I don't feel much pain from it. But the doctor promised me all kinds of final throes."

They reached the porch and Hampton motioned to Will to sit while he excused himself to go inside. Will sat and thought about his family. He did not know anything about his ancestors and he hadn't started a family of his own so he too had no heirs. He had not thought about the Eames or where they came from since he had been a little boy. He remembered that his father telling him once that the Eames family had come to the Eastern Shore and begun farming around 1700, but he realized that he had never seen any evidence of that. He also did not know anything about his great aunt, Anna, except what he had just seen on the gravestone. It was all so distant from him.

When Hampton came back to the porch, Will asked him to tell him something about Anna. "God bless her, Anna, was a sweetheart. She took all the tenderness and loving affection from our mother. She was also quiet and gentle, like mom. But she made a mistake and married the wrong man. A man named Max Bungins, from Bawlimore. He was a grain trader who came once to the farm and swept her off her feet, as the saying goes. I think he seduced her and got her with child. But credit to him, he married her once they found out that she was pregnant. She was seventeen, and he was about twice her age, and even though he was a Catholic, he was already divorced. After they married they went off to Bawlimore and I rarely saw her after that, until she came back that is. Anna had three children. And they looked like little Injuns, like Mena. Dark, bronzed skin, black straight hair. Everyone assumed they were mulattos, being as they lived in Bawlimore where there are so many negroes. Bungins of course assumed that he had been cuckolded, and I was told he detested them. I don't know what became of them, my nephews and niece from Anna's marriage. They have all moved on and disappeared in the great current of life. I suppose they might even be dead by now. Bungins made a lot of money during the war, because he traded in foodstuffs, and the govment was buying. But he didn't get rich because he liked to gamble and drink and he left them when the kids were still youngsters. No one knows for sure when he died. I think I met them once during the war, on a visit to Bawlimore. But he died after Anna's children had all left the home, and he left Anna the house and very little money. So in 1956 or 57 Anna sold her house and came back here and lived with us. She died in 1970 from one of those women's diseases that come on suddenly and kill quickly. One day she was ruddy with health and the next she was dying, and then gone. Her children did not come for her funeral. I didn't know how to find them. They had not kept in touch with their mother after she left Bawlimore, so I just don't know what became of them. But I can't think their fate has been very good. I mean they looked like negroes after all. They were raised in a house without a father, and a scarcely educated mother. They were not raised for success in life, you could say. That's all. Anna and Phyllis got along really well, like two childless old maids. I suppose you were too young to ever have met Anna."

The other Phyllis came through the screen door and asked if they would like some ice tea. When she brought the tea, Hampton took one sip. "Will I have to admit that I orta excuse myself and take my afternoon nap. All this talking had drained me. Too much excitement for an old dying man. I usually nap at four o'clock anyway, so today I'm early."

"I'm sorry. Of course, I should let you go, Uncle Hampt." It was just past three o'clock.

"I haven't shown you the collection of materials I have about mom and her Injun ancestry. You'll have to come back another time to look at it. It's upstairs in my library."

"I'll come back soon."

"And you'll have to bring me an answer about the farm and being the designated heir. Sooner rather than later."

Will drove off after he left Hampton, feeling disturbed and unhappy. He noticed a strange twisting flock of starlings flying over the bare fields of the farm, forming abstract patterns in the sky. Two hawks were harrowing them from the sides, wings flapping desperately. He was disappointed that he would not be offering the farm on the market. The fields along the road all the way back to Bristol looked ready for autumn. As he drove he saw in his mind's eye an old Hampton frail and shriveled shuffling along with a walking stick from the graveyard, so unlike the earlier memories he had from sixteen years earlier of a robust, upright, tall man. It was hard not to be moved by the sight of Hampton's deterioration and aging. He needed to talk with his father.

On Friday morning in the office, Will got a call from the probate clerk. "Will, I need to update you on the sale of the parcel of riverside land you put an offer in for. I'm afraid we can't close just yet."

"Oh yeah, why is that?"

"A lawyer came in here the other day and filed a claim for inheritance from twenty five Injuns who claim to be descendants of Pellmell Randall The list is impressive: it says, and I quote you 'on behalf of the descendants of Pellmell Randall of Wicomico on the Nanticoke near Exeter, hereinafter Mr. Randall, Armand Driggers, Hartly Driggers, Matthew Hartly, Jack Coursey, et al, hereinafter the Heirs or Plaintiffs, all of Wicomico, the Plaintiffs claim to the rightful and sole Heirs of Mr. Randall with the right to inherit the river plot which was Mr. Randall's sole property.' And so on. Looks like there may have to be litigation over the parcel. I'm sorry. There is a first hearing scheduled in two weeks here in the county courthouse. Before there can be a trial on this issue, they claimants will have to establish that they are the heirs of Mr. Randall. That will take some time."

"Dammit. Those damn Injuns."

"They're Indians?"

"Yep, and squatters on that parcel of land, too."

"Was Mr. Randall an Injun also?"

"So I was told, by Mr. Armand Driggers." Almost as soon as Will had said this he realized that he had seen on his great grandmother's gravestone at Hampton's graveyard, the same old-fashioned name, Driggers. "In that list of twenty five plaintiffs—that must be the entire population of adults out there—is there the name Randall."

There was a pause on the other end of the line. "Now let's see. No, not a one. Seems he had no direct family descendants. Wait, here's a curious thing though. The lawyer's name is Jackson Rendall of Exeter. I'm not familiar with him."

"Nor I. But that doesn't mean anything. Just a coincidence."

"So, Will. For now there's nothing we can do. The sale is suspended until we have a ruling on inheritors' claims. There'll be a hearing sometime next month."

"I understand. I'll just wait. Thanks for calling with the information."

After he hung up, Will cursed Armand under his breath. 'Damn shifty rat. Just looking at him, you could tell you could not trust him.' And then the thought occurred to him. He might be related to this shifty rat, a distant relative of his great-grandmother, no doubt. A disgrace. Shameful. He hoped no one would find out. But he was certain that the connections were too obscure for anyone to know. Certainly no one at the probate court would connect this Armand Driggers to his great grandmother, whose gravestone was hidden away behind a distant farm. He wouldn't tell anyone that he was part Indian and related to a living Indian who lived as a squatter on the other side of the county. He wouldn't tell his father either. Bob didn't need to know, and anyway he thought his father would likely tell others, because he didn't think it was a disgrace. This past week had been a shock to Will's identity and a wake-up call about his ancestry. Everything was so unexpected. He had learned that he couldn't build a casino on a land parcel which he, it now seemed likely, was unable to buy. And he was an Indian, probably related to those poor, beggarly squatters on that land. He spent the weekend at home, moping around and feeling sorry for himself. Once again, he was thinking that he was a man —thirty years old, almost middle aged--with no prospects, no aim in life, no family of his own, no future.

His father called him on the land line on Sunday afternoon. "Hey, you've gone silent over the last several days. Are you depressed again? Can you come for dinner tonight? Your parents would like to hear from you." Will agreed. He was hungry. He hadn't eaten anything other than a sandwich since Friday night. In his bad mood he just did not feel any appetite for eating or preparing food for himself, and after he made himself a sandwich on Saturday afternoon his fridge stood empty so he could not graze all weekend.

When he arrived, Will was immediately struck by the delicious aromas of roasting meat coming from the kitchen, and he promptly felt famished. "I thought we'd eat indoors tonight." said his mother as she directed him to the dining table. "Sunday roast dinner. I hope you don't mind." Will hardly heard her as he was already snatching some of the hors d'oeuvres off the table and stuffing them into his mouth.

"No, roast beef would be super, mom." Will mumbled through a mouthful of shrimp in a spicy cocktail sauce. "Everything's ready. Bob will you help me bring the food in?" Bob sat at the head of the table and carved the beef roast and served three plates with meat, mashed potatoes, and succotash.

Will tore into the roast beef with redeye sauce and mashed potatoes as if there was no one else at the table, he was so hungry. Bob watched him bemused, although his mother was a little put off by her ravening son. When he asked for second helpings, Bob broke the silence at the table. "Did you have a nice talk with Uncle Hampton?" "Yes, he talked a lot, about our family especially. And he told me a lot about great-grandma Mena. I guess we do have Indian ancestry." Sue put down her fork. "You mean to say, you really are of Indian descent?" she asked. "Yes, Mar-Sue, I've told you, but you've always chosen not to believe me." Will was sopping some of the red-eye gravy with a biscuit. Bob turned to Will. "Undeniably, Injun ancestry. My grandma, Mena, was a wonderful woman. Very canny, and strong, but she loved us so well." Will was still eating, and his mouth was full, so he simply nodded agreement. "Did you see, Uncle Hampton's news clippings and mementos of Mena and Will Senior?" Will swallowed, and cleared his mouth. "No, but I did see the graveyard. And I was rather surprised to see how much Uncle Hampton has shriveled up since I last saw him." "Well, of course. He's eighty two after all. But you said that Hampton called you to talk about a business proposition. What was it, if I might ask?"

Will put down his napkin. "Yeah, he's thinking about how to dispose of his farm and farmhouse after he has passed. And apparently, he is quite ill already. Fears he will die soon and he doesn't have his final arrangements made yet. He wants to leave the farm to me."

"Wonderful. I hope you accepted. This was what he came to talk to me about sixteen years ago. Remember I told you?"

"Yes, and he raised that issue as well. He wanted me to accept being put into his will as his heir, so that the farm would go to me when he dies."

"And did you accept?"

"I haven't accepted. But I haven't declined, either. I actually don't know what to think. I wanted your advice on this subject. Because I am not sure I'm capable of being a farmer, or want to be either."

"Will, I declined Hampton's offer to inherit the farm those many years ago because I was already middle aged, with a young family, and wife. And I did not know how to be a farmer, nor did I want to move there and learn to become one. But I think you should seriously consider taking him up on his offer and agree to be his heir. And run the farm."

"You think so? You think I can become a farmer when you thought you could not?"

"Look, you were not so long ago complaining of being depressed because you had nothing to live for and saw no point in your life, no future goals. Well, this would certainly give you a whole bunch of goals and objectives for your life. It would keep you occupied for the rest of your life, and I think farming could make you very satisfied. I deal with the local farmers every week, and while they all are constantly challenged, they also seem quite content and rewarded in their lives. Their work is very satisfying, even if they face constant risks."

"Hampton did say how rewarding he felt in his life as a farmer."

"Yes, and another thing: you studied business at college. His farm is a big business. You don't have to be a farmer. You can be a business manager of the farm, and hire the farmers. The farm work can be performed by a farmer for hire, and the heavy labor by seasonal workers."

"Like the lord of the estate?"

"Yes, sure. But you don't need to own and manage slaves like our ancestor did in the early nineteenth century."

"Your ancestors were slave owners?" asked Sue somewhat alarmed.

"Yes, Mar Sue, I have also told you that on occasion. But you don't listen to what you don't want to hear from me. I've noticed that over the years."

"You never told me that one of our ancestors owned slaves here." said Will.

"This was slave territory right up to the civil war. And the big farms from early in the seventeenth century—the tobacco plantations—needed labor. But the Injuns wouldn't accept enslavement, or indenture, and they were dying off so fast anyway, so the big tobacco plantation owners brought slaves here on the Eastern Shore. And when a landowner had a big enough farm, he would get slaves to work it. Our ancestors going back at least two hundred years bought some black slaves to work their farm. The Eames family owned most of the eastern and central part of the upper county back then you know. There was no more slave trade after the 1830s here. And they had to free them after the Emancipation Declaration. Why else do you think there are so many blacks in the county now?"

Will shrugged. He had never thought about the black population of the Eastern Shore and their connection to slavery.

"In any event, I am not going to have slaves. As shameful as our family history is. But you know Uncle Hampton says he does hire Injuns from nearby. And apparently they are related to your grandmother."

"I didn't know that. Really? Grandma's Injun relatives?"

"The self-same Injuns I was telling you about on that parcel of land I thought to buy, on the Nanticoke River, cross the county. And he told me he already runs the farm as a business manager, with a hired man to do the farming and run the farm equipment."

"Well, there you go. He does it. So can you. And you probably can carry on using the same farmer for hire that Hampt does now, after he passes—if you should decide to inherit the farm."

"I wonder what the economics of that farm are?" said Will almost half to himself.

"Did you discuss how much corn and how much soy he grows each year?"

"No, we didn't. We didn't get into the specifics of his farming business as such."

"Or how much acreage he plants in corn and how much in soy?"

"I think he said that he plants one third soybeans, and two thirds corn."

"And how many acres did he say he has under cultivation? He probably grows only field corn and no sweet corn. Did he say what kind of corn he grows?"

"I don't recall. He said his farm is 734 acres."

"Well then, I'll bet you he makes more than a million dollars a year just on his corn, going by the bushel price of corn just now, based what we're paying at the plant today. And I think he would make a good deal more on his soybeans, because chicken demand is growing so strong."

"That's impressive."

"Yes. It certainly is. But you should know what the price was of farms sold in the last couple of years in the region. You helped broker some of them, didn't you?"

"Yeah. I was involved in one sale that was a million and a half. And another that was three million. But I don't recall right off how many acres were in those farms, nor what they planted. I'd have to go look it up."

"So there you have it. I'm just a simple manager, and I can figure out that Hamp has got big business in his farm. Looks like that could be your calling in life."

"I suppose so. I'll have to talk with Hamp a little more about the business of running a farm."

"But you'll have to find a wife if you do inherit the place and plan to live out there." his mother intervened. "Someone to be your boon companion, to make a family with, to care for you."

"Mom, you always say the most important things. But they are always the most difficult things to achieve. You don't think I would like to find a woman to love and marry? It's not so easy in little Bristol, you know."

"Maybe. But it'll be even harder to find a mate out in Roseland. But you need to be more open, socialize more."

"Fine. But all of this is a bit premature. I haven't decided to become Uncle Hamp's heir, and I am not anytime in the near future moving out to the farm to live. So we don't need to worry all about these things now. Maybe I need to go out there again soon, and have another long talk with Hamp."

"So you're still considering Hamp's invitation?" said Bob. "That's good. I understand that it is a life-changing, strategic decision. Needs plenty of reflection. That's all understandable. And commendable. But now it's time for dessert."

"Of course, mom, it's going to be even harder for me to find a woman who would want to marry me and can be my wife, and also prepare a roast beef like you just did. I really needed that meal. You cannot know how much I needed it."

"Why thank you Will. I'll fix it more often and invite you over each time."

Will walked back to his house, which was only five long blocks away from his parents'—a long way in the little town of Bristol-- looking at the stars, and thinking about how he still was not making any traction in his career or in guiding his life. Hamp's offer made everything more complicated. Would he have to give up his brokerage business? Would he have to live out at the Eames farmhouse? Where would he find any social life, if he did live out there? He looked up at the stars in the night sky twinkling coldly but they did not provide him any answers. He thought that it was difficult to understand how the ancients so fervently believed that their fates were written in the stars and determined by the movement of the planets. It was clear that there was nothing in the celestial orb that indicated an interest or even an awareness of Will's fate. The stars did not know the future;

certainly not Will's future, but also not their own. And the stars and swirling galaxies did not provide any structures or direction for human lives either.

The next day in the office mail, Will got a wedding invitation, just as Jackson had promised. In two weeks' time, on a Saturday, Jackson was getting wed to MariAnne McCormick Larsen in Ellicott City, near Baltimore, with a wedding party afterwards at the Woodfalls Golf Club and resort. He called Jack with the initial idea of declining the invitation. But Jack was very insistent that Will come. "But I won't know anybody there, except you."

"You might know my best man," said Jack. "He was in our class at high school. And don't worry. MariAnne will set you up with one of her maids of honor. You'll have a great time." So Will decided to go.

In the rest of the month, Will returned to his normal routines; he went into his agency office, reviewed the press and news about real estate developments throughout Delmarva, he bought the Wednesday issue of the Baltimore Sun to read the business section, he shopped for some food to restock his refrigerator and he resumed preparing his own meals and eating them, he went twice a week for lunch at Poseidon's Palace and had his ongoing conversation with Tony. Tony's father hadn't started building the beer brewery in the back yet, saying he would wait until they closed for the end of the warm season. And he was bored once more and depressed, feeling aimless. The entire period of three weeks was unusually dry and warm, so for three weeks every day looked much like the all the previous days. Monotonous. The only noticeable change Will saw was that the weekend traffic through town and on its way to Ocean City or back was somewhat less heavy.

On the designated Saturday of September, Will drove up to Ellicott City Maryland for Jack's wedding. It took an hour and a half. He followed the instructions that came with the invitation and went straight to the golf club resort. There he checked in and changed in his room into his dark grey suit with a bright blue tie. Outside, the day had blossomed into a warm, bright sunny day, Indian summer before all the leaves had begun to turn color. He drove over to the church and went in and joined the other early arrivals. There were some young women, must've been bridesmaids, making final adjustments to the flower arrangements on the ends of each pew. Will sat by himself in the sixth pew back, until an usher came to ask him if he were from the groom's side or the bride's side. He moved to the groom's side after this point of etiquette was pointed out to him. The wedding was conventional; MariAnne in a tight fitting white gown which promoted her sexuality and not her purity or modesty, Jackson in a dark gray formal jacket with tails which made him look like an attendant at the English Royal Races, the happy families, the organ music which included Mendelssohn, the bridesmaids in pink gowns which bared their shoulders and arms and most of their chests. Everything went according to schedule.

Then most of the attendees piled into cars and drove back to the Golf Resort and reassembled in the small ballroom where all the tables had been copiously laid out and decorated with white and pink flowers, candles and crystal. The guests stood around in clusters looking and feeling awkward, most not knowing the others. Families clung together. The maids of honor were standing closely together and in their puffy dresses they looked a bit like rare pink chrysanthemums. Waiters passed through the groups offering either flutes of champagne or salvers bearing canapes of pate or shrimp. Will felt he was the most awkward and isolated, that he stuck out. But the room became animated when the newly-weds arrived. The orchestra struck up some gay tunes, a reception line was formed and people introduced themselves to each other and to the newly-weds, more champagne was passed around, and everything became more frenetic. When Will shook hands with Jack, the latter turned and introduced him to MariAnne, "You see, another friend of mine from high school days, from Bristol." MariAnne purred at him, "Oooh, I'm so glad to meet you Will. Jack's said so much about you. I've paired you with my friend and bridesmaid, Suzy. You're going to love her." The best man was said to be from Bristol High School, but Will neither recognized his face, nor his name, which was Bruce Johnson. Bruce assured Will that he remembered him, but Will could not understand how. He saw in front of him a plump man with a round face who was already going bald and who looked older than Jack and Will by more than ten years. His looks were not even remotely familiar to Will. Jack asked Bruce if he still lived in Bristol. "No, I work in Warshington. There's no work in Bristol."

MariAnne was right about Suzy. They were seated next to each other at the second row of tables back from the main table where Jackson and MariAnne presided over the party. As soon as they were seated, Suzy began to ooze and flirt over Will. She was blond, voluptuous and with smooth white skin shining from her shoulders, bare arms and an ample exposed cleavage. She immediately asked him all sorts of questions about his background, how he knew Jack, what he did for work, what life was like in Bristol, where he went to university, what he liked to do in his spare time. "And you know, Jack has really caught a special one in MariAnne. She's from the McCormick family, you know. The Baltimore spice family. Her family is rich. She's been my best friend since high school. We went to St. Anne's Girls Academy, very prestigious. And then to St. Mary's College together. I work now in Philadelphia." They both drank up a full flute of champagne together for the first toast to the newly-weds. Will thought it was too cold and very sharp, almost sour. But it was refreshing and he drank it down fast. And he took a second one as soon as it was offered, as did Suzy. And they also drank these down quickly after Bruce made the second toast to Jack and MariAnne and to their future in making many children together. "Oh that's so nice," cooed Suzy. "I want to have many children when I get married." "So you're not married yet?" asked Will.

"No, MariAnne and I used to go shopping for guys at the Naval Academy on big weekends when we were at St. Mary's. But I haven't found the right guy yet. Or he hasn't found me yet, I'd better say. MariAnne told me you're not married, right?"

Dinner was served in several courses, ending with a very flavorful roast filet mignon with a Yorkshire pudding and mushroom gravy on the side. Everything was delicious and Will ate heartily. The waiters filled their wine glasses with red wine and refilled Will's at the meat course. Suzy continued talking to Will, totally ignoring her neighbor on the other side. The room seemed to grow warmer all through the feast, and Suzy looked ever more beautiful and sexy to Will. "How old are you Will?" she finally asked. "I'll be thirty soon." "I'm only twenty-four, but I'll be twenty five in December. Going to have a big birthday party for my twenty-fifth." And she giggled. As the dinner plates were cleared away, Bruce stood up and announced that it was time for the bride and groom to have their wedding kiss. Loud cheers broke out from the guests as they stood. Jack and MariAnne stood up, a little embarrassed, and then enthusiastically embraced and engaged in a long, full mouth kiss. The cheering grew louder and some even made catcalls and loud whistles, as if they were at a basketball game. Then Bruce continued, "And now to show the promise of our love, everyone kiss their loved one next to them." More cheers, and a little embarrassed shuffling, husbands and wives, friends and their boyfriends or girlfriends, mothers and fathers, aunts and uncles in various stages of passion or decorum or awkwardness embraced and began to kiss. Bruce's wife ran up from one of the tables and kissed Bruce. Jack and MariAnne very passionately kissed again, Jack caressing her satin covered shapely bottom. But Will didn't notice as he and Suzy were enthusiastically embracing and also kissing passionately, full mouth and tongues together. It had been a long time since he had felt a voluptuous woman's soft body against his and he didn't want the warm sensation to end. The sensation was like an electric shock running through him. But the group kissing of love did come to an end and the guests left off their embraces and began to applaud, and Jack and MariAnne gradually pulled apart. Bruce's wife, who was not sitting next to him at the front table, rushed back to her seat.

Bruce continued his role as party animator. "And now it's time for the newly-wed couple to have the first dance. Of course we all know that they undoubted have danced together before—maybe even coupled before--but not as a married couple. So Maestro, please strike up the band." In fact it was a small jazz orchestra. They began to play a famous Frank Sinatra love ballad, "little did we know love was just a dance away, a warm embracing dance away." Jack and MariAnne stepped away from the front table and went down to the open space in front of the orchestra and began to sway and dance slowly together. After that tune, played with several repeated versions, again the other guests applauded. Bruce then shouted into the microphone he had, "Now everyone. Time to dance. Everybody, get down and dirty, and dance, dance, dance!" Will could not imagine that Bruce could get down and dirty. He thought that Bruce must be a bookkeeper or maybe even an actuary.

Will turned to Suzy, "Would you like to dance with me?"

"I thought you'd never ask," said Suzy and she jumped up from the table and grabbed him by the hand and dragged him to the dance floor. Suzy was smiling from ear to ear. Will was feeling more and more aroused. She really was very attractive. He hadn't enjoyed himself in the company of a woman like this in a long time, not even with Karen.

The orchestra now started to play popular dance songs with driving familiar rhythms and minimal words or reason. The temperature in the room quickly rose as twenty three pairs of adults and children began dancing with wild and frenzied and bouncing movements. Will's eyes were fixed on Suzy's bouncing breasts. He couldn't help it, they were so prominent. She was shorter than him by a good deal, and her dress did not have shoulder straps so she revealed a very big cleavage. He almost expected that her breasts would both jump out of their pink halter at any moment. But they were too well strapped in. He imagined that she had big rounded breasts and his fingers itched to fondle them. Some of the guests sat back down after three songs when the orchestra changed the pace from rock and rollicking to a slow waltzing type song. And without a word, Will and Suzy fell together embracing closely and began slowly swaying with the calmer music. They continued to dance, rapid pulsating rocking songs alternating with slow songs for hugging and close caressing through the next twenty five minutes together until most of the other guests had sat down again. Then Bruce's wife again ran away from him and he bounced up to the microphone. "Sorry to interrupt the fun. But now it's time to cut the wedding cake!" The dance floor cleared. Suzy plopped down in her seat pulling Will along with her. "Of that was so much fun. You're a really good dancer, Will!" "Really?" he said in surprise. Now he was uncontrollably smiling. "You must have lots of experience." she chirped. "No, I can't say that I do. And it's been years since the last time I danced like we have tonight. You make a good partner too." This answer was almost more than Suzy could have expected, and she blushed, but was tickled from head to toe.

Waiters rolled out a big, six-layer cake with white icing, which was decorated with pink and blue florettes. And then came the posed photo shot of MariAnne-- with a very long knife in her hands, Jack's arms around her as if to support her—cutting the first piece. The wedding photographer stopped them several times and shifted back and forth in front of them getting a seemingly endless series of photographs. Finally when the photographer said he was finished they cut the first piece put it on their plate and retreated to the front table again. The waiters then began to carve up the cake and serve pieces to the other guests. Other waiters went around the tables offering more champagne or white wine in the newly set clean wine glasses. Will and Suzy both took some champagne, and clinked their glasses together before sitting down and waiting for their portions of cake. They had drunk half of their flutes before they got their cake. As they were eating the light and lemony cake, a waiter came by and without even asking 'wine or champagne?' he refilled their glasses with champagne. Will and Suzy's hands were now touching each other often, under and by the table. In the meanwhile a young black woman in a bright red tight fitting satin dress—red that matched her lipstick and gloss—came out and standing like a vamp in front of the orchestra began singing a series of jazz classics into a microphone. Her voice was powerful and clear and she belted out some standards by Ella Fitzgerald and some by Tina Turner, all of them roiling with sexual undertones. "I really adore that song. What about you Will?" "Yeah, me too, I used to listen to it all the time at college." The band asked if there were any requests. Someone shouted out, "'Please release me' by Tom Jones." But others shouted their objections: that was not a wedding song at all. That was a divorce song, totally unfit for a wedding party, thought Will. Will finished his second champagne of the dessert course and he looked around wanting a second piece of cake. After the cake course, coffee and tea was brought out and served. And then the young black woman finished her set of songs and walked off as the orchestra began to play dancing music again. People already finished with dessert got up and the dancing started again. Jackets and even ties came off the men and the children started to dance amongst the adults. As soon as Will finished his coffee, he signaled with his head to Suzy as if to say, 'Some more dancing?' and she eagerly accepted. They danced until they were both hot and wet with sweat. He also had taken off his jacket. From somewhere Suzy had somehow changed from pink high heels to black flats and she danced like a flapper. There were intervals. The orchestra took a break after twenty five minutes and everyone sat down again. Will was feeling the effects of the wine. He was beginning to think more and more, 'She wants it.' and he looked forward to a passionate climax to the party. More coffee and tea was brought out, and the waiters offered cold drinks and liqueurs as well. Will took a brandy, and Suzy with only a little hesitation asked for a Grand Marnier. "Not too strong," she said tipsily. They were both drunk and madly in love, in love with the moment, and with each other's bodies. Will was covered in sweat and his head was unclear. But he remained focused on Suzy: her beautiful face, lively eyes, and her heaving breasts now clearly pearly with sweat. When the orchestra started again, they went back to the dance floor, now with fewer guests dancing. Sometime in the next forty minutes the bride and groom snuck out of the room. Bruce was collapsed in his chair, his wife now next to him trying to restore him. Several other men were passed out drunk at the guests' tables. At the end of a set of slow dances, embraced close and tight together, Will gave Suzy another deep kiss. She went along with the kiss, desperately wanting just that. The party was winding down and the sun was now low in the sky filling the ballroom with long shadows and blinding glare in places. She was now clinging to him, and in the slow songs they were both caressing each other everywhere.

It was after six thirty when Jack and MariAnne came back to the room. They had washed and changed into more casual and comfortable clothes. The waiters were still serving champagne which now tasted exceptionally good to Will. There was the last ritual to perform before putting an end to the wedding party. And that was the assembly of the bridesmaids, including Suzy, and other teenaged and even pre-pubescent girls in front of MariAnne for the catching of the cast off bridal bouquet. MariAnne turned around and tossed it over her shoulder. And of course Suzy caught it and all the girls, Suzy the loudest, squealed with excitement. Then the newlyweds left and the party wound down.

"Do you have to run off, Suzy? Care to come up to my room?"

"Uh huh. Would care to." And they went arm in arm to the elevator with a few other guests, Will with the jacket over his other arm, and Suzy with the bridal bouquet in her other arm and a thin white sweater that Will had not noticed at any time earlier in the day.

It was only a matter of a few minutes before they were undressed and groping and kissing and caressing each other. He feasted his eyes on her curvaceous white body. And then they were in the bed, and then thrashing, making love, Will on top of her. Will was in ecstasy. Suzy seemed to be not far behind. She came in a noisy orgasm shortly before Will did, and released from a full day of seduction and rising excitement, she promptly fell into a deep asleep. Will followed her only moments later in a drunken stupor completely unaware of his whereabouts.

He awoke some hours later, dry and in desperate need of urination. It was fully dark outside. Suzy did not move but she was breathing noisily. He looked at her curvaceous body and finally caressed her breasts and her thighs. Her pubic hair suggested she was not a blond. But Will was still clouded in his mind and after drinking some water, he fell back asleep also. He felt heavy and greatly relieved as if he had recovered from a marathon race. Blindingly bright sunlight entering the room woke them both up around six the next morning. Suzy sat up, pulling the sheet over her breasts-- just like the heroines in the movies always do--looking around the room, briefly at Will, and then she hopped out of bed and began collecting the pieces of clothing and her dress from the floor. With the sheet trailing behind her and her clothes in one arm she ran into the bathroom and closed the door. Will was left with only the blanket to cover himself and he took another drink of water and closed his eyes again. Suzy spent almost thirty minutes in the bathroom. In his hazy mind he could hear the shower running and then the hair dryer's wheeze. When she finally came out she was wearing her pink satin dress and her white cashmere sweater, buttoned up. She sheepishly grinned toward Will. And then headed for the door. "So, it was great. Good-bye Will." Before he could react or even get out of bed she had opened the door and she was gone. He wanted to shout, "Wait!" but he didn't. His mouth was too dry and nothing came out. And he did not want to cause a scene or draw attention to Suzy. He went to the bathroom and relieved himself and then pulling the curtains closed he fell asleep again for another hour. Finally he hurriedly showered and got dressed in his street clothes. He didn't know where to go, but he wanted to find Suzy and talk to her, and hold her, and even to kiss her again. He went down to the reception desk. They said they could not give him her room number, but the operator could call her room. But then he realized he didn't know her family name. Maybe MariAnne had said it when she introduced the two, but in his state of hung over stupor he couldn't remember it. So the operator couldn't connect him. He returned to the receptionist. "Did a blond woman, named Suzy, from yesterday's wedding party, leave the hotel just recently?" "You mean the short woman in a pink formal dress?" the receptionist almost seemed to wink at him. "Yes, she left about an hour ago. In a taxi." "Could you tell me her family name?" "No, I'm afraid not." Will couldn't believe it. He thought they had both fallen in love. Had she seduced him and then discovered this morning that she had been wearing 'beer goggles' all day yesterday? Did she not like their act of passion in the bed? Was that it? Just a one-night stand? Was he part of the wedding entertainment for Suzy, and now that was finished? He was totally perplexed and upset. She was so nice, so attractive, and seemed to be so attracted to him. How could she have run off without so much as a good bye and I'm sorry? After breakfast and packing up it was still early when he drove back to Bristol. He was desolated. And he had a hangover and head ache like he had never had before in his life. As the day was ending he began to think how he could find Suzy again. He wanted her badly, and could not believe that she had dumped him over just a one night stand. He'd have to call Jack, or better MariAnne, after they got back from their honeymoon. Maybe MariAnne would give him Suzy's phone number, and her last name too.

Back in Bristol in the last days of September, just as the weather turned much cooler, Will decided he would talk again with Uncle Hampton about the farm and about how it was run. He phoned him in the early evening to make sure that he did not interrupt Hampton's nap or meal times.

"Yeah, hey Will. I'm glad to hear from you. Do you have an answer for me?"

"I'm getting there. In my mind, I still have to get over some issues before I can agree to your proposal. But that's what I would like to talk to you about. When can I come out and talk with you further?"

"Oh, this is a good time. We're doing the corn harvest just now. So why don't you come out tomorrow for lunch and you can stay the day to watch how the corn harvest is run. We will still have a third of the corn to bring in. The combine is here. Busy working now, as we speak."

Will agreed. The next day was a Thursday, and there was nothing on his calendar that required him to be in the office in Bristol. He went into his office that morning, and looked at the mail. His favorite monthly journal, Real Estate Finance, had arrived, but he did not unseal it. Instead he tossed it on a pile of other journals that he would look at the next day. He drove out to Hampton's farm the next day at noon and they met again on the porch.

"When I came out here earlier this month, Uncle Hampt, I had thought all of your fields were already cleared. But you said last night that you're bringing in the corn harvest."

"Yes that's right, but you saw only the soy fields which had been earlier harvested, cleared and harrowed. The corn fields lie further off the road and you probably did not recognize them. And as usual we harvest dent corn only after they have spent a long time standing on their stalking, drying in the field. So that is usually not earlier than mid or late September, sometimes in October. We've had ideal weather for drying the corn in the field this year."

Phyllis brought in lunch of baked sea bass and French fries. Will again wondered where the fish came from, as it was still not the season for sea bass, and Phyllis must have bought the fish in the grocery store in Bristol.

"So, Uncle Hampt, how did you come to get the farm?"

"I inherited it from my grandfather, Robert, when he died. But I had already been working on the farm since I was a teenager. After father died in 1920, I lived here with my mother Mena, my brother and my sister, Anna. We had moved back here from the house in Bristol. So I basically grew up a farmer. Started working on the farm when I was thirteen or so. Did a lot of the work, especially after Grandpa Robert became too old to do much of the heavy work. I inherited the farm in 1934, when he died. I was eighteen years old. I remember it as if it were only yesterday."

"And you inherited this same farm, namely 734 acres?"

"No it was larger when I inherited it. But it was the Depression and banks could not give credit. Several here on the peninsula even failed. Prices for crops fell through the floor. It was an awful time. So I had to sell 65 acres. Sold it to a man whose farm only three years later failed."

"You said that your father died of Spanish Flu. Do you know anything about that?"

"It's all rather strange. He died suddenly on the second of January 1920. While our family was living in Bristol. The public records do not report anything 'bout an outbreak of Spanish flu in late 1919 in the Eastern Shore. But Mena told me he fell sick around Christmas with flu like symptoms. And although he was a robust man, he died within a week. There were no doctors to help him. She also contracted the illness about the time that Will died. And the press did not report about it, but she told me that there were many others in Bristol who caught the same disease at that time. Especially amongst her Injun folks. She was pregnant at the time and she miscarried the child because of the fevers, not long after Will had died. It was a horrible time. I remember the fear in our family, and I was only four or so years old, my siblings were still infants. I think we all were lucky to even survive. Grandpa Robert and his wife, Harriet, were our saviors. I learned later that no one ever proved that it was Spanish flu that did in our father, but everything I learned pointed in that direction. I have found a press report about the few deaths from a flu-like disease, which doctors called bloody pneumonia, which occurred around the end of 1919 in Bristol. But it does not provide much information really, just that eight people died, including my father and ironically one of the only two doctors in the town at that time. It was a time, after the main waves of the Spanish flu, when everyone was inclined to lie about any further occurrences. Hell, all through that year, everyone was lying in public about the fatal illness of President Wilson, and the devastation of the Spanish flu."

"Do you remember what your father looked like?"

"Sometimes. I have a few memories of being with him. He was slender and it seems to me that he was tall. But then I was not only a little over four years old when he died."

After they finished eating, Hampton called Phyllis and asked her to drive them in the Chevy over to the cornfields to watch Max running the combine. Phyllis cleared everything away and took off her apron, changed into some flat shoes and a windbreaker. She took a jacket out of the closet for Hampton, handing him his stick at the same time, and all three walked out to the porch, down the stairs and over to the car. She very solicitously seated Hampton in the front passenger seat and then got in behind the wheel. She drove over a dirt hard-packed track which was bumpy and bounced and jostled the passengers as she headed the car to the east toward the river. The cornfields started about 400 yards east of the house and as she steered the car closer Will could see that a good part of the cornfield had been already cleared. In front of them in a big cloud of dust and corn stalk litter was the combine with its ominous crab like arms sticking forward, crawling slowly through the upright crisp yellow-brown corn stalks. They scooped up four rows of corn stalks at a time. In the cab was a man wearing a green baseball cap, safety glasses and headphones. "Drive along next to him, Phyllis. And honk the horn to get his attention. But don't get too close." Phyllis did just as she was instructed, seeming very familiar with the routine. She stopped the car, when Max stopped the machine. Immediately the noise level from all the whirring blades inside the machine, which Will had just come to feel even inside the car, fell off and the dust the combine kicked up began to settle. Max climbed out of the cab and jumped down, taking off his headphones as he approached the car. Again Phyllis jumped out and carefully helped Hampton out of his seat.

"Hey Max, you're making good progress so far today." shouted Hampton. "I'd like you to meet my grand-nephew. I think that's what you call the son of your nephew. Will Eames. Will, this is Max Turner. He's our professional farmer. He's from over by Sharpestown." Will saw a strong, weathered man who looked like he could be forty or fifty five, hints of white hair sticking from beneath his cap. He had a very strong handshake.

"Pleased to meet you, Will. Come out to see how the farm works here?"

"Yes, you could say that. I don't know anything about farming. And frankly when I came out here three weeks ago, I thought everything had already been harvested."

"No, then it was just the soybeans thad been harvested at that time. This here is dent corn. We leave it on the stalk for five to six weeks to dry after it's ripe and mature. You might be familiar with sweet corn which is harvested while the stalks and husks are still green. In the mid-summer. For dent corn, the plants remain in the field until they're dried through. I mean all these stalks look dead and yellowy paper, don't they?"

"I know nothing about farming or growing corn, even though I've lived all my life surrounded by all these corn fields. Never even heard of dent corn before."

"It's sometimes called field corn. Used for feed or making fuel. Look there at the stalks. Usually one or two ears of corn per stalk, unlike sweet corn, which might have six or more ears. Corn which you see peddled in all the roadside farm stands all up and down Highway 50."

Hampton cut in, "I don't grow any sweet corn. Haven't done so in many years. It's not very profitable, and it's hard to sell to market."

"You want me to tell Will how a combine works?" asked Max.

"No, Max. That'll be fine without that detail. But maybe if you could answer any of the questions that Will has just now."

"I do have a question or two. Is this combine yours, Hampton?"

"No it is rented for the harvest season only." said Max. "It comes from a farm equipment dealer up in Hurleyville, north of here. When it's driven down here, it backs up all the roads. It's rather funny to see the drivers' reactions and irritation. You can imagine such a big machine drives really slow. And no one can pass it, it's so wide."

"How many acres are planted in corn? And how long does it take to harvest it with this machine?"

"There are seventy acres planted in corn. Think of that as seventy football fields. It takes four or five days to harvest."

"I see corn cobs lying around on the ground. So this machine also shucks and cleans the cobs?"

"Yes, but we call it shelling the corn."

"So where do you take the corn to?"

"We bring in some trucks and we carry it to an elevator in Laurel, in Delaware. They buy our corn and sell it on to different users."

"What's the yield like on these fields?"

"In the past couple of years we've been getting about a hundred and forty bushels per acre. But that can change depending on September's weather. Sometimes we get only a hundred and ten bushels."

"I've always thought of a bushel as a type of basket with ears of corn in it. It's not like that, I guess, now that I can see bare cobs all over the field here."

"No, nowadays a bushel is a unit of weight. Think of a bushel as fifty six pounds of dried corn kernels. Kinda strange, but everyone works with that unit now, not metric, not volumetric. This combine harvester, gathers, husks the ears—that is shells the corn-- and removes the kernels from the cobs. That's why it's called a combine."

"Sure. Thanks, Max. How long have you been working with Hampton as chief farmer?"

"I think this is my sixth year."

"Is it a lot of work?"

"Yeah, sure it is, but the corn is easier to work than the soybeans. They take real effort. But I need to get back to this to clear several more acres before it gets dark. And I still have to load up one more truck. So if you'll 'scuse me."

Max shook Will's hand again and climbed back up into the cab, starting up the engine and the blades. The noise was piercing and deafening, whining blades inside the machine. 'No wonder he wears those headphones.' thought Will. They got back in the Chevy and Phyllis drove them slowly back to the farm house. Will thought that Max was a solid, honest man, and he liked him from the moment he first started speaking. He would hope to rely on him if he inherited the farm.

"How did Max come to work with you? Doesn't he have a farm of his own to work?"

"No. Max grew up on a farm in Wicomico County, across the river. He worked the farm with his father and brother from a very young age. He went to the college of agricultural sciences at the university. But the farm went to his older brother when their father died, so he's been a contractor farmer for the last fifteen years or so. He may not look like it, but he's only forty two. He came to me highly recommended by the state extension service. He worked on some of the university research farms in Caroline County north of here. He knows his stuff. Even vegetable farming. He's done it all. Well, maybe not animal husbandry or dairy farming, but everything else yes."

"So how many acres do you have planted in soybeans, Uncle?

"Let's see. Last year was two hundred and twenty acres. This year, if my memory serves me right, somewhat less."

"But I thought you said you had three hundred and thirty six acres. What's the difference?"

"We try to leave ten percent fallow every year. We rotate that portion. And then there's about three acres for the farm house and outbuildings."

"How much do you pay Max, Uncle Hampt?"

"He gets six thousand or so a month over ten months. But I also pay social security contributions for him, so the cost is more."

Back in the house, Will could already tell that the talk at lunch and the little jaunt out to the field had drained Hampton. He was wilting in front of Will's eyes and his face had become wan. Phyllis helped him up the front stairs and across the porch, whispering to him encouragements. "Time to take your medications, and then take a nap." she said to him as she led him into the main room and seated him on a short sofa. "Will, you'll understand if Hampton retires now. If you're willing to wait here about two and a half hours, you're welcome. Hampton can talk with you again around six. I'll bring you some coffee, if you want. But now I have to take him to lie down." Will decided he would stay and wait. Hampton looked at him as if he were little child apologizing for some accident he did not understand. "Look at the clippings upstairs in my office." he managed to say in a faint voice. Phyllis led Hampton by the elbow and upper arm to a back room on the main floor where he obviously now slept. Maybe he didn't go upstairs at all any more. After twenty minutes Phyllis came back. "Would you like some coffee and some caramel chip cookies?" Will said yes and she brought them. "If you like, when you're finished, I can take you upstairs to Hamp's office and show you his display materials he has put together over the years about his parents. The so-called clippings exhibit." "Yes, I'd like that." said Will.

Half an hour later, Phyllis came back and led Will upstairs where a central stairwell and corridor had five doors leading off from it. There were three bedrooms, a fourth small room which Hampton had converted into an office, and a bathroom. Phyllis took him into the office room. There was a built-in bookshelf on one wall, about half filled with books and box files, a desk in the middle of the room, a steel filing cabinet, and on one side of the room a couple of glass topped display cases. Phyllis pointed to them, "These are Hamp's clippings exhibit. Have a look."

There inside the display cases were about two dozen newspaper articles that had been clipped out and mounted with pins. Some were the original newsprint articles on yellowing paper, but most were prints taken from archive microfilm, which looked in rather better shape than the original newspaper articles. Most of the clippings were obituaries and were short and minimally informative. Harriet's obituary for instance was an original clipping from the Eastern Shore Examiner of Salisbury, was simple,

'Harriet Johnson Eames, wife of the late Robert Collison Eames of Roseland, Dorset County, died in her home last week after a long illness on the 3rd of April, 1963. She was 103 years old. Her three children, William, Albert, and Susan, pre-deceased her.'

Hampton had labelled all of the materials with the source newspaper, the date, and if there were photos the names of the people in the photo. There were about eight Kodak snaps, all black and white, but yellowed and all in poor condition. The longest piece was the obituary of Robert Eames of Bristol and Roseland, Dorset County, which had been published in the Baltimore Sun. It contained details of Robert's wide business interests in addition to his farm, his holdings of the Bristol Grain Elevator, the Delmarva Corn Processing and Milling plant, a chain of farm supply stores and gasoline filling stations in Bristol and around Dorset County, and a stake in a chicken processing and packing plant in Wicomico County. He was apparently a big businessman as well as a farmer and he traded many foodstuffs with Baltimore and Annapolis. The obituary said he died at the age of seventy-four on August 18, 1934 and was survived by his wife Harriet, one child, Lionel Eames of Salisbury—one child who had pre-deceased him, named William Senior-- and three grandchildren Hampton, William Junior, and Anna. It said the funeral would be held at the Christ the Savior Episcopal Church in Shiloh where mourners could gather to pay their respects. This would be followed by the burial at a private service. Will was impressed at the detail and length of this obituary. Robert Eames certainly must have been an extraordinary man.

Next to this article was an archival photocopy of a short article from the Eastern Shore Examiner. It was dated 4 January 1920.

'It has come to our attention that there was an outbreak in Bristol and other places in Dorset County over the Christmas and New Year's holidays of what some have called the return of the Spanish flu to the Eastern Shore. Nothing could be further from the truth. The Spanish flu was last seen in these counties around April of last year. What occurred first in Bristol and then in eastern parts of Dorset County was a localized outbreak of the seasonal flu, followed by what doctors call bloody pneumonia. It was found and quickly confined so that only 18 cases were described in the town and a handful of others elsewhere. The contagious pneumonia, occurring as it did when there was a period of strong cold and wet weather, was rather more serious. Dr. Adamson of Bristol reported that there were eight deaths between the 26th of December and 2nd of January. Included in this group were the following residents of Bristol: James Hunter, aged 40, Bradley Quinn, aged 22, Anna Muffett, aged 26, William S. Eames Senior, aged 31, Harris Randall, 38, Susanna Wilkins, 20, Donald Smith, 29, Victoria H. Harris, 42. We are informed that unfortunately the second doctor of Bristol, Dr. Hanson Williams, aged 54, who so bravely treated the group suffering from these pestilences, also passed away on the 3rd of January from an unrelated illness. It was his opinion and that of Dr. Adamson that the epidemic that was seen during this period was not the so-called Spanish flu of such notoriety, but something entirely different. State public health authorities have been informed and are proceeding to our region to help contain any further outbreaks of these illnesses. The public is not to be alarmed but is reminded to take normal precautions against all respiratory diseases.'

Will couldn't help thinking that this article probably caused more anxiety and alarm among the residents of the Eastern Shore at the time than if they had reported it was the return of the Spanish flu itself, with a rejoinder that in the previous two years it had killed more than twenty million people worldwide and nothing had been found to stop it or cure it.

Along with the article were the eight small black and white photos. Four included Mena, one by herself, the others with her children or standing with Grandpa Robert and Harriet. In all of them, it was hard to clearly see what Mena looked like, but it was clear that she was a pretty woman. The photo merely captured the darkness of her face which was enhanced by a shadow over the front of her face as the camera was too far back and light was coming from behind her. She was faintly smiling in all of the photos and they reminded him more than anything of photos he had seen of Hindu women in the National Geographic. She was not very tall when compared to Robert or Harriet. Her children were ranged around her in the one photo—it was also taken outdoors, probably at the farmhouse, and it was obviously windy at the time as a tress of hair had flown in front of her face just as the photo was taken. The photo's label dated it at October 1927, which meant that Hampton was 12, Will Junior, 11, and Anna 9. Anna's face was the same shape and shared the same features of Mena, but was white skinned. He recognized Hampton, but his own grandfather's face looked unfamiliar to him. He studied this photo the longest. He wondered if his father had any photos of grandma Mena at home. There were also three portrait photos of Will Senior's teenaged children taken for school in all probability. They label said they were taken in 1931. Again Hampton was quite recognizable, Anna looked the same as she had in the earlier photo in 1927, and then the photo of his grandfather, Will Junior struck Will as very familiar. He studied it for some moments and then he realized where he had seen a similar photo. His parents had at their home a color photo of him when he was fourteen years old and it looked identical to his grandpa Will at the same age. He was amazed by the uncanny resemblance. And there was another photo of Will Junior, dated July 1945, in army uniform and green cap, standing by a train wagon but of an unspecified location. Next to it was a color photo that was similarly posed of the young Benjamin in army green uniform, dated 1952, and said to be taken in Bristol. There was a color photo of a robust looking Hampton standing with his arm around the shoulders of a young, smiling very attractive woman whom the label said was Phyllis in 1954. The final photo was also in color and it was said to be of Harriet on the rocking chair on the porch out front. It was the latest in the collection and was taken in 1955. But it did not look like it was a woman related to the rest of the family. It was simply any photo of an aged, shrunken woman suffering from advanced dementia. After he had spent more than an hour examining this exhibition, Will quietly walked down the wooden stairs and returned to the main room to wait for Hampton.

When Hampton woke up, he came shuffling into the big room. His thin white hair was disheveled and he was looking disoriented, or a little wild. "Oh, you're still here, Will? Maybe you'd like some coffee? Or maybe you can stay for supper? Or maybe both."

Will chuckled. "I'd like some ice tea maybe. And if you feel up to it, I would very much like to join you for supper."

Just then a cell phone sitting on the coffee table gave a short ring. Hampton picked it up, looked at the screen and then in a muffled voice cursed. "It's the elevator. This is the time each day when they announce their posted price for corn for tomorrow's purchases. They send me text messages twice every day with the posted prices. And this evening they are down. They take advantage of everyone bringing their crop in at the same time. It depresses prices. Down already 5% since late last week."

Over a supper of pork chops and corn pudding, they continued this discussion.

"Market manipulation?" asked Will.

"No, it's the same with all produce and grain. Everyone brings in their crops at pretty much the same time and the surge and subsequent glut means that there's a momentary collapse in the price everywhere."

"Couldn't you hold off shipping your corn for a few weeks until after the glut?"

"I could if I had silos and could hold it here on the farm until prices came back up. I'd bet you if I sold this harvest in November, I could get that extra five percent back in the price. But I don't have silos, so I can't hold my crops back in reserve."

"I wonder if I could do a cost benefit analysis of the trade-off between the costs of building enough silo capacity, and the extra price you could get for holding back your corn?" said Will almost half-aloud.

"Yeah, that would be interesting. So do you have a feel for the place now?

"I'm beginning to get it."

"A man needs to have a feeling for place. A place where he belongs and where he fits in. Where he comes from. You normally get that in your childhood. I suppose for you, but don't even realize it, your sense of place is related to the rivers and the Bay around Bristol. Water related. Whereas here, it's the flat earth and crops growing here 'round. We have much less reference to the water, even though we're only a few miles from tidal marsh and rivers."

"Hampt, I've been thinking about inheriting the farm. And I think now I have decided that I would consent to be the designated heir in your will. I probably won't ever become a farmer proper, but I can manage the farm and keep it productive. I read the obituary of Robert Eames, your grandfather, and I became aware that he was a manager of many businesses, and was not only a farmer. I think I will take that approach. It's possible that I won't even live here in this house. But I don't have to decide that just now."

"I am so pleased to hear that Will. It's really important to me that this continues to be a working farm, and even more important that it stays in the Eames family."

Hampton took a long drink of ice tea. And then clapped his hands with glee.

"I had really hoped your father would have agreed to inherit this place. At the time I didn't understand how he could have turned down my offer. It upset me, no end. But I have since come to understand better how people might not want to continue family farming. So many of my elderly neighbors have seen their own children walk away from the farm. Didn't want to do the work. Which is admittedly very hard and challenging, and poses unending risks and stresses. But I think you could handle all of that, and build both a more prosperous modern farm, and a family here. You'll find that it is a most rewarding vocation. Tomorrow, I'll call my lawyer and ask him to modify my will accordingly. He should be able to come out here tomorrow, or Saturday."

"Who's your lawyer? Is it someone I know? Does he come from Bristol?"

"No, he lives and practices in Hurleyville. He also keeps an office in Exeter. Although I can't imagine he gets enough work there. His name is Rendell. John Rendell. Do you know him?"

"No, but by coincidence I have run across his name before."

Hampton shrugged. "Will you stay the night here, tonight?"

"I wasn't planning to. But I don't have anything urgent to look after at home, either tonight or tomorrow. So maybe I will."

"Well good. I won't be much company. Because I usually turn in early. But I understand they're going to broadcast an Orioles game tonight starting at 8:30. I get good reception here unless there's a thunderstorm. You can watch it on TV if you want."

That night, after watching the ball game, Will went upstairs to the room Phyllis had shown him. It was a large room with a high ceiling and the same cedar paneling as downstairs with a large double bed standing in the middle of the room. When he lay down to go to sleep, the bed creaked terribly. Must have been audible all over the house. Even the slightest of movements and the springs would sing out and echo, and the frame whined and creaked. After five minutes of making the most plaintive of noises, Will finally was able to lie perfectly still and the bed went quiet. And that's when he noticed the smell of the room. It was an unsettling odor. The odor of dust, cedar, old down in the pillow probably filled with dead dust mites, maybe horsehair in the mattress, all these odors were mingled with the sour smell of old age, and even death. He suddenly realized that he was sleeping in the room and bed where no doubt his great, great grandfather Robert had slept and died, where his wife Harriet after him had likewise slept and died. And maybe even others had slept and died in this old bed. If he inherited the house, he would have to dispose of the bed, at the very least. He thought that he was already looking at the house through the eyes of a future owner.

It wasn't until the next Monday that he went back into his agency office. He had agreed that in the coming month he would visit Hampton several more times to learn about how to run the farm. All weekend long he continuously thought about what he needed to learn about raising corn, raising soybeans, about farm equipment, about planting times, harvest times, markets for corn and soya, about whether he could keep Max on as a contract farmer, about any repairs that the farm house would need, any improvements. When he finally got to his office, he had forgotten all about the Real Estate Finance journal which he had received. In the past he always eagerly devoured all the articles in this journal, even more arcane subjects such as exotic financial tools for building sky-scrapers in dense cities. And when he saw the journal sitting on top of a pile of unread mail where he had tossed it, he at once picked it up and began to look at it. And he immediately spied the first lead article, "The building and financing of the Indian-owned casino, the Firefox Pequoddy Casino and Spa Resort." He turned straight to the article and sat down and excitedly began to read.

The article related the events that lead to the construction and opening of a casino on Indian property. The first point that it made was that inside an Indian reservation or on Indian owned land, the Indian tribes have an almost sovereign right to open and run casinos for their own benefit, free of state taxes and regulations, regardless of the state and local laws that may forbid casino gambling. This had been the secret to Indian tribes being able to develop casinos in the previous decade, often against strong opposition from governors, legislators, and social leaders. The key had been the Indian gaming Act of 1988 which spelled out the rights and limitations for Indian tribes to develop their own gambling operations. This made it incumbent on Indian tribes to be recognized as federally registered tribes having the reservations established by laws or treaties with the U.S. government. This Act allowed a proliferation of Indian tribes around the country to build their own gambling houses. The Pequoddy band of Indians in New England took this lesson and set about getting Federal recognition and a Federal grant of reservation lands as a preliminary step to developing their own casino. They faced much political opposition in their own state—from those who saw unfair competition to their own state regulated casinos, or feared the loss of income, or the spread of corruption and crime where casinos operated--but they also faced the tremendous hurdle of finding financing for building a casino resort. They categorically resisted the advanced of criminal organizations which were interested in financing, building, and running such casinos—the tax free provisions were especially attractive, as were the light regulations of running a casino on a sovereign reservation. After much searching they found an unlikely financier in the form of a Chinese entrepreneur and developer of casinos from Malaysia. He had faced racial objections and opposition to building casinos in Muslim Malaysia, where the minority Chinese community had a long cultural tradition of gambling but were persecuted by the Muslim Malay majority. This man saw the same situation with American Indians versus white American society so he stepped into the financing void. He was an extremely rich man but he did not come with the connections and associations of American organized crime. The article didn't say so, but he was probably the head of a Chinese criminal gang. The terms of his financing arrangements, which did not include contracting construction to one of his own building firms, were not reported in any detail. And arrangements for how his investment would be repaid were also not given. But apparently he provided over four years the funds needed to build a large resort hotel and spa with all the facilities for table gambling, card games, slot machines, and other games. His financing was conducted through the

First City Bank and was counted as foreign direct investment. The results were the new resort which was already earning big funds for the small Pequoddy tribe. Income and earnings that the tribe had never been able to organize before in any earlier venture. This income had already started flowing into the building of a new school, a hospital, and other social infrastructure which had been denied the tribe before. And this income was also already being distributed as a sort of royalty to individual tribe members and their families.

Will put down the journal. He was excited. Here was the solution to his idea of developing a casino to catch some of the huge flow of holiday fun-seekers to Ocean City! Of course. Why hadn't he thought of it sooner? He didn't know anything about the Nantiquak Indian tribe, and the group he had seen at Wicomico numbered only a little more than forty. But he had been told recently by a few people that there were even more tribesmen living on land across the Nanticoke River in the next county. He didn't know even if this tribe had an officially recognized reservation somewhere. He'd have to find out. His excitement built all through the day. This was the avenue to getting his project off the ground. He was sure of it. He would have to look up other Indian owned casinos around America to learn about their experiences and how they got permission and then financing to build casinos. By late afternoon he had written down a long list of questions that he needed answers to, especially so that he could launch his project.

And as if someone, somehow had heard his inquiries on paper, in the late afternoon the phone in his office rang. "Mr. Eames? This is Jenny Johnston, down at the county 'liberry.' Some time ago you requested an inter-liberry loan on a book on the Nanticoke Indians of the Eastern Shore by Mr. Sylvester Alvey, right? Well, I can tell you that we've received this book now and you can come in and borrow it for two weeks, if you still need it."

"Really? That's great. I do need it. What timing! But speaking of which, what time are you open till tonight?"

"Oh we'll be closing in half an hour. You could pick it up now, if you get here before five thirty."

"I'll be right there. Should I ask for you, Jenny?"

"Yes, I have it at the desk. Just ask for me."

"Oh, bless you. I'll be right there. Ten minutes."

Will ran out of the office, even leaving his jacket on the chair behind his desk where the Real Estate Finance journal lay open to the end of the article. He could walk to the library in less than fifteen minutes, but to drive and park by the library would take only three, so he went by car.

"Jenny Johnstone? I'm William Eames, you called me not long ago."

"Oh my, you are quick. Let's see, the book is here. You need to sign this agreement, giving us some details about you, your address and phone numbers. And sign here. Do you have your liberry card?" He was momentarily flustered but he found it hiding in a seldom used cranny of his thick wallet, lodged between a discount card and a store credit card which he never used. Jenny handed him the book with a crispy cellophane cover and a lurid illustration of savage Indians on the front cover. She then added a rejoinder, "Now be sure to get this back to us by the 16th of October. Okay? We have to send it back to the university liberry in College Park by the 18th." "Oh I will be sure to do that, Ms. Johnstone." He had already decided he would photocopy the entire book, cover to cover. "Oh, and Mr. Eames, I have for you the contact phone number for Mr. Alvey, in case you should want to speak to him. He's in Salisbury you know." "Mr. Alvey?" "Yes, he's the historian who wrote this book." And she gave him a slip of paper with the name Sylvester Alvey and a telephone number. "Oh thank you again. You can't know what a lifesaver you are." And Will ran out of the library and back to his car. As soon as he sat behind the wheel he opened the book and began to scan its contents. He decided he would start reading it that very evening, and that tomorrow morning he'd go first thing to the xerox store and begin photocopying all of it. He drove back to his office. Picked up his jacket and the journal, and said good bye to Lucy and then went home to begin reading the book, which was titled, 'The Last of the Nantiquaks, a history of the Eastern Shore Indians 1600-to today.' Not very original, thought Will. He settled in to reading it over a pizza and a beer he ordered, which were delivered in forty five minutes, even though his house was only three minutes from the pizza shop. The book was not an academic history and it made for light reading except that many of the Indian names were difficult, and quite a few different names looked similar in spelling to other unrelated names. But the author fortunately used only the modern English place names and he supplied in the book a good map which pinpointed even small obscure places, especially for places up in Delaware where apparently most of the remnants of the Nantiquak tribe now lived. His main theme was the unbroken chain of deceptions and broken promises that the white men and Maryland authorities hoisted on the Indians. He also carefully laid out the Indian strategy toward the white men who repeatedly were stealing their land: namely accommodation and flight combined with hiding and assimilation. The author carefully laid out the estimated populations of the Nantiquak-Choptiko-Kuskorawaok tribe over the centuries and put the declines squarely on white men's diseases, hunger, and emigration. He even included a chapter on those clans that moved away from Delmarva, including lots of information about what became of those clans. The most important things that Will learned in this book is that the Nantiquak had made a peace treaty with the colonial authorities of Maryland and that this treaty, from 1676, established several reservations for the Indians all along the Nanticoke River and upper Choptico River, including in areas which were at that time still considered part of Maryland, but which subsequently were assigned to the colonial territory of Delaware. His book ended with the setting up of the Nanticoke Indian association which occurred early in the twentieth century. Will finished reading the book by late Tuesday evening, the day after he had borrowed it. As he was reading he made notes of questions he had that he wanted to ask the author. Most were related to the issue of the source of the information. He resolved that he would call Mr. Alvey the next day.

When he called, a reedy voice answered the phone. "Is this Mr. Sylvester Alvey?" The voice confirmed that it was. "I am William Eames of Bristol, Maryland. I have just finished reading with great interest your book on the Nantiquak Indians. It is a fascinating history of the Indians of this region which I had known nothing about before I started reading it."

Mr. Alvey faintly chuckled: "Oh that book. I wrote it ages ago. I am surprised anyone reads it nowadays. It's not a very good book, but it was the best I could do under the circumstances when I wrote it."

Will quickly flipped to the copyright page and checked the date. Indeed the book was published twenty four years earlier. "Well, that doesn't mean that your history is poor," said Will. "But I have a bunch of questions on issues that you raise in the book. I was wondering if I could talk with you to get a better understanding of the history, especially of the last two centuries. I could come to your house and visit when it's convenient for you. How would Friday suit you?"

"No, that won't do. Maybe some time next week, Mr. Eames. I am mostly free on Wednesdays. I get medical treatment on other days. If you like we could meet on Wednesday, next week. I'll have to look at my text and my notes to remind of a lot of things that have disappeared from my mind."

"Yes, that would suit me. What time?"

"Shall we say 11 am?"

"Yes, that's okay for me. It takes me about an hour to drive to Salisbury."

So he had to wait a full week to see Mr. Alvey. He could hardly wait. In the interim Will re-read some parts of 'The Last of the Nantiquaks'. He couldn't help thinking that the title was a deliberate reference to the novel, 'The Last of the Mohicans', which he had read as a teenager. Which he had really liked too. But Alvey's book was not fiction, and there still were Nantiquak Indians living on Delmarva, and unlike the Mohicans whose enemies were other Indian tribes, the main enemy of Nantiquak were English settlers and land grabbers, who frequently resorted to force and violence against the Indians. The general theme and tone of the book was the Nantiquaks as a peaceful people who were victims of continuous injustice and were nonetheless tenacious survivors.

The appointed day came and Will made ready to leave. It had rained early that morning and when he stepped out, everything was still damp and the air was cool and fresh, like a typical fall day. The maple trees were beginning to turn color. Traffic was light on Highway 50, mostly heavy trucks driving through the peninsula. He reached Salisbury in a little more than an hour, and it took him about twenty five minutes to find Mr. Alvey's house. Will was using a navigator that he had recently bought for his car. It was very rudimentary and often was inaccurate. On this morning it seemed it misdirected him a couple times. The database for Salisbury still needed some work it seemed. He went to the door of an old two story house and rang the bell which echoed inside. There was no sound for a long time. He checked the house number and then again his notes about the address. He rang again. He waited more and more impatiently, and was getting ready to leave, when he heard a shuffling from behind the door and then a jingling of locks and then the door opened. A short, white haired man opened the door. Will saw at once that he was in slippers and was dragging along with him an IV drip post on wheels. The man was dressed but also he was wearing a light robe over his clothes. A tube ran from the IV to the man's left arm. "Are you Mr. Eames? Excuse me for not coming sooner to the door. Come in, come in."

"You'll have to excuse my appearance. I'm on this round the clock. It's my torment. But then on other days I have to be in the hospital lying on my back, so I don't complain too much about my days at home." He shook Will's hand. He still had a strong handshake. "I'm the author of the book that interested you. Sylvester Alvey. But all my life I've been called Hank. Don't know why. Come sit down with me in the main room here." And he shuffled off to a room with overstuffed furniture on a bare polished hardwood floor. "Don't be alarmed. I have been on medication for a number of months now. The doctors say it can help me, but I don't know. Hasn't been much change in my condition in recent weeks."

"I hope my coming here doesn't inconvenience you then, Hank—I can call you Hank?"

"Everybody else does. Why not you?"

"Well, then I will try to be brief. I read your book about the Nantiquaks. And I liked it, I might add. And I had some questions. First, how did you come about to write this book?"

"Oh, that's a good question. The long and short of it is that an Indian fellow asked me to. A Nantiquak. He came up to me one day after one of my lectures—I was teaching at Salisbury College then a class on American history in the colonial era and apparently he was a student—and he told me that the Nantiquak's needed a history of their people and if I couldn't write it for them. I wrote it on special request. It turned out that this young Indian was taking my course and studying at the college, the first in his family ever to have gone to college. And he liked the way I portrayed colonial American history, the economic and social struggles. And I had included a good deal about the various conflicts between Native Americans and the first English settlers in New England and Virginia. So he wanted me to apply the same approach to the Indians of Delmarva."

"I naively agreed to do it. Of course, it required a good deal of research, and a lot of work. And of course, I couldn't do that quickly. I became acquainted with the current tribe and the Nantiquak leadership. And they became important sources for my history. Good people, most of them live up in Delaware. I call them the invisible people of Delmarva. They've become invisible because so many of them have assimilated into the white society here, they're intermarried, all have Anglo family names now. They don't have a reservation and so don't live on one. They lost their native language generations ago. Economically they live at the margins, and keep quiet about it. If I look up my notes I can find the name of the young Indian who came to me with the request for a history."

"Yeah I know about invisibility. Maybe part of my interest is that I have distant Nantiquak Indian ancestry, myself. I discovered quite by accident a small group of them living as squatters on land that I bought—or tried to buy—recently."

"Oh, that's interesting. What was the family name of your ancestor?"

"Well, my great grandmother's maiden name was Driggers."

"Yes, that sounds about right. The Driggers were early English settlers on the Eastern Shore. Planted tobacco for three generations until that went bust. Disappeared from history by the early eighteenth century."

"So my great grandmother married my great grandfather about eighty years ago. Under gruesome circumstances. Her mother was shot and killed in front of her very eyes."

"Sadly, that sounds all too typical of the Nantiquaks' history in this region."

"You spoke of a reservation and you mention in your book that they had several over 150 years. What happened to them?"

"The short answer is that white folks stole their land, piece by piece, through connivance and manipulation of the laws. Converted the Indian lands to farm land. But the final story is that the state of Maryland stole the biggest part and sold it in the early 1830s."

"But how did they get the reservations in the first place?"

"Oh that was an interesting story. Because in 1666, the grand chiefs of the Nantiquak-Choptico-Kuskorawaok tribes of the Eastern Shore signed a treaty with the agent of the King of England. Long name for a tribe, isn't it? It is all a confused subject. There were Native Americans living in many small villages all along the Choptank and Nanticoke River. They were all related, that is, all descended from the same original Indian settlers, all spoke the same language—which was Algonkian. But the English settlers, starting from the time of Captain John Smith, all tended to call them different names—names of their residences or their chiefs, as if they were each different tribes. But the treaty lumped a large number of these villages with their representative chiefs as one tribe with this compound name."

"The main chief, a man named Kuskorawaok, who was one of the signatories of the treaty applied for and received three different reservations. One was on the lower Nanticoke. And the other, which I estimated was about 17,000 acres, was on the Nanticoke River and Broad Creek, an area that is now partly in Maryland but mostly now in Delaware. But at that time that territory was claimed by Maryland, and there was a third smaller reservation, north of here and in Delaware also. By the way, would you like some hot tea, maybe? With cookies?"

"Yes that would be nice. The season is suitable for hot tea now." Hank called for Ellen, his wife. An old white haired but vigorous looking woman came, introduced herself, and took Hank's request for tea and cookies with her back into the kitchen.

"The Indians over a period of more than a century mostly retreated away from the settlers, further up river until they nearly arrived in the new Delaware colony."

"You said the state of Maryland stole the last of their reservation in the 19th century? What happened there?"

"Well, it was in the 1830s and overall in the young United States there was a very hostile and widespread social movement against the Indian. And at the head of this was Andrew Jackson, the great Indian fighter. He presided over the Indian Resettlement Act, which was designed to expel the big southern Indian tribes, which claimed lands and sovereignty, from their traditional lands and push them to Indian territory, which became Oklahoma. Thousands died. And under the inspiration of this act and this general atmosphere of hatred toward all Indians, the Maryland legislature, totally illegally, seized the reservation at the Chacowan Creek and Nanticoke, and broke it up and sold the parcels, giving no compensation to the tribesmen that lived there on the reservation."

"You say illegally? Why is that?"

"The reservation had been established by treaty. A treaty that was still in effect at the time, and needed to be obeyed. But the Maryland state government virtually abrogated it without a second thought, and without any justification. But of course, there was no official act abrogating the treaty either."

"I see. But the Nantiquak tribe still exists in spite of that?"

"Yes. After that black moment the biggest numbers moved on to Delaware where they now still live. A big clan—several villages-- moved away to upstate New York and became assimilated with the Iroquois Indians, but that was about at the same time that the Iroquois themselves were driven out of America. And earlier in this century the surviving members of the tribe formed an association. Ultimately it was the association that helped me find so much of the materials to write my history."

"Hank, you've given me an idea to research the Indians and where they lived. I work as a real estate broker in Bristol, and I also sell title insurance. I think, barring fires, all the probate court records of land holdings and transactions should exist in the county seats of all of the Eastern Shore. I would think going back as far as the 18th century. I should look into them to find out whom the state of Maryland sold their land to."

"That would probably be in this county. That's a good idea. One of the most valuable books I've used is a research work called The Tobacco Colony, about life in colonial tidewater Maryland and the Eastern Shore. Full of details and important insights."

"So, there was a treaty. But the state of Maryland unilaterally repudiated it without annulling it or having any legal justification? That sounds interesting. I think I need to speak with the tribal association. Do you know their contacts?"

"Yes and no. I was in touch with them almost a quarter century ago. I'll bet you all my contacts have changed, or died. But the general phone number for the association and their mailing address, I still have them. And it's very interesting. They hold periodic pow-wows as a way of celebrating their existence and as a tourist draw to earn some money. I haven't gone to one of them for fifteen or twenty years. But it seems to me that they hold them every year in September. You should go to one next year, if you're interested. Let me get my directory and I'll write it down for you."

"You say, Native Americans instead of Indians. Is that right? Some sort of political correctness?"

"Well, they were and so they remain. They aren't Hindus, and they didn't live in the Indies. So from the very start, the English speaking world misnamed them. Would you prefer it if I said the aborigines or indigenous peoples? They want to be called Native Americans because that is what they have always been. They do not like being called Indians, and certainly not Injuns as locals round here say, or redskins, or any other racist epithet. In the seventeenth century it was common to call them savages. But they certainly were no more savage than the Europeans who called them savages at that same time engaged in the Thirty Years War, which actually was more like an eighty years war."

"I guess you're right."

"I know I'm right. The Nantiquaks I've met are a very sensitive, gentle people. Historically, they were not nearly as warlike as their cousins the Powhatans or the Susquehannok from across the Bay in what became Virginia colony. Throughout their history, they always chose to flee rather than fight. You know the specialists and linguists believe that as a small tribe they came to the Eastern Shore ultimately from New Brunswick in Canada. And they were chased out from there all the way to here by bigger, more hostile, and more violent tribes."

"When was that?"

"Well, archeological works seem to indicate they only arrived in the Eastern Shore in the early fourteenth or late thirteenth century. So they had only about a few centuries of sanctuary here from their old enemies before the English came."

"What does Nantiquak mean? Do you know?"

"No. I am not a linguist. And certainly no specialist in Algonkian languages. It was probably the name of a village or a chief. But it was not the name they gave themselves. As a collective name for all their villages they used a word which is more like an attribute. I forget exactly how it was said, but it roughly translates as 'dugout canoe people' because they were specialists in making dugout canoes and paddling long distances in their canoes. They paddled up and down these rivers and even across the Bay to trade. But you can ask the folks up at the association if you want to pursue that. Most of the earliest colonialists named the rivers and bays on the bayside for the Indian chiefs they met, or the villages they found, which usually had the same names anyway."

"That's interesting. What kind of tree did they use to fashion their dugout canoes?"

"Cypress trees, mostly. There used to be a lot more cypresses on the peninsula, before farming became widespread. You should know that. There used to be lots of cypresses growing along and in the Wicomico River and the Pocomoke River. And there was the great Cypress Swamp. May I ask you, Will, what is your interest in all these things to do with the Nantiquak?"

"I bought a plot of land on the Nanticoke River and discovered about forty squatters living on it. Unregistered, in makeshift homes. And they were all Nantiquak Indians. I was so surprised, and irritated."

"I suppose you could say that they were hiding in plain sight?"

"Yes, exactly."

"There is a large group, a good sized village living on our side of the river in Wicomico County, who are the same. No official identity. They don't exist on tax rolls, ownership records, school registrations, voter rolls. Anything."

"Yes. And then I got another shock when I learned that I was part Nantiquak myself."

"I think that there would be a lot of white people from the Eastern Shore who would be shocked to learn that they had some Native American ancestry in their blood. They also interbred with a lot of negroes here on the Eastern Shore. This group became true Afro-Americans, to use the newer terminology."

"I am thinking now of a project to redress a little bit the injustices to the Nantiquaks over the past three centuries. I have to figure out how to do it. But I think after talking to you, I need to speak with the Indian Association first."

"But just as an aside, Hank. Are you a down East Marylander? Do you know when your family arrived in the Eastern Shore?"

"The Alvey family, as best I can tell arrived here in Salisbury about a hundred years ago. So not one of the old English farming families from colonial times."

"Good. The Eames, it seems do go back."

"Oh yes. There were Eameses farming in Dorset and Wicomico Counties in colonial times."

"Oh yeah. That's interesting. So meanwhile, Hank, I don't want to wear you down too much. I was not aware that you were so ill when I first suggested coming here. And you've been a big help in clarifying a lot of the issues I had after I read your book. But I think I really should be going now. I really want to thank you. You've been so generous and open. And you've opened my eyes to all kinds of further avenues I can take, I need to take."

"Will, you're most welcome. I retired twelve years ago, but I still like to lecture. And I especially like digging deeper into local history. And I suppose I do go on too much. Excuse if I droned on too much for you. But it's becoming ever more difficult for me. You've stimulated me to give a new look at the book I did—on request—so many years ago. And it's always nice to have company. There's another book about the early years of the Eastern Shore, called The Tobacco Colony. Did I mention that? I recommend that you look it up, if you're still interested."

Will made leave of Sylvester 'Hank' Alvey. He drove to a café he knew of in the center of the old town and had a seafood lunch. On the road home, he was busy plotting and thinking of the next steps he needed to take. He was beginning to think he could develop an Indian casino. Certainly there was the need for it. The demand from Ocean City weekenders would be strong. The need for income for the Nantiquaks was unquestionably there. And the objective of having a worthwhile project to work on and to devote oneself to was very appealing to him personally. He was certain that he could do this project, and he felt certain that the Nantiquak Indians would also want to do this.

When he got back to Bristol, he went to his office to check if there had been any developments. Lucy told him the good news as soon as he stepped in the door. The current owner of a house in the eastside of town had called to say that he wanted to sell his house. "What's the address?" Lucy picked up a piece of paper and read off an address. "That's in East Bristol, isn't it? Did the man leave his telephone number?" "Yes, he did. Here it is." "Hey wait a minute. Isn't that the address of the John Ehrlich house? The writer and Bristol's most famous son? I feel pretty sure that it is. He's not a really famous writer but his reputation could still help sell the place." With the lure of a house sale, Will forgot all about his Indian casino project. Lucy looked at him quizzically. "John Ehrlich is a famous writer? From here in Bristol?" she asked. "Have you ever read any of his books?" "No, I mean I tried, but I couldn't finish any of them. One was assigned reading at university. He's also Maryland's most famous writer. Wrote about the Eastern Shore. But they are strange books." When Will called the owner he arranged an appointment and he also asked if the house wasn't the childhood home of John Ehrlich. When he hung up he turned to Lucy. "It sure is. Ehrlich's grandfather apparently built the house. At about the same time my great-grandfather built the two houses here in West Bristol. And you know what? It seems that John Ehrlich is still living. I assumed he had died years ago." Lucy shrugged her shoulders. "Business, but I'm not sure it will make the house sell any easier." The next day Will went over to meet the current owner, who was unrelated to the Ehrlichs, and after a tour and a long discussion he got the appointment to be the listing agent. The important thing Will saw was that the house had been extremely well built and was still in good condition and upkeep. It should be a cinch to sell before the end of the year, he thought. He put it on the MLS listing that very same evening.

On Friday evening, Will's father called to ask if he would join him fishing for rockfish. "They're running now, and the forecast is for fine weather tomorrow, so we can go out on the Bay." Will agreed to go out and he showed up warmly dressed for a day on the waters. The sun was warm but the air had a chill to it. But the waters of the Bay were still relatively warm so the aluminum boat did not become cold right away. Bob steered his boat out to where the murky waters of the Choptank met the clearer, rougher waters of the Bay. "This should be a good place where we can get some rockfish. They like the colder, shallow waters of the Bay where there are lots of nutrients being dumped in by the rivers." As they threw their lines in and began waiting for some hits, Will started telling Bob about his plans to develop an Indian casino on the land he hoped to buy. He related to him all that he had found out about the Nantiquaks from Uncle Hampton and from Hank Alvey. And he enthusiastically told him of what the next steps would have to be. "So you, who didn't like the Injuns just two or three months ago, now that you know that you have some Injun blood in your veins, you've got yourself an Injun Project." "I suppose you could say that." "And you're not looking to making yourself a huge profit. You just want to do something good for the Injuns?" "Most of the profits will go the tribe, you know. And they need it. I can't see how I would make a lot of money from the project, through the opening. I wouldn't be the manager, just the developer. But it will benefit the Indians and the whole county as well. That traffic of weekenders would stop here and leave some of their money behind, not merely spit on us as they pass by." "You know, it sounds all very well and good. But without the full support of the Nanticokes themselves you won't have no Injun Project. It will be hard enough even with their full backing and support."

After two hours of sitting still in the water, their discussion ended when they both got strikes. Will got a six inch striper, and Bob pulled in a fifteen inch fish, a keeper for bayside fishing. "If we get another like that, we'll have a big dinner of rockfish tonight." said Bob. "They used to say that the rockfish were overfished here, but now they're making a comeback." After another fifteen minutes Will got a strike and pulled in a twelve inch rockfish. "That's a keeper too. Well done, son. Maybe now we can try some trolling along here for a little while or so." Bob pulled the starter cord and the engine roared to life. As they moved slowly along the coast in the open Bay waters, they put on rubber lures on the hooks and threw in their lines. They trolled for another forty five minutes before getting two more strikes, both fish too small to keep. But almost as soon as they tossed them back they got two more strikes, one a twenty inch monster and the other about half that size. "I think that does it for us today. Good fishing. Let's head for home." Bob turned the boat back and slowly made its way back to the Choptico Bay. That's when Will told him the other news about the listing he'd gotten for the original Ehrlich home. "Did you know him, John Ehrlich I mean, when you were a boy?" Bob with one hand of the steering column had to shout above the motor, so his sentences came in choppy and incomplete. "No, --- but I knew of him. ---Everyone in town did.---- When I was in middle school,--- that Ehrlich boy—he was already finishing high school—he wanted to be a drummer, and he performed everywhere. With or without a band. He was a character. And then he left for university, and ----I guess has never come back." At the dock, they reckoned that the four fish together must have weighed over twelve pounds. There would be fish head soup and filets for dinner that night. Will offered to bring beer. 'Injun Project' he thought. 'That's what I should call my efforts. Politically incorrect, but succinct.'

Will got a call on the next Monday afternoon. It was the clerk from the probate court with news. "You know, we had the hearing about the claim from those Injuns on the other side of the county saying they were the Randall heirs. Only their lawyer attended. The long and short of it was that they could not present any evidence that they were directly related to Pellmell Randall. So their claim was denied. That means we can proceed on the sale of that parcel to you.

I suspect closing could be within a week or two. But no later than the first week in November."

Will jumped from his desk and whooped an Indian war cry. Lucy looked up from her desk in surprise. Even from the next door room where the title insurance desk was Marilyn ducked her head in the door to see what had happened. Lucy's eyebrows were raised in question of Will's outburst. "I got it." was all he would say. "That property's going to be mine now." he said as he resumed his place behind his desk with a big victory smile on his face. Lucy shrugged her shoulders and directed her head back to the computer screen. Will needed to tell someone, to share the news. But not his father, not yet. Not Lucy. Maybe Tony. That's it. He'd go to the Poseidon Palace tomorrow for lunch, a day earlier than usual, and tell Tony about his property and his plans. It was not long after he decided that, that he thought he needed to go see the chief of the Nantiquak tribal association up at their offices in Delaware. As soon as possible. He looked for the telephone number that Hank Alvey had given him and the name of the chief and administrator that he had consulted so many years earlier. Will had written it down in the little note book that he always carried with him. But he had to search through many pages before he found the notation. He called the number on his cell phone and asked for the man whose name Hank had given him.

"Oh, I'm afraid you have a wrong number." answered a man with a soft deep voice. "There's no one with that name here."

"Is this the Nantiquak tribal association?"

"Yes, but there is no one here with that name."

"Well, then could I speak with the association president?"

"That would be Mr. Marley Norwood. He's not here just now."

"My name is Will Eames. I'm calling from Bristol in Maryland. Could I make an appointment to meet with Mr. Norwood?"

"Yes. He keeps hours for open consultations on Thursdays and Fridays. Would you like an appointment then this week?"

"Yes, would Thursday morning be possible? I'll drive up."

"Okay, I'll put you in the appointment book for Thursday at 11 a.m. What would be the reason for your meeting?"

"I want to explore some ideas that I got from reading Mr. Alvey's history book, called the Last of the Nantiquaks."

"Never heard of that book. Nor I have heard of a Mr. Alvey."

"Oh, and excuse me. What is the exact address I should come to?"

"Yeah, it's 236 Farm County Road, about two miles outside of North Millville. You can recognize it by the big Nantiquak-Kuskorawaok flag flying outside."

Will thanked the man and hung up. His Injun Project was beginning. He then took out a piece of paper and started to construct a list of the people or agencies that he needed to consult. He tried to put all the possible agencies, but he did not write them in any particular order. There was the Bureau of Indian Affairs, Jackson Parker again, the Indian Gaming Commission, the Maryland state archives, the probate court property records for Wicomico County, the same records office for the county in Delaware next to Wicomico county. And so on. He went to the internet and looked up the address and contact person for each agency. He filled the piece of paper and started jotting down names and addresses on a second piece. He worked slowly as he thought where he might need further to consult. Lucy and Marilyn were leaving the office already before he had finished. He kept at it, trying to think of all the agencies and people that he would need to get either approvals or support from. It was difficult sifting through in his mind all the information he had collected in the previous two weeks. It was already past six in the evening and the waning light outside made the office dim. His cell phone rang, but caller ID did not identify who the called was.

"Will?" said a reedy man's voice. "This is Hank Alvey. I wanted to let you know that I looked up the name of the young man who had requested the book that I wrote. It was one Marley Norwood. A very bright, honest sort, as I remember him. I'm afraid I haven't spoken with him in twenty years or so."

"Oh, thanks. That could be useful. I'll ask for him when I go see the Indian association."

Will put down his cell phone and thought 'What a marvelous coincidence of timing.' Norwood was the same man he was going to meet. Then he went home for the evening. Later that evening as he was watching an Orioles playoff game on the television, he realized he should also call Jack Parker the next morning. And maybe they could both go to one of the weekend's final games. It looked like the Orioles were going to the World Series this year, and he did not want to miss the opportunity to watch a live playoff game.

Thursday morning came and Will drove over to Delaware. It took him about an hour to reach North Millville and he became more and more excited as he approached the town. In the last few minutes his navigator kept steering him the wrong way, and he grew more agitated as it seemed he was moving away from his destination. But in spite of the navigator he found the Farm County Road and after cruising slowly west of the town he saw what looked like a white oversized mobile home set up near the road over which fluttered a large colorful flag. When he pulled up he saw a small sign which said it was the Nantiquak-Kuskorawaok Indian Association. As he stepped through the front door at his appointed time, he was convinced that it was indeed a long, converted mobile home with maybe some additions built onto one side and at the back. It had a very temporary feeling to it. Maybe that was an unintended consequence of building an office on the cheap, he thought. Or maybe it reproduced the traditional shape and function of the Indian longhouses, just using different materials.

The entry was simple: a small room without decoration or wall hangings which had a narrow reception desk next to the entry door, a small round table next to it, a kitchenette on one wall next to the entrance door with a coffee maker on the counter, and three flags standing together in one corner, a U.S., Delaware and Nantiquak flag, and four folding steel chairs standing up in a row against the opposite wall, next to which stood a narrow wire frame coat rack with five empty hangers on it. There was a telephone on the reception desk, but no one behind this desk. A fat, dark skinned man sitting at the table jumped up and went behind the reception desk. "Can I help you?" The man had the same soft, deep voice that Will had heard over the phone. "Yes, I'm here to meet Mr. Norwood. I'm Will Eames from Bristol, Maryland."

The man's face was stoney and showed no reaction. "I'm afraid Mr. Norwood is not here at the moment."

"But I have an appointment with him for this time."

"Yes, it's written right here in the book. But he's not here. Sorry. If you could just wait. Maybe he'll come."

"Wait? What if he doesn't come? Can't you call him on the phone to tell him I'm here? Does he have a cell phone?"

"No. I can't call him. Don't worry. He knows he has an appointment this morning. Take your coat off and just have a seat over there." And he pointed to one of the folding chairs. "Help yourself to some coffee." And the man went back and sat down at the round table which had some magazines and flyers lying across it. The receptionist did not seem to have any work that he was doing. Will hung his jacket, took one of the magazines and a flyer from the table, and he sat down. He was beginning to feel irritated. He began flipping through the magazine, Native American Life, but without paying much attention to the articles or to the copious illustrations. He tossed the magazine back on the table and studied the flyer. It was a color printed advertisement for the Nantiquak Pow-wow, which had been held, it seemed, five weeks earlier. As background to the text were photos of large gatherings of people under pine trees, some in fanciful costumes, some mostly exposing their brownish skin and others in even more outlandish hairstyles. It was already well past noon, when in exasperation Will again asked if Mr. Norwood might be expected. Again the fat man answered laconically, "Oh, I'm sure he will come. And he'll talk with you. He just has to finish some chores first. Are you sure you don't want some coffee?"

Will stood up to stretch his legs and he paced around a few small steps. But he did not take any coffee. The coffee in the pot looked vile, and smelled strong. And then he thought to call Jackson Parker. His Annapolis telephone number was in the memory of his cell phone. He called. After five rings, the same supercilious voice of the officer manager answered again. She again reported that Jackson was not available at the moment, that he was out to lunch. Will left a message saying that he wanted to have another talk on a similar subject, and that maybe they could go together at the weekend playoff game at Camden Yards. The office manager sourly said that she would convey the message and that Jackson would call him back. "On what number?" Will gave her the number of his cell phone, but did not expect any answer soon. Almost as soon as he folded up his cell phone, the front door opened and in came a big man with wide shoulders and a paunchy stomach, long black hair that fell free around his head, and a face that looked like an Englishman's but with a very deep brown tan. He looked around the room, and then came at Will extending his hand.

"You must be William Eames. I'm Marley Norwood. How do you do?" he said in a blustery voice, but with no warmth or friendship in it. "You said you wanted to talk to me about some things you learned from Sylvester Alvey's book?"

"Yes, and some proposals for your tribal association to consider."

"Come with me then." Marley led Will down a short narrow corridor that led off from behind the reception desk. There were two offices on the corridor which ended at an open door to what looked like a large meeting room. There were two people sitting at desks in the first office which had glass upper walls. They appeared to be working on accounts. Marley entered the second office through an aluminum and glass door. Other than a steel filing cabinet, a desk and three folding metal chairs and one padded office chair, the office was bare. There were two bookshelves hanging on the wall behind the desk populated by three framed photos and one book. As he was sitting down, Will recognized the book as 'The Last of the Nanticokes'. Marley turned to the shelf and grabbed the book before sitting down himself.

"This is the book you were referring to?" he said as he showed it to Will.

"Yes, it is. And I even went over to Salisbury and had a long discussion about it with Hank Alvey just last week."

"Professor Alvey still living?" asked Marley with his face showing a more interest. "He's a good man. Understands a lot about the sufferings of the Indians. Especially the east coast Indians which everybody in this country has completely forgotten about. We're the most invisible of the invisible Native Americans."

"That's interesting that you should say so. Not long ago I had a wake-up call, so to speak. I discovered that the Nantiquak people were not so invisible, even though all my life in Bristol I had never been aware of them."

"Surely you were aware of the names of the rivers, the Choptico and the Nanticoke? Both of those are Nantiquak names."

"I vaguely knew that. But I grew up believing that the Indians themselves, your tribe, had disappeared. This book largely documents that disappearance. And then I bought a piece of land on the Nanticoke River and discovered a whole bunch of Nantiquak people living there. Unknown to authorities or any government records."

"Would that have been the people down there who call their village Wicomico?"

"Yes those people exactly. And I discovered there is even a larger group upriver on the other side of the Nanticoke near to Sharpesville in Wicomico County."

"Yes, we know about them also."

"So by a coincidence of timing, I also discovered that I have an ancestor who came from that same village of Wicomico. And that makes me part Indian, one eighth I think it should be. My great grandmother was 100% Nantiquak."

"You and so many other entertainers-- who aren't Jewish anyway-- claim Indian ancestry. Elvis Presley, Cher, Chuck Norris. So what? I guess they feel that it must help their careers some way. Their claim of ancestry certainly hasn't helped the Cherokee, or the Choctaw, or the Creek, or whatever tribes they claim to derive from." Marley was looking at Will with a stony and almost hostile expression on his face. His arms were now crossed on his chest tightly. "With one-eighth Indian blood the Feds would not recognize you as an Indian tribesman. As a general rule we don't often recognize that either for membership in our association."

"Well, I mentioned this just to point out how what was once invisible has recently become quite visible to me."

"So what can we do for you? What is it you want from the until-quite-recently-invisible Indians?"

"I thought of building a casino on the plot of land I bought. But that is not permitted by law. But now I have researched the regulatory and legal background and I have resolved to build an Indian tribal casino that would belong to the Nantiquak tribe."

Marley's expression changed. He showed a little bit of surprise.

"And what if the Nantiquak Indian tribe doesn't want to have a casino?"

"That of course would be the end of the idea and there'd be no project."

"We have discussed this in the past. And we concluded that we would have to get Federal recognition as a living genuine Native American tribe."

"And that's what the Indian Gaming Act of 1988 says as well." said Will. "You would have to be a sovereign entity and recognized federally that way so that you wouldn't have to be constrained by state and local laws."

"And we would need to have our own reservation." answered Marley in a more agitated voice. "And we don't actually have a reservation, and I can't see the Feds granting us one. Certainly not here on the Eastern Shore."

"That's not impossible. You know about the FireFox Pequoddy Casino up in Connecticut? Congress passed a law giving recognition to the Pequoddy Indians. The law also required the Federal government to fund the purchase of lands and buying them as a reservation for the tribe. More than one thousand two hundred acres were bought under that law and put into a trust for the Pequoddys, even though they couldn't find 100 souls who would or could call themselves Pequoddys just fifty years ago. So it is possible. Admittedly difficult, but possible to get recognition and a reservation."

"And you know," Will continued. "I was thinking of putting the parcel of land that I bought into an indivisible trust for the Nantiquaks. Then an Indian casino could be built on it, stepping around Maryland law."

"We'd still have to get Federal recognition. And that is very difficult from what I have come to understand."

"Perhaps. But in any case that would be the first step we would have to take. Getting Federal recognition as a Native American nation."

"We? What makes you think that you have any part in anything that our association decides to do?"

"That is exactly why I am here. I am proposing to you, and the association, and to all the Nantiquaks to lead and organize the administrative and legal processes needed to get Federal recognition as a sovereign tribal nation and to get or restore a reservation on the Eastern Shore."

Marley now looked at Will in apparent dismay. He unfolded his arms from his chest and looked away from Will.

"Look, I am one-eighth Nantiquak. What would it take to be able to join your association? Do I qualify? Is there an annual membership fee? Would you need notarized proof that I am descended from my great-grandmother, Mena Driggers?"

"No, but you would have to apply to the council. You don't look like an Indian, and you obviously haven't any Indian culture. So then you would need to be elected. I don't know of any Indians named Driggers."

"Does the association include those Indians still living in Wicomico or near Sharpesville in Maryland? Because Wicomico settlement still has Driggers living there."

"It could, but in practice it doesn't. It is a Delaware legal entity. But it could be wider in its coverage and membership, I suppose."

Will felt he was getting a very negative reaction from Marley Norwood. He did not understand how he could make his message more appealing. He had never received such a negative reaction to any of the sales pitches he had given in his six years of real estate brokerage. The longer they spoke the more uncertain he was becoming.

"I am proposing to lead and organize the steps needed to get recognition, to set up a reservation, and to finance and build a casino as an interested advisor and consultant. But I am not seeking to get a fee for this from the tribe. There'll be plenty of other fees that have to be paid along the way. Lawyers' fees for instance."

"You've already gone way out in front of anybody here in the tribe. What makes you think that we would want a casino? Or even a new reservation? Our tribal members already own their own lands and houses."

"If you have a reservation that would be the place where you, the tribe, could conduct your businesses and economic ventures free of federal, state and local taxes and regulatory controls. It would also be the place where federal benefits reserved for Indians would be delivered. And of course, if you should decide on building a casino as a money making venture, that would be the place where it would be located. On Indian territory, outside the jurisdiction of state laws."

Marley did not reply for a long time. But he also did not look directly at Will.

"And who are you, really?" he said squinting hard at Will.

"As I said I am William Eames of Bristol Maryland. My family has lived in Dorset County as far as I can tell for eight generations. At the present time I am self employed as a real estate broker in the county. And I also own a parcel of land on the Nanticoke River where a band of Nantiquak Indians are living. Forty five or so souls, living as squatters, in poverty, and with no rights. And, you may find this hard to believe, they are related to me, even if they do not look like me at all."

"So what do you hope to get out of this—helping us change our lives—if you say you don't need an advisor's fee?"

"Well, if there is no casino, I suppose I would not get anything out of this effort, no reimbursement of investment or of the financing. If we don't succeed in getting federal recognition of the tribe, including all of the Nantiquaks who live in Maryland, but might not now be association members, then I suppose I would not put my parcel of land into a trust for the tribe. I would carry on earning my living in a way that remains unrelated to Nantiquaks. And you would carry on as you already do. But if we achieve these goals, I will be rewarded by knowing that the economy of Eastern Shore inhabitants has been enriched, and specifically that my Indian relatives will be better off."

"Sounds very noble. But you know white men have been coming to us over the centuries to trade or to buy our output, saying they would cooperate with us to enrich us, and every time, they have swindled us and stolen from us. They took our lands, they took our oyster and mussel beds, and took for themselves our crabbing and fishing territories. They exploited them until they were stripped bare of oysters, mussels, clams crabs or fish. They developed huge scale tobacco farms on lands they took from us until the land was exhausted and could no longer grow even small amounts of tobacco. Excuse me, if I sound skeptical of you and distrust your motives."

Now it was Will's turn to fall quiet. Both men glared at each other across the desk. Will could hear the faint footfalls and creaking coming from the front room, and he could hear the raindrops that had begun to fall splashing on the thin roof of this converted mobile home. Once or twice he heard the sound of a car swooshing past fast on the wet road outside. Marley broke the silence first.

"So I am not sure we need any freely offered help from the white man and stranger, claiming to be related to us, to help us do what we really have not decided to do for ourselves."

"That's all very understandable. Your association uses the legal services of a lawyer no doubt? Is he a white man?"

"Yes we have a lawyer who is a white man up at the county seat. But I don't think he is capable of providing us with the advice and administrative services that could get us recognition, restore our reservations, or finance and build a casino. Even if we decided that we wanted those things. And I am not sure you have the capability either."

"Well I deal in property, land, and real estate. I also run a title insurance business, which is all about researching legal title to land. That gives me a real insight and experience into just what all these issues of yours are all about. Land ownership. Of course on the legal and political sides of Indian rights, I do not have any experience in that. Very few people do, I would think. And I know how to select and use legal advisory services, especially as they pertain to land ownership issues. I suppose that makes me qualified to be an advisor to the tribe."

He paused. Marley said nothing but he began to look at Will in the face, as if he were looking for something there.

"But you know a lot of these issues are Delaware issues. I think you do not have experience there."

"Granted. That is correct. But all this area, where your association is located, nearly all of Sussex County, they were all a part of Maryland until 1752. Your original reservation was entirely in Maryland and only after the border settlement did a big chunk of it go to the newly formed state of Delaware."

"That was a long time ago."

"And what is more, the reservations for the Nantiquak were established by a treaty between the King of England and the Chiefs of the Nantiquak. Delaware and Maryland, until 1776, were royal colonies and did not have a higher level of authority or jurisdiction than the royal treaty."

"I never thought of our situation in that way before. But all of that is old history."

"I don't think so. Old but still valid. I sometimes still see property and title records going back to the late 1600s."

Again there was a long pause and silence except for the patter of rain.

"So as chief of the Nantiquaks, would you feel more comfortable if I were to perform these advisory and organizational services and to ask for you to pay me for them?"

"I'm not the tribal chief. That is Horace Clark. I'm the president of the association. Not the same thing. The tribe is governed, if you like, by the chief and the council, not by the association. The association is directed by the chief and the council. I am the chief administrator of the association. An employee. All of these issues and ideas are for the chief and the council to decide. Not for me. I am a member of the council, but my word and view is just one of twelve."

"I see. But I gather you're opposed against every aspect of my proposal?"

"Let's say, I do not support it. Just now."

"So would you say that I should make a presentation to Mr. Clark and the rest of the council? In which I can put forward my proposal and all the steps that I believe are needed?"

"Yes, it would be advisable."

"Could you arrange a time when I could come back and make such a presentation?"

"I could do that."

"Would you do that for me?"

"Yes. But the next council meeting is not set for another three weeks. We have to make preparations for our Native American memorial day which occurs on your Thanksgiving."

"There's no rush. I can make preparations for a detailed and thorough presentation. If you think it would be better to give the presentation after Native American Memorial Day, I could do that."

"Well, you do that then. I will call you in about two weeks and tell you if and when there will be a council meeting for your presentation." And with that very abruptly Marley stood up. He did not offer his hand for a shake. Instead he used his arm to direct Will through the door and back to the entry room. Will took his jacket and turned just before the door and offered his hand to shake, which Marley took. "Here's to beginning to work together. Hope to hear from you soon." Will's statement, in front of the fat young Indian receptionist, caught Marley a bit off guard. But he lamely shook Will's hand and he muttered an utterance that sounded vaguely like between agreement and farewell.

The rain had let up by the time Will started for home. The way was all on small back roads, but the traffic was light so that he did not pay too much attention to how he was driving. It was just as well, as he was very agitated, thinking over and over about the hostility that Marley had shown him. Maybe his project was not possible. Especially if the Indian tribe, which would be the principal beneficiary, did not want it. He felt as if he had run up against an insurmountable obstacle. This time even more formidable than the legal proscriptions that Maryland had for casino gambling, which Jackson Parker had outlined for him so starkly. He thought that in every likelihood Marley would not arrange a meeting with the chief and the council, and that he would not call Will back. His agitation built up to feelings of anger by the time he pulled up at his house in the late afternoon. He decided to go for a run, followed by a workout on his training equipment, a routine he had learned while he was in the Marines and which he continued. It was especially useful for dispelling anger. His exercise lasted more than an hour, and after he showered he saw that he had a message from Jackson Parker's office. He called and got Jack's secretary. She told him that Jack would be pleased to join him tomorrow evening for the second playoff game of the Orioles against the Cleveland Indians. It was an important game; the Orioles were pushing for the American

League championship and the right to play in the World Series. Jack had bought the tickets and he would meet him outside Camden Yards at 6. Will asked for Jack's cell phone number and the secretary gave it to him without hesitation. Will felt much better after his exercise and his message from Jack, and he decided to fix himself some dinner and eat at home.

He drove up to Baltimore late the next afternoon. And although there were huge crowds milling around outside the Yards, he found Jack without too much difficulty. They went into a pub adjacent to the Yards and had two high quality beers, what Jack said was not possible inside the ballpark. "They serve piss inside the ballpark. Overpriced and piss poor. These are much better." Jack had bought good seats on the third base line, not too high up in the stands.

"We're lucky to get these seats. I think all 48,000 seats were sold out. Looks like it might be the Orioles' year to go all the way." said Jack as they sat down.

"Yeah, lots of promise this year for sure." replied Will. "But you know with these series, you never have won, until the last ball is thrown and the last batter is put out. And you're not losing until you've taken the last swing of the bat."

"Sure, but that's a rather hackneyed observation. Of course you keep striving to achieve your goal to the very end. As Yogi Berra said, 'It ain't over till it's over.'"

"How was the honeymoon, by the way?" asked Will.

"It was great. We went to Bermuda, and spent a little bit of time on the beach, and lots of time in bed. You know the routine for honeymoons. Didn't even notice the weather or the peculiar architecture of the island. And what have you been doing since we last met?"

"You know, I'm still trying to push forward my casino idea. Because I'm not finished, until I succeed and I'm finished. But now, I'm trying to make it an Injun project."

"Oh yeah? I suppose you could say that the O's have an Injun project on their plate just now."

They watched the first three innings making a minimum of small talk. The Indians took the early lead, but the O's tied up the game in the next inning. Jack came back to the subject.

"What do you mean, Injun project?"

"I hope to build a casino on an Indian reservation on the Eastern Shore. You know the Nantiquak Indians still exist."

"No, I didn't know that."

"And by the terms of the Indian Gaming Act of 1988, they can do this even if it runs counter to state law."

"That's interesting. I think there would still be political opposition to this from the statehouse. Maybe you need to sell the idea to our congressman and senator."

"That's a good idea. Can you refer me?"

"Sure, no problem. Sadly, we have only one representative from the Eastern Shore in congress, but the congressmen still have to pay attention to us eastern-shore people. I didn't know that there were any Indian reservations on the Eastern Shore? Where are they exactly?"

"There aren't any just now. But I'm going to lead an effort to restore them. You know the state of Maryland apparently took away and sold the reservations without any legal justification in the 19th century."

"No, really? How's that?"

"The Indians had a treaty which granted them three reservations. The treaty goes back to the 1600s. And the state of Maryland, after it joined the United States, had no reasons to abrogate that treaty."

"That's interesting. So you're saying the Indians would have a property claim?"

"Yes, I am saying that. Who do you think would be the best lawyer to pursue a claim for wrongful property seizure by the state?"

Jack whistled. "Now that's a hard one. Especially as it is such an old crime."

"Yes, but you know I do title searches that often go back to the beginning of the eighteenth century. Those records all exist in the county court house in Bristol."

"Actually, come to think of it, I know a really good man who you probably already know. I think that Ray McNutt would be your best man to pursue such a claim and suit. He's still working in Bristol and he's handled all kinds of property claims and disputes."

"Of course, I know him. I have used his services on occasion. He's the best property lawyer on the Eastern Shore. I didn't know he was still working."

"I think he is."

They fell silent and resumed watching the game, which was evolving into a tightly fought pitching duel. After forty five minutes, the O's scored again to take the lead.

"Jack, have you ever heard of the writer John Erhlich?"

"Sure, Bristol's most famous native son."

"Ever read any of his novels?"

"Wait, wait. Watch this ball." Jack said as he turned his attention to the field. "It's going to be a hit. Yeah, a double. No, never read anything by him. But he's still pretty well known."

"Well, I got to be the listing agent for his childhood home in Bristol—the house itself I mean."

"That's great. You should write Erhlich and tell him his childhood house is for sale. Maybe he would want to buy it. He lives in Baltimore just now from what I understand."

"Yeah, that's an idea."

After another inning played, Will asked, "Jack, where do you think I can find the copy of that treaty? I would think that there would be a copy in England somewhere, as it was an agreement between the king and his representatives and with the Indians."

"I think the state archives in Annapolis would be the right place to start."

"So all the seventeenth and eighteenth century documents were moved when the capital was moved from St. Mary's?"

"I feel pretty certain that they were."

"Then I will look there. I hope there have not been any fires in the intervening years."

"Will, you know, I think your Injun project is really pretty quixotic. A long shot at best. You think you can sue the state for such an old claim and hope to get anything out of it?"

"I don't know. No one's ever done such a thing in Maryland. That's for certain. But Indians in Connecticut sued and won restitution and even Federal recognition. And they did not have a pre-existing treaty or any reservations either."

"Oh yeah? Well, if you win, we'll have to re-name the Orioles, the Nanticoke Indians." Jack snidely commented.

"And you know, the Indians will have to sue the state of Delaware too."

"No, why is that? said Jack."

"Because of a clerical error. Lord Baltimore it seems agreed to draw the border with the colony of Delaware too far south and the Maryland land that was transferred to Delaware included a large part of the original reservation."

"What do you mean?"

"Penn and his men apparently swindled Baltimore by producing an incorrect map when they were negotiating the agreement for the border of the two colonies. So the surveyors drew the southern east west border from Fenwick Island instead of from Cape Henlopen."

Jack laughed. "That sounds like a swindle that ordinarily peaceful people would go to war over."

"Yeah. But the Indians were the big losers. I can't see that there were any white people living in those territories at the time."

They ordered some hot dogs and some of the stadium's famous 'piss' beer and consumed them without relish. Now the game was reaching its climax. And then one of the Indians' players hit a home run, scoring three players and taking the lead. In the last inning, the Orioles were unable to come back and so they lost, and forty thousand spectators noisily filed out of the stadium upset and disappointed. "I have a bad feeling that the Orioles are not going to win this series." said Will as they filed down the ramp. When they were standing outside the stadium in the crowds who were slouching away into the night, Jack turned to Will.

"I can help you on the political side, Will. But I think your legal strategy is really a long shot. I would guess even longer odds than the Orioles beating the Indians and winning this year's World Series. On the treaty question, that would be a case of constitutional law. I don't think McNutt could help you much there. As for the archives, call my assistant, Hilary, next week and she can get you an intro into the archives. If a copy of the treaty survives there, you should be able to find it."

"Thanks Jack. Thad be a big help."

"I'll ask around to see if I can find a good lawyer who specializes in constitutional law cases."

"That would be a big help too. And if you could arrange an appointment for me with our congressman in D.C. I would appreciate it."

"I'll see what I can do." And with that they parted and went to their own cars and returned home to Bristol and Annapolis. On the road, Will felt a faint pang of sorrow. It would be nice if he were returning home to a woman at the house. And not merely an empty house. But after he got home, he concluded that his feelings were only a consequence of having drunk three beers earlier in the evening and the depressive effects of the alcohol.

The rest of the month slowly dragged by. Will felt depressed again. There was no business, and outside the weather had turned dismal and chilly. In those weeks the Orioles managed to lose their championship series to the Indians. About a week after attending the Orioles' game, Will called Hilary at Jack's office and asked if she could arrange an appointment for him at the state archives. He drove over to 'Napolis' the next week on a rainy Friday morning. He had with him only a legal size notepad and a pen tucked in his thin brief case. The state archives were located in a newly built brick building a fair distance from the state capital and the city center. All the parking spaces were taken so he had to park on the street some distance away. He had forgotten to bring an umbrella so when he got to the building his head and the shoulders of his raincoat were soaked from the rain. The receptionist looked at him with astonishment; that someone so dripping wet would enter the archives. But she dutifully called the collections researcher and took his jacket to hang up. The researcher at her desk carefully listened to Will's request and with an earnest "Let's see." began searching on her computer. After only a few minutes back and forth, she announced that indeed the archives still had a copy of the original treaty. "It is called a 'Treaty of Peace between his Majesty the King of England and Scotland, Charles the Second and owner of the Royal Colony of Maryland, and the chiefs of the Nanticoke nation' and it is dated 1666. We have the one of the original copies. In our rare documents collection. It is handwritten on parchment, and the note says here it is in good condition. And we have in addition made a microfilm copy of the treaty. And we also have a microfilm copy of the copy that is in England—must have survived the wars— and in addition there are addenda that concern the setting up of the reservations."

"That's fabulous. Really that such an old document should have survived intact for so long. Not destroyed by fire or insects."

"And it survived the move from St. Mary's in 1720. A lot of the state probate records and early documents did not survive that move from St. Mary's to Annapolis."

"Can I see the treaty? Can I read it?"

"I'm afraid not. We don't allow people who aren't bonafide researchers look at the physical document. But you can read it on a microfilm reader in the reading room. I'll set you up, if you like."

"Yes, I would like to read it."

"And if you need it, we can make a photographic copy of it on paper. From the microfilm copy that is."

"Really? That'd be great."

"Fine. It costs twenty five dollars a page. And it would take about a week to complete and have ready for you."

"How many pages are we talking about?"

"The treaty and its addenda from 1668, 1669, 1673, and 1681 come to twenty pages. Do you want the copies made?"

"Wow. That's going to be expensive. More than five hundred dollars."

"So, do you want it?"

"Yes, I suppose I do."

"Fine, I can arrange it then. Now come with me, and let me get you set up in the reading room."

They walked down a flight of stairs to a large ground floor room that looked like a typical library room with long wooden tables, except instead of being bare tables there stood on most of the tables large bulky black boxes, with black hoods. These, it turned out, were the microfilm readers. The researcher went to the end of the room to a counter and ordered the microfilm by giving the attendant behind the counter a file number. After a few minutes, the attendant returned with a metal can. The researcher took it and went over to a reader near the window and began setting up the film in the reader. When she was finished she turned on the lamp and there it was: elaborate handwritten text which reminded Will on first sight of the copies he had seen of the American Declaration of Independence.

"Now, here's how you scroll up or down. And how you move page to page. And here is how you can enlarge a piece of text on one page. It's all pretty straightforward. If you need any further help, the attendant there can help. Now is there anything else I can do for you today?"

Will looked at the researcher with gratitude and noticed then that she had a really quite attractive face and a nice figure. But she was dressed very plainly. He hadn't noticed that in her office.

"Thanks so much. Oh and what is your name?"

"Jennifer Oates. Here, I'll leave you my phone number and extension here. Call me when you're finished here and come up to fill in an application for the photocopy. In about a week, if you decide you want them, the photocopies should be ready." And Jennifer left. Will looked after her and watched the gentle rocking of her hips in the tight blue skirt she was wearing until she disappeared through the door.

Reading the text of the treaty turned out to be challenging. Many of the words and letters were hard to decipher, and many of the words were archaic and unfamiliar to him. He wasn't sure what inalienable usufruct meant for instance. And some of the crimes listed which could cause a re-assessment of the reservations were also unclear to him. He was especially interested to see that the treaty was signed on behalf of the most Serene Prince Charles II, King of England, Scotland, France and Ireland, by Cecil Calvert, Lord Baltimore, the Proprietor of the King's colony of Maryland. Every schoolkid in Maryland learned about the Calverts. But reading further down, the signature applied to the paper was that of Charles Calvert, Cecil's son who had power of attorney for the Proprietor, who signed on behalf of the King. Signing for the Indians were six men said to be chiefs of the Nanticoke-Accomack-Kuskorawaok tribe. These names were all unrecognizable to Will, and their signatures were all various squiggly marks or smudges. The treaty outlined the desire for perpetual peace to exist between the subjects of the King and the native tribes in the territory described as the Eastern Shore, with the exception of the territory assigned to the colony of Virginia. Most important it recognized that the Indian tribes were to be recognized as their own sovereignty and not subjects of the King and they would be free to govern themselves, free to practice their own religion, and free to conduct their own livelihoods without consultations or permissions from the Proprietor. It also included several protections for the Indian tribes from English settlers or residents of the Eastern Shore. Will took some notes on his yellow legal pad. There were a few sentences about the regulation of trade and commerce between the two communities. But there was very little instruction on how to resolve disputes between the two communities. And the treaty spelled out what constituted violations of the peace by individual Indians, which could lead to a state of war or a revoking of the treaty. It seemed that treaty could only be revoked from the King's side, and not by the Indians. The treaty ended by laying out an area that would be reserved for the exclusive use and residence of the Indian tribes, or a reservation, which was spelled out in very approximate fashion. "so many thousands of paces to the southeast from the river bank of the Chatacawa River to the Black Creek and then another several thousand paces to the north to the Broad River which drains into the Nanticoke River" and the like. These referred to creeks, and streams and even rivers by names that Will did not recognize. He wrote all of this down and hoped to check out on a detailed map if he could reproduce the coordinates given in the treaty. Reading to the end, he couldn't help but find the date of the treaty to be ironic. It was put as 'Tuesedaye, the 23rd daye of August in the year of Our Lord 1668. He was certain that that date meant nothing to the Indians who had signed, and that, as they were not ruled by the either the Catholic or Protestant churches of the time, it probably seemed a strange way of referring to a day and date. Of course, he assumed that the tribes had no calendar or system for assigning dates.

The first addendum to the treaty was written seven years later and it established a large reservation starting at seven nautical miles up from the mouth of the Nanticoke River and continuing on both banks for another seven miles to the Broad Creek. It was a plot of land measured from the firm land of the river bank to a distance of eight thousand paces out along a line perpendicular to the line of the river bank. And then along a northerly bearing over forty two thousand paces to the Broad Creek on the left bank of the Nanticoke and to an obscure reference point on the right or western bank. There was no estimate made in the treaty as to the area of this land. But Will understood that it was a very large parcel of land. Was this the fourteen thousand acres he had been told about by Mr. Alvey? The other two addenda, dated 1675 and 1683, set up two other reservations further up the Nanticoke in territory which Will understood was now located in Delaware.

Reading these texts on the microfilm reader was hard work and after two hours his eyes were tired and he needed a break. It was also time for lunch. And with the thought of lunch, he suddenly remembered Natasha at the Golden Bull restaurant. He would very much like to see her again. She was really pretty, even sexy, or so he remembered. He turned off the reader and fetched his damp coat and rushed out of the archives. The slanting rain had let up, but in its place there was a very light sprinkle of rain, what his father used to call 'fly piss'. He drove over to the restaurant and at the reception asked if he could have a table served by Natasha. The receptionist, a young acned woman, looked at him askance but led him to a small table deep inside the restaurant far from the windows, leaving a menu behind her. After a few minutes Natasha came over to the table with a glass pitcher of iced water. He recognized her at once. She was still a knock-out; slender with nice breasts highlighted by a tight black top, long blond hair, shapely calves in black stockings. "Hi, Natasha. Remember me? I came here with Jackson Parker about two months ago?" Natasha reacted with mild surprise, and she looked at him for a moment. "No, sorry. I don't. Lots of men come in here. And zey all making passes at me. I know Mr. Parker. Dirty old man. So who are you?" "I'm Will Eames. But I don't live here in Annapolis." "Okay. Do you know what you want to order?" When Will picked up the menu, she said, "Okay. I give you minute to look at it and choose vat you vant." And she abruptly walked away from him. He couldn't concentrate on the menu. He had left no impression on Natasha at all it seemed. He didn't know what he had expected when he rushed over here. 'I didn't think she would jump into my arms,' he thought to himself, but he thought she would have at least recognized and remembered him. He had wanted to see her again, and maybe talk a bit with her. She came back to the table, but did not look at him. She took his order and came back again with his drink. After fifteen minutes she came back again with his order, a Reuben sandwich, and she re-filled his ice tea. But again she refused to meet his eyes. After he had finished eating his sandwich, Natasha came back and cleared away his plate. "Is zere anything else you want? Dessert? Coffee?" Will looked at her again closely. "No, but when are you getting off work? Maybe we could get together over a drink if you're free." Natasha looked at him full in the face, and then shaking her head said, "No. I don't sink so. I get off here at 10:30. And today is my last day working here. Tomorrow, I flying home to Kiev. So we won't get togezer." And she abruptly turned and walked away. A few minutes later she brought the check for his lunch to the table and left it on the table in passing. "Pay at the register." she said as she passed. And she disappeared. He took up his damp coat, put a ten dollar bill on the table and left for the archives. 'Another strike out', he thought in his car on the way back. 'At least she didn't try to humiliate me.'

He had forgotten all about Natasha-- just as she had him-- by the time he came again to Jennifer Oates at the archives. "So I've looked at the treaty document on the machine and I've found lots of interesting information."

"Oh yeah? What are you interested in?"

"I'm doing some research on the Nantiquak Indians from the Eastern Shore. I want to do a big project on them."

"Oh, that sounds very interesting."

"So I do want to make a photocopy of the entire treaty document."

"Fine. Fill out this form. We'll start on it tomorrow. No, I mean on Monday. I'll call you when it's ready if you leave your phone number.

In about a week." She checked the application form he had filled out and continued, "Let's see. The copy will come to $538 including tax. We copy it from the microfilm, not the original document because it's too fragile. You can pay with a personal check when you come to pick up the copy."

"That's expensive. You ought to digitize it. Reproduction costs then would be much less, I think."

"Yes, maybe. But we don't have the money to digitize anything in our collection."

"Yeah, Maryland tax dollars go to building highways here on mainland Maryland. Not to archives. And not to public works on the Eastern Shore either."

Jennifer chuckled and nodded her agreement.

'Really nice woman,' he thought to himself. 'Indefinite age. I wonder if she's married.' He had looked but hadn't seen a wedding band on any of her fingers.

It was November and the Poseidon Palace had already closed for the season so Will suspended his Wednesday routine of taking lunch there while reading the Wednesday business section of the Baltimore Sun and discussing it with Tony. Instead he ordered a submarine sandwich to be delivered to his office. As he was eating it at his desk, he noticed a small article which announced the opening of a new Indian casino. He read it carefully. It was the Cherokee Indians, the eastern Cherokees of North Carolina-- and they had just opened a casino built on their reservation by the Harrah resort and casino company of Nevada. There wasn't much background information, but the news excited him and prompted him to find out more about the background and the terms and conditions under which it had gotten built and financed. Tony had left town for a protracted visit, so he couldn't talk these developments over with Tony. He missed having someone to discuss his plans with, especially Tony's comradeship and his sharp innate business sense. There wasn't much detailed information he could find on the internet—the deep background story on all business and commercial transactions always seemed to be missing in internet sources—so he would have to speak to someone in the know. That probably meant someone there at the casino itself in Cherokee, North Carolina. And probably that someone would not tell him anything, except in a face to face meeting. But he didn't need to go there right away. Not before he had a project and the agreement of the Nantiquaks themselves. But he did find out that the Cherokees did not actually have a reservation. It seemed that the Cherokees had pooled lands that their tribal members had lived on and purchased and combined them into one large parcel, which they called the Qualla Boundary. This they had put into a trust, which the Federal government administered and which functioned for all intents and purposes like a reservation. It was a large area, more than 200 square miles, encompassing large parts of a few counties. The Harrah's Cherokee casino was built on the Qualla. When he finished reading the material he could find on the internet later that afternoon, Will felt a satisfying sense of accomplishment. It felt like he was moving ahead on his Injun project. Even if he had achieved nothing in actual fact.

Later that same evening in the stillness of his house, Will thought he needed to make further research to put together a convincing presentation to the council of the Nantiquak Indians. Assuming of course that the council decided that they wanted to hear a presentation and proposal from him. With a pen and the legal size yellow pad, he sat at a low table and began to lay out a strategy for preparing the presentation, writing an outline and listing the information he needed to get before he could go in front of the council with a convincing presentation. He recognized that he had not sufficiently prepared himself when he first went up to give his proposal to Mr. Norwood at the Association. He would not make that mistake again. But he had to inform himself properly this time. And he had to arrange the information he collected into a coherent sales pitch. That meant addressing any objections that the Nantiquaks might have in advance. Marley had given him some insights to the possible objections they could have. He spent most of the evening laying out the information he needed for his presentation. And the biggest gap in the information he had about the entire project was how to go about getting Federal recognition for the tribe. There was the law of course, but the real issues and regulations were administrative and they all were spelled out and controlled by the Bureau of Indian Affairs in the Department of Interior. That meant he needed to go to 'Warshington' to consult with the people in the Bureau.

It is not so easy approaching a large Washington bureaucracy especially one that was more accustomed to denying benefits or permissions to people than to helping or serving people. And the Bureau was no less like that than any other in the Federal city. Calling someone in the Bureau was difficult, and the general operator did not try to direct his calls to anyone who could specifically help him. Instead several times she directed his call to a computerized answering router, which got him nowhere. He looked on the internet for the Bureau's offices, but while it outlined the structure of the organization, its intricate combination of offices, departments, divisions and directorates what he could find on the internet did not give him names or phone numbers. So he began playing a guessing game where he called the main number and asked the general operator to speak to someone in such and such an office. She would direct his call to another operator or receptionist for that office, who after listening to what he wanted would either direct his call to another person or, more often, would suggest he call a different office, but without redirecting his call. He spent an entire morning this way, repeatedly calling the main Bureau number and getting redirected only to reach dead-ends. It very much seemed to Will that when he indicated to his interlocutor on the other end of the line that he was not himself an Indian or representing any specific tribe, that the answers he got became more dismissive and vague. But finally his inquiry ended up at the receptionist of the acting second deputy assistant secretary for the office of federal recognition, who was not in the office just then. She politely told him that from what he had told her that he had probably reached the right office and that he needed to speak to her boss, but he could not come to see him for another two weeks. So he made a morning appointment to see John Weekes a week before Thanksgiving-- probably a bad time Will thought as everyone was busy in their minds getting ready for the holiday or finishing work that needed to be done before the holiday.

With that appointment set up, Will needed to make another to make his trip a most effective use of his time. For this he called Jack and asked if he could help him make an appointment with the Congressman for their district on that same day in the afternoon. Jack agreed to try, saying he would pitch it to the Congressman such that he would also be coming to the meeting. He said he would call him back to let him know if he was successful getting an appointment. "Too bad about those Orioles, eh?" Jack said before hanging up. "They're probably finished now. Next season will be worse." Will agreed. "But you have to be optimistic in order to succeed at anything you undertake. So I am optimistic that next year, they will do well also." After he hung up on Jack, he suddenly realized that he was maybe speaking about himself and his own project and not the Orioles' future baseball season.

Ten days later he still had not heard anything from the Nantiquak Indian council. So he prepared to make his trip to 'Warshington', a drive of a little more than an hour and a half but a destination that existed as if in another world. He left almost three hours before his appointment. He didn't like Washington at all. It was too big and too heartless. It was a black and white city: white during the day, black at night. During the day it was peopled by white middle class government bureaucrats; a cold bunch, who were almost like automatons suffering from conformity, people who all came from somewhere else. But at night, the city was populated by its real residents: black people who during the day were mostly out of sight but who occupied the margins of the white city, its security jobs, its junior administrators, and its humble service jobs. At night, the black natives abandoned the Federal white city, leaving it like a cemetery. In the rest of the city, they lived a restless, fearful, but vibrant life. Will had always been scared of the city at night—he had been accosted one dark evening on its streets— but during the day the white city left him cold and uninspired. It was a place with little local character during the day. He drove into the city following the late rush hour crowds on a highway which grew wider and wider as it got closer. Once in the city, he had to cross the dead zone within the outer areas of the city—a place of much narrower highways, dirty, littered streets, abandoned houses, crowded residential streets, and people, usually always black people shuffling around with blankets around their shoulders. His first destination was the Bureau of Indian Affairs in the white city, located not far from the Mall. He knew where it was, but he did not know where he could park his car, and he spent some time looking for a public parking garage. He finally found one, about eight blocks away from the offices of the Department of the Interior where the Bureau was headquartered. He had to walk briskly to make it in time for his appointment. His long raincoat made the walking difficult as it dragged on his legs.

When he finally arrived at the offices of the Bureau off of Constitution Avenue, Will had to first go through a barrage of security checks, through electronic scanners, put his briefcase and raincoat through an x-ray machine, and a check for metal instruments and things of any kind. Apparently the Bureau had been attacked not too many years earlier by violent Indian activists who resented what the Bureau did or didn't do. The whole process took longer than an airport security scan. It took a long while. Then he was directed to the main receptionist, who asked him to wait for an escort to take him to the office of federal recognition. It was located on the third floor, and the elevator was not working so the escort led him up the stairs. His raincoat in one hand and his brief case in the other he rushed up the stairs and waited at the top for the escort who was wheezing and gasping by the time he got there. Then he was taken to the receptionist for the office who asked him to sit and wait in the reception room. It reminded him a little of the reception room of the Nantiquak Indian Association; mostly bare, it was decorated only with a large portrait of President Clinton hanging on one wall, a U.S. flag and a flag of the Department of the Interior standing limply in one corner, and a table covered in magazines, all with titles relating to Indians and Indian life. He arrived precisely at his appointment time, but then he began to wait. And he waited, and waited. Forty five minutes passed, and then fifty five before a woman came to the door and called his name. Will wondered if there was something about Indian culture that did not recognize the urgency of the passage of time, or acknowledge the practice of assigning appointments with precise times. She took his raincoat and led him into an office off a central hallway.

The acting deputy assistant secretary of the office of Federal Recognition stood up from behind his desk when Will entered the room and he offered his hand. They shook hands and then exchanged business cards. Will proffered his real estate agent's card.

"John Nighthorse Ward. Please take a seat." Will saw a stocky man wearing a dark grey suit jacket and a blue tie, almost identical to what Will was wearing. The man wore a headband and his salt and pepper hair was pulled back into a long pony tail. It seemed obvious that he was an Indian.

"I'm Will Eames. From Bristol, Maryland." They shook hands. "I'm glad you're able to see me, even before Thanksgiving."

"Thanksgiving is not a holiday for me. I'm a Nottawaysac Indian and we observe Native American Memorial Day in place of Thanksgiving. Please be seated, Mr. Eames."

Will sat and Mr. Ward did likewise, and folded his hands together on his desk looking straight at Will. Nothing was said. Will thought it strange that he was staring at Mr. Nighthorse Ponytail. Still he could not detect any animosity coming from the direction of Mr. Ponytail. Finally Will broke the silence.

"I've come here today to ask you the proper way for a small tribe to seek and get Federal recognition. So far I have been able to find that there is a political process and an administrative process. But I would like you to tell me what the best way is to get recognition, and then all the steps a tribe would need to take to get recognized."

"Yes, I see. You've come to the right place. And I can tell you what you want, even if I have only recently been appointed to this position."

"But first, tell me, Mr. Eames. Are you inquiring for personal reasons, or are you inquiring on behalf of some specific tribe? Are you a journalist?"

"No, I am not a journalist. But I am asking on behalf of a specific tribe which I may be advising."

"May I ask which tribe that would be?"

"Yes. It is on behalf of the Nantiquak-Kuskorawaok-Accomack tribe of Delmarva."

"I see. Sort of an initial inquiry?"

"Yes. I want to understand the difference between a political process and the administrative route to recognition."

"Okay. Well, they are both routes to recognition and they both can result in recognition. Both routes take a good deal of time. But the procedures and steps necessary for recognition through the administrative route are better defined and established by law, and they are administered by the Bureau here. That being said, most of the American Indian tribes which now have recognition have gotten it through the political route, usually by means of a treaty or several treaties with the Federal government. But in the past two decades new tribes have gotten recognition through us, at the Bureau, in accordance with a law Congress passed in the seventies."

"So you would say that the Pequoddy tribe of Connecticut took the political route to gain recognition of their tribe?"

"You mean the tribe which not long ago opened up a casino there?"

"Yes, that one."

"Most definitely. They petitioned their Senator, Senator Dodd I believe, to support the passage of a law which established relations with the tribe. But they also started their process through the courts. As I say, there is no set road map for recognition through the political route. And so taking that route these days is almost certainly to take much longer than coming to us. Our procedures are well laid out."

Ward reached into a drawer of his desk and took out a small booklet with a color printed cover. He handed it to Will.

"This is a guide book which we have prepared to assist tribes and tribal associations and their advisors on the steps and procedures required by the Bureau as established by the law of 1977 in order to get recognition. We advise you to read it carefully to understand what needs to be done by both the petitioning tribe and by us."

Will took the booklet and flipped through its thirty two pages, full of text and diagrams.

"And how long does the Bureau's procedures take to gain recognition?"

"That is a hard question to answer. It depends on the condition of the tribe and data it has, not to mention the willingness of tribal members to undergo the investigations and data submissions that are required. Some tribes have been able to get recognition in less than two years. Others have been working on the process with applications pending more than a dozen years."

"Wow. I suppose there is also a cost to this long, drawn out procedure?"

"Yeah, there are costs to be borne. Legal representation is one cost, and establishing a legal entity is another. Data collection costs. You see I am experienced as I had a leading role in applying for the recognition of my own tribe, the Nottawaysacs of Virginia. It took us a bit more than three years. Not too long considering we have a documented history of nearly four hundred years."

"The Nantiquaks also have such an on-going long history. And they have a state recognized and registered tribal association, which has more than a century of activity."

"That helps the process a great deal. No doubt about it. If the tribe can speak and make all the filings with a unified voice that also greatly helps the process move on to completion quickly and efficiently."

"Is there a formal application document? Or would we need to start the process by a letter and petition and with attached filings?"

"No there are no simple application forms. But your tribe would need to submit a letter requesting recognition and the beginning of the process for getting that recognition. But I am sure you would have a lot of questions. So I would suggest that you carefully read the booklet before we go on any further today. Here's another booklet which sets out the experience of two tribes which recently were granted Federal recognition. It should be very helpful."

"Oh, and may I ask. Are you a lawyer?" said Ward.

"No. I'm a real estate agent. I suppose my business –the buying and selling and transferring of titles to properties—is very similar to getting and disposing of reservations."

"Yes, if you say so. May I offer you a suggestion? You might ask for some free advice about the whole process from a very well qualified lawyer who is currently directing the process for her own tribe. Here. She's Matoaka Warrens, she works for the Bureau, but just now is seconded to the Smithsonian. Here's her contact numbers over there." He handed Will a printed card, which showed the name 'Minny Warrens Office of Legal Counsel.'

"I'm sorry, Mr. Eames. But if you have any further questions right away, you will need to study this booklet and then consult with Ms. Warrens. Just now, I have other things I need to pay attention to, right away and I would ask you to consider our business done for today."

Will thought that Mr. Ponytail, although a recent appointee, was already quite expert at talking in the bureaucratic style. He stood up, shook Ward's hand and bade him farewell. He retrieved his raincoat from the Office receptionist who had shown him in, and now she escorted him to the main entry. Outside, back on the street, the sky was blustery and colder than it had been at the beginning of the morning. Clouds filled the sky and crumpled browned leaves flew about launched by the gusts of wind. It was too early for his second appointment which was going to be at the Congressional Office Building about two miles away. So he decided to re-locate his car over in South East, closer to his appointment and then to grab some lunch at a simple place over there. Once he got to S.E. he started to cruise around in his car, looking for a parking lot with space. The neighborhood around 4th Street looked blighted. There were a number of empty lots all surrounded by chain link fences most of which were dented or rusted. On some of these empty plots paid parking stands offered unsheltered parking, but most of these posted 'Full' signs when he cruised by. On several others there was evidence of the beginnings of new construction but none actually were active on this afternoon. There were no houses or residential buildings anywhere, and neither were there grocery shops or fast food outlets. The sidewalks were wide, but all cracked and hardly any pedestrians were out. 'What a nightmare this place must be at night,' he thought. Still he parked his car at one of the lots situated on E Street between the elevated rail lines and the elevated interstate expressway which both emanated from Union Station. The entire street appeared to be occupied by construction sites or these small parking lots. He figured his walk to the Congressional Office building must be about eight blocks and he despaired of finding any restaurant in the area in between. But he found a place hidden in a new, bland- looking stone and glass building just beyond the metro stop. It was a lunch bar, which served sandwiches, soup and salads for the lunch hour crew and which closed at three thirty. Arriving at one thirty, he was already a late luncher meaning he had the place to himself. He stayed until closing, studying the booklet that Ward had given him. After the lunch bar closed Will walked the final three blocks over a bridge above the expressway to the Congressional Office building. After fifteen minutes Jackson Parker walked up. They then entered and submitted themselves to fifteen minutes of security checks and clearances.

They were meeting with the congressman from the first district of Maryland, one Mr. Morton, a Republican, who to the relief of both Will and Jackson spoke with the slow, southern inflections typical of the Eastern Shore. Jackson led the meeting on behalf of Will setting out the situation of the Nantiquak Indians, their need for Federal recognition, and for the return of their reservation. He did not in this introduction mention Will's project to build a tribal casino. But he did tell him about the history of Senator Dodd's legislation which gave recognition and a reservation to the Pequoddy Indians and the Mohegan Indians. Mr. Morton listened intently to the end. He said he recalled the legislation for the Connecticut Indians.

"And how many Nanticoke—excuse me you did say Nanticoke?—Indians are we talking about?"

"Nantiquak," said Will. "We're talking about twelve hundred Indians living in three different collectives." He omitted to say that most of them lived in Delaware.

"That's not very many."

"No, not from the point of view of political accounting," Jackson retorted. "But that is much more than the populations of either the Pequoddy or Mohican tribes which have gone through legislation to win back their reservations and rights."

"I wasn't in Congress when those two pieces of legislation were passed that you're referring to. So I am not familiar at all with the arguments or political bargaining which got those acts set up as law. Before my time, I'm afraid. And I think that there is very little institutional memory left here in Congress about those cases."

Will moved as if to say something, but Jackson cut him off.

"I think Indian land rights and reclamation is still a hot issue. Maybe more today than they were then. There continues to be both legal challenges and legislation addressing these issues all across the country. And the recent opening of new Indian casinos in several states are testing the Indian Gaming Act even as we speak."

"That's all very fine, Mr. Parker. But you yourself point to a basic flaw in your approach. You see, Congress passed the law for Indian tribes to get Federal recognition, what was it, in 1975. And it established the administrative path to recognition, which has been codified by the Bureau of Indian Affairs. But with all the recent legislation, it is clear to me that we don't need more political action and legislation to solve the Nanticoke's issues. No, you have to follow the administrative path to recognition. Of course you could still chart a legal path through the courts for recourse."

Will now replied, "So that means you would not support a movement to introduce legislation on behalf of Maryland's only surviving tribe? The only tribe which lives entirely in your district."

"No, I think not. Not in today's environment. I could never get enough support for such legislation. Certainly, you may be aware that most of the Maryland delegation in both the House and the Senate comprises Democrats. I doubt I could win much sympathy from any of them."

"Besides I think people here on the Hill are beginning to view the whole issue of Federal recognition of Indian tribes currently as just a front for these groups and tribes to open up unregulated casinos."

"But the Federal government delivers much greater material benefits to recognized tribes than just the permission to build casinos," Jackson replied.

"Yeah, maybe. But look, what are the first budgetary items to get cut when there is a squeeze on welfare spending? Benefits going to Indian tribes. It's easy to cut those benefits, because Indians have so little political voice or weight."

"So maybe we should speak to our Senators?" asked Jackson.

"You're certainly free to do that, Mr. Parker. I won't stop you. But they are both Democrats from the mainland, the Western Shore. I think they will have even less reason to be interested in such an initiative than I have."

Will was beginning to feel very frustrated by Representative Morton's responses. But then he had little experience or insight into the politicking within the Congress or how members of Congress assessed issues that merited support. Congressmen worked to win different returns than businessmen or lawyers or real estate brokers did. Getting re-elected was the supreme return on efforts expended. And Will just did not understand what it took for a Congressman to get re-elected.

"And you know there's beginning to be a sort of push-back on casinos and casino gambling. Everyone recognizes that casino gambling only attracts big time crime. Even if it is closely regulated and monitored and run by Indian tribes.

"So I ask you again. Where are the votes in this initiative? That's a rhetorical question."

With that their meeting was over. On their way out, Jackson muttered the answer to Representative Morton's question: "There aren't any, of course." They stepped out of the building and it was already dark. The wind had died down but now it seemed much colder than it had earlier in the day. Will pulled up the collars of his khaki brown raincoat. It didn't provide much warmth.

"I know of a good bar on Pennsylvania Avenue. Care to join me for a drink? We can hash out where you stand now. It's a long trudge over there, but a nice bar."

It was nearly eight o'clock when he finally left Jack at the bar and walked back across the abandoned Mall to the dark side of the white city, and the empty streets of S.E. He was feeling a little tipsy, but was looking around with a heightened sense of caution. The buildings were empty and shut down and dark. There was a strong chilly wind; he was underdressed for the weather. There was no one on the poorly lit streets, and he feared that there could be muggers lurking in the extensive shadows all around the neighborhood. He just imagined what the condition of his car was in that insecure parking lot where he had left it. He did not like D.C. but he was going to have to get used to the city, if he was going to succeed at his project.

The next day, a Friday, Will received two calls on his cell phone. He was surprised by both of them. The first was from Phyllis, Uncle Hampton's housekeeper and live-in companion. She said that Hampt really would like to have his extended family come over the next Thursday for a Thanksgiving feast. She said that he realized that he had never done this before, but it was his desire to celebrate this holiday as a big family affair before he died. He was also inviting Will's parents, and his sister and brother-in-law, as well as his uncle Ernest (who lived in Yarmouth) and his adult children. And of course there would be a big roast turkey, which she herself would be preparing. Will said he would attend and he thanked her. He asked how Hampton was doing, and Phyllis said simply, "Oh, he's still holding on. Had a bit of a cough last night." The second call came only an hour later. It was from Marley. He said his name in such a mumbled fashion, however, that at first Will thought he had received the call from a crank caller. But after repeating his name a few times, and saying he was from the Nantiquak Indian Association, Will understood. Marley wanted to convey the news that the tribal council would like to hear his presentation, and would be ready to meet with him on the Tuesday, the second of December in the week after Thanksgiving. Could Will come to the Association office at 11 am on that day, he asked. Will said yes and Marley said thanks and hung up without a further word.

These calls reminded him that he should call the woman that Mr. Ponytail had recommended that he speak to. He looked for her card among his papers and finally found it in his briefcase. Minnie Warren. That was strange. Mr. Ponytail had said her name was Matoaka; sounded Japanese. He called the number on the card from his office phone. A woman answered and said that he needed to call her number at the Smithsonian. "Could you give it to me, please?" The woman hmmed and hawed, it was obvious she was looking through papers. "Here it is," she muttered more to herself than to Will and then she dictated it to him. He called the number. There was no answer for some time, so he hung up. He called it again forty minutes later. Again the line rang eight times before a woman's voice answered. "She's not in the office today. She's on sick leave. Try calling again next week, say Tuesday or Wednesday. Better yet, try after Thanksgiving." Will thanked the woman and said he would call back then. He marked down the new number along with Minny's name on his desk calendar for the 1st of December with the message 'to call'. And then he forgot about it. He needed to start putting his presentation together for the Nantiquaks. But before he could start, he had some new real estate business to look after. First, Lucy came to him and showed him a letter she had drafted to John Ehrlich which informed him that his childhood house was on the market, and asked if he would like to buy it. Lucy had chased down Ehrlich's current home address and had put it in the letter. Will approved the letter, which was from him, and when she re-printed it on their letterhead he signed it. "Good work, Lucy. Chasing this down." He patted her on her shoulder as she took the letter back to her desk. Then he turned to two new listing opportunities one for a house in Hurlesville, and the other for a highway store site on Highway 50 in Bristol. These took up the rest of his day, so it wasn't until five that he returned his attentions to his presentation.

At midday on that next Thursday, Robert Eames and his wife, Mar-Sue, and son, Will, in the back seat of their Chevy SUV, drove up the stony lane to Hampton's farmhouse. Kate, his younger sister and her husband, Pat, followed in a white Toyota sedan. They had not spoken during the short drive across the flat, dirty brown country which looked lifeless under the slight fog. There were several other cars parked out front. When they all stepped out of the cars, Will for the first time noticed that Kate was showing the signs of being pregnant. It surprised him. He had not seen her since August and he didn't expect to see such a dramatic change in his sister whose black short quilted jacket accentuated her tummy bulge. Hampton came to the door with his walking stick in one hand and the other holding open the screen door. "Come in, come in, everybody," he shouted in a weak voice which barely carried to them. Will saw that Hampton looked more emaciated than he had the last time he saw him in late September. But his eyes still sparkled he noticed when they passed through the door. Inside his Uncle Ernest stood and walked toward the door, and Phyllis emerged from the kitchen, and they took the new guests' coats and scarves. Hampton was still standing at the door, leaning on his stick. He was looking at the gathered relatives, his very pale face beaming with happiness.

The large dining room had been transformed, with a large dining table set up and laid with a starched white table cloth and tall brass candleholders. It was surrounded by a forest of tall, dark wooden antique chairs, a contrast to the pale teak paneled walls. It did not look like the festive table of a rustic, rural farmer. Will was impressed by the transformation of the house. Will's mother almost at once left the gathered crowd to help Phyllis in the kitchen. In the main sitting room Uncle Hampton sat down in what he said was his favorite yellow Queen Anne armchair, Will stood with his father, Bob, and Uncle Ernest stood next to his daughter, Will's cousin, Jane. Will had only met Jane once, when they were both little, and now she had developed and had become a buxom unmarried woman, rather plain looking in the face, and with a quiet disposition. Ernest was Bob's older brother and was short and stocky, but he looked just as Will remembered him from about fifteen years earlier. Ernest's son, cousin Jeff, would not be coming. He lived with his family in Florida. And Ernest and Bob's younger sister, Will's Aunt May, also would not be coming. Kate sat on the large sofa with her husband Pat solicitously sitting next to her. The group, effectively strangers to one another, mulled around awkwardly searching for something to say, but not finding anything other than short polite observations. Cousin Jane asked Kate very seriously, "So when are you due?" Kate answered her so that no one else heard her, "At the end of February, beginning of March." Uncle Hampt was still beaming with a broad smile on his face, and looking at all his guests in turn. "It's so wonderful to see you all," he said for all to hear. "There hasn't been a big Eames family Thanksgiving celebrated in this house in nearly sixty years. And that last time was held under rather ominous, dark circumstances. War everywhere. Let's see—I think you attended it, last time, Ernie. Do you remember? Oh maybe not, you'd have been still a baby."

Ernest shook his head. "No, no. I do seem to remember now that I seen this house again. But I was young, maybe only six years old."

"Too bad your son and his family couldn't come as well."

"You understand, Hampt. They live so far away. And they were invited today to his wife's family besides."

"Jane, are you married? How old are you?" asked Hampton.

Jane blushed deeply. "No I'm not. And I'm twenty eight."

"No need to be embarrassed, Jane. Lydia and I married too young. Nothing to be ashamed of. Look at Will. He's not married yet either."

Now it was Will's turn to feel the sting of embarrassment.

"But, I see that you Kate are ready to extend the family. Good for you."

Kate smiled and took Pat's arm in her hand. "Yes, we're expecting a boy, very soon. At the end of February. But of course he won't be an Eames."

"That's wonderful," said Hampton, his smile growing even larger. "You will be such proud parents, I'm certain of that."

After a short while Mar-Sue emerged back from the kitchen in the back. "Okay everyone to the table. We're ready. Bob, could you help Hampton to the table?"

Phyllis broke through the swinging door from the kitchen bearing a huge platter with a deep brown turkey on it. "Here it is everyone. A local bird, unlike most of y'awl." She laughed as she set it on the table in front of Hampton.

Behind her Mar-Sue came carrying a large dish of mashed sweet potatoes and a gravy boat. Both women went back into the kitchen to ferry out the rest of the feast, which included buttermilk biscuits and cornbread, fresh butter beans and overcooked string beans, and a large bowl of green salad. Everyone oohed and aahed over the parade of food. Will suddenly felt hungry from the flood of warm aromas. He reached for a biscuit, but his sister Kate frowned at him. "Wait," she said from across the table. Phyllis sat at the table on the right hand side of Hampton. Hampton had insisted. She was more like family, than a servant. Then Hampton called for a prayer of Thanksgiving and everyone grew silent and bowed their heads.

"Lord, we give Thee praise, and thank you with all our hearts for the grace that you have endowed on us. We give thanks for this bounty that you have provided to this family. And we ask that you will continue to show us your favor, protection, and generosity," was part of what Hampton said. Will never paid much attention to dinner prayers, which seemed to him to be filled with cant phrases from dusty church services. But he did hear at the end of this prayer the phrase, "with the time that we have left to us…"

Then it was time to begin eating the feast. There was promptly a huge bustle and clamor around the table as everyone began to dig in with serving spoons and dishes were passed around. It seemed a jolly atmosphere. Hampton tried to take up the lead role in carving the turkey, but soon gave up as the effort was too great for him from a seated position. Phyllis stood up and took over the carving and serving of large pieces of turkey. "Make sure to take some gravy," she said with a big smile. Ice tea served in tall tumblers was already on the table. But Hampton asked if anyone wanted wine as well. "There are also a number of bottles of beer in the ice-box if any of yous are so inclined." he said. There were no takers, neither for the wine or the beer. Will now took his biscuit and right away buttered it and took a bite out of it. It was still warm and delicious. When his filled plate came back to him, he ate ravenously and quickly—everything was so delicious-- and only after finishing most of his turkey did he notice that Phyllis had served Hampton very little, and his great uncle was eating and chewing with some difficulty. After a few minutes of this frenetic activity, a somber quiet mood returned to the room as everyone was intently eating the turkey and dressings. This quiet period lasted much longer interrupted only occasionally by a "could you pass me this?" or a "seconds?" or "yes, please." or "the turkey is so tender." Will thought it all rather strange, forced bonhomie and enthusiastic feasting amongst a group of strangers. He had never before partaken in an extended family Thanksgiving feast, and he suspected that the others, with the possible exception of Hampton, had not either. Thanksgiving while Will was growing up had been a close family affair, just him, his parents, and his sister.

But Hampton was not a fool, even if he nostalgically longed for an extended family. He knew that the family he had assembled for his last Thanksgiving was distant and mostly unknown one to the other. He finished his small portion and put down his fork and watched the others eating, his smile now abated. Hampton intended to direct the conversation around the table.

"So Ernie, could you tell us what you're doing these days?" he said directing a glance at Ernest, the latter nearly dropped his fork at his mouth filled with sweet potatoes. "Are you still working as an engineer?"

"No, I was a civil engineer with the municipal utilities, water and sewerage mostly. In Yarmouth and Talbot County, as you know. But I've retired from there. And now I mostly work on sailing my boat on the Bay. I have a boat moored on Kent Island."

"I see. Does your son-- what is his name, Kenneth—also sail?"

"No. I don't think so."

"You didn't teach him how to sail?"

"No, sadly. I didn't. I took him sailing only occasionally when he was a teenager. We could never get out schedules together."

"And he never took me sailing at all," Jane added taking everyone by surprise at her stern voice.

"That is a shame, Ernie," said Hampton. "You won't have those opportunities again. I don't suppose that Kenneth is a farmer, by any chance."

"No, he's a draftsman. Works for his father-in-law's architecture firm."

"Do you ever go fishing from your boat?" Bob, Ernest's younger brother, asked.

"Sometimes. Not usually. I just get into the wind and go for hours up and down the Bay. I think it's much windier off Kent Island than it is in the Choptico. Remember when we were young, how we had to go way out beyond Tilghman Island before we could catch much wind?"

"Yeah. I remember. I use a motorboat mainly. Never had enough money to buy a sailing yacht."

"It's not a yacht."

"What, you mean it's not more than thirty two feet?"

"No, it is, in fact forty feet."

"A yacht."

"If you insist."

"Enough of your squabbling." said Hampton, smiling again. I suppose you've not talked to one another or met in more than two decades. Am I right?" Both men nodded their assent.

"And Bob, what about you? What have you been doing since I last we last saw each other, sixteen years ago?"

"I was the manager at a large chicken farm-- raising broilers—just outside Bristol. Until it was bought by Perdue about ten years ago and I was let go. Now I work at the feed mill in town, Bristol I mean."

"Well, you're not a farmer either. And I know you didn't teach your son—nor your daughter for that matter-- farming or even raising chickens."

"No I didn't. I was more of a businessman. But my son is in real estate."

"Both of you then take after my grandfather, Robert Eames. He was a businessman, a real estate developer, and farmer in the last century. Very enterprising man. Maybe not very innovative as a farmer, but he made money."

"Before I go on, I did train my son Benjamin to be a farmer. But he wanted to be a soldier and ran off to fight as soon as the Japanese forced war on us. He never recovered from his soldiering. And when he came back he never had a family to teach farming to. You know, I had a series of long talks with my grand-nephew here, and I thought it was important to tell yo'awl –just to make things clear—that all of us have Injun ancestry. That a beautiful Injun maiden wed my father and so our line of the family are all part Injun. I hope that's not too much of a shock to yo'awl."

"I knew," said Ernie. "And I think Bob knows also. We both knew our grandmother—what was her name?"

"Mena."

"Right, Mena. Grand lady."

"Dad, why didn't you ever tell me?" protested Jane, again in an aggressive tone.

"Oh, I don't know. I guess the topic never came up."

"Pa, you never told me either," said Kate. "Were you ashamed."

"No, nothing like that. I also did not think of saying anything about it. But I only told Will for the first time this past summer when he ran into some Injuns from this part of the county." People were now finished eating and all forks were down.

"Would anyone like any more ice tea?" Phyllis jumped it.

"And you know," said Bob. "My son, part Injun, now has himself an Injun Project."

"Oh really?" said Hampton showing more interest and looking at Will as if to say 'you have to tell us about it.'

"Yes, he wants to build an Indian tribal casino on the Nanticoke River." Bob continued. "On land he's bought over there."

"Is that land near here?" Hampton asked. We're right close to the Nanticoke."

"Yes, in fact, it is right close." said Will. "It's between here and Exeter. Maybe four miles from here at most."

"Really? Indians and casino gambling?" said Will's mother. "That sounds like a really bad cocktail, or combination. A way to make poor people, poorer."

"No, mom. The idea is not to provide gambling for the Indians. But to catch a good deal of that flow of money that races through the county all the time, almost every weekend, on its way to Ocean City where it's wastefully dumped in the sand. A casino would raise income for the Nantiquak Indians. And maybe supply some employment opportunities also."

"That seems like not a bad idea." said Ernest. "The flow of sun-seekers and fun-seekers is awfully strong. Through Yarmouth County as well as Dorset County. And they don't leave much money in their wake in either place. 'Cepting maybe at the gas stations."

"I don't like it." said Mar-Sue. "A casino can only attract crime, and gambling, and the drinking that goes with it, can only debase people. And especially the poor. And Indians are the poorest of the poor."

"We'll have to build in protections for the Indian folks, especially for liquor and for gambling." answered Will. "Things like banning people from using debt to buy chips—like their credit cards, or hocking their houses. That has been done elsewhere. There's a fairly new casino in eastern Connecticut and it hasn't debased the poor Indians there, yet. Lots of controls are in place. And meanwhile it is generating a lot of income for the tribe. Financed a hospital for instance. Something the local government was unable or unwilling to do before."

"I can't think that it is a good thing." said Hampton quietly. "But it could make a lot of business sense and I think Will is right that it will attract a lot of income for the Injuns here in the Eastern Shore. And they could use the income. I can assure you that. Several Injuns work for me here on the farm, at every harvest."

Again the other guests were surprised by Hampton's statement.

"So Jane, what do you do?" Hampton continued, changing the subject.

"I work as a legal secretary in a law office in Yarmouth."

"And don't you want to get married?"

"Not unless it's to the right guy," answered Jane. "And I haven't found the right guy yet. Not too many of the right sort in a little town like Yarmouth."

Now Bob jumped in. "Will has a similar problem. It seems he can't find the right mate up to now. Bristol is even smaller than Yarmouth."

"And so many young people leave to find work elsewhere," continued Jane.

"Will says the same thing," said Bob.

"Certainly young people are leaving farming," said Hampton. "They don't want to live and work on farms. That much I can tell you."

Jane then addressed Pat, who was sitting opposite her, in an aggressive tone. "And what do you do besides being Kate's husband?"

Kate started to answer but Pat cut her off and answered. "Actually I write computer programs. I create advertising websites for companies. Something I can do from my home office."

Eyebrows rose around the table. Even Will had been unclear what it was that Pat did. Ernie almost whistled in amazement. "Who buys such things?"

"Actually, one of my recent clients was the Kent Narrows Marina. Perhaps you know about them, Ernie?"

"Yeah? Well I'll be dammed. Maybe then there will be fewer billboards on the highways for that marina."

"That's part of the idea, I think. All those young people who are leaving the small towns and farms of Delmarva, are more likely to look on the world wide web for information about a company or a service provider, than they are to look at billboards."

"So that is the future," said Hampton seeking to cut off this part of the conversation. "For those of you who might be interested in history, I have a rogue's gallery of news articles and clippings, and old photos about our ancestors. Maybe some of you would like to look at it upstairs before we proceed to dessert?" At that signal, Phyllis stood up and started collecting the plates. Will along with several others went upstairs to look at the exhibit again. He especially focused on the photos of Mena. This time under lamp light he thought he could make out a very pretty petit woman with a shy smile and big almond shaped eyes.

Dessert was pumpkin pie with freshly whipped heavy cream. It was a very spicy pie, served cold. When Phyllis gave Hampton a small sliver, he said, "I get such a small piece? Of my favorite pie?"

"All the pies I make for you are your favorites," replied Phyllis. Will had to agree. It was easily his favorite.

On the dark road on the way back to Bristol, nothing much was said. Except after fifteen minutes his mother turned to him and asked, "Are you really planning on building a casino for the Indians? Do you think it can be done?" All Will could say was, "I hope so. I don't know if I will succeed. But I got to try." He was distracted by the thought that maybe this day's Thanksgiving feast was the last time he would see Hampton alive. And the thought made him sad. And as they arrived home, he was thinking that he would have to address in his presentation to the Nantiquak council the arguments people could have in opposition to gambling and casinos. In selling an asset or property or idea you always had to answer and rebut all the buyer's objections to a deal before they could be raised.

On the Monday after Thanksgiving in his office as Will was putting the last touches on his presentation Lucy came in with a letter. "Here, read it. It didn't work." she said.

It was a reply letter from Mr. John Ehrlich, dated on the day before Thanksgiving. In a typed letter Will read:

Dear Mr. Eames,

I want to thank you for thinking of me when you notified me of the imminent sale of my childhood home in Bristol. If not for you letter I suppose I would never have heard the news of its being put on the market. I do remember the house and even remember my bedroom.

However I must decline your offer to buy the old house. I now live in my house in Baltimore and I have no intention in the future to move back to Bristol or to live anywhere else than Baltimore. I have to say that I do not have fond memories of my childhood home or for that matter of my childhood in Bristol. Quite the contrary. I was only too eager to flee Bristol and most of my memories of the place and of my family life are bitter ones which I would rather not remember.

The house itself has little to merit any memorialization. The idea of a house-museum is absurd. The house cannot be said to have contributed anything to my becoming a writer. And besides I am not an American literary giant of the likes of a Faulkner or a Steinbeck, so I doubt anyone would be interested in seeing the childhood house of a mere leading Maryland writer. As far as I know there are no mementoes or documents there in the house that would give any insights into my literary formation.

I wish you luck in selling the property.
Sincerely yours,
John Ehrlich

Will put the letter down on his desk. So this was another sales idea that didn't pan out. Disappointing, but it was of course always worth the try. He wasn't sure who Steinbeck was, though. Was he a giant of American literature? He agreed that Ehrlich was not a giant of American literature. Will looked at the letter again and then noticed there was something strange about it. The typing was at places a little uneven, and seemed jumpy. The letters on the page were not clean and uniform like the correspondence he was accustomed to which all came out of desk jet printers. He realized then that Mr. Ehrlich must've typed this letter out the old fashioned way, on a mechanical typewriter. He could barely imagine it: an old man at a desk typing on a mechanical typewriter. He had only seen that in movies. But then again, Ehrlich was old enough that he probably learned to write using a typewriter like the one that had typed this letter.

In the next week as he was putting together his presentation for the Nantiquak council, he realized he was at the same time putting together a structure and future plan for his own life. This Injun Project could take a number of years to come to completion. And a large part of that time span would probably be just waiting on the deliberations and decisions of other people. Will had carefully read the Bureau's guide to getting recognition and he summarized the steps carefully in the presentation. He put in his proposal to be the lead advisor and director of the overall process, but he was careful to include a tribe member as joint director. He felt confident that he would be appointed as the lead organizer of the effort, but even as he laid out the steps needed, he understood that much of the work would be done by others. All the legal work, for instance. The hardest part of the presentation was trying to estimate how much the monetary benefits would come to the tribe after it got recognition. But he addressed all the issues. His background and qualifications to lead the process. The number and types of lawyers that would be needed. The work and materials that the tribe would have to prepare. The presentation itself was a thick slide show of overhead plastic transparencies, maybe forty five altogether. He estimated it would take him almost two hours or more to present them all. His plan was to take a break after giving the materials about getting Federal recognition and its benefits during which time they could discuss the matter and ask questions. And then this would be followed by a second part of the presentation on building an Indian casino, how it could be done, and its benefits.

Finally the morning of his presentation to the Nantiquak chief and council came. He was from earliest morning excited by the prospect of speaking to the tribe. He had already packed the car with an overhead projector and a screen—he was certain they would not have this equipment at the Association office—and he had also carefully thought about what he should wear and he had laid out his jacket, shirt —no tie-- and slacks the night before. Would they be a receptive or a hostile audience? Would they be stony and unresponsive? Would they be able to make any decisions today? He had no idea on what to expect from his audience. If they were all like Marley, he was sure not to get any decisions or even much feedback today. He wore his brown raincoat over his suit jacket. The drive to the Association took less time than it had the first time and he arrived earlier than the scheduled presentation. The receptionist was still lazily sitting at the round table in the front room. He looked up at Will, as if by surprise, and languidly said, "There's nobody here yet." "That's good," said Will. "I can set up my projector then. Could you show me where we'll meet?" And the fat receptionist got up and took him to the back of the house trailer converted into an office. In fact the meeting room was a separate construction that had been built onto the end of the trailer. It was a large room--apparently unheated--both wider and deeper than any of the trailer rooms, with a raised dais on one side and two big folding tables set up in the middle of the room. There was a chalkboard on one wall. And lots of brown folding steel chairs with cushioned seats. Will set up the screen next to the wall opposite the dais, he just assumed that the council would sit at the table on the side nearest the dais. The projector he put at one end of the table so he could stand by it and feed the transparencies. He tested it, and it worked fine even with the lights on. He took off his raincoat and hung it from a wire coat rack in the corner. About five minutes before the scheduled meeting time, the council members began to arrive, one by one, stocky men, not tall, with weathered dark, reddish faces and noticeably broad hands. All of the eight men looked like middle-aged farmers or watermen. They were all in winter weight jackets and wore hats against the cold. None of them wore their black hair long in ponytails. The fourth man to arrive came over to Will and offered him his hand. "I'm Horace Clark. The elected chief of the Nantiquak." None of the others introduced themselves to Will. Marley was the last to arrive, about fifteen minutes after the designated time. He shook Will's hand and made a small bow with his whole body. His face looked like he was resisting a smile. In all there were nine Nantiquak Indians sitting at the table, including Marley. They all stayed in their coats because the room was cold. They all seemed to be scowling at him.

"Well, Mr. Eames, Mr. Norwood here told us about some of your ideas and some of your proposals for us. So if you're ready Mr. Eames, we can start."

Will introduced himself and handed business cards to each of the nine. "I'm William Eames from Bristol. I work in real estate in Dorset County and some in Talbot and Wicomico County. I am descended from a long line of farmers who have lived on the Eastern

Shore. In 1914 my great grandfather married a young Nantiquak woman and that makes me one-eighth Nantiquak. I've come in front of you today to present to you and the tribe the prospect of getting Federal recognition from the U.S. government and winning back the reservation lands that were taken from the tribe, unlawfully, many years ago. I am proposing myself to help you and to lead the process. I also want to propose to the tribe to develop a casino for the tribe's benefit once we have successfully gotten both recognition and reservation lands."

And with that he started his slide show presentation. The first section took an hour and forty five minutes to present. The council members made no comments and neither did they interrupt during the whole time. Throughout his presentation they all kept stony expressions on their faces and looked as though they were concentrating. Some of them, including the chief, took down notes on yellow writing pads. When Will finished this first section—the most important part about getting Federal recognition—he was feeling quite warm. He was expecting questions in the break. But the council members had no questions for him. Some of the council members stood up and approached Horace Clark and began whispering together. Marley stood and left the room, and shortly after he came back the receptionist came with a tray of coffee in mugs which he distributed to each council member and to Will. As for Will he excused himself for the toilet. He then noticed that the entire trailer-building was quite cold. When he returned to the room he was rubbing his hands together to warm them. Marley noticed: "Maybe you'd like a space heater here? To warm the place up a bit?" Will said he wouldn't mind. Marley went out and came back rolling in an electric heater and he was followed by the receptionist who was pushing in another one. They plugged them in a opposite ends of the hall. "I hope they don't blow out the power," said Marley. The council members were now clustered in three groups and they were talking amongst themselves louder than before. But still there were no questions for Will. After twenty minutes Horace Clark, who had remained seated the entire time, spoke up. "The second part of your presentation contains ideas about developing a casino for the tribe? Is that right? We'd like to hear it, but understand that it would not mean that we have adopted your proposals and ideas that you presented in the first part of the presentation." Will said he understood and he began presenting the pros and cons of a tribal casino and the experience of other tribes around the country that had already built casinos. He cited at length the Pequoddy and the Cherokee casinos. And he addressed the benefits and the drawbacks of having a casino, including the measures they could take to avoid the deleterious effects of gambling and drinking. He addressed the costs and financing for building a casino, again using the experiences of other tribes, mostly in the west and mid-west, which had built small casinos, smaller at least than the FireFox resort. And he addressed the income of the casinos and suggested how much gambling revenues a casino located near Highway 50 could earn for the tribe. In all Will spoke to this topic for about an hour and a quarter, well into lunch time. He was hungry and thirsty by the time he stopped. Once again the council members had no desire to ask Will any questions or to discuss his proposals with him. There was a long pause.

"Very good." said Mr. Clark. "Well gentlemen, I think we have heard what this young man has to propose to us. There may be more information that we need later. But for now I think we have to go back to our people and discuss these issues with them and come up with a response. Mr. Eames could you come back here on Friday afternoon when we might be able to give you our responses?"

Will said he could.

"I think then we have no questions at this time. And we should adjourn. Thank you for this presentation and for the effort and research you put into it. You might be hungry after this long morning's work. I could recommend to you, Mr. Eames, if you go back into Millsville you can get a good lunch of local food at the Waterman's Grill. It's an Indian owned business."

And with that the nine Indians made to leave and Will began picking up his slides and equipment. He did stop at the Grill and had a barbecue sandwich before driving back to Bristol. The entire way, he was thinking about what their responses might be, or about the issues that perhaps he had not addressed enough. He had not a clue about whether he had convinced this group about his proposals. They had given him almost no signals. He thought it was ironic: they would make good poker players. They could clean up in a casino based poker game. He was worried especially that his appeal to them to go for recognition and to build a casino had failed.

In the intervening days before he had to go back to the Nantiquak Association, he had business. He had two closings of properties and on the commercial property he made a really big commission. His business had been dry for nearly six months and now he scored two successes. Still this year would be a bad one compared to his previous years. These successes raised his spirits a bit. But then on the Friday morning before he had to leave for Delaware, he was surprised to receive an offer for the Ehrlich house. And it was a generous offer, ninety-five percent of the listing price. The owner was sure to accept it, especially as he wanted to sell by New Year's. The occurrence of three sales in December was unusual in his business. It marked a huge success for him. He left at midday on Friday feeling very buoyant and cheered up. He dared even to feel hopeful of a positive outcome.

"So Mr. Eames," started Chief Clark, "we have discussed your proposals and your suggested means of achieving the plans you laid out for us. And we have come to some conclusions, but we have some questions concerning the path going forward. First of all, from what you said there appears to be a two track way to win Federal recognition. Through the Congress, legislative, and through the administrative steps run by the Bureau of Indian Affairs. Is that understanding right? And do we have to commit to one track or the other?"

"Yes that's right. I believe that you should follow both tracks. The legislative process is much harder to pursue successfully to the end, and even if successful takes much more time. So going through the administrative path and applying at the Bureau is the first tack we'll take. The process there is bettered defined and laid out."

"So then good. Is it also correct to understand that getting Federal recognition through the Bureau does not guarantee the return of our reservation lands or the granting of a new reservation?"

"That's probably correct. Getting recognition will unlock lots of monetary benefits for the tribe and its members, as I outlined, but the funding to buy reservation lands can only come from Congress. Or by the ruling of a court. My strategy is to go to the courts to win back the original reservation lands."

Another council member spoke up, "But are federal benefits, say like the health care benefits, only distributed to tribesmen living on a reservation?"

"No, those benefits may be distributed on the reservation, but they are for members of the tribe, whether they physically reside in the reservation or not," observed Will. "Obviously relief of property tax would only accrue to those tribesmen who own houses on the reservation. And taxes would not be imposed on Indian owned enterprises that operate on the reservations. Say if you were to open a fish farm on the Indian River. Or a crab packer. Welfare payments could be made directly to both resident and non-resident tribal members."

"But there is another way to effectively establish a reserve for the tribe and that is to put Indian owned lands into a federally managed trust. It is treated then like a reservation. I understand that members of the tribe here near Millsville own collectively a large part of the county. I propose putting the property that I bought where Wicomico is located into such a trust once the tribe gets recognition."

A third council member then asked, "So we will undertake law suits to win our reservations back?"

"Yes, I think that is the most direct route."

"So that means suing the state of Delaware?"

"Yes," said Will. "And the state of Maryland, where a larger portion of the original reservation existed."

Then Chief Clark spoke up again. "You must know Mr. Eames that our Association is not rich. I think that we do not have the resources to be able to pay the lawyers for long protracted lawsuits in the courts. I understand that these can be very expensive."

"I understand. In the case of the Pequoddy tribe and a tribe in Maine, their lawyers were all working for firms that provided their services as a public service, that is, for free. I think we can have reduced lawyer fees by using these kinds of lawyer services. In fact I think we would plan on it for both advice on strategy and for litigation."

"Cost will be a serious constraint for us, you understand. Even if we have public service lawyers."

"I can well imagine. I suggested that I would not be taking a fee for my efforts in directing the efforts to win recognition."

"But also time," said Chief Clark. "All these efforts will take time and input from our tribesmen over, you said, a number of years."

"Yes, that will be a cost that cannot be avoided."

Then another council member spoke up, "What are the first steps we as a tribe have to take? And when can we start?"

Will turned to him. "We can start as soon as you wish. Tomorrow if you like. The first step is to take a census of the members of the tribe."

Marley now spoke up. "The membership of the Association numbers five hundred and thirty people, almost all of them here in the local area in Delaware. That roughly would mean in counting children and minors a population of about eight hundred and eighty persons."

"You should include the Nantiquaks," said Will calmly, "who live in two clusters in Maryland. I estimate they number one hundred and thirty individuals. And then of course you should invite people with only part Indian ancestry to see if they want to be included in the tribe. And you should also consider inviting those people who consider themselves derived from the Nantiquak, but whose forefathers moved away from Delmarva."

"Yeah we have been thinking of that for the Association," answered Marley. "At our annual pow-wows we get lots of people from New York, Wisconsin, Oklahoma, and even Ontario who claim to be descended from Nantiquak. We should count them, if we can get them to reply to our invitations."

"Yes, why not?" said Will.

"But we will not be accepting as tribal members, people with only one-eighth ancestry," concluded Marley. "In your case, Mr. Eames it is just remarkable that your great grandparents weren't prosecuted under Maryland's anti-miscegenation laws. And your ancestors since then were not culturally Indians."

"Well, then, Mr. Eames," said Chief Clark quietly, "I think we can say we have consulted the tribe members and discussed this at length, and we have decided that we will begin the process of getting Federal recognition. And we accept your proposal for you to frame the strategy and lead the process through its various steps. But we would like you to operate with a team. And keep us informed of every step you take and the outcomes, too.

"Sure, I think that is the only way that I could succeed." answered Will trying to suppress his feeling of triumph. He was so elated, that he dared not ask about their thinking about a casino. And as if reading his mind, Chief Clark said next, "We'll put off thinking about a casino or other enterprises until after we begin to see over the horizon with this project."

"If you have time and can stay a little longer, Mr. Eames, we'd like to introduce you to the person who will be on your team as the principal representative of our tribe." said Marley. "It is my younger sister. If you can wait, I'll call her and ask her come over now."

"I can wait." said Will. "Who else will be on the team?"

One of the council members raised his hand as he stood up. "I am one. My name is Bob Hardy." Will shook his hand.

"We are bringing in some food here for lunch now." announced Marley. "To mark the beginning of our effort to become a recognized tribe and to mark the appointment of Will Eames to lead us to that goal."

The other council members all stood now and came to Will and introduced themselves. Some even allowed themselves to smile a little. Chief Clark clapped Will on the back. "We wish you success in this great endeavor. We're pleased to appoint you to lead us to recognition."

After about twenty minutes in came a young dark haired woman and following closely behind her were a parade of seven young men and women carrying aluminum serving pans covered in foil. The young woman went over to Marley who then turned to Will. "This is my niece, Carmine Dovesong Norwood." They shook hands. "She works as a paralegal, will be a lawyer someday." Carmine smiled at Will. "Glad to meet you, Will. Chief Clark told me about the project you proposed. I'm really excited to be working on it." Will did not find Carmine to be very attractive. She was a bit plump and unlike many of the other Nantiquak Indians, tall. Her smile was nice but she had big lips and her eyes seemed to bulge out of their sockets. And her skin color was a pale sandy color, not like Indian coloring at all. But her youth and bright white teeth saved her from looking just plain and ugly. The receptionist, who someone called Albert, then brought in disposable plates, plastic forks and knives as well as serving spoons, while the others set up the serving pans on the long table. Then Albert and three other men went out and brought some more folding chairs. Another person brought in six packs of Coke which he put in a cooler already filled with ice. When all was set up and the foil had been lifted off the pans, Marley invited everyone to begin eating. One pan had corn and beans, which a young woman called succotash. Another pan had breaded fried clams. And in another was fried rock fish filets, and in the next one some sort of greens stewed with chunks of ham. There was one pan of corn bread, and one pan with steamed mussels. Will felt suddenly very hungry and started along with everyone else to plunge in. Carmine said, "You know, all of this is raised, grown, or harvested locally. Some of our traditional foods." "I recognize most of it." said Will. "In Bristol, on the Bay side, we eat much the same." It was the best food Will had eaten since Jack's wedding party. And he ate until he was stuffed. Will was on his way with his 'Injun Project' and he felt delirious. Marley now was smiling for a change. Will looked at him and suddenly thought that Marley looked like a big clumsy child.

"We feast when we as a tribe embark on a new venture, or when we have accomplished something. Or to celebrate a good year." said Chief Clark addressing Will and the group as a whole. "This has been a good year, and now we are embarking on a most important venture."

Chapter 2

November 1997

Minnie finished reviewing the contract and folded it up, saved and closed the program screen, and put the paper draft in a folder in the desk drawer. It was early evening, already dark outside, and well past quitting time for many of her colleagues. But she could still finish another small task before leaving for home.

She could not help thinking bitterly about how Nighthorse Ward had deceived and swindled her. How he had connived and politicked to push her out of the department, while at the same time he had lobbied outside the department and in the halls of Democratic Party members around the city to get the plum appointment as deputy assistant secretary of the Office of Federal Recognition, a post she had been promised by the previous Secretary of the Interior before he had been replaced. Nighthorse was shifty, ambitious, and a classic, deceitful bureaucrat. After his appointment he had then had her seconded to the Smithsonian, because, as he put it, it was an intolerable conflict of interest for her to be working in the same department where she had shortly before applied for her tribe to get Federal Recognition. He did not appreciate that for several years before he had gotten his appointment from the new Secretary he had been working in the same situation in the department while his tribe went through the approval process. But then again he was not the chief of his tribe, the Nottawaysac. She was, and he had argued that that had made her conflict of interest all the greater. She could return to her position in the department once the Federal Recognition was granted. They both knew that could take years, longer even than the Indian museum project at the Smithsonian would take. Now that she was out of the Department, she was as good as forgotten. Bureaucratically she was in effect in a temporary appointment, a dead-end, and as it was she had no prospects for promotions or raises.

But it had always been like that for her. The men around her had always worked against her, not appreciating her talent or experience. Her father had been like that. He had favored his son, Tanner, Minnie's younger brother. Before he died, he had not wanted her to succeed him as chief of the tribe, the Massaponax-Doeg tribe of Virginia. But there had been precedent for women chiefs; most famously Queen Cockacoeski of the Pamunkey in the 17th century. And she had always pointed out to him that he had named her after one of the greatest princesses of the Powhatan Indians.

People in her tribe remembered such things. So Minnie had won the election to succeed him as chief and she then had earned the respect of most of the tribe. But not her father's. Her father had also not approved of her going to law school. "Too assimilationist." he had said. But what he had really meant was that he could not afford to pay for her law school fees, and so he wouldn't contribute. He had also feared that once she went away to university, she would never return to the tribe or live on the reservation again. But she had still managed to get through law school and pass the state bar using her own funds and generous scholarships. And she had gotten that appointment in the Bureau of Indian Affairs. It was through her efforts that she had persuaded the tribe to apply for Federal recognition. But all of her efforts and accomplishments to date had not won her love or appreciation. She got only begrudging respect from her fellow tribesmen. Because they still had not received Federal recognition.

Nighthorse was in a way like her father had been. He did not respect women, and especially not Indian women. It didn't matter that she was a chief of her tribe. He was too full of himself, and his self-importance had always been a matter of friction between them in the department even before he had gotten his promotion. He had pushed her out of the department not because of conflict of interest, but because he was jealous of her. He wanted the top position even though she was better qualified for it. And he did not like her because she was not a submissive Indian woman, like he expected of her and of all women.

These thoughts continued to roll through her mind as she finished up another mindless task. The Indian museum project was going to happen regardless of her efforts. And from her perspective it looked like it was going to be a hash, unfocused, disorganized, and lacking any message. And of course the biggest drawback in the museum project was that there was no way it could properly and fairly portray all 550 Indian tribes in America. Her role in this project was very peripheral. All she was doing was wrapping up some of the details that would address or resolve some of the future controversies and conflicts concerning the acquisition of Indian relicts and artifacts from the Gustav Heye collections, which were being merged into the museum being built on the Mall. There would still be lawsuits and challenges in the future. Most of what Mr. Heye had collected—and how he had collected those materials-- at the beginning of the century was now considered too politically incorrect to even be put on display. All the details she was working on concerned legal mitigation of those problems. She could well imagine that there would be lawsuits and challenges to the collection for decades after it finally opened. That evening was yet another small detail. An item from a Pacific Northwest tribe which had probably been stolen or plundered before it had been sold to Mr. Heye. But then, she thought, everything pertaining to Indian heritage or cultural had been either pillaged or stolen by white men. Setting up this new museum was not going to be able to rectify that legacy. The work she was doing did not inspire her and did not really engage her legal training and background. Any old clerk could do it.

It was past seven thirty when she finally decided to leave for home. She closed up the computer and locked her desk, and put on her middle length dark blue coat. There were no colleagues left in her office, nor anyone left on the floor, no one to wish her a good bye. She stepped out onto the broad sidewalk in front of the building. It was dark outside and threatening rain, the street lights glimmered only dimly. Unlike the stately or historic architecture of the Smithsonian museums on the Mall, the Smithsonian offices where she was now working were located in a bland, characterless building of glass and steel, several blocks south of the Mall. It looked all the more uninteresting by the outline of bare trees which lined the sidewalk outside. The lunch vans which usually lined the sidewalk out front had long ago shut up and moved on. Beside the threat of rain there was a chilly wind which blew between her legs. Both her skirt and coat were cut short at her knees. Perhaps she was underdressed for this chilly November night, she thought. She put up her collar and walked to E Street where she had parked her car. There was hardly a soul out on the streets. Everyone who worked in this district had left for home a few hours earlier. As she walked the six blocks to her parking lot she thought briefly that there might be muggers out. That was why in the evenings she did not walk along Virginia Avenue which was tight up against the wall of the elevated rail line. Too many long shadows there. Instead she would walk down the broad pavement of 7th Street to E Street. On this night she did not pass anyone on the way. There were no cars, only the sound of old leaf litter skittering around in the gutters.

Then almost at her parking lot, on E Street between street lamps, she was suddenly jerked from behind and pulled, almost lifted off her feet into a side alley. Without a word someone grabbed her with one arm around her neck and another around her waist—she was not big- -and he dragged her behind a dumpster where it was very dark. She could not see her assailant. Minnie did not cry out, but she may have gasped loudly. Then she felt a sharp, cold line on her throat. "Doan say a word, Missy. Or I'll slit you throat." The voice was a black man's, she could tell. She wanted to cry but couldn't. A hand was crawling under her coat and skirt. "I'm goan to fuck you, you little black bitch. Real hard." She could feel his fingers tugging at her panty hose but he was not having any success. "Damn, bitch. What are you wearing? Pull down yoa panties." The pressure on her throat of what she now knew was a knife got a little harder. She still did not say anything. "Doan try no funny stuff." She could smell him now. A heavy musky smell of dirt, sweat, and alcohol. She slowly put her hands down below her coat and took hold and began to wriggle down her panty hose which were tucked above the waist line of her skirt. She moved slowly and was only beginning to loosen the panty hose when the man behind her let up on the knife and pushed her down on her knees and he then pushed her shoulders down so that she caught herself by her hands. She could feel the concrete abrade her knees. She was on all fours now and again one of the man's hands was pulling the last tugs at her panties which were under her panty hose. The knife came back to her throat.

She thought she was going to pee with fright, and then she felt like she was going to pass out. She could tell he was now leaning heavily over her from behind. Now she could feel his cold hand directly on the skin of her bared bottom. And then there was a momentary letting up of the knife and a lightening of the pressure on her backside. Maybe he had taken the knife away from her neck, but she couldn't tell. She could hear a jingling as of a belt buckle. And then suddenly....

She heard a distinct thwack, almost a cracking sound like that of a wooden slat breaking beneath a mattress, and the body pushing against her from behind slumped off to one side. She heard the jangle of the knife fall next to her on the concrete. And almost as soon as this happened she could see there were flashing red and blue lights dancing on the walls around her. Someone began to drag the body away from her. She tried to see what was behind her. She heard a different, gentler, calm voice say, "You can stand up now, miss." A white man's voice. And immediately another harsher voice shouted from some little distance. "Stand still! Hands up in the air." Minnie stood on her knees and pulled her panties back up. Footsteps of several men. Then someone put his hand on her shoulder. "Are you alright, ma'am?" She looked around for the first time. Another man was shouting, "Stand over there. Keep your hands up." She looked around and could see the outline of what looked like a lump of rags lying on the concrete next to her. The gentle voice she now heard said, "It's alright officer.

I was the one who called you. The rapist is that one on the ground."
The other officer helped Minnie stand up. "Are you okay, ma'am?"
he said. Before she could answer, there were more lights flashing as a
large white van pulled into the alley and got close to them.

Minnie looked around her, confused and blinded by the flashing
lights. There were two police officers, and two more were running
from the street, and two men in white and red jumped down from the
ambulance. On the pavement next to the dumpster was a black man
in black trousers and a grey hoody sweatshirt. "No I did not see him,"
Minnie muttered to one of the policemen who shouted this question
at her several times. But there was another man she saw; a white man
in a grey suit and blue tie being held up by the gun of one of the police
officers. The paramedics came and stopped by her side and then lead
her slowly to the open rear door of the ambulance. "She has a small
slash cut on her throat. And her knees are bleeding, scraped up." one
of them said excitedly to one of the policemen. Now she could see the
policemen lifting the limp body of the black man, who was beginning
to sputter something. The other was leading the man in the suit, his
hands now down at his side, toward his squad car. Minnie got a good
look at his face as he passed by her, his face caught full in the glare
of the police car's spotlight. A good looking young white man, very
short hair, an open, honest looking face, handsome, strongly built.
The policeman took him about ten feet away to the side of his car
and began questioning him. The other policeman steadied the black
man up on his feet, handcuffed him, and bundled him into another
police car.

Minnie was in shock and she began to breathe much more rapidly.
Everything was so fast, a blur. And against all the walls the flashing
red and blue lights were racing around and reflecting in her face. The
paramedics were trying to ask her questions and inspect her wounds,
but she was trying to hear what the policeman was saying to the white
man who had saved her.

"I saw this guy snatch her off the street, not ten yards in front of
me. From behind. I called you at once. Because he was either going

to murder her with that knife and take her handbag, or he was going to rape her. Or both. I rushed over and watched to see what I could do to. . . "

"Where did you learn to kick like that?"

"No it was with my fist   In the Marines."

"Oh, semper fi, guy. You're one of us. You did a brave thing, man. Good citizen."

She did not hear any more of what the white man said. But she was still straining to hear what he was saying. The policeman was speaking loudly, but the white man was calm and speaking softly. Everything was so confused. One of the policemen was white, another one was black. One of the paramedics was black, the other fat and white. Another policeman looked Hispanic. Meanwhile, the paramedics were asking her insistently something, trying to determine whether there had been penetration by the assailant, or something like that. But she didn't know. She didn't think she had been raped. There was no pain. Not like the previous times.

"Probably aggravated sexual assault without penetration." one of them said to a policewoman who had suddenly appeared next to the ambulance. Minnie realized she was sitting half in half out of the ambulance and one of the paramedics was putting antiseptic on her knees, which now stung intolerably. Another was applying antiseptic to the middle of her neck. He pulled gauze pads off her neck which were bloodied. She suddenly realized that the white man had hit the black man who had been attempting to rape her, and the latter had cut her with a knife. She had not seen the black man's face, or the knife. "She doesn't need stitches." said one of the paramedics. She was becoming numb to everything around her. But she could tell that her pantyhose were bunched up under her skirt and on her bottom, and they were uncomfortable the way she was sitting on them. Maybe they were torn as well. "Where's my purse?" she asked. The paramedic shook his head. He did not know. "Any one seen the woman's purse?" he shouted. A policeman came up holding it in his hand as if it were a dead skunk. "Is this it, ma'am?" It was and it was unopened. The police car with the black man drove off. She heard one of the policemen say, "She's lucky this guy came along when he did. Even though our station is only a block away. . . . ." And then things began to wind down, became quieter, and less frenetic. "Do you need help getting home? Where do you live?" asked the policewoman. Minnie now was shaking hard, and she could not hear clearly or focus very well on what was happening around her. She saw the good looking white man in the grey suit shake the hand of one of the white policemen, and then he briefly looked her way. "Nothing more you can do," shouted a policeman to him. And then the white man walked off. She wanted so badly to talk to him, to say something to him. But in an instant he was swallowed up by the darkness of night beyond the flashing red and blue lights. One policeman, the one who seemed always to shout, shouted to another, "Of course there will be charges." One of the paramedics said, "No she doesn't need to be hospitalized." The policewoman asked her, "Ma'am, can you stand up?" She must have repeated it several times. Then she noticed that the policewoman was a black woman. Minnie tried to stand up. She felt wobbly when she stood up. She felt like she needed to pee, or worse, throw up. "We're going to drive you home now, ma'am. You can't drive yourself home. Is this the address where you live?" asked the policewoman almost hostilely. Minnie could not see the piece of paper she was pushing at her. "My mother's address. I gave you my mother's address." "Fine, fine. Bowling Green? In Virginia, right? Okay. Can you give us a telephone number for her? We'll drive you home now. Do you understand?"

And then everything was over. The policewoman put the purse into Minnie's hands and gently steered her by her shoulders over to a police car. She sat her in the rear seat behind a thick metal screen. Was she under arrest? The policewoman sat next to her. There was a driver in the front seat, but she did not see his face. Then they were moving, over the 14th Street Bridge and then onto the familiar interstate highway south into Virginia on her usual way home. The street lamps glared into her face every other second. It was a long way, but the traffic was light. In just a few minutes the street lamps were spaced farther apart and shone in her eyes less frequently. She still could not focus. But after what seemed like an endless amount of time, she saw something that she recognized on the side of the road. It was a tall roadside sign. And she began to cry. The policewoman tried to console her, but she could not know why Minnie was crying now. The road sign was that permanent marker of the place where Minnie had been raped thirteen years before. It taunted her almost every day, on her way to work, and on her way home. She had grown inured to it over the past few years; always noticing it, but trying not to remember what the sign meant to her. But now in this strange car, after this latest attack, she could not hold back the anguish and she cried the rest of the way home. It was nearly ten o'clock by the time the police car pulled up to her mother's small house, just outside the center of Bowling Green. The police woman helped Minnie out of the car and then slowly led her by the arm to the front door. Her mother opened the door, before they got to it. "Are you Miss Warrens's mother?" asked the police woman, again in an almost hostile, officious tone. "She should be alright. She was assaulted, but we got the assailant before he really hurt her. No, I don't think she needs any medical care." And then she bade good night to Minnie and her mother. Minnie could not talk about the attack with her mother. Just like the last time. She sat silent and brooding for a couple hours—a couple times sobbing-- her mother at her side.

The next morning, a Friday, Minnie's mother called in to her office and told them that she would not be coming that day. As it was, she did not go back to work on that day, or over the next three days before Thanksgiving. She sat at her mother's house brooding and unresponsive. She continued to think about how she had been raped when she was twenty three years old and at law school. In her mind, the events of that night ran over and over: Going to pick her sister up from the brothel where she worked. The late, late night on a highway McDonald's parking lot. The young white man, probably a soldier from the nearby base, who came up to her politely and then violently hit her. The rough ride in the back of his pick-up truck. How he beat her as he raped her. The pain she had felt shooting up through her body when he entered her. How he dumped her on the side of the highway, her clothes torn and soiled. The shame she had felt. How she felt dirty. But above all the intense unremitting shame.

All that holiday week at her mother's house, Minnie thought over and over that maybe she was to blame; that Indian women were the natural targets of rapists, that they were victims who invited rape on themselves. Indian women were always to blame for their victimization. She thought that maybe there was nothing she could have done differently. That her assailant would have still tracked her down, and gone after her, because she looked like a victim, she invited rape, like all Indian girls.

She had not reported her previous rape to the police, because how could she? No one witnessed the event itself. And after all wasn't she near her sister's brothel, the irreputable Motel Eleven? So didn't that make her a prostitute also? After all what was she doing on a lone highway, outside an all-night McDonald's in the early hours of the morning? And the beating and bruises all over her body, well prostitutes had those also. So she hadn't reported the rape. She had just bottled it up inside as a dreadful act against her. And the pain and her shame had lingered. This time the police were right in it even before the man had completed his crime. They were participants. They lasciviously looked over all the details, taking notes. The black man who attacked hadn't undressed her as much as the police had undressed her with their prying eyes. And they would bring charges against the rapist, and there would be a trial where all the lurid details of that night attack would be recounted over again. And she would feel the shame burning inside her again.

During her week at home, brooding, she thought that maybe even the first time she had ever had sex at college, maybe that time too had been rape. What they now called date rape. She had not wanted sex with that red-faced, pimply white kid who had barged into her room after they had had an evening out together. But he had pushed his way in, overcame her, and then penetrated her without any affection or tenderness. And quickly he had left her in her room.

And that time also was painful and shameful. She had cried after that all the rest of the night. Maybe she had invited that attack also. Maybe she had led him on and begged him to take her, poor Indian princess craving the loving of a privileged white man. She had never spoken about this, to anyone. Not to her mother, who had always belonged to the men in her family. Not to her younger sister, who had commercialized rape, even from high school, as a means of escaping her Indian background. Not any of her girlfriends at university. None of them had been Indian. They had all been white girls, who always talked about getting a boy between their legs. Especially the right boy, with connections and prospects, from a proper family. No one to talk to about victimhood, or about the predators of Indian maidens. Maybe she could talk with some of the other Indian women who worked with her at the Smithsonian on the Indian museum project. But she did not feel close even to them. Most of them were married, and coming from another bureaucracy she still did not know them at all. Every direction she turned she felt isolated.

Maybe her experiences could explain why she had never gotten close to a man, why she was still unmarried, or why she seemed to feel afraid of sex, and afraid especially of white men. Maybe because she had been raped, and made to feel she was the victim, she had felt overly sensitized to what seemed to her the excessive attentions of the male professors in law school. The brief touches to her shoulder, innocent as they were, but maybe not at all that innocent. The professor who leaned over her for just a moment too long to look down her blouse at her chest as she labored over an essay exam. Maybe those experiences explained why she always felt as if white men were looking at her with looks that were undressing her, or caressing her private parts. Or dreaming of having a Pocahontas of their own.

The ten days after the assault passed by in misery. Minnie was not recovering from the trauma. She was only trying to figure out how to go back out in the world without being seen or noticed by anyone. The thin linear scab across the lower part of her throat dropped off on the Sunday before she returned to work and it left a thin pink scar. She decided she could hide it with a choker necklace and she had a thin silver one which did the job nicely. She wore trousers on the day when she decided to return and a longer winter weight coat. On the Monday morning after Thanksgiving, her sister drove her up to the commuter train station in Spotsylvania Courthouse and for the first time in many months she went into D.C. by train. It was no faster than driving the 65 or so miles by car, and it cost a lot more to go by train, which was one of the reasons she had chosen to give up going by train in favor of her car. But she was reminded on this morning ride, that it was much more comfortable and stress free. On the train, over the hour and a half it took to reach L'Enfant Plaza, she became lost in thought. She continued to think about the sexual relationship between white men and Indian women. From the very beginning the English had used rape to subjugate the Powhatan Indians, and the so-called Pocahontas, was the very first victim. Taken as a hostage and then given to an Englishman as his bride, even though she was being used as a bargaining chip.

Pocahontas's real name, her birth name, was Matoaka, which was also Minnie's real birth name. For Minnie there was something very symbolic to share the name, the position, and the experience of Pocahontas—although admittedly Pocahontas was the only one of the many daughters of a supreme chief, while she was the chief of one of the subordinate tribes of the Powhatan. But the sexual subjugation of Pocahontas had not lead to peace between the English and the Indians. And the Indians, and especially Indian women had been the losers ever since.

Several times on that Monday she went to the women's room to look at her neck in the mirror. The scar was quite visible, and unmistakably a knife slash. Even with the choker necklace she couldn't hide that. She would just have to hide herself. Instead of taking lunch in the cafeteria in the building, she stepped out to grab a bite at one of the truck luncheonettes. It was run by a Korean family and while she was waiting to be served she looked closely at the Korean woman who was preparing food orders. She must have been the same age as Minnie but she looked haggard and tired, stressed from the demands of her job inside the cramped space of the truck. Minnie wondered how distantly she was related to that Korean woman. After all, the specialists always maintained that the native Americans, the first Indians in America, came from northeast Asia after

the peak of the last Ice Age. She couldn't see any relationship, other than straight black hair. Minnie didn't have the high raised cheek bones, or flat profile in her face. And Minnie's skin color was

rather darker, copper colored compared to the pale, cream colored skin of the Korean woman's. She was so deeply involved in thinking about this that the Korean woman finally barked at her,

"What you order, ma'am?" It woke her from her reveries. She had a hot dog with sauerkraut. Food made little difference to her, and usually she hardly noticed what she ate. But she generally ate only small amounts. And as usual, she ate alone. This time she sat on a square stone column which had been installed in front of the building as a security barrier. The day passed painfully slowly. Finally at five when people in the office began to leave, she decided she too would leave. Best to leave with the crowds. Even though it was already nearly dark outside, she thought, there would be enough people on the streets, even E Street, so that she should be able to reach her car safely. Still she wanted to ask someone to accompany her to her car. But she didn't see any man she knew well enough to be able to ask him. The car was still in its place, although smeared with dust and rain stains after standing eleven days in the open next to the elevated interstate. In an hour and a half she was back at her house on the banks of the Massaponax creek near Guinea. She heated some soup in her microwave and then called her mother on the land line phone, just to check in and report that she was alright and had survived her first day back in the office in D.C.

The rest of the week passed by in much the same way. Toward the end of the week, Nighthorse called. In his leering voice he asked her, even before greeting her, "Why didn't you tell me you had been attacked?" She had told no one except the black woman in human resources. Minnie had to tell that human resources woman, because she could not just take days off. She had to request annual leave, and she had to give reasons for her request. Minnie had tried to keep the justification to a minimum. So Nighthorse must have gotten word from the human resources woman. He loved to collect gossip, he spent most of his time doing nothing else but collecting gossip about everyone around him, gossip which could be used maliciously against colleagues, or gossip about the politicians whose words and attitudes counted for everything about Indian affairs. It was clear to Minnie over the line that Nighthorse was prying for more details. And she wasn't going to give them to him. "Yes I felt bad after I was attacked. It was a mugger. No, he didn't get my purse. It was near where I park. Yes, I'll try to be more careful in the future."

"Well, that's really sad. I'm sorry for you. But I was calling to tell you that I gave your name to a young man who might follow up with you about the details of applying for federal recognition. I gave him our information booklet. He might call you and want to talk with you. You might meet with him and give him the lowdown on how it's done. Okay?"

Nighthorse continued. "I just wanted to give you a head's up. But then I heard about the attack. Hope you're feeling better. Bye."

She hung up. What a despicable person, she thought. Every time I speak to him, he becomes more and more base and despicable. As she hung up, she looked at the calendar and then she saw that she had scheduled a tribal council meeting for that Saturday at Chico's Place next to the county high school in Crossroads in William and Mary County. They met every other month at this restaurant which was located about an hour's drive from her house but half way between— about a twenty five minute drive-- the two principal settlements of her tribe. She had forgotten all about the meeting. She had nothing to report this month. There was no progress at the Bureau of Indian Affairs, and no news. And she did not want to call Nighthorse back to ask him if or when there would be progress.

She arrived at Chico's restaurant a little early, she was the first. So she ordered herself an iced tea and sat in the back corner where the proprietor reserved a few tables for their meeting. The next to arrive was her younger brother who came down from Bowling Green, near their mother's house. He sullenly greeted her and then fell silent. It was the same every time. Tanner resented his older sister being the chief in his place and often participated in the discussions of these meetings only to criticize her or contradict whatever she said or proposed. Finally at eleven the other eight member filed into the restaurant. The other council members were all men. They did not look out of place in Chico's. They all looked as if they could be Mexicans, the immigrant farm laborers who came to the county every fall to help with the local harvests, although their numbers had been declining in recent years. There were handshakes all around and softly muttered greetings, followed by the draping of jackets and coats over the wooden chairs. They were all middle aged men,except for Tanner of course, who was only twenty eight; good men, and they all seemed to like and respect one another. One of the group had even asked for Minnie's hand in marriage a decade before. A waiter came around and took drinks orders from the ten council members. Everyone had either tea or cokes. This was a dry county, but regardless the Indians did not drink much if any alcohol, no beers, nor wine, because they knew it was bad for them. Minnie opened the discussions. There was no agenda. She reported that there was no progress on their tribe's application. But that there seemed the general mood in the Bureau was unfavorable, and no tribes' applications were being processed quickly. One of the council members spoke up to report that they had now nine teenagers at the county high school, after two of their number had left the school. Apparently one had joined the Navy, and the other had quit school and had moved away and was working in Hampton Roads.

Another inquired if they could not organize vocational training— carpentry, auto mechanics, metal turning, computer programming, electricity systems—at the high school. He suggested that as a group the council should request the county board of education to inaugurate such training. Minnie supported that suggestion and asked if anyone knew when the next board meeting would be held. No one knew. One member volunteered to find out and to inform their group. They agreed that three of their number would attend the next board of education open board meeting if it occurred before their next gathering. Then another councilman reported that John Johnson Adams of the upper river settlement wanted to sell his house and move to his brother's house in Bowling Green.

"Doesn't he have children he could leave the house to?" asked Minnie.

"Yeah, he does, but he needs the money for his retirement. And the house is not big enough for all of his children and their families."

"The tribe doesn't have any money to buy it from him." "We know that."

"And his children don't have enough money to buy him out?" she asked. "No, they are mostly unemployed or work only seasonally."

Minnie was pained. This was how the tribe was being dispersed, she thought. "We should try to

raise money from across the tribe to buy Adams's land and house. And then we could put it into a trust. How much does Adams think he can get for his house and land"

"Eighty-five thousand."

"We can ask each tribesman and household—including his children's families-- to contribute seven hundred dollars and then we could buy it out. What do you say we do this?"

There was silence. Everyone knew that would be a difficult request to fill. Minnie again asked. "Shall we give it a try?" Reluctantly everyone agreed.

"I think this again shows that we should file for a legal tribal association." said Minnie. "This would be the vehicle through which we as a tribe could collect funds, borrow money, and channel expenditures like these. The upper river band have a tribal association. But the reservation as we all know is in the lower river."

"We should not let this property fall out of the ownership by our tribe, if we can at all help it." "We could transfer ownership to the reservation." said one councilman.

"Maybe. But it would not get any money to this Adams who wants to sell out. If we bought it we could then transfer it to the reservation."

Everyone agreed with this proposition, but no one knew how to put it into practice.

"If we had federal recognition now, we wouldn't need an association." said Tanner. "Isn't that right?"

Minnie acknowledged that he was right. But she saw the statement to again represent her brother's criticism. Minnie knew at any event that taking up a collection from the tribe members would be difficult. She was well aware that she probably had the highest salary of all the four hundred or so tribesmen from both the upper river and lower river settlements. Economic pressures, she thought, are pushing the tribe apart and weakening the cultural identity that bound the tribe together. Like so many Indian tribes this was the route to oblivion. It wouldn't be long.

The meeting ended with only a brief discussion of when the next meeting would occur. Minnie left very disturbed. She thought she could take a second mortgage and buy this property. But why should she assume more debt for a property that would be put into a trust or into the reservation? Her income was not so great that she could afford such acts of charity for the sake of her tribe. But she wished she could.

The next week, on a Tuesday, back in her office, she got a call. "Are you Minnie Warrens from the Bureau of Indian Affairs?" "Yes, that's me."

"I'm William Eames from Bristol Maryland. Mr. Ward gave me your telephone number and recommended that I speak to you about the process of getting federal recognition."

"Yes, he told me you might call. How can I help you?"

"I was wondering if we might meet, soon, to talk about the process and the ins and outs, you know, of getting recognition for a tribe. I have already met with Mr. Ward, and frankly, he did not seem too willing to give me any advice or insights."

"Are you asking on behalf of any specific tribe or tribal group?"
"Yes, the Nantiquak of Maryland and Delaware."

"Oh, yeah, I've heard of them."

"So, when might I come by to visit with you and discuss the issues involved? I mean before Christmas, if possible."

Minnie thought that was funny. Her calendar was completely empty as far as she was concerned through into the new year. She had no pressing deadlines, and what she was doing could carry on for months, maybe even years, without delaying the Indian museum project.

"So, Mr. Eames, how would it suit you to meet at 2:30 on this Friday?"

"That would be fine by me. Tell me the exact address and how I enter your building, and I will be there."

Minnie hung up, momentarily feeling as if she had accomplished something by scheduling something worthwhile. Someone was coming to consult with her.

The day came around, and at shortly after the appointed time she got a call. It was the front desk reception announcing the arrival of a Mr. Eames. Minnie got up from her desk. She needed to go down the three floors and across to the main entrance desk to receive Mr. Eames and sign him in and then lead him to her office. She instinctively patted herself down, stretched out her dress, and felt her head to check if her hair was in its proper place. Then she went down the corridor to the elevator. She met Eames at the front desk, shook his hand, and without really looking directly at him turned to lead the way back to her office. As she entered her office, still without engaging his eyes, as if she were half apologizing for herself, she said, "You see, I don't have my own secretary to fetch visitors from the entrance desk. This is my little empire here. "You can hang your coat over there.

Have a seat." She stepped around her desk, took a business card from the top drawer, and began to sit down. And that was when took her first look at Will Eames, full in the face. He smiled weakly at her as he was sitting down. She could not believe it. She thought at once that maybe her eyes would pop out. There in front of her was the good looking white man in a gray suit with blue tie, the same man whom she had seen in the poorly lit alleyway off E Street about two weeks earlier. There was no question it was the same man who had apparently saved her from being raped. The former Marine whom the policeman had seemed to admire. She was staring at him, and maybe her mouth was hanging open a little. But he did not appear to recognize her. She nervously grabbed for something from her desk. And then she remembered her business card and she unsteadily proffered it to him. He was smiling a little and he offered her back his card which gave her an excuse to break off looking at him so intensely. 'William Eames, Head Broker, Eastern Shore Real Estate Agency, Bristol, Maryland'.

"So William, you're a real estate broker?" she softly asked still looking down at his card. She caught herself and stopped short of saying, 'And a former Marine?'

"Yes, ma'am. I can sell you a house, anywhere in Eastern Shore, or buy one from you, as you like. I can also sell you title insurance, as I also run a Title Agency. But you can call me Will. It's less formal than William."

Minnie looked up from the card and looked directly at him again. She was relieved to see that he did not seem to recognize her from two weeks ago. But she was certain he was the same man she had seen and heard that night. The same soft assured voice, the same face, the same suit and tie. She was sure of it. She had managed to put her eyes back in their sockets. But she was still looking straight at him, more than most people do in regular conversations where eyes most frequently avoid each other.

"And I can see that you're undoubtedly an Indian. I suppose that's easy to assume seeing as how you're working for the Bureau of Indian

Affairs." He now smiled a big smile, as if contented with his little bit of deductive reasoning. "But tell me. I'm curious. Mr. Ward told me your name was Matoaka, but your card here says Minnie. So what is it?"

"That's right. My proper name, my birth name is Matoaka. But since I was a little girl everyone has called me Minnie. So please call me Minnie." It was apparent to her that he had no idea about the meaning of Matoaka, so it was best left alone.

"Just like me. My proper name is William, but no one has ever called me anything other than Will."

She was certain that he did not recognize her from the evening two weeks earlier. He was the man who had saved her, no doubts in her mind. But now she felt awkward by his presence. She suddenly realized that he must have seen her bared bottom with the skirt and coat pushed up over her back as she was on her hands and knees in the instant after he had knocked out her black assailant. But maybe he hadn't seen her in that demeaning posture. It was just the flash of a moment in a poorly lit alley, at night, with the red and blue police lights rotating wildly around the walls of the surrounding buildings.

"Minnie?"

She had not heard what he had said and repeated.

"Are you alright?" She looked at him again full in the face. "Yes, perfectly. You were saying."

"I was just asking why if you are working for the Office of Federal Recognition, are you sitting her in the Smithsonian?"

"That's a good question. I've been seconded for an Indian project, here at the Smithsonian. They want to build a National Museum of the American Indian. And I am both an Indian who works at the Bureau of Indian Affairs, and a lawyer. And they have lots of troublesome legal issues entailed in making such an Indian museum project. So they sent me here to work on them."

"So you're a lawyer. I would think that that would be of great value in the Office of Federal

Recognition. I can't understand why they would second you here, when the need for legal expertise is so great there. But never mind. I think your insights could be extremely helpful for our efforts to get federal recognition."

"Well, perhaps. They also said I had a conflict of interest, since I organized the application to that office for my tribe, the Massaponx-Doeg tribe, to get recognition, while at the same time I worked there. They said that would unfairly bias my evaluations."

"Yeah, I guess I can see that. I'd still think your legal background and advice could be enormously helpful to our cause."

"But I cannot give you legal counsel or act as your attorney, as an employee of the Bureau." "Oh sure, I can understand that."

"So tell me, Mr. Eames, eh, Will, are you representing some tribe or other? Or advising a tribe in applying for federal recognition?"

"Yes, I am indeed." said Will now breaking into a big smile. "I am representing the Nantiquak tribe of the Eastern Shore. They have a long history, and unlike what most people think in Maryland, they have not disappeared or ceased to exist. But over time they have lost their reservations and they have only just survived by living in remote areas that were not wanted by white men, and by keeping a very low profile. They also have their own tribal association and have kept fairly good records of their four hundred years of existence."

"That's good to hear," said Minnie. "Because those two are some of the most important and most difficult things to compile for the application."

"Further, they are a recognized tribe in Delaware, but not in Maryland."

"And why are you representing them in this process? What is your relationship to the Nantiquaks?"

"That's an interesting story. But to put it briefly, I bought a piece of property on the Nanticoke River that came up in an intestate disposal case. Now riverside properties there on the Eastern Shore are very valuable and rarely available for purchase. And when I bought it,

I found it came with a fair number of Indian residents who had been living on that land for generations. I thought they were squatters, but the previous owner had been a Nantiquak, and that is when I thought the property I had bought was the remnants of one of the original reservations of the Nantiquaks. So I began digging into the situation and found out that indeed it was and that the Nantiquak tribe still was vibrant. But most of them now are living on lands they have owned in Delaware."

"Totally by coincidence, at that same time, I discovered that I had Nantiquak Indian ancestry. That my great grandmother had been a Nantiquak, one hundred percent. And all my life up to then I had assumed I was anglo, pure, through and through."

"And that was earlier this year," he continued, "when I read an article about the opening of large Indian casino in Connecticut. And with coincidence of all these discoveries, I thought it would be good for the Nantiquaks to build their own casino to profit from the huge flow of weekenders who go to Ocean City. You know that lots of people every weekend from Washington and Baltimore go to the beach there?"

"Yes, I do. I've never gone there myself."

"I thought to myself, so why don't the locals, including the Indians, get much or any benefit from that traffic?"

"So you primarily want to build a casino?"

"An Indian casino, yes. But that can't be done unless the tribe get federal recognition, and probably recovers some or all of its former reservation lands. The same as what the Pequoddy Indian tribe did."

"Yes, I know a lot about that case. It really stirred up a huge movement, and helped create Indian civil rights law. And of course the legal case and the act of Congress which started all of that movement, also stimulated the administrative guidelines for the Bureau to give recognition."

"Well that's right. That's what I understand too. And even if a casino is not built, it's the only way for a tribe to get a large amount of federal welfare benefits. The tribe would benefit right away from these welfare benefits. So that is why I am here."

"You're part Indian then, related to the Nantiquaks?" said Minnie almost dreamily, as if she had not listened to much else that Will had said.

"Yes. As the genealogists have it, I am one-eighth Nantiquak." "That would mean we are very distantly related."

"Really? How is that?" he acted surprised.

"Specialists tell us that the tribes on the Eastern Shore and the Western Shore of the Chesapeake were all related when they moved into the region. They were all Algonkian speakers and they all moved from the far north-east. The Nantiquaks partly settled on the Eastern Shore, and some in what is now the Tidewater of Virginia. And apparently one group of Nantiquaks crossed the Bay and set up on the middle peninsula where they are now called the Doeg. Which is my tribe. So you see we are distantly related."

The expression on Will's face seemed to Minnie to suddenly become puzzled and nonplussed. "That would be a really tenuous, distant relation, wouldn't it?" said Will.

"I suppose we could only establish the degree of such a relationship through DNA analysis." said Minnie. "But the courts earlier in this century ruled for the miscegenation laws in Virginia that you could prove racial identity by even one drop of blood. And so an Indian, or a mulatto, couldn't marry a white man even if the Indian woman was generations mixed with whites. Fortunately those backwards, racist laws have all been struck down. They not only were unconstitutional, but they were also poor science."

"Maybe, but I think the Federal government now does not recognize membership of a tribe, if, like me, one has only one eighth of an ancestor. Even less likely if the relation is one-sixteenth. At least that's what the Nantiquaks have come to believe. They won't, I think, recognize me as a tribe member even if I apply to join them."

"In some respects they are right. In our process in the Office, the current tribe members have to show that they have a full blood relationship to an Indian counted in the 1900 census. And if they can show full-blooded ancestry earlier than that, that is even better. This is often an onerous requirement for many tribes to demonstrate. But membership in a tribe isn't just a matter of blood relationship. It's also cultural membership."

"Tell me, Minnie. If these genealogical relationships are demonstrated by the tribe, going back at least ninety years, then why is it that applications take so long to approve? Is there a minimum size for the tribe?"

"That's a really good question. The Office has to corroborate the data submitted, and especially the genealogical data. And actually that is not so easy. For almost a century, racism and racist laws aimed at native Americans, meant that they weren't counted in the censuses. They were excluded from public schools. Also so many tribes didn't have church records prior to the beginning of the twentieth century either. And sometimes, especially in southern and eastern states, the Indians were counted, if they were counted at all, as black people. So records were not kept. Checking data from the tribes often proves to be impossible."

"I'll bet you in Maryland and Delaware, that probate records will show Indian descent through more than a century."

"Maybe, but in the Office, no one knows how to research probate records."

"I do. It's something I specialize in. Probate title searches. And the tribe has had two historians research their background also. They also used probate records in Delaware and Maryland."

"You'll have to demonstrate to us how they are used." said Minnie now impressed by Will's preparation.

"And nowadays there is another way to corroborate Indian blood. You just mentioned it. I mean, the more reliable way is to apply DNA analysis to current Indians and from the relicts of earlier Indians."

"Probably, that's right. But then again, we are not up to date in research methods in the Office. That has proved controversial in the west, where tribes were unwilling to examine the remains of their claimed ancestors because it has meant disturbing their gravesites."

"So the tribe applying has to create a narrative of its recent and ancient history and then provide as much outside corroboration as possible. Is that right?"

"Yes that's right. And there is some acknowledgement in the office that oral histories and family genealogies are all that we can ever get as evidence."

"Well that's good. The Nantiquaks have had their own state recognized association since the 1870s."

"That's very valuable evidence. That also helps writing the narrative."

"And you know this tribe had its own reservations even from colonial times." Minnie perked up at the mention of early reservations.

"How do mean? How were these reservations established?" she asked.

"By the treaty with King Charles of England, a little over three hundred years ago. I have even found the original of the treaty and have a copy of it."

"That's very important. No, I would say crucial for federal recognition. You could make a legal case for acknowledgement based on a treaty."

Minnie could see that Will was very pleased by this. She continued, "And what happened to their reservations?"

"The states took them away and auctioned off the lands in the nineteenth century."

"Sounds familiar." said Minnie. "Something similar happened to the tribe that neighbors mine. The Piscatawico. They had a treaty, also from King Charles, which gave them a huge reservation along the York River. But over the succeeding centuries, white men took most of it away. They should be a recognized tribe, but as of yet they aren't. But they still hold some reservations lands."

"I'm not a lawyer, but that experience sounds very similar to the case of the Pequoddy tribe, which I read about in the professional real estate press. They went to the courts to restore their lands and their rights."

"Well, I am a lawyer, and I also think it sounds similar. But the Indian recognition act and the regulations of 1977 and 1994 were enacted because the Congress did not want so many Indian affairs decided by the courts. They wanted a systematic route to recognition and land restoration. But concerning your initial question about why the process takes so long, the rules and procedures are not so systematic yet."

Will was looking directly at Minnie and thinking about something.

"So you might be suggesting that a legal route would still be a better route for us?"

"I am suggesting that, but not recommending that, as I cannot give your tribe, legal advice as I am employed in the Office which is supposed to process the regulations and see that they are properly complied with."

Will smiled. "An administrative process, but one that could still be influenced and even directed by law suits?"

Now it was Minnie's turn to smile. "Yes, of course. The formative act of law from 1977 makes some matters clear, and leaves a lot of issues undefined and confused." She was thinking of the case of her own tribe's application.

"And could I infer that the process is still subject to political influence and direction?"

"Yes, of course. Everything in Washington is, in the end, political. The implementation of regulations and rules and guidelines always falls in the way of political considerations. Tribes with good political connections, say the Navaho in New Mexico, always get more from the system than little tribes with no representation or political support here in the capital."

Minnie was beginning to feel attracted to the man opposite her. He was taking her seriously and paying close attention to what she said. And his face was friendly and open. And he asked pointed questions: he had carefully read the application instructions and the materials that the Bureau supplied.

"So the genealogical data of the current tribe members for the past century is most important," continued Minnie. "And corroborating data like the census data. But historical and anthropological information about the tribe over the past three hundred years is also important. It sounds to me that there is lots of this material is also. This is very important, and many tribes overlook it."

"Yes, two bona fide historians have written and published well researched histories about the tribe." said Will. "I have interviewed one of them, who is still living. His book was impressive to me—as a casual reader of history. But he told me that the earlier book is even a better work of history."

"That's good. This is often the area where small tribes applying for recognition cannot find much of their own history. And they do not have the means to compile it."

"You said, Minnie, small tribes have more trouble." said Will. "What is considered small by the Bureau? I mean it seems to me that the Pequoddy with only 240 members is rather small."

"But they got recognition by an act of Congress. Yes, 240 members is a small tribe. But my tribe has only about 500 members."

"The Nantiquaks, as best we can estimate now has a lot more than 800 members."

"That should be more than enough. The size qualification is one of those invisible hurdles which the Office does not usually reveal to tribes that are applying." Minnie paused, and then she suddenly realized that they had been talking already for an hour. "Excuse me, Will. I didn't ask if you'd like a coffee or tea, or some cold drink? What will you have?" And she stood up.

"A coffee would be nice."

"Come with me then." And Minnie led him out the door into a large open space office, and walked across this room to a corridor which ended in a spacious open area where there were vending machines, a water fountain, and a coffee maker on a counter. She looked back at him as they walked. He was much taller than she was, and more than ever she was sure he was the same man who had come to her rescue two weeks earlier. But he still did not let on in the least that he recognized her. She was even more convinced by his good looks; lean and sturdy looking. She noticed that he was looking around the office as they walked through both there and back, carefully observing the details. She felt connected to him as they walked through the open space office. It was a strange sensation. She walked with him to the coffee concession area as if she were showing him off to the other people working in the office, as if he were one of her relatives and not a business caller.

Seated back at her desk with their coffees, they both looked at each other for some moments before resuming. She was thinking about that moment in the alley, when she saw and heard him talking to the policeman, like some film flashback in her mind's eye. He was thinking at how attractive she was, and how she somehow reminded him of someone he had seen recently, but he couldn't recall who it was. Finally Will broke the silence.

"So what is the right way to apply for federal recognition?"

"The most important thing is to submit a narrative document which includes all of the information that is required. And to include any other support documents, as well. It's best if all the information that the Office requires are submitted together at the same time. One of the biggest causes of delays is that tribes submit applications documents with incomplete data. And that means they have to provide that information later. The Office sometimes informs the tribes of the deficiencies, but sometimes it doesn't."

"So what you're saying is don't submit an application document until you have gathered all the requested data and information and the document is complete. Is that right?"

"That's the best way, yes."

"Would it be useful to have letters of endorsement from the local Congressmen from the districts where the tribesmen reside."

"No one has done that before, but I think it would be very useful. It could spur things along inside the Office, if the analysts there knew that Congressmen want to see that result. I know it would motivate me, if I were still working in the Office, to handle the application a bit more carefully and to accelerate the approval process."

"Good, then we'll get those letters included. Because I think the Congressmen from the Eastern Shore will want to help the Nantiquaks. They are, as you can probably guess, as a group, a pool of poverty. And all politicians want to help the poor."

"You're right, of course. The whole issue of federal recognition originated from Congress's desire to address Indian poverty. I know that is certainly true in the case of my own tribe."

Will then asked if a tribe stood a better chance of getting recognition if it already had a reservation.

"That's an area where the act of 1977 does not help us much." said Minnie. "It has evolved that it is most favorable if a tribe lives together, preferably on a reservation or tribally owned lands. But most of the tribes in the East or Midwest, do not have reservations. But they may still live in close communities, or several communities scattered over an area in close proximity. So some tribes are applying for recognition so that they can establish a reservation, while others want recognition as a way of protecting their reservation and gaining sovereign rights."

"The Nantiquaks should have a reservation." Will said with some excitement. "They were granted some reservations by treaty, and that treaty has never been revoked by any authority."

"The 1977 act does seem to give preference to tribes that already have a reservation. But then the recognition that the BIA grants them according to the act does give them the rights to establish their own reservations on land that the tribes own collectively and put into trust. So, it's important that you include the treaty in your application document. It is the basic and fundamental recognition that should still be in force."

"But getting federal recognition, it seems to me, does nothing to restore a tribe's historic reservation lands, or to give it a new reservation. Is that right?"

"That's right. In the case of the Pequoddy tribe, the federal act assigned the funds to buy acreage which had not been tribal lands earlier, and used imminent domain to claim the lands. Reserve lands have been recovered using the courts."

"Yes, and I was getting to that. Because I think we want to go to court to win restoration of reserve lands which the states of Delaware and Maryland illegally seized and sold from the Nantiquaks."

"That has been done for a few tribes, especially in the East. I am not as familiar with these cases as with recognition applications."

"But I was thinking that you could steer us in the right direction to get the proper legal counsel."

"Yes, I think I can. There are not many who specialize in Indian affairs law. But maybe we can meet a second time to discuss legal options." She surprised herself by proposing to meet with Will a second time. But she felt that she wanted to see him again. This seemed to have surprised Will a little as well.

"Well sure. We can do that. I'll bring a member of my team who is a tribeswoman and a paralegal. Do you think we can meet again before Christmas?"

"Yes, I think so. I'll make some inquiries. I'd like to introduce you to the Native American Indian Legal Services, or more commonly called NAILS, which has an office here in Washington. They would be the best resource for legal assistance and lawyers for your tribe."

"And I need to ask my team members when they could come with me. So, how about if I give you a call next week and we can set an appointment then?"

"Yes that would be fine. Maybe later in the week." "Do you have a cell phone so I can call you directly?" "No."

"Here, I'll write down my cell phone number. If you need to get in touch with me." Will wrote down a number on a small piece of note paper he took out of his brief case and gave it to her. "You should get yourself a cell phone. Best way to keep in touch with friends and other people. Even outside work hours. Just a piece of friendly advice."

"I see. I wasn't thinking of getting one. But now I'll look into it, if you recommend it."

"Well I do. And if you have one, I can more easily reach you. I can see that we will need your help much more in the future."

She thought this was a bit strange. No one had ever said that they wanted to reach her more easily in exactly that way. Few had ever said that they needed her or her help. It was nice to hear it.

They stood up from the desk and everything seemed to Minnie odd and a bit awkward. As if they were parting as friends, but too early. He also seemed to wait for her lead. Then as if to insert a personal note to close off their professional discussions he said, "Do you have plans to do anything special this weekend?" Again Minnie was surprised by his inquiry. But not annoyed. Maybe he was just trying to make conversation, and he didn't know what else to say. She rarely did anything special or out of the ordinary in her free time or weekends.

"No, I don't think so. Maybe I'll visit my mother." She stepped toward the coat rack and took Will's coat off the hook and offered it to him. He thanked her and chuckled nervously, and then put it on. Then she stepped toward and the door and lead him back to the main entrance hall. On the way down, Will again added a non-sequitur, "I might go fishing. It's rockfish season. They are forecasting cold but clear weather this weekend." Minnie had only once or twice gone fishing before, and that was with her father when she was still a girl many years ago, back in the time when her father still approved of her. But Will's statement was not an invitation. At the reception desk, he turned to her and offered her his hand. She took it and shook hands. It was again strange, as she rarely ever in her office routines or at meetings shook hands with anyone. His grip was strong and his hand warm. "Thank you, Minnie. I'm pleased to have met you and talked with you. You've been really helpful.

And I think we can have further useful discussions. We'll be in touch soon." She didn't fully realize that she was dealing with a salesman, but his manner was pleasing to her and even in some ways comforting. She said simply, "Good bye, Mr. Eames." "Will. Call me Will. Bye now. Have a good weekend." And then he turned and quickly walked out the front doors. She thought maybe it would be nice to go fishing with him.

But then she looked at her watch. It was near five o'clock and she needed to close up and rush to catch her train. After her first day back in the office when she had left early to recover her car from the E Street parking lot, she had started commuting only by train. This meant she had to keep a tighter schedule. She had to leave the office no later than 5:45 if she were to make the last train out to Spotsylvania. And she needed to catch the 7:20 train in order to start work by nine. It was constraining on her work schedule, but she felt safer and more comfortable taking the train. Maybe on this late afternoon she would leave at five o'clock to catch the 5:25 train. But she needed to hurry to be able to leave by then. It didn't matter that she was working much shorter hours these days, after her incident. There was no one who oversaw her output, and there were no deadlines imposed on her so there was no pressure on her to make her own commuting schedule. But she still had to fit in with the commuter train schedule which had only a few departures after 5:30 pm.

On the weekend, she needed to do some shopping. So she decided to drive up to Fredericksburg and go to the mall there. After she had bought her grocery needs she went into the small store of AT&T Wireless. There was a good sized selection of cellular phone handsets all with somewhat alien names like Nokia, Siemens, Motorola or Samsung. The young, pimply man who was the store clerk helping her tried to push a confusing array of different wireless services on her all with different combinations available for different handsets, as if she understood exactly what she wanted. Finally she seemed to be focusing on a Nokia handset because she liked its simple lines and light weight. "Now I can dial on this just like on a hardline phone?" she asked. "Absolutely, ma'am." "Well then maybe I need to see how it works?" "We have coverage here in the store. You can try a call on this model. It already has a SIM card." Minnie took Will's card out of her wallet. "So I call this number, by pressing only these buttons? No code numbers first?" "No call directly the number you see." She tried pressing in the numbers and then held the handset to her ear. The line was quiet for a few moments and then she could hear a foreign ring tone. It rang seven or eight times, and then went quiet. "Hello." It was his voice. She definitely could tell it was his voice. "Hello, Will Eames?" Is that you?" "Yes, yes. Who's calling?" said the speaker. Minnie giggled. "Will, this is Minnie Warrens. You remember, we met two days ago?" "Yes, yes, sure. Hello Minnie. How could I forget you in only two day? How are you?" "Fine, thank you. But I'm sorry, Will if I'm disturbing you. I was just testing out the handsets for a cell phone that I might buy. But the choices are bewildering.

Can you tell me, is the Nokia a good cell phone?" "Oh yes, one of the best you can buy. I would highly recommend any of their latest models." "Okay, thank you Will. I hope that I haven't bothered you. Thanks so much." "No bother at all, Minnie." "Then, good bye, Will." "Good bye,

Minnie. Good luck in your purchase." Now she was giggling more, as she handed the handset back to the young assistant. "I think I'll take it." She paid and then asked the dealer to show her how to set it up and use it for best effect. He showed her how to enter contact numbers, how to insert a SIM card and a memory card. "No, your contacts don't have to be wireless numbers. You can enter any telephone number, fixed line or wireless." So she put into the memory her mother's telephone number, her sister's and her brother's numbers, and her office number. Then she remembered she had Will's cell number so she put that in too. She then felt an impulse to call him again and ask him if he was still planning on going fishing. But she resisted the impulse and did not call. She felt so proud to be the owner of a Nokia cellular phone, probably the first in her tribe. She drove to Bowling Green to visit her mother and show off her new technical acquisition.

The next week, at her office, all she could think of was the next meeting she would have with Will. She started her preparations for their next meeting by trying to look up the attorneys who had represented the Pequoddy tribe in Connecticut and the Pemaquidscot tribe in Maine and who in effect had created Indian civil rights law by litigating for new laws and rules for federal recognition and restoration of reservation lands. By searching the internet she finally found that the original attorney for the Indian Legal Services was a man named Timothy Turino and that he was still active but now working in California. She found several others, like Richard Clark, who had participated in successfully suing states using the Nonintercourse Act of 1790. But all of them had since left the various public legal services firms, where the pay is very low because they provided services to tribes without fees. They all had left this realm for more lucrative legal services outside. But all the trails led to the same place, namely to NAILS. She decided not to call Turino or Clark to ask for references or recommended lawyers, as they would probably only point her back to NAILS. She did find however several articles that Turino and his partners had written which detailed the legal cases he had argued, the reasoning justifying his lawsuits, the legal precedents that he had used and the courts's rulings. They were very helpful guidelines. She then called to NAILS and arranged for herself an introductory meeting that week. They suggested meeting her on either Wednesday or Thursday morning. She asked for Wednesday and they agreed.

On that Wednesday mid-morning she came dressed in her sharpest work costume, a black dress with a white blouse and a black jacket. She also came with her latest professional resume, just in case she needed it, even though she had never worked in a law firm on Indian civil rights law. She left her office on C Street and walked over to the Metro and took the metro train four stops to K Street where she found one of the many plain, non-descript concrete panel and glass buildings where NAILS had its offices. She was met by a young white man who introduced himself as one of the firm's attorneys. He invited her into a small windowless conference room and invited in two even younger people, a man and a woman who were introduced as clerks, meaning they were just out of law school. After the ritual exchange of business cards, she introduced herself and went into depth about her background and her work at the Bureau and at the Smithsonian. Then she introduced the subject about the Nantiquaks and what they wanted to achieve. She ended by pointing out that they were thinking about suing the states of Maryland and Delaware for wrongful dispossession of their reservation lands in the 18th and 19th centuries. The young attorney, who was named Jared Levy, responded very enthusiastically to her story. "That's just the sort of legal assistance we are set up to give, although we aim to provide legal aid to all sorts of low income people. I think we would gladly meet with this tribe's representatives to explore what kinds of litigation strategy and legal advice they will need. Most of our pro bono work is for native American tribes." Levy spoke in a high almost squeeky voice, very rapidly, almost aggressively. She did not like the impression he made with his attacking manner of speech. Levy continued to say that he had clerked with NAILS while he was studying at George Washington University Law School, but that he himself had not worked on Native American legal services. That was the role for one of the more senior attorneys who was out of the office all that week and the next week as well—in other words he would not be available until after New Year's. But Levy said that the office was understaffed and he knew that their office currently had an open position for an attorney for just those services.

"Maybe you have a list of your office's experience in litigation and legal advisory services over the past decade for Native Americans?" Minnie asked.

Levy said that they sure did, and he sent one of the two clerks out to get a print-out of the list.

"So that means," said Minnie, "that we should call your senior partner after New Year's to set up a meeting with the potential client?"

"Yes that would be best."

"Maybe, then I can leave with you a copy of my resume at this time. I would very much be interested in working in NAILS on Indian legal issues." She had not consciously decided that she wanted to leave the BIA and find a new job, but she suddenly thought it was a good idea to find work that was more interesting for her.

Levy took it without even glancing at it, and then escorted Minnie to the front door and wished her a good afternoon.

"Call our senior attorney, Cal Reiner, in early January to set up an appointment. Hope to see you real soon, next month."

On the way back to her office in the Smithsonian Minnie felt that she wouldn't be able to arrange a meeting between Will and NAILS before January. She would have to call him to tell him about the delay and apologize to him. He had wanted to have this next meeting before Christmas, but that was not going to be possible. She also regretted that she would not be seeing Will for another three to four weeks. After lunch, she called Will on his cell phone number. She just wanted to hear his soft, friendly voice. When he answered his phone, she felt immediately relieved. Apologizing would not be too difficult or shameful. She told him the situation with the NAILS and the upcoming holidays complicating any meeting with the attorney who specialized in Indian legal affairs.

"Oh, that's alright, Minnie. But if it's okay for you, maybe we could come to your office and have a follow up meeting this Friday morning, anyway. The tribe's representative will come with me. We are a team. She'd like to meet you as well."

Of course, she had nothing scheduled that could get in the way. She could go through the NAILS experience list and she would have something to talk about with Will. "Yes, okay, so how about if we meet at 10:30 at my office?"

"That would be great, Minnie. I look forward to seeing you then." She felt the same, but did not say so.

"Oh and by the way, are you calling me using your new cell phone? You did buy the Nokia, didn't you?"

"Yes, I did. But just now I am calling you from my office line."

"So you can learn a new routine. Call me back from your Nokia, and then I will have that number and can save it on my cell phone. That is, if you don't mind my having your personal phone number."

"No, no. I wouldn't mind." She already had picked up her purse and was fumbling through it for the small handset. "Okay, I'll call you right back then, Will." She hung up her desk phone and turned on her cell phone and punched in the numbers. It was a little challenging for her as she had not used it much yet and the number pad was small, but she eventually mastered it.

"Yes? Is this Minnie?"

"Yes, Will, so we've connected."

"Alright, so now I've put your number into my phone contacts list. Now whenever you call me from your cell phone, mine will show me caller I.D. and I'll know it is you calling. And you can put my cell phone into your contact list too."

She did not want to say that she already had.

"And when you want to call me, you just select my name from your contact list and press the dial key."

She also did not want to tell him that she had punched in his number directly onto the number pad manually. And as if he knew what she was thinking, he said, "And don't worry. You'll get used to using the features of your cell phone, like speed dialing. It will all come from regular use. So, once again, I look forward to seeing you the day after tomorrow, at 10:30."

"Yes, I'll be expecting you then. Good bye."

"Good bye, Minnie."

She liked the way he said her name. And she liked the way he spoke to her in general. His tone with her was like that of a male friend that she had known for a long time. His was a voice and tone that soothed her and seemed to reach out and support her.

On Friday morning, Minnie found herself waiting for Will's visit with anticipation. She had dressed nicely that morning; she had added a colorful patterned silk blouse to her usual dark wool skirt and jacket. It was a very cold bright morning. So she had also wrapped a heavy scarf around her head and over the collar of her winter coat. On the train ride up to D.C. she reviewed in her mind the legal cases she wanted to talk about. She noted several times that some of the legal challenges would have been appropriate for her own tribe, if only they had had a reservation set up by treaty.

When the phone on her desk finally rang it was just shortly before 10:30 and she snatched up the handset quickly. It was the front lobby receptionist announced the arrival of two guests for her. She rushed down to the lobby and was so eager to see Will that she almost did not immediately recognize him. He was standing next to an unknown young woman, and he was wearing a heavy dark blue long coat which she had not seen on him before. But then when she realized it was Will, she greeted him warmly, and shook his hand, looking intently straight into his face, and then she offered her hand to the young woman. "This is Carmine Norwood," said Will, "a Nantiquak from Millville, Delaware, who I was telling you about, Minnie." "So glad to meet you, Ms. Norwood.

Please come with me up to my office." They followed her up by elevator to the fourth floor, through the open plan office space and to Minnie's office. There they took off their coats and hung them in the coat rack, but before taking their seats, Minnie invited them to go with her to the coffee corner and take their drinks. Minnie snatched a few looks at Will as they moved about, but she also looked at Carmine who was tall and a little plump. Her skin was not as coppery or as dark as Minnie's, it was a little swarthy, and Minnie thought Carmine could be mistaken for an Italian girl. It irked her; Carmine did not look at all like an Indian girl.

Back in her office, she invited them to sit, Will directly opposite her and Carmine at an angle at the desk corner. Minnie looked again at Carmine and concluded that she was not very attractive. She had a round face, big dark eyes which bulged out of her face, a narrow slanting forehead, a slightly bulbous nose, and thick lips. A babyish look to her face. Minnie did not feel that Will would be attracted to Carmine, and that thought made her feel strangely comfortable.

"So, I have looked into the various legal strategies that a tribe such as yours, the Nantiquak, could adopt to gain recognition and to reclaim lost reservation lands. The precedents have been established by several lawsuits already. The most important of which are the cases that you found yourself, Will, the cases of the Pequoddy against the state of Connecticut."

Minnie proceeded to tell them about the various lawsuits that had been filed on behalf of Indian tribes to regain reservation lands. Some had been successful, some not. She reviewed the legal basis of the suits that had been brought. Apparently there had been a number of lawsuits in the 19th century when tribes lost their reservation or were re-allocated other reservation lands. But Minnie said that those precedents were not meaningful for the Nantiquaks, although they had been important for the Cherokees. There were not any lawsuits brought to establish federal recognition, but she pointed out that it was the threat of such lawsuits that caused Congress to enact the 1977 law concerning federal recognition for Indian tribes. And the Congressional act that gave recognition to the Pequoddy tribe was also in reaction to lawsuits. All of this commentary which Minnie gave ran into details and legal reasoning which Will and Carmine knew nothing about and which they found a little difficult to follow. After almost forty minutes of speaking, Minnie began to understand that this was what was happening to her listeners. She paused.

"Maybe I should talk a little about the lawyers who have led these cases and created a whole new area of Indian law. The real leader in this field is Thomas Turino. He was just a young lawyer working for a public legal services firm in New England. He is still working on legal issues that concern native Americans, but he no longer works for public legal services, like Lone Pine Legal Services, where he began representing Indians. He may want to take on some of your challenges. I don't know. Public service legal work does not pay lawyers very well, and he is no longer young, so maybe he wouldn't want to represent the Nantiquak as a pro bono lawyer. But there are others. To name just two there is Richard Clark, who worked with Turino, and Carl Dailey. But there remains the public legal services, who are paid by public monies and contributions. I was telling you Will about NAILS, here in D.C. Next month I will arrange for a meeting with you and them. They are located over on K Street. I think there are more than enough well qualified legal resources that could advise and direct Nantiquak's litigation strategy…" As she was speaking, Minnie became aware that she wanted to be one of those lawyers.

After another half hour she again became conscious that she was losing the attention of Will and Carmine. But her enthusiasm for the subject was growing. She was also conscious that as chief of her tribe she had led the tribe on the wrong strategy by applying to the Office for Federal Recognition. She should have taken the route of lawsuits and legal challenges. Minnie, as a lawyer, had not advised her tribe on taking the most appropriate strategy.

Finally she stopped speaking.

"Well, regardless of what I have told you now, the attorneys at NAILS might give you entirely different advice."

Will retorted quickly. "I think we couldn't do better than if you were our lawyer and legal advisor. You know all the loop holes and ins and outs of the bureaucratic process for recognition as well as the avenues to apply the law to help us. You would be the best attorney we could find, I'm sure."

"That's very nice of you to say, Will. But I am not terribly experienced in litigation, certainly not litigation in the field of Indian civil rights law."

"You know a helluva lot more than the lawyers I work with in Delaware do." said Carmine, her first comment of the morning. She was genuinely impressed by Minnie's preparation.

"Does your tribal association have a lawyer?" asked Minnie.

"Yes, but he's a simple county lawyer, who provides us advice on simple property questions in the county and sometimes on some tax issues related to the association in Delaware."

"I would imagine that the legal entity in your case would be the Tribal Association." said Minnie, half in questioning, half in making a straightforward statement of fact.

"Do we need a different one?" asked Carmine.

"I don't think so. Maybe you could organize some of your litigation as class action, where the class would be all the members of the Association and all other people who identify themselves as Nantiquak Indians. That would be interesting because in effect the court-- and I assume it would be a federal court-- if they accept the class, would be granting recognition to the tribe."

"In that case," said Will, "I would think that could boost our application to the Bureau of Indian Affairs. Don't you think so, Minnie?"

"Yes, it could. Although the office of federal recognition relies mostly on the Act of 1977. It may not feel required to follow the recognition given by a court."

Minnie finished telling Will and Carmine her ideas about legal strategies for another half hour and it was already lunch hour in her office. She capped off her statements with the caveat, "Again, you have to understand these are my views, and the lawyers you get to advice you may completely disregard them and advise you quite differently."

"Minnie, you've again been a great help for us. And all your advice has been generously and freely given. Beyond the usual call of duty. I don't know how we can thank you enough. May I invite you to join us for lunch? I can think of a seafood restaurant quite nearby that serves genuine Nantiquak traditional food. Maybe a fifteen minute walk from here."

"Thank you, Will. But I am not sure I can."

"Surely you can. There is no conflict. You're working on your Indian Smithsonian project. Nothing to do with the Bureau, so our lunching together cannot be seen as an attempt to curry favor in the Bureau's deliberations."

Minnie was flustered. No one actually had ever invited her out to lunch during her time working at the Bureau. She had only sometimes joined work colleagues in going out to lunch. And then it was most usual not to go to a restaurant but to lunch van and eat on the curbside. But on the other hand, she was attracted by the offer. She agreed.

"Good, I am recommending a place down on the waterfront. I first went to it when I was a kid, visiting Warshington as a tourist with my parents. It's a kind of fish market, that serves up meals from their wares. They have great crabs, or oysters, or rockfish that they fix for you. All good Nantiquak food."

"And Massaponax food also."

They walked down 7th Street the five or so block to the waterfront and then over Captain White's Seafood Market. It was a seafood market and Washington landmark for three generations. There were sheltered and heated areas inside the market, where shoppers could make their seafood orders, deciding on how they want their selections cooked and sit down to eat them in warm, but very simple surroundings. It was still near freezing outside with a light steady wind blowing up off the Potomac as they got to the waterfront. Minnie was relieved to get there and go straight inside the market. Inside she was impressed by the number of stalls selling whole rockfish, fish filets, live clams, several varieties of live oysters and mussels—all displayed on ice-- and lots of live crabs in pens. She had never been to this market before and was impressed by its offerings which were much better and fresher than what she usually saw in the supermarkets where she did her food shopping. Will pointed up at a large white board that had a long hand printed list of offerings.

"Here's the menu for today's fresh cooked fish and shellfish. I'll have crab cakes. And the kale."

"And I see they have boiled hominy." said Carmine. "I think I'll some of that with fried red fish."

"That's interesting. Hominy is originally a food eaten by the Powhatan Indians." said Minnie. "The word first appears when the Powhatans, my tribe introduced maize to the English." She chose a dish of steamed clams and hominy.

"Well, then I'll have hominy too." said Will. "And a beer. What will you both have to drink?"

They completed their orders and Will paid. Then they took their drinks and sat on benches at a wood picnic table in the heated area to wait for the orders to be cooked.

"I haven't had hominy since I was a little girl." said Minnie. "I don't see it for sale in the supermarkets."

"Most seafood places and restaurants serve either hush puppies or cornbread with their seafood." said Will. "There's a place in Bristol, a favorite of mine, which serves really good hush puppies."

"Oh yeah, I like those." said Carmine.

Minnie was beginning to feel warmed up. The walk down in the wind had chilled her. Again she sat directly opposite Will at the table. Carmine was now sitting at her side, so Minnie did not have to look at her. She focused her looks and her comments entirely on Will. After ten minutes their orders were ready and Will jumped up to collect them. Minnie followed him and offered to help him carry the six styrofoam boxes back to the table-- the hominy and greens came in separate boxes from the seafood. "That's a lot of food." she said in surprise. "Yes, the more the merrier." said Will. "What you don't eat now you can save for dinner, later."

"I may have to." said Minnie. "And for lunch another day, too."

Over the lunch, Will began to gush over seafood. "And you know, I grew up where almost all transactions, family, social, or business, were accompanied by food. Eating together is the cement of our little society out on the Eastern Shore. And the best food was always the local seafood."

"I think it is the same way with us Nantiquaks." said Carmine. "Maybe it is a shared tradition."

"Or maybe the first English settlers of the Eastern Shore learned it from you." said Will. "After all if the Nantiquaks hadn't shown the first colonists what to eat and how to take it or raise, they would have starved. Like corn for instance. The colonists were not farmers. They didn't know about corn.

And they did not know how to harvest the shellfish which has sustained the Eastern Shore for centuries."

"I'm not sure that we had the same traditional approach on the Western Shore. But the Powhatan Indians were the ones that taught the English how to grow and harvest their own food." said Minnie. "That is well documented. But the English reaction was to take the land away from the tribes where they could harvest shellfish, or grow corn and beans."

She looked directly at Will, "And by the way Will, did you go fishing, as you said you might, last weekend?"

"Yes, Minnie, I did. And we caught several really big rockfish. But it was so cold out on the water. We managed to stay out only two hours before we headed back to the dock. Do you like eating rockfish?"

"I don't know. I'm not sure I know what a rockfish is. I don't think I would know if I were eating one or not."

"It's also called a striped bass. You can catch it in the Bay or in the Atlantic, either from the beach or by trolling from a boat. But it's not usually available in the supermarkets here."

"Do you fish, Carmine?" Minnie asked.

"No, but my brothers do."

"Tell me a bit about your life in the tribe over there in Delaware." Minnie inquired from Carmine.

"There's nothing much to tell. My family is a large one. We own two houses on the Indian River, and one farmhouse a bit away from the water. The waters of Indian Bay at our end of the river do not support either shellfish or fishing. But I am told they used to be very rich in mussels and crabs. But overfishing and pollution has done them in. So the tribe no longer lives off the resources of the waters. I am the daughter of a former chief of the tribe, and I most likely could be the next chief, after the current chief abdicates or dies. But it is rare that women become chief of the Nantiquaks."

"You know in my tribe, it has not been so rare. I am in fact, the chief of the Massaponax-Doeg tribal group, on the Middle Peninsula."

"Really?" Will and Carmine almost asked in unison in surprise.

"Yes, and I've been the chief for almost eight years, since my father died."

"That's amazing." said Carmine. "You have to be my role model, Minnie. Is it hard being chief of the tribal warriors, being a woman as you are?"

"Yes, sometimes there are some conflicts and jealousies. And sometimes some resistance to my proposals, just because I am a woman. But, you know, as I said, our tribe has been governed by a number of famous queens in the past, that is women chiefs."

"And there's some coincidence here too." Minnie continued. "As I already told Will, the Nantiquak tribe and my tribe, or at least the Doeg subtribe of the Massaponx, are related. They came from the same original ancestors in the far Northeast of America. It's just that the Doeg clan moved across the Bay when the rest of the Nantiquak remained on the Eastern Shore, and they began to intermarry with the Massaponx and they never went back. Anthropologists tell us they spoke identical Algonkian languages. Whereas the other tribes of the Powhatan confederation spoke a different dialect of Algonkian."

"You know so much." said Carmine, virtually cooing.

"Study, study, and then lots of study. Preparation for my role, as chief. I suppose that being studious was also not something that was much appreciated by the men in my tribe. They think it is all useless. Book learning. But as we no longer share the Algonkian language we can only learn about our past, our traditions, and our relations with other peoples, all the things that set up apart, from books, what scholars and specialists have discovered and written down for us."

"You are really impressive, Minnie." said Will. "The more I learn about you, the more impressive you appear."

Minnie blushed. No one had ever spoken to her like that, and she was not accustomed to handling either expressions of admiration or flattery. But she liked it coming from Will.

Lunch broke up not long after that. The wind had picked up and it was colder than when they had left from Minnie's office. She cursed herself that she had left her scarf behind, because now she needed it. Her hands were shaking from the cold, even though they were walking fast. After three blocks, at E Street, Will said he had parked the car in a lot there and they would be going straight to the parking lot. Minnie felt a momentary hollow feeling inside. E Street was of course the place where she had been assaulted three weeks earlier. She didn't want to go there again, and she did not like that Will and Carmine were going to the place of her recent humiliation. But they could not possibly know that. They said their good byes and Minnie rushed up the rest of 7th Street to her office. She felt chilled all the rest of the afternoon. But she also thought a lot about Will, and she wanted to work with him.

The next three weeks seemed to Minnie as if they would never end. She was eager to learn about a meeting with NAILS, and she was even more eager to see Will again. Even the interruptions of

Christmas and New Year's did not make the time pass by any faster. Minnie did not have any obligations to prepare for Christmas or the holidays. In her family Christmas was not observed or celebrated. They did not belong to or attend any church. And New Year's Eve was not celebrated at all. Just a day off from her work. Both holidays fell on Thursdays that year, and most people in her office merged the official day off with the Friday to gain a four day weekend, if they did not actually take off a full week between the two holidays. But Minnie was one of those few who went back to work on the two Fridays after Christmas and New Year's Day. It didn't make much difference to her. But she got a surprise on New Year's Eve, when her cell phone made a funny noise. It turned out she had received her first text message. When she finally figured this out and then out to open the message she found a message from Will wishing her a Happy New Year, and success in the New Year with all these Indian projects. She had never before gotten a New Year's greeting from anyone. It made her feel good. She struggled for a few minutes trying to write a message of thanks back to Will on her phone, again having trouble with the small keypad. After New Year's she went back to the nearly empty office and sat morosely working on her Indian museum project. She kept looking at her desk phone. But she didn't really expect to hear from NAILS until after Monday, the fifth of January, and she impatiently waited until the seventh before she decided to call them back to see if Cal Reiner had returned and if an appointment could be set up. By that Wednesday when she finally called, she was told he had returned to the office but that he was away just then. She left a message asking him to call her back concerning a meeting. At the end of the day a call came through on her desk phone. It was Cal Reiner calling.

"Hello, Ms. Warrens. I'm sorry it's taken so long for me to get back to you. I've been very busy this past month. So you are calling about getting together for an employment interview? I've looked at your resume. And it looks very interesting. Do you think you could come in Friday morning to talk about the opening and your background?" He spoke very fast.

"Well, actually Mr. Reiner I was calling about setting up a different meeting."

"That's okay. We can talk about that later. So what do you say? Can you come on Friday morning?" "Yes, I'll be there. I look forward to meeting with you."

"Fine, see you then. Bye Ms. Warrens."

She was overwhelmed. Mr. Reiner spoke even faster than his junior colleague, Mr. Levy. She wondered if she worked for him in NAILS if she would be completed dominated, if she could even get a word in with him. But she showed up, dressed in her handsome dark lawyer's suit with a white blouse, promptly on schedule Friday morning.

It was not so much an employment interview, as a review presented by Reiner of the work the firm had to do in the coming year and her likely contribution to that work. Reiner was an imposing, self- important man. He had not come out of his office to meet her. Instead his secretary delivered Minnie into his office. He was sitting behind a large clear desk with one computer monitor on it, and he was talking on the phone. He was not wearing a jacket and the collar on his white shirt was open and his tie loosened as if he had been working all night. He stood and shook Minnie's hand while getting off the phone. Then he introduced himself as D. Calvin Reiner, or Cal, and gave her his business card. They sat opposite each other and he began with a barrage of questions about what she would like to do, and how much litigation experience she had. She honestly answered that she wanted to help tribes reclaim their rights and to gain recognition, and that she had only limited litigation experience. That she had never led a court case herself, but had worked on several cases for the lead attorney in the Richmond firm where she had first worked after getting her admission to the Virginia bar. Reiner seemed quite alright with her answers. He even waved her to stop. "Don't downplay yourself, Ms. Warrens." he said. She felt a bit intimidated by Reiner's style and intensity.

After an hour, during which Cal Reiner did almost all the talking or posing of questions, he stopped, and asked. "Well, maybe you have some questions for me?"

But before Minnie could ask any, he started again.

"We work nine to five. But of course, that really means you work the hours to fit the workload. As in most practices. I suppose your experience at Petit, Sauvain, and Mason taught you that. And we are a public service firm, paid by government grants and contributions, to do pro bono work. So the pay is not as good as it might be at other law firms here in town, either lobbyists or corporate lawyers. We can pay you seven thousand a month. Plus a possible bonus on completed court cases. You won't get rich working in public service law."

That was about fifteen thousand dollars less than she earned in a year at the Bureau, where she did not however have any prospect for bonuses. It was more than what she expected.

"Getting rich is not a goal that I am working for, Mr. Reiner. I want to work as a lawyer to improve the lot of my people, my tribe."

"Nobly said, Ms. Warrens. And that is why we would like to hire you. When can you start?"

"I think I could get by with two weeks' notice to the Bureau. So I could start here on the first of February, if that is okay with you."

"I like the way you talk, Ms. Warrens, slow and deliberate, and clear. Let's say we have a deal then. You will start as a senior attorney on the first of next month. And I will see you then."

"Except you might see me sooner, if you agree to meet with a possible future client soon. Remember I spoke to you about wanting an appointment to meet a tribe seeking advice and legal representation?"

"Yes? Well that would be good. You will bring in a potentially new client? Well, the sooner the better for that. Let's say next week, Wednesday? Would that be possible? After lunch. What tribe are you recommending to us?"

"The Nantiquak tribe of Delaware and Maryland."

"Never heard of them. And I live in Maryland."

"I would suggest that you have heard of them, if you have ever gone to Ocean City. From here you have to cross the Nanticoke River to get there. That is their name and the place of their origin."

"Oh, you're right. Well done, Ms. Warrens. So we will meet with the representatives of the Nanticoke tribe next Wednesday at two o'clock in our offices. And you'll be coming with them I take it?"

But before she could answer he had picked up his telephone handset and began instructing his secretary to record a meeting for that time in the large conference room. "And tell Mr. Levy, and Ms. Halstead that they are to attend also."

Minnie waited quietly until he was off the phone. "Yes, I will come with them. I recommended them to you, but I am not acting for them. That will wait until I start here and after they appoint us." "Quite right. Very good. So I'll be seeing you then, Ms. Warrens. What is your first name again?" "Minnie. Minnie Warrens."

Reiner stood up and held out his hand. "Let's shake on a deal, Minnie." And then he led her to the door of his office but no further, where he said, "See you then. Good-bye for now." Minnie went to the receptionist/secretary who looked like a true Indian woman, that is a woman from South Asia, who brought Minnie her coat and she left the NAILS offices. Her head was spinning. Her previous three employers were not so easy or quick to get employment offers. They had taken their time, used bureaucratic channels and made excuses about delays. But Reiner it seems had decided to hire her even before she had arrived. She floated back to her office in the Smithsonian, she was so elated. Now she could start working on something serious and with more worthwhile objectives.

She was happy, but did not know whom she could share her good news with. She knew one thing though: moving to work with NAILS would show Nighthorse that he had misjudged her. He would come to regret her departure from the Bureau. There was nothing pressing for her to complete that afternoon, so back at her office she called the HR manager over at the Bureau and informed her that she was quitting effective at the end of the month. The manager, a very sassy and unpleasant young black woman, acted surprised and she asked Minnie was the cause for her resignation was. "I'd rather not say. Can you put without cause? It's plain enough to me that I have no future prospects in the Bureau." "That won't do." the HR girl said harshly. "You have to give a cause." "Well if I must, then I will say the unsympathetic way you handled my request for leave when I was assaulted in November last year. And the way you gossiped about it to other people in my office." Minnie surprised herself as how angry her answer was. But it felt good to get this anger off her chest.

"Fine, we'll prepare all the agreements and forms you need to make, and I put in that 31 January will be your last day. Your last paycheck will be ready for you on the 28th."

Later that afternoon before she left the office early, she called Will on his cell phone and told him about the timing for the meeting with NAILS. Will took the news very appreciatively, and thanked her several times. He said he would bring Carmine, and maybe even another tribesman or two who were on his action committee. She was not going to tell him when she first called that she had gotten an offer from NAILS that she was going to accept. But she couldn't help herself, and she wanted to let someone know that she had gotten good news.

"Oh, that is wonderful, Minnie. I mean, that is such good news. I suspect you wanted to work in such a firm. Congratulations. This is really good for us, too. It could mean that we will soon be working together. I would like nothing better than that!"

He sounded sincerely impressed and pleased by Minnie's news. He spoke with just a touch of excitement in his voice. He had a way of reacting and speaking to her that was always so encouraging, so positive, so appreciative. She had never encountered such a person before.

"So maybe we can meet with you over lunch, before we go over to NAILS's offices. Would that be alright with you?"

"Yes, that would be nice. I don't know if I could add anything useful but we can still have lunch first. Somewhere near their offices."

"Great. That would be really nice. I'll look forward to it. I'll send you the information about who's coming, where we can meet, and the times. I'll be back in touch soon." Will still did not speak fast, unlike

Mr. Levy or Mr. Reiner. But there was genuine enthusiasm in his voice and tone, a steadiness and firmness that conveyed more sincerity than her two future colleagues.

When Will called Minnie back on her cell phone the next day, she had only just taken it out of her purse and put it on her desk in the office. What a coincidence, she thought, I certainly would not have heard it ring if I had left it my purse, and as soon as I took it out, Will calls.

"Good morning, Minnie. How are you doing just now?"

"I'm fine, Will. Just fine. Maybe the rain and overcast skies make me feel a little down."

"Oh, cheer up. The skies'll clear up real soon. I can assure you. And then you'll feel better." But actually she already felt better just hearing from Will. His voice cheered her up at once.

"So I have news for you. There will be three representatives of the tribe coming along with me to

Wednesday's lunch and meeting at NAILS. Besides Carmine, we will be joined by her uncle, the head of the Nantiquak Indian Association, a man named Morley Norwood. And another tribesman, named Ronald Woodson. I also made reservations at a restaurant that serves southern food. A new place. Up off of K Street. Not far from NAILS office. For noon. Is that alright for you?"

"Yes, that sounds nice." said Minnie. But there was some hesitation in her voice.

"Don't worry. It'll be on my tab. And also it is indoors and a regular heated restaurant. So we'll be able to take our coats off, and you won't be cold."

Minnie smiled, as she realized that he had been sensitive to her being cold at Captain White's place. "Fine, that sounds very nice Will."

"Okay, good. I really look forward to seeing you again. On the next step of our journey together." "And I do you, also."

The morning came again when they would meet. It was mid-January and very frosty outside. Once again Minnie found herself thinking what to wear that would most impress Will. She ended up wearing the same outfit that she had worn the previous month. And again she wore a scarf, which she made a mental note of that she would wear also when she stepped out for lunch, unlike their last outing. On the train ride up, this time she did not have to review any materials she might give to Will. On this day, she wouldn't have to speak at all. She was going along for the ride. She thought instead about how Will might react to her on this day. She also thought about why she was so strangely attracted to him. It wasn't merely that he had been her 'shining knight' who had come to her rescue a little more than a month ago. There was more to it. She found him so attractive in many ways, his calm, reassuring voice, his good looks, and yes, his really strong build and demeanor. But most of all the way he spoke to her, with that warmth and what seemed to her to be affection. She wondered also if maybe she was like many Indian maidens just naturally drawn and attracted to white men. She had first become aware of this attraction in high school. There she had fallen for a good looking student athlete, and especially his powerful build, his carrot red hair, and his easy smile. But that boy never took any notice of her. She had confessed at that time her feelings to one of her Indian girlfriends and this girl described it as very typical for Indian girls. She had even used the term 'Indian maiden infatuation for Anglos'. This girlfriend had said, "Don't worry Minnie, I've felt the same way several times, and so has my sister, and all the other girls from our tribe that I have talked to. Maybe we want the white boys to find us attractive. Maybe we are looking at them as men representing power and potential success, something our Indian brothers do not have. You'll just have to resist the feeling. It will go away." But the attraction to white boys did not go away for Minnie. Not until her junior year at VCU, when the white boy she had felt so attracted to forced sex on her in her dormitory room. He apparently knew that she had wanted him. Or so he said. She had not felt the attraction to white boys since then. Not until now. Not until Will. This Indian maiden infatuation for white boys had come back. She wondered if he could notice it in her. She really hoped not. While thinking about this over and over, she suddenly noticed that the time had passed and her stop at L'Enfant Plaza was being announced for the second time. She got up with a start just as the train stopped and left the train as soon as the doors opened. She had been so distracted that she nearly forgot her scarf, which she had taken off.

She left off her work a little too late, and even though she had planned to take the metro, she was running late and she had to dash to the metro station at L'Enfant Plaza. She felt silly, a mature woman almost running along the sidewalk and then through the underground exchange corridors. But when she got onto the metro train she realized that she would be only about five minutes late. If she had to search for the restaurant, then she would be late for sure. But she found the place, "Sweet Gullahh Home", in no time and got to the young black seating hostess just as she could see across the room her visitors from the Eastern Shore were being seated. What a relief. She gave her coat and scarf to the cloakroom and then came up to the table just moments after her four Nantiquaks—counting Will as one of them-- were opening their menus. It was a round table and Minnie sat next to Will who sat next to Carmine on his left. Will made introductions of Minnie to Morley and Ronald, a swarthy looking, middle-aged man with strong rough hands like a farmer's.

The hostess, who was a statuesque and handsome black woman, was explaining to them what Gullah food was all about. She explained how the Gullah people were escaped slaves who lived in the outer barriers islands and the salt marsh islands in Georgia and South Carolina. She added that these escaped slaves evolved a language that was both African and creole. And they merged with many of the native Americans. These peoples evolved a special cuisine that had both African and native American roots. Many of these Gullah people moved to Florida where they were called Black Seminoles. So we are presenting the foods of these mixed cultures. "Hope you enjoy it. And please ask your waiter if you have any questions about the menu items or different foods." It was then that Minnie noticed that most of the other diners in the restaurant were blacks, very well dressed blacks. The food was supposed to be poor people's rustic food but the restaurant's interior was done up very lavishly and the menu prices were embarrassingly high. She thought these must be very prosperous black folks to pay out such prices for the food of poor African American Indians—poor people's food. So she looked at the menu from the point of view of choosing the least expensive items. While the others were discussing the contents and possible flavors of different items, she quickly decided to order the business lunch special of fried catfish fingers with fried green tomatoes. It cost only $10. That would not cost Will too much, she thought.

"Oh look here," said Will, "fried Chincoteague oysters. That's for me. With a side of fried okra."

Ronald, who looked of indefinite age and could have been twenty eight or fifty, smiled and made a lame joke, "Those oysters are said to help your manliness. So I guess you need to eat a lot of them."

"All the better," said Will with a smile, "if the women with us don't object to my acting too manly around them for the rest of the afternoon."

They gave their orders to the waiter, a young strong looking black man with a huge smile, who gave wine recommendations for each dish ordered and also told them of side orders which went especially well with the dishes they ordered. He told Minnie that her chosen dish was intended as an appetizer, but was of ample size. He looked straight into her eyes, but she evaded his. Minnie thought maybe even he was flirting with her. He was good looking, for a black man, she thought.

But she had long thought that all black men thought they were good looking. When he brought her dish out, Minnie saw that it was more than enough for her and she even had trouble finishing it.

Morley, Ronald, and Carmine did not say much during the meal. But when they spoke it was impossible to understand them, they spoke softly and in low pitched voices. Conversation was difficult at the restaurant as it was crowded and very noisy and clangorous. She heard Morley say something about this being his first time to visit 'Warshington'. Will was trying hard throughout the lunch to lead a conversation and expressed surprise at Morley's statement. "How can that be? All your life only three hours away and this is your first time?" "Well, yes. Why would I come here?

I've been to Dover several times." Carmine seemed excited about the visit and especially about the prospect of meeting and appointing the lawyers that were going to help their tribe. Over the food everyone quietly ate, save for Will's exclamations about the food; about how delicious sweet potato biscuits were, or how he loved eating fried oysters, but only ordered them at the beach, or similar statements. Minnie felt oppressed and out of place in this restaurant. She wondered if her Nantiquak guests were not also feeling out of place. When they had finished, she wanted to run out of the restaurant as soon as possible, but the others lingered. As they walked to the offices of NAILS, she moved near Will and told him that she did not want to contribute much to this meeting. That it was for Will and the Nantiquak people to do all the talking. Also the lawyers at NAILS would talk quite a bit, and did not need her input or insights. Will said he agreed with her and understood the strange position she was in, as she was neither their advisor, nor yet employed by NAILS.

"But Minnie you must know how much we appreciate all the help and useful advice you've already given us. You've been a godsend."

That simple comment made her day.

At the office of NAILS they arrived a few minutes earlier than their appointment. The receptionist jumped up and very obsequiously moved about them offering to take and hang their coats. Minnie thought she had not been so helpful when she had come by herself the previous week, and it annoyed her a bit. While the receptionist finished stashing their coats, the five of them stood awkwardly around in the small front foyer for several minutes. Finally she reappeared and directed them to a conference room that was opposite Cal's office. It was larger than the one she had first sat in with Levy a month earlier. The receptionist asked if they wanted drinks, coffee or tea or water. They all asked for coffee which shortly after was brought by a smartly dressed young black woman carrying five porcelain cups of coffee on a tray, with a milk decanter and a sugar bowl. It seemed all very professional and refined. But they waited, and then waited some more. Almost another fifteen minutes they waited in silence.

Finally the door opened and in came Cal Reiner dressed in a dark gray suit and bright red tie and carrying a small folder of papers in one hand. Behind him was another tall white man in a dark navy blue suit and yellow tie, and he was followed by Jared Levy, who was in a slate gray suit also with a red tie. Everyone stood up. The Ms. Halstead that Reiner had asked for last week did not appear with these others. Reiner immediately apologized for making them wait, but his apology sounded insincere and routine to Minnie. Then there followed a very complicated round of introductions and exchanging of business cards, with Reiner leading the NAILS side and Will leading the

introductions of the Nantiquak party. None of the Nantiquak Indians had business cards, and Morley and Ronald looked puzzled with the cards they received. The third NAILS attorney was introduced as Martin Parchesi. "And I believe you already know Minnie Warrens, of the Bureau of Indian Affairs?" said Will. "Yes, we know her and are glad we do." said Reiner almost dismissively. Will continued, "We represent the tribe's steering committee for this meeting, appointed by the Nantiquak tribal council to direct and lead the efforts to get recognition. I am only acting as the chief spokesman in this effort."

"Fine, that is all understood." said Reiner. "Now that we are seated let me start by introducing to you what NAILS is, what kind of work we do, and how we work with our Indian clients." Then Reiner plunged into a twenty minute discourse about public service law firms, how they are funded, the mandate they have, and the support they get from the government. He detailed the nature of the work such as litigation, advisory services, and setting up corporations and other legal entities. He also explained the work they had done for several Indian tribes, one in the East, and four on the Pacific. He included an example of work that the firm could not and would not do. As he put it, it was strange that a law firm based in Washington D.C. by law could not act as a lobbyist for any interest, including Indians' interests. But they couldn't and therefore wouldn't. And he finished by highlighting what he considered to be their biggest successes, and gave them a monetary value. One of their successes that he highlighted was a lawsuit against the state of Connecticut to protect the right of the Pequoddy Indians to operate their casino without regulatory control of the state. Minnie was impressed by the presentation. Reiner slowed his speech down a great deal from the velocity he had used when he interviewed her, and he modulated the items with a differing pitch and volumes and emphasis. He was clearly an accomplished public speaker, and he had powerful persuasion skills. She realized that he would be a formidable boss. But he demonstrated that he commanded the talents to handle the cut and thrust of a courtroom procedure.

Will then began his talk by thanking Mr. Reiner for the clear explanation. He then started to describe the situation of the Nantiquak tribe of Delaware and Maryland. He gave a brief review of the history of the tribe, its treaty with the King of England, the setting up of reservations under this treaty, and the seizure of these same reservations by the states of Delaware and Maryland. He then expounded on the experience in the 19th century when the tribe began to feel pressure from the state of Delaware to dissolve and disburse and to efforts to treat them as negroes with segregated schools and the reduced citizen rights like negroes of that time. This led to the formation of the association in the nineteenth century and finally to state recognition—in Delaware-- as a tribe.

Although they did not receive any state recognition from Maryland.

Will finished his discourse with a summary of what the tribe wanted now. He said that they would begin seeking federal recognition. They wanted the rights to conduct Indian owned businesses free of state and federal taxes, and that included the possibility of establishing, owning and operating a gambling center, as several other tribes have done around America. And that they wanted some restoration of their reservation lands which they had held for nearly a century and a half and which was unlawfully taken away from the tribe over the last two hundred years. And those lands which they could not restore as reservation lands they wanted to put up in trust with the federal government acting as the trustee. Will spoke for about ten minutes and then concluded, "And we are here today to see if you would take our case and act as our advisors and lawyers in the litigation we see in the future to achieve our goals."

"Well said, Mr. Eames. While we do not have any assignments such as yours just now, we have experience in similar cases. And I think we are well qualified to take on your legal services in the coming year. Or maybe several years."

"So how do we proceed? Do we appoint you as our lawyers? Do we sign a retainer contract for your services? And what entity do we need to be to appoint you? The tribal association? Or some other legal unit, say, the individual members of the tribal council?"

"I think in this case, we would go with the tribal association, because while the tribe may be a social entity, it is not a legal, corporate entity. Of course, you could make a non-profit corporation for the Nantiquak Indian People of Delmarva as your legal entity. Maybe we need to think about that for future purposes. We would make a retainer agreement with the association and it would define how we work together and how we make billings. Because we would still charge for the services and advice we give you, but we will not bill you. We get our payment from the foundation which supports this partnership."

"Then I will introduce you to the president of the Nantiquak Indian Association, seated here next to me, Mr. Morley Norwood."

Morley nodded his head in acknowledgement. But he did not say anything. Minnie thought to herself that it was going to be difficult working with him. She had already concluded that he was a deeply taciturn, maybe even sour man who did not care to communicate with anyone. She had come to know many men in her own tribe who were raised to be retiring and quiet, and who as they grew into middle aged, became bitter and almost totally uncommunicative. She didn't like those men, because she did not know how to interact with them. Her younger brother, on the other hand, was quite unlike these reticent men. He expressed his anger and sometimes bitterness.

"I think then, that on behalf of our steering committee, I can say that we would like to appoint you to be our legal counsel for the objectives we outlined to you. Will you take us on as your clients?"

"And we can say yes without hesitation, Mr. Eames. We will agree to act as your advisors and legal representatives. Mr. Levy here can bring us the retainer agreement and we can begin."

Levy left the room quickly and in a few minutes he brought back what must have been a standard agreement. It was maybe thirty pages of dense text.

"I would advise you to read it and study this document." said Reiner. "We need the full official name and address of your association. If you give it to us now we can put it into our signature copy of the document.

"You can see here now the team that will be working with you, and that will be mentioned in the agreement. I will be the lead attorney, and I will be joined by Mr. Parchesi, and Ms. Warrens here, whom you have already met and who will be starting here shortly."

Minnie blushed. Although she had agreed to join them, she was not employed yet by NAILS and she had not signed an employment contract and did not know anything about work in the firm.

"That's great!" said Will still in his salesman mode of speaking. "We already think highly of her, and we can see that it will be a good, experienced team advising us."

Reiner instructed Levy to have the changes made and the specific information filled into the document and to print it out in duplicate. "If you wait a while longer, we can give you two copies which you can take with you and study. They are ready for your signature and when you've signed it, you can mail one copy back to us."

The meeting wound down. Reiner asked if anyone would like more coffee or water. Then he moved over to stand next to Will and began talking with Will and Carmine about next steps. Will offered him a photocopy of the copy of the treaty that he had made, and Reiner took it and immediately set it aside. Parchesi approached Minnie and introduced himself. He asked her about her background, what firms she had previously worked for, what law school she had gone to. Minnie thought he stood too close to her. When he started to talk to her he quickly evaded her eyes. His eyes kept looking down at her chest. She told him some of the main points on her resume. He asked her when she was going to start. She told him she thought it would be on the first of the next month.

Morley took a book out of a bag which he had somehow concealed from everyone since lunch. It was a copy of 'The Last of the Nantiquaks' by Alvey. Shyly Morley waited for Reiner to stop talking to Will to try to present it to him. Finally he got a break when he very meekly offered the book to Reiner who took it, looked at the cover, thanked Morley, and put it down on the table.

It was after four thirty when the group including Minnie left the offices of NAILS. The stood in the main entry foyer of the building and listened to Will.

"I propose this. That we wait out the peak of the rush hour before we set out for the Eastern Shore. Rush hour delays getting from here to across the Bay Bridge can add up to more than two hours.

And they start now. So I suggest we wait in a bar or a restaurant where we can talk around the table, have a coffee, discuss what we need to do next, and then aim to leave after 6:30. What do you say to that? Of course Minnie you should feel free to leave whenever you like. You're still taking the train?"

Minnie was surprised. She did not remember telling Will that she commuted by train. But he had paid close attention to her and remembered it. "I think I will leave now, thanks. I can catch an early train at Union Station. I don't have anything more to add to today's meeting. So if you'll excuse me...."

Will joked, "It'll be hard for me. Parting is such sweet sorrow, I'll miss you until next time."

Carmine giggled. "Quoting Shakespeare is an appropriate farewell. But it's enough just to thank Minnie for all the help she's given us so far."

"Of course," said Will more seriously. "Minnie you've been a big help in getting us launched. We all thank you for your contribution. Have a safe trip home. We hope to see you again soon." The others seconded his gratitude, and Minnie left the group in the foyer. She took a bus to Union Station and in twenty minutes was on the southbound train wondering how she would work in the future, and how often in the course of this future new job she would get to see Will.

The next day at her office desk she got another unexpected call. The woman, with a pronounced black southern accent, told her she was calling from the city prosecutor's office. "Ms. Warrens? Is this Ms. Minnie Warrens of Bowling Green Virginia I am talking to?"

"I am Sharlene Davison, the second deputy general prosecutor for the District of Columbia. And I am calling you to inform you that the prosecutor's office has indicted Edward Booker T. Washington, that is we will press charges against him, on charges of violent sexual assault with intent to rape, attempted robbery, and assault with a deadly weapon. We filed the original complaint on December 1st in the public interest as we had not received your intentions on whether or not you would press charges. Edward Washington was the man who assaulted you on November 20th of last year and who was arrested that same night. I know it's been a long time but with holidays and our caseload, you understand …"

Minnie was alarmed by the woman's statement. Her mind was racing over all the things that could go wrong with a criminal trial. She knew this process could run on and take complete control over her life. She could imagine being harassed by the man's family and friends inside and outside the courthouse. And she knew that everyone involved—as this was a black city—would identify her as a black woman, not an Indian. And black women in this city it was widely believed by the men of the city deserved rape because they were promiscuous. She had read this often in the newspapers. And a trial also threatened publicity, most of which would be sensationalist and intrusive.

"Does that mean I have to attend a trial?" she asked.

"Yes it does, but only if the case goes to court. We don't know yet. You see the indictment came down only yesterday. If he, the defendant, refutes the charges against him and pleas not guilty at his arraignment, then it will have to go to court and you will have to testify. But only about twenty percent of rape cases go to a full court hearing. The arraignment is now scheduled on January 28th. That is less than two weeks from today. But you don't have to attend that."

"But it was nighttime. And everything happened so quickly. He jumped me from behind. So I never got a good look at his face. And the police dragged him away before I even got up off the ground.

How can I possibly testify?" Minnie was panicking thinking of everything that could go wrong.

"Yes, yes. We understand. But the man was caught 'in flagrante delicto'"—it sounded to Minnie over the phone as if she had said 'in fragrant da lick tu'—"and arrested in the act. He, Mr.

Washington, has a previous conviction and several earlier indictments for violent assault, robbery, violence with a deadly weapon, and attempted rape and other sexual assault charges."

Davison continued, "What will probably happen is this: at the arraignment, the defendant, on the advice of his appointed defense lawyer, will plead guilty. We will have struck a plea bargain with his lawyer, and there will be no need for a trial. He will get eight to ten years in prison, minimum, for his guilty plea. But I am telling you all this only as advance notice. Because a trial could still happen. Although it is unlikely."

Minnie was still panicked. A criminal trial would be torment. She would have to testify. Will would have to testify as a witness and thus he would find out in the public arena that she was the victim he had rescued. And a trial would take so much of her time and would drag on, just as she was starting her new position.

"I understand." said Minnie sadly. "So is there anything I have to do now?"

"No, nothin'. But you can give me your current home mailing address. We need it because we have to send you the papers of this process. And you know we can offer counseling for you, if a trial becomes necessary. Most victims find it very helpful."

Minnie gave her her address in Thornburg, not her mother's address and also her cell phone number. Ms. Davison thanked her, said she'd be calling again, and said goodbye. Her call ruined the rest of Minnie's day, and the day afterwards also. She was overcome by worry, and the memories of that night returned to her often. She was spared the physical pain of that night-- memories of bodily pain, the pain of scuffed knees, of a thin slicing knife across her throat, do not linger—but the memories of her humiliation, of the pressure of this man Washington's arms around her, his knife at her throat, her position on the ground, like a dog on all fours, and the memory that perhaps Will saw her bared bottom in the flashing red and blue lights all recurred to her and played in her mind's eye. And they caused her misery again. The misery that had tormented her in the ten days of last November after the incident. On Friday night after she got home she called her mother and asked if she could spend the weekend with her at her house in Bowling Green. She gathered some things and drove over that same night. She didn't say anything about the news of a possible trial—she still had not told her mother anything about November's assault, the rape attempt—but just being in her mother's presence helped her get over the torment. Her younger sister came by with her two children and joined them for Saturday dinner. Minnie always felt as if her sister, Alicia—who had deep knowledge of sex from her years working as a prostitute-- had deduced and understood that Minnie had been raped, that she had had a bad sexual encounter which kept her from having boyfriends or getting married, but as with her mother, she had never raised the subject with Alicia. It was their unspoken understanding. That weekend was an extended break because Monday was Martin Luther King Day and a national holiday.

So it was only on Monday evening before she returned to her lonely house in Thornburg.

For Minnie the rest of January dragged by. There was no more work for her to do at the Smithsonian, as she would be leaving so soon, and she concluded that her contribution to the Indian museum project had been minimal. It appeared to her that it was still a project a long ways away from construction and completion. But it did not inspire her. On one afternoon she had to report to the HR woman at the Bureau's offices to fill in some standard forms. She also gave her a survey exit interview where she solicited Minnie's views about work in the Bureau in general, her experience in particular, and her estimation of how the department was organized and how supportive she felt the human resources office had been. The HR woman asked her if she was leaving for another position that she already had accepted. Minnie answered yes. But when asked if she would tell them what company or office she was moving to, Minnie declined to answer. Most questions were like the multiple choice customer satisfaction questions that service companies so routinely sent out to customers. Minnie thought to herself, 'Can they seriously believe that people departing the Bureau would answer such a survey honestly?' And then after non-committedly answering a number of questions, she thought further, 'How useful can answers such as 'good', 'fine', 'not bad', be for the human resources evaluations'? After that she was looking forward only to her new job at NAILS.

Her final paycheck was sent in an envelope to her office at the Smithsonian and arrived on her penultimate day. She was only relieved that she heard nothing further from Nighthorse.

Her first day at NAILS was on Monday the 2nd of February. Usually, for Minnie first days whether at a new school or at a new job gave her the thrill of excitement and nervous eagerness. But this day started inauspiciously. After her arrival on the first morning she was mostly ignored. The main receptionist led her to a detached office that was furnished with just a desk, office chair, and a coat rack. Minnie was glad that at the very least the small office had a window to the outside. But the room was still dim as the window faced north. The receptionist said a technician would come around later that day to install a telephone and to bring and set up a computer. But that first day passed by with her doing nothing and even though she left her door open no one came to introduce themselves. At the end of the afternoon the technician had just finished connecting the telephone and computer. But he said he would come back the next day and show her how to work in the office local network and make connections. During the afternoon she stepped out of her office and looked around out of curiosity and boredom. The receptionist showed her the kitchenette where the good looking black girl who had served them two weeks earlier was hanging about. She was friendly but was more interested in doing her nails with a small file than talking with Minnie. But she did show Minnie how to operate the coffee maker and stumblingly told her the rules for putting food in the refrigerator. It was apparent that Reiner was not in that day. In one office there were four desks tucked behind cubicles which were occupied by four people who introduced themselves and told her they were clerking for the firm. They seemed busy enough. In another office with two desks was the missing Ms. Halstead, who was Gail according to her nameplate, and Jared Levy. Ms. Halstead, however, was still missing but Jared greeted her warmly, and he chirped, "Welcome aboard." as if she had just joined the fleet, not a law firm. There were two further private offices left. One was Mr. Ronald Parchesi's, but he was out, and the other was occupied by Irine Grieson. Minnie introduced herself to Irine and before they could talk longer, Irine said, "Oh, I have a note for you from Ron. Here it is. I have discharged my obligation." She handed a hand written note to Minnie.

It said simply, 'Organizational kick off meeting. Tomorrow, 3rd February. 11:00 am. Nanticokes.' Minnie thanked Irine and asked what she was working on. "I'm now working on a dispute between the Eastern Cherokees and the Governor of North Carolina over gambling revenues."

So tomorrow would be her first real day of work. The first day had been a letdown. The second started the way new jobs usually should.

A visit first thing in the morning with the firm's financial officer—the title for the firm's sole accountant and bookkeeper—who welcomed her and informed her of the financial plumbing of the firm. He took her data for taxes, pension contributions, and salary payments—which were data that were all specific to Virginia-- instructed her how to claim for expenses on client work and gave her a company credit card to use for big expenses like travel, instructed her on how to submit the monthly time sheets for work allocated to different clients, told her about the health insurance coverage she would get, especially about maternity terms and payments, and all the other financial rules of the firm. And he told her, what he deemed most important, how the senior partners decided on bonus awards at year end. It was all quite complicated compared to work in a government office. He was friendly but he finished his talk with her by saying that she would probably not see him again, unless something went wrong. This meeting was then followed by an introduction by one of the law clerks to the small law library they had. She was a lively, even bubbly, young white girl about twenty five years old Minnie guessed who showed her the special volumes of cases involving Indian rights. She said her name was Tracy and that she always had been fascinated by American Indians. "You are Indian, aren't you? Did you see the movie, Pocahontas? I loved the actress who voiced Pocahontas. Her name is Irene Bedard.

She's wonderful." Minnie thought that Tracy's views on that animated film were typical with all the usual stereotypes about Indians. "I don't know who Irene Bedard is, I'm afraid." "Oh that's too bad. She's a native American too." Minnie thought that Tracy was still quite nice, but very naïve about Indians' lives. "And you're as pretty as Irene, too. I have to say it. She's an actress but you're also an Indian princess as pretty as that actress." Minnie blushed. She herself didn't think she was very good looking, and she had always thought her skin was too dark although it had a distinctly coppery tint. She had always noticed that it was only the completely unobservant, the overtly racist, and the badly uninformed who upon seeing her assumed she was an Afro-American. "Thank you, that's nice of you to say," said Minnie.

It wasn't a big library, but when compared to her previous firm, it contained many more case law volumes on Indian lawsuits and legal decisions. We do a lot of our work using other libraries or through the internet. There are several comprehensive law libraries here in the city which have more volumes than you could ever look at even in a lifetime. We use them all the time." By the time she was finished with this introduction, it was time for her organizational meeting with Parchesi and the others.

She came to the small conference room just as the others were arriving. Parchesi was already seated at the head of the table, without a jacket, scribbling on a legal size yellow pad of paper. The attractive young coffee girl was standing next to him and she took drinks orders as people sat down. Minnie asked for a Perrier. Four people came in, but not Reiner. "Good morning. Everyone I want to introduce you to our new junior partner. This is Minnie Warrens and she comes to us from the Bureau of Indian Affairs, and went to the University of Richmond for law school. And as you might guess she herself is Indian. From a tribe right nearby here in Virginia. Minnie, this is Gail Halstead a lawyer here. And from what I understand she claims she has some Indian blood in her ancestry also, is that right?" A curly brown haired woman said, "Yes, that's what my grandfather told me when I was young. My family comes from North Carolina and lived on the frontier in the eighteenth century and mixed with the Cree Indians." "So there you go, Minnie. And here is John Adamas and Linda Grieves, they work here as clerks." She had seen them both the day before, although they had not introduced themselves then. They looked young like they were still students.

"So this is our team for our Indian Project for the Nantiquaks of Delmarva. We'll use the project name Oyster for all internal communications and documents. But remember not to put Project Oyster on anything we send out to others, filings, letters, correspondence with the tribe and the like. And of course Reiner is the team leader although he can't be here today and may not attend all our team sessions. The rules of the team are that we work together, and separately, and although our tasks may seem pointless at times they will always be pieces of the puzzle which others may eventually need for their task. We need to keep the team members aware of information that we are each working on or may discover. We will maintain a central work file on the computer where we should save all documents and drafts. And one other rule of working is that we are working for the Nantiquak tribe steering committee which will be the sole contact any of us have. No one is to ever talk to or contact a Nantiquak Indian without first getting clearance from Will Eames, the head of that committee. And this Mr. Eames will be always our first point of contact. I prefer that only Mr. Reiner, myself, or Ms. Warrens be the sole authorized members in our team to have communications with Mr. Eames. Is that understood? If you need to speak to him, convey your issue to one of us."

At that moment the black girl returned with a tray full of drinks. "And of course, here is our most important team member, Alie, she will provide with all the sustaining caffeine that you need in the coming months. Her phone extension is sixteen. Important number, Minnie." Alie scowled, distributed the drinks and left.

"We are going to start an advisory assignment for the Nantiquaks, all with the aim of helping them gain federal recognition and restoring their reservations. First thing we need to do is lots of research about this tribe. We have a book here which the tribe gave us, which is a history of the tribe and we need to get hold of two others, one called the Tobacco Colony or something like that and the other the Nantiquaks of Delaware. I recommend everyone read them. We also have here a copy of the original treaty which recognized the tribe and assigned them reservations. We need to find in the archives of Maryland and Delaware everything that happened in the years after this treaty which in the end resulted in the tribe losing their reservations. Records of lawsuits, sales, court rulings for and against individual Nantiquak Indians or the tribe, land seisures, state patents issued on land that was in the territory of the original reservation grants. Whatever we can find. Mr. Eames will be helping us in researching the title records in probate courts. He is a specialist in that field as he deals in real estate and property title on the Eastern Shore. And related to that we need to find any historic maps which may have indicated the bounds of the reservations. We're talking about maps before the 1840s. First place to look would be the University of Maryland at College Park, but also the Library of Congress. Our interest is solely a historical acknowledgement of the presence and territories of the reservations on the maps. But also we need historic maps from Delaware for the same reason. I don't know where to start looking for those. We have to know the legal status and circumstances of the tribe through the last three hundred years in order to give the tribe the best advice. We will also be researching the precedent cases of tribes suing for restitution of their treaty reservations. There have been a few. Some of this research we can do here, but I suspect that we will have to do a lot in Annapolis and Dover—that's the capital of Delaware in case you've never heard of it-- as well as in Millville, Delaware where the tribal association is headquartered, or the county seat there. So some of us may have to travel and stay some nights in those locales. Think about that before you start making your plans for vacations in Cancun or wherever."

Parchesi went on like this for another hour. He divided up responsibilities and he laid out possible time deadlines. Minnie found it interesting that one of the main initial aims he thought the tribe should undertake would be a comprehensive tribal census of all the Nantiquak people of both Delaware and Maryland, not only the ones living near Millville. And that this census should be followed by incorporation as a not-for-profit entity which would represent the tribe in all its filings and possible lawsuits. For him, the legal enforcement of the treaty was one of the key issues. He set out a line of investigation into the treaty's validity and the need to establish that the treaty recognized the tribe's sovereignty which should be acknowledged by the federal government. He wasn't sure how that would be accomplished, but he felt that it would be a lawsuit based on constitutional law—the treaty of the previous sovereign, the King of England, should still be valid, upheld, and in force over the succeeding sovereign, i.e. the United States. And then the next important step was researching exactly how the Nantiquak Indians lost the reservation lands that were laid out in the treaty. Minnie began to regret that she and her tribal council had not received such useful advice when they went to file for recognition. She thought she was only to blame as she had figured she knew enough by working in the Office of Federal Recognition. Parchesi assigned to Minnie the research on how the reservation lands had been lost, especially the so called disposal of those lands by the states of Maryland and Delaware. For Minnie, this was very pleasing to hear because it raised the prospect of being able to work alongside Will.

After another forty minutes Parchesi asked if there were any questions and if everyone understood what task they would start. There were no questions. "Okay then. We now start Project Oyster, our latest Indian project. Right after lunch."

Minnie turned to Gail and asked her what people in the office usually did about lunch. "Oh sometimes we go out to one of the lunch counters on K Street, and other times the simple people here bring their sandwiches and eat at their desks. Or maybe some order take away. And other times when we're really busy, everyone skips lunch and calls out for pizza delivery or something like that. As for myself today I will go to a quick soup and sandwich place around the corner."

"May I join you?" asked Minnie even before Gail had offered.

"Sure, we can chat over some lunch."

At the lunch place, they managed to get a small round table that barely fit the two of them. Minnie had soup, Gail had a tuna and avocado sandwich on a bulky roll.

"How long have you worked with NAILS, Gail?"

"Almost two years. It's been great, although sometimes before a court case it can get really busy. It's what I wanted to do since I was in high school. I mean working for the betterment of Indian tribes. You know with my Indian ancestry. But I'm just faintly Indian, a mixed breed, but with little Cree blood. You are the real thing."

"I suppose so." said Minnie.

"I would've thought before I started here, with the Indian revival movement, AIM and the like that there would be a lot more young Indians studying to be lawyers. But I haven't encountered them yet."

"I guess Indian law doesn't pay well, and young Indians by and large can't afford law school fees. I was lucky: I got almost a full scholarship." said Minnie. But as you know we are public service, here, after all. Government budgets are tight. Working for Indians' civil rights isn't paid like what corporations can pay. But you know, I found out not long ago that there is an national association of native American lawyers. Most of them are young or recent graduates. They invited me to join."

Minnie continued, "And you know most people who claim to be Indians, especially here in the east, are like you, mixed-blood. Those Indians who have survived white man's diseases, and forced eviction, had to assimilate to survive. And that meant they literally melted away into white's man's gene pool. I don't think that's a bad thing as such. Maybe trying to preserve an Indian identity and separateness is a bad thing."

"I can't agree with you Minnie. But maybe my outlook is mostly nostalgic and romantic. I'm mean as near as I can figure it I'm only one-thirty second Cree. And I know nothing about the Cree woman who bore my white relatives. She preserved a bit of her genetic material while most of the rest of the Cree Indians of North Carolina were exterminated or driven out far to the west."

"I've thought about how my own tribe has managed to survive. And I would have to say, they have only just barely managed to by hiding and keeping invisible. Not blending into white man's blood lines for the most part. Some I suppose married negroes. And in some respects, we were allowed to survive by Virginia's Anti-Miscegenation laws and strict racial segregation. They were in place for more than ninty years, although the racism directed at Indians existed for centuries before those laws."

"What tribe is yours?" asked Gail.

"The Massaponax-Doeg of the middle peninsula of Virginia. We were preserved by Virginia's strict race laws which were enacted early, even in colonial times, and by the remoteness and infertility of the land we lived on. We were one of the treaty peoples that were part of the Powhatan confederation. And we lived on treaty land, a reservation if you like, which no white man wanted. Maybe also the swamp fevers deterred the white man from encroaching too much."

"Oh that's so interesting. I have never heard about the Mattapoe –how did you say?" "Massaponax on the Massaponi River."

"Yeah, Massaponax. I've heard of Powhatan, the Indian chief. But I never heard of his name as the name of a tribal confederation. You know all of that is so mixed up by popular literature, film, and of course the movie Pocahantas."

"Yes, I know." said Minnie. She was not going to tell her that her real given name was Pocahontas's name. She also decided she wouldn't tell her that she was the chief of her tribe. She didn't want to share that kind of personal information in her new office. It would come out soon enough. And that information could cause all kinds of jealousies, gossip, and false expectations. It was enough that people knew she was an Indian.

As they finished eating, Minnie asked Gail what was the matter with Alie. "Oh, nothing. But she's not African-American, as you might have assumed. Simply African. She is a Somali immigrant, and she doesn't speak English at all well, so she hides it by acting aloof and grumpy. If you speak Somali with her, I think she would be quite happy."

After lunch the tech man came back and set up her computer to the in-house network. Then he showed her how to access the internet, send documents to printing, and how to use the inter-office messaging software. He briefly showed her how to use the telephone: leaving messages, call holding and forwarding, intercom, conference calling, and use of all the many buttons on the receiver. She had never had such a complicated telephone before. Like Reiner and Levy, the tech man spoke so fast that she wasn't sure she understood all his instructions and as he left, he said, "If you didn't understand all of that, here's the instruction manual for this model. My extension is 93, if you still have any questions or need help using these machines." Almost as soon as he left her office she had a question: 'how do I find the extension numbers of my colleagues here in the office?' She faced her new equipment and immediately she began to feel overwhelmed. There was so much to do, so much to read and to prepare, so much to learn and all of it new, in such a short time. She felt the same thrill and challenge that she had felt at the start of each new semester in university and at law school—when the professors would load them up with all the readings they would have to do in coming semester-- or when she first started at Petit, Sauvain and Mason. It was a thrill that ran through her, at the same time a feeling of panic. How was she going to be able to accomplish all this future work within the time frame being proposed? She didn't know. She didn't know if she could do all. And if she didn't, what would her new colleagues think of her? There was only one thing to do to ease the feeling of panic: to start reading the materials already available. She began by reading the peace treaty between the Nantiquaks and the King of England.

Late that afternoon, before she was ready to leave for the train station, she got a call on her cell phone. Hi, Ms. Warrens? This is Sharlene Davison calling you again from the D.C. General Prosecutors office. Remember we spoke about two weeks ago?"

"Hope I'm not interrupting anything important. No? Good. I'm calling just to tell you that the case against Mr. Edward Washington went just as I told you it might. Mr. Washington plead guilty to the charges against him and the judge assigned him an eleven year sentence in prison, which he has already begun serving. No trial will be needed. So you can be relieved of that, I'm sure. I will be sending the papers which cover the court proceedings. And there's nothing more you have to do or worry about. There will in all likelihood be nothing in the newspapers either. This was all just routine criminal justice and what the newspapers can barely cover in their reports. Justice is done."

Minnie thanked Ms. Davison and whispered to herself. "Thank God, that's over." And she made to leave for the station.

Over the next couple days she was occupied by the peace treaty. The treaty text seemed straightforward to Minnie although it was clear that it favored the English by assigning much fewer rights and protections to the Nantiquaks. She was especially interested in the awards of three reservations and how they were delimited. But the wording was not typical of survey lines and coordinates on a property plat as most property transactions were described in contemporary contracts. Instead the land was determined always in reference to the Nanticoke River bank—so many nautical miles up the river from its mouth, left bank, right bank, a sand shoal, a big rock, a cypress tree stump in the mud, or where a creek debouched into the main stream of the river-- defined by a number of steps away from the riverbank in one direction on the compass, then followed by a turn to the north or south and so many steps in another compass direction, and then a turn and another large number of steps either back to the Nanticoke River or to another large creek which flowed into it. She did not understand the directions and did not comprehend whether these were large plots of land, what their acreage could be, nor could she imagine how they were shaped by the bends in the river. This was clearly an issue for Will to clarify, she thought. He's the property man. What a good excuse to call him and to hear his voice again, she thought.

And on Monday she did just that, calling him on his cell phone. "Hello, Minnie," he answered enthusiastically. "I'm so glad to hear from you." She wondered how she knew it was she calling, and as if he were reading her mind over the phone, he said, "My phone has caller I.D. so it matched your number with the contact name in my phone's memory. And flashed your name on the screen. All in an instant. Isn't this technology marvelous?"

"How are you this fine late winter morning?" he continued.

"I'm fine, Will. Can you talk? I'm not interrupting?"

"No, not at all. Is there something you want to ask about?"

"Yes, there is. I read the treaty and was left wondering about the reservations that were assigned to the tribe. Do you have some idea of the areas of these reservations? And their precise locations."

"Yes, actually. I do. Although exact is not really right, maybe approximate. I was already making a plat map with my interpretation and estimations of the locations and the areas of the awarded reservations. It's fascinating. I was able to find a number of the reference points and I also had fun floating up the river to pinpoint the references that were given as so many nautical miles upriver. The map will be finished shortly, and then I can measure the results and calculate the areas of each plot of land."

"Oh that's good. It can become a document we submit in any lawsuit."

"And we can calculate the areas coming from another angle, namely the plots which the states later sold. But we'll find these when we do the title search. I hope so any way."

Will spoke with enthusiasm that carried even over his cell phone. She had thought since she first spoke with him, that he spoke smilingly always, especially toward her.

"I expect the printer to return the map to me next week with all the tracts included. I will send you a copy as soon as I get it. According to the treaty there were three separate tracts awarded in the treaty addenda, as you probably saw already. At three separate dates, from 1668 to 1698. Then I've included two separate reservations which the Maryland assembly awarded the Nanticoke in 1711 and another in the same year to their cousinly band the Assateague Indians. These latter are not in the treaty and they were given in areas which were later ceded to Delaware. And this reservation was sold by Delaware authorities in the early nineteenth century. The three treaty reservations altogether I've estimated amounted to more than 13,000 acres. "

"That's a huge amount of land." said Minnie. "That's a hundred times the area of what's currently left of the original reservation of my people. And ten times the area of what we estimate was our original reservation."

"Yeah it's a lot. And you can understand why white settlers of the area coveted it and worked so hard to steal the land. From the looks of the tracts that I've estimated it seems that more than 8,000 acres were granted in what is now Maryland and the rest was in what is now Delaware. Although all of it was granted at a time when the entire area was in territory claimed by Maryland." {3,100 acres in lower reservation Chicacoan Creek, 5,520 acres in upper Nanticoke reservation on left bank in Maryland; 2,000 acres on upper Nanticoke continuation of MD reservation, and 3,000 acres on Broad Creek now both in Delaware}

"I will look forward to seeing it. Are you planning on coming to our offices any time soon? Minnie asked.

"No, I don't think so. As much as I would like to—just to see you. But we are going to begin undertaking our own tribal census to see how many people consider themselves to be Nantiquak Indians. That's going to take some time. We also will be collecting oral genealogical records. It seems we're going to have problems with the requirement about representation in the old federal censuses."

"Ok, but please let me know when you plan to begin looking at the old probate title records. I will join you when you start."

"That would be great. Right now I think it will be in three weeks from now. Maybe at the beginning of March."

"Alright." said Minnie, disappointed that she would have to wait so long until the next time they got together. After she hung up the line, she thought about the line Will had said, "just to see you." Was that a throwaway line, something said by real estate agents and car salesmen, just out of courtesy? Or perhaps did he really mean it? He was so nice towards her, and he seemed to always say nice things about her. She wanted to think that he meant what he said, and that he would like to see her and an important part of any visit to D.C. for Will would be seeing her.

As promised, at the end of the next week the modern map with the added tracts of the reservation lands that were described in the treaty arrived in their office. It had modern state and county borders included as well as principal modern roads and highways. Will had added a note saying he had assumed that the river banks of the Nanticoke River, the Chicacoan Creek, the Broad Creek, the Little Creek, and the Iron Branch Creek were probably unchanged from three hundred years earlier, as all of these streams were basically shaped by tidal movements and none of them were subject to heavy flooding or any of the events that moved river courses elsewhere in the United States. When the map came in—addressed to Minnie. Because it was big—it came in a long paper tube-- Minnie spread it out on the conference room table. Along with Ron and Linda Grieves they studied the map for some minutes leaning together over the table, comparing the text from the treaty delimiting the reservations with the physical map. As they looked at the map, it seemed to Minnie that Ron was edging really close and tight to her—almost touching her at the hips and shoulders. And he kept turning his head toward her and obviously trying to look down the opening her blouse. He was not standing like this close to Lisa. A couple times she backed away from him just a small step, and each time he sidled over to be close to her again. It made her feel very uncomfortable. She wanted to examine the map further to see how it conformed to the text of the treaty grants of land, but she was so bothered by Ron's closeness that she said, "Fine. That's clear." and moved away, saying, "We have now a document that we can present with the treaty to the courts." And she left the room.

She had not been leered at like that several years. And she hadn't liked it before and she did not like it now.

The next two weeks passed quickly. Her clerk assistants were finding lots of archival material in the Maryland archives up in Annapolis and each week they brought their findings back to the office and began to paint a tapestry of historic legal dealings between the Nantiquaks and the state deep into the colonial period. But they were also finding informative materials about the Maryland Indians in the 19th and early 20th centuries. But most of the lawsuits did not have anything to do with property rights or improper sales of Indian properties. One of her researchers did find an act in the Maryland Assembly from 1834 which resolved to sell the lands of the Indian reservations of the Eastern Shore. This act did not provide any legal justifications for what was in effect a seizure of Indian reservation lands. She was amazed that such legislation could pass unchallenged at the time. Other clerks on her team found the legal proceedings of the court case against Connecticut. This was very important background material which showed NAILS the proper way to make a claim and Ron summarized it for Reiner to study.

In mid-February there was another short meeting of the working group of Project Oyster. Cal Reiner attended along with all of the rest. Ron ran the meeting first asking everyone for the materials they had collected. He mentioned the map that plotted the reservations, both those awarded in the original treaty and the two others granted later by the colonial assembly of Maryland. Then he reviewed what the Nantiquak steering committee was doing, and specifically that they were undertaking the tribal census in both Delaware and Maryland locations. And when they were finished Will Eames would be ready to start the review of title and probate materials that could still be found for the dates. At that point Reiner came into the discussion and said that he was now of the opinion that the Nantiquaks—all of them and not just the members of the Association at Millville—should file for a new non-profit corporation. And that this corporation, say the Nantiquak Indian Nation of the Eastern Shore or something like that, would then be the agency that would bring file, or submit their application for federal recognition. That he would give this as his lawyerly advice to Eames and he would ask him to convince the Association to consider this plan of action.

But they should not incorporate until they are satisfied that they have included all the tribal people who want to be part of the Nantiquak tribe. Minnie noticed that Reiner was back to his very rapid mode of speech. She had to concentrate to follow him. And when he had finished, Ron asked if there were any questions, any concerns. Gail mentioned that she had read two of the books on the Nantiquak but that they were still waiting for another history from a special lending library. Minnie said she'd like to read one of the books. Gail gave her the book entitled Tobacco Colony, and she gave the Nanticoke Indians of the Eastern Shore to the clerk, John Adamas. And with that the meeting was over. Reiner jumped up and rushed out of the room. He did not like long meetings and he let everyone know it.

In the next week, Cal Reiner called Minnie and Ron into his office. "It's time we spoke to Mr. Eames and give him our views of setting up a non-profit corporation for the Nanticoke Indians," said Reiner speaking rapidly again. "He may have to sell this idea to the Association members, who might not be so receptive to a broader more inclusive tribe. So he has to know that that is our considered advice. And he needs to know it before they conduct their tribal census. All an issue of little tribe or bigger tribe located across two states." Minnie and Ron both nodded in agreement. There was no other answer they could make.

"Okay, I'll call now and put him on the speaker phone." said Reiner. He put the speaker phone on and dialed. The beeps echoed out of the phone's speakers. Will answered.

"Hello Mr. Eames? This is Cal Reiner calling you from NAILS. Are you free to talk just now?" When Will answered that he was, Reiner continued. "I have Minnie Warrens and Ron Parchesi on the speaker phone with me here. We're calling to give you a different advice on the question of which entity would lead the Nantiquak Indians' efforts. We had said at our last meeting that it was probably acceptable to proceed through the Indian Association of Delaware. But we have now reconsidered this piece of advice. And now, in light of your current efforts to broaden the membership of the tribe by conducting a census and recruiting those claiming Indian ancestry and relationship to the Nantiquaks and becoming more inclusive, we want to advise the tribe that it would be better to incorporate a new, not-for-profit corporation that will represent the Nantiquak people and nation in their representations to the Bureau of Indian Affairs and in their possible lawsuits to get restitution."

"I see. And where should they incorporate?"

"I would think it would be cheaper, but just as effective, in Delaware. But as most of the earliest foundation documents are from Maryland perhaps it would be better to incorporate in Maryland. There it would be called a nonprofit corporation. But the name should be inclusive, something along the lines of the Eastern Shore, of Maryland and Delaware, or something like that."

"Alright," said Will. "I'll talk to the tribe and convey this recommendation to them from you. There are some who already are opposed to the broader definition of the tribe. But we are facing that internally first of all. Even before we go out to conduct the census. How would something like 'The Nantiquak Indian Nation of Delaware and Maryland Incorporated' sound?"

"That sounds just fine, Will. It should do for all of our purposes. I'm sure no one else owns that name."

"And another thing, come to think of it." said Will. "I would think that we will need to have an established address for the corporation. And that would mean we would need to incorporate in Delaware because I can't imagine what address we could use in Maryland."

"You have a point Mr. Eames."

"Well, I will get back with you after I have consulted with the tribe up on Indian River and the Association and they have agreed."

"Good, good."

"On another front, I think we can begin looking at probate court records. I was thinking of looking this Thursday and Friday. First in Bristol, and then next week in Princess Mary in Somerville County. Will someone be coming from your office?"

"Yes, I think Ms. Warrens will be coming. Maybe she will come with a research assistant. But we'll see."

"Okay, then I will expect her to come to my office in Bristol at ten in the morning on Thursday. Minnie, are you there?"

"Yes, Mr. Eames."

"You might need to stay the night here to continue on Friday. So you might want to come prepared to overnight here. Alright?"

"Alright. I'll come prepared."

"And I'll send you an e-mail with instructions on how to find my office. You'll be coming by car I presume?"

"Yes, I will probably drive myself. And instructions would be appreciated."

At that they all said their good-byes and broke off the call.

Minnie, right up to the moment she got into her car, could not help but feel eager about her trip to the Eastern Shore and seeing Will again. She would be working close with him for two full days. And when she got underway, her excitement mounted. It was almost like going on a vacation –she was not driving to Washington, but directly to the Eastern Shore via Annapolis on Highway 301. She had never visited the Eastern Shore of either Maryland or Virginia and this trip was like an adventure; traveling for the first time into new territory, crossing the broad Potomac River near the traditional Doeg home territories, going over the high Chesapeake Bay Bridge, seeing Maryland's eastern tidewater areas, so much like the tidewater regions of her own home on the Virginia side of the Bay. She was not after all going with either of the office research assistants, so she was on her own. The drive did not take long. She left at seven on a frosty morning shortly after sunrise, and pulled into Bristol on the Choptank River at 10:30. The weather was mild and clear, in Bristol it was much warmer than in Thornburg. Without too much effort—Bristol was a small town after all not much larger than Bowling Green—she found the Eastern Shore Realty Agency, just as Will's instructions described it. She stepped into the office, and she suddenly felt overwhelmed by a surge of unaccustomed happiness. She found herself smiling more than she usually ever did. Will was there in the office waiting for her and his greeting was ebullient, as if he were greeting a long lost special friend, not the greeting of two professional work colleagues. She continued to smile a lot.

"Oh, here she is, at last. We've been expecting you sooner. Hello Minnie. Welcome to Bristol on the Eastern Shore." Will came over to her and gave her a hug. Then he offered to take her coat. "I'm glad you made it safely here. No troubles on the way, I trust?"

"No, it was easy. No traffic really. But the Bay Bridge is so high, it nearly took my breath away."

"Yes, isn't it a marvel?" said Will. "But the important point is that you did not fall off, and you got here safely. Would you like a coffee?" She nodded yes.

"This is my little business here, two rooms." he said after handing her a mug of coffee as he led her around the office. "This is my assistant, Lucy, who does all the real work for me. Lucy, this is Minnie Warrens who is our attorney for the Nantiquaks, on my Injun Project." The two women shook hands. Minnie was a disturbed to hear Will calling their work the Injun Project. But she kept it to herself. Then with a sweep of his arm he directed her to go through a wide door in the middle of one of the rooms. "Step in, this is the title insurance office, also one of my businesses. This is Marilyn, who runs the office. Marilyn, this is Minnie Warrens from Washington, who is going to be joining us today. I think we'll be ready to go over to the court house archives in about ten minutes."

At the archives, Will, Lucy, and Minnie began their search. Will had brought with them a copy of the map he had had prepared, which showed the locations of the original Nantiquak reservations. Will showed the clerk of the probate property office his map and the clerk suggested that they search backwards. The clerk brought out the plats of the current ownership of the farms in the county which overlapped where the reservations had been. Once they knew the present owner of such a plot they could find his deed and title transfer that he had acquired or his father or grandfather before him had acquired. Will had looked at Maryland history and was looking for a sales date somewhere after 1832 but earlier than 1840. These dates were after the Nate Turner rebellion in 1831, a black rebellion of both slaves and freedmen which terrorized the white population in those days, especially in current and former slave states, as Maryland was. They looked first at a large farm just outside of Exeter which overlapped where the Nantiquak "capital" of Chicocoan had stood. This area was occupied now by a two hundred acre farm, two other small farms of less than 40 acres each, and a five hundred acre farm. They looked first at the title history of the five hundred acre farm. It had been held for several generations of Roscoes, and the current holder's grandfather had expanded it greatly during the Depression. They struck success on this very first property; finding that the Roscoe family had bought the largest share of it in the 1890s, and that the previous family had bought it in 1864 from two families that had bought the property and established the original title in 1836 from the state of Maryland. There was no earlier title on the property, meaning the state had sold it for the first time and had considered it state property prior to 1836. This was a demonstration of the state of Maryland seizing and selling Indian reservation land without recompense to the Nantiquak Indians. The records showed that the two properties were sold for $58 and two hogsheads of tobacco each, an interesting insight which showed that as late as the 1830s tobacco was still a currency in the Eastern Shore of Maryland. These sales of the two parcels amounted to more than three hundred acres, but from the coordinates given in the probate record they did not include the marshy lands right down to the Nanticoke River banks. In fact they sold only the lands west of the Chicocoan Creek. "This corresponds with the situation as it is today," said Will. "Except that I have now bought the marsh lands down to the Nantiquak River and the state claims most of that territory as wildlife reserve land." Will's excitement in finding this historic information in the crisp yellowed paper archives of his county courthouse was clear. And it was exciting for Minnie also as it went a long way in establishing their legal case of the Nantiquaks against the state of Maryland. "It just amazes me that all these old records still exist, in such good shape." said Will.

Minnie couldn't agree more. Such records in Virginia had largely been burned up during the Civil War in courthouses across the Virginia Tidewater and elsewhere across the state. She had not been able to refer to any historic records for her own tribe when she had compiled the application for her tribe's Federal recognition. And she realized how much a handicap that had been. This search had taken fifty minutes. Will asked the clerk to make a photocopy of the page, so he put a thin marker on this page in the ledger book.

The second and third properties which currently overlay the territory of the former Chicocoan reservation did not lead to any older titles. Those records were clearly missing. Although these tracts did appear in the records also in the 1890s, there were no earlier records of title transfers in the archive. The four of them, including the clerk, were leaning over the large plat maps on a huge low table. Minnie was leaning on her elbows, and almost snuggled against Will. It gave her a warm feeling. Every now and then the clerk would get up and return to a very large ledger book which contained the title records from the second half of the nineteenth century. He consulted it and then returned to the map to check the coordinates of the tracts described. The entire process of research moved slowly. For the first half of the 19th century there was a smaller but still substantial ledger book, and for the second half of the 18th century there were three ledgers which were even smaller, but which each held fewer transactions. After two and a half hours of searching, Will proposed that they take a break over lunch. "Let's reconvene in an hour." Lucy excused herself and went home for lunch. Will took Minnie to the Cedar Island Bar and Restaurant. Minnie felt strangely secure that she was deep in Will's territory. All the landmarks were his, and each and every one were new and strange to her. Over lunch Minnie had to ask. "Why did you call this project, the Injun Project.

Don't you think that is a little bit objectionable to your clients? Or to me?" "Oh that, no offense meant. Certainly not for you. My father gave this name to my efforts for the Nantiquaks and for building an Indian casino. You see, in this part of the world people call Indians, Injuns. Not disrespectfully. Kind of a vestige of old days when Indians were still seen around here, and a sloppy way of pronouncing the word. Many people around here use the term. My father and my grandfather only referred to Indians as Injuns. And my father meant it for me as a kind of a snide name, making fun of me. But I liked it, so I use it. I'm sorry if it upset you. No harm or disparagement meant." "It's racist and outdated. So could I ask you not to use the term any more, Will?" "Yes, I won't. I'm sorry." "Maybe I can get over it, Will. But it is politically incorrect these days. You should not use it when you're talking to Indians." "I understand, Minnie. Forgive me."

He looked at her repentantly. She smiled. "In our office, we call this assignment the Oyster Project." "There's a point, our local patois here on the Eastern Shore. We would say Oyshtyur Project. Funny, eh? We speak differently here from the people in Warshington." Minnie chuckled and let the subject go. She forgave him and did not mean to make a fuss about the word Injun. She wanted to impress Will, not offend him. She had always reasoned that Injun was not as offensive or demeaning as the word nigger was to African Americans, although they used the term among themselves. And even in the old westerns, the term was not used with the same amount of contempt and hateful baggage as the n-word, or even the term redskin. But Injun still represented the old racist days and white contempt for native Americans.

In the afternoon back at the archive they started by looking at a property which overlapped the reservation on the north side. As they started, Will suddenly declared, "This farm borders up next to my great uncle's."

"Your great uncle has a farm?"

"Yep, a big one, about 15 miles from here, and only six miles from the original Chicacoan village." "That's interesting. But his land was not originally Indian land?"

"Not in the sense we're examining today. Not reservation land. But before the white man came here, three hundred and fifty years ago or so, all the land around here was Indian land. But none of it had title or deeds. I understand that Indians here had a very different concept of land tenure from the English."

The archivist was looking at them strangely and impatiently. "Can we continue?" she said. Lucy chuckled and said: "In the past eight months Will has really been taken by everything about Injun history."

Minnie looked at Will and they exchanged faint insiders' smiles.

This tract passed through many hands until it was the property of John Whitehead in the mid- nineteenth century. And then the record showed that he, or his father, had bought the property from the state of Maryland in 1833. This was another property that was sold out of the reservation. But only a small part of it according to Will's map. Perhaps four hundred acres. "So it looks like we have a another piece of the puzzle." said Will. "And just like the others, this man Whitehead only bought the land that was above the tidal marsh. Land he could drain and cultivate."

"So this is another tract that Maryland seized and sold illegally from the original reservation." said Minnie. "We can include this in the claim against the state."

"That's good, Minnie. Really good."

The archivist then noticed that there was more probate information included with the state sale of this parcel. "I can read here the handwritten note that the buyer, Mr. Whitehead, bought this tract of land, some 380 acres, from the state of Maryland for $685 in silver, and two hogsheads of tobacco."

"Really?" said Will. "That seems cheap. I'm surprised they were still using tobacco as currency, as late as then. I wonder where the market was then?"

"I think that could be important information for our case, Will." said Minnie. They asked to photocopy these pages as well as the page with the sales record.

They continued searching the ledger books, but through the rest of the afternoon, they did not find any more parcels which had been sold in the 1830s. The clerk was eager to close up at 4:45 so she could go home; their first day was finished.

"We might be finished for Dorset County." said Will. "We might have to search in Somerville County next. But we'll come back her tomorrow morning to see if we can find any other tracts that were taken. It's curious you know Minnie. The tract that I bought last year seems not to have been sold by the state. Maybe it was still held as Indian reservation, even though the state maps show it as wildlife reservation lands."

"Maybe the state of Maryland considers Indians to be wildlife." said Minnie with a faint smile.

Will looked at her with surprise. She was making a derogatory joke about Indians. And it seemed so unexpected. He smiled too.

On the way back to Will's office, Will asked Minnie if she wanted to stay overnight there in Bristol and then continue the next day, or if she wanted to return home and come the next day. Minnie said she would stay the night and finish up on Friday. Will then asked Lucy if she could contact the property archivist at St. Mary's in Somerville County to see if they could come the next afternoon.

"I thought we could have dinner at my parents' house." said Will. And then you could sleep at my house while I stay at my parents'. You'll be more comfortable that way."

Minnie felt relieved in some ways about that proposal. She had worried a bit about staying with Will overnight and the possibility that he might seduce her given her proximity. But the prospect had also given her a tinge of excitement. She was not so sure that she didn't want to be seduced by Will.

At six o'clock, Minnie took her overnight bag from her car and they got into Will's car. Just as she sat in the front passenger seat, Will touched her hand gently. It was the first time he had touched her. But it was just momentary. He drove across town to a large, white gingerbread house with a high porch and tall gables set on a street lined with linden trees. Minnie thought it looked charming. "This is it. My parents' house. Come on in. Mom cooks the best meals in town." To Minnie it all seemed a little awkward, as if he were taking her as a serious girlfriend for the first introduction to his parents. But inside, the mood was casual and welcoming. Will's father asked her if it was her first visit to Bristol and if Will had bothered to show her around. Will's mother, Mar Sue, asked her where she worked and how she got to know Will. When Minnie said that she was working for the Bureau of Indian Affairs when Will had come by to ask some questions, Bob said simply, "Oh his Injun Project." without the slightest bit of condescension or even awareness that she was herself an Injun. Will's mother cut in. "He's always ribbing Will about his ambitions for the Indians."

"Actually, I appreciate that. I myself am an Indian." answered Minnie.

"I'm fixing baked oyshtyurs for dinner, Minnie. I hope you like them."

"I can't say I do, as I have never had them before. But I like oysters."

Over the table Bob was chatty and Mar Sue was quiet.

"Where are you from, Minnie?"

"I'm from Bowling Green, Virginia. But just now I live in a small town outside Fredericksburg."

"I can't say I know those places. Never been there. I never have gotten much chance to visit in Virginia. 'Cepting maybe Accomack or Assateague Island here on the Eastern Shore."

Mar Sue jumped in. "And you said you were an Indian. What tribe do you come from?" she asked. "My tribe is called the Massoponax tribe. It was once a part of the great Powhatan confederation." "Oh, the same Powhatan that was the father of Pocahontas?"

"The same one."

Will jumped in. "You know she is actually the chief of the Massoponax tribe."

"A woman Indian chief?" his mother queried looking as if that was the oddest thing she had ever heard.

"That's right. But it is not so unusual in our history." said Minnie demurely.

"Did our Will tell you that we have Injun ancestry in our blood?" asked Bob taking another piece of oyster from the serving platter.

"Yes, he did. Almost as surprising and unusual as a female Indian chief." said Minnie looking at Will. "And from what he told me," she continued, "it makes us distantly related."

"Really?" said Bob excitedly. "How's that?"

"You see my tribe includes the Doeg people who were a band of the local Nantiquak people, five or six hundred years ago. And from what I understand you all are related to the Nantiquaks. So that should make us related. With some English mixture, of course."

"I'll be damned." said Bob. "This Injun Project of Will's is getting more and more interesting. Maybe you two should tie the bond and close this circle of relationships." It seemed to Minnie that Bob said this with the most innocent of intents, but still she blushed a little. Will did not say anything to scold his father. But his gaze turned to Minnie's and he smiled abashedly. Bob looked around the table seeking some support for his statement, but he got none.

Just after she had cleared the dishes and brought in a pudding dessert, Mar Sue continued to ask more about Minnie.

"And what is your last name Minnie?"

"It's Warrens." Minnie answered quietly.

"Oh," said Mar Sue as if she were surprised. "I was expecting that you would have an Indian sounding name. But Warrens, isn't that an English name?"

"No, my name is an Indian name, only anglicized. You see the local Indians here on the Eastern Shore and in Tidewater Virginia spoke the same Algonquian language and the word for chief was, and still is, weroanse. Warrens is a rough Anglicization for weroanse. The chiefdom of my tribe has been in the family for several generations now and so all of my ancestors were called weroanse, or Warrens for Anglo records."

"Oh, how interesting." said Mar Sue.

"But you know mom," said Will. "most of the local Indians in this region have English names. They adopted them often from the local English farmers in the 18th or early 19th century. Our ancestor, my great grandmother, and pa's grandmother, had the family name of Driggers. That was an old English family that owned a tobacco farm just north of Exeter."

"I see," said Mar Sue. "I thought maybe Warrens was a married name."

Again Will jumped in. "But Minnie has a real Indian first name. It's Mataoka."

"Yes, that sounds like an Indian name." said Mar Sue. "Does it mean something?"

Minnie did not think that the Eames would make fun of her name so in an instant she decided to tell them. "Yes actually. It means the same as Pocahontas. In fact it was Pocahontas's real name."

"I've heard of Pocahontas." said Bob finishing his pudding. "We all heard stories about her in school. I think she married a man named John Smith, or something like that."

"No. She married an Englishman named John Rolfe. They went to England, she had a son there, and she died from some horrible local English disease. But her son came back to Virginia and owned a farm on the James River and had a family. And Pocahontas's descendants live in Virginia to this day. There's a legend however that Pocahantas saved John Smith's life by putting her head on his as he was about to be executed."

"Wow. Now that is interesting." said Bob. "I didn't know that part of the story at all." "And are you married by the way?" continued Mar Sue.

"Mom, it's like you're running an inquiry of the future bride, or something." complained Will. "That's alright Will." said Minnie calmly. "No. I have not been married."

"Oh, that's too bad." said Mar Sue off-handedly. "But no offense intended. It's just that it's important for a woman to get married and have children."

"So I've been often told by many people in my family and in my tribe. I've nothing against marriage. But I went to law school after university, and just never had the opportunity nor have met the right guy to marry." Minnie smiled a little. It seemed to her that Will's parents were really old fashioned, and straight-forward, but simple and sincere in their questioning. They meant no insult, and they did not seem to hold any prejudices against Indians.

After dinner Will suggested that they walk a while and then walk on to his house. Minnie took her bag. It was not far to Will's house about six blocks, less than half a mile, through bare tree lined streets, but it was frosty and dark outside so they did not dally. At the house which was poorly lit by the street lamp, Minnie suddenly recognized a small cottage which appeared just like the one she rented in Thornburg. "That looks like my house, Will."

"Really? It's a common style of bungalow that was built all around the Eastern Shore in the 1930s. It's very comfortable. But rather small. So I'll stay tonight with my parents so you can rest here at ease."

Inside, he showed her around the small place. He showed her where there was coffee, eggs and bread, and yoghurt and fruit which she could have for breakfast. Then he suggested that they watch TV. He turned on his set with the remote and turned the channels settling to a culture channel which was showing a piano concerto. They sat together on his couch. Minnie was feeling close and comfortable with Will and she longed for him to touch her, perhaps embrace her. But he didn't.

"Do you like classical music, Will?"

"No, I don't understand it actually. So I usually don't listen. And there are never any concerts here in Bristol as you can understand. But this is nicer than anything else they're showing on the tube tonight." After a short while Will asked her if she would like a beer, but she said no. He did not get one for himself.

They fell silent for several minutes watching the screen. Minnie liked the music, but didn't know what it was; she wished they would put the name of the piece on the screen. The camera panned over the pianist a couple times as she was playing, and the subscript on the screen said the artist was named Martha Argerich. Then there was a long close focus on Martha's face. Suddenly Will jumped up from the couch.

"Hey look at that, Minnie. You look just like her, like the pianist. In the face I mean. You look like this Martha Argerich woman. Look for yourself."

Minnie was surprised. She had not taken much notice of the pianist. And she then had to wait several more minutes for the camera to focus again closely on her face which was intensely concentrated on the keys.

"You see? You look just like her. Maybe she's a little lighter in facial color than you but the resemblance is uncanny. Don't you agree?"

Minnie looked closely this time.

"Maybe there's some resemblance. But I don't know, Will. She's so pretty. I'm so dark."

"And so are you, Minnie. I mean pretty. Really. You're very pretty. You look just like her—in the face. And even her figure is like yours."

Will was standing up now near the TV screen, waving his hands excitedly.

"Maybe that is why I thought you looked so familiar before when I first met you. You look like this famous pianist who I may have seen some time before, in a concert or broadcast, or on an album cover. My mother has a big collection of classical records, you know, where I might have seen her photo before. I really mean it. You're very pretty, Minnie. Just like this Argerich woman."

Minnie felt herself blushing.

"Did you feel that you had seen me before when we first met, Will? Did I seem familiar to you then?"

"I don't know. There did seem to be something familiar about you shortly after our first meeting. But I thought it was because you were so naturally attractive."

"You seemed at once to be very familiar to me." said Minnie. "But in my case, I had seen you before. But you didn't remember it."

"What do you mean, Minnie?"

"I saw you on an early night in mid-November about three months ago. You saved me from a rapist in D.C."

"I did?" Will said in disbelief.

"Yes. I remember your face distinctly. I saw you in the light after you had knocked out my attacker. You were talking with the police. And you told the police man that you were a Marine, and that in the Marines you learned how to hit a person like you hit that black man who was on top of me trying to rape me. In an alley, near E Street. That was you who came to my rescue."

"Yeah, I guess I remember that incident. I didn't even think much about it afterwards. After they took my witness statement. But wait, I haven't told you I was in the Marines."

"That's exactly right. But I overheard you telling the policeman that. A big black policeman."

Will paused and thought about what Minnie had said, trying to recall the events of that November night. "Yeah, you're right it was a black policeman who interviewed me. And he was a former Marine, too. So that was really you?" Will said now calmly.

"Yes, it was me on the ground, on my knees."

"But I don't recall that I saw your face then."

"I figured you hadn't. It was dark, wasn't it? And everything happened so quickly. Didn't it? And maybe you remember that my attacker had a knife to my throat?"

"Yes, I recall that. I waited for him to put it down from your neck before I hit him."

"Well, he left me a little souvenir of his attack. Look here." said Minnie and she moved aside the upper part of her shirt collar to reveal to him a faint, pink, thin line drawn across the windpipe of her throat.

Will leaned close and looked at the scar for a few seconds. "Sonovabitch. Should ov hit him harder." he hissed. "I guess that really was me and you in that alley." said Will looking intently at Minnie.

"Yes, I recognized your face again when you first walked into my office. I thought I would fall off my chair. And I recognized your voice too. Quite distinctive. I will never forget it. You were my savior and hero, since that night."

"Just doing what any self-respecting citizen would have done."

"I don't think so. It took bravery to follow me into the alley against an armed attacker."

"But why didn't you tell me before, Minnie? If you knew all along that I had saved you there in November."

"I don't know. I thought maybe you would eventually recognize me. But I didn't want to push it, because it was my shame that night, you know."

"Well, I'll be damned. I have been thinking about what an attractive woman you are for the past few months, that I was somehow drawn to you, when in fact, I bumped into you a couple months earlier even. Although we weren't introduced."

"No, we weren't introduced. Were we? People dispense with introductions at the scene of an assault and rape."

"All this sounds like fate, doesn't it?"

"Yes, I suppose so. Especially if that lazy, oily guy, Nighthorse Ward, who used to be my boss, had not sent you my way rather than giving you the help he should have done."

"So you don't think much of him either?"

"No, I despise the man. Kind of the ass-licking, shifty, politicking, measly mouthed, bureaucrat who thinks only about how he can get ahead in his office. Stepping over other people in the office. Especially the women."

"That about sums it up. You came to a very accurate judgment of him very quickly."

"It was easy to do. But I am serious Minnie. I do feel drawn to you. Have felt attracted to you, maybe better to say. I thought it was only because you were pretty."

Will was still standing next to the TV screen, and Minnie was still sitting on the couch maybe three yards away. An embarrassing silence fell over them, as the piano music continued to pour out of the TV speakers. They had reached an impasse. Will did not know what to say further. And Minnie was afraid she had already said too much.

"And you know, I really like working with you too." said Will.

He moved toward the front door. "Now maybe it's time for me to leave you to get some sleep." Minnie stood up. "You don't want to stay to the end of the concerto?"

"Well maybe. Thad be nice." Will came back to the couch and sat down. Minnie sat again. She reached over and took his hand in hers, and they sat together silently watching the screen. But the concerto was over in only another five minutes. Will slipped his hand out of Minnie's and slowly stood up. "Well now it is time to go I think." He moved toward the door, took his winter coat from the hook, and reached for the door knob.

"I will come around here at about 9:30 tomorrow. Okay?"

"Yes, I'll be ready." said Minnie and she approached him and then leaned closer and gave him a light kiss on the lips. "Good night, Will."

"Good night Minnie. Sleep well." Will then ducked out of the door into the frosty night air and began to walk to the street. Minnie watched him until he disappeared into the shadows and then she shut and locked the door. She then went into the main room and turned off the television. She picked up her overnight bag and went into the bedroom. She looked around and realized that the bedroom everywhere had the characteristics of a background in the Marines.

The double bed was made tight, with the corners folded under the top mattress and the blanket stretched taut. She wondered if it was true that a quarter dollar coin had to bounce up and flip over from the bed when tossed on to the blanket in the middle. The walls were bare of decoration except for a large glass framed copy of William Eames' Marine Corps commission. His desk was empty of everything except for an upright computer tower and a monitor. IBM of course, she thought. For a moment she felt that she was trespassing and that she couldn't sleep in this bed. For one thing, she thought she couldn't re-make it so well again in the morning. The bathroom was also clean and uncluttered of bottles or tonics or soaps. Finally, she decided to undress and get into her pajamas. She turned out the light in the bedroom and stepped into the bathroom and changed. She then loosened the covers and slipped into bed and lay there in the dark for what seemed like a long time. She could not sleep. She was too excited. She felt she could smell Will in the covers. They had confessed their attraction to each other, and all she could think about was getting closer to Will. In her mind's eye she kept reviewing the few moments when she had first seen Will in the alley, and the times they were together leaning over the plats table earlier that day. All of those memories were from cold days, but she felt very warm and snug in the bed. She felt as if Will was holding her close. It took her a long time before she fell asleep. Her mind was spinning. She wanted Will to hug her; she wanted to kiss him again. Sleeping In his bed, already warm under the tight sheets, she felt really close to him, and she wanted things to stay that way. She wanted him there in the bed by her side. She had never slept with a man before, and now she was feeling it was what she most wanted in life. She wondered if he would stand close to her tomorrow over the plats table. Maybe Lucy would notice. Will had already confessed that he was drawn to her, as she was to him. She had revealed a lot about herself to him that night and he had appreciated it, not mocked or scorned her. He truly was a hero. And then she was already regretting that she would return home tomorrow, and that there would be a long time until she saw him again. Eventually in this active state of mind she dozed off and had strange, pleasant dreams filled with sunlight, and Will's smiling face.

When Will came the next morning to pick her up, it was overcast, cold and raining a thin drizzle. She had already cleaned up the kitchen after her breakfast, and to the best of her ability she had tried to remake his bed as he had, but had failed. On her bed at home she had a puffy feather comforter which didn't need much effort to spread over the bed, nothing like the taut, military efficiency of

Will's bedmaking. She stepped out into the morning air and was immediately chilled. She suddenly remembered that she was wearing the same short lightweight winter coat that she had worn on that fateful night when she had been nearly raped and had first encountered Will. She shivered in the damp and cold air. She hoped at once that Will did not recognize or remember the coat. Maybe she needed to throw it out when she got home, never wear that coat again, she thought. Will had a large golf umbrella which he leaned over her head. "Good morning, Minnie. Did you sleep well?" "I think so. It's a comfortable bed."

"I know. Nothing like the beds I slept in in the Marines."

He led her to his car and sheltered her as she climbed into the front seat. Lucy went directly to the archive offices and was waiting for them there already inside ready to resume. The archivist seemed to be moving slower than the day before. Will was looking for records of two pieces from the original reservation at Chicacoan which they had not found the day before. It took only about forty minutes to find the current owners of these two tracts. They owned farms that overlapped the former reservation in only twelve acres each. So they then tried to follow the owernship and deed transfers for these farms back in time. For the first piece they could not find much of its history. The present owner's family had bought it in 1948, and before them the previous owner had bought the property during the depression. Apparently the farm had fallen victim to the Depression and the lack of credit. But as for the owner back to 1933 they could not find any records of him and there were missing records of the title for that plot in the

19th century. As the four of them were standing around the plat table, Minnie shifted her stance and for much of the morning she stood rubbing up next to Will, nudging her hips and upper thigh to his. Will made no effort to stand off from her.

The second piece yielded more information and gave information about the changes in ownership all the way back to 1834 when the first white owner, one Roger Whitehead, bought the small fifteen acre parcel from the state of Maryland and added it to his farm plot that he already owned further west. They had this page photocopied, and then tried to continue tracing Whitehead's farm back further. They found that the records gave ownership of the small Whitehead farm back to the 1760s when, presumably, a grandfather or great-grandfather of Roger's first bought the property. "Undoubtedly, a man like Roger Whitehead, coveted the land in the Nantiquak reservation adjacent to his farm long before Maryland decided to sell it." said Will. "All indicators from the Indian's history showed that they had by and large abandoned the reservation long before."

With this discovery, they agreed that they had concluded their title search on former reservation land within Dorset County. It was already time for a late lunch and they thanked the archivist and took their photocopied pages and left. At the door Lucy reported that the probate archive center in neighboring Somerville County was not open that day, but that they would be able to see them on Tuesday in the next week, the third of March. "Okay, let's make a date to visit them then at 10 am." said Will. "Will that be alright with you Minnie?" "I can make that date available, Will." answered Minnie. "Fine, then probably you would need to plan to spend two days here then as well. The reservation lands on the other side of the Nanticoke River were much larger than what we researched here in Dorset County."

Once again Lucy went home for her lunch and she said goodbye to Minnie. Will then drove with Minnie back to the Cedar Island Bar for lunch. This time Will ordered himself a burger and Minnie decided to eat a fried crab cake. They sat opposite each other and Minnie looked straight into Will's eyes. He smiled back at her.

"I think we're making some good progress. And most important we can see that the records are intact, even if they are more than one hundred and fifty year old. Some even more than two hundred years old."

"I've never done this before, and I've never been involved in litigation against the state for restitution over improper seizure and sales of property. Seems to me though that we've collected some important evidence for our case against Maryland. But I'm sure all this would not be possible in Virginia. All such old records were burned up during the Civil War. Certainly this has hurt the case for my own tribe, but it helps the Nantiquak."

"I feel confident we'll get some more next week too in Princess Mary." said Will as they ate their lunch. Outside the drizzle had changed into a steady rain and the skies were very dark. It made the inside of the restaurant seem like it was night.

"How old are you Minnie?"

"I'll be thirty six in September. And you?"

"I'm thirty later this year. I was born in 1968. To Mar Sue and Bob Eames. Right here in Bristol. Lived all my life here, except for the couple years that the Marines took me around to see the world, as they say. And the three years I was at university." Will looked as if he were proud to have said this. Minnie thought it was a well-rehearsed line. But he suddenly looked cute to her.

Changing his expression to a more serious one, Will asked, "Minnie, you told me your father took you fishing once when you were a little girl. Is he still living?"

"No he died about seven years ago. He died suddenly of a heart attack. I was away from home when it happened. At my work in Richmond. By the time my mother got hold of me to tell me, and by the time I got to the hospital, it was already too late. He was dead."

"I'm sorry for you."

"You don't need to be. He had always seemed so strong and robust. But inside it seems he was a wreck it seemed. All his life he had been a heavy smoker. And apparently he had heart disease for many years."

"But your mother is still living?"

"Yeah, she lives in Bowling Green. My father had worked on the army base there, as a general repairs and maintenance man. For more than thirty five years. On that income he was able to buy the house there where I grew up. He was the chief of our tribe before I succeeded him. Mother now lives alone. But I usually stay with her on weekends."

And do you have any brothers or sisters?"

"Yes, I have a younger sister who is married to one of our Indian men and lives at Whitebank Landing, near our reservation. She has two little girls. I see them often. Now when you mention that I'm pretty, they are really pretty. And I have a younger brother, who envies me and wants to be the chief of the tribe. He runs a towing company. He's just like my father. Rather short tempered, smokes heavily. And you? Do you have any brothers or sisters?"

"Yes, I have a younger sister, who is married and who just had her first little girl, my niece. She lives with her man up in East City in the next county north of here."

"That means we're both the oldest in our families."

"Yep, I suppose so. The advantaged ones, by our tradition. But I am not a chief." said Will smiling mischievously. "But as you suggested, I am distantly related to you."

"Yes, I suppose so."

"So, if your father can no longer take you fishing, I might propose to take you out in our little boat to go rockfish fishing out in the Bay. It's the season soon. Would you like that?"

"Not in this weather. Maybe later?"

"Okay, understandable. But in March, the weather already begins to turn mild and sunny. And if it is rainy and cold we wouldn't have to go out."

"We'll see." She was mixed in her mind. She wanted to jump into the boat with Will right then and there. But at the same time, she also felt a frisson of fear about being out on open water and an aversion to the chill and cold weather.

"What do you like to do in your free time, weekends for instance?"

"On weekends I usually go to my mother's house. We just visit, and sometimes my sister comes too with my nephew and niece. But we don't do much of anything special."

"Do you like going to the beach?"

"No, not especially. But I have only gone to the beach once in my life. The surf scared me to death, just looking at it. I really don't know how to swim. And I don't like to sit in the sun, just to get darker. I don't need that."

"I don't like sunbathing either," said Will.

As they finished eating their lunch, they fell silent. Minnie did not want the moment to end, but what more could they do? It was already 1:45. They were the only two customers left in the restaurant or at the bar. She liked just talking with Will. In those two days she had told him more about herself than she had ever told anyone before. He made her feel warm and close and she wanted to tell him all about herself.

After a long pause, the waiter came and cleared away the dishes, and then asked them if they wanted anything else. Will relayed the idea, "Would you like a coffee?"

"Yes. Maybe a cup of coffee, before I hit the road."

"Do you have to go back to the office?" asked Will. "I don't have anything planned for the rest of today. There are never any buyers looking for property on rainy, late winter Friday afternoons. Maybe on Saturdays, but doubtful even then."

Minnie hadn't even thought of things in that way. It was a Friday afternoon. She didn't need to rush back to Washington to her office. Nothing pressing to do there. She could just drive straight back home. That would take two hours or more. But still she did not want to rush off.

"Probably it makes most sense for me to drive straight home. Maybe, if I leave now I can get home before it's completely dark."

So they ordered two coffees. And Minnie looked deep into Will's eyes, and then looked down to stir the sugar into her coffee. She did not want to leave.

"Tell me Will. Really, what's your motivation in doing this 'Injun Project' of yours?"

"Maybe it sounds strange, but I needed something to do in my life, something to aim at and work for. A life project to work towards. Something more than just floating along through life."

"But why this for the Indians?"

"I first thought the project was to build a casino to capture some of the Ocean City traffic. It would be good for the county. And I could put it on my land on the Nanticoke River. That's what initially excited me. But casinos are not legal in Maryland. And then I learned about the Nantiquak Indians. The squatters on my property that I had planned to use are Nantiquaks, and as poor as they come. And then I learned that I was descended from the Nantiquaks. That came as a shock. But I think there are a lot of people on Delmarva who are descended from the Nantiquak Indians, or other tribes. And don't even know it. So then I thought I could do something good for the Nantiquak Indians and for the county, and for myself. Maybe I won't succeed, but at least I will have some clear objectives and purpose."

"And then one thing led to another. The Nantiquaks needed to be federally recognized in order to be able to develop a casino. And they needed reservation land. So we are going to go after all those things. Of course the hardest part is getting their agreement and cooperation.

But I like challenges. I like persuading people to buy things. That is why I am in real estate."

"But by this you mean you don't have any general idea of improving the lot of Indians?" asked Minnie.

"No, I never have had any generalized feeling that I had to do something good for Indians. My concern is only local. My neighbors here in the county and in Maryland, the Nantiquaks, and as it has unexpectedly turned out, my distant relatives. I don't concern myself with other Indian tribes."

"I see. So you wouldn't be interested in what happens to the Massoponax-Doeg tribe?"

"Only inasmuch as I am now interested in what becomes of a certain female chief of that tribe. Let's face it, if I had not embarked on this project I would never have had the opportunity to meet you."

"You say the nicest things, William Eames."

"No, I mean it. After all, it was fate and coincidence that you saw me for the first time in that alley off E Street. If I had not gone to see Nighthorse that day, I would not have been there. And we both would have been worse off for it. Really, I am glad I met you properly later. And as it turns out, I am glad I was there and saw that bastard grab you and that I could give him a good whack before he did anything hateful."

"I often thought this way when I served in the Marines." Will continued. "The bullet missed me, because fate at that moment took me to some other space where there were no bullets flying around with my name on them."

"So I am extremely lucky, that you were flying around on that evening like a bullet with my name on it?"

"Yes. Kind of. But if I was a bullet that night, I was meant to hit that rapist. It was fate, and I was also extremely lucky that Nighthorse, bastard that he is, shucked me off from his office and sent me your way. As it turned out, I came across you even sooner than I could have expected, even though I did not know it at the time."

Minnie agreed that she was lucky, but said nothing.

"I've never given much credence to fate." said Minnie. Fate for the native Americans has always been cruel and unforgiving, early death. I've been extremely fortunate compared to other Indians. But I've still felt at times I've been dealt a bad hand."

Will thought for a moment, and then said, "Then don't go into the casino. By design the house deals out only bad hands."

"So why do you want a casino for the Nantiquaks?"

"Not so they can gamble. No, I can assure you. I would have it that the Nantiquaks themselves would not be allowed to gamble. But that won't happen. But if they take the role of the House and gain the benefits of others' bad cards and bad luck, then it can bring them income that currently just drives by and is thrown away on the sands of Ocean City for the benefits of others."

There was a sudden tapping at the window from a windblown dourpour of rain which ran on and raked the streets. Its sound broke the mood. I was already well past two o'clock. Through the window it could be seen that the dark clouds were breaking up and along with these last splashes of wind driven rain, there were streaks of sunlight gushing through the remaining clouds.

"I should be going, now, Will. I could stay and talk all afternoon and evening."

"I wouldn't mind talking with you all afternoon and evening too. And into the night as well." "You're so nice to me, Will."

He smiled at her, and quipped in a mock cockney accent, "I aims to please. Madame."

He took the check for the lunch. "These are our expenses, not NAILS's." Then he drove her over to his office, which was not at all far from the restaurant, just off Highway 50. Before she could step out of the car, Will had already whipped out the large golf umbrella from the car and was holding it over her head. "Always have to ready for rain when a customer is in the car with you." He helped her put her overnight bag in her car and then gave her a light kiss on the cheek. "Drive safely now. Hope to see you on Tuesday." "I'll be here. Early." Minnie replied as she started her car. On the road home, Minnie was preoccupied by her fate, and the good fate that had made her cross paths with Will. Maybe it was her fate that he could be her man. She wished it so. And she was so pre- occupied by the idea of being with Will all the time, that she did not notice the height of the Bay Bridge on her return journey. Could she talk about him with her mother that weekend? Maybe with her sister? She didn't know. But by the time she arrived at Thornburg, she decided there was too much she didn't want to reveal to her family, so she decided she would not tell them about Will. She felt certain that Tuesday could not come soon enough. Throughout the weekend she ached from longing to see Will. And from having to keep a secret locked up inside her from her mother and sister. They did notice that there was something eating her up inside, but they were both discrete enough not to push Minnie to find out what it was. They certainly would not have been pleased to learn that she had fallen in love with a white man.

Finally Tuesday morning came and Minnie threw her overnight bag into her small, blue Ford Escort and set out for the Eastern Shore. It was still very chilly that morning and overcast so she had dressed warmly, in wool slacks and a tight fitting knit top with a sweater. She had remembered to dispose of her light weight winter coat, so she wore the long winter coat. Over the weekend she had looked up some history about Princess Mary's and Somerville County. It seemed to her that the town was a place that history had passed by, it was a very small, like Bowling Green, only without the adjacent army base. She was a little surprised at how far it was from Bristol to Princess Mary, it was another hour further along the road down the peninsula. She had not suspected that the Eastern Shore was so big. And she was also surprised to learn that Princess Mary had been founded as a port city. From the map she could not see that a river flowed from the town to the Bay. But there was a small creek there in the center of the town, and as the old towns were only founded as shipment points for tobacco, it must have been able to float the tobacco down to the Bay on this creek. She arrived in Bristol just after nine o'clock and drove straight to Will's house which she found without difficulty. Sun was just breaking through the clouds.

Will came to the door without a jacket or tie on. "Minnie! I'm so glad to see you! But I'm not quite ready yet. Come on in. Would you like some coffee?"

Minnie stepped in and took off her coat. Will rushed around first to pour some coffee for Minnie— "Cream and sugar?"—and then to grab his tie and start tying it while popping into the corridor washroom to consult the mirror. Minnie sat in the kitchen, which was open to the living room and watched Will as she sipped at a mug of coffee. Will went back to the bedroom and came back with his gray dress jacket. Minnie was amused by Will's jerky movements around the house. She recognized the gray jacket.

"You'll have to excuse me. I was late coming back from my morning run. The weather was nice, so I ran farther than usual. Do you practice any sports?"

"No," said Minnie. "I don't. Never have. Although I wanted to be on the athletics team when I was in high school. I liked running. But I wasn't good enough to make the team." She had to shout her answer to him for her voice to catch up with Will as he dodged from room to room.

"Okay, we're ready to go. Was your drive over here nice, and uneventful?" he said as he took Minnie's coat off the hook and helped slip it onto her shoulders. "Maybe, your coat will be too warm for today, if the forecast turns out to be correct." So he noticed her coat, Minnie thought.

Maybe if she had worn the other one, he would have noticed that one too, and where he had seen it before.

In an hour they were at the county courthouse for Somerville County, in the very middle of the somnolent grid of streets of Princess Mary. They had come once again in Will's car, a silver Oldsmobile, much bigger and plusher than her small Ford. They drove through Salisbury on the way and Will pointed out that this was Maryland's largest town on the Eastern Shore. And was also the place where the author of the history of the Nantiquaks lived.

"You know, Minnie, I think our application for Federal recognition will be helped by his book. Have you read it?"

"Yes, I have. A bit sketchy on the history, lots of gaps in the history, but informative enough. I think you're right. Having a history of the tribe does help the application process. And the Nantiquaks have three such published histories."

"You and your tribe could perhaps benefit from commissioning a history to be written and published. You know this professor I'm telling you about was approached by one of the Nantiquaks who was a student at the university here in Salisbury. He had been so impressed by his history of the colonial period here on Eastern Shore Maryland that he asked him to prepare a history for his tribe."

"I'm not a historian by training, but I think it would be hard to research and write for our tribe. Too much of the historical documents have been destroyed in Virginia."

"Maybe. You met this young man—who's not so young anymore— Morley Norwood, when we came to D.C. in January. He was the one who offered Cal Reiner the copy of that history book that he had requested. Maybe there is some history professor in Virginia who is interested in more accurate depiction of the Virginian Indian tribes."

"You mean a more accurate history than all the popular media depictions? Than all the legends and endlessly repeated stories?"

"Yes, and a history specifically of the Massaponax-Doeg tribe."

"Will, that's a good idea. We can see if we can find such a scholar willing to write out history."

At the brick courthouse, they were directed to the records and archives department which was housed in a brick annex building sitting just across the street. There they met Lucy and all went into the archive together. The building looked like it was something built in the sixties or seventies, all the corridors and rooms had long fluorescent bulbs providing all the lighting. Lucy asked for the archivist that she had made their appointment with. They were taken to a large room which had two large plats tables in the midst of steel shelves filled with file folders and ledger books. The place smelled dusty and looked unused. Will introduced the objective for his search and put out his map on the table.

"You see, there was for more than one hundred and fifty years a large Indian reservation located here on the Nanticoke River and Broad Creek. In what used to be part of Somerville County. In the mid-1830s, the state of Maryland, considering the reservation to have been abandoned by the Nantiquak Indians, and under pressure from local farmers who wanted the land, broke up the reservations into tracts and sold them. Illegally. So we're looking for the records of these sales. And the records which established first title to these lands."

"Oh, but that area is now part of Wicomico County." said the archivist, looking very concerned. "Yes, I know. But the sales took place in 1833-34 or later, and Wicomico was not split off from

Somerville County until 1867. Wouldn't you have the original records for that period here? We are also looking for the land grant records from the time the reservations were granted by the King through the eighteenth century."

"I don't know, is the exact answer. We definitely don't have the earlier property ledgers or probate records from before 1812. The original courthouse burned down then and all our county documents were burned up with it. And then the wooden courthouse that replaced it burned down in 1830.

Apparently some of the records and property ledgers survived that later fire, but not a lot. The brick court house you see outside was rebuilt at the beginning of this century from an earlier reconstructed brick structure."

"Were the remaining ledgers and documents for the northwest section of Somerville which became Wicomico County transferred to Salisbury at that time?"

"I don't honestly know. No one's ever asked for those records before, since I have been working here."

Minnie was thinking that this was just the sort of problems she would have researching for her own tribe. Fires, relocated records, and decayed paper.

"Well, then we will have to look to see if we can find some records." said Will. Minnie was amazed at how continually optimistic Will was. He always pushed forward, feeling assured of success. She thought again maybe it was his Marines background, a 'gung-ho, can do' outlook toward life.

"How are your property sales records arranged? By district or by years?" asked Will. "Most of the ledgers are arranged by year, or years."

"So let's begin our search in reverse, so to speak. From the 1830s when we know that Maryland sold off parcels of the Nantiquak reservation."

This proved to be a very time consuming process. They started with two huge ledger books: one for the years 1826 through 1834, and the other 1835 through 1847. Apparently the original scribes had recorded transactions until a ledger book was filled and then opened a new book. The group decided to split between them the survey of both books to make the work go quicker: Lucy with the archivist and Will with Minnie. The archivist had the advantage in that she was accustomed to reading the handwritten entries from the nineteenth century. Will and Minnie went to a long desk and sat down close to each other and started scanning. It was not easy for either of them. The entries were often abbreviated, and land transactions were mixed in along with legal rulings, sales of livestock, and notes on costs or other notable property transactions of the time. Minnie found it very hard to understand what the words were, while Will seemed to catch on quickly. He patiently showed her some of the handwriting tricks, and which flourishes to ignore and which were short- hand devices. Still it took them more than an hour to survey the year 1832, which Will had decided was the earliest year during which the state of Maryland might have sold off Indian reservation land. They found nothing of what they were looking for. The next year there were very few entries, but there was one long entry of a land transaction in the southern part of the county which was very detailed informative and which revealed to them the type of information that they were looking for including survey coordinates and title transfer. There was also an entry referring to a township called Massoponax. "Hey, that's the same name as my tribe, and the river that runs through it," said Minnie with some delight. "I wonder how that name ended up here on this side of the Bay." After more than two hours of scanning, in a land transaction from September 1834, Will spotted just what they were looking for: the sale of a large parcel in the area of the east bank of the Nanticoke River to the Delaware border. The entry put the property sold at 1,700 acres of "swamp and well drained land" which was formed from a "line opposite the midpoint of the tributary stream called the Tannocock Creek or Marshy River drawn due east about 5020 steps to Delaware, and from another point two and half miles upstream or north near Tilghman's Wharf a line drawn due east parallel to the first line and also to the Delaware state line, a distance of about two thousand steps. "The small stream called Plum Creek flows down the middle of this property," was recorded almost as a footnote. The entry did not indicate the original title owner of this land nor the seller. But it did indicate the buyer, one Mr. Samuel Cousey of Salisbury. The ledger also indicated a price of $1,800, which was paid entirely in cash dollars issued by the Merchants Bank of Baltimore. As he was reading the entry out loud, Will was getting more and more excited. His excitement was infectious and Minnie felt as if they were making great discoveries, although the data were just a small part of evidence which would be incorporated into their lawsuit against Maryland. Will laid out a copy of the map he had made and tried drawing lines to match the coordinates that the registry entry indicated. They almost exactly corresponded to the markings he had estimated from the treaty coordinates given for the reservation, except of course they did not include the north-south Delaware border line, the handiwork of Messieurs Mason and Dixon.

"Look at that, will you." he yelped. "We have a match. Proof that the state of Maryland was disposing of Indian lands!" Minnie felt pleased as well. Another small step in the legal process of reclaiming the Nantiquak reservation was accomplished. "And Maryland sold this for a pittance it seems," said Will. "Only about a dollar an acre. I would have thought that they could have gotten much more than that."

"Still, even at that price," said Minnie, "I'm fairly confident that no Nantiquak Indian got any of those sales dollars."

"You're probably right, Minnie. But I had a look at current aerial survey maps of that area and it's clear that a very large part of that land has not ever been cleared for farming, or may ever be as so much of it is situated in swampy territory."

At about the same time as Will announced his discovery, the other team of the county archivist and Lucy, claimed they too had found a sale that looked just like what they were looking for. It was late in 1835, about a year after the first sale. The archivist announced it with a simple, "This is it." And she began to read out the registry entry. "Sale of a tract of land in the nose of the county in the far northwest lodged between the Nanticoke River and the Delaware state line. On the 13th of September, 1835, the state of Maryland disposed of 570 acres of land to Henry Charles and Ashton Davies both of Salisbury, Maryland. Its southern boundary is an east west line of 2200 steps from the banks of the Nanticoke to Delaware. Its northern boundary is the left bank of the River. It is a tract adjacent to the earlier patented Cousey tract. They paid 500 dollars in notes drawn on the State Bank of Somerset to the state treasurer in Annapolis. Registered this day by J.S. Stevens, esq."

"That is as explicit as you want." said the archivist.

"Yes it is." said Will. "And these gentlemen paid even less per acre than the on the other tract. Must have had fewer takers in the interim year since the first sale. But I have to confess it looks to me like this land never was attractive for farming. Maybe they thought to use the plot for lumber."

Will asked that this second reference be photocopied and proposed to Minnie and Lucy that they drive out to the main highway which bypassed the town and grab some lunch. "The by-pass has effectively preserved the historic heart of this little town, and all the highway strip malls and fast food outlets are situated out here on the highway. But we don't have much choice of food. Only fast food staples, no local food or home cooking at all." They had lunch at a clean Kentucky Fried Chicken place which was mostly empty. "I wonder if KFC sources any of its chicken from the big processors here on the Eastern Shore?" asked Will as they sat down with their red trays at a fixed table for four. After eating they headed straight back to the records building—it was only a mile and half away. "This county is even smaller in population than Dorset and I think its population is in decline. Seems it would be rather expensive to maintain all the county court documents."

"I'm glad they do, for our case anyway." said Minnie. "Do you know what the population of this county is?"

"It is about twenty-two thousand," answered Lucy. Minnie thought Lucy had been very discrete all morning. She had apparently not noticed Will and her rubbing up against each other, or at least she had not made as if she had noticed.

"So it has a bigger population than the county my tribe lives in." Minnie addressed Lucy. "King's County was long noted as one of the only counties in Virginia with no traffic lights. I know a lot about the stretched finances of an underpopulated county. Schools go begging, road repair is put off, and there are no paid firemen. No business investment."

They continued scanning through the second ledger, but found no more references to property sales of land which would have been Indian land. At three they decided that they were finished. They collected their photocopies and thanked the archivist, who apologized to them as if she had overheard their earlier conversation. "Sorry I could not help you last week. Mine is only a part time position.

The county only pays for two days a week for this position. More important to have a county clerk."

"I'll be going off to the office. See you tomorrow there? Good bye Minnie." said Lucy before she drove off.

Will and Minnie got back into his Oldsmobile and started the drive back toward Bristol. Will took the business route this time, through the very heart of Salisbury. Minnie noticed many large Victorian brick houses from the end of the last century which suggested that Salisbury was more prosperous than Bristol. "It probably is, and has been for a long time." said Will in response to Minnie's observation. "It has benefited from the peninsular rail line up to Delaware and it's at the junction of the two main highways on Delmarva as well. They've got a university too."

When they got back to Bristol and stopped in front of his bungalow next to her Ford, they sat quietly in the car for a moment facing the question they had not wanted to address up to then: Would Minnie stay the night? Minnie wanted Will to invite her and he was thinking how to put the question to her correctly. He wanted her to stay the night also. Finally after a long pause, he offered, "How about if tomorrow we visit the county records office of Sussex County in Delaware to see what we can find there? It's also about an hour away from here. And after that we could stop in and pay a visit to the tribal association offices at Indian River?" This was the perfect solution to invite Minnie to spend the night and she quickly accepted his suggestion.

"I'll have to call my office and tell them and find out what else might be up there." she said. "Of course." said Will. "I need to check in at my office too. Although I do not expect any new business has blown in the door today. And I'll call my mother to tell her to expect two guests for dinner tonight, like last week."

They stepped out of the car, and Minnie took her overnight bag into Will's bungalow. After they had made their calls—Will also called to members of his executive committee at the Nantiquak Association--it was nearly six o'clock, and Will suggested that they watch the evening news on television. There was only local news broadcasts either from Washington or Baltimore. Both broadcast consisted of almost exclusively a litany of short notices about violent crimes, robbery, shootings, fatal traffic accidents, assaults, most often young black men perpetrating these crimes against other young black men or women. "There's no news, except for this. Nothing ever reported on happenings on the Eastern Shore. Rarely do they report anything about the inauguration of new construction, or new businesses opening up. If you watched too much, it would depress you." Minnie agreed. The local news she would watch from Richmond, showed the same kind of fare.

Will then proposed that they walk to his parents' house. As they stepped out onto the street, Will took Minnie's hand asking gently, "May I?" and they slowly walked the short distance together hand in hand. Minnie in all her adult life had never walked with a man hand in hand, not at school or at university, nor afterwards. Not since she was a little girl, maybe five or six years old, but for only a few years her father would take her hand when he walked with her in the evenings around the streets of Bowling Green. She found it now a strange sensation, but she liked the feeling. At first her hand did not seem to fit in his comfortably, but then they found a comfortable position that did not require her to hold her arm in a strange position. The key was to relax her hand and take a light grip on Will's. It was completely dark by the time they arrived on the well-lit front porch of his parents' house. The house had the warm aroma of roasted meat when they entered. Mar Sue came to the door and greeted them, directing them straight to the dining room, where Bob was already sitting at his place at the head of the table.

"Oh, ho." said Bob, acting a little surprised. "Looks like as long as Will's Injun Project continues, we are going to have a new member of the family." He said this and finished with a big smile. Then he stood up and with his arm he directed Minnie to sit at his left, with Will further down the table next to her. "I want to sit next to the pretty women in this house. Not my hangdog son," said Bob continuing to smile broadly. "So glad you could come and join us again Minnie."

And with that Bob sat down again. Moments later Mar Sue came into the room carrying a platter of roast pork with potatoes. "It sure smells good." said Will. Minnie agreed. She was thinking to herself what a nice family the Eames were.

Over dinner Bob and Mar-Sue no longer questioned Minnie too much. Will told them what they had been doing this week and last, and he especially stressed the state of the historic property documents, which amazed him. He was very excited to see title registrations of properties from the nineteenth century, and even from the eighteenth century. He told them about the talent for reading hand written text of the part time clerk down in Princess Mary. And he told them a little bit of the history of how today's counties were carved out of the original county of Somerville.

Mar Sue turned to Minnie and asked, "So what are you going to use these records for?"

"We are organizing a lawsuit against the states of Maryland and Delaware for the unlawful disposal of the Nantiquak Indian reservations." answered Minnie.

"You can do that? You can sue the state for sales it made more than a century ago?"

"Certainly. It may not be easy. But it has been done for other Indian tribes and they have won." "So that means you're a lawyer, right?" asked Mar Sue in dismay. "How did you come to be a lawyer?"

"It wasn't easy. Not many Indians can get into law school. Because you first have to complete undergraduate studies at a university—and not many Indians do that--then pass the entry exams, and the hardest of all is to pay for law studies. I was fortunate in that I got very generous scholarships because I was a qualified minority student and where I went to school was a state law school."

"Well congratulations to you, Minnie. You obviously are very talented and hard working to pass all those hurdles."

"Thank you, Mrs. Eames." said Minnie. "It was hard work, but perhaps the biggest hurdle for me was the lack of support I had from my family. You see I was the first member of our tribe ever to go to university, much less law school. And my father did not approve of either. He was afraid it would cost them too much."

"Minnie, please call me Mar Sue."

"What a coincidence." said Bob. "Our Will here was also the first one ever from the Eames family to go to university. But we supported him to the hilt. The only difficulty we had—and it was expensive for us—was that he wanted to leave college before he finished. To go join the Marines. Of all the stupid things. If you can imagine."

"I for one certainly did not support him in that little lark." said Mar Sue. "You know he could have gotten himself killed when they sent him off to Iraq."

"He went to the war in Iraq?" asked Minnie, a little surprised.

"Yep, I served one tour of duty there. Fate let me get out alive and unscathed."

"Yeah, and he learned a little lesson too." said Bob. "Like the advertisement says, 'the Marines want a few good men', but they don't much care if those few men come back alive or dead. So he returned and finished college."

"It was fate," said Will smiling at Minnie. Minnie thought again about fate bringing the two of them together.

"So do you work for a law firm, then?" asked Mar Sue.

"Yes, a sort of law firm. It is a firm that provides public service legal services to the poor or disadvantaged. In this case we provide legal advice and legal aid to Indian tribes. Our bills are paid from public monies and charity contributions."

"That's interesting. I've never heard of such a law firm before." said Mar Sue.

"Well it is the same concept as when a court appoints a paid defense lawyer or public defender for accused people who cannot afford a defense lawyer. It arose out of the Civil Rights movement. The Congress—most of whom are lawyers by background—recognized that poor people were not receiving any of the legal services or advice that they needed. So they voted to set up public service law firms funded by budget monies. Including those firms that work on Indians' rights."

"I see." said Mar Sue now baffled and more informed about the situation than she had wanted to be.

"I'll bet you make a damn good lawyer too." said Bob.

"It's very difficult work, I'm coming to learn." Minnie replied. "Difficult and tedious." "And we couldn't do our project without her." said Will.

Minnie noticed that he had dropped the word Injun.

"So we're so grateful that we have her services. As well as those of the others who work with her," said Will.

They finished dinner and Mar Sue announced, "You two will just have to stay longer now. You gave me such late notice, Will, that I had not time to finish making a pie for dessert. But I think you can wait here. It'll be done in an hour or so."

"Can I help you clean up?" asked Minnie.

"No, no need. You visit with Bob and Will." Minnie helped clear the dishes from the table.

When Mar Sue emerged again from the kitchen she came in smiling and bearing a large pie which smelled of cinnamon. "So apple pie it is, hot from the oven," she said. "Come on back to the table."

So they came back, and sat at the same places and Mar Sue served out the pie. Bob immediately asked, "Is there any ice cream to top this off? Pie a la mode, as they say."

"No there isn't. And besides, Bob, you don't need the extra calories. But there is coffee if anyone wants some." Everyone did, so Mar Sue left the table again and brought out four cups of coffee with a creamer and sugar bowl.

"You know, this could be a family affair." said Mar Sue. "Too bad Kate and her baby and her husband couldn't be here."

"So you have a sister Will?" asked Minnie.

"Yeah. But I told you that. She's two years younger than me and married to a guy who works up in Kent County. She just had their first baby a month ago or so. I haven't seen them since she delivered. So I have one niece."

"I have one niece too." said Minnie as she finished the last piece of pie. "And two nephews from my younger sister who is five years younger than I am."

"Would you like another piece of pie?" Mar Sue asked Minnie.

"No thank you, Mar Sue. As you said, I don't need the calories."

"Mom, I wanted to ask you. You know the big collection of records of classical music that you have? Do you recall if you have any recordings by the pianist Martha Argerich? Apparently she's an Argentinian pianist. Very famous."

"No, I believe so. But I don't remember the records I have except by the name of the composer, not the artist."

"I ask because last week, we watched a concert on the public television station. And this Argerich woman was playing a concerto. And I thought that Minnie bears an amazing resemblance to this Argerich woman. Although Minnie didn't think so. What do you think?"

"Oh, I don't know. Minnie's very pretty, and I think most successful woman pianists are usually pretty. But I can't think what Martha Argerich looks like. I think I've heard of her before. But I know of Van Cliburn, and I couldn't tell you what he looks like right now."

"She never looks at the album covers." said Bob. "And these days she hardly listens to the albums either."

"And you've never ever taken me to a piano concert, Bob." said Mar Sue sharply.

"Not too many ever come this way to Bristol." said Bob protesting with both his hands up. "Nor in Eastland either for that matter. Maybe Bawlimore. But that's an awful long way to go for a concert."

"I've never been to a live classical music concert," said Will. "Neither have I," retorted Minnie.

Mar Sue acknowledged them then turned to address Will. "You're welcome to look through my records albums if you like. Maybe you'll find one where she is the artist and there is a photo of her on the cover. But most of the time, when they put pianists' photos on the jacket cover they are photos taken in profile."

"Let's do it." said Will. He and Minnie went back to the big room and found a cabinet with shelves filled with record albums. They began looking through them, looking both on the front and back.

"You know, mom, these vinyls are rather an obsolete medium nowadays. It's obvious you don't buy music anymore because you don't have any CDs."

"I guess I'm kind of obsolete then. Or old-fashioned. And I don't buy CDs because I don't have a CD player. I have a perfectly good record player. Maybe you would like to listen to something while you're looking.?"

"Oh no, please, no music now." protested Bob, who went to the television set and turned on the knob on the set panel. "This is kind of obsolete too. We're just two obsolete people, Will."

Mar Sue ignored her husband. "I have some more records upstairs. I'll bring them down."

Minnie and Will continued looking. Minnie pointed out to Will that they needed to look on both sides of the album jacket because the artist's biopic was often on the back, and was often a full face photo. But after looking through about eighty albums they did not find any with a photo of Martha Argerich on it. But Minnie did find one album where Argerich was the principal pianist on the recording, playing in an ensemble, although there was no photo of her on the jacket. The same situation occurred on the other dozen albums that Mar Sue brought downstairs.

"I guess I have never seen a photo of Martha Argerich before that concert on the TV." said Will looking disappointed.

"Why is that important?" asked Mar Sue.

"Because he thinks from when we first met that I looked familiar to him." answered Minnie. "That he had seen my face or likeness before. And then when he saw her he thought that Martha Argerich and I look a lot alike. Or so he thinks."

"Oh, that's too bad we don't have a photo of her. We could compare it with you." "We'll just have to look on the internet to see what we can find." Will said to Minnie. Bob interrupted again, turning his head away from the television program.

"Minnie, that just means he recognizes pretty women. All pretty women. And he recognized you because you're pretty."

"Thank you, Bob."

"Think nothing of it."

After nine thirty, Will suggested that it was time he walked Minnie back to his house, but he also said he would be back shortly. Minnie felt disappointed at once. She would once more spend the night in Will's bed, but without Will. And this time he advertised it to his parents. She sighed as they left, although Will's parents were effusive with their goodbyes. "Be sure to come and visit us again, real soon, ya hear?" said Bob. "You're always welcome at our house, Minnie," said Mar Sue. She felt embarrassed. She sensed that they were trying to treat her as if she were a favored girlfriend of Will's. But she did not know if she was, or if Will had any other girlfriends. She couldn't ask him, and she could not think of a way of indirectly questioning Will about whether or not he currently had a girlfriend. They walked slowly back to Will's bungalow. Once again he took her hand in his, but at first he did not say anything.

"That was very nice, Will. You have such a lovely family. I'm glad you've invited me to join them this past week."

"You'd like my sister, Kate, too." said Will.

They reached the door of his bungalow and Will unlocked it, but paused in front without entering. "I'll leave you now Minnie, for tonight. Everything's set up for you as it was last week. I'll come by tomorrow at 9 and we can leave then." Minnie was disappointed but even before she could react or respond Will stepped closer to her, wrapped her in a hug and began to kiss her on the lips. His tongue then pushed into her mouth and the kiss became heavy and deep and arousing. He was holding her tight to him and she could feel the contours of his body even through her heavy coat.

How long does a lover's kiss last? To Minnie it seemed to last forever. His one hand pressing her toward him on her back, his other holding the back of her head. She nearly forgot to breath and broke off momentarily to catch her breath, but resumed kissing immediately. All the impressions-- her tongue and his wrestling inside her mouth, his lips pressing against her teeth, the pressure from his hands, her feeling aroused throughout her body, the feeling and scent of his face rubbing so close to hers, the warmth and snug feeling of the hug, her legs feeling weak—all were new impressions she had never felt before. After maybe six or seven minutes she felt excited and tingly, almost tipsy, as if she would faint. But she wanted more. And then Will pulled away, taking a big breath, and looking into her face.

"Good night, Minnie." he said tenderly. "Sleep well. I'll see you in the morning."

Her hands were still reaching for his, trying to hold on to his arms as he withdrew. If only the moment wouldn't end, she thought. But he had already stepped back and reached to turn the door knob and open the door. He nudged her into the house. She couldn't speak. She wanted him to come in with her, to continue to hug her, to continue to kiss her. But she couldn't say anything out of the jumble of feelings and emotions that were sweeping through her everywhere.

"It was a wonderful day with you." he said taking another step back.

"Good night, again. Lock the door behind you." And in the next moment, still in an elated daze, Minnie found herself inside the house looking through the porthole window in the door at the retreating silhouette figure of Will as he slowly walked away until he had completely disappeared into the murk of the night. This night it was even more difficult to fall asleep than it had been the week before. She was too aroused, thinking about all the little details of the day just passed, going over in her mind's eye the expressions on Will's face as he had said something, whether simple or explanatory. She finally slipped into a dreamless sleep, but it felt to her as if it were after hours of flailing and hearing over and over again Will's words, 'wonderful day'.

The next morning Minnie awoke moist all over and with feelings of deep satisfaction, rapture, and contentment. She had not experienced anything like the feelings she had in those first minutes after she awakening. She felt almost as if she had had a nocturnal visit by an unseen tender lover. It was all about Will, and her emotions began to stir as soon as she thought about him. He was coming soon to meet her. This was his bed, his warm covers, his spare room. She was surrounded and seemingly held close by him even in his physical absence. She felt joined to him. When she washed herself, she felt sensitized. She could not wait to touch him again, to hear his voice again, to be next to him. What yearning she felt in those few hours until he knocked on the front door again.

"Morning Minnie. Are you ready to start?" said Will as he stepped in the door. She was ready, all she had to do was to grab her brief case and put on her heavy coat.

"I hope you slept well last night. I certainly did. The extra bed in my parents' house is more comfortable than mine, I'm afraid. And I had such pleasant dreams."

He took her coat from the hook and helped her put it on. And they stepped out and got into Will's car.

"So now we're off for Centreville, Delaware. I've never been there before. It's more than an hour away because of slow roads. I had to do some research on the history of Delaware because so much of our tribe's story occurs there. And there was a lot I did not know about Delaware and especially

the southern Suffolk County where we're heading now."

As they got underway they drove through the town's main highway "strip" on Highway 50 and turned off onto a secondary highway that followed the Choptico River. Will continued, "It seems that shortly after Delaware became a state it was decided to build Centreville as a centrally situated county seat. It was called that because it is the very center of the county. It is supposed to be at a point where no place in the county is more than sixteen miles from the county seat. And they built it with a circle at its very center. The courthouse is located on that circle."

Minnie recognized that Will had fallen into his lecturing salesman mode of speech. She didn't mind. He delivered this information with the enthusiasm of someone who's made a recent fascinating discovery. After about fifteen minutes driving on a flat three lane road that ran along a fair number of single story white clapboard houses standing amongst oaks and maple trees and with bare, plowed fields behind them, Will pointed to a road that exited to the right. "Down that road just a short ways, is my grand uncle's farm." The sun was

"Your grand uncle is still living on a farm here?" asked Minnie. "I'm a little surprised. How old is he? He must be ancient. And still a farmer?"

"He's living; must be about eighty five plus some. Didn't your late father have any uncles?"

"Yes a few, but I never knew any of them. The last of them must've died while I was still a little girl."

"Well, mine is still living. Just barely. When you come here again, I'll have to introduce you and show you the farm. He's the oldest surviving son of my Indian great grandmother. He'd be pleased to meet you."

"I'd like that. Indian families in my tribe may be big, but they are not so extended. Because life expectancy is so low, especially for the men."

After passing that road to the farm of Will's great uncle, the road became a wide two lane highway. On both sides of the road were an unbroken series of bare, dirt fields, some large reaching far beyond the road on both sides off to woods, some fields were small. On some fields there were tractors working with small crews of men kicking up clouds of dust. "They're preparing the fields for planting." Will shouted. Minnie had been closing scrutinizing the landscape and found it surprising. The land for the past twenty miles looked both more populated and prosperous than the hardscrabble empty lands in the counties around her tribe's own reservation. They passed through a small town with one traffic light in the middle of the town and three gasoline stations. And then they were promptly in the countryside again. Five minutes passed by. "And there's the sign saying we've entered Delaware." said Will pointing at a green roadsign. There appeared to be no interruption in the landscape. If anything the roadside fields became larger and the houses fewer and farther between. Minnie had to ask as she had continued to see these strange spindly looking structures in the fields that seemed to be doing nothing. "Oh those. They are irrigation pipes on wheels. They can be tugged around the fields by tractors to cover your entire field. They wouldn't use them this early in the season." After another five minutes they came to another set of traffic lights on a divided highway that crossed their road from the north and south. It looked to Minnie like a crossroads in the middle of nowhere. "That's the main Delaware highway that runs down the middle of the state. Oh darn. I forgot to check my odometer back there at the border crossing. I wanted to see if Centreville really was only sixteen miles from any point in the county."

Slowing down, they drove into a small town of single story wooden houses sitting on tree lined streets. They passed a brick school, and few brick churches, a glass and steel car dealership with flags flying over a large yard of gleaming cars, and a couple of gasoline stations. There were occasional concrete buildings that housed equipment rental and car repair businesses, and all the businesses that supported agriculture.

"We are here."

"That didn't take long." said Minnie. "It's farther from my house in Thornburg to our tribal reservation." And almost before she finished saying it, they were at the central circle in the middle of Centreville. Around the circle were imposing red brick buildings, a bank with its white Doric columns, a hotel, the historic court house, a church. In the middle of circle were bare trees not yet recovered from winter. "I guess we can park here and we walk from here." said Will. It was only a quarter past ten and the sun which had been shining was not screened by high pale clouds. The air was warm when they stepped out of the car. They had only a short ways to walk. They first stepped into the imposing courthouse building and a police guard standing inside the door directed them to the Court of Common Pleas which was behind the main courthouse about forty meters off the circle. Minnie could not exactly put it into words but the town looked unlike any small town that she had seen in Virginia. Will was thinking the same in comparison to Maryland towns.

After asking several people in the smaller court building, they were directed to a second floor office which had painted on its glass fronted door in gold lettering, Probate Records and Deeds Archives. Will introduced himself and Minnie to the clerk that was standing behind a tall, black counter directly in front of the door. He gave him his card from his title insurance business in Bristol and introduced Minnie as a lawyer working for NAILS in D.C. He explained the story of the reservations that were granted to the Nantiquak Indians by the treaty of 1682 from the king of England and his colony of Maryland. He then showed the clerk the map he had drawn with the approximate boundaries of the reservations, the one granted in 1692, the two granted in 1711, and the one established near Millville in 1705. "You see, we've been led to believe that these reservations were sold by the state of Maryland, or more likely Delaware, beginning in 1760 through the beginning of the 19th century illegally, without legal cause, and without the sales monies going to the Indians. We would like to see if the records of these sales still exist in your archives." The clerk looked perplexed.

"I'm not sure we have any property records going back that far here in Centreville," he said reluctantly. "As for the reservations, and when they were granted, I think you'd have to go the Maryland archives to find if those records still exist."

"You mean in Annapolis?" asked Will.

"Yes. I think the earliest records we have extant here are from the late 1760s, a few years after the county seat was moved here from Lewes."

"Maybe we can work backwards then from the current title holders to the original owner of current plots? You see here these areas along the Nanticoke River right next to the Maryland border, can we find out who the current owners are? On contemporary maps they are shaded green, as if they are parks or reserves. I have looked at those lands and they are all swampy areas next to the riverbank."

"Oh that should be easy enough," said the clerk. He then offered them to step around the counter and to enter a map room with a table in the center and chairs. "You can hang your coats there.

Have a seat. Wait a few minutes for me here."

"Maybe we've hit a dead end, Will," said Minnie.

"I doubt it. Don't give up too soon. This is just a snag. Probably he just doesn't know what all is in his archive."

After five minutes, the clerk came back in the room with a plats map of the southwestern most part of the state. "The property records are organized by what we archaically call here 'hundreds' which is most like the old English district name, township. The Nantiquak Indians for example live on the Indian River Hundreds."

He laid out the map on the table and pointed to the area which he called Cyprus Hundreds. It showed all the property boundaries between the small town of Laurel and the Maryland borders, west and south. With his finger he pointed out the property borders along the south bank of the Nanticoke River and the Brant River.

"Well, these you can see are as you guessed, state owned wildlife reserves and state parks. And these are privately owned. With these coordinate numbers we can find the current owners and then begin searching for when they, or their ancestors, first acquired the properties. I'll start with looking at these two properties between the reserves and this county road 20. Presumably they are farms. Be right back."

After a short while, the clerk came back carrying two file folders.

"Here are the records. This property of 150 acres belongs to a Mr. Simpson who inherited it from his father in 1970. It says here the records for his father's property are in register number 47, which I've brought with me. And if we find the reference page, here we are, it says the property was bought by a Mr. Albert Simpson in 1908 from a certain John Willingsby. And he's in register number 4. Be right back. You understand none of this has been entered into computer records yet."

"This is going to take a long time, isn't it?" asked Minnie quietly. "These records are not as easy to follow and find as they were in Maryland."

"Yes, it seems so. Different state, different system. Different property laws also. We'll have to be patient to see what we can find."

The clerk came back with two leather bound registers, one with the number 20-4 printed on its spine and another older looking one with the number 19-17 on its spine.

"Don't be misled by the numbers. This refers to records from the nineteenth century, and is register number 17, and so this is twentieth century, fourth register."

"All rather tedious isn't it?" asked Will half in jest.

"Yes, extremely so. But I didn't design this system. I only try and interpret it and find data."

By this slow procedure they followed the parcels that comprised these one hundred and fifty acres near the Nanticoke River to the very beginning of the 19th century, 1801 when a hundred acres were sold for $125 of notes drawn on the Bank of New Castle. The buyer's name was indicated but not the seller's and there was no indication of a prior title being passed. The registry entry also carefully included the coordinates and gave detailed reference points and number of steps, although it was clear the plot had not been surveyed.

"So this entry doesn't indicate the seller or show any transfer of title?" asked Will.

"Yes, that very strange." said the clerk. "I haven't seen a record like that before."

"Maybe that indicates the state was selling the Indian reservation lands?"

"Maybe. We can see here a transaction which occurred in the neighboring farm plot where clearly the seller and buyer are indicated. So this entry is clearly missing that information, intentionally."

So Will decided to put that line of property sales aside and look at another neighboring property. This next property took more an hour to trace it back to its original buyer. Again it showed no seller, but the buyer's name and the cost and the year, 1798, were entered along with an interesting detail which described the one hundred and twenty acres as "mostly swamp and forested land." This entry also included the plot's boundaries and entered them in a very similar form to the previous property entry, as if they were done by the same clerk.

"I'm not sure this information will help our case in a suit against the state of Delaware," said Minnie. "But we will need copies of these entries to take with us."

"We're finished with these tracts of original reservations lands, maybe we can find something on the sales of the plots on the Brant River." said Will. "Would your archive include records from the 1760s?" he asked the clerk.

"I'm certain they don't. The colony was only formalized and surveyed in 1760, and the county seat organized here in 1793, after statehood. You can see the old courthouse not even a hundred yards from here. Just beyond the brick zone. But we have no documents from the time of the old courthouse even. You'll have to search in the Delaware public archives up in the capital, in Dover. And I feel certain that all those records are on microfilm only."

"So, I think we've hit a dead-end here," said Will looking at Minnie.

"We'll have to send a researcher to those archives, then. Sounds like it would take a lot of time to search for records which may not even exist any longer." said Minnie somewhat disappointed.

"Let's catch a bite of lunch and then we can go on to meet with the Nantiquak team." said Will. If he were disappointed, his face was not showing it, thought Minnie.

They arrived at the Nantiquak Association building at about two thirty only to find no one else from the operating committee had arrived yet. In fact there was no one there but the heavy man-- whose name was Rick-- who manned the reception desk at the front of the trailer building. He was his usual unreceptive self who pretended he still did not recognize Will. Rick invited them to sit at the wobbly round table and wait, and he disappeared into the back of the building.

"What have you and the committee been doing in the past month when you haven't been doing this title research?" asked Minnie after they were left alone.

"We've been conducting the internal census of all the possible members of the Nantiquak nation, especially those who don't live here in the Indian River area and are members of the Association."

"How is that work coming?"

"It's been also very tedious and time consuming. And surprisingly we've met some resistance. Both from the Association and its members and from the other Indians. And it's slow work, because we are trying to collect family genealogical information from those who preserve the memories of their ancestors. We've collected a lot of information already. I'm afraid that we won't have sufficient federal census information for our application to the Bureau for recognition. The race laws of the last century pretty much precluded Indians from the census."

"That was a problem we had with our application. From what I can gather from some of my former colleagues, it is the major obstacle in the way of getting our recognition approved." said Minnie.

"Yeah, I guess our biggest task in all this is to build a tribe out of the shadows of their history, most of which is not recorded history, even when those who survive and think of themselves at Nantiquaks do not want to promote the tribe."

"Maybe they do, but maybe they resent the effort to build up the tribe being led by an outsider." Minnie said gently. She did not want to offend Will. "In the case of my tribe, there was also resistance, even though I was leading the efforts. There is some ambivalence about whether the Indian identity can or should survive."

A short while later, Carmine, Morley and Ronald, and another Indian man arrived. Minnie and Will stood up, the small reception room was cramped with six people in it. Rick poked his nose in from the corridor. Morley told them to move to the back conference room where there was more space. "And bring your coats along with you," he said almost as a command. In the conference room, the four took off their coats and threw them in a pile on a chair. "Rick," commanded Morley, "Bring coffee for everyone. Carmine, sit over there." He pointed to the dais table. "Miss Warrens, this here is Jack Stoner. He's also a member of the executive committee. Jack, Minnie Warrens is on our team of lawyers helping us with our legal needs." Will deferred to Morley, even though he was the director of the executive committee. Morley was the older man, and he was of course the manager of the Association. But Morley indicated that Will should sit at the head of the table and he himself sat to Will's left next to Carmine, and directed Minnie to sit to Will's right side. Ronald and Jack took seats further down the table. Morley continued to take charge.

"Well, we appreciate that you've come to check on us, Miss Warrens. I understand that you've been working with Will on the lawsuits to reclaim our reservation lands. Maybe you can tell us a little about what you've found out so far."

"Certainly, Mr. Norwood. As you said I have been assisting Will Eames in looking at the archival records which prove that the states of Maryland and Delaware sold the reservation lands that were granted to the Nantiquak Indians by treaty. A treaty by the way that should still be in force. The states were not compliant with that treaty and it seems starting in the late 18th century they began to auction off the reservations. The reasons and justifications why they did this are nowhere recorded from what we've been able to find so far. We could speculate that the states believed at the time that the reservation lands had been abandoned by your ancestors. And there is certainly evidence that large numbers of your tribe emigrated away from the Eastern Shore, for reasons that are also lost to history. But that is speculation. A more likely reason for their sale was greed, and the petitioning of local white people to the authorities to take these lands for their own use. There also seems to be no records of expulsions of any Indians who may have remained resident on the reservations, but we do have evidence that much of the lands sold from out of the reservations were eventually converted into farm land, some of the swamp lands were drained, canals were dug, and the forests cleared. And that these farm areas continue to this day. But we also see that a large part of the acreage, especially along the banks of the Nanticoke River and Brant River, remain in the ownership of Maryland and Delaware and have been reassigned as wildlife reserves or park lands.

So these were lands that they were unable to sell and which remained under the control of the states. One interesting fact that Mr. Eames and I were able to find is that the state has never established title to these lands, which were only a small portion of the total acreage of the original reservations tracts. So from this information we are working on two lawsuits that will seek to annul the legitimacy of those sales, and require that restitution be made to the Indian tribe." Minnie paused as if that was all she was going to say.

"This work is still ongoing," continued Will, filling the momentary silence. "We still need to search some more archives in Dover and Annapolis to see if we can establish cause or the states' justification. I expect we will not find that, and that will actually help our cause and complaint against them. So if I understand from Miss Warrens correctly we still have some ways to go before our lawyers will be ready to bring suit. But also if I understand the situation correctly as of now we have already establish cause for a claim of improper seizure and disposal of the original reservations. Am I right in this, Minnie?"

"Yes, you're right, Mr. Eames. And we've also discovered lands the states may have to restore to your tribe, lands which will not cost them much to transfer. That will help us in case we win our court case and compensation or restitution is required."

"So we're still working on this front." said Will. "Now we can report to Minnie what progress we are making on other fronts. First Carmine can you tell us about our internal tribal census and how far we have gotten?"

"Sure, Will." said Carmine. Minnie looked at Carmine and thought she saw in Carmine's eyes the same kind of admiration and attraction for Will that she herself felt for him. Then Carmine became more serious and concentrated. "We have started a comprehensive census to find all those individual families in Delaware and Maryland who might count themselves amount the Nantiquak. We have started by talking to people who can claim at least one quarter Indian ancestry. And we have identified places where these people live as they were reported in the recent U.S. census results, which were from 1990. From this data we concluded that around 5,000 people claim Indian descent in Delaware, and in the Eastern Shore of Maryland, all the counties, some 3,800 people claim Indian descent. Now not everyone in Delaware can claim Nantiquak ancestry. We estimate out of that 5,000, roughly 2,800 are descended from Nantiquak lines. The rest are probably mixed races or Lenapi Indians. As we have more than 650 members in our Association, we could be looking for almost 2,500 other possible Indians with Nantiquak ancestry. We've concluded that the overwhelming number of these live here in Suffolk County. But our problem is that this group probably does not live in the towns or cities of the county. And perhaps a large portion of this uncounted group were declared by the state or the courts of the time to be Negroes in the 19th century, to be in compliance with race laws. This was a split in our Indian River tribe that occurred at the time when the Association was first set up, to get a separate school from the state funded Negro school, where much of the tribe at that time sent their kids to school. So we are looking for these people who may still be in the Millville and Indian River region and we are searching them out by the family names which were identified in records from more than a hundred years ago. Once we find them and contact them we ask if they want to be included in tribe and if they would submit to a detailed interview about their immediate ancestry. We do not consider that they ever were Negro not when they sort of seceded from the tribal to keep their school, nor now through intermarriage. You can look at their faces and see that they do not have any negroid features."

"So this has been a long, slow process so far. We have interviewed thirty two adults so far who claim a quarter or more of Indian blood in Delaware. Most of them would gladly join the tribal, or so we've been told. So we're doing anthropological work, kind of."

Carmine continued: "We are conducting census interviews a little differently in Maryland. We started with recognizing that the Nantiquak tribe in the seventeenth century was not one village, and the next village was another tribe. No, we recognized that the Nantiquak tribe consisted of bands that lived in different villages all along the rivers on the western shores of what is now Maryland. And these bands sometimes had multiple settlements, usually based on clans, but these settlements and clans were not different tribes. So there were the Chicacoan band of the Nantiquak, the Manochkin band, the Annemessex band, the Assawoman band, the Pocomoke band, and the Askecksy band in what is now Delaware. But anthropologists have pretty much established that the Assateague Indians were not a band of Nantiquaks. They moved into the Maryland territories and then to Indian River fleeing English settlers in what is today Virginia."

Minnie was wondering about the scope of the Nantiquak internal census. What Carmine was describing was amazed her. It was clear to her that the situation with the Nantiquak tribe was much more complicated and the tribe much more diffuse than her own tribe. For one thing there was not the issue of racial intermarriage with her tribe, certainly not with black people. And her tribe was much more compact, living –if not on the small reservation itself –then in a very restricted area surrounding the reservation. But of course, the numbers of Massaponax were also much smaller.

Other tribes lived next to them either across the York River or on the next peninsula. They had all been once members of the Powhatan confederation almost four hundred years earlier, but they still considered themselves today to be separate tribes.

"So we have identified four small settlements that represent different bands scattered across three counties in Maryland, but all near Delaware. And we have started interviews at one of these settlements. These are places where previously there lived many tribesmen and their families, but from where most of the clans emigrated away from the Eastern Shore to New York or Canada, or to the West starting from about one hundred and eighty years ago. But although the histories say— histories written by white men— that they all emigrated away and have never come back, some few clans remained in place. They apparently were never evicted by the buyers of the reservations, neither by the original buyers nor their successors. And in some cases, they remained on lands that the states of Maryland and Delaware assumed because they could not sell the tracts. Their numbers did not expand. We estimate we are talking about two hundred people, including young children and the elderly. They seem to have culturally merged their small communities into the neighboring ones, primarily by joining a nearby church. Some send their children to schools but others don't.

We have begun the census interviews near a settlement called Indian Town in Wicomico County, which used to be called Injun Town and we should finish this week or next. We will next week begin at a small clan settlement on Will's plot of land. We'll call it Driggers Plot for convenience."

"Before I finish I want to convey to everyone that so far we have found that there are some who for various reasons are not too keen to join the Nantiquak tribal nation, especially if the main group are the Indians who live here in Indian River area."

"Even if they stand to gain recognition, legal addresses, and social benefits?" asked Will. "Have they been told what benefits they stand to gain if they are members of a federally recognized tribe?"

"Yes, we do that first. Although that is also a contentious issue." said Carmine.

"We've collected a lot of material already," said Jack quietly. "It's remarkable. Lots of genealogical materials that these clans have preserved. Mainly orally.

"It can all be used in your application to the Bureau," said Minnie.

"They are less intermarried than we are here." continued Jack. "It's amazing really what they hold in their memories."

"And they are uniformly poor. Very poor." added Carmine. "Just barely scraping by on subsistence incomes. They do not participate in the formal economy at all."

"That's why it is so important to get them into a tribe that is federally recognized," said Minnie. "To help them get out of such poverty and be sustainable as a small minority society. To help them with schooling, finding employment, getting medical services, getting food aid."

"Carmine, you and your group are doing a bang up good job," said Will. Minnie noticed that Carmine's face literally brightened up and her smile spread clear across her face from ear to ear. She suspected right away that Carmine was attracted to Will. And it caused her a small pang of jealousy.

"Remember, I'll be joining you next week when you come over to Driggers Plot."

"Yes, I remember." said Carmine blushing through her ruddy complexion. "I can't wait to work with you again."

"Yes, we work well as a team," answered Will. Now Minnie felt distinctly jealous. How could Will be publicly so nice to Carmine? She was so ugly. Was it just his way with people to encourage them and make them feel good about themselves. His salesmanship character?

"So what has been done about getting incorporated as a non-profit Indian tribe?" asked Minnie.

"I can answer that too." Carmine answered eagerly. "We have told the lawyer for the Association up in Centreville that we want to do this. He says it is not difficult at all and it can be done in no time.

And it's not expensive either. But he said it would be best if we held off until we have finished the census and we can include a list of all of the adult members of the tribe both here in Delaware in the Association and outside in Maryland, and those living in the clan settlements in Maryland. And we will have to put in the rules for tribal membership, such as minimum one quarter Nantiquak blood. And some indications of governance and functions of the tribe across the two states. This corporation can include structures such as the Association or our museum, or any other Nantiquak owned businesses, and the management and running of any future reservation lands. So we can give him our data and he'll make our filing for incorporation in Dover sometime in June. That's what we estimate anyway"

"That would be good," said Minnie. "We cannot make our lawsuit filings earlier than then, but we will need to have the incorporation done before we start."

"We understand. We'll have it done by then," said Will looking at Morley and then at Carmine, and finally into Minnie's eyes. "I guarantee it."

"All this is very good," said Minnie softly.

"No," said Will smiling like the cheerleader that he was. "We're doing a great job! Soon everyone in the Eastern Shore will know about the Nantiquak Indian nation. We will make sure that the press reports on it when we get our incorporation."

On the road back to Bristol Minnie forced herself to ask, "Will, do you like Carmine?" He flippantly answered, "Oh yes, she's a good girl. Quite capable."

"No, I mean…"

"No, I don't Minnie. Not like I like you. Not at all like that. She's just a young work colleague who's working with me on this project. Just like Lucy. I respect her, and encourage her too, in her work. You understand."

"She seems to really like you, though."

"Maybe. I give her lots of encouragement and approval. Which I feel certain she does not get from the men in her life. Certainly not from her uncle, Morley."

"Is that all you give me. Encouragement and approval?"

"Minnie, don't you get it? I really like you, I want to be near you all the time. I love hearing your voice, I love looking at your face, and being close to you. Do you get it now?"

Minnie felt upset. Already she was looking ahead to her departure back to Virginia and to her office, and the upcoming uncertainty of being away from Will for an unknown period of time. Her coat made her feel hot inside the car, but also she was feeling flashes of warm emotions. She could cry, but she tried not to. She couldn't face the long drive back to Thornburg. She couldn't face the emptiness of the long commute tomorrow on the train. And two days of sitting in the office, isolated, reading law texts. And next week more of the same.

Will changed his grip on the steering wheel and with his right hand took her hand. And then as if he could read her mind, he said, "Minnie, all I can think about right now, is when next we can be back together again. It makes it hard for me to keep concentrating on the road, like I should be."

Now Minnie began to feel her eyes tearing up.

"What would you say if I asked you out on a date?"

"I could like that. But what do you mean a date?"

"Nothing conventional. Not a movie and dinner. I was wondering if you'd like to come back out here next weekend and go fishing with me for rockfish? And then maybe we can have a fish fry. And if you really like fishing, we can go a second time on Sunday. And if you'd really like to go to a movie, we could do that too. What do think of that idea for a date?"

Minnie took a kleenex out of her purse and wiped her eyes. "That sounds like it could be a lot of fun. I'd like that."

"Then let's consider it a date. You drive out here next Friday evening after work and we can spend the weekend together. Fishing if you like. But most important being together. That would be Friday, the 13th. What do you think of that? An inauspicious day for a long date?"

"No. Not at all."

"But you'll have to bring jeans and outdoor wear, windbreak, sweater, topsiders or waterproof sneakers. Fishing can be dirty you know. And wet and cold. You know, I've never seen you in jeans or casual wear."

"I'll have to see what I have that is appropriate." she said thinking that she full well knew she did not have any clothes she could wear to go out on the water and catch fish.

As they drove into Bristol, Will suddenly proposed, "Before you leave, let's have a coffee at the Cedar Island. Okay?" She agreed. She could not think of a better excuse to spend a few more minutes with Will. They drove to Will's bungalow and Minnie put her bag in her car and together they drove to the Cedar Island situated on Highway 50. Inside it was a bit brighter than it had been the last time they were there and it had been raining, but the place was still empty, not yet Happy Hour. They sat at a small table next to the bay windows and ordered double expressos. Minnie draped her heavy winter coat over the back of her chair.

"I think we got a lot done in just four days," said Will. "I'm really pleased that you could come and join me and see our beautiful country here. And now I look forward to seeing you next weekend on our little 'date'."

"I do too. But I'm warning you I don't know anything about fishing. Or being in a boat, for that matter."

"Don't worry. There's nothing to it. And we have life jackets on the boat in case you're scared of the water."

And then almost as if Will was reading her mind, he said, "I know it's a long time until we see each

other again, but we can always talk on the phone in these coming days. I'll call you. And you can call me any time. I know I will call you. Just want to hear your sweet voice."

When they stepped out and approached Minnie's car, Will again read her mind. "Maybe you wouldn't be so hot if you took your coat off and put it in the back seat before you take off." "Good idea," she said and she did just that.

"Now how about a sweet send off?" And Will took her into her arms and began to kiss her passionately. Minnie felt her breath was taken away. After what seemed a long time of bliss, she pulled herself out of the kiss and said, "Maybe enough for now. Or I won't leave ever." She opened the car door. "I wouldn't object to that." said Will. For the second week in a row Minnie felt as if she were floating back home down the long road and over the Bay Bridge and the Potomac Bridge.

It was dark by the time she pulled up to her cottage. She suddenly felt that she was very alone in the world. She longed to be with Will that very moment, in his bungalow which looked so much like hers. But she would not see him again until a week from Friday, in nine days. It seemed to her like a chasm in time.

When she returned to her office the next morning, it seemed for a while as if she had been away not for four days but for weeks. This strange sensation took almost the entire day before it faded away.

That weekend Minnie drove up the short way to the Walmart mega-store in Spotsylvania. She was looking to buy a pair of jeans, a warm flannel shirt, a fleece pullover, a rain slicker and a pair of flannel lined waterman's boots. She had to try everything on because she had never bought or worn such clothes and she was not sure of her sizes for these items. The jeans looked funny to her and seemed to exaggerate the wrong features of her figure, making her hips and bottom look fat, and her legs looking like heavy columns. The flannel shirt did the same thing but in reverse, hiding the shape and size of her breasts, and exaggerating the width of her shoulders. And she had trouble finding a shirt with sleeves that were the length of her arms. Either they were too long or too short. Selecting the clothes that fit and looked good on her took a very long time, and in the end, she gave up and bought what came closest, but which she knew still made her look funny. The boots were hard to find because she did not know what would be best in the boat, which she assumed would have water sloshing around in the bottom of it. Finally she needed to buy a carry-on travel bag, because she would be taking clothes for fishing and a change for work and her overnight bag was not large enough for two sets of clothes.

After shopping she went to her mother's house in Bowling Green. There she modeled her new clothes and had to tell her mother that she was invited next weekend to go fishing in the Maryland Eastern Shore with a work colleague of hers. Her mother made no issue of the fishing trip, but she could not help laughing at Minnie in her new clothes. "Those look so odd on you. Like a Wall Street banker showing up to work in a garbage man's overalls." Minnie blushed. But there was nothing she could do. "Maybe they look funny to you just because they are brand new," said Minnie in a huff. "Have you ever gone fishing before, Minnie?" her mother asked still chuckling. "Do you know what to do?" "No, but father took me fishing two or three times when I was a girl. He said I was a terrible fisherman and never took me again."

On Sunday afternoon, Minnie got a phone call at her mother's place. It was her brother. He had been looking for her to remind her that the next Saturday they had agreed to have their quarterly tribal council meeting. The reminder struck her like a bolt out of the blue. This meant she couldn't go to Bristol on Friday, and couldn't go fishing with Will. The council meetings usually started at 11:30 and usually lasted about two and a half hours. What could she tell Will? She couldn't get out of the meeting. She'd have to postpone their fishing plans, and that meant she wouldn't get to see him for another week or more. She was so upset that she forgot that her brother was still on the line. "Minnie?" he finally shouted at her. "Did you drop the handset? Are you still there?" "Yes, sorry, sorry. I remember now. Thanks for reminding me." "Okay. Then we'll see you next Saturday at our usual place, at the usual time." And he hung up.

This was awful news. She would miss her weekend with Will. And for what? A meeting where she had no news, no developments or ideas for programs, and nothing to report. She could only face criticism. How could she tell Will? She spent the rest of the afternoon and early evening fretting about how to tell Will this bad news. Still after lunchtime on Monday she hadn't called Will with the news. Finally she got up the courage to call him in mid-afternoon.

Will answered his cellular phone in his usual chipper voice, greeting her straight away. "Hello, Minnie. I'm sure glad to be able to hear your voice."

She told him about the conflict of commitments that had arisen, and how she had forgotten about the meeting on the Saturday, and she apologized and apologized. And she asked if they couldn't postpone their fishing adventure right away to the next weekend. Will would have none of it.

"What time does you tribal council meeting normally end?"

"Usually no later than 2:30, sometimes earlier." said Minnie.

"Well, as I see it, you only need to miss Friday evening here. You could still drive out here on Saturday after your meeting? It should take two hours, maybe a bit more."

"Yes, I could do that."

"Fine, then we could go fishing on Sunday instead of Saturday. And on Saturday night we could go up to my great uncle's farm and spend the night there before we start the next day. You have to meet him. You'd really like him. And he has a housekeeper who is a super cook. She'll fix us a really nice dinner. And you could stay Sunday night as well, and leave directly for work on Monday morning, like a lot of other commuters from this county. So if it's alright with you, please do come on Saturday afternoon."

Minnie felt greatly relieved. "Yes, I could come then. I'd like that. Sounds like a good idea. Thank you."

"Oh, not at all. I want to see you, and this weekend I will only get to see you if you come for half of the weekend. And you know, I checked the long-term weather forecast and right now they're saying we'll get a lot of rain on Saturday. We can do without that. We'll see then what Sunday brings."

"Okay, that all sounds fine. Thanks, you've cheered me up. I thought we'd have to postpone fishing entirely."

"No, and with all the fish you catch on Sunday, mom can fix us a nice fish bake dinner on Sunday. You'd like that, no?"

"I really would, Will. But are you sure we'll catch enough for dinner for the four of us?"

"I'm certain of it. So certain that I think I will ask Kate and her man and baby to come along. Then you all will get to meet."

"That sounds nice. I'd like that."

"Good. So we'll make that our plan. And I'll see you on the 14th, instead of on the 20th. I like that." "So do I."

"And most important I get to see you again, sooner rather than later." he said enthusiastically.

Minnie felt so uplifted after the call ended. She had worried that he would quickly postpone as she had first suggested to him. But his optimism had shown through. He had not hesitated in changing the program and insisting that she come anyway. She had not ruined his plans at all.

During the rest of that week, she worked on some points of law for the Project Oyster. And she sent one of their research assistants to Annapolis to hunt through the Maryland archive to see what might be there documenting the Nantiquak reservations and any other legal transactions with the Indians in the previous 250 years. On Wednesday, Will called her. She instantly worried that he was calling to tell her of another change of plans, or a cancellation, but right away he quashed those worries. He just wanted to talk about things in general, and to report about their internal tribal census. She mostly listened, because she did not have anything to report to him. But she enjoyed listening to his voice and the endless enthusiasm he had for his project. On the few occasions she saw him in the corridors of the office, it seemed again that Ron Parchesi was making eyes at her, preliminary to flirting. She did not appreciate it or acknowledge his attentions. She did not think he was at all good looking. Finally Friday came and she left early to catch the first train out of Union Station.

Saturday's meeting was thankfully short. As usual she was the first to arrive, and after the others came in the day's agenda was shortened because no one had investigated the issues that they had agreed on in the previous meeting. She raised the issue of conducting an internal tribal census just as the Nantiquaks were doing at the moment. There was no support for the idea, but there was opposition to surveying for a wider membership in the up county for example. So she let it go. She would propose it again at the next meeting. She did not stay for lunch but excused herself to get on the road. It was rainy outside just as Will said had been forecast. That would add some extra time to her trip. She had laid her rain slicker ready to wear in the back seat. So it was not even 1:00 when she started out. She decided to call Will and tell him she was on her way. He was pleased to hear it and said he would forward to her arrival before four. "Drive carefully. There's a lot of wind with this rain." he cautioned before hanging up.

It was not to be. As she passed through Dahlgren near the Potomac River bridge, suddenly the traffic headed to the bridge slowed and came to a complete halt. In no time there were three lanes of cars standing behind her, everyone was boxed in. Within five minutes a few emergency vehicles came racing up in the left southbound lanes, which had been empty. So it was clear that traffic was not crossing from either side of the bridge. She estimated that she was more than a mile from the river. There apparently had been an accident on the bridge, but there was no information offered for the delay. She stood there for an hour, an hour and a quarter before a state policeman in an incandescent yellow rain coat came up to them on foot. "There's been an accident on the bridge. Traffic will resume shortly, but will be slow for several hours yet. We advise you to advance to the next turn and return back and find alternative ways across the river." he shouted out through a hand held megaphone. Almost at once the lane of cars in front of her began to move slowly. But apparently most of these had decided to turn back at a turnaround about two hundred yards from the bridge itself. Then the line of cars stopped again. But after ten minutes, her lane began very slowly to move forward. It took thirty minutes to get onto the bridge and over the water. She could not see anything in front of her. But after another fifteen minutes she saw that there were flashing lights, and people in orange rain coats and hats directing traffic one lane at a time past a spot where there had apparently been an accident. She was still on the part of the bridge where there low trusses, only three meters or so above the waters of the Potomac which looked black today. At that point where the two lanes alternated into one lane, to the far left she saw that a vehicle, a truck or something large had crashed and pushed its way through the concrete wall barrier on the side of the bridge where a shoulder would usually be. When she was just passing the accident site she saw that the truck had in fact pushed a car through the barrier and into the water. There were rescue vehicles still there near the gaping hole in the barrier wall. After she passed the accident site, traffic speed picked up and she was across by three o'clock. She shuddered at the thought of falling off a bridge, begin pushed off by a big truck behind you. The sight remained with her as she crossed the much higher and bigger Bay Bridge. She would be much later than she had said so she stopped once she was on the Eastern Shore and called Will to tell him to expect her at six. She was very upset. "Don't worry, Minnie. Relax and drive carefully and don't worry at all about when you can get here." said Will. "Situation beyond your control. Just take your time. And I'll see you real soon." His words soothed her a little, and at the same time the rain tapered off and it was clear that the winds were pushing the clouds off to the south.

She arrived at Will's bungalow at a quarter past five, frazzled and upset by the long delay and long drive under trying conditions. Will came out to her car. There was a light shower of rain falling. "Come in for a moment, Minnie. Maybe you want to rest or compose yourself before we go to my uncle's place." Minnie gratefully accepted. "I'm glad you made it safely even if that accident was serious enough to close the bridge."

Inside he gave her a big hug and a brief kiss, offered her a coffee, or the use of the bathroom. "No need to apologize. It's not your fault. We're still not late. What's important is that you're here safe and sound. In one piece. Maybe you want to rest for a while?" he repeated. After a short rest and a cup of hot tea with some cookies, they went back out to Will's car. It was not yet twilight. Will moved Minnie's things into his car and they set out. "Don't worry, it only take twenty minutes to my uncle's place." She recovered her calm sitting next to Will and began to feel comfortable for the first time that day. "This is where we turn, and in eight minutes we'll be there." said Will pointing to the place he had pointed out when they had driven up to Centreville. Then he turned off the highway onto a gravel road, the tires crunching hard on the wet gravel. They came up to a cluster of mature trees still not with leaves. And inside the trees was a very large wooden two story house with nine bays in front and high covered porch. "This is it." said Will. "You see we're not late at all. Not quite six and still a little dim twilight."

"This house is much bigger than I had envisioned," said Minnie.

"Yeah, and for a house that is a bit more than a hundred years old, it is in great condition. It is real top quality piece of construction. Come on in."

Before they could open the door, Phyllis opened it for them and stood there on the porch smiling.

"Welcome Will. We've been expecting you this past hour. Your uncle especially is anxious. Glad to see you again."

Will introduced Minnie to Phyllis in the front foyer and took off her spring weight coat and hung it on hooks. She was dressed as she usually was for work and Will did not notice that the coat was new.

Minnie was looking around the well-lit interior of the house. She was impressed by all the yellow maple paneling, trim, and woodwork.

"Come this way, Hampt is waiting for you."

Hampton was sitting in a wheel chair in the front sitting room; a light lap blanket was covering him. It looked like he was dozing, and the wheelchair perhaps exaggerated the appearance that he had shrunken. His head was very white and he had almost no hair left on his scalp.

"Uncle Hampt. We're here. Wake up. Here we are."

"I'm not sleeping. Already had my nap today. Just waiting here for dinner."

"And it's ready to be served whenever you all can get over to the table." said Phyllis.

"Uncle Hampt, first I want to introduce you to my friend, Minnie Warrens, chief of the Massaponax Indian tribe of tidewater Virginia."

Hampton looked up, with an expression of lively interest in his face. And he extended his hand. He looked into Minnie's face. And the smile faded away, and a look of consternation slipped over his face. He took Minnie's hand and said, "Come a little closer, my dear." while pulling her gently toward him.

"This is amazing, Will. This woman looks just like my mother, Mena. The spitting image as I remember her when I was young. Even her eyes are the color of my mother's eyes. Where did you find this Injun princess, Will?"

Minnie felt embarrassed and felt as if she smiling awkwardly and blushing at the same time. Hampt was still holding on to her hand.

"She's not an Indian princess. She's a tribal chief."

"Same thing, young man. Minnie, is that your real name?" "Well no actually. My given name is Mataoka."

"You see there. With a name like that. She's a princess. Or an Injun queen."

"One of my ancestors was the Queen of the Powhatan confederation." said Minnie.

"You don't believe me, Will? Run upstairs to the exhibit and have a look. There is a portrait snap of my mother dated 1918. It's in good condition. Look at it closely. And even though it's black and white, you'll see. Go on. You can go with him, young lady, while Phyllis serves out supper."

Will led Minnie up the stairs to the study where the exhibition had been laid out. He snapped on the lights. In one of the glass display cases, in the very middle there was a three by four inch portrait photograph of Mena. And that was when Will suddenly knew.

"When we first met, I thought there was something very familiar and attractive about you Minnie. And this is it. I had come here in November and looked closely at this photo. And it stuck in my memory. That is why you looked so familiar to me. Uncle Hampt is right. You look just like she did."

Minnie was amazed. She was looking into the face of an unknown Indian woman eighty years earlier, who was looking back at her as if she were the reflection in a mirror. She even had the same guarded smile. Perhaps she looked to Minnie somewhat younger. But the quality of the photo did not allow her to see the skin quality or exact coloration.

"It's remarkable how much I look like her. Maybe not quite as dark, but the lines in the face, the shape of the eyes and the cheeks…"

They went back down to the dining room, where Phyllis had finished serving all the plates and had just sat down.

"You're right Uncle Hampt. Spitting image as you say."

"Of course I'm right. I may be invalid and sick, but I am not demented and blind. Minnie you are the very angel of my mother, come down to call me up to heaven."

Minnie giggled. "No, I can't be your mother's angel."

"Will, you didn't answer me: where did you find this Injun princess, my angel?"

"I was sent to her because she is a lawyer who is helping out on my Indian Project."

"And if I might say something," said Minnie. "He came to me the first time as a kind of guardian angel, who rescued me from something I dread to remember. Just in the nick of time, too."

"Well, that all makes perfect sense. Destiny," said Hampton.

"Yes, and you know Will and I have determined that we are distantly related through the relations of my tribe with the Nantiquak four hundred years or so ago."

"Of course, of course. Will, you have to marry this girl. Close the ring, so to speak that started with my father and my mother. Right away. This is a very good harbinger, come to life." Hampton paused, looked at his dish, and then resumed: "Eat up. This is smothered chicken. Phyllis does a bang up job fixing it and it is delicious."

They began eating. Hampton ate slowly and kept looking up and staring at Minnie, who smiled at him each time. Will ate fast, as if he were very hungry, but said nothing other than complementing Phyllis for the delicious chicken.

"You know, when Will came up here last weekend to help me start the planting season, he told me he would bring a friend as a guest. He didn't mention at all what a very special guest she would be."

"Has Max started yet? With the planting?" asked Will between bites.

"From what I could see, just yesterday. The seed arrived on Wednesday. He's got some of the Injuns from Wicomico out on the fields even today. They should be finished planting the soy tomorrow or Monday, and then they'll start with the corn."

Minnie noticed that Hampton was eating very slowly and seemed to have trouble chewing. The very small portion which Phyllis had put on his plate was still mostly there. Hampton kept interrupting his bites by looking closely at Minnie.

"Miss, are you going to marry Will? You should. He's a good man, needs a beautiful woman like you to keep him out of trouble."

Will protested, and Minnie blushed.

"Well actually, he hasn't asked me, so I guess I would have to say no to your question."

"So what's keeping you, Will? Can't you see that you obviously are fated to have this woman for your wife?"

Phyllis laughed and before Will could react, she chided, "Hampton, you're misbehaving again." Minnie thought that was the reason for Hampton's mischievous expression on his face.

"Oh, all right. You're saying I too often try to arrange things for other people in my family?"

"Well of course you do. And the less often you see them the more you try." answered Phyllis now sternly.

"Fine. So I'll change the subject. Minnie, as you are my mother's angel sent to call me home, I want you to promise that you'll come to my funeral. I can assure you it will be soon. And I'll arrange it to be on a Sunday. In a church. You go to church, don't you?"

"I'll come, but really, it can't be soon." answered Minnie seriously. "I haven't gone to church in a long time."

"What do you know? I've made all my final arrangements. And otherwise I'm at the very end of my tether."

Minnie didn't know what exactly a tether was, but she guessed his meaning.

"So I am so pleased that Will brought you here, young woman, before it was too late for me." Will, Phyllis, and Minnie had finished eating, but Hampton's plate was still half full.

"I don't want any more, Phyllis. I'm just about ready for bed again." Then Hampton turned his gaze once again to Minnie. "You like this old house? I was born in it. I lived here with my mother and my grandfather when I was a child. And when I die, Will's going to get it. Did he tell you that?"

"No," said Minnie somberly.

"That's right and the entire farm too. This irresponsible rascal's going to inherit the whole pile. Quite soon, I assure you."

Phyllis now cut in. "Would you like some pudding now, Hampt? It's chocolate, your favorite." She turned to Minnie and said, "This old man's got a terrible sweet tooth."

"Yes, that would be nice. You can take this away. I can't eat any more of it." "Thank you. It was delicious, Phyllis." said Will.

"Yes," added Minnie. "What do you call this dish? I've never had such a delicious chicken dish."

"It's a braised chicken called 'smothered chicken'. I use the chicken's blood which I collect when I kill it and mix it in with the other liquids." Phyllis said as she was collecting the plates from the table.

Minnie didn't really understand those instructions. She didn't do cooking of any complication for herself, and she only occasionally helped her mother cook meals on the weekend. Again almost as if he were reading her mind, Will said to no one in particular at the table, "I don't do any cooking myself. Just heating food or re-heating things. I do grill burgers and fish on the grill outside, but nothing fancy. Oh and of course I do crab boils—but that's hardly cooking, is it?"

Minnie smiled at Will. He suddenly appeared to her to be much younger than he was. She wondered how it was he was able to seemingly read her mind so often.

After Hampton had his chocolate pudding, Phyllis wheeled him to his bedroom which was in a room in the back of the house on the first floor. "Well, good night youngsters. Hope to see you in the morning," Hampton said weakly as he was pushed out of the dining room. "Don't worry about making any noise. I can't hear it. I've been practicing sleeping like the dead for a while now."

That left Will and Minnie facing each other across the table confronted by a momentary silence. Will was the first to smile.

"He's a character, my great uncle. Isn't he?"

"He's charming," said Minnie thinking that was the only word that came to mind. "Adorable, I mean."

"He's long been a promoter of the family. Maybe because so many of his immediate family died prematurely and left him alone. His father died before he reached the age of five. And his first wife died young, as did his only son, who went off to war and was killed there. You saw upstairs the memorial museum he maintains of his family members who have passed away."

"It's interesting. Because he keeps the paper documentation of his family and ancestors. In my family and in my tribe, we keep only oral memories of ancestors. And that's so easily lost. I should write down all the ancestry information that my father told me about, before I forget it and lose it."

"Definitely you should."

"It's sad to hear him talk so openly about his imminent death."

"He's really very ill. Over the past four months I've seen him deteriorate very quickly. The doctor gave him only six months to live—and that was almost twelve months ago."

"Oh dear." said Minnie. "My father died of lung cancer. He seemed very robust and strong until he started coughing constantly.

And then from the time he was diagnosed till his death it took only four months, and he was dead."

"I'm sorry. I think in father's case we could say he died prematurely. Uncle Hampt has had a very long life and now everything is worn down and failing inside him."

There was another long pause. Minnie did not look at Will but instead was looking down almost into her lap. She was momentarily seeing in her mind's eye the scene where her father's body was laying on the bed in their small Bowling Green house. She remembered that she only regretted at that time that he had never had the chance to tell her he approved of her. Or to say in the last months of his life that he loved her and was proud of her studying to become a lawyer. She also recalled scenes of the burial, of her tribesmen digging into the hard sticky red clay in the churchyard near the reservation.

"There's no place really to go, but maybe we can take a walk down the lane." said Will.

"Let me clear the dishes to the kitchen."

"Fine, I'll give you a hand."

When they stepped out onto the porch, it was very dark. The skies had not cleared of the clouds although a chilly fresh wind was blowing. Minnie shuddered from the cold. There were no lights on the lane nor any street lamps on the road beyond. "I think we could use a flashlight." said Will. He stepped back in the house and in a moment came back out with a large beam flashlight. They stepped down the stairs and onto the gravel in front of house. There was water standing in puddles all around. Will took Minnie's right arm into his and with his right hand directed the flashlight's beam down the lane. They slowly moved off into the inky night.

"Is it true, what your Uncle said that you stand to inherit this farm?"

"As far as I know, yes. I haven't seen his will, but he told me he intended to do that some months ago."

"He's your great uncle. Why would he leave it to you? Were you close to him?"

"The short answer is he does not have any direct close descendants or heirs. He initially wanted to leave it to his nephew, my father. But my father did not want it, so then he decided to leave it to me, if I wanted to maintain it as a farm."

"So you'll become a farmer?"

"I suppose you could say that. Although I am not a farmer by background or upbringing as you understand. I'll be the owner and manager of a farm hiring professional farmers to work it."

"And you'll live out here?"

"I don't know. I haven't thought that far out. I don't think I could out here all by myself, like Hampt has for god knows how many years. Of course he hired Phyllis to live out here these past fifteen or so years, as a housekeeper and live-in care giver."

"It would be hard for me to live all alone out here so far away from everywhere."

"I agree, Minnie. Uncle Hampt knows that. I told him I might not live out here. At least not full time. We'll see."

Their feet made cracking noises as they walked across the coarse gravel, otherwise it was deeply silent. No crickets chirruping, no birdsong, no wind in the leaves, and no traffic on the road which was still a couple hundred yards away. The cloud blotted out the stars; the night was as if they were buried under a thick blanket. Minnie was thinking that she wanted to live with Will, but she could not see herself living out here on this farm. Will extinguished the flashlight and pulled her around toward him close into his arms and he hugged her. She felt her as if her heart were aching from the evening's talks; the story of Uncle Hampton's imminent death, the possibility that Will would move out here, her desire to be with Will, to love him and live close to him which did not seem possible. She was confused, but she felt secure in Will's arms. She never felt so deeply satisfied as when Will embraced her as he was embracing her just then. They stood in that embrace for what seemed like twenty minutes, but it was only four. They walked with his arm around her waist, his left hand swinging the beam of the flashlight down the lane. She was maybe three or four inches shorter than Will when she was wearing these flat shoes; she thought that they fit well together when they walked so close together, no awkwardness or bumping because of the different size of their steps.

She leaned her head onto his shoulder for a while, and that was comfortable too. They came to the road, and they started walking down the middle of the road back in the direction of Rosedale. They walked another hundred and fifty yards until they came to a woods on their left and the road made a slight bend. He tugged her over to the side and they stood under the even darker shadow of a tall oak. They hugged again and he began to kiss her and caressing her breasts under her jacket. But after only a few moments she pulled back from his kiss and pushed away his hands.

"No, not here. Let's go back to the house," she said. She was no longer thinking about Uncle Hampton or living in the farm house. She was feeling aroused and yearning to show her love to Will, but did not want him to make love to her there on the cold ground in the deep shadows next to a lonely road. They strolled back to the lane and up the three hundred yards back to the house, arm in arm again. The light was still on in the porch and they tried to quietly enter the house but shortly after Will closed and latched the door, Phyllis emerged from the back of the house.

"I wanted to show you your rooms upstairs and the facilities. I've laid out some towels for you as well."

They took off their jackets and followed her upstairs, Will carrying Minnie's carryon bag and a small bag of his own.

"This can be your room, Minnie." Phyllis said as she open a yellow, solid wood paneled door. "The former master bedroom. It has an antique four poster bed from the last century, but the mattresses are fairly new. The bathroom is that second door down the corridor." Phyllis took five steps further and on the opposite side of the corridor opened a similar door. "And this is your bedroom, Will.

There's a doorway inside to the study. I'm going to retire now to my room downstairs. I'll prepare breakfast at eight thirty if you are ready." Phyllis turned and went back downstairs. Will threw his small training bag into his room and then suggested to Minnie that they go back downstairs.

In the main room, he turned on the TV and tuned through the channels looking for something suitable to watch. But there was nothing. And the signal from the public television channel was too weak to be able to watch. He finally found a channel showing an old black and white movie. It was just at the point where Humphrey Bogart's face was held in close up getting ready to kiss a young woman whose face was not showing. "This will do nicely," said Will and he came over and sat on the couch next to Minnie.

He turned to her and moved in to kiss her. And then he began to caress her as he kissed her. Minnie was taken by surprise at the energy he threw into his kissing and his hands moving all over her body. She had to push back to catch her breath. And then she continued the kiss. His right hand opened her suit pants and soon he was gently rubbing her vulva. Again she reacted with surprise and alarm and had to take another breath. She also needed to push her hair out of her mouth. She had no idea where her own hands were; they were groping at the air. His kisses were intense but he interrupted to change his position and with both hands began to undo the buttons on her blouse.

She broke off the kiss once more, and again had to push her hair out of her face and mouth. Out of the corner of her eye she could see that he had a big erection that had raised his trousers. "Wait," she gasped. "Let's go upstairs. Not here."

Will got up, went over to the noisy TV and turned it off, and then he switched off the lights in the main room. Minnie straightened her clothes and stood up too, moving to the main foyer. She started up the stairs, while Will switched off the last of the downstairs lights and switched on the upstairs hall. At her door she paused. "Maybe you go to your room first." She whispered. She did not want to undress in front of Will with the lights on. And she did not want him to tear off her clothes and damage them. "I'll change into my nightshirt. And you then come back in five minutes." "In three," said Will and he headed to his room. She pulled her nightshirt out of her bag and quickly undressed, and pulled the nightshirt over her head, switched off the overhead light and got into bed with the covers pushed to one side. Then she switched off the lamp on the nightstand. She was already breathing fast and her heart was also beating hard.

Quietly Will pushed the door open. He moved very slowly probably because he couldn't see where he was stepping. Minnie was faintly aware of his black silhouette approaching. Then his arms hit the side of the bed. "It's so dark in here." He paused another moment, and then Minnie could feel him move onto the broad bed. It made a slight noise as it compressed under him. Then Minnie felt his hands touching her and tracing the outline of her figure. When they touched her bare skin, they were cold. She immediately felt goose bumps rise over her arms and even her thighs. Her hands were now reaching for Will, touching him and lightly stroking him. She realized he was completely naked. He pulled himself up onto her and began to kiss her again. One of her hands was scratching his back which seemed smooth and muscled. But after only a few moments he arched away from her and with both hands began to roll up her nightshirt. Once he had pulled it over her head,he began to kiss her breasts and nipples. Thrills shot through her body, she seemed everywhere excited to the touch, sensitized beyond anything she had experienced before. And suddenly she became aware that his fingers were stroking her labia and then her sweet spot, and the level of pleasure shot up even more. His tongue was inside her mouth again and once more he was on top of her. She shivered with pleasure from the soles of her feet to her scalp. It seemed her arms and hands were flailing in the air, but instead they were rushing around Will's body, touching, scratching, even pinching him. And then he made a move to enter her. The bed creaked.

"Careful," she whispered. "It hurts sometimes." She remembered the two previous times a male penis had penetrated her and she remembered what a tearing, searing pain she had felt both those times. But she did not resist his advance. And he slipped into her so gently and slowly that she hardly recognized what was happening. There was a little pain and then he began to thrust while at the same time he stroked her clitoris. She almost swooned from the pleasure. The sensations were so intensely pleasurable everywhere that she lost track of herself. Her mind was swept away in a flood of feelings and pleasures like she had never before experienced. He was no longer kissing her, she was aware of that much, but still she could hardly breathe fast enough. She lost all sense of time and even sensation of her physical presence. Instead she turned in a bright shimmering ball of electric pleasure, throbbing, shuddering, vibrating like a bell, thrumming. Inside her was a warmth that ran to her very core. Ecstasy! All the bands of control and self were stretched to breaking and beyond. An earthquake had run through her body. Love! unlike anything depicted in art. And these overwhelming sensations seemed to last forever, a thrumming in her head put out all thought of time or place.

But Will eventually slowed and then dropped off of her. A film of moisture covered her everywhere and she immediately felt a shimmering, the cooling effect of the sudden evaporation. She was breathing heavily, but shallow. But slowly her breathing and fast beating heart recovered. She was luxuriating in the continuing vibrations that pulsed through her. She lost all consciousness of Will who was snug against her. She had never felt a pleasure so intensely and she wanted it to continue, to last forever. After what seemed an eternity, she turned a little to look at Will. He was dozing and oblivious to her. She began to run her fingernails over his chest, gently, softly. The dark was so deep she could hardly make him out at all. "I love you, Mr. Eames." she whispered. But he did not respond. So she continued to study him, looking at his body and continuing to gently scratch his skin. Eventually she wanted him to embrace her again, caress her all over. She lay like that for some time, until eventually she felt a chill. She reached for her nightshirt, but it had fallen onto the floor and when she moved to get it, Will awoke.

"Come here, my love. Let's do that again." He was reaching for her. But then she noticed her mouth was dry and shortly after his caresses started again, he moved and then excused himself. "I'll be right back," he whispered. And he left the bed, put on his boxer shorts and left the room. Minnie had such thirst. She got out of bed and found her nightshirt and put it back on and got back into the bed just as Will came back into the room. "I brought you a glass of water." he said quietly. They groped toward each other until she found his hand and she took the glass and drank. She lay back and then heard the noise of the bed groaning again as Will got back in the bed. He reached for her and began to caress her again, pulling himself up close and tight to her. But now she was overcome by a profound torpor, a deep lingering gratification. She turned in the bed and fell asleep, Will's arms wrapped around her, his body pressed against her back.

She awoke to the faint puffs of Will's breathe on her neck. The room was twilit and dim but she could see all the features and furniture of the room. Will was still holding her. It was the most comfortable, secure feeling she could imagine. She turned toward him and he moved, still in his sleep. He was naked and she now could look at him and study all his features. She suddenly realized that she had for the first time in her life made real love. Now she knew for certain that pimply undergrad had raped her. Now she knew what real love making felt like, and it was the most wonderful thing in the world. She continued to look at the dozing Will, especially at his long limp penis. She touched it with her fingers and it promptly moved. She resumed scratching him lightly with her fingernails the skin on his chest. Eventually he awoke. She kissed him a darting quick kiss, and then kissed him again. With one hand she took his penis and squeezed. "Let's do it again Will." And they made love again, more slowly this time until they both reached a climax of delight and shook the bed and made a lot of creaking noises which she hardly noticed.

When they recovered, Minnie asked what time it was. Will did not know. He was not wearing a watch and he could not see a clock in the room. But it was increasingly light outside behind the window drapes. "Must be late." he said. And he jumped out of bed, slipped on his boxer shorts and stepped out of the room. When he came back, he was in a robe. "Good morning, love of my life.

It's after seven thirty." He came over to the bed and sat next to Minnie and gave her a kiss on the lips. "Maybe you would want to use the bathroom? Or maybe we can make love all morning? Over and over again." She snuggled against him and held his arm. He caressed her breast. It tickled her. "No, let's make love again, but not now." And Minnie pushed his hand off her breast, and swung her legs off the bed. "Such lovely brown legs. Why didn't you want me to see them?" She ignored him and stood up. She picked up the towel on the chair and went to the bathroom. When she took off her nightshirt, she at once smelled the odors of love-making all over her body. The musky, the salty, the salivary, the sweaty animal aromas. She took a shower to wash them all off. She was certain if she could smell them, everyone around her could smell them as well, and know what those scents were. As she washed herself, she became more aware of her body, and she inspected herself to make sure she didn't have any blemishes or deformities that would not please Will. Her breasts were too small, maybe her hips just a bit too wide, her vulva too hairy, her belly a little too brown, a little too round. She looked all over and to her alarm saw that the labia of her vagina were swollen and red, as if from too much rubbing. She could let Will see that. She was very self-conscious, especially of her brownish-coppery colored skin. Not white and as shapely as the white girls they always showed wearing bikinis in promotional ads for Caribbean cruises or beach vacation trips. Will would not like her once he saw her fully naked. She felt sure of that. She did not wash her hair because she thought it would take too much time to wash and dry and brush out. As she dried herself she checked in the mirror and saw that she was smiling, virtually beaming and not even aware of it.

Back in the room she dressed in the same clothes she came in. Then she went down to the dining room where Phyllis was already laying out the places. "Have a seat, here, Minnie. I'll bring out

Hampton now." After a few moments, she came back pushing Hampton in his wheelchair which she then parked at the end of the table next to Minnie. "Good morning, my dear. Did you sleep well?" "Like I never have before." said Minnie with a smile. "Of course, it's our clean, fresh country air."

Will came in a walked around the table to Minnie and gave her a kiss on the cheek and then went to his seat opposite her. It was the first time he had ever made a display of affection so publicly.

Hampton noticed and smiled but did not say anything. Minnie wasn't annoyed though with Will. She wanted to kiss him that very moment.

"So I understand that you're going fishing today. For rockfish. That's great. It should be a good time for it. The weather will be just right for you."

"I don't know. I haven't really ever gone fishing before out on the water."

"I suppose you could get wet. But Will will take good care of you. Don't worry. But you're going to go fishing in those clothes, are you?"

"No I will change into fishing clothes in Cambridge."

"That's good. Have you instructed her on how to dress for the boat, Will?"

"Yes. But we'll have to see what she has. She's told me that she's never gone fishing as an adult." "So that means she'll catch more than you. Professional that you are."

"No doubt."

Phyllis had made waffles for breakfast, but she gave Hampton two softboiled eggs with a slice of bread. She excused herself by saying, "He prefers that. Easier to chew for him than the waffles."

No one had ever prepared waffles for Minnie before. She was beginning to marvel at all the firsts she was experiencing since she first met Will. She found them delicious, much tastier and crisper than the waffles sold at the Waffle House in the Fan in Richmond where she had sometimes eaten when she was a university student there. "You'll have to show me how to make these, Phyllis. They are delicious." "Why thank you, Minnie. My mother taught me how to make them on a cast iron grill that we put over a wood burning stove. The electric waffle iron is much easier. Next time you come, I'll show you."

After breakfast Minnie and Will went back upstairs, packed their bags, and came down prepared to leave. In the meantime, Phyllis had pushed Hampton in his chair over to the foyer in front of the main door. They stood in the foyer for a few minutes saying their goodbyes. "Time for us to go, Uncle Hampt. Phyllis do you have my cellular phone number?" At first Hampton was all smiles, but soon he began to blubber and when he started Phyllis began to sob as well.

"My Angel Minnie, I'm following you out. Mother sent you and I will obey. Maybe, God willing, we'll meet again here on this earth. But you promised to come to my funeral for the final send off."

"Uncle Hampt, you're being too maudlin."

"And you young man, look after Minnie. Love her, and hold her close. Make a family with her. There's no better person anywhere that you could meet to love and care for than a real angel. She's a much better catch, than any rockfish you could ever hope to hook."

Minnie giggled. "You're really sweet, Hampt." And she kissed him on the head.

"Thanks, Uncle Hampt. I'll do my best. And if we catch a large rockfish, I'll ask Bob to send it up to you."

"We'll put it in the ice box for your next visit. But I'm serious, Will. You've got to take this woman and marry her, make a family, and love her forever. Don't let her go."

"I won't Uncle Hampt."

Then they left and got into Will's Oldsmobile and drove off. "He's a real character, isn't he?" asked Will as they turned off the lane onto the blacktop road.

"Yeah, and he really likes me."

"Of course. You're adorable. And you look so much like his beloved mother. I mean, I love you. It's not surprising that he sees the same things in you and loves you too."

"Do you?"

"Yes, Minnie. I do. I think I loved you at first sight. Just like Hampton, at first sight." "You always say the nicest things to me."

"I'm serious. From that first time, I could not take my eyes off of you. And I couldn't stop thinking about the next time I would see you."

Minnie couldn't bring herself to say that she had had the same feelings of longing for him and yearning to see him again whenever he was absent from her.

They got to Will's bungalow and took in their bags. It was ten o'clock and the weather was bright and cloudless with cool air. In Bristol she could smell the marine air which was not noticeable at

Hampton's farm. Minnie went into the bedroom and changed into her new clothes. She carried the slicker in her arm and stepped out to show Will.

"Is this more appropriate?" she said.

He looked at her, and to her surprise he chuckled.

"What is? What's wrong?" she asked feeling self-conscious again.

"Oh, nothing. It's just looks like you're wearing brand-new clothes straight off the rack. They look brand-new stiff, and they hide your figure completely."

"Well, that could be because they are brand new." she answered a bit huffily. "That's nothing. I think they'll do just fine. And I hope you'll be warm enough." "Me too."

"If it rains, with your slicker, you'll be plenty warm. And dry too. Let's go now to dad's house to pick up the gear and the keys to the boat. The bait and ice we buy down at the docks. I'll put the cooler in the car now."

Will loaded the cooler, and they left. At Bob's house Will jumped out of the car and quickly moved to the shed behind the house. He came back bearing three maroon colored rods and a long handled net. The lines on all three rods were stretched tight and the hook attacked near the reel. "These go in the back seat."

Mar Sue came out on the porch. "Hi, Minnie. So you're going fishing with Will? Bob is so jealous. Be sure to bring back some good sized fish. Remember, what you catch is what we eat this evening. And Kate and her family are coming tonight and look forward to meeting you."

"Does Minnie look like a lawyer now?" Will asked facetiously. Mar Sue did not understand. "No. She looks like she is a model for a female waterman." Bob had come out of the house. "Do you think she looks like an Indian chief in that get-up?" he asked also smiling broadly.

"Maybe not." said Will. "But maybe Indian chiefs out in the Northwest or Alaska who go out on the tuna boats look like that."

"Well, then. Minnie good luck catching some tuna."

"I'll try. But I thought we're after rockfish."

"Of course you are. On the Bay, as well."

They drove on a little further down to the wharf and parked the car in front of a shed like structure. "This is where I get our bait." said Will. "And there is the ice machine. Could you get two eight pound bags out of the freezer?" Minnie took the ice and put them in the back of the car. Will came back with two plastic tubes of bait and a sack full of drinks, beer and soft drinks. "Menhaden fish, this morning's early catch. You could eat these if you caught nothing else." Then he drove onto a bare jetty that jutted into the river and stopped next a wooden dock. The boats were bigger than Minnie had expected. "We unload everything here and then I have to park the car back off the jetty." He took up the bags of ice and the cooler from the trunk and took them out to the third boat out on the dock. "We need to hurry, because the tide is beginning to move out and that's when the fish bite the most. Bring the rods." In short order, they had moved everything from the car to the well of the boat. "You can get in the boat while you wait for me to move the car. Be right back." Minnie sat down on a bench inside the boat and wondered to herself what had she gotten herself into. She didn't know anything about fishing. And once she felt the buoyancy of the boat, she again felt a small panic. Her fear of the water. She would be out in deep, murky water. What would she do if she fell in?

When Will got in the boat he said, "There now, we are almost ready. But first some lessons."

"Here the back of the boat is the stern. The front of the boat is the bow, and you're now sitting in the well. This is a twenty three foot boat, very reliable. Whenever we're underway, that is moving fast through the water, you'll need to sit down here. Or you can sit on the bench next to me where I'm steering. The sides we call beams, and for now, this is the left beam, it's left relative to our moving forward in the water, and this of course is the right beam. There, under the benches, are the life jackets. You need to put one on and you'll wear it as long as we're out on the water. If it starts to rain and you want to put on your slicker, you still put the life jacket on over it. Here is the engine starter. You turn it like that to start the engine. The anchor line is forward near the bow. If the boat should capsize, that is turn over, or fill with water—that is very unlikely—you should stay with the boat. It won't sink. There are floatation cells built into the boat and we will have to stay with it until rescue comes. But it won't capsize, because it's my father's boat and he wouldn't allow it. We have flares there in that box if we need to indicate that we need help. That's all. Basic."

Minnie paid close attention, but she imagined from the manner that he gave these instructions what Will must have been like giving commands to his Marines. So self-assured, so confident.

They soon pushed away from the dock, and Will started the engine on a low blubber and the boat moved through very slowly through the docks and then into the open river. The sun was hazy and not warm, but it wasn't cold either. They left the marina and were out in the river when Will revved up the motor and turned sharply to the left. Minnie was surprised at how much bigger the river seemed to be when she was down on the water than when seen from the bridge or the riverbanks. Soon they were moving fast through the water and bouncing slightly sending spray off the bow and both sides. Minnie's heart started beating fast. She could hardly keep her bottom on the bench.

She was clenching her teeth and holding on to a gunwale railing tightly. The rods which were laid out on the floor were clattering. She was trying to suppress her fear. But it was fear mixed with thrill. Will's back was to her; he was standing at the wheel. They couldn't talk over the noise of the boat. For the next half hour they surged down the river, which seemed to open up and become wider, greener, and muddier in color.

The river banks continued to recede away from them. After a little longer, a low point of land approached them a little. Will pointed at it and shouted something but Minnie couldn't understand what he said. Then suddenly the water changed color to a bluish slate color, there were little wavelets running through the water, and the boat began slapping and bucking harder over them, sending much more spray off the beams. The noise became much greater. Her fear was redoubled and she held the railing tighter until her knuckles turned white. She began to pray that they would be safe. After another twelve minutes of this Minnie was almost ready to scream. But suddenly Will turned down the throttle and the boat slowed and then stopped in the water. It was rocking very distinctly from right to left. Minnie thought water would spill into the boat. "So now we're in the Bay. Think of it as a gigantic flooded canyon. The waters here are about forty to forty five feet deep and there is a branch canyon here that continues the bed of the river and falls into the Bay canyon. This is a very good place to fish for rockfish, especially as the tide is running out." He looked toward Minnie and seemed to understand that she was not paying very close attention. "You've turned paler. Poor Minitoaka." It was the first time he had ever used this diminutive name for her. She wasn't sure she liked it, but she let it pass. "So we'll drift a little while and then maybe put out the anchor a bit later." He picked up the rods. "And now we can start, the second most important business of the day." He set one rod down angled on each beam. He opened a bag of ice and poured most of the ice in the cooler. Then he opened the bucket with the menhaden bait. It let loose a big stink. "Whew, not so fresh. So look out there, all those other boats are doing the same thing as we are. It's a good time and a good fishing spot. Now let me help you put the bait on the hook." He released the line from the reel and pulled up a deeply curved hook. It seemed to Minnie to be too big. "Now in your left hand take the menhaden, hold it tight, it's slippery." Indeed it had a very oily feel. "In your right hand like this hold the hook and pierce it through the fish here, just below the gill opening and then out through its mouth. Only a small portion of the hook showing.

The fish apparently can see the hook if too much is exposed." Minnie suddenly saw in her mind's eye the time when she was six or seven and her father bent over her the same way and in the same assuring manner showed her how to put the bait on the hook while floating on the York River. It was one of her cherished memories of her father. But as her mind wandered a bit into her childhood memories in a moment of inattention the bare end of the hook snagged her thumb and pierced the skin enough to draw blood. She let the rod and line drop and in the boat and let out a little shout and took her thumb into her other hand, looking striken.

"Oh you've caught yourself. Have to be careful." said Will. He grabbed her hand and without a moment's delay pulled the hook out of her thumb and put it into his mouth. He then pulled a clothe handkerchief out of his pocket and had it wrapped around her thumb tightly in no time.

"All fisherman at one time or another in their careers catch themselves on their own hooks. You just started early. Fortunately the hook did not get deep and the barb did not get set. It's no different than a wound from a needle."

"But it stings."

"Exactly. Like a bee sting." They spent a few minutes waiting for the shock to wear off of Minnie's face and the hook's sharp arrow to fade. "So first time, a false start. Ready now?" Minnie nodded but looked sad. He re-baited her hook.

"Now you have to stand up, I'm afraid. Get your balance as the boat rocks. Take the rod in both hands here on the butt end handle, and let the line hang out over the water. That's right." Minnie still felt the rocking and funny sensation of buoyancy was unsettling. "We're not going to do any casting today, so don't worry you won't hook yourself. You're going to swing the line out a few feet from the boat and let out about thirty five feet of line. You see there in the middle of the line is a sinker. That's a weight that will take the line to within five feet of the bottom of the river bed. Here I'll help you." And he put his arms around her and held her and the rod. She immediately felt more secure and the rocking seemed to recede.

"Is this right?" she asked.

"Yes, perfect. Now you will swing the rod side to side and when the line is at its full arc, you throw it out like this." And the hook, bait, line, and sinker flew out about six feet from the beam and made a plonking sound. The reel squealed and ran out line. Will waited what seemed like forever, but in a little more than a minute he showed her, "Now with your thumb move this latch here and the reel stops. The hook will hang in the water above the floor of the riverbed. Don't let go of the rod.

That's always important." Then Will pulled his arms away from Minnie and he stepped back. "Put your finger on the line here, Minnie. Can you feel the tension coursing through the line? That is the water running by the hook and the fishing weight."

"How will I know if I've caught a fish?" said Minnie tentatively.

"You can't mistake it. We say the fish strikes the bait. And believe me you can feel right that through the line and rod."

Will moved to the other side of the boat and picked up the other rod and began baiting the hook. But he hadn't stood up to throw his line in before Minnie felt her first strike of the day.

"Oh, Will!" she almost screamed. "I think I've got one."

Will looked around and saw her line bobbing in the water.

"Okay. It does look that way. Now you need to set the hook in deep." And he took hold of her rod with his arms around her again. "You will jerk back hard like this." And they made a short jerking pull on the rod. The line again began to run a little away from the boat.

"Okay. You've got him now for sure. You can start reeling him in. Don't drop the rod." Minnie began turning the reel handle.

Will stepped over and picked up the net. Minnie was laughing with excitement, like she hadn't in years. She tried to turn her head to see Will but the rod kept bouncing and tugging back. It took what seemed like forever to reel the fish in. But then she saw the silvery line of the fish dodging through the water. "Yep there it is. Keep pulling it up." And then the fish was splashing as it broke the water, and Minnie pulled the rod so hard it jumped up in the air almost to the level of her face. Will put one hand on her rod and with the other waved the net under the fish and snared it. Then he turned Minnie, the rod, and the fish in net over into the well of the boat and dumped the fish onto the deck. It flapped and jumped, jerked and made a noise bumping around on the deck floor. Minnie was laughing almost uncontrollably. Will caught the fish in his hands. "Bravo, Minnie. The first of the day. Here sit down, hold it tight with both hands." The fish was cold and slimy. And it was still writhing hard. She feared she would drop it. The spines in its dorsal fin pricked her hand. "Ow, that hurts." "Yes, you have to be careful of the fin bones. This fish is about six inches. It's too small for us to keep so this is what we do." And in a quick motion he twisted the fish and the hook came out, and in one movement of his arm he threw it back into the water. "Will it live?" Minnie asked a little surprised. "Oh, probably. As you felt it was a long way from being dead. And it can still breath in the water. Congratulations. Now we start the whole process again. Need help again rebaiting the hook?" Minnie nodded yes. And they began. She loved Will standing and rubbing against her, holding her arms, or with his arms wrapped around her as they put another bait fish on and then tossed the line in the water again.

"Now you know what to do, it's my turn to bait up." said Will. Minnie could not remember a time when she was so happy doing something like this. She was so elated; she could no longer notice the boat rocking or the funny sensation of buoyancy running through the boat. Only moments later Will dropped his baited line in the water off the right beam. This time she had to wait before she felt anything other than the tension of the running water.

"You said six inches is too small. What size fish can we keep?"

"We won't keep anything less than twelve inches. But you know, there's been a moratorium on commercial fishing for rockfish. To try and let the fish numbers recover. We should only keep fish bigger than fifteen inches. The Indians here on the Eastern Shore couldn't sustain their traditional lifestyle, even with reservations, because the waters were fished out, and the shellfish all harvested until none were left."

"Our tribe's reservation certainly isn't sustainable, either with farming or harvesting fish and shellfish." Minnie thought how could something as big as the Chesapeake be fished out. She could not imagine the scale of industrial fishing, or shellfish collection.

"Will, I sometimes feel soft bumps on the line. What's that?"

"Fish nibbling at your bait, but not going for it."

After ten minutes like that Will suddenly jerked his rod back.

"Got one." Minnie turned her attention to Will and watched how he brought in the catch. He reeled it in and with one hand on the rod and one on a net pulled it to near the surface and netted it and put it on the deck. It was a much larger fish than what Minnie had caught. "Twenty inches I reckon." said Will as he grabbed it and pulled the hook out of its mouth. "Our first keeper today.

Take a look." Minnie turned around to see the fish's mouth gaping at her. Then Will tossed it on the ice. It was a pretty silvery fish with long dark green lines running down its sides and two yellowish dorsal fins. But she did not have time to study it too long. She felt a distinct strike on her line. "My turn." she said. "Remember to jerk the rod back to set the hook." said Will as he was re-baiting.

"Yeah, and this time it seems heavier than the last one." She began reeling in the fish and was aware that it was tugging back on the line, resisting. "Will, this one seems heavy." Will put his rod down and came over next to her. "I'm having trouble holding on to it and reeling it." "Here let me take it." said Will as he took the rod from her hands. He began turning the reel furiously. The rod was bent over like snared sapling, and it was jumping from side to side. "Minnie, you got a big one for sure. You know the biggest rockfish are about your size and weight, believe it or not." "Really?" "Yeah, and I believe in the last century they were even bigger, veritable giants. Sometimes you see their jaws on display."

Then Minnie could see the long silver line flashing in the water. "They don't fight all that much, but getting the bigs ones out of the water can be hard sometimes," said Will. The rod was bent over it seemed to Minnie almost to the water level. She thought for sure it would break. And then Will landed it inside the boat. It was big and it made a huge racket as it flopped and jumped and jerked over the deck. "Wowee, Minnie. You caught a monster. This fish alone is our dinner." said Will. He hung the fish from the line until it stopped wriggling. Then he took out a measuring tape. "Look at that, thirty one inches! Must weigh twenty five pounds, if not more. Minnie, you're a champion."

"No. Beginner's luck." She was so excited. "I wish I had a camera to take a photo of it." "Too bad they haven't put a camera into cell phones. That would be very handy."

So Will took the hook out and laid the fish on the ice in the cooler. It nearly filled the cooler by itself. Minnie couldn't help herself stare at it. Its mouth was still gaping for air. She had never seen such a beast, up close.

"Need help hooking some more bait, Minnie?"

She didn't but she liked the attention and the closeness. So they together put another menhaden on her hook and threw it in. Then Will went back to his rod and threw out his line. "We generally don't try to cast or throw our lines over head. When I was young, I once snagged myself with the hook in the back of my head. I can tell you, that hurt. Doctor had to cut it out with his surgical scissors." "I'll be careful."

They had twenty minutes or more when nothing happened. Then Will caught another fish, about the same size as the first one. And after another ten minutes he caught a third which was a little bigger. And not long after that he caught a fish that was too small and which he threw back. After almost an hour, Minnie again felt a distinct strike. She jerked the rod, and felt the fish resisting and running. She had it hooked. She began reeling it in. It was clear to her it was not as big as her whopper, but it took her a long time to bring it into the boat. Will applied the net and lifted it over the beam. Again she had caught a keeper. It was eighteen inches, and maybe weighed five pounds. "That goes to the ice," said Will. "And speaking of which, would you like a beer, a drink?" "No beer, but a Coke maybe." Will opened the second cooler and pulled out a can of beer for himself and the blue can of cola. "We usually drink RC Cola here." said Will as he handed it over to her.

"Are you having fun yet, Minnie?"

"You can't imagine. This is such great fun."

"It's especially fun when the fish are striking. There are times when you can sit for hours waiting on the fish to strike. Not fun at all when the sun is scorching."

"It's not too bad today." said Minnie. But the sun was still warm through the hazy white cloud. "There's still enough that we'll both have some sunburn by the end of the day."

"I don't need it."

"Do you turn darker or redder when you burn?" asked Will.

"Redder. But I burn, unlike say a black person."

"So do I. I was stupid not to bring some sunblock for today."

"Let's see if we can catch one more fish each." said Will and he returned to baiting his hook. Then Minnie put a piece of fresh bait on the hook and threw in her line too. This time, they waited. And waited. Will finished his beer and took another out for himself. "Another Coke for you, Minnie."

"Yes, please. I'm feeling dry today."

They sat forty minutes, and then both caught two small fish that had to be thrown back.

"I think that's all for today. The fish have moved on. The tides are changing. Ready to head back?"

Will put up the rods, closed the buckets and coolers and started the motor. It blubbered to life and they were soon rushing back over the water. This time Minnie did not object as much to the slapping and bouncing of the boat. Maybe it was less than in the morning.

They delivered the fish and the tackle and gear to his parents.

"Wow, you caught a monster here." said Bob upon seeing the large fish that Minnie had caught. "We certainly will have enough for a big dinner this evening."

"Minnie caught it." said Will.

Bob looked a little surprised. "And was she able to land it herself?" "She could use a little help. So I helped her."

"So she's already a better fisherman, or fisherwoman, than you are son?"

"Seems so. I promised we'd send a fish to Uncle Hampt. So put one aside in the freezer for him."

"Well, it seems I've got a lot of scaling and fish cleaning to do this afternoon. You should ask mom, if she has anything you could have for a late lunch." It was already well past two thirty. Mar Sue gave them some smoked fish on crackers along with some pickles and two stout glasses of iced tea.

Minnie felt ravenous, and still very dry. She drank two teas.

"Thanks, mom. We need to go to my place and get washed up." "Be back here before six for dinner."

Minnie was feeling as if she had fish slime all up her arms. And she felt sweaty as well. So she was ready for a shower. Again as if reading her mind, Will said, "And, you know, if you clean and scale the fish you really get dirty, it seems all over. The stench seems to cling to you for a couple days.

And the mess goes everywhere. Usually we scale the fish right there on counters down by the docks. Maybe we'll do that next time."

"I'd like a next time."

On their way over to his parents' at six o'clock, Minnie asked Will, "Did you buy a new hair dryer for your bathroom?" "Yes, I did. I thought last weekend you couldn't wash your hair because I didn't have one." "You were right. Thank you for that." She felt much more comfortable after washing her hair, especially after spending the day out in the salt spray. She did not want to feel self-conscious about her hair in front of Will's sister. When they arrived, Kate and her family were already there, and Kate was with Mar Sue back in the kitchen fixing the meal. Will introduced Minnie to his brother-in-law, Pat, and his five month old baby girl, who was cooing in a fabric leaner chair on a low table in the main room. Minnie looked at the infant and cooed along with her for a few moments. "I have two nieces and one nephew. You know?" she said to Will. "But they are not as cute as this little girl." "She's trying to cut her first tooth," said Pat, beaming with pride. Will led her by the hand to the kitchen to introduce her to Kate. Kate wiped her hands on a dish towel.

"Oh, I'm so pleased to meet you Minne. My parents have told me so many nice things about you. You are working with Will? How long have you known Will?"

"We met more than two months ago. And we're working together on a project to get the Nantiquak Indians recognized by the federal government."

"That's wonderful. But I didn't know there were any Nantiquak Indians left anymore." "Most of them live now in Delaware." said Will.

Minnie was feeling a little self-conscious. She was wondering if Kate could obviously see that she was much older than Kate.

"I understand you caught the big fish today that's going to be our dinner tonight. Is that right?" "Yes, but I thought it was perhaps too big for dinner."

"So you upstaged Will. Well done. He's so boastful about his fishing and crabbing achievements." said Kate.

"I don't know. Is he boastful?" said Minnie looking at Kate and then at Will. "I find him rather charming." Minnie was thinking that Kate did not like her, or maybe it was just that she did not approve of her. Was it because she was an older woman, or a dark Indian woman? She did not feel the empathy that she felt from Mar Sue or Bob. Maybe there was some kind of long term rivalry between Will and Kate, or resentment, like what her own brother felt toward her.

"Well, that's good. Anyway, we're having rockfish baked in foil. It's mother's specialty."

"Mar Sue is a great cook, but she still has not shown me how she prepares even one thing. And now I've missed how she put the fish in the foil and in the oven."

"You'll just have to eat it and guess." said Kate in a tone of voice that again seemed to Minnie to be less than friendly.

At the table, when they were all seated after Mar Sue had brought in the fish on the platter, it was Bob who took over the role of master of ceremonies.

"So Minnie, our guest tonight, was the one who caught this wonderful fish which Mar Sue cooked up for us. So Minnie gets the first and most delectable piece. And Mar Sue gets the second piece. The rest of you will have to scrap for what's left."

"It was Minnie's first time fishing in the Bay, and it was only the second strike of the day." said Will proudly.

"Beginner's luck, I have to say." said Minnie blushing.

"No, no," said Bob. "It's in your nature. You're instinctively a first class fisherwoman. You know, Minnie, I was real jealous when Will told me he was taking you out in my boat to go fishing, but that you wasn't going to take me. I could have seen your secret for landing such a big 'un."

"Next time, if Will takes me again, we'll take you too."

"Oh, thad be fine." said Bob serving another plate and passing it to Mar Sue for the potatoes and vegetables.

"No one's even mentioned that little Susan is on her first visit here." said Kate. "You're all ignoring her."

That was it, thought Minnie. She was jealous of the attention Minnie was getting from the rest of the family. Kate did resent her brother's latest girlfriend. And maybe even worse because she was an Indian. She was now on her guard.

"Oh I guess you're right, Kate." said Bob looking at mother and daughter who was kicking her legs in the air and ignoring the proceedings entirely. "But it's a little early to take her out fishing just yet.

Remind me in fifteen years and I'll be sure to teach her how to fish like Minnie does." "Why? You never had the patience to teach me how to fish for stripers." said Kate.

"You never said to me that you'd like me to take you fishing," said her husband, Pat. "Just say the word and we'll go fishing."

"In any case, we can't do that until Susan's old to leave with her grandmother. And she isn't now."

As people began to eat, Minnie was feeling self-conscious. There was a tension in the family and her presence seemed to bring it out. She felt a little warm on her face.

As soften happened Will seemed to be reading her mind. "Minnie, it seems you got a little sun today. I hadn't noticed earlier. On your cheeks, they are pinker than usual. I for one noticed that I got a sun burn noose around my neck."

"I do sunburn. Easier than most people would think. I don't have that melanin protection in my skin that black people have."

"I think the extra blush looks good on your cheeks," said Will.

A lull in the conversation fell over the table as everyone was busy eating. Minnie was strangely still feeling dry. She drained her tea and asked for another. It seemed she had been drinking without pause all day, but in fact she had sat in the wind and sun for almost three hours before she had had the cola earlier in the day.

After a little while, Will broke the silence.

"We had dinner with Uncle Hampton last night and stayed the night with him. Sad to say it, but he is failing fast now."

"That's really sad to hear." said Bob. "I'll take that fish up to him tomorrow. I'll tell him Minnie caught it especially for him. Phyllis knows how to fix fish in the way he likes it."

Kate now broke in, "Mom tells me you're working on an Indian project with Will. Never mind that there are no Indians here tell me what that project could be, Minnie."

"It's a project to restore the treaty status to the Nantiquak Indians. I'm a lawyer and we're going to go to courts to try and get compensation for the reservations that the tribe used to have."

"But I thought they all left the Eastern Shore or died out, or assimilated."

"Will tells me that this is apparently not the case. I myself I'm not from this area. I'm from Indians who have lived on the Western Shore in Virginia. We're a small tribe, but we have survived intact."

"So, then if most of the Indians here have either died, left or been assimilated and none of you speak your original language, what makes you an Indian?"

Minnie felt aghast at the hostility of the question. She had not heard such a question since a professor queried her when she was in law school interested in studying the laws on Indian rights.

"My looks for one. The long black hair, the ruddy dark skin, my Indian facial features—they are a racial identity as pronounced as the African racial characteristics."

"Almost Asian," added Will.

"That's right. And my family given name, which is an Indian name. And the stereotype things are true, as well. I like eating succotash—which is corn and beans mixed together. And other Indian traditions that my parents taught me. How to hunt, how to cook, how to make clothes from deer hide—I'm just joking about that. And like all Indians we can't hold our alcohol, and so we're hopeless drunks. So I don't drink—that's an Indian tradition; trying to be a teetotaler. But you're right, we don't do pow-wows or wear feathers in our hair. My tribe lived primarily by farming, raising corn, tobacco, beans and tubers. And by fishing for shellfish and fish that we caught in large sieve nets in the rivers, but not on boats. The Nantiquaks I understand were watermen and boat people. And apparently they still are, although they no longer make log canoes. In our tribe we caught and ate the fish that we used today for bait. Sometimes we even used the fish to fertilize our fields. And most of our tribe are now farmers. Is that enough for you?"

Minnie was almost angry at Kate. She was surprised to find someone who was so racist in a family that had seemed to so openly accept her.

"What's gotten up your nose, Kate?" said Bob. "You know the days of cowboys shooting up yelping Injuns are long gone, and those stories were all made up legends by Hollywood, anyway. Do you resent that you share Injun blood from my side of the family? You've never seen or heard me talk about scalping white people. Minnie's a great girl. And she is Injun because she was born in an Injun family. That's enough."

It took a long while for any conversation to return to the table. There remained small talk about Pat's job, which apparently did not pay very well for a growing family, clearing the dishes from the table, and the dessert Mar Sue had prepared, and the one that Kate had brought. On the walk back to Will's bungalow he apologized for Kate. "I don't know what got into her."

"She doesn't like Indians it seems, and she especially doesn't like me."

"Yeah, but she has always disliked the girlfriends I've had; even in high school. I don't know why exactly. Jealous of my love life?"

"She'll get to like you. But it doesn't matter to me one bit, if she likes you or not. Her views don't change my feelings for you at all."

Minnie took Will's arm and rested her head against his shoulder as they walked slowly. It was very chilly outside and wind rattled the bare trees which lined the roads all the way to Will's bungalow.

Once inside, Minnie straight away began preparing her travel bag for her departure in the morning. "What time do you think I need to leave here to get to my office in D.C. tomorrow?" she asked.

"I think 6:30 is about right. I don't know about how long it will take you to find parking once you get there, but point to point it will take two hours. There is both commuter traffic and the last stragglers from the Ocean City weekend bunch."

"So we need to set the alarm for 5:30?" she said.

"Sounds about right. Enough time to get dressed and have some breakfast before you have to leave."

She was feeling apprehensive about the drive and getting up early enough to make it. But she was suddenly apprehensive about making love again with Will. She wanted again to do it with him, she especially wanted his hugs and caresses, but she was still self-conscious about the opening motions. And when they went to his room, she still did not want to undress in front of him, and she did not want him to see her completely naked under the lights. She also still feared that there would be pain as he first penetrated her. And she wasn't sure that Will's bed was big enough for the two of them. But she wanted him, she ached for him, and when he hugged her and began to caress her still with her clothes on, she almost swooned, and then a shudder with the goosebumps again rushed through her. She passionately wanted him again to reprise last night. But she stopped him after only a short while kissing and fondling. Will was also aroused, but he was willing once again to leave the room and let Minnie undress herself and get under the covers and extinguish the light before coming to her. She did all that in a hurry, and loosened the sheets from under the corners of the bed. The sheets were cold when she climbed in and she turned off the light hoping Will would slip in with her soon and warm her up. And shortly after thinking this he came back into the room carrying two plastic bottles of water. He undressed there in the room which was not as impenetrably dark as it had been out at the farm so she was able to watch him. And then the pleasure she first felt the night before resumed. He was very careful and gentle as he started. But it seemed to Minnie in no time she was rolling in spasms of pleasure and she even was aware that she was moaning. The bed shook quite hard, but she did not take any notice of the noises they made. This was love. The love she had never had before and she now knew that Will was her one and only. She did not know how long they coupled, or when the passion climaxed, or when the tickling and electric currents stopped running through her body, but after a long time when her normal breathing returned, and Will had moved off on top of her, she was again dying of thirst. She drank from the bottle Will had brought in with him and fell asleep. Throughout the night, she in her half sleep, felt the embrace and warmth of Will's body close against hers. It was the most comfortable feeling, just what she had yearned for the previous weekend when she had slept alone in this bed and he was at his parents'. His warm presence even crept into her pleasant dreams, but she could not remember them after the alarm went off.

It was still before morning twilight, so there was only the dimmest light in the room when the alarm went off. She skipped off to the bathroom and dressed there in her office clothes. When she stepped back out of the bathroom, Will had switched on the light and was dressing. He was not at all shy of revealing his naked self in front of her. He was dressing in running shorts and in a thin, sleeveless athletic shirt and socks. He planned to take his morning run after she left for Washington.

At breakfast, before she could say anything about what was bothering her, Will jumped straight there. "Maybe you can come out here on Friday after work and spend next weekend here as well. I'd like that. Wouldn't you?"

She agreed that that would be nice. "There's nothing I can see that requires your work presence here during these next few days. And I just have to be with you. I think you understand that. So if you came we could have a nice weekend just being close. I like nothing more than being close to my Minni-oka."

"I feel the same, Will." said Minnie. He had made up a new name of endearment for her. She liked it enough. In university, some guys mocked her by called her Minnihaha. But Minni-oka was a clever combination of both her names.

"Kate doesn't like me, does she?" Minnie asked as she finished drinking her coffee.

"Seems that way. I don't know what got into her yesterday. It was both rather aggressive and obnoxious. I suppose she doesn't like the fact that she and I are both one-eighth Indian."

"Maybe. I wonder how she will be in future meetings. Does she like you?"

"You know, I've always had a hard time understanding the answer to that question. When we both little we scrapped a lot, like two tomcats going at each other with their claws. All the time. I had thought that we had outgrown that antagonism. But that doesn't matter. What matters is that I love you. And she can go off to Yarmouth, and maybe we never have to see her again."

"I would miss my sister if I had to do the same."

It was twilight when they finally stepped out to leave. Before she opened the door to get into her Ford, Will gave her a hug and a long kiss. She thought they must have looked funny to people in the neighborhood. She in her dark, winter clothes and short coat— going off to her law office-- and he, in his bright orange track suit, going off on a jog around the town's streets. As she climbed behind the wheel, he also gave her another bottle of water. "In case you get thirsty in the traffic." And after another quick peck of a kiss through the open window Minnie slowly drove off. As she drove the skies grew brighter and soon the sun was rising in her rear view mirror as she approached Kent Island in slow dense traffic. She suddenly felt a wave of happiness come over her. She felt so good and was feeling a delightful pleasure coursing through so many parts of her body that she almost did not notice the Baybridge rising up in front of her. She felt as if she floated to the office in the center of D.C. It was 8:40 when she was leaving the parking lot near her office. She decided to call Will on her cellular. "Will. I've arrived safely. I just wanted to say I love you and I miss you already."

"I love you too Minnie. You're the most special woman I have ever met."

"Well, that's all. I wanted you to know. Friday evening seems like such a long time from now."

"Yes, I know. I will be busy, but I will be wishing you were near me. Just like when we worked on the title searches."

"Me too."

The rest of the week at her office dragged by. She was completing her contributions to a lawsuit against Maryland after one of their researchers came back from two weeks search at the archives in Annapolis. There was another researcher working still in Dover Delaware at the state archives and the picture there was not so clear. The case against Maryland looked strong and on precedent 'winnable' but up to then they did not have a case against Delaware. During the week they had one meeting of the Oyster Project team, and not long after the meeting Ron Parchesi made a lewd pass at her, grabbing her by her buttocks. She was furious. And she reacted strongly and cursed him, telling him it was a criminal offense to sexually handle someone in that manner. Her strong reaction shocked him at first, but then he recovered his sense of self-importance and he laughed it off and went back to his office. At that moment she suddenly realized that when Nighthorse had done something similar and had propositioned her for sex in the office at the Bureau only a few years earlier she had been unable to react at all and show him her anger. She had that time only meekly retreated, feeling humiliated and powerless. Maybe her new love relationship with Will had changed her, steeled her to the unwanted attentions that she had lived with and tolerated earlier throughout her adult life. During one of their telephone conversations that week she even told Will what had happened, what Ron had done, and how she had reacted. "Good for you." he said. "He's a swine for trying to goose you. In your offices no less. He's trying to demean you by doing it where your colleagues could possibly see it. If you want, I'll come there and knock his block off for you."

"No need, Will. I think now I can handle him. Before I wouldn't have been able to. But I've changed I think."

On Monday after work she drove back to her Thornburg house-- the cottage which looked like

Will's—and began thinking about what Kate had pointed out. What was Indian identity in this day and age? And specifically, what were the things that made her Indian. Her answers to Kate were too flip, too off the cuff while sitting there at the table. She began to think about whether being Indian was a racial identity or a cultural one. The ideas swirled through her head through the entire two hours it took her to drive home. When she pulled up, her house looked forlorn and abandoned and that evening she did both some cleaning and the laundry of her new fishing outfit and her clothes of the last four days. Late in the evening she tried to think some more about the Indian identity issue, but she was tired and she thought about Will and her affection for him. But she also tried to think if it was right for a pure-bred Indian should have such feelings for an Anglo, even if admittedly he had some little bit of Indian blood. It was clear her was not Indian. So she thought it was primarily a cultural identity. She fell asleep before she could think out the issues in a more thorough fashion.

On Tuesday she resumed her commuting by train to D.C. leaving her car near the Spotsylvania train station. She called her mother to tell her that she would also not be coming over to Bowling Green on this coming weekend. "Must be you have a love interest in your life?" her mother said. "Your nieces will miss you. I miss you. But come when next you can." Finally on Friday morning she drove up all the way to Washington and parked in the nearby garage where she had parked on Monday.

She had packed her casual non-work clothes, a change for the office for Monday, and she brought also her new set of jeans and checked flannel shirt. In addition she brought her own toiletries, shampoo, and lotions which she would leave at Will's house after the weekend. On the drive up I-95 on Friday morning she was already getting excited at the prospect of seeing Will soon. The day passed by slowly and at three she called Will to tell him she would be leaving at five pm. "Great, you can probably get here by seven, before dark."

And she did. But the commuter traffic got in her way. It was moderately heavy for the start of a weekend, and there was only a short backup over the Bay Bridge. This time the length of her Friday drive and the slow congested traffic irritated her. She was in a hurry to see Will, and the crawling commuters and weekenders were holding her back. She rarely could drive at even forty-five miles per hour. It was five of seven when she pulled up to the curb in front of Will's bungalow. Will did not step out of the house to greet her. Minnie took her bag from the trunk and walked up to the door and knocked on it. He answered right away, but did not stay at the door. Instead he rushed back to the kitchen. "I've got some things going on the fire." he shouted as he retreated. Minnie did not stand long in the doorway. She took off her coat and hung it, then took her bag to the bedroom, used the bathroom, and walked to the kitchen, as if she had always lived there, and it was her regular return from work, and she was not simply a visitor, not even a special visitor, but rather a resident who always commuting workdays to work. Will was busy frying fish filets in a large pan. "Minnie, you made it just in time!" said Will and he leaned over from the stove and kissed her.

"Everything will be hot and ready to eat in just a few minutes. Are you hungry?" She was a little bit. But it was more accurate to say that she was feeling a little rattled by the drive in heavy commuter traffic. "Maybe you'd like some ice tea?" She sat down at the kitchen table and watched Will finish up at the stove. "Yes, I'd like some tea."

"Surprised to see me cooking? Tonight we're not going to get fed at mom's house. I thought I'd fix something. I've made fish with hush puppies, brown rice and succotash. Something I think you'll like."

Will brought over two plates to the table and after setting them down, he gave Minnie a big kiss. "I'm so glad you came back, Minni-oka. I've been feeling a bit empty since you left on Monday."

"Me too. No one to hold and hug, when you're not near me."

She looked at her plate as she started to eat the fish. "What are hush puppies?" she asked.

"They are corn fritters. And actually, they are very popular throughout the south, and especially served with seafood. But I've been told by people who should know, that they're originally a way that Indians prepared a corn mash. So as you can see I have tried to prepare an Indian derived meal."

"I already like succotash, you know that. So I am very pleased you made it specially for me. I like fish too. These hush puppies are very tasty. I've never had them before. I think I like Indian derived meals."

"My friend over at Poseidon's Palace makes better hush puppies. We'll go there soon, after they re- open for the season, to try them. Which should be soon."

"I've been thinking since last week's confrontation with Kate, that I should look more into Indian identity. You know before I started at NAILS I was working for several months on this new museum in D.C. for native American Culture. Maybe they should include Indian food and cuisine. I think they would have a lot of material if they included the native peoples of all of North America."

"That's a great idea. Food is certainly part of a people's identity. Everybody learns in school that it was Indians that gave the first English colonists in America corn and turkey. So presenting native

American foods in the museum should attract interest. You should pursue that idea."

"Yeah, I think I might." She was still thinking about how to answer Kate's challenge about those things that made her Indian.

After dinner, Minnie changed into her more casual clothes. Will liked them. "You look really attractive in those clothes, Minnie." He proposed that as it was mild outside and not yet fully dark that they take a long walk to the riverfront. Minnie accepted and they set off at a strolling pace, hand in hand.

"I suppose a lot of people here in this small town recognize you Will, and even know you by name."

"I reckon so. My face is on billboards on Highway 50 about four miles east of here and five miles to the north. But I don't think many people will recognize me in this faint twilight dimness. Are you feeling embarrassed, a dark skinned Indian girl, walking with a white man who is someone well known in the community? It is obvious to me that you are often self-conscious."

"Is it obvious?"

"Yes, I am afraid so. It shines out like a neon advertising sign. That you're shy and ill at ease with yourself, especially with men. Your face so often says that. But you don't need to be self-conscious. I mean you're so good looking. You're really smart and accomplished. You're the chief of your tribe, for God's sake. And you know, I'll let you in on a man's secret. Most men are really attracted to pretty girls who act demure and unsure of themselves or shy. They believe they can more easily assert themselves, even impose their aggressive selves on the girl. I know, I'm a salesman. I see the behavior all the time. I pitch properties to self-conscious women buyers entirely differently from how I pitch them to assertive, self confident men."

Will, you know you so often seem to read my mind. Understand my thoughts when I am having them. How do you do that?"

"By careful observation. I have learned that people's facial expressions don't reflect emotions—as is widely believed—but that they reflect what a person is thinking about how to proceed, how to react to the situation they find themselves in. So those expressions instead say things like, 'How do I get out of here', or 'I want to hit this guy', or 'I'm so confused', or 'this conversation has got to stop', or 'how can tell this guy, I want him to kiss me'"

"So you used these techniques then to seduce me?"

"Yes, of course. I was attracted to you, from the first moment I first saw you. And I thought I saw pretty quickly that you were likewise attracted to me too. But I couldn't figure out why. You

weren't flirting, but you were sending signals. So I was paying very close attention to your words and your expressions and body language. Everything to give me some insight. But everything I've said about you being pretty and talented, and all that. I really mean them. I haven't been flattering you and manipulating your self-consciousness."

Minnie stopped where they were and threw her arms around him. "Then you know, William Eames, that I especially like it when you hug me and I'm in your arms."

"I've come to realize that. And what's more I like it too. You can hug me as much as you like. I'll always reciprocate."

They walked along the river, but the path did not get closer than twenty feet. From the pavement there was marshy trimmed grass growing on soft ground which was generously supplied with worm hills. It was not suitable for sitting on and there were no benches. They walked past the wharf and the marina, which were well illuminated. Although the air was chilly there were already insects whirling around the lamps. After almost two hours stroll they went back to the bungalow. "You can understand this is a small town, and there really is not much night life at all. Except maybe at the McDonalds on Highway 50, or the Cedar Island Bar and Restaurant. They might have a singer on Friday nights. Soon the softball season will start and they play in the evenings under the lights."

"I understand, Will. The town of Bowling Green where I grew up is even smaller than Bristol and is also without much of any nightlife. It's so small it doesn't have even a movie theater or a hospital."

"Neither do we here. We have a small hospital but if you need serious medical help in an emergency you have to go to Yarmouth which is about fifteen miles away."

"We have to go to Fredericksburg for our healthcare. It's twenty miles away. I'm a little closer to my doctor from where I live now in Thornburg."

"The community is shrinking, there can be no doubt. And the main street business district is shutting up. I'll show you tomorrow."

As they walked away from the river and back to his bungalow, Minnie looked at the stars now twinkling in the moonless sky. "They say our fate is written in the stars." she said. "But I have never met anyone who knew how to read the stars."

"I'm highly skeptical that the stars can tell us anything about a person's fate, his or her future, or much of anything useful. I mean understanding about quasars or the formation of galaxies, or black holes or supernovas or stars billions of light years away, that may excite astronomers and physicists but it doesn't give us a clue of what we will do tomorrow."

"When I was a little girl one of my great aunts told ancient stories that she had preserved from our tribe. One was about the great hunter in the sky, lassoing stars and racing on constellations. It was nice, but it wasn't a creation story, or as you say, it didn't explain much about our life. And it didn't inspire me—or anyone else in our tribe for the longest time—to become an astrophysicist."

At home, Will asked Minnie if she wanted a coffee to arm herself and some cookies his mother had brought over. They sat at the kitchen table eating the cookies with the hot coffee. Will was rubbing Minnie's free hand. "Your little hand is so cold, Minnie. We have to warm you up."

"It was really cold outside. I think I got a bit chilled."

"Yeah, it's a strange season now. You definitely can use a coat and sometimes gloves at night, but in the day it can get quite warm. But not warm enough for the beach yet. Warm enough that all the trees are now in bud. You'll see that tomorrow."

They continued for a long while just talking about life in their respective towns. And after 10:30 Will led her to the bedroom. Will began to caress and kiss her and even tried to start undressing her.

She once again stopped him and retreated to the bathroom with her nightshirt in hand. He undressed himself and opened the bed. She came out of the bathroom bashfully, put her neatly folded clothes on a chair and got into bed. She averted her eyes from looking at Will standing there completely naked. "Turn out the lights please." she said shyly.

Under the covers Will slipped off her nightshirt—"Now we'll really warm you up."-- and they made love again until they both dozed off to sleep exhausted. Throughout that night Minnie in half sleep felt Will's body near hers and she often felt secure and comfortable, and sometimes she felt a pang of arousal and a desire for more sex. But these were fleeting moments, interrupted by dreams, or movements by either her or Will in the bed seeking space.

As twilight crept through the windows the next morning, Will slipped out of bed and went to the bathroom to pee. He came back, took a long swig of water, looked at the clock which showed six- forty five, and then he slipped back under the covers. Minnie sighed and turned on to her side facing him. He only half covered her and spend a long time looking at her breasts and down onto her belly which gently rose and fell with her breathing. He did not touch her but his gentle steady breathe fell on her and after a while she opened her eyes and looked into his face. "You're looking at me. I'd rather you not." "Why? what I'm looking at is marvelously beautiful. You are beautiful and shapely. And perfection to admire." "But my breasts are too small. And they are too brown." "Not at all. We've agreed you are native American, not African American. You are definitely not too brown." She started to leave the bed, "Now, really. Don't look. You won't like what you see," she said. And completely naked she stood up and rushed to the bathroom holding one hand over her pudendum and the left arm over her breasts. She came back the same way and quickly slipped under the sheets again. "You looked." "Ah yes, and I saw a lovely bum. Suitable to copy as a statue and put in a museum next to Venus de Milo. I have never seen a lovelier bottom." She did not know who or what Venus de Milo was, but she smiled. Will now began to lightly caress her breasts. She felt they were very ticklish and she shivered and wriggled. Then she pushed his hands away. "No wait." She turned to her side of the bed and took a long swig of water, and then chased it with another. "That's better. You're lying Will, about my bum. It is not so beautiful." "I strongly disagree with you Minni-oka. Besides, when do you ever see it?" Will began lightly rubbing his hands over her belly and breasts. Then he suddenly lunged forward and licked the tip of one of her nipples. It tickled and Minnie recoiled as she giggled. "Don't do that." "Then missy, you'll have to kiss me on the lips." She did, and he rolled toward her and shortly after they were making love again.

They spent much of the morning in bed, alternating between copulation and play, examination and discovery of each other's bodies, dozing and resting. Giggling and occasionally kissing, teasing, and caressing. Will continually re-assured her that she was beautiful, shapely, proportional, and in every way a delight to the eye. Minnie also snuck looks at his anatomy, looking with some curiosity as his penis deflated. "I know, I know." he said. The male penis is not very pleasant to behold. In fact it could be said to be ugly. I myself have never seen a good looking penis on another man, and I don't except mine either." Minnie giggled. "But then genitals in general are not very good looking, on either man or woman. Maybe that's why so many peoples around the world mutilate them in one way or another." At another time she was tracing his shoulder when her fingers came over a large jagged cicatrice. She followed it down and there was another red scar on his upper arm. "How did you get these?" she asked. "In the Gulf War, near the Kuwaiti border with Iraq. I can't tell you what happened exactly. I was in an unarmored vehicle and there was an explosion quite nearby. And the shock waves threw metal shrapnel our direction and two small pieces hit me on my exposed right arm, which wasn't in body armor. I was kind of exposed you could say. That shrapnel sliced right through my shoulder, taking a big piece of skin, and a small piece landed in my arm. It was the most hideous pain I ever felt in my life. Fortunately I was in a field hospital being doped up with pain killer and patched up in less than two hours. But I was missed. You can look at me today, because I was spared."

"And I am glad of that, Will Eames. Do the scars ever hurt you?" "No. They're just not very smooth, and they are unslightly."

"Here's my scar," said Minnie as she drew one finger across her lower neck. "The one I got on the night I first met—or encountered—you."

Will had to look very closely to see it in the low light. "Like the thinnest of silver chains." he said and he kissed it tenderly.

Another time Will said, "I don't understand how you keep such a trim shapely body, Miss Minnie, when you don't practice any sports." "I don't know," said Minnie shrugging. "I don't eat a lot. I have never eaten as much as I have in the past three weeks with your family. I guess I should watch it." "More water?" Will asked.

It was well after ten thirty when they finally decided to get out of bed. They took showers in turn. Minnie emerged from the bathroom after her shower and she was positively beaming in Will's view. Her smile was not in the least constrained or bashful. "Maybe you're hungry now?" asked Will.

"After all that love-making, you could say so."

So they went into the kitchen and Minnie offered to prepare a breakfast of eggs and toast. "I'll show you what I can cook." she said. And with a little bustling, and confused searching to find all the ingredients and equipment needed, she cooked two very nice omelets for both of them. "You see I can do some things around the kitchen." "You're a super woman, Minnie." Will drawled at her. "You're going to have to show me more of your hidden talents." Minnie watched Will as he rapidly ate his omelet. She was transported to a time almost thirty years before when she had similarly cooked a meal for her father and then had watched him as he voraciously ate what she had given him. She had not thought about the times when she would cook for her father, in many, many years. But then she also thought that her father would not approve of her undressing and shamelessly making love like she had to a white man. It had always been like that; he seldom showed her his approval of almost anything that she did.

After breakfast, Will suggested that they needed to do some shopping for food and for other unspecified things. Outside it was a bit warmer than it had been on Friday. But it was blustery and was a day suited for sweaters and windbreakers. And Will said those would be their first items to find and buy. Will drove over to the Walmart on Highway 50 and in no time found a lavender windbreaker and a loose knit white sweater that fit Minnie just fine. He insisted on paying for them. She put them on before leaving the store, and looked at her reflection in the sliding glass doors as they left. She thought the jacket looked super on her. It seemed that shade of lavender was just her color. Then Will announced that they'd go to Salisbury, about a forty minute drive away, but when pressed by Minnie to say why, he would not say. Except to say it was a surprise. When they pulled up in the parking lot in front of a Mattress Warehouse store she knew exactly what the surprise was.

"Yes, we need a queen sized bed for the two of us. The double sized mattress we're sleeping on now is too small." Minnie wasn't so sure. She liked how snug it was with Will in the double sized bed.

Together they tried out several different mattress styles. She thought it was funny to plop down together on their backs fully clothed there in the store, but apparently that's what mattress buyers did to judge which one of a wide assortment to buy. They agreed on a deep mattress with an extra soft top liner mattress. It would be delivered to Will's house on the next Tuesday.

Then Will drove into the downtown section of Salisbury and parked at a diner where they had a lunch of crab cakes and cole slaw. As they were walking around the streets of Salisbury Minnie did notice that nearly all the trees were in bud, as Will had said they would be. "In a week or a little more, the first fruit trees will be in bloom too." said Will. As they drove back to Bristol, Will said he was feeling tired. Minnie was also from all the exertions of the night before and that morning.

When they got back to the bungalow they both took naps, Will on the couch in the main room, and Minnie on the bed. It was late afternoon when they got up. Will suggested that they take a walk again down by the small creek that split the town and flowed into the Choptico River. They walked down his tree-lined street and then turned left on Bridge Street which was bare of trees and soon they were on a concrete truss bridge over a large still creek.

"This is where I have made a lot of my money, and expect to make a lot more in the coming years." He waved his arm to the creek banks where there were one or two recently built apartment buildings, and where there were another five construction sites.

"They will build these condominiums with boat docks, a great place to buy a second home for people who like to go out in their boat or yacht. There are plans for dozens of these apartment complexes all up and down the creek here. I expect I will be the broker selling most of them."

"So that's your alternate project to the Injun one?" asked Minnie with a faint trace of sarcasm.

"You're teasing me? Well yes. It's the biggest development in Bristol town in years. Almost as big as the resort there just east of town. And the developers need to sell the apartments they build. But it will be over maybe the next five to six years. It won't be all at once."

They walked down to the Choptico River where there was a green grassy park right on the riverbank and squeezed up against the Sunburst Bridge over the river. A Dorset County visitor's center stood in the middle of the park. They stepped in and looked at the exhibitions and display materials.

Minnie was not very impressed by the display which consisted mostly of tawdry advertising flyers and pamphlets.

"The County sees that its future is in development of waterside properties as second homes. I think that's mostly right. The fish and shellfish industry is exhausted and farming is in decline."

"You think there could be enough demand? I thought you said that vacationers were mainly heading to Ocean City for the beaches."

"It's surprising how much demand there could be. The Nantiquak Indians over on Indian River in Delaware sold off most of their bayside property over the past thirty years to developers who built second or vacation homes on the water. They all sold out to people from upstate Delaware. There are scores of houses there. And now the Indians don't have access to the Bay's waters."

They walked further on a boardwalk directly on the riverbank. It wandered under the Sunburst Bridge and to a second smaller bridge.

"I wanted to show you something. This was the original bridge built across the river. You can see it was a low truss bridge. There was a swinging bridge in the middle to allow boats going upstream to sail through. They took it out when they built this big bridge behind us. Now this old bridge is a bridge to the middle of the river on both sides. It's now a fishing dock. It's where I first learned how to fish."

"Maybe I should have started fishing lessons also from this bridge to nowhere."

They strolled slowly up the length of the low bridge which was quite narrow for a road bridge. There was only one small black boy with a simple rod fishing from the bridge near its end. It was almost six hundred yards to the end. When they got to end where there was a barricade, Will asked the boy, who looked like he was seven or eight years old, if he had caught any fish. "Yeah, five menhaden.

Ya wanna see them?" "No, that's alright. Good luck. Maybe you'll catch a striper." "Thad be great, misteh. Is that you girlfriend?" "Yes she is. Why?" "She don't look likes she's from around here."

Will chuckled and said to Minnie. "She isn't." As they strolled back the sun began rapidly descending.

"How about if we go to the Cedar Island for some supper?"

"That would be fine by me." said Minnie. "Or should I say, 'Thad be fine.' and smiled at her mimicking of the local parlance.

"Yeah, we do speak peculiar." said Will smiling back.

They walked another four hundred yards to where the neighborhood began to look drab and bare of all trees. It was an empty area behind the strip malls and stores on Highway 50. They crossed an empty lot that was covered with gravel and broken concrete and crossed the highway at a crosswalk protected by a light.

"This area is rather ugly," said Minnie.

"It certainly is. Typical of how so many towns and cities across American have developed along a main highway. Ugly is the right word. The proper setting I suppose for drive-thru fast food restaurants."

"In Bowling Green we have the same thing. Everything is tacky, looks very temporary, built to serve the army base next door."

On that west side of the highway two lots further was the Cedar Island Bar and Restaurant, where they had had coffee a few weeks earlier. The lights inside the marquee on the highway went on just as they approached. It was deep twilight. The marquee said there was a band playing that evening. "Do you know this group?" asked Minnie. "No, never heard of them." They sat inside at the same table as had they had before. There were more diners inside this time than last. A waiter came, offered them menus and filled their glasses with iced water. They ordered: a hamburger and fries for Will, and some soup and a seafood salad for Minnie. Will ordered a beer, and Minnie said she'd stick with the water. There was no music although two young bearded men were setting up equipment next to the bar.

"Are you still feeling dry?"

"Yeah, a little." said Minnie. "You aren't?"

"A little knocked out. But not too dry. You don't drink, do you?"

"I try not to. I don't like alcohol, and I should say, alcohol doesn't like me too much."

Their food was brought out but the band still was not playing. Minnie thought her portions were too big. "I'm not going to be able to finish all this food." "Don't worry. You don't have to. No one's going to be upset with you if you don't." It was a family restaurant for the locals, not really a place for the weekenders heading to or from Ocean City. Minnie had been afraid that people might stare and gawk at her, a "colored" woman sitting and eating with a white man, but she needn't have been. None of the other diners paid them any attention. There were no blacks in the restaurant or any at the bar at the other end of the place. Yet she felt comfortable.

"This is still a fairly segregated place, isn't it?" she asked as her half full plate was taken away.

"Yeah, I'm afraid it is. You know that Maryland was a slave state until the 1840s, and Jim Crow race laws remained in force until World War Two. There are no conscious efforts to segregate and isolate blacks and colored people here, but it happens none the less."

"In Virginia I guess it's worse. People would not like that I, a colored person, would be eating with you in a public restaurant. Some might even take action to try and stop us. And if they knew that we were lovers. Well, you know it was quite recently the miscegenation laws were struck from the books. Most of those were aimed at blacks mixing with whites, but in practice the law struck at all races having sex with the white race, and that included Indians. I don't think I would feel so comfortable in Bowling Green or even in Fredericksburg."

They ordered some coffee. But Minnie passed on dessert.

"You were poking fun at the local dialect. That gives me an idea. Tomorrow we could go down to Crisfield and take the ferry to Smith Island. Now there they speak in dialect. I'm told it is a regional

British dialect from the 17th century. Sounds very strange to my ear. Would you like that? A day on the water?"

Minnie remembered the slapping and bouncing of Bob's twenty-three footer and she must have turned wan. Her expression told Will she was uncomfortable being on the water.

"Don't worry. It's a big boat. You won't feel the water at all."

So the next morning after rising early and taking showers and eating breakfast they left around eight to drive to Crisfield. She still had doubts, but she was willing to explore. The drive to Crisfield took an hour, and the boat was scheduled to leave thirty minutes after they arrived. Crisfield itself looked like a once prosperous place that for many years had fallen into hard times. Most of the houses were old and in bad need of paint or repair. Many were abandoned altogether and one street looked like a ghost town. There were very few tourists waiting for the cruise as it was still chilly spring weather, but the water was smooth in the sound during the forty five minute crossing. For the first fifteen minutes Minnie and Will stood arm in arm on the deck, leaning on the railing and watching the banks and salt marshes float by. Will was right; Minnie did not feel too much bouncing or heavy rocking of the boat on the open water. The last four miles of the cruise were in an area of flooded marshes where reeds and cordgrass grew on land that was submerged during high tides. It didn't seem to Minnie like habitable land. She imagined houses all built on stilts above the high water line. Finally they floated into a narrow creek and the docks of the island's sole settlement appeared. There were a few fishing trawlers moored, only a little bit bigger than Will's father's boat, and one long narrow boat with a very low stern and gunnels. "That's a boat for the watermen who harvest clams and mussels. They stand on the stern and use giant tongs to pick them up out of the muck on the bottom. They have to work in rather shallow waters."

On the island itself there was not much to see. The people in the main settlement where they landed were attending church, the men who fished or collected shellfish were already many hours back home and their catch already in the processing plant. This gave the village an abandoned deserted look. They walked through the narrow quiet streets until there were no more streets to be seen. At noon, the bell in one of the church steeples began to peal out. They went into an empty restaurant down next to the docks and had lunch of crab cakes. Minnie noticed that the waiter spoke a strange way, but she could understand her. As they were eating a second tourist ferry arrived and it seemed its entire contingent poured straight from the boat and into the restaurant. They made noise like a yard full of startled geese.

"I think the locals don't eat at this restaurant." wondered Minnie out loud.

"You're probably right. The people here just barely scratch out a living. Eating out would definitely be a luxury. Probably eating meat, which has to be floated in over the water, is too expensive for their budgets, as well."

After lunch they hired two bicycles and slowly began pedaling to see the rest of the island. It was easy pedaling because the island was absolutely flat. In several place the road went right down to either the water of the Bay or the black water of the tidal marsh. "This is scary place to live in when there are storms accompanying high tides," said Will. "I think the entire island is plunged under water in those times. And such storms occur two or three times every winter. But those who hang on here, I think, are a very hearty bunch."

They bicycled about two miles out, which pretty much ran out the entire length of the paved roads on the island. They saw one or two more houses, which looked derelict, a church, a number of docks some occupied by trawlers, an old graveyard, and not much more. Their return ferry ride was at 3:15 and they got back to the village with twenty minutes to spare. Minnie noticed a post office, and was a little surprised. "Probably the most important building on the island." said Will. "And kind of a federal subsidy. I'm sure it loses tons of money being here. But the locals order a lot of their purchases for mail delivery. So it's where they are supplied from."

At the dock there were obviously some local men working. Minnie could tell by their dress, and she heard them speaking amongst themselves. She could not understand a word they said. The pronunciations were strange, the intonation foreign sounding, and they spoke with a kind of deep throated mumble.

Back in Bristol, Will got a call on his cellular. They were invited for dinner at his parents. He accepted without even asking Minnie.

She must have given him a puzzled look. "Don't worry, Kate will not be there."

"Could you call Mar Sue and ask if I can come early and watch how she prepares tonight's dinner?"

They went over early and Minnie went into the kitchen to watch Mar Sue preparing a beef pot roast. Will sat in the front main room with his father drinking beers and talking about the upcoming Orioles baseball season. Over dinner, Minnie did not talk much. She was watching Will and imagining him last November coming to her rescue. She was also looking forward to getting into bed with him that evening. They made small talk around the table and then Bob began talking about the old dialect of the watermen. When I was a boy there were still a fair number of watermen here in Bristol. The packing plants were still working. And the watermen here spoke that same dialect as on Smith Island. Blacks and whites alike. It was really pronounced how they spoke. And their women folk worked in the plants doing the canning. They spoke the same way. They're all gone now. Don't know where they all went."

"Probably the same direction as the oysters." said Will. "They were depleted and died out. I don't remember anyone around town speaking that dialect when I was in school. Well, maybe a few black kids spoke something like it. But not many."

"What about you Minnie? Do you remember anybody speaking your Indian language?" asked Bob.

She didn't catch the question at first because her mind had drifted off. Bob repeated his question.

"My tribe spoke an Algonkian language. I'm told by specialists that it was very much like the language that was spoken here. But we have a tradition that the last speaker of that language died more than one hundred and sixty years ago. It was an old woman."

"And of course no one wrote that language down, right?" said Will.

"No, not systematically. There are historical records of people writing down a few words, a few phrases, and some equivalents. But not enough to recreate the language."

"So do you think that there might be a vestige of the language in your tribe's dialect?" asked Will.

"I don't think so. I was never aware that we spoke any differently than the white kids at school. No one ever thought my English sounded strange when I was at university."

As they walked back to Will's house after dark, Minnie was thinking about how much she wanted these weekends to continue. She felt a deep need to be with Will, to sleep with him, to make love to him, to walk alongside him. They didn't need to talk about it after they got back. She merely said: "Next Friday night, I will come again straight from work?" Will's answer was reassuring: "I will count the minutes till then." He was very tender in bed that night and he drew her along in her rising passion for what seemed like a prolonged time. She was so elated that she even forgot to set her alarm.

But Will woke at five thirty, just as the week before. It seemed to her disorienting because it was still so dark outside, not even a trace of dawn's twilight. At her own little house in Thornburg, she was close to the highway and there were the lights and always the traffic noise. She rushed through her shower and washed her hair and dressed for work while he prepared coffee and a simple breakfast. He again saw her off in his running outfit at the very beginning of dawn's earliest light.

And then over the next eight weekends they lived together following no routine or fixed schedule, but each weekend getting to know each other closer and deeper. Minnie learned about Will's likes and preferences, his strange habits, and his enthusiasms. He liked films and they would go to the Blockbuster and rent a video to watch on his television on Saturday evenings. They shared cooking responsibilities.

But not every weekend was the same.

The very next weekend started with sad news. Will called her on Wednesday to tell her that his great-Uncle Hampton had died and that the funeral would be on Sunday. And that of course he wanted her to be with him at the funeral at a church near Hampton's farm, the burial at the farm, and the funerary supper afterwards. Minnie of course at once agreed. She told him how sad for him she was to hear the news. She quickly began to think if she had an appropriate black suit or not.

She'd have to go to Macys' to buy herself a new outfit, and that meant it would have to be on Thursday after work. At the same time she bought herself a black long raincoat. She had never had a dress raincoat and it was lined so it was perfect for going to work during the chilly seasons.

She didn't tell Will over the phone on that occasion that she was going to her gynecologist on that Friday morning to get a long overdue check-up, to ask about her complaint of dryness and pain, and to buy some birth control pills. As it turned out her doctor in Fredericksburg conducted a few tests and suspected that her complaint about dryness was related to a low estrogen level. It had always been very difficult to talk with the gynecologist about her sexual activity and her private parts. But she forced herself. It was at that appointment that Minnie confessed that until just the last month she had had no sex life for many years. The doctor said she would have to confirm that suspicion after she got back the test results. Minnie also asked her about the pain she had felt when she first had penetrative sex almost sixteen years earlier. The doctor reassured her that it was probably down to the circumstances, which both agreed had amounted to rape, although the first time was date rape. The same was probably the cause of pain when she was violently raped, which had occurred six years later. Minnie realized that that was the first time she had ever told anyone about those two horrible sexual events in her life. Not even her sister, who was sexually very experienced, knew about the rapes Minnie had suffered, and certainly not her mother. She was able before driving away from Fredericksburg to buy the birth control pills that the gynecologist prescribed. And as if to mark this weekend for its sexual complications, during the work day her monthly period began, perhaps one day earlier than she had expected. This put her in a bad mood and made her uncomfortable during the entire drive over to Bristol that evening. The weekender traffic did not help her. And as if to re-enforce the premonition of a dark and sad weekend, it began to rain just as she approached Bristol. She hadn't brought her rain slicker with her and she did not have an umbrella.

After a light dinner which they prepared together, when Will began making advances, Minnie had to tell him for the first time that she didn't want sex that night because of her period. He didn't take the news too badly. She had hoped he would still be affectionate and close, and without asking he was. He went out and rented a few videos and when he came back he put on the film Titanic. They snuggled together on the couch the rest of that rainy evening and cried over the sad love story. That night she noticed that the new mattress was in place and that it was much more generous in space for the both of them. Will also had bought a present for her: a satiny green night gown. He had laid it out on the new bed as a surprise for her. When she saw it, she was surprised. His only response was to shrug his shoulders and say: "I didn't know when your birthday was, so I got this for you." Later, when she slipped it on in the bathroom, she felt its satiny finish against her skin, and she again felt sexy and tingly. They slept in the new bed; at first she snuggled in Will's arms, but later they moved away into the extra space of the mattress.

Saturday was also dark, chilly, and blustery, but with only occasional lashings of rain. They spent the day in the bungalow. Minnie did not feel well, as her period was especially bloody and painful with cramping. Will acting embarrassed, especially as there seemed there was nothing he could do to relieve her discomfort. They went out to run one errand: they had to buy flowers for the funeral.

The florist shop would be closed on Sunday. By coincidence they ran into Mar Sue at the florist shop who was also buying flowers. She was pleased to see Minnie again, but annoyed by the thin selection of flowers. "I should have planned this better," she said. "Maybe I should have gone to Yarmouth to buy a proper wreath." Later, the two of them went again to the Cedar Island for supper. On Sunday morning Will asked her if she went to church.

"When I was still living in Bowling Green, before I went to college, I went with my parents to church. But I have not gone much since. I would say I am not really a believer."

"What denomination?" he asked. "Baptist."

"That's interesting. It seems that the Methodists made a special effort to convert Indians. Most of the churches here on the Eastern Shore are Methodist. And many of them are located at places near the former reservations. And apparently many Nantiquak still go to Methodist churches."

She dressed in her new black suit, and showed it off to Will to get his approval. "Seems very elegant to me." he said. "I don't really know the etiquette for a funeral. This is the first one I have gone to." It was not the first funeral for Minnie. Will had a very dark gray suit also which he wore with a white shirt and black tie. They left the house at twelve and arrived at the little Methodist church that stood on the road to Hampton's farm, about three miles distant. The cars were already gathering around the church and people were debouching into the small church which was built on the crown of a small hillock. The scene appeared to Minnie like almost the stereotypical portrayal of funerals: a dark, overcast, windy day with mostly bare trees clacking in the wind, a small church on a knoll, people in dark clothes walking up the gravel to the church, hunched over, an open coffin in the church nave, people dressed in black putting flowers on the coffin. She took Will's arm. He supported her, as her heels made her wobble over the loose gravel. In the church people, only a few of whom she recognized, quickly took their places after the flowers were in place and the service began. There was no music. A minister in purple robes gave a eulogy and a farewell, ending with the promise of resurrection and life eternal, and very quickly it was over. There was a file by—few tears were shed. Minnie didn't want a final viewing, but Will pulled her along. "Remember he said you were the angel sent to take him away." She was struck by how transformed the head and face looked in its coffin. He did not resemble at all the old man she had met so recently. Then the coffin was closed and Will and Pat, his brother-in-law, Bob and another man heaved the coffin onto their shoulders and carried it out of the church and slid it into the back of a long van. Everyone then drove on to Hampton's farm, up the gravel lane, and parked in front of the farm house. The van went further around the farmhouse and drove to where there was a line of gravestones between two big oak trees which still did not have any signs of leaves breaking out. There was a large fresh hole in the ground. The men took the coffin out of the van and put it on ropes lying next to the open grave along with the wreaths. On the other side was a large pile of reddish clayey earth. Skulking behind the one oak were two men who Minnie barely noticed, but she thought that they looked Indian. They were clearly trying to hide from the others. They did not open the coffin a second time. Now Minnie saw Phyllis. She was crying quite openly and seemed to be the only one in the small crowd crying at all. Bob stood at the head of the grave, and gave a short oration about the triumphs of Hampton and his many sufferings. Kate's baby girl began to squawk and make noises demonstrating her impatience or hunger. Then they lowered the coffin into the grave with the ropes and Bob took a handful of clay and delivered a short message ending with "from earth to earth, and dust to dust". Then the two men, who clearly were Indians, came out from behind the oak with shovels and began shoveling the earth onto the coffin. Now Minnie felt like crying. This was just like the burial of her father with the two Indian grave diggers shoveling orange clay into the grave. She couldn't help herself and she began to sob. Will put his arm around her shoulders. The rose that had somehow ended up in her hand she tossed into the grave before it was filled. And then everyone slowly filed away. But just as she turned to go, she saw Will go over to one of the gravediggers, shake his hand, and slip him a few green bills. They all went around to the farmhouse, up the wooden stairs to the porch and with a great stomping and wiping of feet, they proceeded through the great door. Inside, Phyllis had prepared a large spread of food as a buffet, which was displayed on the dining table along with dishes, flatware, glasses and tumblers, and with several open bottles of wine. People served themselves and then milled around either in the dining room or in the big main room next to it. Minnie had no appetite and took only some sliced cucumbers and a small bread roll, and a glass of red wine, which she did not drink. She tried to stay close to Will, but he was constantly pulled aside by relatives wanting to express their condolences. Bob came and spoke to her a couple times, Mar Sue also on her own. But Kate did not, nor did her husband. Will one time brought a middle aged sturdy looking man over and introduced him as Max, the farm manager, 'the one real farmer on this farm'. Max shook her hand and nodded his head as if she were Hampton's widow. But he drifted off without saying much of anything. Phyllis came by and greeted her and called her Hampt's angel. She was still teary eyed and said she would miss the old man immensely, and that he had told her again shortly before he died that he had seen his mother's angel sent to come take him back to her. "You cannot understand, maybe, how much your visit pleased him, Minnie." said Phyllis who then began to sob again. Minnie couldn't console her, but she said, "You managed to prepare all this on your own?" Before the repast had ended, Bob came back to her with Will at his side. "We're so glad you came, Minnie. A funeral is never enjoyable. And Will here tells me it's not your first. But you know, the farm here is now Will's." Minnie had been told that by Hampton, but could hardly have believed it at the time. Now she thought how strange that this big farmhouse and farm should become Will's. That Will was a big landowner. On the drive back, Minnie asked Will who that Indian looking fellow who had been slinking around the grave. "Oh, him. That's my distant cousin. Armand Driggers."

That evening back at Will's place, Minnie continued to feel sad and miserable. Her period was very different and more painful than in past years before she had started taking the birth control pills. She did not want to watch any films, but she did want to keep still in Will's arms on the couch. She sobbed several times. Will had brought one of the bottles of white wine back with him and they slowly shared its contents through the evening. And then they went to bed early. All night she had disturbing dreams, of separation, loss, and tears. But in the morning she could hardly remember them.

Two weekends later Will asked her over the phone if she would not object to going to Easter church services with him and his parents. Once more Minnie needed to think of what she had that was appropriate to wear for Easter. But as she began to object, saying she had nothing to wear, Will cut her off. "We'll go buy some Easter clothes for you. Maybe even an Easter bonnet."

Another weekend that was a little different from their routine, came three weeks later. She spoke to Will over the phone during the work week. He had called to report to her the results of their internal census. Then she asked him for a date in D.C. "Come to D.C. for the weekend. I would like to see the cherry blossoms with you on Saturday. They should be at peak. And further, there's a recommended concert at the Kennedy Center and I would like to go to it with you." Will agreed promptly. "And I'll get a hotel room and we can spend the rest of the weekend in relaxed luxury. Enjoy a leisurely Sunday brunch together." He drove in on Friday afternoon and left his car at the hotel up on M Street and then he met Minnie outside her office at five. He took her carry-on bag and together they walked first to the hotel to drop off the bag, and then to the concert hall in time for the seven o'clock start. They had time before going in to buy some sandwiches and wine.

Looking at the program, Minnie did not know the music, but the conductor, Leonard Slatkin spent some time introducing the pieces to the audience. The concert led off with a piano concerto by Beethoven, and was followed by a short piece by Aaron Copland which seemed full of American folk music. Will was studying the program to learn more about the pieces and their composers. After the intermission the concert concluded with the three suites from Prokofiev's Romeo and Juliet ballet. Neither Will nor Minnie knew the Romeo and Juliet story in detail, but Minnie knew the general outlines of the story and tried to tie the music to the scenes from Shakespeare's story, but she was unable to tie the emotional thrust of the pieces to the incidents.

The program helped very little. Except for the death of Juliet scene: when Minnie was saddened by the music. Will applauded loudly at the end. And then they walked back to the hotel. The weather was almost balmy and the skies clear, but the city lights were too bright to see many stars, so they strolled slowly under the trees which now mostly had their first young tender leaves. They sat in the lobby and Will ordered a bottle of white wine. After only a few sips Minnie was already feeling happy and a little high. She began to laugh. Over a couple hours they finished off the bottle between them. Minnie's head was spinning and she felt warm and flushed. She had only been drunk once before in her life, at a weekend party with some of her college friends more than fifteen years before. She had regretted that evening, but on this occasion she felt happier and sillier and even safe until finally Will half carried her up to their bedroom. Once inside she began to giggle uncontrollably, and she continued giggling as Will undressed her while she was still standing up, a first in their love affair. When she was completely naked, still giggling uncontrollably, Will heaved her over his shoulder and slung her into the bed. She couldn't remember making love that night, but she knew the next morning that they had. She slept in a deep dark sleep, seemingly without dreams except she was still on and off throughout the night faintly aware of Will's arms around her. She awoke in desperate need for some water.

The next morning over breakfast she confessed to him that she had achieved another first last night. Not only had she gone on a date with her lover to a classical music concert, but she had gotten thoroughly inebriated and made love to that lover under the influence. She smiled at him and said, "And it was wonderful." They took a taxi down to the Tidal Basin off the Mall. The sun was smiling and the air balmy and crowds still hadn't gathered yet. But Minnie was totally unprepared for the glory of the copious pink cherry blossoms gleaming in the early morning sunlight. The aroma once they got under the trees was overpowering. There was a very low hum of bees in the blooms. "Isn't it glorious?" she trilled.

"It certainly is. In all my life I have never seen anything like this. It was such a good idea to invite me to see them. I haven't been to the

Mall since I was a little kid with my parents. And the cherries weren't in bloom then."

"It's a first time for me too. I seem to have so many first time experiences with you."

They spent the next several hours strolling hand in hand around the Tidal Basin. They stopped frequently along the way to take in the different views, or to swing underneath low boughs, or to visit the memorials to Roosevelt and Jefferson. And after the Tidal Basin they walked further down the street along the Washington Channel, also lined with heavily blossoming cherry trees.

"We'll have to plant some cherry trees at the farm." said Will. Minnie noticed that he used the word 'we' but it didn't seem to be the royal we.

That evening Will suggested that they go back to that southern Gulle restaurant they had gone to for lunch back in February. It was nice, but she remembered it was expensive so she tried to decline. "Well then, we should go to that monument of jovial society and nightlife in Georgetown, Claude's. But we had better call for a reservation." They could only get a table at nine o'clock.

"It's a noisy place, with music. But lots of fun. And they serve fresh oysters on ice."

Claude's was packed with young people. And it was indeed noisy. There was a band comprising a guitarist and drummer playing behind one side of the bar. Occasionally the guitarist would sing through a microphone. On the other side of the bar was a large ice table displaying oysters from all up and down the Atlantic seaboard, including the Chesapeake. There were five screens above the bar each projecting a different sporting event: ice hockey, basketball, an early season baseball game, soccer. Even in the adjacent dining room the tables were all occupied and there was a great clamor in the room. Minnie looked at the menu and could not see anything that would be a small portion, other than soup. Will suggested that she have a half dozen oysters, so she ordered those. He ordered a dozen for himself followed by a burger and a beer. They could not hear each other even across the small table without shouting. Will leaned over and spoke in her ear: "The oysters are to boost my virility for later tonight." Minnie blushed. "And what about me?" she answered him. A waiter with a smeared white smock apron proudly brought out two trays of oysters on the half shell on ice and dramatically put them in place. From his pocket he took out a bottle of tabasco sauce and plopped it in the middle of the table. "Enjoy!" he shouted. Minnie tried the first oyster, said to be from Prince Edward Island. It was cold and briney, and smooth and light. She liked it much to her surprise. This was another first: eating raw oysters. Will was adding lemon to his, and he gulped down quickly three oysters and chased them with a swig of beer. Minnie's second oyster had a distinctly different flavor, she liked it less. But the Chesapeake oyster, her third attempt, had a sweet and mildly salty taste and was firmer than the first two. She liked it also. They finished off their oysters and Minnie shouted to Will: "They were delicious. This was a great recommendation." After they had finished their meal they sat around with their coffee and listened to the guitarist trying to wail over the sportscasts and the crowd noise in the next room. The Saturday night revelers slowly began to clear out. But a boisterous crowd remained at the bar. It seemed young people everywhere were desperate to have a great time and be jolly. And their jollity spread good cheer to everyone throughout the. Minnie felt especially content and happy. They walked back along M Street over the Rock Creek Bridge and then on to their hotel. It was nearly midnight when they got back.

After a leisurely brunch, Will suggested that they spend the day visiting Alexandria. He had often heard that it was a scenic town just down the river from D.C., worth the visit. They spent the afternoon strolling around the brick paved sidewalks. Minnie thought the town looked like a larger version of downtown Fredericksburg, late nineteenth century two story brick buildings and houses with large windows. Will stopped at the display window of a jewelry shop and motioned her to go in with him. He was looking for something; that was clear. He asked to look at an emerald pendant and then he asked the saleswoman for the very finest silver necklace they had.

She brought out several. Will wanted a short one. "Now hang the emerald on it and let's see how it looks on my girl here." Minnie was surprised. The saleswoman helped her try it on. "Green to match your eyes, Minnie." said Will. "And thin silver to draw people's eyes away from your line." Minnie was surprised. She looked in the mirror. The chain sat directly over her thin line scar and the emerald gleamed just below on her lower neck. "You mean you're going to buy this?" "Absolutely. For my Mini-oaka. Just a small token of my love." She was amazed and taken aback. "But it costs " "Yes, I know." Will cut in. "I hope you'll wear it often." Minnie gave him a kiss and a hug right there at the display case of the shop and she wore the pendant and chain out of the shop and for the rest of the day. The rest of the day she kept seeing Will in a different light. This was a very generous man who loved her. She realized that his efforts to restore the treaty rights to the Nantiquak Indians also sprang out of his generosity.

The next morning after breakfast, they reversed the usual Monday commute. They checked out of the hotel at eight thirty and Minnie left by foot for her office which was only a few blocks distant, and Will got in his Oldsmobile and drove off to the east back to Bristol. His parting words as he went for the car were: "It was a fabulous date, Minnie. I'll remember it for the rest of my life."

The weekend after their 'date in D.C.' Minnie again had to come late to Bristol on Saturday afternoon. Her gynecologist had called her and asked to see her, but the only time they could agree on an appointment was on Saturday morning. So she called Will who was duly disappointed but admitted that he did not have hard and fast plans for Saturday, so as soon as she could come he would be happy again. "But miserable on Friday night and Saturday morning until you arrive and are in my arms". he said. "You say the most romantic things Willeems." she answered over the phone. (She had started calling him Willeems as a diminutive of William Eames.) She also had to go to Bowling Green and finally tell her mother.

"I have a boyfried, momma. He lives in Bristol Maryland, and that's where I've been going all these past weekends."

Her mother looked directly at her for a few long moments, staring at her as if to bore the full truth out of her. "And is he an Anglo?"

"Yes, he is. And I love him."

"And I suppose you will tell me he loves you too." Her mother began the classic diatribe, "You have to marry an Indian. You can only get heartache from white boys. They just want sex from you and if you get with child with them they will dump you like a hot ember. For heaven's sake, you're the chief of the tribe, and you can't get yourself hooked to a genuine Indian."

"Mother you know. I'm already too old. There are no men in our tribe who want someone like me, an old woman who is a lawyer, working and earning a salary bigger than they will ever have. Maybe there are no Indian men anywhere, who would want to marry me." She did not tell her mother that Will was younger than she.

"White men are bad. Mark my words. They can only do you harm. And how long has this affair been going on?"

"For about two months. We met in January and I fell in love with him in February."

"I suppose you can't tell me what he does? He's a mechanic, he's unemployed, he pumps gas?"

"No. You could say he's a farmer. But he also dabbles in real estate. He's working with me on the legal case for the Nantiquak Indians."

"Oh, worse and worse. A farmer." her mother said in disgust. "You know, Mataoka" –since her childhood her mother had only used the name Mataoka when she was angry with Minnie—"you're a disgrace. I thought your father and I raised you better than this." And for the rest of Friday evening and into the next morning before Minnie had to leave for Fredericksburg and then on to Bristol, her mother bore her an angry grudge. Minnie apologized on her way out. She had expected that reaction. "You'll be sorry." said her mother. "I know, you'll be a real sorry case when you come crying back here when it's all over with him. Don't even tell me his name."

The doctor on the other hand was very solicitous, concerned and gentle with Minnie. "Your tests show as I suspected that you have a slight deficiency of estrogen. Nothing serious. It's within the range of normal indicators, but on the low side. It can explain both your vaginal dryness, and even the occasional pain you described. And by the way, have you noticed again the pain since we met, three weeks ago? We need to give you a course of estrogen supplementation for a month or two."

"I don't get it." said Minnie. "Does being on the estrogen low side mean I can't have children? That I am already on the verge of menopause?"

"No, oh no. Not at all. This is just a treatment that will actually enhance your sexual experience, and maybe even make you want to have sex more. It's not extraordinary. Women in their thirties often need this."

So then Minnie had to buy the prescription and of course she worried about all the possible outcomes she could think of with her condition all the way to Bristol. This time there was no accident at the Potomac Bridge and no delays anywhere along the way. The weekenders for Ocean City had already all passed through on Highway 50. Her visits to her mother and her gynecologist threw her off for the rest of the weekend. Saturday night Will noticed and he tried extra hard to get her to respond affectionately to him. But she would not tell him what had transpired. She was too ashamed, and afraid of those unfavorable outcomes that her worry and imagination had created.

He tried to fondle her, and kiss her, but she did not cheer up. He took her out to hire the film '10' from Blockbuster that evening. Will had already seen it, but he thought a little comedy might help Minnie get out of her funk. He was completely prepared. After the film he led her to the bed, and undressed her very slowly, and then the two naked lovers skin to skin, as they began to make love in the new bed made up with freshly laundered and ironed satins sheets he slyly asked, "Shall I put on Bolero now?"

It was in May, on week nights in her cottage in Thornburg that Minnie began to notice that she was having trouble sleeping. She missed Will's touch, his warm body next to hers in the bed. She would awake on many nights, suddenly conscious that she was alone in the bed. But that it was not in Will's bungalow, but hers. And then she would hear the sounds of the night, the creaks, the rustling of leaves outside, sounds of the house complaining against its footing, all sounds which spooked her and which in Bristol she would ignore and snuggle up to Will. She wanted to be with him every night, and every day if possible. She was only really comfortable when he was next to her. This arrangement where she visited him every weekend was not enough. She needed him even more.

On other weekends in Bristol, Will and Minnie went fishing off the truncated bridge to nowhere— the so called fishing dock. Another time, he took her out in the boat and introduced her to crabbing.

She especially liked that, even though the crabs nipped her fingers several times. She liked

especially that they didn't have to run far down the river at speed or go out into the Bay with its choppy, even rough waters. They went on two different weekends crabbing and had a good catch both times. And afterwards they ate the catch in a crab boil along with Bob and Mar Sue. Bob again complained that he wasn't included, but only facetiously. Minnie enjoyed eating the crabs almost as much as catching them. She especially liked cracking open the shells with the wooden mallet. She threw herself passionately into banging on the crab legs, sometimes she even missed and banged the table instead. Mar Sue was shocked at how wild Minnie was with the crab mallets. "Will, you should lock those mallets up after you're finished eating crab. So she doesn't get any ideas about using them in cracking your head." she said half in jest. Later in bed together, Minnie chuckled and said, "To think that your mother could think I would crack your head with those wooden mallets."

Will smiled and said, "You mean you haven't thought of it before?"

One week in May Minnie called Will and told him that they were finishing up the court filing for the suit against the state of Maryland. But she would need to include in the filing estimates of what value the lands would have that the Nantiquak would be claiming. So she needed from him the land values from recent sales. He said that he could compile that without too much problem, but that there would be three different figures: the price per acre for farmland in the vicinity, the price per acre for undeveloped marsh or forested land, and the lands that were currently set aside in nature or wildlife reserves along the Nanticoke and Broad Rivers. As for the latter he thought there would be no comparable prices available, but as the state was the owner of those reserve lands they would be better able to estimate how much a sales price would be. Will called back on Friday before end of her day to tell her that he had compiled the current sales values per acre for all the lands, and had put together a total land cost for the acreage that they wanted to be restored. He had compiled the figures from farm sales of the past several years in Dorset, Wicomico, and Somerville Counties.

These data had given him a sound basis for the estimated sales price for the land. The total came at in excess of ninety five million dollars. Minnie thanked him and said she would thank him again later that evening, in a more personal, intimate manner. "I look forward to that. As always." said Will before he hung up.

The weekends of May were quite warm and all the trees had developed their fully green manes, making Bristol look much nicer, and in fact, making the all roads around Dorset County and the Eastern Shore more attractive. Memorial Day weekend came early that year, as the holiday was supposed to be the last Monday in May, which was the 25th, and could not fall on the Monday following the last weekend, which would be the 1st of June. It was a time when the Ocean City gang would greatly surge in numbers and come out from the 'Western Shore' for the long three day weekend (many even making it a four day weekend by coming on the Thursday before the holiday itself). All the forecasters predicted a very, preternaturally warm May weekend. That meant swimming weather and even bigger crowds rushing through Bristol on their way to Ocean City's beaches and boardwalk. The forecast and the mass migration, and then the arrival of the heat itself excited Will as well. But he had been already extremely excited on the Friday after Minnie arrived. "We have to celebrate tonight, you know. You cannot guess, Mini-oaka, what good fortune has come our way." (Again Minnie noticed that he used the inclusive plural.) "We have to get some champagne, or something really special to mark the news." Will's enthusiasm was infectious and Minnie was dying to know what was up.

"What is it, Willeems, that can be so important?" asked Minnie a little uncertain about what was coming.

"Wait, I'll get the champagne out of the fridge. I've prepared a little."

He came back out of his kitchen with a chilled bottle of Californian champagne –"It was all they had at the grocery store earlier today."— and two champagne flutes which clearly he had just bought as well as Minnie had never seen them before in his kitchen.

"Oh those, nothing special. They're plastic after all. See you put them together like this." "So when are you going to tell me what's so special about this news you have?"

"Well, Minnie, my love. I am now officially a farmer."

"But that's not the special news, is it?"

"Part. You see in Uncle Hampt's will, he also left me a million dollars. So that makes me a millionaire farmer. We're rich, you see. The executor sent me the check yesterday at the same time that he called me with the news of the terms of the will. It's already in the bank. We can drink to that, no?"

Minnie's breathing skipped over one breath. "You're kidding me, aren't you?"

"No, Minnie have I ever kidded you about the important things?"

"I don't think so."

"Right, only playful chiding. But this is worthy of drinking champagne." And Will opened the bottle and poured out the bubbly yellow wine in both glasses. "We drink and then we dance."

Minnie drank her glass of champagne and began to dance in Will's arms. But she was confused and suddenly a fear ran through her mind that by inheriting the farm and so much money Will would no longer be interested in the Injun Project or in her. That he would drift off with other occupations and interests. What would a rich farmer want to do with a poor, working Indian woman? she thought.

But Will continued to dance, spinning around with his arms around her waist, and laughing. It was hard for Minnie not to feel the joy and she was smiling and feeling the effect of the bubbly drink. Will poured himself another, but Minnie declined to drink more. After a few more turns to the unheard music Will stopped and pulled Minnie over to the couch.

"Uncle Hampt had promised to leave me the farm in his will. That I already knew. No surprises there. But I had no idea that he intended to leave me money. I mean so much money. I knew he intended to leave a smaller sum, for running the farm for the rest of this year. But a million dollars. I did not in my wildest dreams expect that. You know we grew up reading about the rich uncle leaving an inheritance to an undeserving nephew. I never believed that ever happened, except in fairy tales. But it has. For the grand-nephew. Hampt also left a large sum for my father and his brother. As well as one hundred thousand dollars for Kate, and sixty thousand for Phyllis. But I didn't reckon he had so much savings. I have always thought in general it was very difficult for a farmer to get rich only on his farming activities."

Minnie's expression must have conveyed her anxiety, her trying to figure out what her future might include. Will looked closely at her. "And you're thinking 'what's to become of me?' I suppose." Minnie nodded her head and she couldn't suppress tears coming up in her eyes. "What's to become of us?" asked Will. "Don't you still love me?" Minnie again nodded her head affirmatively. "This doesn't change my love for you, Mini-oaka. We can do more together than before, we have more options. I would think you would want to be with me now more than ever. I'm still charming and dashing. Don't you think so?" Again she nodded her head. "Come on Minnie, smile for me. Smile for *our* good fortune."

Minnie continued to sob and tried to smile while Will tried to wipe away the tears from her cheeks. Will tried to kiss her, but she turned her head away. "I'm so happy for you, Will." she said while still sobbing.

"Of course you are. Now let's go out before it's too late tonight and celebrate with a fine meal.

Maybe at the yacht club? Maybe ma and pa could join us. They're pretty happy just now too. You'll feel better."

Minnie allowed Will to pull her up from the couch by her hand. "I'll call them to see if they'll join us. You're dressed just fine as you are, but I need to put something nicer on. We can walk there; remember the place?"

Once they started walking outside, Minnie quickly felt better, the effect of the champagne blunting her mind cleared. And she began to think that nothing really had changed yet with Will. And she still adored him and hungered for his presence as ardently as before. She took his left hand, after he moved the champagne bottle to his right. "You don't want to leave me, do you?" asked Will. "No, I want to hold on to you, whether you're a rich man or not." she said. Bob and Mar Sue met them at the Bristol Yacht Club, where even though it was a Friday evening of a holiday weekend there were few diners. It was eight o'clock, and that was considered a late dinner. The kitchen closed at nine, even though it was Friday. Bob was in a jolly mood, and Mar Sue even broke from her normal outward serenity to smile broadly at Will and Minnie. They ordered a bottle of French white wine which Bob poured out to all but Minnie who declined. Then he raised his glass and proposed a toast to Uncle Hampton Eames, and his overflowing generosity.

"We're in the winner's circle now." Mar Sue said. "Good cause to celebrate. Have you two begun to discuss how you might employ your windfall?"

"No, not yet. We've barely had time to grasp the news." said Will. Minnie only shook her head as if to say no.

"We might take a long overdue vacation to some tropical beach where the fishing is wonderful." said Bob. "And I might buy a new boat."

"I'd like to finally re-model the kitchen," said Mar Sue. "And maybe take a vacation to Hawaii with Bob. Is there anything that you might want, Minnie?" Minnie answered simply, "Happiness."

"And you should add, and a large family." said Bob chuckling as he said it.

They ordered dinner all around; Bob a steak, Mar Sue and Will the rack of lamb, and Minnie ordered the appetizer portion of baked oysters—"They were not as good as Mar Sue makes."—and a salmon salad. The wine made Bob feel giddy.

"Ordinarily, I'm only a beer man." said Bob.

"And too much beer, at that." said Mar Sue.

"But this is a special occasion, once in a lifetime. So I drink to everyone's happiness with white wine."

"And I want to finish this bottle of champagne." said Will as he poured himself a glass of the not so bubbly drink.

"As we're eating here—in the yacht club, I'm reminded of the only Indian joke I've ever known. I have to tell you." said Bob again chuckling to himself. Mar Sue kicked him under the table. Minnie braced herself for something unflattering. She always thought that people who laugh at their own jokes, either before or after the telling, did not tell very funny jokes.

"What? When I was growing up as a young kid there was a popular song called Red Sails in the

Sunset. My favorite was Nat King Cole singing it. I must've been a teenager. I always thought it was about an elite rich yacht club on the Pacific. But, anyway. The story goes that the two sons of a leading Indian chief were invited and given membership in this yacht club. Which I thought was only possible if you were rich and owned a large yacht. So the press goes to the Indian chief asking if he was proud and if he had any comments he might share with them about the news. And the chief without smiling points out to the Pacific and the setting sun and stoically says, 'Red sons in the sail set'." Bob paused, looked around and said, "Get it?"

"Yuk, yuk. Some one really had to stretch to get that play on words." said Will. Minnie did not find it too offensive.

"Oh, it's funny. And it's harmless." said Bob. "I liked it, anyway, when I first heard it." "Eons ago." said Mar Sue.

Minnie didn't see any harm in the word play. But the delivery was rather stereotyped. And the joke hinged on the total implausibility of two young Indian men ever getting into an exclusive rich man's yacht club, which of course would be assumed by all the white men that heard the joke.

"Wasn't Nat King Cole a black man?" she asked.

"Yeah, why?" said Bob. "He had a fabulous voice."

Will had insisted that they order the baked Alaska, and he had asked the waiter to tell the kitchen to prepare it for after their meal. When the dishes were cleared, the waiter proudly brought out the white, toasted meringue cake and set it in the middle of the table.

"It's got ice cream in the middle, yet it's a baked cake." said Will to Minnie. "Very special. For celebrations."

Later that evening on the walk back home, Will suggested that they go to the beach on Saturday, and on their return they could stay two nights at the farm. He would call Phyllis and she could ready the place and cook dinners.

"But I don't have a bathing suit."

"We'll buy one tomorrow before we leave." Trying on and picking bathing suits was one of her least favorite activities. "A simple one piece black bathing suit, not too revealing, shouldn't be too hard to find." Minnie thought all bathing suits were too revealing.

"But you know I don't really know how to swim."

"Oh that's no matter. We would just splash in the surf a bit." Minnie did not tell him that really she was scared to death of the water, and especially the surf, which she had seen once before in her life.

"We wouldn't go to Ocean City beach. We'll go to Assateauge Island, much quieter there."

The next day, again at Walmart, Minnie spent more than an hour trying to find a bathing suit that fit. Her figure may have matched the golden rule in terms of its ratios of chest to waist and hips to waist, but the suits at Walmart seemed to be designed only for women of gigantic proportions: either huge breast cups or huge hips. There was one racing suit for girls that fit but it clung super tight to her figure--and it had scooped away large areas of fabric so that nearly all of her buttocks were exposed and all of her back and under her arms, the sides of her breasts showed—way too revealing. She finally expressed her dissatisfaction to Will and they left. He suggested a sports store in Salisbury might have more appropriate options. So they drove on there and he was right. She tried on several and found a fit that was not either much too big or much too tight and revealing, not a suit that was a special Sports Illustration selection. She found a purple one that was perfect for a mature and modest woman, and suited for wear on the beach. Will bought it and he also bought sunscreen, flip-flops, sunglasses, two sun hats, a beach wrap for Minnie, and an umbrella and folding chairs.

They set up on the beach by 11:30. The sun was already intense and the air was very hot, although there was a steady fresh breeze blowing strong off the ocean. The beach was extremely clean and had bright yellowish sand for as far as you could see. There was not much of a crowd, and few people were in the water. There were no lifeguards on duty, although there were flags fluttering. The wind had kicked up the surf so that the breaking waves had high foamy white manes which came crashing and pounding down on the sand right near the water line. Minnie saw this and immediately was scared to death. They changed into their swim suits, Minnie under her wrap, Will contorting under his beach towel. He led her by her hand down to the surf line. And he made her put her feet in the foam which ran up the beach. It seemed very cold to Minnie. She did not want to enter the surf. After much wheedling and pleading, Will convinced her to step with him into the water. "But don't let go of me." He held her hand tightly and they stepped slowly into the water up to a depth of just above her knees. The onrushing waves looked terrifying and she wanted to run back and they seemed to fall right on them when in fact they crashed down about two yards in front of them. That was enough though to get them both wet from their shoulders down and for Minnie to feel the oncoming force of the water. And the water was cold. "This is no fun Will. Let's go back." she shouted. He turned around and pulled her back out. When they got to the end of the foam line, he looked at her and recognized the terror on her face. The effect was heightened by goose bumps that formed as the wind ran all over her wet body. "That's alright, Minnie. You don't have to go in the water. Besides it's cold still."

"You stand here, while I swim a little." he said. And he plunged back into the next big crashing wave. Minnie watched as he jumped and splashed and plunged under wavetops. She thought he looked like a dolphin. She especially liked how the water glistened off his lean body as he jumped and arched over the waves. He was so fit, so good looking. It pleased her to watch him play in the water as he did. But then she got concerned as it seemed he was too far out. He was swimming well beyond the waves' fall line where the water was dark and choppy. She tried to call to him, but the wind and sound of crashing waves swallowed up her voice. He spend fifteen minutes or so in the water before coming out, but to Minnie it seemed like an hour. "We can walk along the foam line," said Will and he took her hand and everything was at once pleasing and attractive. They walked a long ways, kicking the occasional shell, watching the sand fleas trying to plunge back under the sand, or the seagulls picking off worms or tiny crabs between the ebb and fall of the foam. After a long walk they went back to their beach chairs and towels. They were both completely dry by then.

"You don't like that much, do you?"

"No, not at all. You knew that."

"But you were willing to come with me, because I like it?"

"Yes."

"Well, at least you tried. This was your first time to the beach?"

"Yes."

"We don't have to stay. And we don't have to come here again."

The spent thirty minutes lying in the sun, and then Will got up, had a drink of water, and announced he would go in the water once more and then they could leave. "But you have to get under the beach wrap and the umbrella now. The sun's way too hot." He went down to the water line and ran into the surf. Minnie watched him: a tiny figure, barely visible rising in and then sinking away into the water behind the waves' crests. She had trouble following him. And then suddenly she had a flash of fear run through her. He had disappeared. Where was he? Had something happened? But then she saw his head and shoulders re-emerge with a splash a long distance from where she thought he had been last. His arms started stroking strongly and steadily, no sign of distress. But now she was afraid for him. Minnie only felt relief finally when she could see him stand up in front of the waves and head toward her.

"No I don't like this at all," she said half aloud.

They changed back and picked up all their beach equipment and left. A few miles beyond the inner estuary, over the bridge from the island, Will stopped at a crab house restaurant and they had lunch.

"So you were willing to try out the beach, just for my entertainment?" asked Will at the table. "Yes. But maybe better to say just barely willing."

"Minnie, you're super."

They drove over the farm and found Phyllis was already there. The spent much of the afternoon walking around the fields of high corn stalks, with their green and clacking leaves, the fields of dark green soy. It was the first time she got the impression of how big the farm was. From the house to the corn fields was a long walk, it took an hour to walk there and around them. Walking around the soy fields also took almost forty minutes, even though they could be seen from the house. They ate the dinner that Phyllis had prepared for them and when she had finished cleaning the dishes, they said good night to her as she left to go to home. The house lay silent as the long day and twilight slid away. And then the grasshoppers and cicadas unleashed their chirruping roar that invited the night in. Later in bed, as Will slipped off Minnie's green night gown, he suddenly chuckled. "Well you did get some sun even in that short time. You have a distinct body print of lighter skin where your swim suit was." "That's not funny," said Minnie as she pushed away his hand that was tracing the sunburn line on her body.

The next day, they spent the morning examining the press clippings and photos of the exhibition that Hampton had put together in his study.

"So Mena was there when there was this robbery at the store? And she probably saw her mother gunned down?"

"That seems probable. But the articles don't say so. Hampt told me that that was what his mother, Mena, told him."

"And this says here, the black man was hanged in Bristol several months later?" "Right."

"That was after your great grandfather, Will, married Mena?"

"Yes, Hampt also told me that the town was a bit scandalized. There was only the briefest mention in the newspaper of their marriage. They married in the church in Rosedale."

"Why would a white man, in that day and age, want to marry a young Indian girl? What, she was only eighteen at the time?"

"He fell in love with her?" Will offered. "I don't know myself. And neither did Hampt. He didn't know his father very well. He died when Hampt was only four or five."

"And that was presumably from Spanish flu?"

"It sounds like that."

"You know, the Spanish flu killed a lot of my tribesmen in 1919-1920. But nobody wanted to help the sick Indians at that time. They scarcely wanted to help those whites who were sick."

"And who is this in the photo with Mena, which seems to have been taken out front of this house?"

"That was my great-great grandfather, Robert. He brought Mena and her four kids out here from Bristol after Will died. He looked after them. So Hampt was raised out here on the farm. I don't know much about Robert Eames, except that he owned a lot of properties and businesses around the county. He built two houses in Bristol, the one where my parents now live. He owned a chain of stores and gasoline stations around the county, even though it's hard to believe there were many cars then. He owned several businesses in Bristol."

"I like these photos of Mena. She looks like a very kind woman."

"She was. Hampt adored her, and says she was very kind and always happy. I suppose it's understandable, he was her son after all."

After they had thoroughly examined the materials in the display, they went out and looked at the little family cemetery. They looked at each stone and connected the individuals in their relationship one to the other. Minnie noticed that the Hampton stone had new chiseling on it. It was his death date, from April. "This is already done?" she asked. "Yeah I found the stone inscriber in Exeter and he did it right away. He told me that he was part Nantiquak, you know. And that he wanted also to be enrolled in the tribal census."

That night in bed in the deep dark of the farm house out in the dark countryside ripped by cicada choruses, after they had made love, Will asked Minnie if she would come live with him, full time. Not just on the weekends.

"I'd like that, but I think I couldn't face the daily commute from D.C. It knocks me as it is, just on Fridays and Mondays. We couldn't live here, though. It's too far and too isolated."

"No, you're right about that. So we should just continue doing this? Weekends in Bristol or on the farm?"

They next morning, the Monday holiday, they were just finishing breakfast when they were surprised by a loud knocking on the front door.

"Armand. Good morning." said Will. "What are you doing here?" Will stepped out onto the porch, and shook Armand's hand.

"I'm working just now in the soya fields. Max sent me to ask you to come out there to ask you about a few issues."

Minnie came to the door and asked through the door, "Who is it, Will?"

"This is my distant cousin Armand Driggers. You'll notice the same last name as Mena's maiden name."

Armand looked at Minnie and addressed her. "Are you a Nantiquak Indian maiden too?" "I am an Indian, but from a Virginia tribe."

"Is she your squaw?" said Armand in his usual snide way. "You could say that?"

Armand turned toward Minnie and asked her, "Are you married to Will, or are you just doing him intimate favors?"

Minnie turned and went back into the house, throwing the door shut behind her. "That was unjust and really insulting Armand." said Will.

"It's what Indian maidens do."

"Yeah but you don't need to insult Minnie. She's the missus of the house now. And you need to be respectful of her to her face. If you don't like that she lives with me, you can go home and don't come back here. You understand? Now, can we drive to where Max is, or not."

"Yeah, we can."

Will went back in the house and looked through a few rooms before he found Minnie weeping in the kitchen.

"Minnie, don't pay any attention to that asshole. He insults everybody, just out of habit." But Will couldn't soothe her. He tried to kiss her but she turned her face away from him. "It doesn't matter what other people think about us. What Armand thinks isn't true, so it doesn't harm us, or harm you." He held her in his arms for several long silent minutes.

"I have to go out to speak with Max about some of the farming business. It must be important, or need a decision. I don't think I'll be long, but I'll come right back as soon as I can."

Will was gone for forty minutes. When he came back in again he had to search through the house to find Minnie.

"Are you alright now?"

"No how could I be alright. Does that guy hang around here all the time?"

"No, he's only an occasional worker. And then, he usually only works in the spring, during the planting, and does weeding in the soya fields."

"I don't want to see him again. You understand. You're aware about white racists and how they might look unfavorably on our relationship. But Indians also look at our being together in a racist, hateful way. They aim it especially at me. I didn't tell you but my mother strongly disapproves of our being lovers."

"I don't give a dam about what he says to me, or what anybody says. If it really gets under my skin, I can more than give that person a stinging response that will leave him writhing on the ground. Shall I administer the same to Armand? I can ask Max to fire him and ban him from returning to the farm, if that would make you feel better. I already told Armand in front of Max, he's not to approach the house again when we're here. Do you want me to punish him more?"

"No, he's poor and powerless and it wouldn't change his views, or the views of so many other Indian men."

"Well precisely. But you tell me if someone decides to abuse you for your love for me. The hostile opinions of others won't drive us apart or keep us apart. They can't shame me. And you don't anything to be ashamed about either."

But Minnie remained upset through the morning. Phyllis came to prepare a dinner. And after dinner, Minnie asked if they could go back to Bristol for the night. She still did not feel comfortable.

The next day, the Monday holiday, in Bristol, Will proposed that they rent a canoe and paddle up the Choptico River above Bristol. Minnie thought that sounded interesting. She had never gone canoeing in her life. Again it was warm and sunny, so she wore her broad brimmed sun hat and covered her arms. She also wore the new pair of shorts that they had bought on Saturday. Will took a cooler with drinks and a picnic lunch, which were the leftovers from the previous day's dinner.

They drove up to a point called Indian Creek which flowed into the main river. Down on the brown green still water, there was a dock and canoes for hire. He loaded up a green aluminium canoe, gave her a life jacket to put on, and pushed the canoe into the water from the sandy shore next to the dock. He gave her a paddle and showed her the basics, but the hardest part for Minnie was getting into the canoe and maintaining it stable. It wobbled precariously when she took her first two steps into the bottom of the boat. She went to the front gunnel seat. She calmed down once she was seated and she turned around to see Will get into the stern of the canoe and push off. Then slowly and silently they were sliding through the water; Will initially doing all the paddling.

"This was one of my favorite activities when I was a boy." he said. "Now you try paddling, just the way I showed you. That's right, but not so deep next time, and you don't have to pull so hard. The water's still here and yeah, that's enough to power us through. You're mainly paddling to keep us straight. That's why you paddle on the opposite side from me."

They soon paddled into the main stream of the Choptico which had not any current but which was pulled by the tides up and downstream depending on the time of day.

"I think on our first go, we won't try to paddle across the river. It's more than a mile across just here and the tide will pull us a long way either up or down, depending on which way it is running."

They headed upstream and soon Indian Creek seemed a far ways behind them. There were big herons wading in the shallows and among the canes and reeds of the boggy shore. Red winged black birds were shouting out everywhere.

"I should've brought my binoculars." said Will.

They paddled what seemed like a long time to Minnie, but they had gone not even two miles upstream and it was getting hot. Will steered the boat to what looked like a sandy spit, almost like a beach, and said they would get out there for a rest and drinks. The bow of the boat ground onto the sand and Minnie put up her paddle. "Now, hold on tight, Mini-oka." She felt Will hop out of the boat and heard his feet splashing in the water as he pushed the canoe further up onto the sand. "That's fine. Now you can step out and keep your feet dry." He picked up the cooler and walked across the ten yards of the partly muddy, sandy beach to where there was one good sized oak tree growing which gave good thick shade. They sat down straight on the damp sand on the verge where wild grasses grew tangled and spread out into a field beyond the tree. "This is a nice place for our picnic." said Will. "What is it called? The painting. Lunch on the grass by some French painter?" "I don't know it." said Minnie. "Yeah well you don't have to get fully undressed like the woman in that painting was. We'll just sit as we are."

"Oh, I think I remember seeing that painting too once in an illustration. Strange to call it lunch on the grass when the woman is naked, and the man, presumably the artist is fully dressed, smirking at her. And none of them are eating."

"Maybe she was going to go into the water to bathe, as they say. You're welcome to here, if you want. That is go skinny dipping. The water's really calm, and probably warm, and no one's around."

"No thanks. I didn't bring my bathing suit."

They ate the leftover cold fried chicken and carrots and cucumbers, and drank some cokes. After a short while, the heat shimmering all around the shadow they were sitting in, Will began to doze off. Minnie looked at him for a long time while he slept. Here was a man who was so good to her, who respected her and tried so hard to please her. What was wrong with loving him? Just because she was a different race, raised an Indian? She owed him so much already. He had introduced her to so many things. And really he was largely responsible for her landing in the job she was currently doing which was the best and most meaningful employ she had ever had. And he was so tender with her, and affectionate. Why should she care what other Indians think? She thought all this, but she felt like she wanted to kiss him. In his sleep. That if she kissed him he would wake up a prince. But then she realized since Friday, he had already become a prince. No, now her main task was to hold onto this prince.

When he awoke, the locusts were still rattling and chirping loudly and the heat was still overwhelming.

"We should head back I guess."

They stood up and started picking up their picnic things and the cooler and packing the canoe. It was a very hot mid-afternoon for late May and they felt it after they stepped out from the oak tree's shade. Minnie put her sun hat in the canoe and was getting ready to step in, when Will suddenly jumped at her, picked her up and ran into the river and dumped her like a sack of stones in water that was only three feet deep. Minnie came up spluttering and shaking and awkwardly trying to find her footing in the muck. Will splashed down like a log next to her and came up all dripping wet as well. "Oh sorry, Minnie. I must have slipped. And we don't have towels." Minnie wanted to be angry, but then she started laughing, and she began to splash him with her hands cupped in the water. "But we're not hot anymore." said Will smiling broadly.

They floated back to Indian Creek, wet but quickly drying out, and drove back sadly and quietly, windows wide open, to Will's bungalow. First thing after they got back in the house they had to throw off their damp clothes and take showers. Will let Minnie go first. She did not want to shower with him, because she was still a little bashful, and the shower stall was small. She didn't like intimacy in a small shower stall. He took the damp clothes and put them in the washer. After Minnie came out of the shower her long black hair still dripping wet, Will took a quick shower. He came out with a towel around his waist, saying, "Now you can use the hair dryer."

They put together a cold dinner with iced tea, and after cleaning up they sat on the couch and began watching one of the films Will had rented. When the evening wore on, she wanted more than anything to make love to Will. She began purring and cuddling up to him on the couch and slipping her fingers under his shirt. He began to kiss her, and before she knew it they were coupled right there on the couch in the full light of the main room in front of a running TV screen. In the lull afterwards, Will stood up, naked and limp, and went to the kitchen and came back with two fresh bottles of water. He put them on the side table, and then picked up Minnie and carried her into the dark bedroom. He put her in the bed then went back for the water bottles. And then they started again their passionate horizontal tango long into the night.

The next morning, they followed the usual routine, although it was a Tuesday instead of Monday early. She had her packed carry-on bag and was dressed in her professional clothes, and he was standing by her side in his running outfit, but without the orange track suit because of the warmth. They kissed and she was off soon joining the flow of weekenders also returning from the long holiday weekend in Ocean City. She thought briefly about how unsuccessful their visit to the beach had been. How could all those people spend an entire weekend, every weekend on the beach in Ocean City, she wondered.

The next day, Minnie called to tell Will that she would be coming back on Thursday after work because the legal team planned to come to the Nantiquak Association near Millville on Friday morning at eleven to make a presentation to the tribal council and Will's operating committee. The purpose was to consult with the tribe, as they were ready to file their lawsuit against the state of Maryland for restitution of reservation lands. Will already knew about the meeting and had already gotten the agreement of the tribal council and the members of his team to attend because Cal Reiner had called him on Monday to inform him of their need to meet with the tribe. Will deliberately set the meeting for Friday at eleven o'clock so he could spend Thursday night with Minnie. The tribal council did not object to that time. She told her bosses, Ron and Cal, that she would drive straight to the meeting on Friday morning and meet them there. They had no idea that she was spending weekends and all her free days and nights with Will in Bristol. Before she finished her call Will told her that he would be coming the next day to Washington to work at the census bureau's archives and they could make a dinner date and stay at that hotel they had stayed in in April.

When she arrived on Thursday night, she was in a good mood, excited by the preparations for the lawsuit and for the fact that the time had come to submit it. To launch the project. She spoke about it through supper and on into the evening. "It's really interesting. We're doing what has only been done once before. In Connecticut. We're following their model. And we think we have actually a better case and a better chance of success than that first suit had. We even consulted with Thomas Turino to get his advice." Will was pleased and he listened carefully to her. He was looking at her and thinking what a smart, capable profession Minnie is. He even felt that for the first time he was proud of her. "So I wish you all success." he said. "When and where are you filing this suit." "In the federal court in Baltimore. And we're ready to file as soon as the tribe gives us the green light.

That's what this meeting tomorrow is all about."

They took a long walk in the warm June air. It only became fully dark around ten o'clock and they strolled hand in hand to the riverside and down the river all the way to the outskirts of the town. Each street lamp was festooned with thousands of moths and flying bugs looking like so many living, quivering halos.

"These lamps remind me of summer evenings in Bowling Green." said Minnie. "Except there's no big river there."

"I wonder why there aren't more mosquitoes tonight." said Will. "They usually don't bite me."

"Well, they do bite me. They don't bite you because you have a different aroma. They bite me because they can smell the sugar in me."

Minnie was excited right to the time when they went to bed. "Let's play Bolero again." she asked Will. Their loving making was very passionate. She remained passionate long into the night because of her excitement.

Early the next morning, Will kissed her, and slipped out of bed and took his usual training run. He got back, hot and sweaty, just as Minnie was finishing her shower. When she stepped out of the bathroom all wrapped in towels, Will exclaimed, "Minnie, you're positively shining this morning!" And it was true, she felt love and at the same time she was very excited, even little nervous, about the upcoming meeting. She felt elated and happy, and that was what Will was seeing. After Will washed up, Minnie prepared a simple breakfast of eggs and toast and they sat discussing all the future steps of their project. Minnie was dressed in her serious, smart dark gray lawyer's suit. Will thought she looked great. Will did not wear a tie, but wore a light blue summer jacket and matching slacks. At the appropriate time, they left each in their own car for Delaware, kissing and hugging before they left. Will wished her luck during the presentation as they got into their cars.

Minnie followed Will all the way and they arrived at the Association building in only fifty minutes, before Cal and Ron arrived, but while members of the Nantiquak council were driving up in their cars. It was a warm day, so Minnie and Will waited outside. They greeted

Morley when he arrived, but he answered in his usual dour manner before entering. Chief Clark was friendlier and hailed them with a halloo and handshakes before also going inside. Minnie was so excited she could hardly contain herself. She stepped inside twice to use the facilities and check that her hair was still alright. One time when she came back she saw Carmine standing with Will chatting. But this time Minnie did not feel jealous at all with Carmine displaying her affections for Will.

Cal and Ron finally arrived in a stern looking black Toyota Camry just at the hour. On getting out of the car, Cal started his routine of acting as if he were in charge of everything and leading this event. He commanded that Will and Minnie go inside, but neglected to greet them with a good morning or anything. He even neglected to shake Will's hand. But Cal's driven, aggressive character immediately ran into clusters of sullen Indians—most of whom he had never seen or met before-- standing in the corridor of crowded trailer who were in no rush and certainly in no desire to be commanded by Cal. He almost immediately was exasperated. "We need to start this meeting now." Cal said to no one in particular. Then to Will he blurted out in a quieter tone, "Where is the chief?

What's his name? Where will the meeting be held?" Will calmly led the lawyers through the corridor, greeting each Indian by name on the way, he even pushed his head into Morley's office and greeted him a second time and told him that the lawyers from NAILS had arrived. And he made a joke with Morley about his new shirt. Morley grunted at that and stood up from his desk. Then Will continued on to the back hall where there were another six or seven men mulling around quietly talking to each other. Cal was pointed to the chief and he went over to him, said 'Good Morning,

Chief Clark' and shook his hand perfunctorily. It was a professional but cold and impersonal greeting. "Now we can get started. Where do you want us to sit, Chief?" Minnie was appalled. It was Cal's first meeting with the tribesmen who ran the council and the tribe, and Cal was not making good first impressions at all. Morley came up to them and said that not everyone had arrived yet so they would wait until everyone was there. He showed the lawyers where to sit on the dais behind a long table. Will sat with the other Indians in the three rows of chairs facing table. Shortly after Carmine came in and sat next to Will and began to talk to him in a low voice. Some of the other Indians wandered in without rush and took their seats, and sat silently. And then they all waited.

Minnie took out a yellow pad of paper and a pen, and then sat patiently looking at Will. Ron sat between Cal and Minnie, embarrassed by his boss's apparent impatience, but not brave or rash enough to tell his boss to cool it and relax. The Chief sat next to Cal on the other side and occasionally leaned forward and in a very low quiet voice gave some instructions to a young man who was sitting directly opposite him. Morley stood at the door. Over the next ten minutes one or two more tribesmen entered the room from the corridor and languidly took their seats. And then two more after fifteen minutes. This was Cal's first meeting with the tribe, and he was clearly showing his agitation and impatience and complained several times to Ron. Finally at 11:25, when Cal's exasperation was about to explode, one last man walked slowly into the room, waved to those in the room and took one of the last empty chairs.

Chief Clark remained seated and now spoke up, but still in a steely quiet voice. "I think we are ready now. Everyone's here. Today we have the honor of a visit and presentation by our legal team from NAILS in Washington. They are here to tell us about the progress they have made on our behalf.

And I am sure you will all find it interesting. Here is Mr. Calvin Reiner, the managing partner at Nails, to tell you something about our fate and one of the important steps in becoming a federally recognized tribe. "

Cal now puffed up with self-importance. "Shall I stand or remain seated?" he asked Chief Clark. "As you like." Cal stood up and began addressing the assembly. He started speaking slowly and with clear enunciation but as he progressed he began to speak faster. He told them about how the state of Maryland had appropriated and sold the Maryland lands appointed by treaty to be reservations in perpetuity for the Nantiquak Indians, and how these seizures and sales were illegal at the time. And that they remain a crime and a tort that should be remediated. He said that the law made it clear that the newly incorporated Nantiquak Nation had the right to sue the state of Maryland for restitution, and even damages. He told them how he and his team, and he introduced Ron Parchesi and Minnie Warrens, Chief of the Massaponax tribe, had put together a legal complaint and that it was ready to be filed in the Federal District Court in Baltimore. He then asked Ron to put up a map that they had made showing the size and location of the reservations which had been seized and sold. Ron unrolled a large sheet of paper and then held it against the back wall. It was map of the Eastern Shore focused on Maryland. It had highlighted in color the various fragmented reservations along the Nanticoke River, the Broad Creek, the Wicomico, Manikin, and Pocomoke Rivers.

"In total all these reservations came to more than 13,000 acres." Cal said seriously, raising his voice for dramatic effect. "A very serious appropriation of treaty lands. Ranking up there with the other seizures of Indian lands elsewhere by the administration of President Andrew Jackson, all of which were later to be found to be illegal and in violation of treaties and laws."

Cal continued, waving his arm in Minnie's direction but not looking at her, "And Chief Warrens here, who is also a respected lawyer with our firm, has compiled the likely value of these lands today. And her estimates indicate that the market value of these lands today amount to more than one hundred and thirty million dollars. Gentlemen, you indeed have a very serious grievance and claim against the state."

Someone in the middle row spoke up, interrupting, "We have lots of grievances." Cal stopped and looked up. There was a mutter of approval around the room, which took a few moments to settle down.

and then as he would say in the office, 'get out of Dodge.' Discussions and questions continued a little longer, and finally Cal asked Chief Clark, "Could we make a poll on whether the tribal council approves of moving forward with this lawsuit?"

Chief Clark nodded his head, and said simply, "We're doing that now. Consensus building."

Another tribesman stood up and asked if they could ask the state of Delaware to recognize their properties on Indian River as being in a reservation. Again Minnie answered.

"Once the tribe gets federal recognition your members can join their properties together and put them into a trust where the federal government would be the trustee. This is just what the Eastern Cherokees have done to form their large reservation. And once this trust is formed the tribe could buy any privately held lands that are within the boundaries of the trust—if the owners are willing to sell-- and add them to the trust. The trust lands would be in every respect like a reservation. The members would still own their properties within the trust, but could not sell those properties to someone outside the trust. And the trustee would guarantee the ownership and control of the lands by the Indians resident inside."

Finally after more than forty five minutes of discussion which to Cal seemed really off the main point of his visit, Chief Clark said to the group, "So is there anyone here who would be opposed to starting a court case as Mr. Reiner has so kindly outlined to us?"

There was a silent pause. No one raised a hand, no one raised an objection. After a minute, Chief Clark then turned to Cal and said, "So there you have it. We give you our consent to file our complaint against the state of Maryland. When might you do it?"

Cal paused momentarily, "Let's see today is Friday, May 29th. I think we would go to the clerk of the court on Tuesday morning, the 2nd of June."

"That's great. So we're all for your efforts, and you'll let us know if you need any support or additional information from us for this lawsuit to move forward. We want to thank you for your efforts up to now and for your visit today."

And with that the meeting ended. Cal was ready to bolt out of the room, but Ron and Minnie had to put some of their materials back in their briefcases. Will came up to the table and congratulated Cal and shook his hand. "We feel confident that you have done the best job possible in preparing this complaint. So we think we should prevail. I trust you'll keep us informed about the progress of the case in court. Once the court decides to take on the case." Cal shook Chief Clark's hand and turned to leave. No one came up to the table wanting to put additional questions to the lawyers except for Carmine. She went to Minnie as she stood up to leave.

"Thank you so much, Minnie. You were great. What you said was so clear and made so much sense. And you've done so much preparation. Can you tell me about the steps that will take place in this case, step by step?"

"I'm afraid I can't Minnie. I've never brought a complaint up to a federal court, especially one against a state. I suppose the court will review the case and decide whether they will hear it or reject it. After that the details of the steps—well, I just do not know what will happen when. What the court does in sessions, and what the attorneys do in sessions. Or in what order exactly."

Carmine looked disappointed. But she gave a big smile to Minnie, and then turned to Will and said, "We'd like to follow the steps as they go. But I suppose the court hearings will not be like we see in films or on TV. But keep us posted."

Cal and Ron rushed directly to their black Toyota almost neglecting to say farewells to Will. Minnie went over to their car and told them that she would not go back to the office that day. It would be after three by the time either she or they could get there. Cal excused her and drove off as if he had to catch a plane. Will then turned to Minnie and said, "You want to follow me back also?" He was joshing her and his smiled showed it. Minnie nodded her head and got into her Ford and drove behind Will out of the parking lot, followed by a dozen or so cars and pick-up trucks of the Nantiquaks. A little over forty five minutes later at one fifteen they drove into Bristol. Minnie was still following close to Will's car and soon she realized that he wasn't going straight to his bungalow off Market Street near the river. Instead he stayed on Highway 50 until he signaled and turned off to the right. Minnie followed and parked next to Will's car. When she stepped out of the car, she asked, "What's with the detour?"

"I thought that we would try the seafood in this my favorite restaurant in Bristol, Poseidon's Palace. It's just opened for the new season. Best seafood on the Eastern Shore. And good craft beer made on location."

They went in. "And the owner's son is a friend of mine from high school days. Here he is. Minnie meet Tony Giannis. Tony meet the love of my life, Minnie." Tony shook Minnie's hand. "Isn't Will a super guy?"

"I couldn't agree more with you." said Minnie smiling.

The interior walls were decorated with antique crabbing, oystering, and fishing paraphernalia, clam tongs, large posters of enlarged antique lists of fish prices, prices for crabs, and announcements of new consignments of seafood for sale, old photos of the town, fishing trawlers, watermen standing on the sterns of their flat boats with piles of oysters behind them, and large colorful cans.

"What are those cans Will?"

"Those are oyster cans. It used to be that oysters were shucked and canned here in the old canneries. And then a fast ship would take them to Bawlimor or Warshington where they would be sold without the shells. Bob when he was young used to work in one of those canneries. Maybe you noticed that the parking lot was all oyster and clams shell bits and fragments."

At the table Will said the crab cakes were especially good. Tony added that the new beer they had brewed last night had to be tried. Minnie said she would taste Will's, but she ordered the appetizer portion of the crab cakes with a side of hush puppies which she had now come to like. Will ordered a pan fried rockfish filet with some fried oysters as a starter.

Some moments later Tony again came over to their table offering iced tea in large plastic tumblers. "Have you begun to reel in the Ocean City weekenders yet in this new season?"

"Yes, you may have seen that we put the words 'stop in for homemade craft beer' onto our marquee outside. Memorial Day weekend was a big success. Since then we have reeled in a bunch of new customers on their way to the beach. We should start seeing this weekend's customers in a couple hours now. How's your Injun project going?"

"Minnie can tell you. She's a lawyer acting for the tribe."

"So she's not merely your newest girlfriend?" said Tony winking at Will.

"No, she's very talented in so many ways, but she's also learning the life of the Eastern Shore people every day."

"We're making good progress on the Indian Project, Tony." said Minnie. "We had an important meeting with the Nantiquak tribal council just today."

"You mean up in Delaware?"

"Yes. We're going to court on their behalf next week."

"Great. So be sure to tell me when you're going to start the Indian casino part of the project."

"Sure," said Will. "But we're still some ways away from that stage, sad to say. More than a year I think. Maybe more than two years."

"So Minnie, do you come now often here to Bristol?"

"Every weekend for the past two months. Or almost every weekend." "Like Bristol?"

"Yeah, and I like Poseidon's Palace too."

Minnie tried a taste of Will's beer. She was surprised. It was the first time she liked the taste of a beer. Normally she wouldn't touch beer. Will agreed with her that it was a very tasty and smooth beer. He ordered another pint.

Later that afternoon, after Will had checked in at his real estate agency office and Minnie had changed into her fishing clothes, they went to the abbreviated bridge to go fishing. It was a hot and sticky afternoon, without even a faint breeze, so they spent only an hour fishing, catching three small croakers and one sheepshead. And that evening together they cleaned and cooked their modest catch and ate the fish with hominy. The next day the weather was cooler and the skies overcast so Will proposed that they go hiking through the Black Marsh reserve. "You'll see what most of this land looked like when the first white settlers approached it from the Bay. What wasn't marshland, and especially tidal marsh, was all pine forest."

They drove down to the reserve and went to the visitors' center--which thankfully was air- conditioned--and saw the exhibitions. Then they took the driving loop through the marshes. There were lots of sea birds and tall herons. Minnie even saw a black snake lazily squirming across the road. "Keep your eyes peeled. Ther'r all kinds of wild animals here. You can see them everywhere." said Will. Further on this drive, Minnie also saw a raccoon waddling in the middle of the road. As they passed, it idly went to the side of the road on Minnie's side of the car as if to let the car pass.

"It looks like it has a frog in its mouth." she said excitedly. There were several places where the road came right down to open water. On these large ponds were ducks and geese floating about, and on all the verges were reeds, thrushes and cattails.

"Let's count the species we see." said Will.

"I don't know the names of the birds. I've seen a lot of them before on our reservation. But I don't know what to call them."

"Just point them out to me; I know a lot of them by name."

Not long after Will spotted a lumbering mass on the side of the road which looked like a walking rock. As they approached it froze looking at the coming vibration of the car. "It's a snapping turtle." said

Will. "Very archaic looking." After completing the loop, Will parked the car. "Let's take a short hike."

They walked about three hundred yards toward what was indicated as an overview, but were swarmed by clouds of tiny biting mosquitoes. "I forgot the bug spray." moaned Will. They were slapping themselves from front to back and top to bottom. The mosquitoes drove them back and they at the end ran back to the car and jumped in, still swiping at daring mosquitoes which flew into the car with them. "Look, Minnie. I've drawn blood here, here and here. My own!" One had bitten her on the forehead even and two bites on her ear especially itched. "I suppose it's always like this?" she said. "Except in winter. Sorry I forgot about it. You know in the town, they spray against mosquitoes." "Really?" "Yeah, when I was a little kid, it was pretty bad in town. And my pop told me when he was a boy there was still yellow fever in Bristol carried by the mosquitoes." Minnie shuddered. She remembered that when she was little on the reservation, mosquitoes had been bad, but not so bad as what she just experienced. "I can imagine that there are not a lot of tourists who visit here, other than the road tour and the visitors' center." she said.

That evening Will found a voice mail message on his phone. It was Jackson who was inviting him for a party next Saturday evening at the Bristol Yacht Club. Will told Minnie about Jack and his party invitation and suggested that they go together. She agreed.

"In that case, tomorrow we need to go to the mall in Salisbury to buy you some party clothes." So on Sunday they drove over after spending a leisurely morning in bed together. They went to a stylish shop, Ralph Lauren and Tommy Hilfiger were featured, and Will pressed her to buy several colorful blouses, some light weight slacks, and one casual but smart looking summer-weight dress. He led her through the whole process, selection, fitting, and trying on for him. Minnie protested every step of the way, but at the end she was surprised at how much she liked the pieces she had selected with Will's encouragement. When they were finished in the clothing store, Minnie had five boxes of new clothes tucked into three enormous shopping bags. Will led her to a jewelry store. "I want to buy you something to go with your new clothes and that matches your eyes." He went straight for the stones, and quickly found a pair of emerald stud earrings. "These I think will match your emerald pendant." The pair he selected were priced at seven hundred and twenty dollars. He asked for a ten percent discount on the posted price, and he got an eight percent discount.

"Will, really, that's too much." Minnie protested mainly at the price.

"Besides I don't have pierced ears, Will."

"They can take care of that here, right now." "Won't it hurt?"

"I'll hold your hand, if you like. I assure it won't hurt more than a bee sting. And then it will be all over. It will hurt maybe even less than that fish hook in your thumb a few weeks back."

"But I don't want to be stung by a bee either. I've never liked that."

"Mini-oaka, you will look so beautiful in them tonight when we go to my parents for dinner. Wearing your new outfit and your emeralds. And next week at the party every girl there will be envious of you."

She gave up any further protest and she went to a sheltered corner of the shop where the woman sales assistant took out an instrument that looked like a modified paper hole punch and a bottle of alcohol and a cotton pad. She put some alcohol on the pad, whipped Minnie's ear lobes, and then real fast it was over. She told her to hold the cotton pad tight on the ear lobe while she punctured the other one. The second time Minnie yelped a little. It certainly seemed to her that the pain was more than a bee sting. With her fingers and the cotton pad she pinched down on both ear lobes for several minutes. Each came off after those few minutes with a tiny drop of blood. And then the assistant wiped the earring studs also with the alcohol and offered Minnie one of the earrings to try putting it on. It felt strange as she pushed the stud through her ear lobe. The second ear lobe hurt more when she put in the other earring. And then the assistant offered her a mirror. Minnie caught sight first of her thin white scar on the lower neck, but then she focused on the earrings. They were dazzling and beautiful, quite large translucent green stones set in white gold. She had never had jewelry in her life and now she had an emerald collection.

"That looks just as I thought, Minnie. Stunningly beautiful. Sparkling. Mother will be really impressed tonight."

And at dinner Mar Sue was impressed by the makeover in Minnie's outfit. No longer sober grey or black. And then Mar Sue noticed the emeralds.

"Wow! Minnie they're so beautiful. They offset your beautiful black hair so nicely. Did Will get them for you today?"

Minnie blushed and nodded yes. "And the blouse and the slacks too."

"You're a lucky girl. Dressed up like that, you look beautiful. I suppose I should say that it's Will who is lucky."

Over dinner Bob asked about the Injun Project, and much to his surprise it was Minnie who answered in depth and at length. She outlined first the objectives for the Nantiquak, then she went through all the key objectives, and then she explained the steps and preparatory tasks that everyone needed to complete in order to fulfill the objectives. She finished with the possible outcomes, chances of success, and finally she outlined what the Nantiquak nation could do with federal recognition and new reservations. She concluded by describing the lawsuit that they were going to file that next Tuesday.

After dinner as they walked back to the bungalow, Will thanked Minnie for that outline and detailed explanation. He told her that his father had been very skeptical of the whole project, and thought that what he was doing was a pointless waste of time, but that her presenting it the way she had obviously impressed Bob and added credibility to the project. "He saw that it was your project too," said Will. "And I appreciate that you did that. He saw that you were committed and serious about carrying it out." Minnie snuggled against Will and they strolled even slower. In bed together cuddling and maneuvering and caressing each other into foreplay Will kissed each earring on her ear lobes and whispered to her, "I love my green eyed girl."

On Tuesday evening, Minnie called Will from her office and told him that the suit had been filed. And that the court would take it and vet it and put it under consideration to see if the lawsuit could be pursued. They were told it would be about a week to ten days before they heard whether the court would accept it for a hearing.

"And I have a surprise for you. The next weekend, on the 13th, I got tickets for us to go see a piano recital that is being given by Martha Argerich herself. On Saturday night. Would you like that?"

"Yes, super. We can see and hear her, a little close up. Closer than we have up to now. And then you'll see how much you two look alike. And we can have a weekend on the town like we did last month."

"That would be great."

"Shall I book the same hotel?" "Yes, it was very nice."

"Fine. I'll come on Friday afternoon. But you have to agree to wear your emeralds when we go out."

"I agree, and I hope I remember too to bring them with me on Friday morning."

They spoke over the phone again on Wednesday and again on Thursday. For Minnie these were the most important moments of her work week. To talk to Will, hear his voice, dream about what they might do that weekend, to shorten the time and distance until she could see him next in Bristol.

The next weekend was like most of the others except that they went to Jackson's party at the yacht club. They walked over there for the five o'clock start. Minnie wore one of her new outfits, with a new pair of loafers and of course with her emeralds. They walked hand in hand. Will apparently did not know what the motive of the party was, and he was eager to ask Jackson what it was. All he told Minnie is that Jackson, or Jack as he called him, was a friend from high school who was a lawyer and a state deputy in Annapolis. And he told her that he had attended Jack's wedding to a Maryland girl named MariAnne, the previous September, so it couldn't be a one year anniversary party for the two of them. They walked into the yacht club and at the front were a well-dressed couple acting as greeters.

"Hello Jackson," said Will. "MariAnne, how are you both? I've come with my girl, Minnie Warrens of Bowling Green, Virginia."

They were all smiles. Introductions and hand-shaking.

"I'm glad you could come Will. And happy to see that you've brought an Indian princess with you."

"I'm so happy to see Jack's good friend, Will." said MariAnne. And you look lovely Minnie. Don't worry Will, Suzy won't be here."

Minnie looked at Will as if seeking an explanation. Will went wan for a moment, but then continued. "So you're not going to tell us what occasions this party, Jack?"

"No, it's just a party, having fun." said Jack. "The Assembly is no longer sitting for the summer, so we've moved back here until the new session in October. So you could say a welcoming party, a house warming, for the two of us. It's the first time we've lived here in Bristol together. We're having steaks and a little later there'll be a band, so dancing the night away. Come on in, grab some wine, introduce yourselves around."

There was a buffet table set up along the back wall in the main party room. A barkeeper stood behind one table next to the buffet serving cold drinks and wine. The sliding glass doors were open, leading out to the patio and the lawn on the riverbank. There were clusters of young people standing around, chatting, waving their wine glasses and around the patio were a about a dozen small round tables covered in white table cloths, each table provided with two chairs. On the lawn several men were setting up a large grill and loading it with charcoal briquettes. "Do you want a wine?" Will asked Minnie. "No maybe an iced tea would do for now." She sat at one of the tables that was already half in the shade as the sun was fast descending into the lower Choptico. Will came back with the drinks. He had a chilled white wine which had already coated its glass with condensate.

"I don't know anyone here," said Will. "I think we're the only ones here from Bristol, besides Jack and MariAnne."

"Who's Suzy," asked Minnie.

"Oh she was one of the bridesmaids at their wedding party last September. We danced for hours. But she was from Philadelphia. Don't need to be jealous. You're my only woman, only love in my life."

"But you've had other girlfriends too, haven't you?"

"Yes. A couple of them even live here in Bristol. But I haven't seen either of them in almost a year or longer. And what's more I don't want to see them ever again, either."

"Oh, that's good to hear. I've displaced all the previous contenders."

The band was setting up. Then people took up plates and lined at the buffet table taking salads and potatoes, and taking drinks. Then they returned outside and lined up at the grills and chose their grilled meat, either steaks or pork ribs. Will took another wine and while loading up inside he spoke briefly with Jack. Back at the table when they had sat down again, Will told Minnie what the motive for the party was. "It's funny. For Jack and MariAnne this is their second anniversary of the day they first coupled. Apparently their sex life is the calendar of their life together." Minnie thought that was a funny moment to commemorate, but she realized that her life was also highlighted by her new sex life with Will.

Not long after everyone was finished eating, the band began to play. There were three people in the band, no singer, and they played dance hits of the previous twenty five years. Will with his hands invited Minnie to join him with the others dancing and scuffing on the patio floor. "I don't know how to dance. I'll embarrass you and me too."

"Come on, Minnie. Just follow the rhythm and step simply."

She let him lead her onto the floor, holding both her hands and looking into her face. She did not resist but she moved slowly. Will began to dance a simple dance step, first one foot and then lifting the other and turning his shoulders back and forward, still holding her hands. Will was smiling.

Minnie was feeling as if everyone was looking at her, but of course, no one was. She looked shyly around and saw that everyone was dancing in his or her own style, each couple quite different from the other. "Just let yourself go with the flow." Will spoke into her ear. Minnie wasn't quite sure what that meant but she did warm up to the activity. And after a few songs Minnie began to loosen up and felt that she was indeed flowing with the music. Her motion, in unison with Will's, even began to feel pleasurable. They danced five songs together and then retreated to their table which had been cleared away except for the glassware. They got more drinks, Minnie took a glass of white wine. The sun was chasing the horizon to its orangey finish over the green river. It was the most pleasant early summer evening Minnie could ever remember. And in this small group of maybe 16 revelers, no one seemed to recognize that Minnie was an Indian. No one seemed to care or even notice her. She was with Will, by his side or in his arms, and that was all that anyone noticed, that was the only thing important now to her. She especially liked the slower dances when Will took her into his arms and pulled her close to him so that her figure was pressed against his contours. The slow swaying and turning was like honey. Once again she was experiencing something delightful— this time it was dancing with a man she loved—which she had never done before.

The next day started out sunny and warm. They resolved to go out crabbing, and Will called his father by his cell phone to ask for the boat and to ask if they would like to share in a crab boil later that afternoon. Everything agreed they drove over to Bob's house, Minnie did not even get out of the car as Will bounded up the stairs to the grand entry door. Bob handed him the key to the boat and the dockside locks. Mar Sue ducked out the door and waved and smiled to Minnie. "See you soon with your harvest," she shouted over to her. And then they were off. Will bought a bucket of smelly chicken pieces, and a big bag of ice. Minnie put on her broad brimmed sun hat. He filled the motor with gasoline there in the marina and they then slowly put-putted out into the river which was between tides and fairly calm. Will steered across the river about a mile down from the marina near Foy Point and there he anchored the boat.

"So now for good luck, you'll kiss me." said Will as he leaned across to Minnie and planted a kiss on her lips. She pushed her tongue into his mouth and the kiss lasted a long time, with Minnie's fingers lightly tracing across Will's neck and jaw.

The good luck kiss worked charms. In an hour and a half they had caught thirty good sized blue crabs, and Minnie didn't get her fingers pinched even once, even when she worked the scoop nets.

When they had caught three dozen crabs, Will said it was time to get out of the sun and go back to

the dock. "Anyway, we're out of stinky chicken bait." On the dock he separated the crabs, twenty to one cooler and the rest remaining on the mostly melted ice in the original cooler. "I can sell these crabs to Tony at the Poseidon Palace. We don't need so many for our crab boil this afternoon."

Later in the back yard at Bob's house, they sat down to eat boiled crabs, steamed corn, steamed clams and mussels, potatoes all accompanied by drawn butter. Minnie once again really enjoyed slamming the wooden mallet down on the crab legs. Everything tasted so good to her. Bob and Will had beers, Minnie stayed with an ice tea, and Mar Sue drank white wine and soon everyone was in a happy mood. In this high state of jollity, Mar Sue raised her wine glass.

"We can consider this an early birthday party for you Will. Congratulations to Will on becoming a full grown man."

"So when exactly is your birthday Will?" asked Minnie.

"Next Wednesday, the tenth of June. But it's nothing special and I hadn't thought about doing anything. No party or anything. It's mid-week."

"You'll be thirty, right?"

"Yep. So I'm no longer a youngster for you to take advantage of," chided Will. "Just kidding."

"What do you mean nothing special? Your thirtieth should be a milestone, no? I'll have to get you something special for your birthday."

"You already have. You bought tickets for next Saturday night's concert."

Minnie thought she heard a gentle reminder of her being older than Will. She felt again that perhaps she was too old for him. Mar Sue did not miss it.

"So when is your birthday, Minnie?" she asked. "September 3rd. I'll be thirty-six then."

"Oh, we'll have to write that down." said Mar Sue. "We have to have a birthday party for you then."

"What day of the week is that, Minnie?" asked Bob.

"I don't know." she said.

"It's a Thursday." said Will. "I know because it's just before Labor Day weekend, the biggest weekend of the summer."

Will paused and smiled at Minnie and then as usual said the right thing. "She says she'll be thirty six. It's hard to believe when she has the skin, face and figure of a twenty two year old. When almost everything we do together are first time experiences for her. She's still a young girl of twenty something who only pretends to be thirty five, because the calendar in her case is lying."

Bob smiled at something he thought up. "Yeah, Minnie, you look so young and innocent, that I bet you they still card you, whenever you ask for a hard drink, or buy a bottle of wine."

Minnie thought what Will had said was sweet. But again it was his way as a salesman. She knew he was wrong. Her biological clock was not mistaken. And maybe later he would come to resent her being so much older. She asked for a glass of wine.

"I raise a toast in advance of Will Eames's birthday." she said. "You will always make me feel younger."

On Wednesday, Minnie stepped out of her office for lunch. But first she called Will on his cell number. He answered at once. "Hello

Minnie. Are you at lunch?" Minnie sang 'Happy Birthday' to him over the phone, except that she used the word 'dearest' instead of 'dear Will'. She giggled a little when she finished. Will was ebullient in his thanks.

"You know they need to invent a way to send things through the microwaves. You could then send me a birthday cake straight through my cell phone!"

Minnie did not quite know what he meant, or whether he was joking.

"But I could order one for delivery for you." she said. "In fact I can do that now. Why hadn't I thought of that before? Is there a bakery in Bristol?"

"None that I know of. Other than mom."

Back in the office on Wednesday, Minnie looked in the yellow pages on the internet and found an advertisement for a bakery and cake shop which offered delivery in Bristol. She called the shop and spoke to the woman who answered asking if they could do a delivery that same day, there in Bristol. She answered that they could, but only for cakes that were already prepared. And there were only three left. One was a wedding cake, clearly not appropriate, and there were two others, one a chocolate cake with double chocolate icing, the other a white cake with lemon cream frosting.

Minnie asked for the lemon cream cake and asked if they could write Happy Birthday on it. The saleswoman agreed and they then made payment arrangements directly over the phone with Minnie's credit card. Later that evening, as Minnie was on the train to Thornburg Will called her on her cell phone to say thanks and that he had just received delivery of the cake. He would enjoy it and would have to share it with his parents as it was more than three pounds. More cake than he could eat in a week. Maybe even in two weeks. But he said it was delicious. He loved chocolate cake. When she got off the line, Minnie wondered how the bake shop could make such a mistake.

On Friday late afternoon, Will was already waiting for her outside her office when she got off work. They drove her car over to the hotel and parked it in the courtyard parking lot. As she stepped out of the car, she suddenly remembered the day's big news. "You know, Willeams, I have really good birthday news for you. The court in Baltimore accepted our petition and will try the case." "So we get a breakthrough. Wonderful news. You've done a good job and I'm sure our complaint will win." They then took her overnight bag up to the room that Will had already checked into and when Minnie started to undress and change into her more casual clothes, Will grabbed her, half undressed, and rolled with her on the bed. They made love together earlier than their recent routine, in the daylight. Will said that he could not wait any longer for her. Minnie felt the same way from the first kiss. "So maybe that was a starter for my birthday gift for you?" she said as they lay in bed recovering. After they got up, after they had freshened up and gotten dressed, Minnie gave Will a birthday present. It was a book by a famous Wall Street financier entitled, "How to Invest Successfully in a Volatile Market". He thanked her with another hug and kiss, and promised that he would heed the author's advice.

"I didn't know what to get you, Willeems. You're a man who seems to have everything."

"Almost everything. But the important thing is that you give me your free time and your love; that should be enough for anyone."

"Do I please you?"

"Immensely, enormously, stupendously, lovingly."

Later, they stepped out and walked across the Rock Creek Bridge to Georgetown. As they passed along the wooded streets of brick townhouses which comprise Georgetown, Will pointed out to her all the houses which had signs showing that they were either for sale or for rent. There seemed to him to be a lot of houses on the market which was odd as 1998 was not a presidential election year. They went to Claude's for dinner. He'd made a reservation earlier for eight o'clock. They ordered oysters again as their starters. They both drank iced tea with mint.

Over dinner, when there was a lull in the Friday night hurly-burly, Will said:

"I've been thinking Minnie about a way to solve our little problem. I mean about beginning our life together, living together. I think we could rent an apartment and live here together in Washington.

I would commute between DC and Bristol on Monday thru Thursday, and on Fridays after your work, we could both drive out to the farm for the weekend. Or to my little house in Bristol. That way we could live together all the time. You wouldn't have to commute the long way. What do you think of that idea?"

Minnie thought it was a brilliant idea. But her answer was reluctant. "Really? You would do that?"

"Yes. In a snap. But the question is, 'Will you do it? Move in with me here in DC?'"

"Yes. Yes, let's do it." she said. She felt immensely relieved, she committed to living with Will.

"Well, we can shack up, as the saying goes, as soon as we find a suitable place. I propose we start looking tomorrow. We can call it our Nike project."

"Why? What does that mean?"

"You said, let's do it. 'Just do it' has been the advertising logo for the sports shoe company, Nike, for a long time. So let's just do it."

Minnie giggled and agreed. "Yeah, let's do it. Again and again." She was thinking of making love as she said this, let's do it was often said by Will when he wanted to start making love to her.

When they got back to the hotel room, late that evening, Will surprised Minnie with some of the chocolate birthday cake which he had brought with him. "Let's order tea, or liqueur or something from room service to go with the cake. Oh, forks and plates too. What will you have?"

"Milk. With chocolate cake I like milk."

So he ordered and in twenty minutes they sat together eating their cake and drinking tea and milk.

On Saturday they started looking for available apartments to rent. Will knew exactly how to get the property listings and he had brought a street map of Washington with him. So first they did some research together over the map, matching available units with the neighborhoods and seeking proximity to the metro stops. They chose six places that offered the best combination of reasonable rent and conditions along with a good location near a metro station or a main bus stop. One of their selections was complete small house, and the rest were apartments. All of the offered apartments were unfurnished. They finished their morning search by calling to the rental agents to set up viewings. They arranged to see three that same afternoon and the other three on Sunday.

Inspecting the apartments Minnie saw for the first time Will's professionalism as a real estate agent on display. He amazed her with his ability to recognize problems or needed repairs straightaway where she saw none. He understood how the places were built, their quality, and the level of wear or past repairs that had been implemented just by looking. He knew his stuff. And he applied it.

Two of the apartments he ruled out almost immediately as he identified that they had mildew problems in the walls of the apartment building, which pointed to unpatched roof leaks and a problem with the heating system as well. As it turned out on Sunday, they liked the house best of all, although it was the oldest property that they visited. "The owner has kept up this property really well. I think he's spent a lot on repair and maintenance." The house was located on a quiet tree lined street in the Cleveland Park neighborhood, and was available because the owner was leaving on a four year diplomatic posting overseas. The price was a reasonable $1,400 a month for sixteen hundred square feet. And they could move in immediately. Will said right there to the agent that they would take it and he would pay for the advance on the spot. Minnie was overwhelmed. Her cottage rental was not due to expire for another two months.

"Well in that case, your renewal notification is probably due any time now. You just tell the manager that you don't intend to renew. We can move you out next weekend. Maybe we can strike a deal with the owner of your cottage to enable him to rent it out for those two months. Especially if we evacuate the place and have it all cleaned up."

"And you don't need to worry, I will be paying the monthly rent, and for the moves. We know what we're going to be doing next weekend."

Minnie was amazed at how quickly Will decided everything. For her, pulling up house, packing, moving to a new city, setting up full time life with Will, dealing with the movers and unpacking and setting up a new home, these all seemed like major moves and changes, life changing and important, requiring lots of time and slow careful preparation. For Will he was able to organize the implementation of all these changes without the slightest of doubts or hesitation. It seemed to him all easy, just a matter of execution and will. It was all exciting and a little breath-taking for Minnie.

On Saturday evening, before they had rented the house in Cleveland Park, they went to the concert at the Kennedy Center. They took a leisurely stroll to the Center from their hotel through the warm summer evening. The concert itself was splendid but Minnie was a little disappointed that she hadn't bought tickets closer to the stage as the view of Martha Argerich was not so clear. But Will did not mind. He had brought his binoculars (not opera glasses) with him, and after the maestra came out onto the stage he was able to look at her and he confirmed that although clearly older than Minnie and not as ruddy skinned, the two bore some close resemblance. Not as close as Minnie and Mena, he added, but close enough to make him think he saw Minnie when he looked at Argerich. Will even liked the music; a concerto by Franz Liszt, a composer whom he had never heard of before and whose music he had never heard either. Minnie loved the music and adored the way Argerich performed it. She had not heard the concerto before either, and she was swept away by its drama and romantic power. Using the binoculars she did recognize a certain similarity between her face and Argerich's. But that recognition did not excite her much. And especially as she read in the program notes about the artist that Argerich had not long before recovered from a long and painful bout with cancer. This saddened her and made her think of her own mortality and made the romantic highlights of the music seem more poignant. The rest of the concert comprised a symphony by Tchaikovsky and the fifth symphony by Sibelius, something about swans flying south in the Fall. Will saw that musical image at once. "Just like the geese that fly over the Eastern Shore on their way south. But maybe swans and geese don't fly the same way." Overall she enjoyed the concert immensely, and was pleased that Will seemed to enthusiastically respond to the music as well. At the end he kissed her and thanked her for the most beautiful birthday gift imaginable.

After the concert, they stopped in a small restaurant claiming to be a French bistro and they had a quiet dinner. Will continued to be effusive in his praise for Argerich and her performance. "She is so beautiful, so graceful. Her long fingers running through the notes. What a wonderful woman, a wonderful artist on the keyboard! Of course I've never seen a live performance of a piano concerto before, but this was clearly top class."

As they walked back to their hotel, Will said simply, "We should do this again. I mean the concert. And often." Minnie agreed although she was feeling a little tipsy and flushed from the glass of red cabernet wine she had drunk.

Sunday evening they spent dining on the outdoor terrace of Tony DeLuca's seafood restaurant down near the Watergate on the Potomac. It was a hot sticky evening, typical of humid Washington in the summer. When they first were seated rowers were still out training on the river in their long slender shells making tracings across the still waters of the river as the last of the sunlight glinted off and reflected back off the white marble of the Kennedy Center. Minnie ate a small salad and a large bowl of clam chowder and Will had oysters as a starter and a grilled grouper filet. After the dishes were cleared they sat closer and started plotting the tasks they needed to do the next weekend.

"So we need to plan to pack up your house on Saturday the 20th." Will started writing on a yellow legal pad Minnie had brought with her. He wrote at the top of the page: Nike Project. "I will drive up here on Friday afternoon with some things from my house in Bristol and I can move them in there before you get out of work."

Immediately Minnie knew there was a problem.

"The 20th? That's the day of our tribal council meeting down the peninsula. I don't think I'll be able to get out of it."

"Can you be finished by two?"

"I think so, but it is still forty miles away from Thornburg. I would also like to introduce you to my mother. She thinks you're a poor dirt farmer, taking advantage of me."

"Well I am, Minnie. As often and as much as I can. And loving every minute of it."

"Don't joke like that, Will. She's not going to like you at all. Because you're a white man. It will be hard for me. She thinks I will cease being an Indian, too assimilated, by being with you."

"No. I think it's the other way around. I will become more Indian. But, okay, so after you get out of work we can drive down in my car to Thornburg on Friday night after I pick up the keys and drop things at the house."

"But then don't forget we would have to go pick up my car at the Spotsylvania station." "Right."

"And then where will we stay?" Minnie asked. "Friday night? Why at your place, no?"

"The bed's too small, I think. The place is too small." "You mean it's a twin bed?"

"No, it's a double, but it's small."

"So we'll be closer than usual. That is after we stop making love together. Don't worry. We'll manage to sleep in each other's arms.

"And the place is such a mess."

"Not a problem. The next day we're going to throw everything into boxes and into a truck and then the place will be quite neat. Now of course, you will need to tell the landlord or the manager that you'll be evacuating the place from the 21ˢᵗ."

"I'll do that."

"So, maybe we should make introductions to your mother on Friday evening, if it won't be too late." "That should be alright. She lives twenty five minutes away."

"Good that way, we can get all the upset and tears out of the way so we can begin packing on Saturday. The movers could come first thing in the morning. Do you have a lot of furniture that needs moving?"

"No, not really. A chest of drawers, a kitchen table, a couch, some chairs, one overstuffed chair. Not so much really."

"So you'll have to think what I might need to bring from Bristol. You can do that over the coming week. Fine. Then I'll stay at your house supervising the packers, when you go to Central Garage for your council meeting. We should be all finished by the time you get back."

"That sounds good."

"So I need to book a proper moving company for a small house move to come on Saturday. And deliver to Cleveland Park on Sunday, or Monday at the latest. I'll do that, then, first thing tomorrow morning."

"So I understand that on Saturday night we would need to stay in a motel somewhere near Thornburg." said Minnie.

"That's right. Although if they pack everything and take off by Saturday afternoon, we could drive back to D.C. and spend the night in a hotel there."

"Wouldn't that cost more?"

"Yes, but we would avoid people who might still think the miscegenation laws are in effect in Virginia. And other racists who might object to us rooming together."

"You're right of course."

"And then on Sunday we open the house for the movers when they arrive. And while we wait, we can go to the zoo, which is practically next door."

"Why would we do that?"

"Oh, I like watching the monkeys copulating for the visitors." Minnie hit him with a light swipe on the shoulder. "Oh stop it." "Beat me, beat me. I'm in heat."

"Stop it. Not here."

"And then when the movers are all through, we kiss them goodbye and go to buy some groceries for supper or breakfast, and spend the rest of the year unpacking boxes and putting things away. Trying to sleep there that evening, and trying to sleep there comfortably during the rest of the week too.

So ends the Nike Project." "Sounds doable."

"Yes it does. So let's do it." "You mean, the Project?"

"Also." By the time they were finished it was dark and the rowers had all retired for the night.

The next morning they left at eight forty after checking out of the hotel: she set off walking in her professional lawyer's uniform and handbag, he dressed casually getting into his Oldsmobile. He did a wolf whistle at her as she walked away. It did not upset her. She liked it, from him. Their life was about to take another major change.

The week flashed by, they kept in frequent touch by cell phone with updates on the arrangements. Friday came and Will called Minnie that he had packed some things in the car and was leaving Bristol. Next time he called a few hours later saying that he had already unpacked them in the house and he was heading to meet Minnie in front of her office. Another two hours later they picked up her car and drove on to her Thornburg cottage. Will had brought two large suitcases for Minnie to pack up the clothes she needed for work the next week. They grabbed a light dinner at a greasy spoon on the intersection of two highways that defined the center of Thornburg about half a mile from Minnie's place. Minnie had decided not to ask her mother for dinner, because she thought for sure it would be too stressful and maybe even her mother would refuse to prepare dinner for a white man who was exploiting her daughter. But her mother did expect them and they arrived at her Bowling Green house just as twilight's last glow was slipping away.

Minnie's mother laid out an icy reception for both of them. She answered the door and turned away from it even before they could enter the house. She did not smile at seeing her daughter and she barely muttered a greetings. With her arm she waved them on into a little front sitting room where they sat together on a small sofa. She did not say much besides, "Would you like some coffee?" she asked sternly. Then she left them in the room while she went to prepare the drinks. The house was silent and in a general rundown condition. Minnie hadn't really taken much notice of the sad state of the sitting room in her most recent visits. But now she did and she felt ashamed. She feared that Will would judge her mother unfairly. How much of this shabbiness and dust was due to poverty, how much to the indifference of living mostly alone in her old age, and how much to a general Indian indifference to cleanliness and orderliness Minnie did not know, but she was afraid that Will might conclude the house's condition was due to an Indian predisposition to slovenliness and disorder.

She at least had shown Will a neat and clean cottage. When Ma Warrens came back in with the coffee and a sugar bowl, Minnie made the introductions. Ma Warrens remained standing in an opposite corner.

"Mom, this is the man I was telling you about, Will Eames of Bristol Maryland. He's down here now because we are moving house up to Washington where we will live. He runs a real estate agency in

Bristol and runs a large farm further up in Dorset County. Will this is Genna Warrens, she's a purebred Massaponx Indian."

Will stood up and leaned over toward Genna. "Pleased to meet the mother of my beloved Mataoka. She's the finest woman I have ever met or known. You raised a wonderful, talented woman."

Will offered his hand to shake, but Genna did not take it. She did not smile. In fact, she scowled even harder. There was a long moment of silence.

"Mom, be polite."

"Why should I? Are you two getting married? No?" "No."

"But you're going to live together, unwed, in Washington, a city full of dangerous negroes. You don't demonstrate that you're going to take very good care of my girl."

"I'll take real good care of Minnie, Mrs. Warrens."

"Yeah, right. The first pretty white blond girl with big tits who flirts at you, and you'll be gone in an instant, leaving Minnie in misery."

"No. That will never happen."

"Mom. Be nice, for a change." "Fine."

They finished their coffee.

"You're right. Minnie is a good girl. Don't ruin her. It was a white boy who seduced her younger sister and then pimped her into prostitution. She was lucky to escape and find a husband. But most are not so lucky."

"Mom!" said Minnie in alarm.

"White men have never done any good for Indian women. They don't even protect them from black men."

"Then it must be hard for you to live in this town of white men, so far from your tribesmen." "I look after my grandkids."

"Wouldn't you like to live on your reservation? Closer to your brethren?" "Can't afford to move. And there are not any houses available there." "Well, then maybe we can help you."

"What for?"

"To relocate to a place where you'll feel more comfortable."

Genna did not say anything. She frowned and looked away at a different corner of the room.

"Mom, I didn't want to upset you any more than I already have. We have to go now." For the first time Minnie noticed how old, ashen-skinned, and shrunken her mother had become. Her hair had a lot more silver in it. Had this occurred just in the past four months since she had been spending weekends on the Eastern Shore? Or was this the first time in a very long time that she looked closely at her mother?

"Mrs. Warrens, here is our address in Washington. And our telephone numbers, both cell phones and home phone, our work phones. If you ever need anything, feel free to call us."

"I'm not going to send you even a postcard. And I won't send one to you either, Minnie." So they left after a very brief visit. Minnie was very upset; she cried most of the way back to

Thornburg. She was upset with her mother's angry rejection. And she was ashamed that she told Will about her sister's period of working as a prostitute. She did not want to make love that night, but she did want Will to hold her. He tried to sooth her, but to no avail. They fell asleep after a long bout of sobbing by Minnie. Will held her in his arms, it seemed all night.

The next morning the movers came not long after they had finished breakfast. Minnie had already set aside her clothes in suitcases to take that night to D.C. After the movers had already constructed a dozen cartons and boxed the mattress, it was time for Minnie to leave for her tribal council meeting at the café. Will saw her out to her car and put two of the suitcases in the trunk of his car. He gave her a kiss, and patted her on the bottom. "Be brave, Mini-oka. See you in a few hours back here." She felt immensely sad as she drove across the summer landscape. She had prepared a program of items to present to the council, but her mother's harsh reception last night still shook her. And the empty abandoned landscape across to the peninsula, failed roadside businesses with their rusted signs hanging outside, fallow fields, houses with caved in roofs, and empty farmhouses, all weighed on her. These were outer signs of the curse of poverty that so afflicted her tribe that chose to remain in these lands.

She started the meeting with a review of the progress of their application to the Bureau. Unfortunately she had nothing to report. Nighthorse had told her over the phone only that the tribe's recognition application was still in process and had not yet been approved. But a conversation with one of her former colleagues in the department told her that Nighthorse was blocking the application for reasons that no one could understand in the department. She, of course, could not tell that to her tribesmen. She changed the subject. Again she brought up the recent experience of the Nantiquak tribe in conducting an internal census. That census had included a lot of interviews about family histories and ancestry and in the process had uncovered genealogical links to Indians living in the 19th century and as well as lot of tribal lore, legendary history and stories and information that had not been put into the written historical record. She suggested that the three bands of the Massaponax-Doeg tribe undertake the same kind of census and interviews.

"This is especially important now to avoid any further assimilation and to collect the unwritten records of our people. We have to uncover and promote the cultural relics that give us our identity besides our racial identity, and make us uniquely a tribe of the eastern Tidewater. These relics could be little things, like remnants of Algonkian words or phrases that are still known or the story of our last Algonkian speaker. The Nantiquaks have lots of information about that that they have compiled over the years and preserved. Or like a recipe for one of our traditional foods. Or a dance step that our ancestors used to perform for one occasion or another. The Nantiquaks have initiated an annual powwow to show some of those traditional dances, maybe even if they are only recreated."

"This is especially important as our three bands live so far apart, and of course are drifting apart. This kind of effort also would be something that we can completely control. Unlike our negotiations with the school system. And it would create a kind of database of information about our tribe that would be a source to future generations."

The other members of the council were not prepared to hear Mataoka's proposal. They were not sure what the census would entail, how it would be conducted, or what benefit it would have for the tribe. And they of course could not understand what such a program would cost, and who would do it. All this got into complicated and pained discussion, with a lot of digressions and subtle objections to doing much of anything. Minnie tried to stir up enthusiasm and support from the other men, but was frustrated by their stubborn refusal to understand the entire concept. Until finally Tanner broke into the discussion.

"All this identity research you're talking about sounds just fine, except that it won't stop any further assimilation and loss of our identity. You yourself have started living with a white man. Can you really expect to remain an Indian? Your assimilation is complete. Maybe you should no longer be our tribal chief?"

"Tanner! I have not ceased to be an Indian because the man I love is an Anglo. But that makes it even more important that we find out more our people and our ancestors. And in fact nothing is so clear cut. He himself is one-eighth Nantiquak Indian."

"Yeah, we'll all become mixed breed if we follow your example. And we'll cease to exist—just fade away. No more Indians. The white man's ideal solution to another race problem."

Minnie appealed to the other eight tribesmen of the council. "Do you want me to step down as chief?"

The other men reacted startled and confused and mumbled among themselves, but did not answer clearly one way or the other.

Minnie let it go. "I think our meeting is over. I won't be staying for lunch—again—because I have other things I have to do today."

"So why don't you resign, right now, Minnie?" taunted Tanner.

She ignored him. And she asked if the others were willing to end the meeting. All agreed, and she left without sharing lunch with them. The meeting made her mood even sourer. She should have resigned right then and there, on the spot and let Tanner clean up the mess. But she hadn't. She had missed her chance and her proposal to conduct an internal census had for the second time that year met the opposition of indifference.

When she got back to her cottage in Thornburg, Will was standing outside haggling with one of the movers. The truck was closed up and the front door stood wide open. Will waved to her and smiled. Just seeing him like that lifted her spirits a bit. It looked like the movers were already finished, and indeed when she approached close to Will, he turned to her and said just that. They were negotiating when they could deliver to the Cleveland Park house. Finally the young man with whom Will was negotiating agreed for a delivery the next day at three o'clock. He was a scruffy looking white man, but his lifting partner was a huge, muscular black man. She could imagine that he carried all the furniture out of the house and into the truck by himself, including the mattress and bed frame.

"I'm really soaking." said Will. "I have to take a shower. How did your parlay go?" "Not well. Maybe I'll tell you about it later."

"Okay. I brought a towel and some soap. Do you need a shower too? We could try together, save water."

Minnie looked in the direction of the movers who had already climbed into the cab of their truck. Maybe they hadn't heard. "No I'm fine for now without a shower."

"Well, then I will do a solo cleaning job, and then maybe we can grab some lunch. Come on in and have a look around to make sure we've missed nothing."

Minnie followed Will into the house. He closed the door behind them. Minnie was struck by how different the place looked when it was completely empty of furnishings. She had thought she would be upset by moving out, but in fact in her nearly five years of living in this isolated small house, she had not grown attached to it at all. She saw some large spiders emerging from newly exposed corners. They made her shiver. She wondered if there were any dead mice. Will went into the bedroom-- which she had shared only once with him that previous night-- threw off his clothes in the middle of the room and from a sack on the floor picked out a towel and a shaving kit. And then fully naked he stepped into the bathroom. Her eyes followed him the entire way. He was good looking; she kept thinking how much she liked looking at his bare body, with its rippling muscles, shoulder scars, small buttocks, and his healthy genitals. When he stood up fully naked, he looked his full height of six foot one inch. Somehow when he was dressed he did not look that tall. But he was five inches taller than her and she snuggled under his shoulders comfortably. There was no place left to sit down in the entire house. So after moving between a couple rooms, Minnie stepped out the front door and sat down on the stoop. The truck was already gone, and the traffic flitting up Highway One made a small racket across the eighty feet of grass and weeds that was the front yard.

They arrived at the Cleveland Park house at about four thirty on a sweltering, humid summer afternoon. They both found parking on the street right in front of the house. Minnie took her suitcases out of her car, and Will came over and took them from her and they walked together up the brick stairs to the house. Once inside, Will turned on the central air conditioning and he took the suitcases to what would be their bedroom, the larger master bedroom with a full bath attached and a walk-in closet. The house was almost as empty as the Thornburg house they had left a few hours earlier, except that Will had brought some simple furnishings the day before such as a pair of chairs, a set of towels, a small kitchen table and some cooking utensils. They actually had rented the entire second floor of a large three story brick townhouse. Will had said it was seventy years old. Still it had a private entrance, two bedrooms and a separate kitchen and dining room, and even a utility room with a new washer and dryer, altogether more than 1400 square feet of living space. It was very spacious. The carpeting showed everywhere the outlines of the landlord's earlier furniture. "This will be our home for the near future." said Will. "But it sorely needs furniture." They did not stay long, it was far too stuffy inside and it would take hours for the conditioner to cool the place under the broiling sun. Will had made a reservation for the night at the same hotel they had stayed in the previous weekend. After eating a small meal at a small ethnic restaurant—it claimed to be Salvadorean but Minnie couldn't tell from the menu-- on Connecticut Avenue they took the metro down to the West End.

Sunday as promised the moving truck arrived and three different young men started promptly unloading it and carrying the cartons up to the second floor. In about two hours they were finished and had set up the bed and mattress, and carried away some of the larger cartons. Will gave each of them a twenty dollar tip. They now had some furniture in the house. A full size dining table for the kitchen, a couch, a television, a wardrobe, one overstuffed chair, bedside tables. And a bunch of unpacked boxes. They began the very tedious process of unpacking and figuring out where things should go and by evening they had a pile of cardboard by the front door.

"I would stay tomorrow and continue unpacking," said Will, "except that I have people who want to see some houses. I always have to attend to potential buyers. So I will start my commuter routine tomorrow. And come back tomorrow evening. But we've unpacked enough that we can sleep here tonight and get dressed for work tomorrow. Don't you think so?"

"Yes, but it looks to me that we will be unpacking for a long time."

"Yep. We'll have to make a list of our needs for this new house. But anyway we can begin our life together here tonight. You'll have to tell your office manager that you have a new address. Taxes will be different, unfortunately. This week we'll have to make arrangements with our banks, and the post office, and the power company."

"There are lots of things we have to do to start this new life together, aren't there?"

"Yeah. For starters, right now, we need to buy some food, coffee, an electric kettle. So we can start fixing our own dinners and breakfasts here. Maybe we can do that now before going back to that place we ate at last night for dinner tonight. I saw that there is a grocery store on Connecticut

Avenue, not too far from us here."

"And then I can become a housewife."

"Precisely. My lover and housewife. And tribal chief, and lawyer, and Argerich look-alike. Multiple roles for you, Mini-oka. I don't have so many roles."

"I guess it should be enough that you are my man."

The next morning, Will started their new city life with an early morning run around the neighborhood. He was back by seven thirty as Minnie was just finishing drying her hair. He took his shower. "It's really humid here, and the terrain here is not flat, as it is in Bristol. So I am soaking wet." They had breakfast and were ready to leave the house at eight thirty.

"Today on our first day, I'll walk you to the metro station."

"You don't have to. But it would be nice if you did."

It was a five minute walk down the hill to Connecticut Avenue and then to the metro stop. "I think you'll appreciate the air conditioning inside." said Will. And then he kissed her goodbye.

That week he commuted back and forth every day except Friday and came home at around six o'clock. Minnie came home at the same time and they met at the house. Monday evening after emptying a few cartons, they inaugurated the house by making love –hot and sweaty-- first in the living room on the couch and then in the bedroom, and fell asleep completely exhausted. Friday afternoon, Will stayed in Bristol and waited to meet Minnie there in the late evening. They stayed that night in the Bristol cottage, and they planned to move out to the farm on Saturday afternoon.

Friday, Will stayed in the house all day, and that afternoon he met Minnie outside her office with his Oldsmobile idling on the street out front. Then they joined the heavy stream of weekenders heading for the Bay Bridge and Ocean City. "I never thought I would become like those weekenders heading for the beach. How life can change." said Will as the traffic began backing up before the bridge.

"We'll jump out of this heavy stream before the beach though." They were in Bristol by seven o'clock and he stopped at Poseidon's Palace for dinner. Minnie already thought of this small restaurant as a familiar and welcoming place that was part of her life.

"Maybe it would be nice out at the farm. We haven't been out there for a while. And I could become more accustomed to living there." They pulled into the gravel lane just as twilight was beginning to lose its last gleaming.

They both had overnight bags with them. And on the porch, fiddling with the keys to open the grand front door,

Once inside at the farmhouse, after driving through a frightening thunderstorm, Will saw that the house was very clean. But the windows were closed and it was warm and very stuffy, in spite of the thunderstorm.

"And there is no air conditioning in this house. That's a shame. Good thing it's not as humid here as it is in Washington. But we'll have to get some fans for each room. Maybe some air conditioners, for the windows. And I'll call Phyllis. She can come tomorrow and make our meals."

That night as they lay naked in the big bed on the main bedroom on the second floor, Minnie became aware of the intense deep voice of the surroundings. On the one hand, the night seemed deeper and darker--absent any jarring city noise like car motors, burps from motorcycles, or distant sirens-- than in Cleveland Park, as if they were on an uninhabited island in the ocean. But on the other hand she came to notice that there was a huge background noise of chirruping and clicking of cicadas and locusts that never ceased. But this noise was calming, consistent, and lulling, not alarming like so much of the city noises which crashed in on them from time to time through most every night. It was almost as if there was no noise at all. Minnie thought she stayed awake far into the night but when she woke for a drink of water she saw that it was only one o'clock. She slipped back into her green night shirt and went back to sleep.

Early the next morning, a Sunday, when the sun was already bright, she tiptoed out of the room without disturbing Will. She went into the study and began to look again at the photos of Mena. She agreed that she looked a lot like Mena, except it seemed Mena was much darker skinned. She thought that she had probably been sleeping in the same bed that Mena slept in seventy years earlier. Not the same mattress that was clear. The thought gave her a curious feeling that she somehow belonged to this house. She wondered if Mena would approve of her. At least as much a Hampton had. Mena would understand Minnie's fear of assimilating away from her Indian roots.

And Mena would approve of her love for her great grandson, Will. And probably Mena had been confronted by much more racist contempt than Minnie so far had experienced. She spent nearly an hour looking at the photos and reading the articles. She noticed that the articles about the black man who had murdered Mena's mother nowhere gave his name. And one article suggested that in addition to shooting dead Mena's mother this criminal had violated Mena. Minnie thought that meant he had raped Mena. And from the notes that Hampton had put together it seemed that Mena and Will Senior had married less than nine months before Hampton was born. Had Will Sr had sex with Mena before they got married? Could that explain his attraction to her and his desire to marry her even against all the opprobrium of the society around them at that time? Perhaps they were lovers before they got married. But Minnie saw that Hampton clearly could not have been the child of the black man who assaulted Mena and murdered her mother. As he was born eleven months after the incident, but only seven months after Mena and Will Sr got married. Around seven thirty, Minnie crept back into the bedroom where Will was still sleeping. She quietly went back to the bed and took his penis in her hand and began to stroke it. She suddenly wanted his love so badly.

Later over breakfast Will suggested that they go out canoeing on the river again. Minnie agreed at once. "But I will wear my swim suit so we can go in the water and keep our clothes dry."

"And don't forget to wear your sun hat." said Will.

They went back to the same rental place on Indian Creek and got the same green canoe they had the last time. This time Will suggested that they try to paddle upriver to a point opposite Goose Point and there where the Choptiko was only about six hundred yards wide they could try to paddle across. "There are some sandy beaches on that side of the river where it's a little nicer to swim."

"So the answer is Nike: Let's just do it." said Minnie grinning at Will.

"Sadly there is no oak tree to give us tender shade on that side of the river."

So when they got to the place opposite Goose Point they began paddling strongly against the tide. She clearly felt its tug once they were in the middle of the river. It was strong enough that Will had to keep turning them to the right, but the tidal pull was only in the middle and soon they were approaching the white sand beaches at Goose Point. And there they put the canoe in, Will jumping out in the water just as the bow of the canoe began to scrape against the sandy bottom. He pushed it far up onto the sand and invited Minnie to step out on to dry land.

"Now first we have to have some drink." said Will opening the cooler that sat in the mid ships of the canoe.

They had drinks and then Will suggested that they step in the river to cool off. Minnie consented and took off her clothes revealing her swimsuit. Will changed into his swim suit, undressing fully before stepping into the swim trunks. Then he took her hand and together they stepped slowly into the water until they were in up to their thighs. The bottom was not mucky as it had been on the other bank, but instead there was sand and clay. He led her out a little ways further until the water was up to her hips. She could see her feet through the green water which was not cold at all.

"And now, we take the plunge. One, two, three."

And he sat down in the water. And pulled her down into the stream with him. The water was refreshing, not quite warm. He splashed her. And then he sat on the bottom and she moved over to him and sat down in water up to her chin, her black hair curling around her head on the water's surface.

They remained sitting, sometimes splashing, for some time. Minnie was often giggling.

"You know, I've been told that almost a quarter of the Chesapeake is shallow enough that I can stand in it with my head above water at middle tide."

Later they got out of the water and dried off with the towels that Will had brought this time. But they did not change back into their clothes. Minnie put her big brimmed sun hat back on. Will brought some food out of the cooler and opened a can of beer for himself and a lemonade for Minnie and they had lunch sitting on the sand.

After they finished and Will had put the containers back in the cooler, they sat talking about what they still had to do for the house in Cleveland Park. He said they would have to put together a wish list of things they needed to do for their own comfort. "Like putting in ceiling fans in the farmhouse, or spot air conditioners to help us get through the summer."

It was then that Minnie apologized for not doing anything for his birthday, two weeks earlier.

"What do you mean? You bought me that book and sent me a lemon cake that was chocolate. And it was delicious."

"No I mean we could've had a party for you."

"I didn't have any plans. And having a birthday party is not all that important for me. I don't have a big group of friends in Bristol insisting that I hold a party. I didn't expect anything."

"Could I do something for you? If you could have gotten your wish at your birthday, what would you have wished for?"

Will paused to think a bit. "What I wished for my birthday? Or right now? Honestly, Minnie, it would be to marry you."

Minnie was caught off guard, and she must've blushed. She didn't know what to say.

"Let's put that in a different way." He reached over with his hands from where he was sitting, not very close to Minnie, and took her hands. "Mini-oka, will you marry me, plain old Will Eames of Bristol Maryland? There, that's more like a proposal. I don't have a ring just now, but my proposal to you stands just the same."

"Really? You're not pulling my leg?"

"No, not pulling. It would be better than any conceivable birthday party or birthday present, if you were to say yes." he said earnestly. "I'm really sincerely serious. I want to marry you." And then he smiled, and mischievously said with a change in his tone: "And if you don't say yes right now, I will leave you right now as they say round here "up a creek without a paddle" and it's a long walk back to Bristol."

Minnie chuckled but wanted to cry at the same time. His proposal took her so much off guard. She shook her head as if to say no. "I can't marry you." she said almost under her breath. "I'm too old for you. Maybe we couldn't have children. I'm a dark-skinned Indian who people around here don't accept or respect. Indians shouldn't marry white men. And what's more, I'm an Indian tribal chief, who would not be respected by her own tribesmen. Your parents wouldn't approve of me as a wife. My mother is opposed. I wouldn't make a good wife for you. I would disappoint you in so many ways. There are so many obstacles." The one obstacle she didn't mention but which was one of her biggest fears was that if she married Will, she would in no time cease being an Indian altogether.

She also hadn't told him that her only sex prior to their love making had been two rapes. She feared that Will would change his feelings about her if he knew that she'd been raped twice in her life. And she did not know how she could tell him. She was crying by the time she finished reciting her list of obstacles.

Now Will pulled himself up close to her and planted a kiss on her cheek. "I don't have a ring just this moment, but Mini-oka," he whispered. "will you marry me?"

Still Minnie was crying. "I'm crying from happiness. But I'm sad."

"You don't want to marry me?"

"No, I do, it's just that I can't. I don't see how it's possible."

"So you'll have to think about it?

She nodded her head. She was now afraid that if she didn't agree to marry Will he might not want to carry on living with her, even though they had just started.

"So, I understand. You want to marry me but just now you can't for reasons that you find unexplainable, or are not fully understood by yourself. Am I right?"

"Yes, yes, yes. You're right." she said and wrapped her arms around Will's head pulling him against her chest, and kissing the top of his head. "I won't say no, but just now I can't say yes."

"So I will have to find out the ways to get you to say yes. To overcome your obstacles. To make your wish equal to my wish for us. So that you will soon come to me and also say you want to marry me."

"I can answer your first objections right now, Minnie. My parents would love to have you as their daughter in-law and would not object at all to our marriage. In fact I think they are rather expecting it and even encouraging it. Maybe there will still be opposition from your mother, and the rest of your family, but we will have to work on them to come round to me. The local society in Bristol would not be opposed and neither scandalized and would hardly even take notice of our marriage. We certainly don't have to show off or broadcast it widely in Bristol. And besides we will mostly be living in Washington. As for being an Indian chief of a tribe across the waters, I think that can be addressed but I don't know how just now. And for sure there are no more laws that ban marriage between Indian women and non-Indian men. And you are certainly not too old. I don't think of you as too old. I mean just look at your figure. I think we can still have babies, but maybe we will have to work at it. And as for being a good wife, I think that probably is not the case. But maybe being a good spouse requires effort, and we will just have to put in that effort. After all you yourself said last week that you have become a housewife."

"But I was only talking in terms of setting up the house." said Minnie.

"Mini-oka, you can be a lover, a sexual partner, and a housewife and my wedded wife all at the same time without any conflicts between those statuses."

"And of course we are really only talking of formalizing what we already have. We are already joined in conjugal partnership. You are my lover and I am yours and I think we both want to plot our future life together, for as far as we can see. Am I right?"

Again Minnie nodded, but she did not look up at him.

"I pledge to you that we'll have to overcome all these obstacles that you believe prevent you from saying yes to me right now. I will resolve to do this. It may be as difficult as converting the Nantiquaks into a federally recognized tribe, but I doubt it. And you will help me. I've seduced you and convinced you to love me and live with me, so now I must convince you to commit to me as I want to commit to you. Minnie you will be my new Injun Project. We will work together to overcome your obstacles and defenses and tear down the walls of your reluctance and fear of unfavorable social consequences. Right?"

Minnie nodded and they kissed and then he began to kiss away her tears from her cheeks. Her hands were caressing his back and head.

"And most important of all. You love me don't you?"

"Yes, very much. You're my Willeems, my one and only love."

"Well that sounds like a formula from a marriage ceremony. All you have to say further is 'forever'." They sat closely and quietly for several minutes, hands wrapped together over Minnie's lap, her fingers nervously rubbing against his.

"Minnie, you can't be crying because I say to you that I love you. Can you?"

Minnie shook her head in the negative.

"I'm so confused." she said and she started to sob again.

They remained sitting next to each on the sand for some time, until Minnie began to calm down. "We'll resolve this later." said Will and he stood up and jumped into the river and swam a ways out and then back. He stood up. "Want to get wet again? Cool off?"

Minnie stood and walked carefully into the river and repeated the sitting posture in the water.

They got out but remained silent. Will had another beer, and then said it was time to head back to the farmhouse.

"But first you will have to paddle us back to Indian Creek, okay? Meanwhile I'm going to have a cold drink—just don't think of me as too callous. I mean letting you do all the paddling while I drink. You could have a cold bottle of water too if you like."

Minnie's mind was tied up in rational calculations and raw conflicting emotions. The rational arguments threw up obstacles to marrying a white man. But her feelings and emotions ran in opposite directions; they made her feel as if she would explode and she yearned to get married to Will as soon as possible. Tonight if possible and let the calculations go hang. She could barely contain herself.

Later that night as they went to bed, Minnie pulled Will up to her. "Keep on loving me, as you have loved me before. Keep on saying you love me, just as you have said before, Willeems. And I can love you again and again, over and over. Because I love you, Willeems. I am still learning what that means. But I want to keep on loving you as long as I can. And take me into your arms at all times, now and forever. Please, say that you will."

"Minnie, I will. I am yours, now, and forever. You have all my love."

Chapter 3

Near Indian River, Delaware, early 1998

"We didn't include them in the tribe in the last century, so why should we want those half-breeds and Negroes in the tribe now? You know, we set up the Association to distance ourselves from them. And they haven't been part of our community ever since. Even though they are our neighbors. They were willing to give up their Indian identity and go to the school and church for the Coloreds. They submitted to being called colored and Negroes. And they still do. So why invite them to return to the tribe now?"

"Uncle, we're half breeds too."

"But we're not colored or Negroes. Now are we? They haven't any cultural or racial relationship with us. So how can you conceive of them as Indians?"

"They may conceive of themselves as Indians in spite of their inter marriage or what we think about them. After all we consider ourselves Indians in spite of our mixed heritage. And besides they don't look like blacks. Or at least most of them don't. And many of them demonstrate that they consider themselves Indians since they participate in your powwow every year since it was started."

"Maybe they don't look black, but they don't look like Nantiquaks either."

"And what is a Nanticoke Indian supposed to look like," interrupted Chief Clarke

"You know what I mean." said Marley.

"No, I don't. Tell me," said Chief Clarke now sounding a little irritated. "At the last powwow there were dancers from the Shawnees, one or two Oneidas, a black Cherokee from Oklahoma. And several Ojibwai. They all looked like Indians to me, especially in their traditional clothes. Even if they weren't especially authentic. We don't have any such traditional clothes and I can't think of anyone in our Association who looks like those other Indians. So does that mean that Nantiquaks don't look like Indians? We have photos of the founding members of the first Association. And I can see in them that they look like they are related to each other, but I can't see that they looked so different from our neighbors who didn't join the tribal association."

"Yeah, everyone always tells me I don't look like an Indian." said Carmine. "I'm too fair and too tall and don't have the high cheek bones. But I think I am no less Nantiquak than you Uncle."

Marley was clinching his teeth and letting anger well up inside him.

"Well, let's say we conduct the census of those eastern Indian River people and use that as an invitation to the tribe." said Will. "We can try to extract information out of them about their ancestors, maybe even where they married with blacks. Of course only if they know. That way they can make the decision if they want to be included in the Nantiquak tribe, instead of us making the decision for them. Maybe after one hundred and twenty years of exclusion they will not want to join up with the tribe."

"But maybe they will, when they learn that we are trying to get federal recognition for the tribe and all its bands and clans." said Carmine.

"So does anyone else object to extending this census to a wider band of Indians?" asked Chief Clarke. "I think there might be later objections when you go to invite the bands of Indians in Maryland to participate in the census and to join the larger tribe."

No one in the room spoke up.

"Fine we'll vote on it then. All those opposed to extending our invitation to the Indian River Indians to join the Nantiquak tribe raise your hands." The eight members of the tribal council and the four members of the operating committee all remained silent, and then four people slowly raised their hands, including Morley.

"Yes, and all those who favor including the others in our tribe and extending an invitation to them so we can conduct a broader census, now raise your hands." Eight people, including Chief Clarke, timidly raised their hands looking around the room to see who else was voting in favor.

"Will, I think that means that you can proceed with the census." said Chief Clarke.

"We will, but how will we find the members of this "lost tribe?""

"I think we can start at the AME Church where they still go." said Ronald.

"And the eastside school where the separation first started." said another, who Will did not know by name.

"What's the story with the school?" asked Will.

"It was back in the 1840s when the state of Delaware said they would only pay for a school for our community if they considered it a school for the coloreds, and the teacher they appointed was a negro from Dover." said Carmine. "Our group of families that later set up the first association objected and said they did not want to be classified as negroes. So they pulled their kids out of that school and set up the Heritage School, which they paid for out of their own pockets. All the names of that group then agreed to set up an Association which they registered as the Nantiquak Tribe in Centreville. The two groups have been separate ever since. But those that remained behind in the black school and black AME Methodist church did not continue to call themselves Nantiquaks. In fact I do not know what any of them call themselves. But they remain to themselves, like an Indian tribe."

"I guess we can start then on Sunday at the church, and at the school on Monday." said Will.

Morley looked sourly at all the others. He felt that if they invited a broader number of people into the tribe and then incorporated it, it would mean the end for the association. But he had already expressed this concern a number of times and Will had reassured him that the association could carry on, but it would change its objectives and maybe even its organization.

"Then once we get the names of the families for this eastern band of the Indian River Indians who want to join the broader Nantiquak tribe, we can start the census questionnaires with them. Maybe we can even find some genealogical links with today's tribe. And maybe they will unveil to us their black ancestry, if they indeed have any."

"They won't." said Ronald. "It would be too much of a disgrace for them."

"How's that? All the race laws that penalized the tribe in the 19th century have been struck down."

"You'll see. No one here in this part of the state wants to be considered to be colored or black. Including the negroes themselves."

"And what if they were considered Indian or native American?" said Will.

"And they also don't want to discover that they are only one-eighth or less Indian by blood." said Morley. "We should not allow people with such weak claims and distant blood relationships to be members of our tribe."

"You mean people like me?" asked Will, now getting fed up with Morley.

"Not just you. But people with even less of blood claims."

"Pardon me, but all of this is bunkum." said Will sharply. "Do you all have detailed enough genealogical information back six or more generations to be able to verify your blood ancestry? Is it written down as historical documents anywhere?"

Chief Clarke tried to calm matters. "No we don't." he said dryly. "Some families maintain oral traditions, but most don't have memories going back much more than four generations, and then they can't confirm that non-Indians entered into their bloodlines even in those four generations."

"Maybe there are church records?" asked Will.

"Nobody's asked about church records," answered Carmine. "But I doubt that the local churches have any documentation. The oldest ones are just simple wooden structures. No offices, no residences for pastors, and so no records or files."

"Maybe not marriage or birth records, but gravestones?" asked Will.

"There is a church historian for the Methodist church who lives in New Castle, upstate." said Carmine. "It seems the Methodists starting in the 1820s made the biggest effort to convert all the Indians on the Eastern Shore, and that means the Nantiquak and all its bands. So checking gravestones might work. If they can be found and read."

Will had a sudden brainstorm. "But the real way to confirm genealogical descent would be to check the DNA of today's Nantiquak with the DNA of those of the eighteenth or nineteenth centuries. A gravestone does not indicate what race a person was. But their bones might."

Once again Chief Clarke interrupted calmly, "Are DNA tests accurate enough to indicate a person's Indian ancestry-- what tribe, what band, what clan they belong to?"

"From what I've read, I think they do." answered Will. "Certainly more accurate than the censuses that the federal government conducted in the nineteenth century when racial policies and Jim Crow laws distorted everything."

"So then, we can ask people to identify gravestones of their ancestors in Methodist churchyards at the same time that we conduct these census interviews." said Chief Clarke.

"And then we'd need to ask people who feel they are related to the bodies in the graveyards, if they would permit us to dig up the bones of their relatives and examine them for DNA information." said Carmine who seemed most familiar with the issues.

"Yes, and all of this is going to take a lot of time." said Morley as if that made the effort not worthwhile.

"So to establish a baseline for the Nantiquak Indian DNA," said Will, "I propose that right away we can exhume the bones of my great grandmother and run a test for Nantiquak DNA on them. And maybe also the bones of her mother can be found and tested as well. That would establish the genetic line from the nineteenth century for the Nantiqauk band who still live down on the Nanticoke River. And we can ask them if they know of older gravesites of their ancestors also."

One of the tribal councilmen raised his hand seeking to contribute. Chief Clarke nodded to him.

"I'm Jimmy Walker. Since I was a little boy, my parents and grandparents always pointed out to me the gravestone of my great, great great-grandfather lying in the graveyard up at the Heritage Methodist Church. He was a John Walker. If I remember correctly it says he died in the 1850s. I can volunteer that his bones be dug up and tested for his DNA."

Another man stood up, "And I can offer the same for my ancestor grandfather and grandmother. Their stone is located in the same churchyard. They died in the 1870s. They are in the Coursey family plot."

"Of course we can start DNA and genetic testing from our own ancestors' remains. If people don't object to exhumation. I recall there are a lot of gravestones in the Heritage Church graveyard from the early to mid-nineteenth century." said Carmine.

"But we will need to find the laboratory that can reliably do this DNA or genetic testing for the ancestry of the Nantiquak line." said Ronald.

"I think I can do that." said Will. "It seems that there are laboratories offering these services as genealogical investigators, commercially. Some are advertising over the internet. But I read quite recently that some universities have started this kind of genetic testing as well. So I will start looking into that this afternoon."

There was a long quite pause in the room then Chief Clarke raised his hand, "We are agreed then. That we will begin our surveys—this so called internal census—of the other bands of Nantiquaks in the Eastern Shore. And we will extend an invitation to our neighbors here in the Indian River area to see if they want to be counted as Nantiquak Indians and if they will participate in the census. And we will start that this weekend. As soon as we have the resources we will begin the censuses among the bands located in Maryland. We are not concerned at this point to make decisions about the degree of blood relationship of the individuals we interview to the greater Nantiquak tribe."

The meeting adjourned and the men from the tribal council including Chief Clarke quietly filed out of the large meeting room of the Association building. None of these said good bye upon leaving. Will spoke up asking the members of the operating executive to remain a short while to discuss next steps. At that Morley stood up.

"I'm not going to stay, because I'm not going to assist in the census. Most certainly not in the invitation to our black neighbors who are not Nantiquaks."

And with that Morley left the room also and went to his office in the next room. Four people remained with Will, including Carmine, the only woman, Ronald and two young men named Jefferson and Rob Johnson.

"So I see we will have more work to do with even less resources."

"It's not such a loss," said Carmine. "He's my uncle, but you know, in general he does no work because he is so lazy, and he wouldn't be much help to us, even if he participated."

"So what are we going to call these neighbors? The black Nantiquaks?" asked Will. "The non-Association members? The separatists? Maybe we need to make a public invitation to find the names of those who would like to join the Nantiquak tribal corporation."

"We who are in the Association were probably the separatists," said Ronald. "But perhaps that is the easiest way to refer to them. We don't know their numbers, nor their names—other than a few names that existed in our history a century ago."

"I think we should make a public invitation to a meeting for all those living in the Indian River area who want to be counted as Nantiquaks." said Jefferson. "That way we will get a response that fits with our needs. We don't want people with no Indian ancestry coming from all quarters. So we need to make the invitation a focused one."

"But I think we should still make announcement at the AME Church and at the separatists' school." said Carmine.

"Fine, let's take this combined approach." said Will. "We will print up flyers and then put them up across the community. At the public high schools, at the AME Church, or the other Methodist churches, at the large grocery stores. And these flyers will announce a meeting of all who feel they have Nantiquak ancestry and who would like to join the tribe. We should also look for people with the last names of those identified in Professor Vyner's book on the Nantiquaks who accepted the black school teacher, and accepted being called negroes or colored. There were about a dozen families that he identified by name, if I recall."

"Then we need to arrange a date for the meeting, and a meeting place large enough to accommodate them."

"What about the high school gym?"

"That would be good." said Will. "How about if we aim for Thursday evening, the 12th for the meeting date?"

Everyone nodded their consent.

"Fine, so who can print up the flyers and who will post them all around Millsville and Indian River?"

"I'll draft up the flyer and print up sixty or so copies." said Carmine.

"We'll help post the flyers around the community." said Jefferson and Rob.

"Good. I think I will contact the Nanticoke band early next week to see if we can start our census there." said Will. "So our work is cut out for us for the next ten days. Call me if you get any information between now and our meeting a week from Thursday. Otherwise, I will be coming up here late that afternoon to participate in the meeting."

"I'll send you a draft of the flyer through email." said Carmine smiling broadly at Will.

He smiled back at her, but was thinking that she was not at all pretty even when she smiled.

"Yes, you do that, and I'll get right back to you with any comments. Just remember to make it legible from a distance. And use color, big bold letters and colors."

As Will was driving back to Bristol, he tried to put Carmine's smiling face out of his mind. He wanted to envision Minnie. When she smiled at him, his heart seemed to soar. She was not only much prettier than Carmine, she also looked much more like an Indian, an Indian maiden such as the ones always portrayed in the Hollywood movies. For him, Minnie was an Indian princess. He ached to see her in person again. He couldn't understand why she attracted him so much. It was probably her smile that she seemed to reserve for him. He would see in the next few days. He was glad that she was coming the next day for their first archive search together. He spent the late evening giving his house a thorough cleaning. He had already stocked the kitchen with breakfast food. He was hoping that she would stay the night before the next day's continued research. He would stay at his parents, but still he wanted to impress her in every way he could imagine.

Carmine sent a draft of the flyer to him early the next morning. Will was able to run through a few iterations through electronic mail until they agreed that one version was going to work. They agreed that they would start putting them up around all the public places starting on that weekend after they had canvassed the church.

His research with Minnie later that day went far more successfully than he had hoped. But he was also titillated by Minnie's close physical presence by him. He kept feeling that he wanted to hug her, but of course he couldn't. After two days working with her, walking around Bristol with her, eating with her he felt he knew that he loved her. He was captivated by her, the way she walked demurely, her willowy figure, the smooth skin on her face, the way she talked both confidently and softly, but above all he was entranced by the way she smiled at him. A smile that was reserved only for him, it was clear. He ached again when she left for home, but felt relieved to know that she was coming back in only a few days to resume the same kind of archival research.

Will drove over to his plot of land in the salt marsh of the lower Nanticoke by Exeter to talk to Armand Driggers or anyone else there about the census. It was a cool, overcast day, the last day of February, and a chilly breeze blew steadily in from the northwest. Last season's leaves blew across the road and even across his windshield, and the fields down to Exeter were bare and still untilled. He took notice this time how few pine trees remained, unlike the large stands of pine in Wicomico County across the river. He drove slowly up to the settlement which like the last time appeared abandoned. The houses were more exposed and appeared more desolate as all the deciduous trees were black, their branches as if dead without leaves, and the chest high weeds and nettles that he walked through the previous summer were beaten down by the winter's rains and snow. He stepped out of his large car. Only a couple of cars were parked outside the houses. No one moved around outdoors, but there were some houses which he could see had interior lights burning. The fluorescent gleam of TV screens showed on the windows of several of the houses. He walked over to one of the houses—one of those older mobile homes that had been converted into a fixed house and had grown into the earth around it—and he knocked on the metal door that was probably the main entrance. After a long pause, the door opened outwards a crack. "Is Armand Driggers here?" Will asked. "No, not here." a heavy middle aged woman answered through the crack. "Not here, go away."

"Where does Armand live?"

Will could see the woman wave her hand in a direction that was unclear. "Two houses down that way."

And then the door shut with a metallic clang. Will went down to the second house, a place that was littered with broken or discarded plastic toys in the yard. He knocked at the door. It was also aluminum and it had at eye level a bent over metal scar, which looked like someone had used a screwdriver to try to force the door open. Again there was a long soundless pause, but finally the door opened and a teenaged boy in a faded tee shirt and dark blue sweat pants was standing opposite him.

"Armand's not here. Maybe he'll be back in an hour or two." The boy did not look at Will, instead his eyes looked beyond Will at an indefinite horizon.

"Is there anyone I could talk to here in this settlement?"

"If you're trying to collect electric bills, good luck. No one's here who will pay you. All the men are out fishing or at work." There was a slight tinge of anger in the boy's voice.

"Is there no one here that can tell me something about you people here?"

"Maybe old man Sockum will talk to you. He's in the next house over."

"Are you Armand's son?"

"No. His step son. Who are you, asking all these questions?"

"I'm Will Eames. You could say I am the landlord here."

The boy slammed the door shut in Will's face. He trudged over to the next house and took a look at the electric lines which hung loosely above his head, looking as if they had been strung up from house to house by amateurs or power thieves, or both. It reminded him of the poor neighborhoods he had seen in the Middle East where all the power seemed to be supplied by lines that were illegally tied into the main lines.

Will knocked at the door of the next entrenched mobile home. Again the aluminum resounded sharply. This time Will could hear movement inside as a seemingly heavy object began to shift around the house causing it to groan and creak. The moving object slowly came to the opposite side of the door. Will could hear a bolt being drawn back and then the door swung out toward him. Opposite him was a dark skinned, very fat older man with long, unkempt white hair falling down to his shoulders. The old man cast a quick look at Will's face and then looked down at the ground.

"Are you Mr. Sockem?"

"Yes."

"Are you a Nantiquak Indian?"

"Yes. Who's asking?"

"I'm Will Eames. I own the land around these parts. I've come to speak to Armand Driggers, but he's out working or something."

Sockem said nothing and continued to avoid looking at Will. He stood blocking the door so Will could not see anything inside the trailer home.

"I need to talk to someone here in this village. About joining the Nantiquak tribe and becoming a federally recognized Indian tribe."

"We are Nantiquak Indians. So what? We have a tribe."

"Do you mind if I wait for Armand over there in my car?"

"Do as you like. I won't stop you. Just don't ask me anymore questions."

Will waited in his Oldsmobile for a little more than two hours. In that time no one ventured out of the mobile homes, and no one came from outside. Then a brick red old Chevy drove up quickly and parked abruptly in front of Armand's house. Armand himself stepped out of the car and looked around and focused on Will's Oldsmobile.

Then, just as he had the previous time, he strode over to Will's car and stood in front of the driver's door, confrontationally.

"So you've come back?" Armand said. "What do you want this time?"

"I have a few questions for you and for the others here as well, Armand. Maybe we can sit down and talk."

Armand shrugged his shoulders as if there were no worse alternatives. "Come on then." he sulked.

Inside Armand's trailer home, everything was cluttered and things seemed to be piled on top of things so that the house appeared at first like a warehouse of burlap sacks stacked in formless rounded piles. Only the television set stood free, except for a rabbit-ears antenna. When they entered Armand's step son like a feral animal, slid off one of the piles and slinked away deeper into the house.

"Have a seat, Mr. Eames. I was up at your uncle's place doing some odd jobs today."

"How long have you worked there?"

"Oh, it's only occasion work, and seasonal. But maybe over the past twelve years."

Will sat down on what seemed to be a gigantic rabbit hair coat, or a large hairy dog, or a synthetic blanket, he couldn't tell which, but it didn't move out from under him. Then he told Armand about the project to get federal recognition and restore the reservations for the Nantiquak Indians. And that they were now getting ready to incorporate all the Nantiquak Indians, in all their bands, and clans, from Delaware and Maryland into one tribal non-profit corporation.

"You mean those Indian River Indians that claim to be Nantiquaks up there in Delaware?"

"The same. You mean they aren't Nantiquak?"

"Not really. Even less than you are."

"And we need to compile a list of all the Nantiquak Indians, by bands and include them in the tribal corporation when we apply for federal recognition. And to do this we need to conduct a survey of the surviving Nantiquaks everywhere in the Eastern Shore. And that includes this little band of Indians here on this plot. By the way, what do you call this place or your band of Indians here."

"Kuskowarok is our band. I already told you that we call our place Wicomico. So what if we don't want to join that tribe, whatever they claim they are?"

"You're entitled to do that, I suppose. But you stand to benefit if you are officially recognized. And as a bigger tribe you will all have more voice in making claims and righting wrongs. You will get the right to live here without hiding."

"What? The feds will send us lots of surplus subsidized peanut butter, sugar, and canned peas?"

"You have to pay for those things now, don't you, if you want to eat them?"

"We don't have to. As official Indians will we have the right to fish and crab without the controls of the state wardens?"

"All that will have to be negotiated I suppose. I understand that the Indians in Oregon can take salmon, which white people are banned from fishing for."

"I suppose that would be something. If we only had salmon hereabouts. Or oysters."

"So we will bring a group of the Nantiquaks down here," continued Will, "to conduct a census and do some interviews of all the adults in your settlement here. And we will be asking people to relate –if they remember anything—all they know about their Indian ancestors back as many generations as they can."

"Those fraudsters will do that? I'm serious. They are so intermarried up there in Delaware—they all look like white folks—I doubt if they have even a drop of Nantiquak blood flowing in their veins. I'm sure they don't know where they come from, from niggers, or moors, or white escaped criminals, or Lenapes. They need us to join them to have a half decent claim to have legitimate Nantiquak descent. They dance around at their powwow, pretending it is Nantiquak dances and in costumes borrowed from Western Indians like the Sioux and Shawnee, and wearing feather headpieces that have feathers from birds that don't live anywhere around here in the East. From Brazil, I think."

Will looked at Armand. He had to admit a lot of the Indian River Indians did not look very much like Indians at all. Carmine for one, could pass for an Anglo, on any street, anywhere in the States. And maybe she tried to as well.

"You mean you won't cooperate and participate in our census?"

"No, why should I? They aren't real Indians. They'll never get federal recognition."

"I don't know about that. But we want to make this Nantiquak Indian corporation to include Kuskowarok and your neighbors across the river in Wicomico County."

"The Puckamee."

"Yeah, that band. The Puckamee." said Will. "So I would ask you to help prepare the adults here to help with our survey. We'd like to start in about two weeks."

"It will have to be in the evenings. That's when almost all the adults are here in this settlement."

"Okay."

"And maybe you could tell me," continued Will. "Those Indian River Indians told me that in the 1820s or 30s most of their ancestors converted to Methodism and to this day they attend churches that were built for them primarily. The first in the Eastern Shore. Is that the same with your Kuskowarok band?"

"Yes. We attend the two Methodist churches that are near here. One is the church where your uncle goes to services. I don't always go. But when I do, I attend church there."

"And are your ancestors' graves in graveyards of those churches?"

"Some are. There are several gravestones of the Driggers in the Asbury Church between here and Exeter. It's not even two miles from here. The graveyard there includes Jemima's gravestone, the mother of your great grandmother, who was murdered by a black man."

"Really? Now that's interesting. Any older Driggers buried there?"

"Yeah I think so. From the last century. Jemima's father is there. He's our shared great great-grandfather."

"I'll have to go have a look."

"You do that."

"And are there gravestones from the Kuskowarok at the other Methodist Church up by Rosedale?"

"Yeah some. I reckon a dozen or so. Fewer burials up there these days. No so many of our people go there anymore. It's five miles away."

"Do you have a cell phone, so I can call you to arrange our meeting?"

"Yeah, but there's no signal here, nor in most of the places where I work out in the fields."

"Well then we will have to make an agreement for our first meeting in advance. How about Wednesday, March 11th at six in the evening?"

"Fine by me. I'll tell the others to expect you all. You say your group will only be people from the Nantiquak Association?"

"And me too. But only them. No outsiders, and maybe I will not stay if you think people here don't like talking to white folks."

"No, they don't much care for answering questions from white folks. So maybe that would be a good idea."

"And if you could tell people here about the project to include them in a Nantiquak Indian corporation."

"Yeah, I'll do that. But they won't like it if they have to pay for membership. Like the yearly fees for the Association."

"No, they do not have to pay for membership in the corporation. And they don't have to pay to get recognized as a tribe. And they won't have to join the Association either."

As he was leaving Wicomico, Will thought again about how hard it was getting cooperation from these Indians. They really only wanted to be left alone. They did not want any improvement in their lives and certainly they feared change, and tried to hide from it. But he thought that trying to hide and to be left alone was increasingly a route to extinction for them as poverty and bureaucratic regulation would increasingly crush them. It was nearly dark so he did not stop at the Asbury Church just then, but he came back two days later.

He walked slowly through the small graveyard and looked closely at the headstones. Most were of a worn pale limestone, covered in lichens. They were all hard to read. He could make out the names but sometimes he could not make out the dates, especially for the nineteenth century stones. After much examination, even from some of the stones he had to wipe away the detritus of age, he finally found the stone of Jemima Driggers with her dates 1872-1914. He did not notice her at first because she was included on the stone below the names of her father and mother, Hanbal Driggers, 1850-1901 and Gayla Walker Driggers, 1868-1908. It suddenly seemed almost miraculous to him that he was looking at the grave of his great great-grandmother, and her parents, people who lived beyond the living memory of the oldest members of his family. There were several stones with the Driggers name, and also Walkers, Johnsons, Buckhams, and the Couskers. And there were two stones with the Randall name inscribed. They were dated from the beginning of the century. But Pellmell Randall's stone was nowhere to be seen. He'd have to ask Armand where Pellmell was buried. He took notes of the names and the dates that he could read. None of the death dates on the stones appeared to be earlier than 1850, and that stone appeared to belong to one Jos. Hanscom. Will was a little surprised to see that there were no recent stones, none later than 1969. Had church attendance fallen off he wondered. And none of the stones indicated that the "dearly departed or the herebelow" were Indians, or Nantiquak. But from the names it seemed most of the graveyard served the Kuskowarok. A look at the announcement board out front of the church did not have a very recent event listed. Maybe the church only had occasional services. There was an Exeter telephone number, however written at the bottom. He'd call it later. The bare lands, some fallow, some plowed last season, surrounding the church and the distance from any trees gave the whole area of feeling of desolation and howling emptiness. The parking area had no recent tire tracks other than those from his own car. The place looked long abandoned.

When he was finished at the Asbury Church he drove the four or so miles up toward the Methodist Church at Rosedale. Immediately the appearance of this church struck him as an active living church. It was well painted, white clapboard with a red main door, and the announcement board out front had notices about upcoming Easter season services and activities, still about a month away. The grass and weeds had been cut at the end of last season and had not resumed growing yet. There was a low iron fence around the graveyard, painted not long before with black paint that still shone. He entered the cemetery and began studying the headstones. It immediately stuck him that the death dates were up to current times, and there was even one new grave moldering under freshly upturn soil. He noticed at once that many of the stones were in much better condition than any of those at the Asbury Church. Perhaps they used higher quality stone--more well off people used this church and cemetery-- there were even some stones in dark marble. He searched for names he recognized but did not find any. Here the earliest death date recorded was 1843 that belonged to one Mr. Charles Talbot. He was surprised even to find a gravestone for Mr. Andrew Eames who died in 1873. Perhaps one of his ancestors, he thought, somehow related to Robert Eames. But he was not sure if any of the names were Indian or not. There were no Driggers buried there that he could find. He left after an hour, his search apparently coming up with no Indian graves that he could identify.

The late winter was a time when usually Will had no real estate business at all, no buyers, no sellers, and this year was the same. He didn't mind this year, because it left him a lot of time to work on his Injun Project. Now that he had launched the Nantiquak internal census and wakened the Kuskowarok tribesmen to their efforts, he turned to doing other research on the background of the Nantiquak, material and historical information that would be needed for their application to the Bureau for recognition. In his brokerage office in Bristol he sat thinking of the measures he could take next, and he began making a list. He needed to solicit a letter of support to the BIA from Congressman Morton for recognition. And he needed to visit the Delaware congressman to get the same thing, a statement of support in a letter which would point out that the Nantiquak's were already a state recognized Indian tribe that needed Federal acknowledgement. As Will saw it, a visit to the Congressman during the work week in D.C. would be a great excuse to call on Minnie also, and that made the project very worthwhile. He could not get enough time with Minnie as things now stood. He'd have to find someone who could introduce him to the Congressman. Maybe he could ask the Association's lawyer-- what was his name?--if he could introduce them and help set up a meeting. He also added to his list calls to the numbers that were listed for both those Methodist churches. He was not sure what he could find out, but he would pursue the line of discovery of the Indians families buried in their graveyards. He also wanted to find the name of the historian of Methodism on the Eastern Shore. It was important to talk to him to understand the extent to which Nantiquaks took up Methodism and when. And of course, if he had them, to get more names of Nantiquaks in the mid-nineteenth century. And maybe he needed to visit with Professor Alvey again to ask him about Nantiquak burials and whether there were any archeological findings with old bones. Thinking of bones, he then added to his list of things to do to find the commercial firm or university that would extract and test genetic DNA material from bones of any of the bodies of Indians he was able to exhume. And then he remembered that he needed to start looking through the U.S. census records for 1880 and 1900 for any listings of the Nantiquaks. He did not understand why 1890 data were not required, but he could ask when he started the search. These census data seemed to be an important requirement of the Bureau's application process. But he did not have a clue about how he could go about researching the old census data. He needed to call around and find someone who could advise him on that count. And maybe the archives were located in

Washington. He could not find any information through the internet at that time about what might be included in the reported census information about Indians. He'd have to ask the archive what kind of information he could get. The only easy part it seemed to him was searching the census records for Nantiquak names in Delaware, who were at that time already members of the tribal Association. All these data should be in the archive. And finding the data would be another excuse to go to Washington on a week day, to see Minnie and to consult the census archive. But especially to see Minnie, whatever the pretext.

There was no order or priority to the list he had constructed. He didn't even attempt to put timings or target dates on getting the items completed. He thought he would proceed with what was easiest first, and what would take a long time, would wait. Unfortunately that meant his possible trips to Washington, when he could arrange to see Minnie, would also come later rather than sooner. So he started by calling the phone numbers of the two Maryland churches he had picked up. The first one he called, the Rosedale church, had a recorded message, and requested that he leave a message and wait for a call back. The phone number for the Asbury Church did not answer after twelve rings. He'd have to try later. He then tried calling Hank Alvey. Again he waited a long time, twelve rings, before hanging up the line. He'd have to call again that evening. In the meantime he looked up the name of the Delaware Congressman from the Sussex County district. Then he called Carmine on her cell phone.

"We can start making contact with our political friends in Washington. Like your Congressman Yeates. Does anyone in the Association know him? Maybe your lawyer up in Centreville could give us an intro. We want to visit him in his office in Warshington sometime later this month. Can you look into that?"

"Yeah sure. I think our lawyer might well know Congressman Yeates. I understand he is from Centreville."

"Okay I'll leave that with you."

A few hours later Will got a call.

"I'm John Francis, the pastor at the Rosedale Methodist Church. I'm returning your call Mr. Eames. Are you any relation to Hampton Eames?"

"Yes, he's my great-uncle, in fact. I have something I want to talk to you about concerning him. But first I want to find out if you have any number of Indian members in your congregation. Nantiquak Indians."

"We don't usually class our followers by race, Mr. Eames. But I happen to know that we have several older members who are Indians. You can tell by looking at them. Why does that interest you?"

"Well as it happens my great uncle and I are both part Nantiquak. And I am currently leading a project to establish the genealogical history of the remaining Nantiquak Indians who live on both sides of the river in our county and in Wicomico County. Specifically I am trying to establish from the graves sites in your cemetery how many Nantiquak Indians have been buried there since the 1830s."

"Oh that's from the very beginning of our church here in the county. I don't know exactly about the graves. There are some names of course which are the same as some of our current members. But I don't know much about them. I actually don't know much about the contents of our cemetery."

"Fine, maybe I can come out there—I'm based in Bristol—to consult with you at the church and we can look at gravestones and maybe you can relate any history that you might know about your Indian membership."

"You can do that of course. I'm usually only here on Wednesday afternoons and Sundays until about two o'clock. If you want you can come out here on one of those days."

"So how would this coming Thursday, the 12th, at three thirty do for you?"

"Yes, that would do just fine with me. I will be in the sanctuary. Just walk in the main doors when you get here."

"And just by the way, do you keep records at your church of births, baptisms, marriages and deaths from the nineteenth century?"

"No I think those went to archives of the Maryland Methodist Conference. We have vital records of our members only from the thirties, nineteen thirties. But again I think they do not indicate race. Even though we long had many Nantiquak members, there were probably no marriages here by Indians because of the state law banning interracial marriages."

Will momentarily thought again about how his great grandfather and namesake married Willemena in 1914. How was it possible? Were there civil marriages recognized back then?

"Okay. Now I also wanted to talk to you about arrangements for a funeral service for Hampton. He's quite near death now and I need to make plans for his final remains."

"Oh yes. I'd understood he is very ill. We can talk about it when you come. Will you want to bury him in our graveyard also?"

"No. We will bury him in the family plot on the farm. All of his closest family are there."

"Understood. So I will put down in my appointment book that you'll be coming next Thursday in mid afternoon."

It was late afternoon when he called Hank Alvey's number again. This time the line answered, but it was not Hank, it was his home nurse who answered.

"Hank's taking a nap just now, Mr. Eames. Can I have him call you back when he is up and around again?"

"Is he very ill?" asked Will.

"Yes, he's in a pretty bad way. But his mind is clear as a bell."

"Okay. I'll wait for his call."

Alvey called back about an hour later. Will caught him up on his Injun Project and the steps they were taking to get Federal recognition for the Nantiquak tribe. Hank agreed to talk some more with Will at his house on the next Tuesday, in the early afternoon. He would look up his notes and papers for his book before Will came to refresh his memory.

Before he finished that day he tried calling again to the number he'd written down for the Asbury Methodist Church. Again there was no answer.

At the end of the day, Will felt mostly defeated. He had accomplished very little and had moved his larger project forward hardly even one step. He felt hungry and did not feel like preparing anything for his dinner so he put on a light jacket and stepped out to go to the Cedar Island to get a bite to eat. He had two beers with a cheeseburger and cole slaw. He was sitting by himself in the dining section and at one point out of the corner of his eye he thought he saw the unforgettable figures and dark wavy hair of Karen standing at the bar. But when he focused his vision there he saw that there was no one at that part of the bar, either male or female. And then he began to think about Minnie again. He had to see her again, soon. She had only left the day before after their research up in Centreville. But he ached to hold her in his arms, to look into her greenish-brown eyes again, to kiss her lips. He wouldn't be seeing her this weekend. But maybe he could see her the next weekend. That is when he had a eureka moment. He'd invite Minnie to come to Bristol the next Friday night to go fishing with him on Saturday. She had said that her father had only rarely taken her fishing when she was young, and she had said as if she had all her life yearned to be taken on a fishing trip again, preferably with her father. And they could arrange to go to Uncle Hampt's house for dinner one night, and maybe have a fish fry at his parents' house after their fishing trip. It could be a date. Not conventional, admittedly. But he liked fishing and the season had just begun, and maybe she would like to learn how to fish with him. Even before he finished eating he took out his cell phone to call her. But he checked the time and realized that probably she was commuting home from work. He would wait to call her after he got back home, maybe in an hour and a half. She had seemed quite receptive. Maybe she would accept a date, a weekend out on the Bay or on the river, fishing for striped bass. His hopes started rising right away. If she said yes, that would compensate for a frustrating day. He could hardly wait to ask her, to hear her smooth voice over the phone. He was a little surprised when she quickly accepted his proposal for a date on the water.

Will decided to go fishing that weekend to prepare for Minnie's coming on the next weekend. His father, Bob, went along with him. They went to several spots that traditionally had yielded up lots of bass in the past, but they caught only four decent sized fish, just enough for a meal for them and Will's mother. Then on Sunday the weather turned rainy and blustery, so he spent the day loafing around his bungalow. He didn't feel like running. His traditional stand-by, a broadcast of a Baltimore Orioles game, was not available as the season still hadn't started. There wouldn't been any baseball to watch until April.

But Monday morning dawned bright, clear and cool and Will went on his usual training run of about six miles around the town and down the Choptico River. When he returned he already felt optimistic for the week ahead of him; great things would happen that week, and then Minnie would come for the weekend making everything sweet and unforgettable, even if they caught no fish. Later at his office he again began making phone calls and computer inquiries. He finally got an answer to the number from the Asbury Church.

"Oh, you got my number from the announcements board at the Asbury Church? I'll have to update that. I'm Mayron Rattel and I'm afraid to say that I no longer work for the Methodist Church. I was pastor there until about a year ago, but I was also covering the Methodist Church in Exeter. It proved too much for me, and attendance was falling at Asbury. So the Methodist Conference retired me. I no longer work at either church. I don't know if the congregation still attends there at Asbury. Actually you caught me just in time. Because I am planning to move to Florida next week. So how can I help you?"

Will told him about his interest in the Nantiquak Indians being early adopters of Methodism and his relationship to the Indians at Wicomico. They arranged to meet to talk through all of Will's questions the very next morning. But Rattel told him a similar story about archival data.

"I never saw any old data on the vital records of my congregations at that church. Or any other of my former churches, either. Certainly none from the last century. I think everything was sent to the Conference up in Dover, Delaware. In the past almost five years when I was pastor there, there were no funerals, no baptisms, and no marriages. So in any event I had no data to record or to send to the central Conference."

They met the next morning in a small coffee shop in the middle of Exeter that must have been the only point in the town where the Nanticoke Memorial Bridge was not visible. Will had not visited Exeter in many years and it seemed to him it had fallen on hard times. It looked shabby and poor, with many derelict houses, and shuddered businesses. The coffee shop was empty when Will stepped in, the front window faced to the northwest, so no direct light entered the place and it gave the impression to Will that he was stepping into a dim, dark cave. There was only one client sitting at one of the booths facing the front door; an older, white-haired man with a newspaper laid out on the linoleum table in front of him.

"Mr. Rattel?"

"Yes, that's me." said the old man as he stood slowly in a gouty sort of way. "And you're Will Eames, I presume?"

They shook hands and Will sat down opposite the former pastor. "So you found the place alright. I think I'm the last customer who ever comes here. Now you wanted to talk to me about the Indians who attended or used to attend the Asbury Church."

"That's right. While you were the pastor there did you know of a Mr. Driggers or a Mr. Randall?"

"Yep, those wily characters from Wicomico: they would attend sometimes and bring their extended families with them, and all their neighbors. And they would be most of the congregration. But when they did not attend, no one would come from the settlement. It was before my time of course, but I understood that when the blacks stopped attending and organized their own AME church a couple miles further up the road, the congregation was cut in half and never recovered. Almost no white folks attended there nowadays. And the Indians who did attend were none too literate. All except that half breed lawyer, Mr. Rendell, who went there from here in Exeter."

"You say this Mr. Rendell is a lawyer who lives here in Exeter, and you think he is a half breed. Half breed Indian, you mean? How did you know he was half breed?"

"He would tell everyone he ever met. He said his family had once lived in Wicomico, and that his grandfather was an Indian, and his grandmother a black woman. How he got schooling and training as a lawyer I will never understand. But apparently he did and he was all the time looking for work from the Indians. He would come to church and hand out his business card. His sort of advertising for tort claims and that kind of business."

"So maybe his family name was actually Randall, like Pellmell Randall?"

"Could be."

"Old man Randall died last year and apparently did not have any heirs, so that was how I was able to buy the plot of land around Wicomico…"

"Mosquito territory."

"Right. I wanted to ask you if you know where the records of the burials might be located for the grave sites in the Asbury Church graveyard."

"I believe they would be up at the Methodist Conference for the Eastern Shore in Dover, Delaware. They were my employers."

"So you're not from around here? You don't know about the Nantiquak Indians."

"No, I'm originally from Elkton, up the peninsula. I've worked all over the Eastern Shore, but mainly in southern Delaware, occasionally in Kent County and in Warwick County in eastern Maryland. In Suffolk County in Delaware I first got to know about the Nantiquak Indians of Indian River. Even had some in my congregation I held there for about six years."

"You know the Nantiquaks have a history with the Methodist Church here in the Eastern Shore."

"Yes, I know. They were amongst our earliest adopters. Our circuit riders went out of their way especially to convert them. And freed slaves too. Evangelism, you know, reaches out to the poorest. I think that the Indians back then were most impressed that the church preached and practiced strict temperance. The Indians believe it was white men that started them down the path of alcoholism. The Conference has put together a little history of the Methodist Church in these parts."

"Do you know the name of the historian who wrote that history?"

"Not off hand. But if you call Mr. Dimpleton at the Conference offices in Dover, he'll be able to put you in touch with him."

"So do you know much about the family names that lie in the Asbury graveyard?"

"No can't say that I do. I maybe looked at them once while I was working there, but not closely. You know Mr. DImpleton should be able to help you with archival records of the churches in these parts. They all should have survived. There have been no big church fires on the Eastern Shore, and there was no fighting around here during the civil war. From my experience in Warwick County and Suffolk County as well as here, the vital records were all sent to Dover."

"Here let me give you the phone number for Mr. Henry Dimpleton."

Will finished the last gulp of his coffee and thanked Mr. Rattel and made to leave, wishing him luck for his move south and hoping he wasn't too much of a bother just before his move.

"Oh think nothing of it. The most interesting conversation I've had in a long time."

It was while Will was on his way to Salisbury that he got the call from Minnie, all upset that she would not be able to come fishing on Saturday because she had to attend a tribal council meeting at midday. She sounded as if she were on the point of tears. She had prepared for her first fishing trip as an adult and had bought everything she needed for the weekend. And now she was afraid she couldn't come for Saturday. She said it was her fault because she had forgotten about the previously scheduled meeting, and she had to attend, because as tribal chief, it was technically her meeting. Will tried to calm her down. He asked her about how long the meetings usually ran and when the meeting could be expected to adjourn. And then when she told him that they adjourned the meeting no later than one thirty and had lunch afterwards, he saw the answer.

"Maybe Minnie, you would still want to go fishing on Sunday? If you drove out here after your meeting we could meet for dinner here, spend the night and go fishing on Sunday morning. That would still work for me, and my family, and for the fish, too. They can wait for our baited hooks another day."

So it was settled that way. Minnie was so thankful that Will adjusted the fishing trip to fit her obligated meeting.

"The important thing is that you get here. On Saturday late afternoon. I can take you out to my great uncle's house to meet him and to have dinner there." The date was still on, and he would see her on Saturday late afternoon, instead of Friday late afternoon. Maybe the traffic would be better for her coming from Virginia on Saturday, instead of with the weekenders going to Ocean City.

At Salisbury, Hank Alvey did not come to the door. Instead a woman who looked like a home care nurse answered the door and showed him in to the sitting room where Alvey was sitting in a wheel chair with his back to the door.

"Hank is expecting you, Mr. Eames." said the nurse as she then moved away.

"Oh, there you are, Mr. Eames. Come let's shake hands." said Alvey.

Will stepped around to face Alvey and shook his hand before sitting down on the couch.

"I'm glad to see you again, young man. But I'm sure the sight of me does not gladden you. I look a wreck and I seem to be failing fast now. No strength left at all. And I cough usually all night, so I don't sleep unless I'm sitting up. But never mind me. How can I help you further in your quest to learn more about the Nantiquaks?"

Will told him that they were now conducting a census and interviewing Nantiquak Indians to find out about their ancestors from the last one hundred and sixty years or so, the period after they lost the last of their reservation lands in Maryland and Delaware.

"I particularly wanted to ask you about the adoption of Methodism by the Indians here in the Eastern Shore. Because we are now also searching the graveyards of Methodist Churches to get an idea of Indian families in the nineteenth century. We seem to have a disconnect between records of Indian family names in the eighteenth century with those in the late nineteenth century."

"You know when I was putting together a history of the Nantiquaks, I noticed this gap also. This was the exact period when records tell us that large numbers, if not all the Nantiquak bands began to move. Most of the Nantiquak numbers apparently left the Eastern Shore. Some moved to southern New Jersey and joined their cousins the Lenape. Others went to the north, to New York and even Canada. And they joined the Iroquois or other tribes that shared the Algonkian language. Many of those eventually ended up moving further to the West. But also those that remained moved deeper into the peninsula. Into the woods of Warwick County and the area that would become part of southern Delaware."

"And of those that remained on the Eastern Shore was it at this time that interbreeding with black people and poor whites began?"

"Yes. But you won't find much documentation at all of this occurring. Probably because the race laws of the early nineteenth century did not recognize Indians as a separate race. They were always officially lumped together with other coloreds, that is negroes, who were either freedmen or slaves. All I was able to find were elaborate legends which some anthropologists of the early part of this century collected. Some interesting stories, maybe family legends or maybe contrived genealogies."

"But I've noticed that records of Nantiquak Indians of the nineteenth century seem to universally refer to them using English surnames. Was this due to their conversion to Methodism in the early nineteenth century?"

"I don't know much about that. You'd have to look in Church records, if any exist still. I don't think anyone has researched the Nantiquaks and the Methodist Church here in this part of the Eastern Shore."

Alvey paused and reached for a glass of brown liquid to drink.

"Excuse me. I drink whiskey in the afternoon. Helps me relax and take my nap a little later and suppresses the pain and the coughing." Alvey continued.

"There is one legend about the mixing of Nantiquaks and freed blacks quite near here in southern Delaware. It seems that some entrepreneurs decided to log the great cypress swamp that existed between here and Injun Creek in Delaware around the beginning of the nineteenth century. Freed black men with their families moved there and local Indians joined together in the work crews and cut down nearly all the cypress trees over a fifteen year period. And it seems that black men married Indian women, and Indian men married black women. And when that industry petered out, this work group all moved together towards Injun Creek and what is now Millsville."

"I was thinking about investigating the genetic DNA of Indians buried in Methodist cemeteries."

"Yes, yes, that's possible. But I don't know how you'll know which graves to examine. I think none of them indicate white, Indian, or Negro. There was another interesting story that was collected about how the Dutch from New Amsterdam decided to establish a colony in what was empty land in Maryland colony on the Delaware River coast. They sent a large group of Dutch Mennonites, men and women and families too to a place near what is now Cape Henlopen. They called the place Hoorekill, which the English called Whore Kill. This was during a time when the Dutch were at war with the Catholic French and the English. Well a little later the English, at war with the Dutch, forced the surrender of New Amsterdam and they sent a military force to destroy the colony at Whore Kill. The English records said they burned down all of the houses and killed all the men and scattered the boys and women. The local Indians say they found the remaining colonists lost in the forests and they took them back and adopted them into their tribe. And they bred with them. Or so they say. I think the numbers of people would have been small if such a thing did happen, no more than a dozen white women and children. Probably less."

"Yes, Hank. This interbreeding question does concern me, and the Nantiquak Indians up near Millsville too. That is why we are going to try to do some DNA tests of the bones from Indian graves. I think we can establish the Indian surnames in Methodist graveyards. Some of the families still attend Methodist services in the churches where their ancestors first did. But I was thinking that today's remaining bands of Nantiquak all have mixed blood, some going back as you say more than three hundred years. Blood mixed with both whites and blacks, and although it sometimes does not show in the facial features of today's Indians, sometimes it does. To the point where the Indians today are not sure at all of their racial identity or their genealogy."

"There was another story. That the Nantiquak Indians adopted a small group of shipwrecked Spaniards who were just barely surviving on what is now Assateague Island. At the end of the seventeenth century. This would have been the Asksesky band, or sometimes they were called the Assacompak band. That group later moved up from what was Virginia and through Somerville County, and what became Warwick County, east of here, and then further into what became southern Delaware. The first records of them by the English, said they looked whiter than most Indians."

"So I was thinking, if it would be possible to find the bones of Indians from the eighteenth century or even earlier, before the Nantiquak became Methodists."

"But as I was saying," continued Alvey, trying to catch his breath, "the stories of their interbreeding all seem legendary, but they are often interesting. There was one story of a Jesuit Spanish attempt to colonize the Eastern Shore in the sixteenth century. They came up from their colony in Florida. But when they tried to build a colonia, the local Indians attacked them and drove them off. But the Jesuits took a young Indian boy with them—the Spanish records of this story do not indicate what the Indians of these parts were named, this was long before John Smith and the English at Jamestown, you know. And apparently this boy even went to Spain, became a Catholic, married a white woman there, and he came back with another colonizing expedition. He was supposed to help the colonists translate their wishes into the local language. He and his wife escaped and were never heard from again."

"So do you know of any earlier Indian grave sites in the Eastern Shore? Have Nantiquak bones been found by archeologists in old burial sites hereabouts?"

"Oh, there is more information about old Nantiquak burial customs. I do remember finding information about that. The English found them very curious and several people wrote about them. They did not bury their dead, it seems. Instead they put the newly dead bodies on platforms and let the birds and the elements consume the bodies. And when the bones were bare and dried, they apparently collected them together in ossuaries which they kept underground in custom built houses in their villages. And when they migrated between villages they would take the bones with them." Alvey cut himself off, and tried to breathe but it was clear that he was short of breath. After a pause to get his breath back, he continued. "And you know what, when the biggest number of Nantiquaks left for the north, they took those ossuaries along with them just as they did when moving between villages here on the peninsula. English settlers in the late eighteenth century wrote of seeing these Indians trudging northwards carrying the bones with them. They thought it was a grisly sight. So I think you won't find any early graves for the Nantiquaks. I myself don't know of any archeologists who have found graves in their digs of Indian settlements that have been found. At least I didn't come across any reports of such findings."

"That's a shame." said Will. "If we can't find older bones of Nantiquak Indians, from the eighteenth or even seventeenth century then we can't do any genetic DNA testing. And we won't know about how closely all the different bands of Nantiquak Indians are related. And so we won't clear up the matter of inter-breeding with other races, either."

"No, I guess not." Alvey said as he reached for his glass of whiskey and took another very small gulp. He coughed a little bit before settling down. "But have I given you any information that might be of help to your project?"

"Oh yes. But then we still face the problem of establishing the continuous line of ancestry from two or three hundred years ago to today."

"Well, if you don't have any further questions I can help you with, I'm afraid, it's time now for my nap. I wish you luck with your efforts to get official recognition as a tribe for the Nantiquaks. They have a difficult and obscure history, and it remains mostly hidden to this day. Only legends and tall tales. Susanna, my keeper, can show you out the door. Farewell, Will Eames. It's always a pleasure talking to you."

At the door, Susanna whispered to him, "He's in the last stages of emphysema. It does not look good for him. But I think your visit probably cheered him up. He doesn't get any visitors these days. And he loves telling stories."

"I can tell. He tells good stories too." said Will as he stepped onto the porch. It saddened him to think that he probably was seeing Hank Alvey for the last time.

The next morning Will called Mr. Henry Dimpleton up in Dover at the Methodist Conference. He explained to him how he got his name and the investigation he was undertaking about Nantiquaks who became early converts to Methodism in Maryland and southern Delaware.

"Oh yes, we do have archived records of those first churches. Some even from churches that no longer exist. Much of the vital records data are kept up to the present day. You'll have to come up here to look at them. And as it so happens the historian you're looking for is the archivist here. So you can come meet him and ask your questions. When would you like to come?"

"How about this next Monday morning?"

"That would be fine. Our address is …in Dover, near the Amoco gasoline station and the Wesleyan Methodist Church. See you then."

Will hung up uttering a little whelp of success. He felt so good that he decided he would start the search for a firm or university department that could perform a genetic DNA search. He started with a search on the internet for firms doing ancestry research. He found only one that claimed to use DNA analysis of an ancestor's genetic links. It was a firm in Utah called Genetic Tree of Life. He needed to wait a few hours to call them. In the meanwhile, he called the University of Maryland and asked for the genetics sciences department. After a few turns around the campus switchboard, his call was taken by someone saying that she was in the bio and genetic science department. He told her he was looking for some department or agency or commercial firm that would be able to extract and study the DNA of the old bones of presumed ancestors and judge the genetic relationship to current living people.

The woman—she sounded young to Will—listened patiently and finally gave him a quick answer.

"You mean DNA profiling. No, no one here does that sort of research. And no one at this university does either."

"Could you tell of some university that does that sort of research--DNA profiling for genealogical research—that might be able to run a profile on the old ancestors of local Indians?"

"You might try Johns Hopkins. Or maybe the University of Utah. They are big on genealogical research using DNA."

After noon Will then tried calling to Genetic Tree of Life. Will explained to the person on the other end what he wanted and that he first wanted to examine the DNA taken from the bones of his great grandmother and compare it with his own and with the DNA of another man to see how closely they were related. He told him that he was seeking to begin to establish the genealogical links and relationships between different bands of Indians who lived over a wide area of eastern Maryland.

The man on the line, who said he was a sales technician reacted very enthusiastically.

"This is just the sort of work we were set up to do. And we have even done work for Indian tribes here in the Four Corners region. But we have not ourselves done DNA extraction from old bones, not yet. We can put you in touch with several forensic archaeologists who do that sort of work and who have supplied us with DNA materials in the past."

"Have you been doing this sort of work for a long time?"

"No, only two years. But we've gained a lot of experience and we have now done DNA profiling on more than a thousand customers' DNA with the aim of helping them establish their ancestry and origins. We are now working with the Mormons to help expand their database of ancestors using DNA analysis methods."

"Suppose we were to contract your services, what end result could we expect to get? What steps would I need to do? And how much would all this cost?"

The man from the Utah firm then embarked on a rapid fire accounting of the work they did, of the insights into genetics they reported on, on the haplogroups, on the ways of taking DNA samples, of the key genetic points, on comparing genetic lines between different people from different centuries, how the work was very time consuming and required a great deal of computer power, and so on, very technically, using precise jargon that was way beyond what Will understood. And it would also cost a lot, depending on which level of detail Will wanted in the reports he chose.

"Twelve thousand dollars. That is a lot." Will whistled under his breathe. How was he going to pay for that?

Then Will asked about the actual steps of getting DNA samples sent to the firm's office, especially the DNA extracted from exhumed bones. When he was satisfied that he understood all the steps and procedures and the contracts and the timing required he thanked the man on the other line and prepared to hang up.

"No wait. First I said I would give you the names and contacts of several forensic archeaologists. I will send them to you through the mail. And I need your address also to send you all our promotional materials and the descriptions of work that we just spoke about."

Later that afternoon he drove over to Exeter where he waited in the parking lot of the Speedy Food Mart-- which was a combination of a fuel filling station, a quick food restaurant and a small grocery shop-- to meet a carload of census takers driving down from Millsville. The skies were overcast, and the twilight seemed to arrive early. They arrived only ten minutes later than the appointed time. Carmine hopped out of the large pick-up truck and came over to Will's car.

"Hi Will. There are four of us, and we're ready to start."

"Well good. I think today we'll have to first spend some time selling these Indians on the idea of joining a larger Nantiquak tribe. We'll be doing that today. I know of one fellow who doesn't like the idea at all. We'll run into him straight away. Get in with me and let's go over there."

The two cars drove the less than four miles over to Wicomico off of Old Indiantown Road. The skies were dark but it was still only half an hour before sunset and the entire settlement barely appeared out of the murk. The entire way from Exeter there had been no street lamps—it seemed they moved into a darker and darker land-- and now at Wicomico none of the trailer homes seemed to have either exterior or interior lights on. Will parked his Olds on a grassy patch and the big rust red truck parked right next to it. The four Delaware Nantiquaks got out of the vehicles and stood quietly, with large note pads in their hands. Will motioned them to stay there while he went to find Armand. In the dim light he knocked first at the wrong door, but at the second Armand came to the door and told him they were ready, but they had only very cramped space. They would meet in Sockum's house. Will went back to the executive committee—Ronald was there and two other young people he did not know—and told them they were ready to start. They traipsed over to Sockum's trailer home and Armand motioned them inside where a few dim lightbulbs were burning. Armand then went out to invite the other adult members of the Kuskowarok to come. He brought back twelve adult men, and seventeen adult women, about half of those were white haired and shriveled. The group crammed into the small area of the main room, most were standing close to each other. Mr. Sockum, who was both tall and obese sat in an overstuffed highbacked chair in the middle.

Will's group introduced themselves: the two newcomers were Bob Johnson and Stan Hancum. Will asked Carmine to lead the meeting and he stood to the back.

"We're Nantiquak Indians just like you." she started. "We have started a project to get official recognition for our tribe from the Federal government throughout its original territory on the Eastern Shore. As a first step we are going to set up a non-profit corporation for the greater tribe to include all Nantiquaks wherever they live here in the Eastern Shore. We are also starting a process for the states to restore our legally granted reservations. And for these objectives we are inviting all of you to sign up to be members of this corporation and to put your names to the list of all our tribesmen and tribeswomen. And then we want to ask you if you could identify your forefathers and mothers going back over the past century or longer so we can show that the tribe has a living heritage continuing from our ancestors. We, the Nantiquak Indians of Indian River in Delaware are participating and will be part of this corporation and we sincerely want you the Kuskowarok band to join us along with the Puckamee band, and the Askesky band and others in Delaware to join us."

The locals who stood cramped in the room around Carmine and her three co-tribesmen shuffled uncomfortably but did not say anything. Most of them scowled or looked baffled. Their body language it seemed to Will was very negative, the men stood with their arms wrapped tightly around their chests. The women all seemed to be looking at the floor. After a long pause, Carmine continued.

"So then, who will sign up to join us in the Nantiquak Corporation? We would like you to write your names to a petition which we have here. It says simply, "We, the undersigned, affirm that we are Nantiquak Indians and desire to be included in the rolls of the Nantiquak Indian Nation of Maryland and Delaware which will be incorporated and officially recognized." You can sign it now as we file out. And before we begin to our interviews to collect information about your ancestry. We'll conduct our interviews over the next several days, one at a time, in your homes."

Then suddenly Old Man Sockum cleared his throat with a loud froglike sound. "I am proud to say that I am a Nantiquak Indian. And I want everyone to know it and want the U.S. government to acknowledge that I am a member of this proud but much abused tribe. So I will be first to sign. Bring me this list."

Will was surprised. But he saw that Sockum's announcement swung the sentiment in the room. A small portable folding table appeared from somewhere and was set up in front of Sockum who then looked at the page carefully, looked at the pen, and then scratched out his name, Ebenezer Hank Sockum, and his signature and added the words, 'born in Maryland in 1939'. When he finished he looked up and beamed.

"Can we smoke the tobacco pipe now?" he said.

"I will." said a man near the front. He took the pen, wrote and signed his name in the same manner as Sockum and then slowly walked out the door into the darkness outside.

A man and a woman—obviously married-- then took their turn and filed out of the house. It was already very stuffy inside and the opening and closing of the door brought in much relief from the cool air outdoors.

And then, without a word, everyone lined up to sign. The house seemed to breathe a sigh of relief as the weight moved off its floor. After six or seven people had signed, Armand made a flourish as he picked up the pen.

"I add my name with the profound feeling that all of this is useless effort and will not gain us one bit of change or improvement in our lot." It was not clear whom he was addressing. He wrote his name and signed with a flourish, and put his date of birth as June 1949. But he did not leave the room. Will again was surprised by Armand's acquiescence. He had felt sure that he would speak against participating and try to convince others not to join. As the list grew, Will noticed that several of the older looking women did not write their names. Instead they asked Sockum to write their names on the list, and then they put an X sign next to it as their signature. And they did not put their date of birth. In all there were eight couples out of the total who signed as married couples. Armand Driggers did not have a wife who signed as Driggers, but a woman who resembled Armand's stepson did sign up after Armand did and she left the house. The entire process of signing up the thirty one members of the Kuskowarok band of Nantiquak Indians took about forty minutes, until there were only Sockum, Armand, Will and the four Delaware Nantiquak Indians left in the house. Will wanted to ask Armand what he had told the others that convinced them to sign up, but he decided against it and left Armand to his inscrutable self.

Carmine, appearing very satisfied with the result said, "Now we can start our interviews. Perhaps we can start with you, Mr. Sockum. And Ronald can interview you, Mr. Driggers, at the same time. And then we can start interviewing other members of the community. How would that be?"

"It's fine by me." said Sockum.

"Now that Old Man Pell has left us, Sockum is our living book." said Armand. "You'll get lots of information about our ancestry from him. Let's go to my house to have my interview. One of you can interview my wife at the same time." He pointed at Bob Johnson and then made to leave with Ronald and Johnson. "And you, Mr. Hancum, you can come to the house next to here and interview John Hartly."

As he stepped out the door, Armand turned back to Carmine. "And by the way for your census, there are sixteen children who live here in Wicomico. You should include them in your count. Names, ages, all that."

Carmine pulled up a stool next to Sockum and spread her writing pad on the folding table and said, "Let's see. What was the name of your parents?"

Will looked at Carmine and then interrupted her. "Excuse me, I think we can carry on until about 9:30 tonight and do the rest on Friday or Saturday. Okay?" Carmine nodded her head. "That sounds okay," she said. Will wanted to leave for home. Maybe he could speak to Minnie after she finished her commute home. But he stood around listening to some of the more interesting details that Sockum had to share. He was especially interested to hear that on his maternal side he had Driggers ancestry. After more than an hour listening to Sockum's answers to Carmine's questions, Will excused himself. "Give me a call after your meeting tomorrow evening to let me know how things go. I won't be coming for that." When he got home he called Minnie just to hear her voice. He told her about the beginning of the census and how well it appeared to be going.

On Thursday afternoon he drove over the thirteen miles to the Rosedale Methodist Church. Pastor Francis was the only person in the church. He seemed to be dusting. Will introduced himself and reminded him of his errand. Pastor Francis was middle aged and short and slender. He greeted Will warmly and led him over to a side alcove.

"I've put this list of names together of the six Nantiquak Indians who periodically attend services here. I thought since you were interested. There are four different family names for these six people. See here: Buckham, Gibson, Grieves, and Jackson. I went and checked in the graveyard and there are two gravestones with the same family names. I'll show you."

Will did not recognize any of the names on Mr. Francis's list. "You know they are Indians?"

"Yes, some of them have told me. But all of them look like Indians, not at all like your usual black people."

They stepped out to behind the church where there was the graveyard. It was maybe three times the area of the church, it was surrounded by a low black iron fence and in the middle stood a large oak tree which cast a shadow over nearly the entire graveyard. Pastor Francis walked to a whitish gray headstone that was standing vertically at a slight angle. "This is one." he said pointing at the stone. Will looked closely. The shallow inscribed letters were difficult to read. Pastor Francis rubbed his finger in the letters which were filled with pale green lichen. Will could follow and he read out: "Francis Buccham. 11 June 1847 aged 49. His wife, Jemima Buccham. Died 1843, aged 32." Further down on the stone in a slightly different style of chiseled inscription he read out. "John Buckham. 12 February 1866, aged 36. His wife Mina. Died 1879, aged 41."

"There are two other Buckham graves here. One, just over there is for a John Buckham who died in 1915. And there is another on that side for Robert Buckham, who died in 1961, and according to my member is her father." Pastor Francis was talking from notes he had made on a small scrap of paper.

"This is great. But I don't recognize any of the surnames." said Will. "Do you know where these people, your current church members, live?"

"Yeah. They all come from across the river just beyond Sharpesville."

"Would that place be called Puckamee?"

"I don't know. Sounds vaguely familiar to me. But I don't know really."

Pastor Francis continued. He walked over to a gravestone just behind the oak tree, hidden from sight from the church. He pointed at a more deteriorated stone.

"And this one is James Grieves's stone. It's a little harder to read. But I think it says James. And that he died in 1850. And his wife is listed here below his name. As Bonnies Grieves. With a name like that maybe she was a white woman. I don't know. It says she died in 1845 aged twenty five. And then there are two further generations of Grieves in the graveyard. There and there. And a quite recent one. In the far corner. That black one, that also says Jimmie Grieves." They walked over to it. It looked new, but it was from 1984, only fourteen years before.

"I didn't ask the current Grieves congregant how this Jimmie is related to her. But he probably was. You see he lived eighty-six years. But his wife, Jemima, lived only fifty years."

They went back to the church and stood outside the main doors, which looked freshly painted in red contrasting with the white clapboard. Will asked him how to arrange funeral services.

"You're thinking of Hampton, right? Will it be open coffin or closed?"

"I think from what I saw that his cancer is going to get him within the next month. He's been failing fast this year. I would prefer open coffin."

"In that case you would need to embalm the body first. I can recommend a good funeral home in Bristol that can both pick up the dead body, file the death notice, and do the embalming and deliver the body in the coffin here for the service. Here's their number. Maybe you've heard of them."

"Yeah, I've always noticed their home, right next to the old hospital."

"You should contact them now and pick out the coffin you want. They can supply a big choice but they have to order most of them in."

"Thanks, Pastor, I'll do that this week."

"And I understand you want to bury his body out at his farm?"

"Yes. As I told you we have a family graveyard out there."

Pastor Francis gave Will the pages with the names he had written on them, then shook Will's hand and wished him well. "Call me when Hampton passes away. We can arrange a funeral service just past noon on the next Sunday." Then the pastor opened the door and went back into his church. It was just beginning to rain lightly.

On Friday morning he called Carmine to ask for a report about the meeting of the previous evening.

"We met at the gymnasium of the local high school. Seven couples from the other community came. They said that their grandparents never renounced their Indian heritage or roots. That is was our community that left them, because our group was unwilling to have a Negro schoolteacher for their children. They did not buy that claim to be Negroes or half-breeds with Negroes. They, unlike us, just acknowledged the Negro as a separate but equal race to the Indian race. But they four or five generations later still consider themselves to be Nantiquak Indians. They never assented to being classed as Coloreds for the U.S. Census. Which our Association did not and also has not accepted. They said they would join the tribe to be incorporated, if our group in the Association were to apologize for more than a century of estrangement and exclusion."

"I had to admit they did not look as if they had much if any black racial features. In size they looked like we do, but they are fair skinned, if anything. And also they do not have many Indian racial features. So we need to get a meeting of the tribal council and 'smoke the peace pipe', so to speak, with them and Chief Clarke will issue an apology."

"They in turn agreed to share their records and memories of their ancestry as far back as they know it. I'm sure we will get some interesting materials from them. Some of them have the same last names as the traditional leaders in our group. Johnson, Hanscom. But they acknowledge that they are a mixed breed. They just are not very sure what part of their ancestry derives from non-Indian parents, nor who those parents were."

"It's interesting of course to learn that they have clung together right next door to us for one hundred and fifty years. Our neighbors. Acting just like an Indian tribal village. You would think that if they had not felt they were shared a racial identity as Indians they would have all moved away and their community would have disappeared long ago. But they didn't. And they adopted Methodism at the same time as we did. I think we will expand the Nantiquak tribe. But I think we will not be able to identify how much Indian blood flows in their veins."

"Maybe you can find ancestral gravestones at their churches?"

"We can ask them and try to make genealogical connections. And then we can look for the gravestones."

"Send me, if you can this weekend, the names of family ancestors they believe are buried in those churches and also the names of the churches and their addresses. I'm going to Dover on Monday to consult the Church archives about Indian Methodists."

"Meanwhile," Will continued, "Did you get a lot of genealogical family materials from our Kuskowarok band on Wednesday?"

"Yes a lot of material, but we in the end only interviewed seven people. We're planning now to go back there tomorrow, maybe we can finish up. But I doubt it."

"Sounds good. You're doing a good job for sure. I might come over and join you around noon then. Will you already have started by then?"

"Yes we should get under way around eleven. So see you there."

On Monday, after Minnie left, Will was feeling elated. So much in love with Minnie, so much loving Minnie the previous two nights. He drove up to Dover in a cloud of arousal, replaying memories of things she had said, of her smile, of the contours of her breasts, of the taste of her mouth, of the sweet sounds she made in her sleep, of the tender and passionate moments, or the wildly passionate heaving and rocking together, of kissing her sternum and licking off the sweat. He was so elated that he sometimes lost track of the road and very nearly lost track of oncoming traffic. He drove up as if on a flying carpet, the car seeming to be racing onwards two feet above the road surface, and he floating another two feet above the car. He only came down from this pleasurable cloud when he finally drove into Dover and needed to start searching for the offices of the Methodist Conference. After some time turning around blocks, going back and forth over the same stretches, and searching for road names, Will found the building, which from the outside was not marked, but was standing next to a well-marked Methodist church building with a large parking place in front of it. Inside he asked for Mr. Dimpleton and was taken to his office. Mr. Dimpleton, who looked like a stereotypical plump middle-aged pastor in a three piece suit, stood up, with a beaming smile, and offered his hand. His handshake was very nearly limp.

"Welcome Mr. Eames to Dover and to the Methodist Church Conference in the Eastern Shore. I'm glad you could make it. One moment, I'll call Mr. Woodburn to tell him you're here." He sat back down behind his desk and dialed an old-fashioned rotary action phone.

He hung up and smiled again. "Let me take you there. He's ready for you." As Mr. Dimpleton stood up, he said further, "By the way, Mr. Eames, are you a Methodist by any chance?" Will answered. "Yes, but not practicing much." "A shame." As he led Will through a short corridor toward the back of the building and then up a flight of stairs, spoke to him with his head turned over his shoulder.

"You know, I'm actually from Suffolk County. I've known those Indian folks for a long time. Some of the churches I went to when I was an active pastor had Indian members." He stopped at a door with a brass plaque on it with the words Church Records written on it. "Here we are."

"Bob, I'd like to introduce you to Mr. Will Eames, whom I told you about."

From around a table that was cluttered with several piles of papers, bound folders, and a large computer screen, a thin, white-haired man stood up and came around the table. He was wearing a brick red wool sweater with holes in his elbows. As he approached it surprised Will to see that he was much taller than he.

"Glad to meet someone coming to do research on our records and archives." he said, offering Will his hand.

Mr. Dimpleton, who was still smiling broadly, excused himself and closed the maple colored wooden door behind him. It was then that Will noticed the distinct smell of age and dust in the room.

"Tell me now what you are looking for?" said Bob. But even before Will could start, Woodburn asked, "Maybe you'd be interested in this article I wrote on the history of the conversion of the Indians of the Eastern Shore to Methodism. I published it not too many years ago in the national Methodist Church monthly journal. I have a copy of it here for you."

Will took the article. It was three pages of double columned text, photocopied out of the journal. He then told Mr. Woodburn what he was looking for, namely records from the 1830s to the 1880s of baptisms, births, marriages, burials which indicated explicitly that the subject was an Indian. Woodburn shook his head.

"I don't know. I don't think that race was indicated by anyone, but let's see. Let's start by searching the oldest records for a specific church. You say the Asbury Church near Exeter in Dorset County? Let me check." He looked at his computer screen and began moving around the mouse and pressing a button or two. "So I found it. Come with me."

There were glassed-in steel shelves with large spaces between each shelf, arranged in rows. They were labelled with the years. Woodburn went all the way to the back of the room, where the long shelf was labelled 1820-1845. He went to the third door and produced a key to unlock and open it.

He pulled out a bound folio sixe file. On the spine was printed simply 1825-1850. Woodburn took the book to a high table set against the wall next to the stacks. He opened it gingerly and opened it to the third tab set amongst the pages. "These are the records of the Asbury Church. The first page is a modern addition, as it lists all the ministers and circuit riders who worked at the church. And as you can see it is typewritten. This list also indicates that the church was first built as a wooden structure in 1829."

The records began from 1830, and were entered by year. They began with records of baptisms, followed by marriages, followed by births, and finally by burials. Woodburn pointed at the ledger page on which was written lines of text with details arranged by columns.

"This looks like we are lucky on our very first strike. You see these baptism records show us that these first Methodists adopters were adult baptisms. And look, it shows birth name and the name taken on at baptism. You see: 'On 24 October 1830, one man and his wife were baptized. He took on the name John Johnson, and she Jenny Johnson. His birth name was Black Owl Hakankuk and he is about twenty eight years old, and her birth name was Clear Water Blanrushcomb, she is twenty two, so she estimates.' Now that doesn't say explicitly that they were Indians, or Nantiquaks specifically, but I would bet you that this is pretty convincing evidence that these were Indians who were converting from their traditional religious practice. And that required that they be given English names."

Will felt a thrill of excitement. Here he was finding convincing historical documentation of the presence of Nantiquak Indians there on the Nanticoke River near Exeter. And the family name of these Indians were the same as ones that survived at Wicomico to this day.

"This is great, you know. This will help support our application for recognition."

"It's strange I didn't notice this when I was doing research for my little history of the spread of the Church on the peninsula. Let's look at the other baptism documents."

They read the next several records; they were all given the same date—the 24th of October-- and they all seemed to indicate adult baptism into the Methodist Church. The fourth record, also indicated what were clearly Indian birth names which were replaced by English given names. The picture emerged that the minister of the newly built church at that time performed a mass baptism of new converts and followers. Then in the tenth record, the entry read, 'On October 24, 1830, I baptized one young man. He took the name Andrew Jackson Driggers, giving up his birth name of Fire Earth Chacagoan-Puhaola. He claims to be eighteen years of age.'

"So there it is!" shouted Will. "The first appearance of my ancestor in history! And proof that he originated in Wicomico, near the old settlement of Chacagoan." Will felt overjoyed by the finding.

"It seems to me that you've already done a lot of research on this particular subject." said Woodburn.

"Yes, and I know a lot of the current inhabitants of Wicomico."

In all for the Asbury Church, on that fateful October day in 1830, ten out of twenty seven people baptized were Indians, although the records did not mention Indian or Nantiquak explicitly. The next recorded baptism was in April 3rd, 1832. But it was written in a quite different hand, and it did not record a mass baptism. Then, also in this different hand, the record for June 2nd 1832 listed the baptism of Butler Randall, aged estimated to be 24, whose birth name was White Buck Cusckorwaroak. It was unmistakably the Randall descendant of Old Man Pellmell Randall.

"Our records show that one Francis Westbury was the minister in the church then for about four years." said Woodburn. "He had been earlier a missionary and circuit rider in the middle peninsula, and he earned a little bit of fame for us Methodists. I wrote about him in my little history. He converted apparently lots of Indians and black people to Methodism. My records did not show who was the minister of the Asbury Church earlier in 1830.

They continued reading the entries for baptisms. It seems that after Butler Randall there were no more adult baptisms and no further indications of Indian names changing into English names. A little later they did discover listings of child baptisms of the newborn children of the John Johnsons, and the Driggers and the Couskeys. But none of these indicated that the infants were of the Indian race. Then they began to search the records of marriages and births. For the twenty year period of this archive there were recorded neither any marriages nor any births from these familiar Indian surnames.

"Maybe they did not come to the church for these rituals." Woodburn suggested.

Finally they concluded their search by reading through the entries for deaths and burials for the period. There was one record which matched what Will had found, and seemed to be an Indian name. It was a burial in February 1850 of Joseph Hanscom. Again there was no indication of his being an Indian or a Nantiquak.

All of this took about an hour and a half. Woodburn moved to pick up and replace this archive.

"Do you want to look at records of other churches? I need to take a break now for lunch. Maybe we can resume in an hour."

They agreed to resume at two o'clock. When they did resume, Will asked to see the archive records for the Rosedale Church.

"But maybe we can take a little detour." said Will. "Could we look first at marriage records from 1914?"

Woodburn said sure and once more looked on his computer for where to find those records. He went to a different part of the stacks and pulled out a quarto sized ledger book which was marked 1890 to 1920. This book held the records of four churches in the Eastern Shore of Maryland. One of them was Rosedale Wesleyan Church. Woodburn quickly scanned through the records and soon found the section on marriages. Then he turned a couple pages and found the year 1914. And then he found the entry. 'November 2, 1914. Marriage of William Eames and Mena Driggers service conducted by Oliver Reece.'

"Well, that certainly verifies a personal family milestone. It indeed took place in spite of the ban on interracial marriages and in spite of the social disapproval of this particular wedding."

"You mean, this Mena was an Indian?" asked Woodburn.

"Yes, and a fairly dark skinned one. You could not mistake her for a white woman. But the church married them regardless."

"So, in fact, the local minister was knowingly breaking the law to wed them?"

"It would seem so." said Will. "Although the law in Maryland may have been a little different from Delaware's."

Then they began to look in the early records from the Rosedale Church. Again in the folio sized bound ledgers there were the records of five churchs, all in the region of the middle Nanticoke River in Maryland. This one also had compiled a typewritten list of the earliest ministers and preachers of the various churches. Rosedale's records began from 1825. Once more starting in 1828 there appeared to be a mass conversion of Nantiquak Indians to Methodism through adult baptism. Will had the list of names that Pastor Francis had given him from the cemetery and he looked for those first. The handwriting was difficult to read as it was very fine, slanted, and loopy. Woodburn also struggled with reading the scripts. This time the recorder did not give the original names of the individuals, just the English surnames of the baptism recipient.

"And look here." pointed out Woodburn. "It seems in these earliest years, the man writing these records was writing them outdoors. You see, these smudged marks are signs of raindrops falling on the page. That might indicate that they did not have a church building yet even though they had organized a congregation. That happened often with the circuit rider missionaries."

Throughout the records of the Rosedale Church from 1825 to 1850, there were only two explicit indications of a recipient being Indian, and both of these were infant baptism records with the standard entry, 'Indian child of Walter and Mariam Hately'. Those two entries from the early 1830s established only two Indian surnames who were members. Will was disappointed. They finished up their search at four o'clock. He had established from church records the definitive presence of Nantiquak Indian families bearing nine English surnames, all of which had graves at the two churches and which had continued well into the twentieth century. It was discouraging. As he was leaving, Will began to think whether membership in the Methodist Church would have in the eyes of the 19th century census takers inclined them to number those as racially colored or white even. As a sign that the Indians' conversion to white man's religion ended their cultural identity as Indians. His last question for Woodburn was to ask what he had for the earliest records of Methodist Churches in Suffolk County. Woodburn looked again on his computer and answered, "The earliest records for the establishment of a church in that area is the Francis Asbury Church near Beaverton, not far from the Brant Creek. Established in 1822."

"That could indicate ministry to the Nantiquak Indians who lived on the old Brant Creek reservation. Is there also a church on the Old Gum Road where all the Indians were working felling cypress trees?"

"Yes, there was one. It shows here that records started from 1824."

"Fine. I'll send some of my researchers from the Indian River community here to do further research on the Delaware Churches. They'll be coming soon."

On his way back home, he called Minnie and told her the news of what he had found at the archive center of the Methodist Church for Delmarva. He was excited by his findings, but as much he was excited to hear her voice and report to her.

"It's only too bad that our tribe doesn't have anything like the same history as the Nantiquak." she said. "It would help our cause with our application in the Bureau."

"I understand. But you said you went to church when you were little. Was it an old church that your tribe had joined early?"

"I don't know. I certainly don't recall ever seeing an old church graveyard of our ancestors. Maybe I just didn't look for it. I'll have to ask around. I don't think we went to a Methodist Church. I think it was a Baptist church. It wasn't old, I can remember that. It was a newer brick building."

"I can hardly wait until I see you again this Friday, Minnie."

"I feel the same." she said softly.

All he could see in his mind's eye all week was Minnie's green-brown eyes, her aquiline nose, and her direct smile for him.

Later that week, Will received through the mail the materials from the firm Genetic Tree of Life. He enthusiastically reviewed all the materials which helped him understand some of the methods that were used by the company, and he gained some more understanding of the terminology and what it all meant, and what he could expect to get in terms of uncovering ancestry. But at the end he was still confronted by the price for the services. At $12,000 he just could not afford to undertake this kind of investigation. And that price did not include the cost of the forensic recovery of DNA from old buried bones. The materials also included the names of some forensic archeologists who had worked on recovering Indian DNA.

He would not go ahead with a DNA profiling of his great grandmother just now because of the expense. But he was still curious about the process. So he called the phone number of one of the archeologists given in the list, a certain Dr. Houlder. It was the number of a man in Colorado; a man affiliated with the university in Boulder. He did not reach him with the first call, but left a message on his answering machine. Apparently Dr. Houlder, his message said, was out in the field on a dig. That he checked his messages every day and he would get back to him if Will left his telephone number on the machine. Will did not get a call back the rest of that week, and Will forgot about Dr. Houlder. But toward the end of the month, he got a call from a number that he did not recognize.

"Have I reached Will Eames? This is Dr. Houlder calling, Jack Houlder. You called me."

"Oh yes, thanks for calling back. I was calling you to ask about the process of extracting DNA from old buried bones. Specifically, about DNA recovery to uncover American Indian ancestry."

"I'm working on such an investigation just now for some Navaho people in Utah. But extraction is a trade secret. No just kidding. The process of finding and extracting viable DNA from long buried bodies is just beginning really, as the sequencing of DNA and profiling is still fairly recent. So what can I tell you? How we do it? We drill into a bone that should have contained marrow and we carefully extract material inside that we find. Then we send it to a laboratory that cuts it up, mixes it with some liquids to be able to search for the DNA strands. And so on. For Indians' bones, none of that is difficult. Any more so than for examination of pharaonic bones or those of recent mass graves. The hard part is legal and political."

"I see." said Will. Then he explained to him the context of his investigation. And that he wanted to do DNA profiling on his great grandmother who was a Nantiquak Indian of Maryland's Eastern Shore. He was trying to establish the genetic relationship and continuity of the Nantiquak people with the original Indians of the peninsula. But he did not have the old bones to test, other than his great grandmother's and her parents from a century earlier.

"Wait a minute. You said Maryland's Eastern Shore? You know, three months ago there was a significant find there of buried Indian bones. It is a huge and exciting breakthrough for our small community as it comprises the only old bones ever found there and from first examination it looks like it is ancient. At least five hundred years old. A friend and colleague of mine is working on this find."

"Really? That's very exciting. Undoubtedly Nantiquak Indians' bones. Or similar ancestors. Do you know where this find was made?"

"I don't recall exactly. Does the name Salisbury sound correct to you?"

"Yes, of course. It's not even thirty five miles away from where I am standing now."

"I'll have to look into it."

"Is your friend going to try to recover DNA to better identify these bones?"

"I don't know. The short article I saw said that no one so far claims them as their ancestors. They may try DNA extraction. I can call my friend and ask."

"Could you? I think in that area of Maryland we can probably claim that those represent the bodies of Nantiquak Indians or their ancestors. We need to establish a genetic baseline from as far back as we can, and I think this could do it for us—I mean for the Nantiquak, whom I'm representing."

"Okay, I'll ask and get back to you, Mr. Eames, with more information."

On Thursday evening that week, Will drove over to Shapp's Landing and started looking for the exact place where Puckamee was situated. He had only the sketchiest of instructions; 'about half a mile from the gas station outside town, toward Manning Springs, a small turn off onto a dirt road'. And he had to try several dirt roads which looked like farm tracks before he found the one that 'turns west and then north and leads into the woods'. He continued slowly driving, bouncing along a dusty road in the woods of stunted oaks and occasional pine trees. He finally found a squatters settlement in a large clearing in the wood that was bounded with a treeless marsh on one side. The day had been warm and breezy, and some of the trees other than the oaks were beginning to show leaf buds. The settlement looked similar to Wicomico, only larger with more trailer homes built into the ground arranged in a shallow V shape and with a second row of houses built parallel to one arm of the V. Some of the trailer homes had TV antennas, there were power wires hanging haphazardly from house to house, and the yards were cluttered with discarded junk and lawn chairs. There were several cars parked helter skelter around the settlement, and another half dozen parked nose first up to the edge of the marshy area. Will stopped his car in a cleared dirt area at one side of the collection of houses. Almost immediately little children poked their noses out to look at him with curiosity and they were shortly followed by three or four men who emerged from different houses. All of this horde started slowly approaching Will, some of the men tried to shoo the children away, directing them back to their houses. Will could see that all of them looked like coppery skinned Indians; he had found Puckamee. He waved to the assembled crowd as they came closer.

"I'm Will Eames." he shouted. "I'm looking for Nantiquak Indians and the settlement of Puckamee or Wicomico."

"You've come to that place, mister." said one man taller than the rest. "We are Nantiquaks. We've been expecting you."

"Then you might know that I myself am part-Nantiquak and that the Nantiquak tribe in Delaware is organizing all Nantiquak Indians across the Eastern Shore to make an application for the larger tribe to get recognition from the U.S. government as an authentic sovereign tribe."

"And why are you here?"

"We want to include all of you as tribesmen whose names will be given to the government. We want to recover the reservation lands that the Nantiquak lost many years ago. We want you to be part of a larger tribe that will receive Federal aid and health care and schooling."

"And what if we do not want to be part of a larger tribe, based in Delaware?" said the tall man.

"You will continue to live in hiding, to work on the side, and to always be wary of the tax man or police who will want you to move away from these lands that aren't yours. Are you the leader here?"

"No, that would be Jack Buckham. But's he's away just now. I am Albert Heyden. Reverend Francis told my mother that you might come looking for us."

"Do you know the Nantiquaks at Wicomico on the other side of the River?"

"Yes, we know of them, but do not much interact with them."

"You are all from the same tribe. And your two groups used to own reservations in these parts. We think we can with your assistance recover them to you. You would have legal ownership of your homes then."

"That would be good."

"The group of Nantiquak Indians living near Millsville in Delaware want to count your numbers and enter your names into the list of all Nantiquak Indians. Sort of a census. Can we talk about this?"

"Sure, come to my place."

Will followed Heyden across the small patch of dirt and the other men folded in behind them, and the remaining children followed them in a crescent formation. Heyden opened the door to his trailer home and invited Will in. Much to his surprise, the interior was very neat and orderly and surfaces all seemed clean. The main room was sparely furnished and the walls were all hung with dark blue curtains. There were only folding chairs in this main room and two long benches; it seemed as if this room had been primarily used for meetings. Four men had followed them in and they all promptly sat on the benches without uttering a word. Heyden offered a canvas folding chair to Will and pulled up a padded folding chair for himself.

Then Will started his pitch, much the same pitch he had made to the Nantiquak Association about four months earlier. He highlighted the benefits of getting federal recognition. He spent a little time on what that process required. And then outlined how joining together with the Nantiquaks of Delaware and Wicomico, and others would strengthen the tribe and strengthen their claim for greater rights. He suggested how the larger tribe might work together, how they would be free of many taxes, how the tribe might be governed, and how it would be organized by bands. Then finally he raised the issue of Indian owned companies and enterprises that could be set up on their reservations. But he did not mention the casino at that time. Then he outlined the steps that they would need to take. And he introduced the census and ancestry survey they would take of all the adults who wanted to join the larger tribe.

"We will be hoping that you can identify your ancestors going back to the middle of the last century. We'll need this information to apply for federal recognition. We've already done this with the Kuskowarok band."

"And have the Askesky band given over their information?" asked Heyden.

"Askesky?"

"The Indian River tribe you have spoken about. They are Askesky, no?"

"I don't know. Where did the Askesky live before moving to Suffolk County by Millsville?"

"Not too far from here. On the other side of the Brant River reservation on what is now the border between Delaware and Maryland. Near the Great Cypress Swamp."

"How do you know this?"

"It is in our tradition about the bands who left. Askesky also became a reservation. They were related to us originally and lived near the Pocomoke at what is now St. Mary's, before they started moving north. We learned about them again when they started advertising for their annual powwow."

Heyden continued, "I think you need more information from them to establish their authenticity, than you do from us."

"I'm beginning to appreciate that." said Will.

"They are true half-breeds."

"Have you ever gone to one of their powwows?" asked Will.

"Yes, once. I thought it comical, and very unauthentic."

"So, will you all here in Puckamee sign up to be members of the Nantiquak tribe?"

"I don't know. We'll have to discuss it together. Maybe I'll call you next week to let you know if we want to participate. I think we will not like the idea of being governed by the Delaware Nantiquaks."

"I am not sure that you will be. I think you all will have to meet and agree on how the different bands will be lead."

"So then, Will Eames, I will call you after we have consulted and made our decisions. Let me have your telephone number."

"Do you have a cell phone?"

"Yes, here it is." said Heyden, reciting his number. "But our signal coverage here is not very good so you can't always reach me on it."

"Let's try it to see if it works now." said Will. He tapped in the numbers and waited. Heyden's phone began to ring with a funny staccato ring tone. "It works alright."

Heyden smiled. "So now, for a change, I get to say to you the white man's favorite expression: 'Don't call me, I'll call you.'"

Will thought of that expression as he called Minnie later that evening, at a time by when she had usually gotten home. He wanted to tell her the news about the Puckamees. Even though she was supposed to come the next evening, he couldn't wait to hear her sweet voice.

The next day he called Carmine to get any report from her about the census interviews they were doing with the 'Black band'—the name they had started using to distinguish the smaller neighboring group of Indian River Indians whom they were inviting to join the corporation. She told him that all total they had interviewed sixteen adults, and there were still seven more to interview. In addition their population had eighteen children. She also told him that they had finished the complete census of the Kuskowarok band in Wicomico. Their total population, she said, came to forty six men, women, and children, and that there were only five surnames in the entire settlement—although the name Randall did not survive. So that they were closely related to each other. He told her about the Puckamees and that maybe they represented eighty or more Nantiquaks.

As she was speaking he noticed for the first time how similar her manner of speaking, the tone and pitch of her voice, and her intonation were to Minnie's. It was uncanny. And it especially struck him over the phone, when he could not see Carmine as she spoke. It made him ponder long afterwards that day if there was a vestigial uniform Algonkian women's mode of speech that had somehow survived and was passed on from mother to daughter, even across long distances like the distance between the Massoponax and the Nantiquaks at Indian River. He'd have to look more closely at Minnie when she spoke to him up close, and then he would try to look at Carmine when she was speaking in the room with Will some time. But before then Will spent that weekend luxuriating in the arms of Minnie, loving her like he had never loved a woman before.

The next week, there was little to do. That week there was still no real estate sales or purchases to tend to, and none in sight. Will decided the most useful and necessary thing he could do while waiting for some business was to drive to Salisbury and buy a new larger mattress to better accommodate loving and sleeping with Minnie. He went to the new shopping mall outside of town and quickly found a mattress discount store and was able to select a very comfortable, queen sized mattress that the merchant agreed to deliver and install the very next day. Before returning to Bristol, he strolled through the huge corridors of the new mall. He was lured into a Victoria's Secret by a shapely, willowy manikin wearing a sexy satiny emerald green nightgown. "That's just the thing for Minnie. To go with the new bed. For me to take off of her." thought Will. He went into the store, almost without embarrassment, and bought two such green nightgowns, a long one, and a short night shirt. "I hope this doesn't upset or embarrass her." he thought as he left the store. As he started to drive away from the mall, he thought maybe he could stop in at Hank Alvey's and tell him about the finding of Indian bones not far away. But then he thought against it. Hank would not care to be disturbed by such news. It made no difference to him at this late point.

The next day, late in the evening, he got a call on his cell phone from Phyllis. She was sobbing.

"Will, I don't know what to do. Hampt is dead. He died not long ago, after I last checked on him. He hasn't gotten out of bed for the last three or four days. And now he's passed away. There was no one else I knew to call. Max is not here. So I'm calling you." And then Phyllis began to cry uncontrollably.

"Relax, Phyllis. There's nothing more you can do for Hampt, now. I'll come out there now. I've made already many arrangements for his funeral, and I will call the funeral house first thing tomorrow morning. They will pick up the body and prepare it. Do you know the number for Hampt's doctor? He needs to see Hampt and issue a cause of death certificate. I'll call him and see if he can do that tonight. Do you need a lift to your home for tonight? Or would you rather stay there?"

Phyllis quieted somewhat with Will's words. Some of the responsibility was passing from her shoulders to Will's. "I think I would prefer staying here tonight." she said in a choked voice.

"Fine, I'll be out there in about forty five minutes. I'll call the doctor now and see if he can't come also."

Will was not prepared to see Uncle Hampt when he got there. He hugged Phyllis and comforted her for some minutes. Her eyes were swollen and red. Finally she led him to Hampt's sparely furnished downstairs bedroom. Will was shocked to see Hampt's body. Not only was it ashen white. But also it was as if, like a punctured tire, Hampt's body had surrendered most of the gases which had sustained it. He had shrunken so much from even the last time he saw a fortnight earlier. It was sight like no other Will had ever seen before. And he had seen the lifeless bodies of his slain colleagues in Iraq, several of them. They had not been deflated and shrunken like this. Nor ashen white and waxy. Thought shot dead, they had remained in appearance as lifelike and vital as when they had been alive, at least until they began to swell in the Kuwaiti heat of the day. He thought to himself that maybe the decay of death had already started in Hampton long before his final passing.

"Well the doctor says he'll be out here by about nine-thirty. He can issue the death certificate. But the funeral house people will move the body not before ten tomorrow morning."

"Fine. So shall I cover him--his head I mean—with a sheet?"

"Yes I think that would be enough. But we'll do whatever the doctor instructs us to do. Is there much ice in the icebox?"

"Not too much. A couple pounds or so."

"I think we should put some bowls of ice around his body. Or plastic bags if you have any here. And start making some more ice. Tomorrow is supposed to be warm. And I will spray the room with bug repellant to keep the bugs away until tomorrow."

The doctor came. Took one quick look at Hampt. And took out his notebook. He had the declaration of death form with him in his doctor's bag. "He lasted so much longer than I had ever predicted." he muttered. "Amazing. Almost three years longer than I had told him. Shows you the strength of a positive outlook on life. His will was much stronger than his flesh."

Then the doctor made to leave. Will asked him, "Do I owe you something for this house call?" The doctor shook his head. "Have you arranged for the mortuary people to pick up the body?"

"Yes."

"Well then, you'll need to show them a copy of this." he said as he handed him the certificate. "Maybe twenty-five dollars would be enough."

Will took out his check book and wrote out a check to the doctor, who handed Will a business card. 'Dr. Walter Grimsby, GP' it said. Will thought a doctor with the word 'grim' in his name was most inappropriate.

With the bowls and bags of ice placed all around the body, Will saw there was nothing more to do. Phyllis stood at one side of the room, staring silently. He let her stand like that for some time, before he gave her a hug and said he would leave. She whispered, "Just like my Ken. He looks now just like my Ken when he passed away."

Will left and found that he was surprised by the shock he felt when he got home. He felt like having a drink of something strong. The Cedar Island bar was probably already closed and he had nothing in the cupboard. He called his father and asked if he could come over and share some of his whiskey. There he told him the news about Hampt's death. Bob scowled and poured out a dram of whiskey in two glasses. "Here's to my uncle: a great man, and that I did not know well enough." Bob said. Mar Sue had already gone to bed. Bob and Will talked in low voices about what they knew about Hampt's life. "All his life, he lost the family members that were closest to him. But he bore up through it all." said Bob as Will prepared to leave.

The next morning early, he went out on his training run, showered and ate a light breakfast. As soon as it was eight thirty he called again to the funeral house to remind them of the arrangements for the day. Then he left again for Hampt's farm. He arrived as Phyllis was in the middle of putting out fresh ice bags around the body. She seemed a bit recovered, although she looked exhausted. There was beginning to be a strange and unpleasant odor in the room. The mortuary team came promptly at ten, looked at their copy of the death certificate, and bundled Hampt's body out of the room to a gurney they then carried into the back of their black windowless van. "So now we need to activate all the arrangements I made with your director." said Will as they left.

He turned to Phyllis and gave her another hug.

"Next? We'll hold the funeral on Sunday, at the Rosedale Church. I think you know it. Reverend Francis will preside, open coffin. That will probably be around 12:30. Then we'll come over here and have the burial. And then afterwards, a funeral dinner. Can you think of anyone we should notify, who might want to come. His friends? Neighbors?"

"Max, maybe."

"Certainly Max. I'll call him. He can contact the guys that will dig the grave. So do you think you can handle the preparation for the funeral dinner? I don't know how many will be coming. I think maybe five more than came to Thanksgiving last year. But you don't need to buy a turkey. Keep things simple. Buffet food."

"Yes, I can handle it. I can ask a friend of mine from Shapp's Landing to come over and help me with the cooking. And I think there might be some friends of his at the Church who might want to come. Reverend Francis can announce his death during services, before the funeral."

"So. Do you think if I gave you forty dollars that would be enough for the food? I'll buy flowers and some red wine in town."

"Yes that should be plenty. I'll clean up his room now and set up the dining room now. Would it be alright if I take his car to run the errands I need to?"

"Yes, of course. Here's thirty dollars now. Did he owe you any wages for the past month or so?"

"Yes, he had not paid me March's wages yet."

"Fine I'll write you a check for that, now. How much do I make it out to? And what is your last name?"

"Marlon, spelled with an 'o'. Two thousand, two hundred."

Phyllis started to cry again. Will knew that there was nothing he could do to console her. He gave her another hug. "You did so much for Hampt. We in the family are so thankful to you, even if we don't say it often enough."

During the drive back to Bristol, he thought about Minnie's upcoming visit that weekend. Maybe she would not want to attend a funeral. Maybe they would not make love because the funeral upset her, or it didn't seem appropriate to her. Maybe she would be spooked by Hampt's calling her the angel of death, or something like that, less than two weeks ago. Finally as the afternoon began to wane into evening twilight, he decided to call her and tell her about the funeral, and that he would be very pleased if she came. He got her just as she was riding on the train home. He told her that Hampton really liked her, and of course that she really, truly looked like his mother. They had seen that themselves. So she reminded him of his mother, whom he obviously dearly loved. Minnie said of course she would come. But she needed to get the proper dress for the occasion and she would do that the next day. Over the phone she sounded sad and she spoke very softly. Will decided that was in part because she was on the train and did not want to speak out too loudly. "I'm sorry for you, Will." she said in almost a purring voice. He wished her a good night, and kissed into the phone speaker.

That evening Will called Max and told him the news and invited him for the funeral.

"And could you ask Armand, "asked Will, "and one of his mates if they could come over Sunday morning and dig a grave in the family plot? You know the place, right?"

"Yeah, but I don't see him until Friday when we have some work to do at the farm."

"Fine. Is twenty dollars each enough for the two of them to dig?"

"I think so. It should take them only about two hours, including back-filling. But you always pay them more."

"And do you know, Max, if there is any rope in the barn?"

"Yes there are several coils of rope."

"They'll need them for lowering the coffin in the grave. And while I'm talking about the grave, do you happen to know who did the inscription work on the gravestone that includes Hampton's name and birthdate?"

"No, I'm afraid I don't. I've seen it, but I didn't see the fellow who did the work. And I can't think of any monument engravers anywhere but in Salisbury. Unless one of the Puckamee Indians do that sort of thing. It is remarkable how talented they are."

"Interesting. Did Hampton use any of them for work around the farm?"

"Yes. And they were always more skilled than Armand and his gang. I don't know why that is."

"Well I'll ask out there later this week."

Will called Albert Heyden straight after hanging up on Max.

"Hello." came from the other end, rather gruffly.

"Hello, is this Albert Heyden on the line?" asked Will. It seemed he did not have caller ID on his telephone unit. Will's telephone did not recognize Heyden's phone number, even though he had put it in his phone memory.

"Yes."

"This is Will Eames. Remember me from earlier? I have the opportunity to call you first, breaking your rule of 'Don't Call Me, I'll Call You.' I presumed you were talking about potential employers who so frequently said that to you?"

"Yes. That's right. So why are you calling?" Heyden said in what seemed clearly in an irritated voice.

"I am looking if perhaps there might be someone in your settlement who does incriptions of headstones for cemeteries? You know, stone carving? If there is someone like that I have a job for them."

"Yes, there is a man here who over the years has done a lot of work for the Salisbury Monument Company."

"Do you know of my great uncle Hampton Eames near Rosedale?"

"Yes, I met him once or twice at the church there. And several of our people have worked for him. He's well known hereabouts."

"Well he's died and he needs the inscription on his gravestone to be completed. Maybe your man could do this kind of work?"

"Maybe our man did that work in the first place, earlier. And you're saying it now needs to be finished?"

"Yes, I'm saying that. So how can I contact this man of your tribe there to come and finish the job he started?"

"His name is Mannuel Hately. Maybe he can come to the farm and look at the stone and see how much it will take to finish the job."

"Good. Then you could tell him if he can and he would like to get the job, he can come out to the farm on Friday early afternoon. And if he's interested I will be there and will hire him. No need for him to call me."

"I'll talk to him, tomorrow. And I'll text you if he cannot or won't come."

Without another word Heyden abruptly cut the line.

Late Friday morning when Will set out for Hampton's farm, the skies were dark and rain clouds were menacing. He found that no one was at the farm. Hampton's car was gone; Phyllis must've taken it. He had a set of keys and he let himself in. The house was quiet and very chilly inside. Phyllis had turned off the heating, it seemed. He went into the kitchen which faced out the back toward the family grave plot in the oaks. He put the kettle on the electric stove to prepare himself a cup of coffee and he looked in the refrigerator while he waited for the water to boil. . There was almost nothing in it, no milk for his coffee. He couldn't find the sugar either in the cabinets. He sat down at the kitchen table and waited for Max to arrive. What a strange, big house, he thought. And for so many years only one person lived in it. It must have been hard, so isolated and quiet, to live out here all alone. Especially after Hampt could no longer do the farming work himself. Will had not finished drinking his coffee when he was surprised to see the figure of a man in dark coat walk across the back yard over to the oaks and then to the family gravesite. The man knelt down and was looking at something. Will jumped up and opened the rear door which made a cracking, tearing sound as if it were protesting being opened after so many years of being sealed shut. The noise was enough that the man, twenty five yards away, stood up suddenly and turned toward the house.

"Hey, you there." Will shouted from the door. "What are you doing there?"

The man did not answer, but took several steps toward the house. Will moved down off the back porch and started walking fast toward the intruder.

"Who are you? What do you want?" Will shouted. At he drew closer he suddenly realized that the stranger was an Indian. Will slowed down. The man put one hand up in front of his chest, almost like the stereotypical peace gesture that Hollywood productions always used for Indians.

"I've come to cut the stone."

"Oh, are you Hately?"

"Yes, that's me. Who are you?"

"I'm Will Eames, Old man Hampton's nephew. I was the one who spoke to Heyden about a stone cutter for this gravestone."

"I know about it. I cut this one for Hampton. About two years ago."

"Sorry I shouted at you. I wasn't expecting you just now."

"Heyden told me to come today."

"Oh, yes. So can you do the job?"

"Yeah. I can start now, I brought my tools. If you give me the date of Hampton's death."

"When can you finish it?"

"By tomorrow. I figure it will take sixteen hours or so."

"You work fast. So the death date to use is 24 March 1998 so that it matches the form of his birth date."

"Hm." Hately grunted. "So he lived eighty four years. Long life."

"Eh, yes. He was an old tiddler."

"The stone is in the barn. So you need to open it for me and I can start."

"I don't have the key to the lock on the barn. But it's coming. The farm manager is supposed to be here any time now."

"I'll wait out front then." said Hately.

"Oh, and one other thing. How much do you want for the work?"

"Three hundred dollars, cash only."

Will balked. He thought it seemed like a lot of money.

"I usually get paid in advance."

"I don't have that much cash with me just now."

"You can get some at the ATM in Shapp's Landing. Or you can go to Secony in the other direction on the Choptiko. There's an ATM there too. More reliable service."

Max arrived at the farm about half an hour later, and he knocked on the house door until Will answered it.

"So I'm here now." said Max. "I wanted to consult with you with some questions about the planting."

"Fine," said Will. "First we need to unlock the barn so the stone carver can get started on Hampton's gravestone."

"Oh sure. I'll do that right now." And Max stepped down off the porch and went over to the barn and opened the padlock on the barn door. Then he came back to the front door of the house, at the same time that Armand Driggers came walking up the lane. Max told Will of his plans for the planting season, plans he had agreed with Hampton earlier in the month. He said he would need three farm hands over five days to help him, first with the soybean planting, and then another two days for planting the corn. He would need some cash to pay these guys once they had finished.

"And how much do you think it will come to for these guys you're going to hire? You mean Indian workers, right?"

"Well here's one just now," Max said as he pointed toward Armand. "I think it will come to about $500 each. I work 'em hard. Ten or twelve hour days. It's not really very expensive. I pay them less than they could earn in a MacDonald's, if a MacDonald's would hire an Indian that is."

"Why won't MacDonald's hire Indian workers for their staff?"

"Racism. They resisted hiring blacks for the longest time until not so long ago they lost a lawsuit against discrimination. So you go to MacDonald's now in Salisbury and it is full of black people serving white people. But Indians will have to sue the chain to get work there for themselves."

Will was thinking that suddenly the Hampton's farm was a big drag on his funds. He didn't want to ask Max if Hampton had paid him for March. That would be six thousand dollars, and at that moment Will didn't have that kind of savings. He had not discussed any of the current operating costs of the farm with Hampt and of course he did not know how Hampt took care of his books. He'd have to talk to Phyllis about that. But worry about how he would finance the continuing operations of the farm began to creep into his mind.

"Fine, fine, Max. That's what you agreed with Hampt. Then it's alright by me. I'll get the money to pay them. When? In ten days?"

"Yeah, I'd say by end of day next Saturday. That's the fourth."

"Okay."

Max then stepped away and down the porch. "We'll get started now." he said.

Will motioned to Armand.

"Good afternoon, Armand."

"It doesn't look so good just now. Rain."

"Yeah, maybe. Did Max tell you about my need for you to dig a trench out back?"

"You need two gravediggers? Yeah, he did. You got one. Driggers the gravediggers."

"So could you come here on Sunday morning a dig a grave for old man Hampton? It will have to be ready by one thirty or so."

"Yeah. I got a friend and we can do that, no problem. And we'll even shovel the clay back in after Ol' Man Hampton is in the bottom of the grave."

"Fine. Then I'll I pay you twenty dollars each to do the work. How's that?"

"I can't say that's too much. Maybe twenty five would be better. Urgent work you're asking for. Tight deadline. You understand."

"Okay, I agree."

"Okay massah. Now show us niggers where we needs to dig."

Will gave him a harsh look. Armand was always snide with him. And he didn't like it. He had after all just agreed to pay him more than slave's wages.

Will lead Armand over to the gravesites. He saw at once, that it wasn't clear where a new grave should go. Putting a grave on either the far right or far left sides of the graves that were already there was not going to work, because it would be too close to the trunks of good sized oaks. If it was dug in front of the line of the five graves already there, nearer to the house, would it be best on the right or the left, or in the middle, in front of Robert Eames's grave? Will paced around a little. He decided on symmetry. In the middle in front was where the grave should be dug.

"Here. Let's put it here. I get some string and pegs and I'll mark it out for you."

"And leave the shovels out of the barn, while you're at it."

When Will came back, Armand was sitting with his back against the trunk of one of the bigger oaks, so that Will could not see him.

"Armand," Will shouted.

"I'm here. Just 'laxing. It's a long walk up here, you know."

Will started to lay out the grave with the string and a measuring tape he had brought.

"Seven feet is not long enough," said Armand. "It should be eight and half feet minimum. Coffins are mighty big for shriveled up white men."

Will pulled the peg back to eight and half feet long.

"And it needs to be at least three and a half feet wide. I know from experience."

"So that's it." said Will standing up again. It looked to him like an awfully big plot of earth to dig up.

"And we dig to five feet deep. Any shallower and the foxes will be digging it back up. Any deeper and it will be lying in the ground water."

"If you say so." said Will.

"I do. I know from experience."

"I'll see you Sunday then. After you've finished digging this hole up."

Will then left to go to the ATM. When he got back he was surprised to see that Armand had already dug a half foot of the sod and soil off the complete outline of the grave that he had pegged out.

"Very unfriendly Injun, there in the barn." said Armand. "Wouldn't talk to me. So I started the digging. A backhoe would be faster you know."

Hately was standing at a bench in the barn, tracing out the letters of the stone onto some heavy paper. Will paid him the three hundred dollars cash and then left for home. The rain had started lightly and the landscape looked everywhere desolate, gloomy, and bare, almost wintry. Today he felt fleeced by all around him. Hard to grieve when you feel fleeced.

All afternoon the rain continued to pick up in force, and the streets in Bristol were covered with rain run-off, looking like waterslides. He desperately was looking forward for Minnie's arrival. She would cheer him up. But she didn't. When she finally arrived late Friday evening, it was raining steadily and she seemed glum and distracted. But they still embraced for a long time inside the house. They ate out at the Cedar Island and she told him about the somber black suit she had bought for Sunday's funeral. Later as they headed for bed, she whispered to him that they couldn't make love that night, or maybe the entire weekend because she had her period. Maybe that was what was giving her a headache and general discomfort. She adored the new green night gown, and as she got into bed she noticed it was a new wider mattress. But their affection was limited to caresses and hugs. She fell asleep in his arms with her back to him.

On Sunday morning, when Will first saw Minnie in the new suit that she had bought-- black blouse, black jacket and black long pleated skirts that fell to the middle of her shins longer than her usual skirts--he was wowed. He couldn't help think she looked like an actress he had seen in a funeral scene in a Hollywood movie, or several actresses playing the same scenes. It was as if she were wearing a standard uniform. And she was beautiful, just at those actresses were in all the films. Her straight black hair that fell to her shoulders enhanced her beauty and her funereal costume.

After the memorial meal, Phyllis asked Will to step to one side.

"I should have told you earlier. Hampt left me this ATM card with instructions to use it for the expenses for the funeral. You shouldn't have had to pay for all those things earlier this week. Here you take it, and go to the bank in Salisbury and draw out the funds. The pincode is 4444."

"And here are two checks that he filled out for Max's wages for March and April. You can give them to him right now, before the probate court takes control of the accounts."

Will thanked Phyllis and said she had done a wonderful job on the meal.

"But I wouldn't have expected anything less. Everything was delicious. Do I need to pay your friend something for her help?"

"Thad be nice, Will. Maybe twenty dollars would be enough. She was here all morning helping out. Oh, and one more thing: you need to take a copy of the house keys, the car keys and the key to the lock on the barn." And she handed over to him a large keychain with the eight keys.

"Max doesn't have keys to house or for the car. And I will keep only a house key until arrangements on the house are settled. But I wonder if I might take the car for the next several weeks?"

"Yes, sure. Otherwise it will just sit here rusting. No?"

As his family began to leave the farm house, Will felt so comfortable walking arm in arm with Minnie. He needed her by his side, and even though she appeared sad and somber, she lifted his spirits immensely. He was so in love with her.

Heyden did not call Will back until late in the next week.

"Buckham and I spoke about your proposal and invitation. And we have decided that our little group wants to be counted in the greater Nantiquak nation. So what do we need to do next?"

"We will send a group of Indian River Indians to Puckamee and they will start a census and conduct interviews to see if we can reconstruct your ancestors back for three or four generations. Some of this information we will use in our application for recognition, and some we need to enumerate the tribal members for our incorporation application."

"Yes, I see. When would that be?"

"We can start next week if you like. The head count and interviews should be taken in your village there."

"But we often aren't here until after six, because of our work schedules."

"That is why we start in the evening. Four interviewers will come down from Millsville. Interviews take about an hour, but sometimes more depending on how much genealogical information and memory the individual has. Only adults will be interviewed, men and women."

"So maybe we can start on Tuesday evening."

"I think that would work for us."

"Oh, and by the way," Will added, "Hately did a really bang-up good job on the headstone."

"He always does. He's a master craftsman in stone."

"And I will come to start things out. But I do not conduct the interviews. Only Indians will be interviewing Indians at your place."

Not long after Heyden hung up, Will got a call from Carmine. She reported that they had completed the interviews for both the Kuskowarok and the 'Black band'.

"We got really good genealogical information from both groups, although most of it is from family memories. Surprisingly some few actually had documents for their ancestors. And their memories of ancestors in most cases match up with the Church and gravestone records you found. It's looking real good for our incorporation of the tribe."

"That's great news, Carmine. Sounds like real progress. What was your head count of those two groups?"

"Including children, the Kuskowarok come to forty five, and the Black Band comes to thirty two souls."

"Now we can start with Puckamee. They're ready to begin on this coming Tuesday. Will you and our team be ready to start interviewing again?"

"Sure, starting at five thirty like before?"

"Yeah, we can meet in the parking area of the Shazzam gasoline station and convenience store, on the Beaverton Road at the entrance to Shapp's Landing at that time. Think you can make it then?"

"Yes. See you then. I'll call the others and tell them to be ready."

"And one more thing. I propose instead of driving back to Indian River late that night, you all can spend the night at my great uncle's farmhouse which is about six miles from Puckamee. I'll let you in when you all are ready. There will even be a bed for yourself, so you don't have to sleep with your mates coming with you. And you can then resume the next day interviewing the women."

"Sounds good. I think everyone will prefer doing that."

"So I'll see you at the Shazzam at five-thirty on Tuesday. Call me if you run into problems or are running late."

That Friday, when Minnie arrived at his house, Will felt he was ready to burst. He escorted her into the house and immediately began caressing her, kissing and cuddling her, and making it clear he was eager to make love to her straight away. She gave in and they went to the bedroom, but it was still light outside as the sun had not set yet, and she was still shy about undressing in front of him. So he suggested that she undress in the bathroom and wear the new bathrobe he had bought for her. Then after she came out and jumped under the blanket, he snuck in after her and they began rollicking in bed, he burying her in kisses and trying all sorts of techniques to excite her. They came up for breath only an hour later, when both were too parched to continue. "You're pleased to see me?" she said with a tone of irony in her voice as he retreated into the bathroom to bring some water. It was late when they got to the Cedar Island for supper. There, after ordering drinks, Will answered: "Yes, Minnie. I was dying to see you and get you into my arms again. Hampt's funeral was too big of an interruption to our loving." Minnie seemed to blush.

When Will and the operating committee arrived at Puckamee the light was turning dark because of low cloud, although the sunset was still about an hour away. It was stuffy warm and mosquitoes were already active. Heyden came out to meet their cars and he led them back to his trailer home. It seemed hard to believe but he had even more chairs in the main room. The room was well lit, brighter than what Will remembered from last time. There were about a dozen men and women collected there, sitting quietly. He noticed this time that the Puckamee Indians uniformly had the dark, copperly tint on their faces that seemed stereotypical of Indians. The same tint as Minnie's. They were much darker than any of the Indian River crew that came in with him. Will wondered if that meant there had been so much more mixed breeding with white people than had occurred here down west on the Nanticoke River. The women in the room had the same black, straight hair as Minnie, but they were all plumper and had more rounded faces and in Will's view they were not nearly as pretty as Minnie. Will then thought he saw Hately among the crowd, although he wasn't too sure. The man did not acknowledge Will—when their eyes met, he continued to look on dourly at Will, so maybe it was just someone who bore a resemblance to Hately.

Carmine had brought two more people to help with the interviews, both of them were young women who looked duskier than Carmine. Carmine told him that they would help in the interviews of the women. She had learned that having men interviewing women did not get results, especially if the women were unmarried, although at Kuskowarok there were not too many of those. It was clear that there were too many people in Heyden's main room to interview that night. Carmine figured that the six of them could at best interview fifteen or sixteen people that evening before it started getting too late. Then it was a question of how to ask some people to leave and come back in an hour or two, and to ask ten others to come back tomorrow. Carmine thought it was best to ask women to delay until tomorrow, because the men had to go for in search of work during the day. Heyden agreed. Heyden then turned to the crowd and addressed them in a stern voice, "Who wants to be interviewed first? Six of you can come up here and wait. Then ten of you women folk can leave for tonight, but will have your interviews tomorrow during the day. In this same place." Ten older women stood up to go and made for the door, and then the six select stood and stepped to the front of the room. "Now the rest of you can wait at home. These on this side of the room, you come back in an hour and a half. And the rest of you come back at nine-thirty." There was a great shuffling of feet and moving of bodies around the confined space. The floor of the trailer house groaned and squeaked. Then the door opened and people filed out of the trailer house, until there remained only six local and six Indian River tribesmen and women, plus Will and Heyden. The room immediately breathed a sigh of relief, and became less stuffy.

"Now, we can start." said Heyden. The interviewers one by one took up their notebooks and picked out a candidate and together they went to a far corner of the room. There were three local women, and three local men. And in low voices the interviewers started by taking the individual's name, date of birth, marital status, and number of children, if any. Carmine had found it was best to coach genealogical information out of their subjects by first asking these simple questions and then spending some time explaining to the subject the purpose of their inquiries and how they wanted to demonstrate the continuing history of the Nantiquak tribe and bands. That they knew their ancestors. And that way they could make a story of the survival of the tribe thought the decades and centuries. Heyden took Will by the elbow, and led him down a short corridor to the kitchen. "Maybe you would like some coffee?"

"Maybe I owe you an apology Mr. Eames." said Heyden. "As you understood from the start I was very skeptical and even dismissive of your project. But I learned from our cousins in Wicomico that you are seriously pursuing this. Buckham also spoke to me and said that this is the time for Indian tribes all over America to get official recognition and get on the gravy train as they say. So we will cooperate. And we'll open lines of communication between our different bands. We have not spoken with the Indian River band for years. Never thought there was any point to communicating with them. Now maybe they have something to offer that can help us."

"And I think we can send one of our braves, soon, to Beaverton to pick up some pizzas for your team. Even Indians eat pizza."

"Let me pay for that." said Will. He took out fifty dollars from his wallet and gave them to Heyden, who refused to take the money and pushed it back at Will.

"No, we can't accept that. It's not part of our tradition of hospitality. Although the food may not be so traditional."

The four pizzas were brought just at the time when the crew was ready to start the second shift, just before eight o'clock. Will took a slice for himself and washed it down with a coke. After this small supper, when the interviews resumed, Will stepped out and called Minnie. He mainly spoke about their progress, but he wanted most of all to tell her how much he missed her. But he didn't in the end. It was enough just to hear her voice. The last interview of the evening was with Heyden. It did not take long because he did not know much about his ancestry beyond his parents. So he had little information to share. He had no idea where his surname Heyden came from or what it meant, and he hadn't been given an Indian name when he was young. Carmine reported that, in general, the women had better knowledge and memory of their distant ancestors than the men. "They are better at remembering names and relationships. Even of ancestors they never knew or met." At ten Will was ready to take the six interviewers over to Hampton's farm and once there he showed them the bedrooms and covers, and he showed Carmine the kitchen and what was available for their breakfast. Will had brought a few loaves of bread and some coffee along with him and he left them on the kitchen table. "I'll come tomorrow morning after eight thirty to let ya'll out and take you back to Puckamee." Then he headed back to Bristol for the night.

The next morning, after his training run, Will came back to the farm and picked up the crew. On the way Carmine, who was riding in Will's car, told him that they had mice and the mice appreciated the bread on the table. "But they left some for us this morning. And we found some really nice strawberry jam in the fridge. And some eggs too. So we girls cooked up breakfast for the guys. I think everyone got enough to eat."

"Oh, I hadn't thought about mice." said Will.

"They gnawed their way through the plastic and into one of the loaves. Left a nice symmetrical hole in the loaf. Is this your house?"

"No, it was my late uncle's. He died only a fortnight ago. He never told me about mice, but I think they come with the property. It's a farm after all."

"Oh, I'm sorry to hear about your uncle. Looks like he had a really big farm. Impressive really. And there were people out working in the fields first thing this morning. And it looks like your windmill could use some repairs."

"Some of those workers are no doubt your Indian cousins from Wicomico, who you interviewed last month."

"Oh, so you're one of those exploiters of Indians?" she added sarcastically. To Will it sounded like something Armand or her uncle would say, but not Carmine.

"No, actually we pay our Indian slaves." he answered back with the same tone of sarcasm as Carmine's.

At Puckamee, they were able to start interviews at nine o'clock. It was then that Will first met Jack Buckham. He was quite different from the other Puckamees. He was short, stocky, and had fair, sandy colored skin, and brown wavy hair. Heyden introduced him.

"I'll do my interview first. I've got to go to Salisbury soon for some work." said Buckham.

"Maybe I can sit in on your interview?" asked Will.

Buckham shrugged his shoulders as if to say 'why not'. Ronald was the interviewer. First off, Buckham's name was Johnson, not Jack, which Will thought strange. He was married and had three children, and had had a fourth who had died in infancy. He worked at odd jobs, and at the university in Salisbury. Then Will perked up his ears when Buckham said that just recently he had worked as a digger at an archeological discovery of a Nantiquak Indian burial mound just outside of Salisbury. "Yeah, should be interesting," said Jack when Will asked him further if the discovery uncovered bones. "Big discovery and all that. Lots of bones all neatly stacked together but in a tangle. But the works sucks, and they paid me $5 an hour and I had to buy my own water. The white school kids got paid $8 an hour because they were studying archeology at university. They didn't even know which end of a shovel to hold." Then as the interview progressed it appeared Buckham knew a lot about his ancestry. He knew that he had several great great somethings in the graveyard at Rosedale. He even named one Francis Buckham lying in the graveyard. He knew the names of their wives, and sometimes even the years of their deaths. And yes he was the grandson of Robert Buckham. He even related a story of how his family had gotten the name. The family legend had it that they had attended a camp meeting of a Methodist circuit rider sometime around 1816 (or at any rate after the war with Britain), and they had converted then to Methodism. When asked where that ancestor came from he said Puckamee, and from that the preacher said, 'Your surname will be in English Puckham. And we'll give you the first name of Francis in honor of Francis Asbury.' And after that after they started going to the Rosedale church, even though it was hard to reach in the 19th century before there was a bridge across the Nanticoke River. Jack didn't know when the name became Buckham. And he said as well that his ancestors in that first generation still spoke Algonkian and only pidgeon English. He knew that because of stories he had learned about the various misunderstandings his ancestors had in that time with their white neighbors.

"Well, if you don't need to know more, I need to be off." said Jack standing up even before Ronald had finished writing his last answers. Ronald looked up surprised, but Will excused him. "You've given us a lot of vital information, Jack. But could you tell me why were you named Johnson?"

"Because I am the son of my father, whose name was John. Thus Johnson, just like in England. Weren't you paying attention?"

At lunch time, Will told Carmine he would be leaving for home. Carmine also said that they would also go home in a couple of hours, as they would be finished with all the interviews of women, so they didn't need to stay at the farm again, and they didn't need to come back until the next evening to finish with the men.

It was then that Will saw Hately come into the house. Hately scarcely acknowledged Will when their eyes met, no smile of recognition or greeting.

"Yes, it's my turn." he said in a low, dour voice.

Will knew now that the man he had seen last night was not Hately. Simply someone who looked a lot like this man Hately. When he took off his coat, Will suddenly realized that Hately was quite slender and not plump or stocky as he had remembered him from that rainy day at the farm.

"Hately," said Will as he offered him his hand to shake. "I want to thank you for the very nice job you did on the finishing the gravestone. And so fast too."

Hately emitted a sound more like a grunt than an acknowledgement.

"Good progress, I think." said Will turning back to Carmine. "Yo'awl are doing a great job. Let me know when you get here tomorrow. I'll come over."

Will drove back to Bristol thinking that they were making advances in their first step and that he had overcome the reluctance to participate by these outlying Indian bands. He wondered how much more effort would be needed to complete the application for recognition. Three months, four? Maybe more. Back at his office in Bristol, Will discovered there were still no signs of new business in spite of the warmer, sunnier weather of April. It was still a long way to the summer real estate season. Just had to wait. But waiting for Minnie that Friday was harder. When he called her that evening he asked if she would come with him to church that coming Sunday for Easter services. He said he was that kind of Christian, "attending at Easter and Christmas only." She said she was probably even less than him, but she would bring some dress clothes for the occasion. "Maybe I can buy you some nice spring outfit for church this weekend? Would you like that? Don't need to wear black again, although you really looked great in your black mourning suit." She demurred, "We'll see." "Probably my parents will join us." said Will. "So I'll see you Friday evening? Usual time?" "Yes. But it's hard to figure out what the usual time is with the weekend traffic." "I'll fix dinner then for eight. Okay?"

On Saturday they got in Will's Olds and drove the thirty minutes or so to the Salisbury Mall. Once inside, Will lead her to the Hecht's department store.

"I think we can find a nice colorful outfit for you here." said Will. "They have conservative tastes, not too racy at all. But no doubt we can find something in daffodil colors."

Minnie was overwhelmed by the large selection, organized by the different brands names.

"I don't know how I can choose, Will. There's too much here to even be able to focus."

"In that case, Minnie, I'll help you select some things that I think would look nice on you. And you can try them on in the fitting room and then model them for me."

And in only a matter of a few minutes Will had led her around a couple of sections of the store and found five different spring colored dresses and outfits for her to try on. The suits were with jackets and long skirts. She modeled them all for Will to see. He could tell she was embarrassed. She had probably never had a man buy her dress clothes before, he guessed. She ruled out two straight away, and the third one Will said was not right for Easter or for spring. But there were two that looked really nice on her she noticed before leaving the fitting room to show Will. Will liked them both.

"It's easy to pick out pretty clothes for you when your figure is so –willowy-- just right for the clothes. And both of these enhance your dark hair."

She asked him which one he preferred: The dark lilac colored dress, or the pale yellow suit costume, with a yellow and black patterned skirt. He liked them both. But she couldn't decide between them.

"So then let me buy both of them for you." said Will.

Minnie tried to object,--they were too expensive she thought, together they would cost almost two hundred dollars-- but Will would have nothing of it. "Now get dressed again and we'll take both." he said. He took the outfits to the register and paid for them with his credit card. He would not hear of accepting any contribution from her.

The next morning as they woke up to the sunny morning, and before they got out of bed, Will began caressing and stroking Minnie, trying to arouse her. "Mini-oka can't you tell that I want to love you again and again? And right now?" he whispered. While he was on top of her heaving back and forth, in the bright light of the morning sun, he thought he noticed something about her for the first time that seemed unique. But he could not focus on what it was as he was too close to reaching climax and too gripped by passion. They made love then until both were wet and exhausted, and then they fell into a doze, Will's right hand draped across Minnie's chest. He woke suddenly from the deepest of sleep and looked abruptly at the clock. "Minnie, it's past ten o'clock. Let's get up, we'll have to hurry." Minnie jumped up, pulled her green nightgown up shielding her modesty and ran into the bathroom. "I'm first she said." Will had to piss badly and he ran to the toilet next to the living room and after relieving himself he walked back, still naked, and sat on the bed waiting for Minnie to finish her shower. She came out finally with the towel wrapped around her still moist body. "Now is this appropriate behavior for Easter morning, Will? You take your shower while I get dried and dressed." "I want to watch you." said Will. "No, you know I don't like you to see me naked." When he finished showering and shaving, and drying, Minnie had already put on a slip and was about to put on the yellow suit. "Oh good, I get to watch you put on your Easter clothes."

They walked arms locked together to the church, which was located only a few blocks from Will's bungalow, and arrived just as Bob and Mar Sue were beginning to enter the main doors. Will hailed them and they waited for them at the landing at the top of the steps. Mar Sue took one look at Minnie and coo-ed. "Oh Minnie you look absolutely beautiful. What a pretty Easter suit." Minnie was beginning to like Will's mom. Inside during the service, Will became aware that Minnie wasn't singing, and she didn't appear to know the typical hymns sung at Easter services. Instead she mouthed the words or pronounced them with barely any sound at all. He looked at her and smiled. She tried not to notice him, and shrugged her shoulders.

After the service let out and they were standing in the sun out front of the church, Mar Sue asked her, "You don't usually go to church?"

"No, I'm afraid to say. I haven't gone to church since I was in high school. And in Bowling Green, our family went to a Baptist Church."

"That's alright. Here on the Eastern Shore, it seems everybody is a Methodist."

"Yeah," said Bob amused by Mar Sue's comment. "And a lot of church buildings too. It also seems there is a Methodist Church here in Bristol almost on every other block. I guess Methodists cannot agree with one another, so they leave one church and go and build another one."

At his parents' house, afterwards for dinner, Will told his parents about his research of the Methodist cemeteries in the eastern part of the county, where he had found lots of Indian gravestones from the nineteenth century. Mar Sue had put a roast of lamb on the timer in the oven and when they stepped in the whole house already smelled warm and meaty. As she was bringing out the dinner she brought a panier of buns. "These are hot cross buns I baked on Friday. We can still eat them as part of the Easter tradition." The sweet smell that permeated the house however came not from the buns with their sugary white cross on top, but from the sweet potatoes that baked in the oven with the meat. "It's too bad that Kate and her family couldn't come." said Mar Sue. "I invited them, but as you can see they decided not to come. To have a big family celebration would have been nicer."

"Yes," Bob said. "We consider you part of the family now Minnie. You have certainly improved Will's behavior. In just a short time, too. And we're glad you joined us for church. Easter services are the most important family event for us."

"When I was a little girl, we all went as a family to Easter services too." said Minnie. "There were mostly other members of our tribes at the service then. Unfortunately I have not gone to church in a long time."

Will was staring at Minnie throughout dinner. He was completely taken with her looks, the way she sat so dignified and pretty, her handsome profile framed by her black hair, and her aquiline nose, and her shy smile which she occasionally sent his way. He also was noticing how differently his parents were responding to Minnie. They were addressing her quite differently than they ever had to Karen. They were indeed, he thought, treating her as family, as if they had already married and were living together as man and wife. He thought maybe at times it was a little presumptuous of his parents, but he liked the tone and the assumption: that Minnie and Will were life mates, bound to each other. That seemed very appealing to him. He wondered how Minnie might feel about it. He also wondered how he could find out.

The next weekend, at the Washington date that Minnie had arranged, Will felt from the first moment he saw her leave her office a heightened sense of arousal. During the music, especially the first half when it was music he did not understand or recognize, he continued to turn to Minnie and admire again the profile of her face, the sloping neck, the slightly high pronounced cheek bones, her small ears, her aquiline nose –he had noticed among the Nantiquak people there were many with more typically Roman noses—the smoothness of her facial skin. It wasn't until they had returned drunk and giggling to their hotel room later that evening that he finally recognized what had momentarily struck him as unique the week before in his bed with her. Standing giggling under the bright light, letting Will completely undress her, he saw that she had almost no body hair, other than the long straight hair on her head. None on her arms, not even faint hair or black hair under her arms, none on her legs. Not even much if any pubic hair. He had never seen a woman like that ever before. She was smooth and hairless as a marble statue of Venus, except she was not white like marble. Was it possible, he thought, that she shaved all over? It just did not seem possible. By comparison he was a hairy beast.

The weekend date was for viewing the cherry blossoms, which were then at their peak bloom that Saturday. He was completely overwhelmed by their beauty, and especially by the powerful, sweet fragrance that the blossoms lent to the entire area around the tidal basin. He learned from the information panels around the park that theses cherries were a gift of the Japanese who called them sakura. As he and Minnie strolled under or around the trees, Will became so enamored of their aroma that he wondered if he could find a perfume that used cherry blossoms. He would have to find out and buy a bottle of such perfume to give to Minnie. It would be their special scent. He would always thereafter associate her with the fragrance of sakura.

At the end of the next week Will got a call from the probate clerk of Dorset County. She informed Will that they had verified the validity of Hampton's will, and an executor had been appointed, and public death notices had been issued and published which gave creditors forty days to make claims against the estate. So the process of disposing of Hampton Eames's estate would begin.

"Who is the executor, if I may ask?"

"A certain Mr. John Rendell of Exeter. He was apparently Eames's lawyer and he brought us the will."

"There will be a reading of Hampton's last will and testament at our office on Wednesday, the twentieth of May, where the estate executor will be introduced and the distribution of assets, net of debts, will be announced. All of Mr. Eames's heirs can attend."

"You can't tell me what I will be receiving now?"

"No, only the executor, Mr. Rendell, can do that. And the exact amounts won't be known until all debts and taxes are paid. That's why there's still this one month delay. We're still in the discovery phase."

"Thanks. I'll be sure to put that date in my calendar." said Will. He was more curious about meeting this character John Rendell, than he was about receiving the news that he had inherited the farm, which he already knew. He did not think that this call told him anything new. But he marked his calendar anyway.

By the end of the first week of May, they had finished the census and all the interviews. Carmine reported to Will that they had now a tribal population of eight hundred and thirty six souls, including women and children. Nearly all of these people lived in Delaware and Maryland, although they had included a dozen individuals who had in recent years moved to Philadelphia or Baltimore and who still wanted to be counted as Nantiquak Indians. They organized the tribe into five bands: by far the most numerous was the Indian River Band, followed by the Puckamee Band, the Makadewa-Ninda Band the name in translation into Algonkian meant Black Face which the interviewers had given to their neighbors on the Indian River who were supposedly intermarried with African-Americans, the Kuskowaroak Band, and the smallest group was the Asksesky Band in the vicinity of Gumboro and north Salisbury. With that information they were ready to consult the Association's lawyer in Centreville. This lawyer, who was named Beardsley, told them initially that incorporating as a non-profit was very easy, and inexpensive. But there were a lot of preliminaries needed, and these would cost some money. For one the corporation would need to have a registered office and an address, and that it would have to propose its board members and officers in advance. And furthermore it would need to have articles that would allow the corporation to apply for tax exemption from the IRS and from Delaware state taxes. And it would need to set out the corporation's rules for membership, and its bylaws, "In other words," said Beardsley over the conference call they had with him, "how the corporation would operate, and how individuals could apply to become tribesmen or women and members of the corporation. I can do all this for you, but of course that would be chargeable work." Will agreed that all of these preliminaries needed to be discussed with the tribal council and representatives of the new Bands.

"And that will take a great deal of time to arrange. We'd like you to attend and give us advice on the corporation bylaws, and appointing officers."

"Certainly, I can do that. But I will have to charge you my rate. And we both know that discussions with the Nantiquak can take a lot of time. You let me know when this meeting can take place and if you need me to attend. It would be best if they decided what they wanted first before I come into the equation."

Then Will thought that perhaps Minnie would know all about setting up tribal governance and incorporation. So he decided to ask her if she could help. And he thought too she could contribute her insights and advice as work paid through the contributions made to NAILS. Public service funds. .

"Oh, and before we hang up, Mr. Beardsly, I wanted to ask you if you know the Congressman for the south Delaware district. If you do, maybe you could help us get an appointment with him in Washington? We want to solicit his help in getting federal recognition for the tribe."

"Yeah, I know Bob Morton. Real well. We're brothers in the County Masonic lodge. I'll call him now and arrange a meeting. Would anytime next week be alright with you all?"

"Yes, Wednesday or Thursday would be fine with me, if it's okay by him."

"And Wednesday would be fine for me too. And probably Ronald also." said Carmine.

"Fine, I'll take care of that." said Beardsley. "He needs to do more to support and help our Injun friends and neighbors in the state."

After getting off the phone, Will called Minnie at her office.

"Minnie, I have more work for you if you want to do it. For the Nantiquaks of course. I think you're probably the best qualified person anywhere to advise them on governance. We're at the stage where we're ready to incorporate the tribe as a non-profit and there is the question of the rules and bylaws of the corporation. Do you think you could help?"

"Will, maybe you over-estimate my experience. But I have seen how governance issues are handled in other tribes, and I have experience with my own tribe—which is not incorporated. I will be glad to advise the tribe."

"Great I have a commitment from you then. We'll do it then. But would you be able to sacrifice our weekend together to have a consultation meeting on a Saturday? I will still be near you, participating."

"You are a driven man, Willeems, but I like you that way. So set up the Saturday meeting then and I will do it. And afterwards we can go fishing, if you agree to fish with me again on one of our shared weekends?

"It's a deal. I'll let you know when we have this meeting. It will be sometime in May."

"Okay, but we're still on for this Friday, right? See you then?"

"Of course. Always want to see you, ma'am."

But as usual it was difficult agreeing on a meeting time with the Nantiquak, even without the added complication of inviting representatives from the Maryland bands. That weekend, the first weekend of May, it was not possible. Will and Minnie were free to pay attention only to each other all weekend long. Finally they were able to arrange a meeting for the third weekend, a Sunday, at the Association headquarters, provided they arranged rides for the distant representatives of Kuskowarok, Puckamee, and Asksesky.

In the interim time, Beardsley called Will and said that Congressman Morton would be able to see the Nantiquaks on Wednesday, May 6th in his offices in D.C. Will told him that they were having their meeting with the Nantiquak to discuss all the issues he had raised with them around getting incorporated on the Sunday, the 17th. And if at that meeting the tribal council could reach agreement they would come to him during the next week to submit the information needed for the application. Beardsley said he'd be ready.

On the day of their meeting with Congressman Morton, Will waited at his agency office for Ronald to drive down from Indian River, bringing Carmine and Morley with him. They then continued in two cars up to Kent and then over the Bay Bridge, and on to 'Warshington'. Ronald in his car followed Will all the way into the parking lot, not far from the Republican Congressional Office Building, the same one that Will had used that fateful night last November, as Will realized as they were walking up Third Street to the Office. They went through security and were escorted up to the congressman's office where they were left to wait in his reception room for almost forty minutes. Finally they were invited in, just as two men dressed like high class lawyers crossed the room to leave.

After introductions, Will told the congressman that they were there representing the Nantiquak Indian tribe.

"Oh, I'm very familiar with the Nantiquaks of Delaware. They live in a strategic location in my district, and they are important constituents." said the congressman, who looked like his morning make-up was coming off.

"So we are seeking to get federal recognition for the tribe and to restore the reservations that were granted to the tribe by treaty, but which were sold by the colony and later the state of Delaware."

"When was this treaty signed?"

"The first treaty was signed in 1667, and there were additional treaty agreements right through 1698."

"So long ago? And you think they are still valid?"

"Legal opinion is pretty much united that the treaties are indeed still valid."

"My word. They don't teach you much about the law of Indian treaties in law school."

Then Will outlined to Morton the current steps they were undertaking and then he concluded that the tribe would also look to a legislative solution to see if Congress could not declare the federal status of the tribe.

"Oh, I'm not sure about that. You know, ever since Reagan was in Washington, our party, the Republicans have been trying to curtail the rights and independence of Indian tribes and especially the financial support and promotion of programs for the benefit of Indians and only Indians, not other poor or indigent races and minorities. I would be hard put to try to stroke against the stream in my own party, as they say. That wouldn't do me any good and ultimately wouldn't be very helpful for the Nantiquak people either."

"So, maybe then the courts will have to decide our fate."

"Maybe. That's right. The courts."

"So then, we would ask you first to write a letter to the Bureau of Indian Affairs stating your support for our application for federal recognition, and how much you would like to see our tribe get recognition, and your desire that the Bureau expeditiously make a ruling on our case. Do you think you could do that for us?"

When confronted so bluntly with a request for a concrete action leading to a written document, Congressman Morton now became more concentrated and thoughtful. He was a man who had learned to be very wary of putting his signature to any kind of document that other people, especially there in the halls of Congress, could point too and challenge. For the following twelve minutes he spent the time hmming and hawing, thinking in fragments half aloud about the pros and cons of drafting a letter, how it would be seen, how it should be written, whether it would effective, what tone he should take, whether he could get in trouble with the members of his caucus. He was talking and arguing a case in his own mind, almost as if Will and his three Indian friends had left the room. Finally Congressman Morton found the formula that was most mealy-mouthed, which seemed to promise enough to these petitioners and enough to make them go away.

"Okay, I'll see what I can do."

Carmine jumped in, rightly seeing that nothing had been conceded in that answer and unwilling to let an answer go unformed: "That means, you're against writing such a letter of endorsement?"

"No, I didn't say that, young lady. But you see I have to consider all the different perspectives of your request and your tribe's objectives. And, of course, the law for getting federal acknowledgement. Don't want to step on any toes, inadvertently, trespass into other departments' domains. That's the worst of all crimes here in Washington."

Shortly afterwards the Nantiquak delegation left Congressman Morton's inner office, unsure whether they would get a letter of endorsement and support for their efforts. But they stopped in the outer office at the desk of his administrative assistant and Morley gave her the mailing address and contacts telephone numbers of the Association. Will left his business card. They also gave her the name of Nighthorse Ward and his title and address at the Bureau. Morley was nearly on the point of blowing up as they left the Congressional Office Building.

"There's no understanding the spinelessness of these politicians." said Morley. "They come to us before every election with their begging bowls out but when you ask something from them, they cannot even formulate a simple yes or no."

Carmine was next to Morley and tried to distract him to keep him from shouting. Will had to admit that it was completely unclear what Congressman Morton might do for them, if anything.

"I suppose we'll just have to wait and see if he gives us any consideration. On the whole I think he was trying to find a way to give us such a letter without appearing to be committing anything."

Will asked if these group wanted to go out for lunch, maybe to the Gullah place again. They all politely declined and so they separated. Will called Minnie and asked if she would join him for lunch now as they had discussed. Of course, she did. And she was waiting for him outside her office by the time he got there. They went to a small French bistro off K Street where Will ordered mussels: "Let's see what the Frogs make of a shellfish dish." he said.

"Frogs?" asked Minnie a little confused. "But you're ordering mussels."

"Yes, but no. The French are called Frogs, because traditionally they used to eat lots of frogs."

"Really? They eat real frogs?"

"Yep, frog legs and snails too."

Minnie winced. "I think I will have the Dover sole. The menu says that it is a flat fish."

"Yes, but I wonder if it comes frozen from Europe."

Over lunch they talked about Congressman Morton and his prevaricating. Minnie thought it was funny. She had seen before the consternation in the Bureau when tribes tried to mix political means with administrative means. It caused her to laugh a little, now that she was no longer in the Bureau. But she didn't think in the end the congressman's endorsement letter would help one bit.

"Not as much as the threat of a lawsuit." she said. "The congressman was right. The executive departments pay more attention to courts. And courts often take over where legislation prefers not to go, especially in the questions raised by our minority, native Americans. Our numbers are just too small for there to be really any political commitment or drive."

"Yeah, but we still need to push at all doors."

When their main courses came, Will cut off:

"You know, maybe you thought I hadn't noticed, but that lilac dress you're wearing looks smashing on you. It fits your color spectrum just right. It's the first time I've seen you wear it since we got it last month."

Minnie smiled warmly at him. "You saw me try it on then in the store."

"Yes, but this is a real demonstration. It looks stunning on you. You're so beautiful today. With that dress on you could hide in one of the azalea gardens outside. You'd blend in."

"Just spring colors." Now she blushed a little.

As they left the bistro, Will remarked: "Now that is a different way to fix mussels. White wine makes a real difference. We'll have to try it sometime with our local Bay mussels."

He then changed directions, and walked over to the garden he'd seen where the almost purple azalea were in full bloom. "You see how you fit in with them. Too bad I don't have a camera with me. I'd like a photo of you and the azalea as a keepsake." They walked on, arm in arm, around two long blocks before Will left her again at her office.

"We'll have to do this again sometime. Maybe I should stay here in D.C. for dinner with you." he said as he kissed her goodbye. "We can do this often."

"That would be nice, Will, but I had promised to go see my mom this evening after I get back from work." I don't see her on weekends anymore, as you know. I see you."

"Well then I will look forward eagerly to seeing you on Friday." Will gave Minnie a brief hug and kissed her on her cheek. She looked around, still sensitive that someone from her office should see them acting so openly affectionately.

After he left Minnie outside her building on K Street, he walked over to Hecht's. It wasn't far. The lunch crowds had long ago left the sidewalks clear and the home-bound commute hadn't yet started. It was a warm, brilliantly sunny day and the trees were fully green along

K Street, heavily shading Farragut Park and Franklin Square. It was a pleasure to walk along the twenty five minutes to the department store. It was the first time that he had ever strolled along the streets of Washington on a work day and really enjoyed it. He felt safe and the city was so beautiful in the sunlight with the greenery in full display. At Hecht's he went straight to the cosmetics department which occupied most of the first floor. He was looking for a cherry blossom scented perfume for Minnie, as he had resolved the previous month. The customer service representative was a pretty middle aged woman dressed in an all red outfit and who looked to him like she was from Iran or an Arab country. She told him to ask at the De Rene display. Once there he asked again if there were any perfumes they had that were based on cherry blossom essence oil. "But of course, sir." said the very svelte young woman also dressed all in red. "Our best-selling brand here in the spring, Sakura." And she pointed to a display of the Sakura line of perfumes and eaux de perfume and toilette. Will asked to see the perfume, and the young woman handed him a box that nicely fit in his hand. It said Sakura and had a woman in a kimono kneeling under a blooming cherry tree. It also said 3 oz.

"Just what I am after then." said Will.

"Here, smell this sampler." she said handing him a long strip of white paper.

Yes, he thought, it was the exact aroma he remembered that he found so wonderful in April. What he wanted for Minnie.

"That's it. That's what I want. How much does this cost?"

"That particular sized bottle costs three hundred and nineteen dollars before tax. But you can get a five percent discount if you buy it using our store credit card."

How very expensive he thought, in alarm. More than three times greater than what he had thought he would spend on such a perfume. The young woman in red had the exact presentiment that the perfume was too pricey for him; the same reactions had occurred to a number of men before.

"But, sir, you might be interested in the smaller bottle, here. One and a quarter ounces of the perfume. It costs only one hundred and forty dollars."

Will looked at the bottle she was offering and was beginning to feel out of his depth. He had no idea that perfume was so expensive. And this bottle looked so small. Again he demurred. And once more the sales woman had the answer, as this was a path she had gone down with many men without their wives looking for a gift.

"The eau de parfum is less expensive because it more diluted and has less of the cherry blossom essence than pure perfume. It is less concentrated with the pure essence of the perfume. Here is a three ounce bottle for two hundred and twenty dollars, and a one and a half ounce bottle for eighty nine dollars. Here smell this. You'll notice that there is only the faintest of differences. In effect the essence of perfume lingers longer on the woman's skin than the does the eau de parfum." the woman pronounced these terms as if she were speaking French.

Will now was in a panic. Could he afford so much? What if Minnie wouldn't wear perfume or eau de parfum? Up to then he had not noticed that she wore perfume, and he had never seen her apply any. She did agree with him that the scent of the cherries in bloom was intoxicating and wonderful. So he bought the three ounce bottle of Sakura eau de parfum. He'd have to think of the right way and the right time to present it to her. So he left Washington for home smelling the fading scent of the cherry blossoms on the paper sampling strip and dreaming of anointing Minnie with the new eau de parfum. What pleasure, he thought.

On Sunday the 17th, Will and Minnie—she dressed in her professional wear-- drove up together from Bristol to the Association, on the way picking up Old Man Sockum from Wicomico. He was so fat that they—and two young tribesmen-- had a hard time shoe-horning him into the car, even though the Oldsmobile was a spacious car.

Once underway, Sockum said, "I'm going to go see my long lost cousins today. Who would have thought that possible? Will, you are driving this process along. And I'm thankful. It's long been needed."

"Well, let's see what happens once we get there." said Will. "I think Minnie will be the star of the show today."

"And who is this lovely looking lady?"

"She's Minnie Warrens, the chief of the Massaponax-Doeg tribe of the middle peninsula of Virginia. And she's a first rate lawyer working for the Indian legal aid services helping us with our ambitions. She's going to give a lot of useful advice today."

"Glad to meet you Miss Warrens. And really pleased that you're helping out your fellow Algonkian tribesmen. We certainly don't seem to be able to help ourselves."

"So Armand couldn't come today as another representative of the Kuskowarok?"

"No, we wouldn't want him to come. He's no good. He's just an obstructionist. So snide. One of those, as I was saying, who always objects to trying to do anything to improve our life. He always just gets in the way. He's got real problems. And besides he really hates white people. That's not helpful, if you're asking them for favors."

The meeting in the Association included the entire tribal council from the Indian River Band, two representatives from the neighboring Makadewa-Ninda Band, and Jack Buckham from the Puckamee Band along with another representative whose name was unknown to Will, and Old Man John Sockum from Wicomico. There was a representative also from the Asksesky Band, but Will did not meet him. Carmine was the only woman representative from the whole Nantiquak tribe. It was a big group, and they spent some time standing and introducing themselves to one another and talking in hushed voices about their lives and their interests and the program that Will had launched them on. There was an excited agitation in the room, which Will had never seen before among these Indians. Will led the meeting but Chief Clarke called all the men to order for the discussions to start.

Will said they were there to formulate rules how the new larger tribe would be governed in the future and what the non-profit corporation would mean for the tribe's operations and functions. And the first order of business said Will was to agree on a legal address and offices for the tribal corporation. He suggested that the offices should be located in a central location between all the bands, and that location was Beaverton, which was about twenty miles from all the main settlements. He had already checked and they could rent a small empty two story brick building there for almost nothing. This building could provide the space for all the administrative functions of the corporation including accounting, communications, and meetings of the board of directors which would be in effect the executive tribal council of the combined tribe. It would become one of the regular operating expenses of the tribe, but there would be needed some repairs and build-out needed in order to occupy it. Not to mention furnishing and equipping. He called for a vote of the representatives to decide on getting this building and establishing it as the official headquarters of the Nantiquak Tribe. There was muttering around the room. Chief Clarke asked if there were any questions or objections. There was only one, as a man from the Indian River stood up and said that that location was so far away from Millsboro and Indian River. Others expressed their agreement. Another then asked how much the rent on this building would be to which Will said it would come to two hundred and fifty dollars a month. But buying it would cost about twenty five thousand. So when Chief Clarke asked for a vote to set this building up as the offices of the new tribal corporation the vote was in support, twelve to four.

Then Will spoke about the need to name a board of directors for the corporation, and that at the moment of application only a chairman of the board needed to be named. The board of directors would in effect be the tribal council for the wider tribe and only tribal members could be directors. One of its members would also serve as the president of the corporation. And the composition and selection of the board would be defined in one of the bylaws of the corporation which they would discuss next. Then he introduced Minnie to the group, saying that not only was she one of the lawyers working on the effort to restore the Nantiquak reservations, but that she was also the chief of the Massaponax tribe across the Bay in Virginia. Those who didn't already know that issued interjections and soft grunts of approval.

Minnie, who was sitting at the head table to the right of Will, cleared her throat.

"I am pleased to be here today to give you all advice on the future governance of the Nantiquak tribe. I am giving you this advice based on my experience advising other tribes, as well as my own—which is much smaller than yours and which is not incorporated. I am going to suggest as well some language and actual rules which I have seen in tribal structures around the nation. I expect that today's meeting will not end with a complete list of the bylaws and operating principals and rules, but that we will end with general understanding and some minimal principals which can serve as governing rules. That way, in later meetings with the participation of fewer people, the remaining bylaws can be established and accepted." She spoke steadily, but softly. Some of the men in the back asked her to speak a little louder.

Then she began to refer to several pages of notes which she had prepared. She addressed the issue of the foundation members of the corporation which comprised a list of all the adult men and women above the age of eighteen, and the qualification for new members in future. Members were like shareholders in the corporation, but that no member could own more than one share in the corporation. About new applicants for membership she discussed the issue of demonstrated blood relationship to the Nantiquaks: whether new tribesmen or women would be accepted into the tribe by one-quarter blood relation or whether one-eighth would be enough to qualify. Children of current members would become full members upon obtaining their majority. People who applied would also have to be residents of Delaware or Maryland, and those applicants who belonged to one of the several emigrant groups in New Jersey, Canada, or the old Midwest or Oklahoma would not qualify for membership in the corporation. Residence in one of the future reservations would not be a requirement for membership. Members would share equal rights to any distributions made by the corporation. But no member of the corporation, or grouping, such as bands, would bear responsibility for the liabilities of the corporation. There would be an annual 'shareholders' meeting where the board of directors would report to any members who wanted to attend about the corporations actions, accounts, and future operations.

As for structure, she offered the following basic idea: The tribe, which would officially be the Nantiquak Nation of Delaware and Maryland, would be comprised of five bands, the largest of which by population was the Indian River Band. Each band would select its own chief for periods that each band determined and by the vote of one vote per one man or woman. These chiefs would also serve as directors of the corporation. Four additional representatives would be appointed to the board of directors from the Indian River Band. The chairman of the board would be selected by the other members of the board and appointed for a three year term. This chairman did not have to be a Nantiquak or a member of the corporation, but all other board directors must be Nantiquak Tribe members.

The board of directors would act as the greater tribal council and it would meet at least once a quarter at the corporation central offices to conduct and direct the activities of the corporation and to make decisions about the disbursement of funds on expenses, distributions, and liabilities as well as the purchase of assets or the establishment of Indian owned companies. The board would also make appointments for the four officers of the corporation. These would be a corporate president, vice president for finance, vice president for communications and chief accountant. The board of directors would decide the pay for these officers and would also review their performance and they would receive twice yearly report on accounts from the officers.

The corporation should be capitalized and its assets enumerated. Any future reservation lands assigned to the tribe would become trust lands and be accounted as assets of the corporation, but governed by a representative of the U.S. government. The corporation would not be free to dispose of or sell these trust lands or reservations. Assets include the Nantiquak Tribe Association of Delaware, the Tribal museum where entry fees are charged to visitors. The corporation can acquire or establish other assets, the net income of which would go to the corporation. The corporation will be organized and registered as an entity that is exempt from state, local, and federal taxes. Any net income after payment of debts and in excess of the authorized capitalization and reserves set aside for coming year expenses, should be distributed to the members in equal shares once a year. The corporation can take on short term debt with outside entities and remains solely responsible for paying these debts back.

"Now, for example," she said in a change of tone, "say the board of directors of the corporation decided to set up a casino, it would become an asset of the corporation and its net profits after reimbursement of debt and payment of operating expenses would go to the corporation for distribution. But on a smaller scale suppose that it set up a souvenir manufacturing company that makes handicraft souvenirs for sale to people who come to visit the powwow, that company would also give its net profits over to the corporation and it would count as an asset of the corporation."

She continued to outline the activities that the bylaws would permit. For example, the corporation could also set up services, such as a health clinic, or a police force. And it could also contract for the building of houses or public centers on reservation territories.

In this manner Minnie continued to outline the bylaws that could be put together for the corporation. She spoke for more than an hour and a half outlining these rules and giving details and examples of wording for each article. Will was watching her closely as she made this presentation. He had a strange feeling, one he had never felt before with any girlfriend. Even though no one in this crowd knew or had any reason to suspect that he and Minnie had intimate conjugal relations, he suddenly found himself feeling proud of her. It was a strange feeling, but very pleasing and gratifying. On their way back to Bristol later that afternoon he told her about it, about how his admiration of her translated into this feeling that he could think was pride for Minnie's talent and expertise. She thought it was strange. She could understand the sensation of admiration; she felt that about Will often. But she thought you could only feel pride in your loved one only in relation to other people who know of that relationship.

After she finished the room again filled with interjections of satisfaction, wonder, and confoundedness. Some felt they should applaud, but no one did. They did not know how to express their appreciation, especially as so many of the participants were unsure of what they understood or of what they needed to do. Finally Chief Clarke said:

"So again, Minnie, on behalf of all of us, I want to thank you so much for the preparation you have done and the presentation of how we should run our tribe through the bylaws of this new corporation. I am a little confused myself that someone outside our tribe should bother to make so much effort on our behalf. But I am thankful for your thoroughness and your help. Maybe we can give you applause to show you our appreciation." And Chief Clarke led the tribesmen, along with Carmine, in a short applause for Minnie. Will noticed that she blushed. As far as she was concerned she was simply delivering legal assistance and advice to help set up the corporation, it was simply a matter of professional delivery of advice.

"And now, I think we can also say that we can accept a lot of what you have outlined for us, as well. In fact not too much changes from the way that we have been running the Indian River Band. So I think we can agree that we can adopt several of the articles which you proposed for concerning membership, structure, and the governance of the tribe within the corporation. If I understood everything correctly, I would continue to be the chief of the Indian River Band of the Nantiquak, and as such I would have a director's seat on the board.

Our tribal council could continue as is, but four other members from it would also move to being on the board of directors. Isn't that right?"

"Yes, that's right."

"And the other bands need to more formally designate their own chiefs and representatives. And they will also become board members, effectively the new larger tribal council of all the Nantiquak peoples here in Delaware and Maryland."

"That's also right."

"So today for our application, we need to have our official name as we want it, to have our address for a registered office and corporate headquarters, and the name of our appointment for Chairman of the board of directors of the corporation. Is that enough?"

"And we need to have two hundred dollars for the filing fee, and corporate name search." added Will.

"So do we agree with the official name: 'The Nantiquak Indian Nation of Delaware and Maryland, Incorporated'?" said Chief Clarke.

"Maybe it is enough to just be the Nantiquak Nation of Delaware and Maryland?" asked Ronald.

"Or maybe we should limit it to southern Delaware and Maryland only?" asked another man who stood up. From his appearance, Will surmised he came from the Makadewa-Ninda band. "We don't want the people who claim to be Moors from upstate or the Nantiquak-Lenape from northern Delaware and New Jersey to be demanding membership."

"That's right. And I don't think that name conflicts with the name of the Association, either." said Morley.

"Certainly, we do not want to include the Moors." Chief Clarke repeated. "They are not from our tribe at all."

"If I may," said Carmine, jumping to her feet enthusiastically, "I would like to nominate Minnie Warrens to be the first chairwoman of the board of directors of this corporation."

This surprised many in the audience, not least of all, Minnie herself. Will thought it was a brilliant start for the new tribe and corporation. But Minnie, while flattered, thought it was another impossible task, a lot like her position as the elected Chief of her tribe. She wasn't really the leader of the Massaponax tribe, she knew, because no one on the tribal council listened to her, and none of them cared to adopt her proposals or pursue her initiatives.

Chief Clarke stood up now. "I want to second that nomination. I think Miss Warrens would be best to lead our tribe as she is already working on restoring our reservations and winning us federal recognition. All those in favor of appointing Minnie Warrens, raise your hands." Chief Clarke and Carmine had their hands up even before he finished speaking. Slowly around the room, most of the men raised theirs. Only a few did not.

"So I think that is settled," said Chief Clarke. "Minnie Warrens will be the first chairwoman of our board of directors and we'll put that in our application."

"There's also the matter of the initial capitalization of the corporation." interrupted Will after a short delay. "I would like to propose as an appropriate starting level, a sum of twenty five thousand dollars. Can the tribe swing that?"

Chief Clarke acted a little surprised. He looked at Morley Norwood. "What do you say, Morley? Does the Association have that kind of money that it could put to the starting capital of the corporation?"

Morley looked even dourer than he usually did. "Yes, we have, but we cannot pay it over just now. We would not have enough to stage this year's powwow if we did."

Will now jumped in. "The starter capitalization does not need to be paid in full when you all make the application. I think Beardsley made that clear. But we can indicate the sum in our foundation document. And then it can be paid in full after the powwow. But the tribe will still need to pay the filing fee up front."

"Fine. We'll pay cash at the filing time." said Chief Clarke.

"Maybe a bank draft would be better," answered Will. "You can get one for maybe five or ten dollars, and you won't have the risk of cash not being accepted. After all Beasley will file at a registrar's office, not a chance that a cashier would be there. He will supply the name of a registered agent and we agree to use the address of the property in Beaverton as the official registered office."

"So, I think we can adjourn today's meeting." continued Chief Clarke. "We have everything we need to file for incorporation. And following that filing we can apply for our tax exempt status. But now let's eat. Morley, is everything ready?"

Morley nodded his head. "I think so. Let me check." He stepped out of the big room and after a moment he came back and signaled to Clarke that everything was ready. Except for Old Man Sockum (Will had noticed that Sockum was the only truly fat man in this group of fifteen men and two women), everyone had already stood up, some stepping out for a smoke. But following Morley two young men carried in a long folding table, and behind them a young man and woman carried in a second table which they began setting up. Then the four young people left and returned carrying aluminum heating trays of food. Two middle aged women carried in some heating trays as well. They were putting on a feast just as they had six months earlier when the tribal council had agreed to embark on this program. There were trays of fried chicken and fried chunks of fish, a tray of hominy stewed with tomatoes, a fourth tray of beans in tomato sauce and the last one contained boiled kale. There was finally a large plastic box filled with squares of corn bread. They set these out with serving spoons and brought out paper plates and plastic forks and spoons and cups. The men in the room, now all standing formed into a line and took up plates and utensils. One of them stepped over to the raised dais and invited Minnie to go through the line first, which she did. The young people brought out canned soft drinks and large plastic bottles of water. Then the remaining men began serving themselves filing down both sides of the tables. The entire process was remarkably quiet, Will noticed. After Will got his plateful, he came back to the table and sat next to Minnie.

"They are a generous bunch, aren't they?" he asked Minnie. "The women prepared all this food in their own homes this morning. They don't buy take-away."

After they dropped Jack Sockum back at Wicomico and Will steered the car back toward Bristol, Minnie turned to him. "How did I do? Did they understand what they need to write for their bylaws?"

"Minnie, you were super. You impressed them no end. I was so proud of you, you cannot imagine." He took her hand into his right hand and brought it up to his lips and kissed it.

"I didn't seem too nervous?"

"Not in the least that I could tell. It was cooly professional and very suited to the audience. As I said, I was super impressed. How did you know all those things?"

"I took a course on corporate law also at law school. And I've seen a number of tribes which have applied to the Bureau that also have governance rules and bylaws."

"Did you incorporate your own tribe?"

"No, I could not convince the two different tribal groups to agree to do it. I was not persuasive enough. But they could not agree to merge into a unified tribe. And like the Nantiquak, one band lives far away from the other and they would rather remain independent of each other."

"That's too bad."

"A catastrophe really. It will probably make our application for recognition fail."

"Well, let's hope your contribution today and the incorporation of the Nantiquak helps them succeed in their application. And you know, now you are, in effect, the Chief of two tribes. We'll have to drink to your promotion."

Minnie's excitement lasted into the evening and he noticed that it added to her passion in bed later.

The next day, after Minnie left for work, Will drove over to Beaverton and found the agent who was offering on lease the unused brick store. The rent was really very low. He was able to agree a monthly rate of $400 because it had stood empty for such a long time. And the area of the building even though it had two stories was also very small; only one thousand two hundred square feet, the size of a large apartment. He called Carmine and gave her the details for the building, including the mailing address so she could put it in the application for incorporation.

Three days later Beardsley took the Nantiquak application and filed for a non-profit corporation

During the next week, Will got a call on his cell phone from an unidentified caller.

"Hello, hello. Is this Will Eames? Jack Houlder on the line here."

"Yes, this is Will Eames." Will said a little hesitantly as he did not remember right off who Jack Houlder was.

"Remember we spoke early last month about DNA extraction and a find of Indian bones in Maryland?"

"Oh yes, I remember now. Yes, how are you? Do you have some news?"

"I'm very well, thank you. And yes, I do have some news that I thought would really interest you."

"Okay. You've got my attention now."

"I inquired with the archeologists who excavated that find we spoke about. And they have invited me to come to Maryland and to see if I can't recover some materials which might have DNA. We'll then take the samples back here, to my university and the biologists will see if they can recover and sequence the DNA."

"Really? Where's that that they will try to do that?"

"At the University of Colorado here in Boulder, where I am now. But I will be coming to Maryland in the first week of June for a day or two. I thought you might like to meet me in Salisbury and watch me as I try to make a few extractions. Would you like that?"

"I sure would. You have to know I really would. When are you coming exactly?"

"Right now, I'm scheduled to fly into Philadelphia and drive down to Salisbury on the third of June. I will be going to the site on the fourth. So we should arrange to meet then."

"How much does your DNA extraction service cost?"

"Oh, I don't know. I'm paid by the university. It's part of my duties."

"And what about the DNA analysis? How much does that cost?"

"I don't know that either. I don't think they will be charging anyone for their research and their report.

Only a few moments after Will hung up, after the rush of elation passed, he suddenly realized there was more he needed to ask Dr. Houlder. He called back the number that was in his cell phone memory.

"Dr. Houlder? This is Will Eames again. The thought occurred to me. Would it be possible, would you have time during your visit, could you do DNA extraction on the bones of my great grandmother which lie buried only about twenty five miles away from the Salisbury mound that you're going to visit? She was also a Nantiquak Indian, just like those older bones are presumably from Nantiquak Indians. I'll pay you for your service."

"Eh, well if I have time, ..." Houlder's voice reluctantly came over the phone. "You want the DNA for profiling of your ancestor?"

"Yes that's it. I'd give the DNA to a commercial firm that does DNA profile for genealogical research."

"Well, I don't see why not. I guess I could. Will the body be exhumed already when I get there?"

"Yes, yes. I can have that all arranged. Again, how much would you need for this immensely important service?"

"We can talk about that then, but I don't think I would charge you more than $100 for my time and materials."

"Fine, fine. Then I'll make it a plan for the 4th of June, two weeks from now. I'll meet you at your hotel in the morning."

Will got on the phone again and called Minnie. He had to share this news with her right away. But he didn't get her on the first attempt because she was in a meeting. She called him back on his mobile about an hour and half later. He told her of the DNA profiling and the coming of Dr. Houlder to Maryland who would try to extract DNA from the ossuary pile that Will had already told Minnie about. And that he would meet him, and maybe he could extract a DNA sample from his great grandmother's bones as well. Minnie was pleased to hear the news. It would be important information for establishing the credibility of the current Nantiquak to show that they were genetically related to the people whose bones were placed in that ossuary, and to show that there was continuity of residence by the Nantiquak tribe.

"But, just now, Will, I'm pretty busy. Could we talk about this some more tomorrow after I get to Bristol?"

"Sure, sure. Sorry to interrupt. I just think this is such exciting news."

"It is. I'm glad you called to tell me. Maybe you can call me tonight after I get home. Bye for now."

Not long after Will got off the phone it rang again. (He thought he really needed to change the ringtone on his cell phone. As he was fiddling with his cell phone to open it he also thought it would be nice to have a ringtone assigned for Minnie and a different one for everyone else.) It was Carmine calling. She said she was simply calling to inform him that they had filed for the non-profit earlier that day. And that they should have an answer and notification early the next week. She had just gotten back from Dover where she and Beardsley had gone to file with Department of State.

It was on Friday morning that he got the news from John Rendell of his inheritance from Hampton. And with that news, Mr. Rendell told him that not only was the title to the farm transferred to him, but that unexpectedly he was going to send Will a check for one million, one hundred thousand tax paid. Will was astounded. After he hung up he whooped out loud in his office. So loudly that Lucy and Marilyn both stood up and came and looked at him, as if he had gone loony or just scored a big sale. They wanted to know the news, especially if it was of a big rich sale of property, but Will was not saying anything right then. He wore a smile that looked to them as if he really had gone crazy, happy and demented at the same time. They continued to press him to tell them what had happened to make him become so ecstatic. Finally he said only, "It's confirmed. The farm's mine." And Will left the office, stepping out into the warm sunny air. He called Bob on his home line. Mar Sue answered the phone, probably the beige phone hanging on the wall by the kitchen door.

"Yes, Will, a Mr. Rendell called us and told us that Hampton left us a very sizeable legacy. And that the check in is the mail."

"Yes, and he told me the same thing. I wasn't expecting any money, other than the funds for the farm. But he left me more than a million dollars. Can you imagine?"

Mar Sue almost screamed with delight and she called to Bob to come to the phone. Will heard her, "You know what? Our son is a millionaire!"

"I think we should celebrate together tonight, don't you?" said Will. "Minnie's coming in a few hours. I haven't told her yet. I want to leave the news as a surprise. We can all meet together at the Yacht Club. Say about eight o'clock? We can have champagne and steaks and cake. Have a real celebration feast."

"Yes, yes. Let's do that. I'll call them and make reservations for us. I'll call Kate also and see if they might come, because I would imagine that they got some legacy money too."

"Yes, probably. Call her. It's short notice but she and Pat might be able to come."

So they agreed to meet at the Yacht Club restaurant at eight. At the restaurant they had a gay time and perhaps he drank too much champagne, but he could not understand why it seemed that Minnie was less than pleased by the occasion for their celebration. But her reserve, he thought her usual public outlook and behavior was reserved, did not put him off. He tried all evening to make her happy, what could he do to please her? That evening she did not confess to him the reasons for her reservation. She said several times, "I'm really happy for you Will." but it was said with little enthusiasm or elation. But the holiday weekend was overall very enjoyable for both of them. They both liked the extra day, the Memorial Day Monday holiday, and night together. And on Tuesday morning, when Minnie left for work, they both commented at how soon Friday evening would come. It was a shortened week of separation.

But Will still was looking for any excuse to go to Washington and carry on work there and see Minnie during the week. And on Tuesday morning he realized what it was. He had listed a search of the census records for the Nantiquak Indians in the nineteenth century. And those records were located in the National Archives in Washington a place where he did not need an appointment in advance. He decided to go to 'Warshington' the very next day. He called Minnie and told her he was coming again to D.C. the next day and he would spend the night with her at the same hotel they had stayed in April. She was pleased with the news, but she told him that Cal had decided that their lawsuit was ready and that they were going to come make a presentation to the tribe, possibly that Friday. So she would be coming to the Eastern Shore even earlier. Perhaps Thursday evening, and so she could drive up to Indian River with Will on Friday morning. And then she lowered her voice. But you know, tomorrow we won't be making love. I still have my period."

"That's definitely sad news. But I can still hug you till you sleep, no? Caress and tickle you until you die of laughter, right? And you can still kiss me until you drive me crazy with desire, yes?"

"Yes. You're right. I think I will still like to be in your arms tomorrow night."

Things were happening quickly now, it seemed to Will. As soon as they reported to the tribe, they were going to file their lawsuit in Federal Court in Baltimore. As soon as next week. He hung up and then called Carmine and asked if any of the others in the operating committee could also come to D.C. to search the census records. Carmine couldn't, but she thought that Ronald might be able to. She would ask him. But then she reported that they had finished typing up the genealogical relationships of the various families in the different bands which they had collected during their internal census surveys. It was a lot of materials, but of varying quality. Some families had detailed memories back four, and even five generations, with names and sometimes even dates. While other families could only remember back as far as to their grandparents. Carmine said that they had also compiled the Methodist church baptism and burial records and put them alongside these genealogical lines of descent. The report came to more than forty-five pages of text.

"The only thing that is a shame," said Carmine, "is that other than the church archives, we have very little documentary corroboration of the ancestors that our current tribespeople have identified in the oral memories."

"Right. That has been the principal problem we have been facing all along. Minnie tells me it is one of the key lacking data that disqualifies petitions from tribes. In other words, without white man's records, the Indian oral histories are not considered to be reliable evidence. But we all know that white man's records over the past two centuries were badly tainted by racism, and deliberate non-reporting. And we have even less about the Indians from the eighteenth century."

Carmine called back a while later to tell Will that Ronald could join him on Thursday in D.C. but again that she could not on attend either day because of her work. Will thanked her and asked if Ronald had a cell phone. She gave the number to him.

Early the next morning after his training run, Will set out in his Olds towards 'Warshington'. He was surprised at how heavy the commuter traffic was, especially for a mid-week morning, and especially after he got to Queen Anne's County. It took him two hours to reach the outskirts of D.C. and another forty five minutes to find a parking place near the National Archives. Still he was able to walk in the building by nine forty five. And he found the archive research office in only another fifteen minutes. They had him set up on the microfilm reader by ten thirty reading the census results for the 1880 census for the state of Maryland and the counties of the Eastern Shore. When he told the librarian there that he was looking for information about Indians in that census, the woman had an immediate response for him.

"Oh that is such a sore spot in the census taking over the centuries that a special report has been written about it. I'll go get it for you. It is the annex examination of the American Indian in U.S. censuses since 1790. It will answer a lot of your questions before you can even ask them."

He started scrolling through the microfilm. He had only just gotten to the section for Dorset County when the librarian came back with a pamphlet which turned out to be almost forty pages long.

"As you're doing research on Indian mentions in the census, you can keep this booklet." she said.

He read the first dozen pages of the booklet and realized that the U.S. long had a policy of deliberating neglecting Indians and not counting them going back to the Constitution. The reasoning was that acknowledged Indian tribes even back then, living on reservations, were thought to be sovereign nations and not a full part of the United States, so they should not be counted. And then after the racist reaction to Indians in the East which led to the passage of the Indian Removal Act of 1830, the Indian got caught up in racist views and census takers began to count Indians only if they lived off reservation, but if they counted them at all, they did not class them as a separate race, but counted them as Colored people, like negroes and slaves. Then Will read that it was only after 1880 that the Census Bureau decided to try and enumerate Indians both on and off reservations (although not in the western territories of the U.S. or in Alaska). And most alarming of all, the first census where the policy was clear to enumerate Indians as a separate race, the 1890 census was entirely lost in a subsequent fire at the Census Bureau. So the first census to attempt to count all American Indians was the 1900 census, but even then especially in former slave states, there was the latitude given to census takers to classify Indians as Colored people and not their own race. The booklet was helpful also as it indicated that Indians, if counted, were counted separately on the last pages of each county. That saved Will some time in looking through the microfilm, which turned out to be very slow going. But for the 1880 census he did not find any Nantiquak Indians, neither in Dorset County nor in the neighboring Wicomico County. By the time he made that conclusion it was time for him to leave to meet Minnie for lunch. He got to the front of her office building just as she was stepping out.

"Let's go a bit further away for lunch this time." said Minnie as she warded off his attempt at a kiss. "I think I shouldn't be seen by my colleagues having an affectionate rendezvous and lunch with our client. We need to be discreet just now, both here and at with our Indian client."

They walked four or five blocks back east through the sticky, moist D.C. air and then, finding that they were at McPherson Square, Will suggested that they go again to the Gullah restaurant, and have a business lunch. Minnie consented. The air conditioning struck them as soon as they stepped in, like the open door of a commercial freeze box. It was Washington summer for sure; hot and muggy outside, frigidly cold inside.

"I wish I had a light sweater," said Minnie.

"What color would you prefer?" asked Will.

"I don't know. Maybe we can stick with green?"

"I'll go out and get you one right away. But you'll have to carry it on your arm most of the time."

As they were being seated their waiter came over to the table, and Minnie immediately recognized him as the same young man who had seemed to flirt with her the last time they were there three months earlier. He didn't seem to recognize her this time and paid no special attention to her. The restaurant was already packed full with the lunch crowd so they got a small table that wasn't in the direct blast of the AC. And that and because of the noise they sat snuggled together.

"Maybe you'd like to put my jacket over your shoulders." It was a light khaki cotton suit jacket. Will had come dressed for summer.

"Maybe, yes." Will slipped out of his jacket and draped it over her shoulders.

"Let's see. Summer time means no oysters. But maybe they'll have soft-shelled crabs? I like mine fried."

"What's a soft-shelled crab?" asked Minnie feeling Will's warmth that his jacket carried along with it.

"It's a normal blue crab that has molted its outer shell, which is hard and has begun to grow again. So you eat the crab whole."

"Oh, so no hammering then? I'll try them."

After they ordered—two plates of the soft shelled crabs and a side of fried okra-- Will began telling her about the census situation.

"Yes, I know too well." said Minnie. "It's as you might say a Catch 22 that is guaranteed to stymie Indian tribes petitioning for Federal acknowledgement. The regulations call for official documented evidence from the nineteenth century from the U.S. census that tribe's people existed and lived as tribes in late nineteenth century or one hundred and twenty years ago. And that means only the census. But as you saw the census takers in those decades did not count Indians, or recognize them as a separate race. And if they lived on a reservation, they were not counted at all until the 1900 census. That disqualifies scores of petitioners. It's annoying. Isn't it?"

"Very. And so far, I'm looking at the 1880 census, I cannot even find the names we know existed then. They were simply neglected altogether."

"The same occurred with my tribe. And of course, half of our tribe in that time were living on the small remaining area of our original reservation and the other half were living off reservation further up the peninsula, just as they do now."

The waiter came back with their dishes and set them in front of them and then came back and poured iced tea in their glasses. It was then that he looked closely at Minnie and said, "Hey I remember you. You were that sweet looking girl who came in here a couple of months ago. You said you were Indians, right?"

Minnie smiled and said, "So I guess you don't see all that many Indians in here?"

"No, ma'am. It's rare indeed. And none as good looking as you are."

"Careful, young man." said Will. "Don't get too fresh with my woman."

"Oh, yessir. Sorry. You've got a right good-lookin woman. For sure. Hope you enjoy your dinnah."

Over their meal they continued talking about the injustices of the census system.

"And you know what we discovered, Will, when we started our research? It seemed even when they gave out instructions in 1880 that census takers indicate Indians as a separate race or color, that it fell to individual census takers to determine the race of the Indians. And with Jim Crow prevalent, many census takers in the South called Indians colored people, meaning black people. So you might not find listings of Nantiquak Indians except as Colored."

And later that afternoon as Will continued, he found that to be manifestly true. They parted with a kiss back on K Street and 15th, she having already given him back his jacket which he carried then in his arm. Will turned around and dived into the Metro and was back at his microfilm reader in twenty minutes. He found that in the Delaware listings all the names of the original Nantiquak Association members were recorded, but they had all been entered as Colored: the very crime and insult that had split them from the Makadewa-Ninda Band a few years earlier.

Will then began looking at the 1900 census report and he quickly found that the situation was somewhat rectified with regards both the Makadewa-Ninda and the Indian River Bands in Suffolk County, Delaware. He found most of the names that were in the tribe's own genealogical records for both bands. But most important now they were listed as race 'I', as in 'I' for Indian. He noted it down. This was the first official documentation of the Nantiquak Indians by the U.S. government, although by that date the Nantiquak Indians of Indian River were already recognized as an Indian tribe by the state of Delaware. And importantly for both the Bureau and its processes and for the Indian River Band in their century old dispute with the Madakewa-Ninda Band, these data showed the latter to be counted as Indians, not Coloreds. That would make their recent inclusion in the new corporation more palatable to Morley Norwood and the other opponents to inclusion. Will then eagerly began looking for the data from Dorset County in Maryland. Again he looked at the end of the entry for the county but he was disappointed to find only a few names enumerated as Indians. But this was the surprise: the names of Indians in 1900 in Dorset County were Conty Randall and his wife Irena, and John Rendall, presumably the ancestors of Pellmell Randall and John Rendell, both of Exeter. There were two other names indicated and shown as Indians, but they were shown to reside in Bristol and they were names that Will did not recognize. Of course the census data, while listing the race as 'I', did not indicate Nantiquak. Apparently no where did the census indicate the name of the tribes that enumerated Indians belonged to. Then when Will looked in the data for Indians in Wicomico County, there were only a few family names he recognized. There was the Hately family and the Heyden family both listed as residing in Shapp's Landing. And then the important listing there was the Pucckam family, which was presumably Buckham's ancestor. He had to admit that he was a bit disappointed by the results of this review. But before he could look further in the 1900 census data, he had to leave because it was nearly five o'clock and closing time for the archive.

He called Minnie and asked if she was ready to finish work and meet with him. She said she still needed another hour as they were putting the finishing touches on their lawsuit filing. So they agreed to meet outside her building at 6:30. In the meanwhile he left the archive and walked over to Hecht's. This time he was surprised not by the humidity and stuffiness, but by the crowds on the sidewalks. Everyone left work in D.C. at the same time—except for Minnie— and they were all rushing off to home, or to Hecht's which he found also packed with rush-hour shoppers. It took him only five minutes to find what he was looking for: a cashmere shamrock green sweater. He paid the cashier and rushed off with his briefcase in one hand and the blue Hecht's bag in the other. He walked fast to the parking garage where he had left his car and drove over to the hotel and parked it there, leaving the bag with the sweater and his brief case in his car. He still had time to slowly walk down to the K Street entrance of Minnie's building, where he was waiting for her, drenched in sweat, at 6:30.

"We have to go to the garage first. I came in today by car, so no one would see my overnight bag." said Minnie after greeting Will. When they got into her car, they kissed, long and affectionately. "It's so nice to see you again, Mini-oka."

"Yeah, I feel the same way about you."

And she drove over to the hotel up near Dupont Circle and parked it again in the hotel garage in a space right next to Will's Olds, his "boat" as he called it. Will took the Hecht's bag out of his car and then they went up to reception and checked in.

"Here, this is for you. A summer gift for all those frosty places you go to in D.C." he said while handing Minnie the Hecht's bag.

In the room, she threw the overnight bag next to the bed, and looked into the Hecht's bag and pulled out the sweater.

"Oh, it's so light. Really, you didn't need to buy this." said Minnie as she started to try it on.

"It's never a matter of needing to, Minnie. Everything I do for you is out of desire. It looks really good on you."

"And it fits me well, too. How did you pick out something that fits so nicely?

"Easy, the label says it is medium. I would say that you are outstanding, not merely medium. But none of the sweaters had that size, outstanding, I mean."

"I won't be needing it this evening if we go out for dinner."

"No it's much too humid for that sweater and I think the restaurant we're going to in Georgetown will be hot and bustling also."

He hung his jacket in the closet and she left the sweater neatly folded on the bed and they set out to walk the ten blocks to the J. Rob's restaurant in Georgetown. The place was rocking when they walked in, bustling, crowded, and noisy with young people at the bar shouting at the top of their lungs at each other to be heard, the music of a three man band in the back corner almost imperceptible. They tried to find a table in a far room where it was a little quieter, but it was still noisy, as the music was piped into the room and all the tables were occupied by diners who also had to shout to be heard. The large dinner crowd and all those at the bar also heated the place, so that the air-conditioning was scarcely noticeable.

"You were right not to bring the sweater with you here." Will shouted.

This being summer, there were no oysters on offer. And they also did not have soft-shelled crabs. So Will ordered a hamburger and Minnie asked for the caesar salad with chicken. They drank iced tea and no wine this evening. By the time their orders came to the table, dinner visitors had begun to leave and the restaurant became a little quieter. But still it was hard to converse even across their small table. After dinner they strolled over the Rock Creek Bridge on M Street and then up Connecticut Avenue to their hotel, the long way. As they were getting ready for bed, Will finally asked what was bothering Minnie.

"I feel uncomfortable staying in a hotel, you know, making love in a hotel on the sly. It feels a bit tawdry—if I'm not drunk. It makes me feel too much like a prostitute, or a mistress hiding an affair from her husband."

"Oh come on. You are most certainly not a prostitute, and you do want to make love with me, no? As my lover?"

"Yes, with all my heart."

"So you should move in with me, and we start living together. All the time, not just on weekends. And that way I can be like both your lover and your husband."

He took her into his arms and began to caress her as he helped her undress.

"But you live so far away. And I live so far away in the other direction."

"But if we lived together, then we wouldn't have to meet together in a hotel on work days."

They got in bed, and soon their caresses and kisses gave way to coupling, heaving and thrusting, and their personal erotic exercises. Minnie was quickly aroused and brought to climax with much elated sighing and moaning, and exclamations of love. Again that day, the air conditioning was insufficient to douse the heat of their love making, and when they separated they were covered in sweat. Will turned on his side facing Minnie still luxuriating in her sensations and began to lick the pools of sweat off her chest. "Yum, salty. I'm working in the salt mines." he said in jest. Then he began tracing curlicues with his finger in the beads of sweat on her tummy until he had traced out an elaborate scene of many interlocking treble clefs all over her skin. "I love you, Mini-oka. I want to live with you and make love to you every night and see you every morning, like Aurora arising."

"Aurora?"

"The goddess of the Dawn."

Minnie was surprised by this obscure reference.

"You mean you're calling me the Goddess of Dawn? Aurora? A new name for me? How do you know about that?"

"My commanding officer in the Marines told me about the meaning of Aurora. We were at the time based in a camp called Aurora, Camp Aurora, somewhere in the desert. I asked him what Aurora meant and he told me. He was a very cultured man."

Minnie rolled up on her side against him and began fondling his penis in her hands. "You're such a remarkable man, Willeems. I keep learning so much from you. I want you so badly all the time." And they began again the erotic foreplay to love making. "Tomorrow you can love me at your home, but for now I will love you here."

The next morning their morning routine was a little different than usual; they dressed and Minnie packed up her overnight bag, and they went downstairs for breakfast together. Will did not go jogging, and Minnie was not going to drive off into commuter traffic across the Bay. Instead they slowly ate breakfast together. Will felt very happy for some reason. Minnie looked glowing, but she seemed to be preoccupied until she slipped in a word between the coffee and orange juice:

"I would like to move in with you Will. But I don't think I could handle the daily commute to and from Bristol. In fact I know I couldn't."

Will knew at once, that the conversation from the previous night had not finished. But he did not want it to end this way.

"Maybe we can think of something."

They finished breakfast, paid, and checked out at the front desk, and then walked down into the garage and put Minnie's bag in her car. Then, after kisses, both of them drove off to re-park their cars nearer to their workplaces for the day.

"See you this evening, in Bristol," said Will as they got into their cars.

"Call me when you are leaving D.C." answered Minnie.

Back in the archives Will resumed searching the 1900 census data. First he looked up the Wicomico County entries. As there was no coda for separate Indian entries, he looked for family names that were the same as the names they had collected from family genealogies from that turn of the century period. The census data was organized first by residents of cities, towns, and smaller municipalities, and then there were entries for all other rural residents of the county which were arranged strictly alphabetically within county districts. This was slow going, because Will had to read a number of pages to get past the entries for towns, and many of the county's rural areas were included in the listings for the towns. He had searched for a little more than an hour, when he got a call from Ronald. He had arrived and was outside the archive building asking Will where to enter for the census archives. Will went down to the sidewalk to meet him and show him the way in. Then he explained how he was searching and got Ronald set up on a reader also searching the 1900 census for Suffolk County. He didn't mention to Ronald that he had not found much if any entries for the Nantiquaks in Maryland, either in the 1880 or the 1900 census. He did not want to discourage Ronald from the start. But Will himself was already somewhat discouraged by the lack of results. After another hour's search he found six names in entries that their ancestry interviews had uncovered for them, but they all indicated the 'W' for the white race. Four of those were married and with children, and all six of the names and families lived in the woods near the Delaware border in what used to be the great cypress swamp, or the Gum Swamp or Wimpissoccom as it was called by the Nantiquak in the eighteenth century. Will thought that these entries presumably indicated Indians, but they were not proof, and the fact that the census taker had called all of these individuals 'white' could just mean that the names coincidentally matched what the current families had given them, so Henry R. Barnley, claimed ancestor the contemporary Asksesky family of Barnsleys near Delmar, could have been an Indian or an Anglo. There was no telling from the census data, no proof.

Will worked on this until about two o'clock.

"How are you coming, Ron?" he asked.

"I'm finding a lot of interesting information. So far I have found twelve entries that match our information for the ancestors of the Black Face band. And even more interesting they are all shown as being not Colored but Indian."

"That is very interesting. That means at that time, less than thirty years after being shunned for accepting a black minister and black school teacher, and then being excluded from the Nantiquak Association, these people continued to self-identify as Indians."

"Yes, so it seems. Maybe our bunch has been a little harsh on them. You could even say racist. But if you want to know, if you look at them-- their faces-- today you'd say they were 'whites', not Indian, and certainly not blacks."

"This is probably going to be a problem with our petition to the Bureau."

Will made ready to leave. He was very disappointed with the findings. "Carry on, Ron. I'll see you Friday at the presentation by the lawyers at your place." As he was walking up the sidewalk to the garage, he looked up and saw a Apartments For Rent sign in a fourth floor window. It didn't look like a residential building, but there was a phone number printed on the sign. On the way home, Will thought about what the housing market in D.C. was like, what rents were like, and what property prices were like. He resolved to look into it through his realtor networks. Next week.

Almost as abruptly as the switching on a ceiling lamp in a darkened room, Will's real estate business started on the first of June. People started calling asking for help finding a house, a second home, or wanting to sell out their house in Bristol. It had always been like that; eight months of twiddling his thumbs at his office waiting for work or clients, and then bang the real estate season started on the first of June. June and August made up most of his income for the entire year. And so that first week in June Will was busy, meeting new customers, showing houses, advising sellers, arranging meetings and advising on buying or financing. Making lots of friendly talk, passing information on to the customer, and selling the attractions of Bristol and Dorset County to people who were moving in from elsewhere, people usually moving from the Western Shore who wanted to be near the waters of the Bay. He didn't make any sales or purchases that week, but he did get some interest and he would have to wait to the next week to see if he could make a sale.

On Thursday morning, as agreed, Will drove over to Salisbury to meet Professor Houlder at a Holiday Inn there. He was a man about five to ten years older than Will, taller than Will, and with a bushy red beard and reddish wavy hair. Will thought he reminded him of what he expected a geologist or a gold prospector would look like. He saw at once that Houlder spoke softly but that he tended to bite on his lower lip so that he was in effect speaking through the beard on his lower lip and chin. The two of them drove out to the archeological site which was located in the same area that Will had been combing through the census records the week before. There Will was surprised to see how animated the site was. So many people sitting on their knees in the orange earth. Houlder, with what looked like a carpenter's hard plastic tool kit, walked boldly up to one of these crab-like diggers and asked for the chief of the dig. He was pointed to a lean-to that was covered with a tarpaulin far off to the side. So then Houlder led Will to the lean-to and he introduced himself to a man who looked a little like Houlder only with a brown beard.

"So I want to introduce you to a representative of the Nantiquak Indian tribe. Will Eames. He's here in an interested capacity as they would like to get a DNA profile of the people who once lived in these bones. This is Carroll Keppling."

Will shook hands. "Yes, I was extremely interested in learning about this project when I, by coincidence found Professor Houlder and he told me about his coming out here."

"So where are the bones you want me to operate on?" said Houlding

"Over here. We have cleaned two thigh bones here on the table."

"Have you reached a consensus of the estimated age of these bones?"

"We think they are at least five hundred years old. The wigwam they had been placed in had enough wood material that we've sent a sample for carbon dating to get a more exact date."

Houlder opened up his plastic tool kit on the table alongside two long femur bones which appeared as if they had been roasted. Will was surprised to see that the box was indeed just an ordinary tool box containing what looked like ordinary tools. The first tool that Houlder drew out was a hand drill. Then he took out what looked like a drill bit for drilling concrete, encased in a plastic tube. And finally he took out actual test tubes and very long thin pincers which had plastic covers on the tips.

"You see, we have to sterilize everything that we use which comes into contact with the target material, so we don't introduce any contaminants. We're aiming to get material from what would have been the marrow of the thigh bone near the hip socket."

Houlder put the drill bit into the chuck of the drill, and then pulled off the plastic tube covering the end of the bit and promptly he set about gently drilling. Slowly, gingerly, obviously holding back to feel when the very tip of the bit broke into the marrow chamber. Then he quickly pulled it out.

"Here, hold this, if you could, Will." said Houlder, handing him the drill.

Then he pulled off the covers of the tong arms of pincer. It was very thin and narrow and he pushed it slowly into the small hole he had made. Then he pulled out a wad of stringy brown and ash colored material and plopped it into one of the test tubes and quickly sealed up the tube and wrapped tape around the seam. Then he took a small thin swab on a long wooden stalk and put it into the hole and appeared to be swirling it around. He withdrew it and put it into another test tube, broke off the wooden stick and again closed and sealed the tube.

"Now, we have I think two good samples. Maybe they will have viable DNA. But we maybe need a molar. Carroll, do you have any skulls with teeth in them?"

"Strange thing about this mound. In all the bones we found piled up inside what was obviously a mortuary wigwam, there were no skulls. Not a one. So I'm afraid to say, no molars for your efforts today."

"Oh, that's too bad. Especially for bones this age. Very often only the molars still contain readable DNA."

"I'll let you know if we find any skulls or molars, Jack. We're still digging here. We've uncovered a number of residential wigwams. It's strange. They are arranged around the ossuary wigwam. I haven't seen anything like that before on Algonquin sites."

"Well, we're still learning," said Houlder. And he took the test tubes and placed them in a wooden box with sponge depressions for cushioning the glass tubes. Then he re-packed the tools, placing the pincer and used drill bit in a separate small box. "And so we're off. I'll send you the results, Carroll, when the lab finishes reading what I've extracted here. Thanks for the invitation."

He turned to Will. "And so now on to your ancestor. We'll do the same on her. When did you say she died?"

"About forty five years ago."

"Oh good. We'll have a fresh specimen. I don't often get to work with those in my usual line of business."

They went back to their separate cars and Houlder followed Will the twenty five or so miles to Hampt's farm. They drove up the lane, through fields that were filled with spring green sprouts, and stopped the cars around the back of the farmhouse.

"Nice place here. It looks like a well-run farm."

"Except for the broken wind mill there."

"I grew up on a farm that looked not nearly so nice. Of course it's the time of year too."

Will saw Armand slouching by the oak trees. Then he saw that he had dug up Mena's grave and that there was on top of pile of soil, a heap of rotten boards. He saw the small skeleton only when they drew close.

"I don't like this work." complained Armand. "I'm not a gravedigger by background. Don't ask me again to do this."

"Ah, alas Yorrick. I knew him well." replied Will. "The important characters in Shakespeare's Hamlet."

"I don't give a hang about Shakespeare or Hamlet."

"So here we have the specimen, obviously a woman." said Houlder. Not very big I can see right away. And you said she was your great grandmother." He glanced over at the gravestone. "I understand, your great grandfather married an Indian woman. Rather unusual I would think."

"And she was probably my great grand-aunt." added Armand.

"So you think she came from the same Indian tribe, as those people who left the pile of bones back there near Salisbury?"

"I'm pretty certain of it." said Will. "We're all related to the Nantiquaks hereabouts."

"Some more than others." added Armand in his snide sneering voice.

"So let's see. Slightly different working conditions here. Not a clean site." Houlder went back to his car and took out a black plastic bundle and unfolded it to where it was clear that it was a large ground cloth. On this he set his tool kit and pulled out two other test tubes, a new clean drill bit in a tube, a new pair of long slender pincers, and then the drill. Then he put on a pair of blue rubber gloves. He reached over the wooden remains of the rotten coffin and took hold of one of the femur bones and began his drilling. "In life, women would never let me handle them like this so close to their private intimate parts." joked Houlder. "I always wanted to be a gynecologist when I was young." Will didn't know whether he was joking or not. In ten minutes he was finished and got two samples that were—much to Will's surprise—still pinkish. Then Houlder turned to Will. "Now did anyone call a dentist?" he said as he reached into his tool box and pulled out what looked like dental pliers, along with a small box from which he peeled off some plastic tape. "Now this is really appropriate for today's subject. These are called arrowhead pliers." Houlder laughed at his own joke. Armand scowled. "Will, can I take one of your grandmother's molars?" Will said yes. And in a flash Houlder reached over to the skull, holding it in one hand and with the other breaking off a small molar from the upper jaw, and then again he plopped it quickly into the small box. He threw down his instruments and closed and sealed up everything. "Don't want to get too much pollen in there along with the DNA. Now do you have any teeth that need extracting, before I have to go?" Houlder had hardly disturbed the pile of earth or the wooden remains, or indeed the skeleton. He stood up smiling with his hands on his hips, and now he reminded Will of a northern woodsman; Will half expected him to sling his axe over his shoulder and walk away with his bright blue ox.

"Armand, so now you can respectfully put great grandma back where she belongs." said Will as he stood up. Then he turned to Houlder.

"Jack, maybe I can treat you to lunch? I will drive you out to Highway 13 at any rate."

"Well, I do need to catch my return flight in Philly at 5:30. Do you think I have time for lunch now?"

"Sure, if we don't drink too many beers." joked Will. Then turning to Armand who was looking in disgust at Mena's remains, as if he couldn't figure out how to put the skeleton and scraps of wood and dirt back into the open hole, he said:

"Armand, I'll be back here in an hour or two. Will you still be here?"

"I won't be going anywhere. There's work I need to do for Max."

Will slipped Houlder two fifty dollar bills just before they got into their cars. "I really appreciate your service. It was great watching a master at work. Now follow me. We're going to Beaverton, about nine miles from here."

Over lunch of steamed mussels and fries, they discussed about how the profiling would be done, and how Will would get a report on the results and findings. "Ah science. Amazing what scientists can discover now." said Will. Houlder agreed. "It really is. But I'm just a handy man in the equation. You should get word on the results in about three weeks." After they finished, Will lead Houlder out to Highway 13 and waved him goodbye, pointing him to the north.

The next day, Friday, Will called a couple of real estate agencies in D.C. They dealt with him very respectfully when he explained that he himself was a broker, but that he was looking for himself for an apartment. One even agreed to send him electronically the rental listings for the "decent" parts of town. Will got it that day after lunch and spent an hour studying the offerings. Then he saw that it was already at ten past three and he jumped up. He needed to rush and leave for Washington at once to be sure to get there by five thirty. Fortunately his overnight bag was already packed and in the car, but he still needed to take the left over cake from his fridge back at home. Fortunately, the rush hour traffic was all in the opposite direction to him and he had no traffic delays all the way into Washington and when he pulled into the parking garage of the hotel it was only five twenty five. He then rushed down the hill to K Street as he called Minnie from his cell saying he would be there in eight minutes.

The next evening as they prepared to leave for the Argerich concert, Will finally found the right opportunity to present Minnie with the cherry blossom scented perfume he had bought her.

"In April, I was so enamored of the aroma of cherry blossoms, while at the same time so completely enamored of you that I had to get this for you, Minnie. I've been waiting now for the most appropriate moment to give it to you. And that moment has come."

Minnie again was flustered. No one had ever given her perfume in her entire life. And she had never thought of buying perfume for herself; she didn't wear it. She didn't wear much in the way of cosmetics at all. Just a little eye liner, and some colorless lip balm. She leapt into Will's arms and kissed him on the neck.

"The woman at the cosmetics counter said you apply it to the heat points. Just a dab. Here, here, here, and here." said Will as he pointed with his finger to her wrist, her lower neck, behind her knee and one ear. "And also here," he said as he reached down into the top of her blouse and touched a point on her sternum midway between her two breasts and above the wire joining the two cups of her bra. "So will you try it on now?"

"Of course. I'll be the lady of the ball tonight."

"Yes, maybe people will mistake you for Martha Argerich."

Minnie looked at him with a disapproving expression. Then she went to the bathroom and opened the perfume and applied it in all the spots Will had pointed out. She came back as if on a pink cloud.

"Hme, let me smell you. Here, here, here. Did you put some on you belly button?" And here. Deliciously fragrant. I could eat you up."

All through the concert, when he wasn't looking through the binoculars at Martha Argerich, he was looking at Minnie's profile, and sniffing the fragrance of her new perfume. He pinched himself several times. He could not believe he was so in love with this woman next to him, who did not look, he confirmed, so much like Martha Argerich. For one thing Argerich must have been at least 20 years older than Minnie. Throughout that concert, Will was overwhelmed with the feelings he had for Minnie.

Will sprung the other surprise of that weekend on Minnie. His proposal to set up house together in an apartment in Washington. On weekdays, he would do the commuting, back and forth to Bristol. And evenings they would both come to the same house. It didn't take Minnie long to agree, although she was taken aback that Will thought they could find and rent a place and move her out of her Thornberg house in only two weekends. "I've already looked at the sort of places that are ready and available, in nice neighborhoods. So all we have to do is go see them and choose the nicest one. Once that's done, we can spend the next weekend moving you out and releasing your place there in Thornberg. It can be done. Believe me." So it wasn't until the morning of the 22nd of June, a Monday, that Will started a dramatic change in his daily routine. He left their new house in Cleveland Park with Minnie next to him, and then they kissed and separated: she walked down to Connecticut Avenue and he got into his Oldsmobile and drove off to Bristol. And this time, for the first time, he was very aware that it was a long ways. Time behind the wheel on those roads in the summer sun just did not seem to move. Or more precisely, the longer he drove on, it seemed the longer he still had to go, that he was not getting any closer to his destination. Unlike ten days earlier when he rushed off to meet Minnie for their date weekend, this first day of commuting to work seemed very much like a heavy burden. One hundred miles was no doubt a long drive, and especially long drive just to go to work. It took a little more than two hours, door to door. And coming back in the afternoon was, it seemed, even harder, especially with the sun glinting in his eyes or reflecting off the asphalt. And he was tired when he started out from Bristol for the return trip. He could set his own hours—that was one solace. On that first day, he left at 4:15 and was back home, key in the door at 6:20. Only shortly later, he heard Minnie coming in. Now the real test began to set in. They needed to change clothes, then dinner needed to be prepared, but wait, maybe a drink. Ice tea would do. Will was parched, and Minnie didn't want any alcohol. And eating dinner on the new dining table, followed by washing the dishes. And then it was already after eight thirty. Maybe they needed to buy some more food for the rest of the week. So they walked down to a small grocery store in Woodley Park to buy some supplies. And by the time they got back and put everything away it was already well after ten and dark outside. And both of them fell on the couch, exhausted. Minnie cuddled against Will.

"You're my superman, Willeams." she purred.

Will felt tired. The exertions of the previous weekend and today's commute were catching up with him. It didn't help that the couch was plush and deeply cushioned and soft.

"Not feeling so super just now. Moving house and setting up house seems a lot easier than merely living in a house, especially if your place of work is nearly one hundred miles away."

Will got up and flicked on the TV. He came back to the couch and began browsing through the channels. "The broadcast service selection is much wider here than it is in Bristol, that's for sure." At one channel he saw some familiar flashes of colors and he paused.

"Hey, this is an Orioles game."

"What's that?"

"A baseball game. They're playing up in Camden Yards in Baltimore. Right now. This is live."

"I know nothing about baseball. What's special about the game?"

"Nothing, when you ask it that way. Looking at it on TV must seem especially baffling. I played baseball in high school, and so I am familiar with the ins and outs of the game. But it still has to be completely obscure to an outsider. Special? For a spectator, the special thing about the game, is sitting outdoors in the stands in good weather for a couple hours, gabbing with a friend, having a beer or two. And occasionally something happens. We'll have to go up to Bawlimore sometime soon and watch a game. Then maybe I can explain to you how it all works. And you'll get the feel for the atmosphere of an outdoor game."

But Will did not watch it. He instead rolled over closer to Minnie and began to very gently caress her.

"Maybe I'll go to bed. I'm bushed, Minnie."

"I'm tired too. Let's maybe retire to our second new bed."

"Good idea."

The next morning, very early he went out on a training run. The morning air was already humid and the sun was heating the atmosphere quickly. But what especially hit Will in comparison to his training runs around Bristol, was that there were hills all around. One street went steadily up and the next down, even plunging down into the steep, narrow ravine where the Rock Creek flowed. But there were lots of streets and potential running routes to explore and Will was just beginning. The important thing on this day was that he run no more than an hour. When he got back to their new home, Minnie was partially dressed and preparing breakfast.

"What's ya fixing for breakfast?" he asked as he looked into the kitchen, still hot and sweaty.

"It's ready. I made corn meal mush. Ever had it?"

"No, can't say that I have. Do I have time to shower before we eat?"

"No, let's eat now and then you can shower."

She served him a large bowl of the mush and offered him a pot of honey to go with it or a small bowl of brown sugar. Then she brought coffee, served herself the mush and sat with Will at the kitchen table.

"It was a family breakfast staple we ate when I was young, in hot weather and in cold weather."

"So this little hausfrau will cook breakfasts, and we can share the task of fixing dinners here?"

"What's a hausfrau?"

"It's German for housewife. I learned that in our German base when I was stationed there with the Marines. All the TV advertising is aimed at the hausfrau. Most of it related to cooking and cleaning as far as I could tell."

"You learned a lot in the Marines, mister. Both useful things and interesting trivia."

"You bet. But I didn't get much cooking practice."

"Fine, but I told you and your mother, I will need some instructions about fixing dinner. I've not done a lot of cooking in the past. And I only know how to prepare a few dishes which I did with my mother's help. I suppose we will need to make menus and do meal planning. And then we can go food shopping together to fit the plan."

"Yeah, let's do that."

But instead of cooking dinners only at home that week they began a different routine. Twice that week in the evening, they walked down to Connecticut Avenue and dropped in at a small ethnic restaurant for dinner. Once, they tried an Italian place, family owned and run, and the other time a Mexican cantina. The problem for Minnie at restaurants was always the same; portions were generally too big for her, far more than she was accustomed to eating, or could eat. The Italian restaurant with its curious name, Nel boschetto di Cupido, became their regular hang-out because it was snug and comfortable, reasonably priced, and because it served Italian versions of seafood and the staff adjusted their servings to Minnie's appetite when she told them of the problem. It was also good for them because it served dinners even after 8:30. They became regulars on Wednesdays throughout that summer. Minnie also learned to prepare a couple of simple tasty dished at home from ones she was served there. Spaghetti with clams in white wine sauce, which they both enjoyed, was one that became a favorite of both Minnie and Will.

They made love on Monday and Will fell asleep, exhausted, almost at once afterwards. They made love again on Wednesday before going to sleep. But Will became aware in the nights of their first week in the Cleveland Park house that at night it was not as dark as it was in Bristol. There were street lights on their street and there were even more on Connecticut Avenue which made the night's darkness seem only partial, glowing as it was with all the lighting in Washington. And the sounds of the city were always apparent. He woke up several times during that week and in the weeks that followed hearing the shrill scream of a distance ambulances siren, or occasionally of a car revving its motor. And in the earliest hours before sunrise he would hear the groaning of a garbage truck on its neighborhood rounds.

On Friday that week Will changed the commuting routine from the previous four days. He stayed in Bristol in the afternoon and waited for Minnie to drive out to him. They would spend the night in his Bristol cottage because he had an appointment on Saturday late morning with an interested buyer. He decided he would make dinner, but he kept it simple; hamburgers and potato salad. After dinner, they took a long slow walk along the riverbank and got back after ten and were thankful for the air conditioning in his cottage. Will did feel knocked out by his first week of commuting, but his desire for Minnie was unabated. He led Minnie to the bedroom and began the slow dance of seduction, kissing her here and there and removing one piece of clothing after another.

After his appointment, late the next morning, Will went back to his cottage house to find Minnie making lists. She was arranging things in the kitchen and one of her lists was the kitchen equipment and eating utensils that they needed to buy for the Cleveland Park house. She had already made a list of clothes that she needed to buy in order to have a reserve for Bristol, mainly casual wear and summer weight clothes, so that she wouldn't need to haul an overnight bag back and forth every weekend. Her work wardrobe would stay in D.C. but she still needed underwear and socks, and walking shoes and sandals, for the Bristol home. And they needed to buy towels and washcloths for the bathrooms in Bristol and at the farm, as Will had taken bathroom linens to the D.C. house from the Bristol bathroom.

"And if you want to spend more time at the farmhouse, I suppose we'll have to buy some clothes to have in reserve for me and you there. I think I can leave my swimsuit here though. We won't need beach towels in Washington."

"I hardly think so." said Will.

They went for a late lunch to Poseidon Palace. Tony was there and hailed them both as long lost friends.

"We've brewed a new sort of beer. It's an amber ale. You ought to try it." said Tony.

Looking at the menu and the specials on the chalk board, Minnie this time knew just what to order for herself.

"Tony, I'll have the fried soft-shell crabs with hush puppies. And maybe I'll try a glass of your new beer."

"I'll have the fried rockfish and okra. And a pint of the new ale as well."

"So you two are here only on weekends?" asked Tony.

"Yes, we are renting a house in Warshington and I commute here on weekdays."

"Wow." whistled Tony. "That must be a challenge."

After lunch, Will proposed that they move to the farm for Saturday night after going to Salisbury Mall to buy some of those needs that Minnie had noted. They drove out to Salisbury in Will's car and spent a couple hours buying linens, simple basics for clothes to put in the farmhouse, as well as a pair of sneakers and some sandals for Minnie. Will bought himself two pairs of house slippers for the farmhouse and for the Bristol house. And he insisted on buying some summer weight blouses for Minnie—because they were so pretty, he said. When they finally were ready to leave, loaded down with several large bags each of necessaries, they were both surprised to see how dark the skies had become while they had been inside. To the west they could clearly see a massive thunderhead raising up its fury high into the heavens over the flat lands. It was approaching fast and was already sending gusts out in its advance, shaking the leaves on the trees and stirring up dust and grit from the roads in the area around the mall.

"I think we're going to have a storm dumped on us, before we get to Rosedale and the farm. It wasn't in the forecast for today."

They set out and in only ten minutes they began to see the wind whipping up dust and leaves and the detritus of fallow fields in front of them. Then they could clearly see a slate gray sheet of water falling down not even two hundred yards in front of them. There was a sudden bright flash nearby and a tremendous crack and roar. The cars in front of them on the highway put on their brakes as if to better greet the onrushing torrent. Will braked as well.

"That was close." He meant the lightning strike.

And then they were plunged into a downpour like Minnie had never seen before. Large drops of rain were hissing down on them, hitting the car with a sound like snare drums right over their heads. Will switched on his wipers to the fastest speed, but they scarcely could clean the windscreen of water, and he turned on his high beam lights and slowed to a bare crawl. There was almost no visibility in front of them. They were in the full fury of this thunderstorm, so noisy that they could not hear each other. Minnie felt afraid. She could see just to the side of their car that the raindrops were hitting the road and shoulder and bouncing back up almost a foot and a half in height. In what was only a minute the drainage trenches on the side of the highway were filled to the brim and overflowing. Then another blinding flash and the skies again exploded quite near them. The road almost instantly was under several inches of water, and it seemed to Will that he was hydroplaning in several places. But he slowly continued up the highway.

"Maybe we should've stayed in the mall." Minnie whimpered.

But Will could scarcely hear her over the sound of the furious wipers and the beating from the rain drops on the car roof.

This torrential rain continued for a full fifteen minutes as they slowly moved up the highway. Some cars along the way had pulled over to the shoulder and were standing with their emergency light blinking wildly. Finally the downpour began to abate a little bit, although they were still under dark clouds and whirling winds. They continued to creep forward as the onslaught from the thunderstorm lessened to a mere spate of rain.

"Here we are, at Shepp's Landing, now." said Will. And soon they were crossing a low hump-backed bridge over the Nanticoke River at a narrow point, not even three hundred yards across. The river looked black—not the usual green of the Choptiko-- and the waters were still being pricked by the rain, making it seem to have a living sheen. And then they were surrounded by the low growth of salt marsh and then a hard wood forest. "Nearly there, Minnie. Don't despair." Very soon, the woods gave way to flat open fields that were a covered in spring time early green. Minnie noticed that the torrent of rain was still running off the fields in muddy rivulets. And all the green crops were beaten over and crushed flat onto the ground as if rolled over by a road roller. Will made a sharp turn, and then after another three hundred yards he turned onto the gravel lane of the Hampton farm. The lane was filled with puddles which splashed when Will drove over them. All around the green crops in the fields were beaten down and water was either standing in big puddles drowning the young plants, or running off with mud. It was lightly raining when Will pulled up to the farmhouse. And the western skies were beginning to lighten.

"Well we've survived that battering." said Will smiling at Minnie. "Although the fields don't look like they have. We don't have umbrellas so we'll have to make a dash for cover under the porch."

When they stepped out and grabbed their bags, it was immediately noticeable how the thunderstorm had lowered the temperature by twenty or more degrees and the air seemed fresh and clean. Even as they stood on the porch looking out over the battered fields the rain finally stopped altogether and the landscape fell to a quiet symphony of dripping sounds. Will unlocked the front door. As he swung open the grand entry door, Will turned to her and said. "Maybe I should carry you over the threshold to our second new home?" Minnie was surprised. "But we're not newlyweds."

"But it is our joint house and home. At least for weekends."

"We'll save the wedding traditions for another time. You can carry my bag instead."

So he let Minnie in and then returned to the car and brought the rest of their supplies and bags in. Inside with the windows all closed, it was very warm and stuffy. It remained very warm inside through the night and it made it difficult for Will to sleep. The next day they decided to go canoeing again on the Choptiko River. It was sunny and hot again. As they were leaving in the mid-morning they saw Max walking the fields not far from the house. Will stopped the car and stepped out to speak to him. Max walked over through the muddy and still wet fields.

"Looks like yesterday's downpour did a lot of damage. I don't like what I'm seeing. I think the crop will be way down this season." said Max.

"Will the crops stand up again?"

"Yes, some might, but a lot are damaged beyond repair."

They drove on to the same canoeing center they had used before.

That evening, they moved back to the Bristol house. They had to retrieve Minnie's car, and sleeping in the air conditioning was much more comfortable. They went to Will's parents for dinner. Both of them seemed sad and it showed. Will because Minnie inexplicably had turned down his marriage proposal, and Minnie because she had felt she had to decline for a bunch of reasons that she did not entirely understand, even though she wanted nothing more than to marry Will. They sat at the dinner table, moody and pensive, and there was nothing that Bob or Mar Sue could say that drew them out.

On Monday morning, Will saw off Minnie at six-thirty and then went on a run. He was trying to concentrate on what it was that made Minnie turn down his proposal. But he could not really understand what was standing in Minnie's way. Maybe he thought she couldn't understand. Maybe she couldn't accept living in Bristol or on an isolated farm. Of course that would only be possible if she stopped working at NAILS in D.C. To the end of his run, the issues Minnie had remained a mystery to Will. It was obvious to him that on a physical level she was already his woman and passionate partner and she wanted him badly always. But on some rational level she was struggling against the idea of marriage. Maybe her rejection was related to what her mother had said. And maybe, he thought, she couldn't marry Will because he was not an Indian. He couldn't think how he could overcome that objection. He got home and was feeling upset and hurt. He had some client calls that day and they distracted him a bit. And soon it was four o'clock and time to drive back to D.C. and to Minnie.

He worried on the way that maybe Minnie would still be morose about Sunday's events on the river, but when she came home he found that she was in a fine mood. She was so pleased to see him, all smiles, and generous in her early kisses. She proposed that they walk to small grocery on Connecticut and resupply their pantry with food for the week, and that afterwards they could go out for dinner at "Cupido's". Their love making late that evening made him forget completely about his worries about Minnie. Her desire for him was so rampant and passionate that he couldn't believe she would not soon submit to marrying him.

During the rest of the week while he was in Bristol Will contacted a HVAC vendor and arranged window air conditioners to be installed on four windows in the house, two downstairs and two in the upstairs bedrooms. The contractor agreed to do the work but only after that Saturday, which was the 4th of July. That convinced Will that they would have to stay that weekend at his cottage in Bristol. But that wasn't bad; they would be at his parents for the barbeque and watch the fireworks display set off over the Choptiko. Kate and her growing family came as well. Kate was no longer unfriendly to Minnie. She was simply too busy taking care of an infant and a new baby to pay any attention to anyone else.

Will brokered two sales of properties—both the new riverside houses—during July. It was not a great return, but it required him to be in Bristol on most weekdays. At the same time he started composing the petition document that the Nantiquaks would submit for federal recognition. He went one day to the Association headquarters to consult with Carmine who began helping writing the document. They would draft the document at long distance and share it over the computer lines. On the week after the 4th he went to Beaverton to kick off the build out of the headquarters, meeting with Chief Clarke at the same time. And on several other days through that month and the next month he went to Beaverton to oversee the refurbishment of the building.headquarters of Nantiquak Corporation's. The tribe's officers decided to completely rebuild the interior two floors to have it ready and open in time for the powwow in September. In the end they built a large entry and reception room with space for displays and even a video screen showing films of prior years' powwows. And behind that front room they built three offices, and a board room, as well as a small kitchen. Upstairs they built three more offices and a bedroom for guests, along with a full bathroom with shower. They had to build a new staircase to make the upstairs accessible and they added a second staircase to the roof. Will hired the contractor to lead the work with the stipulation that he would in turn hire three tribesmen from the

Indian River Band who regularly worked as builders. They found out as they started the interior work that they needed to repair the roof as well and resurface it. Will convinced the owner of the building—a nice elderly widow who lived by herself in the town—to contribute half of the funds for the upgrade and refurbishment. But during his negotiations with her he could not convince her to sell the building outright to the Nantiquak Corporation. She wanted to have it as she said to leave to her nephews when she passed away.

That summer on the weekends after the 4th of July, they would stay at the Hampton farmhouse. The air conditioners made it much more comfortable and made sleeping upstairs possible. Ever since that heavy downpour in June, the weather stayed very hot and dry and in fact the dry hot conditions hit the already damaged crops especially the soy beans and each weekend Will could see that a drought was growing deeper and more punishing. Max once or twice called on the house to tell Will that things looked bad for that year's harvest. It was clear that Max was very concerned and upset by the poor growing season. By the end of July he began insisting that Will needed to put in an irrigation system, but that it was probably too late to save that season's crop.

While they were staying at the farmhouse over that summer, Will found more and more things around the house that needed either repairs or replacement. Fortunately the boiler had been recently replaced. And a quick inspection also fortunately did not show any signs of termites. He did contract a mechanic to come out to repair the wind mill, a four day job. He saw also that the outside needed a new paint job, but he decided that could wait to the next year. All the demands needed by the house exceeded what his usual yearly income from his realty and title businesses could support, but they were one-time expenses. Up to August Will had been paying for the rent of the Cleveland Park apartment along with half of the costs of building-out the Beaverton headquarters out of his inheritance money. Minnie was concerned by Will's outlays and one Sunday in late July she insisted that she contribute to the monthly rent payment of the apartment. They discussed it at length, Will at first not willing to let Minnie spend her money on the rent, but finally he relented and they agreed to split the rent fifty-fifty.

"After all," she said, "you spent your money for all the new furniture we got for the apartment. And you're spending to upgrade the farmhouse. As we are living together as one household, why don't we pool our resources for the monthly expenses?" She almost said "like a married couple would" but she didn't.

It was on the Saturday after the 4th that Minnie was invited to attend the first board meeting of the Nantiquak Corporation in her capacity as chairwoman of the board. She was reluctant to go because she didn't feel right as an outsider and a woman leading this group of men who were all strangers to her. And she feared that the meeting could become like the problematic meetings she had held as chief of her own tribe. Only on the 4th of July weekend had she formally "abdicated" as chief of the Massaponax-Doeg. And she did not want to attend without Will's attendance. The other board members assured her that Will could attend as an "interested" observer. They said that "after all, he's one-eighth Nantiquak."

The new board met in the meeting room of the Association's building near Milltown. Chief Clarke was there--but he reminded everybody that he was now only the Chief of the Indian River Band, "so you'll have to call me Charlie Clarke from now on" he said—as was Morley Norwood, and John Buckham from the Puckamee Band. No one had come from the Kuskawarok Band, and the Black Face Band sent a representative that was unknown to Minnie and to Will. The remaining members of the board were three representatives that had previously served on the tribal council of the Indian River Band. Minnie surprised Will by taking the lead and announcing that the meeting was now convened on "this day, 11 July 1998", and that as the first order of business they needed a recording secretary to keep the minutes. She herself took out a yellow legal pad and kept notes throughout the meeting, but there were no volunteers to serve as recording secretary. None of the other Indians in the room had with them either pens or writing pads, except for Will. So Minnie asked him to be the recording secretary for this meeting. "But at the next meeting, Carmine will have to come and act as the recording secretary" said Minnie. "Because the rules of this new Corporation require that minutes be kept on all board meetings and be prepared so that they could be presented to outside auditors or for later review. We need to run this Corporation as a professional business."

Then Minnie asked for a roll call to be taken and she started by introducing herself. Will was writing furiously trying to keep up with the names, especially as most of the men mumbled their names. The representative of the Aksesky Band introduced himself as Michael Burnley of Delmar, Maryland.

"And we note that there is no representative of the Kuskaworak Band in attendance today, but do we know who the designated representative will be? The representatives from Kuskaworak, Puckamee, Asksesky, and Makadewa-Ninda bands will effectively be the chosen weroance from each band. And the Chief of the entire tribe will be elected from the members of the board."

No one knew who would represent Kuskaworak. And they couldn't assume it was Jack Sockum.

"Fine. Before we leave today we'll need to get the contact information for each of you. Phone numbers, cellular phone numbers, mailing addresses.

"The order of business for this first meeting is above all to set up the rules of how the Corporation is run. And they will also address tribal governance and tribal membership rules. We can start with the formation of the board, and the scheduled meetings of the board, and the powers, rights and duties of the board. After that we need to select the officers of the Corporation and again we need to define their duties, obligations, and rights, and what they are authorized to do. And then we will at every meeting we will review operations, activities, investments, and projects and cultural programs, including authorization of expenditure for these. And finally we will review the Corporations finances."

"So I propose that we start by establishing that the board will be obliged to hold quarterly meetings at a place to be designated, but we presume in the future in the Beaverton headquarters. Does anyone object to this?"

No one objected, and no one proposed a different schedule. There were a few comments about how far away Beaverton was. Chief Clarke answered that, "We are a dispersed tribe. And actually this is a very central location for everyone."

Minnie capped the distance issues by pointing out that the Navajo Nation covered a much bigger territory and people had to travel much farther for their central tribal council meetings, which were held monthly.

They appointed the officers of the Corporation. Chief Clarke would be President, Carmine Norwood would be Vice President for Communications which included communications with the Bureau of Indian Affairs, and Morley was appointed as Vice President of Special Cultural Projects, which was limited at that time to the powwow. And the surprise was the post of Vice President for Finance, because Chief Clarke proposed and firmly insisted that this position be held by Will Eames. After a bit of back and forth—the representative of the Black Face Band asked rhetorically "Shouldn't the officers of the Corporation have to be Nantiquak Indians and only Nantiquaks?"— it was resolved that Will would be appointed as that VP for a two year term. And the issue was repeated when they discussed the office of Chief Accountant. "Here is a case where we must insist that we have an experienced and professional accountant in this position. And if we can find one that is a Nantiquak then that is good." said Minnie. "But if we cannot we need to fill this position through a profession search." It was agreed that none of the officers, except the Chief Accountant, would receive a salary for his or her work.

Likewise there was some discussion and differences on the qualifications for membership in the tribe in the future. It was easy to agree that children of current members of the Corporation were automatically eligible for membership and they became full members at the age of eighteen. But then the issue of automatic tribal membership going to a child born of a Nantiquak woman and a white man caused the beginnings of some arguments. There were some who said that the automatic right to membership should not convey to future half breeds. They said that only those who lived in an Indian family and lived an Indian style life should qualify automatically. They left the issue in a compromise; such a child would be eligible, but he or she would have to show that intended to live as an Indian. Morley brought up the issue of eligibility in general and proposed that no one who had less than one paternal grandparent who was Nantiquak could be a member of the tribe, and that that person had to have lived his entire life within the drainage areas of the river basins of the Nanticoke, Choptiko, Indian, Wicomico and Pokemoke and Manokin Rivers. It was pointed out that this represented the Dorset, Wicomico, Princess Marie, and Suffolk Counties, but Morley argued that those were white men's political boundaries. Chief Clarke came into this discussion saying that as a tribe they needed to be geographically defined, as geography was destiny, defined how you lived, and established your values and preferences. It was their ongoing ties to this land defined by the rivers flowing either to the Bay or to the Ocean that was an essential identity of the Nantiquak people as opposed to Iriquois or the Cherokees or the Lenape tribe in New Jersey. And such a definition also disinherited all those generations of Indians who had left the Nantiquak lands as much as two hundred years ago and assimilated with other tribes or white men in so many different parts of the U.S. So the consensus was that new members had to be able to demonstrate ancestry that made them not less than one quarter Nantiquak from the riverine lands of the central Eastern Shore. The vote on this was still not unanimous. Four people voted against. The objectors especially did not want any future disqualification of their membership if they could not show one quarter blood ancestry.

And so on, Minnie steadily and firmly with a planned agenda led the board through one item after another. At the end of four hours, with only two breaks for coffee and smoking, they reached the point where they were ready to discuss the current project to build out and furnish the headquarters for the Corporation in Beaverton, including the estimated budget. Chief Clarke presented the outline of the build-out, the offices they would build, the rebuilding of the upstairs. As he had not brought any presentation materials, he drew out on the chalk board what the floor plans would look like. Then Will took up the presentation about the contracting, the expected costs, and the financing of the works. His estimates was that the work and the materials would cost in total about eighteen thousand eight hundred dollars. That would include paying the wages of three builders from the Indian River Band, who would be hired and paid by the contractor. And that Chief Clarke had nominated these three and they had accepted the work at normal rates for builders in the region. He said further that they would buy the building materials and bathroom and washroom fixtures at the Home Depot in Salisbury, and that they would themselves be responsible for delivery of those materials in their own trucks, as a way to save money. And he estimated a building period of six to eight weeks would be required. And these expenses would be funded half by the owner, and half by a loan from himself to the Corporation. So with that as the presentation, Minnie polled the board for their authorization and approval. And they all did approve the project with the understanding that they would come back to the board to get its approval for the additional expenses for furnishing and equipping of the headquarters at a later date. The board then asked Morley if the Association had the spare funds to be able to pay the first three months' rent for the headquarters, or fifteen hundred dollars. Morley said it had sufficient funds and he would arrange to pay the rent in the next week.

Finally Minnie asked Will if the foundation capital for the Corporation was paid up. He said no, but that he himself was willing to advance a loan for twenty thousand dollars to the Corporation for that foundation capital, and the rest of the capitalization should come from the Corporation members. Will mentioned that they needed to do that because in the next month he was going to file the papers with the IRS and the State of Delaware to get tax exempt status for the Nantiquak non-profit Corporation. Minnie asked for a vote of approval for this approach to financing the Corporation in its start stages. It was unanimously approved, with the only dissenters saying before the vote that they did not want to have to pay dues or annual fees to the Corporation on top of the small annual membership fees they already paid to the Association.

The last order of business was to hear Morley report on the preparations for that year's powwow. He said they were well under way. Charlie Clarke then interjected and said that there needed to be some changes as the Association needed to invite the participation of the four outlying Bands. To see if they could contribute to the activities, shows, or crafts that made up the powwow. Morley said he understood and he would have to go with some of the organizers to talk to the members of the other Bands and invite them. He would start doing that this month.

By that time, Minnie was feeling very exhausted but many of the other members of the board were also tired and did not have the stamina to carry on. She proposed that they set another board meeting for the first weekend in September, but not on Labor Day Monday. "That would make our next meeting for Saturday September 5th. So everyone take note. It will be our first quarterly meeting. Will will get the minutes of this meeting typed up and copies will be sent to each of you in the coming weeks. They will become part of the Corporation's records. And by this I now adjourn this meeting."

Morley then, as he had at last December's tribal council meeting, stood up and said that there was a buffet dinner ready for everyone to eat together and that they would bring it in right now. The food had been prepared by the wives of the five representatives of the Indian River Band, including Mrs. Clarke, and they carried in the serving platters loaded with fried fish, succotash, corn bread, stewed beans and tomatoes. Minnie didn't feel up to eating, she was so tired, but Will who was shaking off writer's cramp from his right hand, was hungry and wanted to stay and eat and socialize. They didn't get away until after six in the afternoon. Will hoped that no one took too much notice of the fact that Will and Minnie came together in Will's car.

The next day they went out crabbing again down the Choptiko River and again they were very successful. They brought in so many crabs that once more Will sold the excess to Tony at Poseidon's Palace. They went to his parents' house and ate the rest of the crabs with white corn on the cob, all washed down by the ale they bought at Tony's. Soft shell crabs were by then out of season so Minnie got back into the swing of smashing and bashing the shells with the wooden mallet. She did it was so much enthusiasm that it caused Mar Sue to laugh several times.

In the first week in August Will got a call from Dr. Houlder saying that the DNA profiling had been completed and he could now send Will the report with the results.

"And I think you'd be interested to know that your grandmother, Mena Driggers, was a direct descendant of the people whose bones we tested." he said in his muffled way through his beard.

"That's great news. Now I can maybe see about DNA profiling of other tribal members to see if or how they are also related to the people of the Salisbury tell."

"Yeah, I don't see why not. You're going to use a DNA genealogical research firm?"

"Yeah, they are a little expensive but we can start with that."

"Oh and by the way, the archaeologist on the site told me they got the test results back for the dating of the bones. He was surprised to learn that the bones are between six hundred and fifty and seven hundred years old. A lot older than they had first estimated." said Houlder. "Well good luck. You should get this package in a few days." Will was whooping up the triumph in his office as he hung up, again causing amusement and consternation in his employees. But this time they did not make any inquiries as to his outburst. "Just another big breakthrough in the Indian Project." Both women nodded their heads and went back to their desks.

He then called Minnie as soon as got off the line with Houlder to share with her the exciting news. She was also excited by the news and enthusiastically responded.

"You'll have to put those findings into your petition to the Bureau." she said calmly. "It will be an entirely new approach to establishing descent and tribal continuity. Much better than the current methods which rely on old fashioned concepts of race and nineteenth century anthropological frameworks and definitions of what comprises a tribe."

"We can drink to this wonderful finding tonight, after I get home. Now I need to extend research into the genetic lines and relationships to all the other bands of Nantiquak Indians."

After he got off the phone with Minnie he saw that it was already a suitable time to call the firm, Genetic Tree of Life. So he got out the promotional materials the firm had sent him earlier that summer and found the name of the man he had talked to: Mr. Bradley Webb.

"Is this Mr. Webb? I'm Will Eames. We spoke about three months ago about doing genetic DNA testing to undercover the geneaological relationships of members within an Indian tribe. Remember me?"

"Oh yes. I do remember we talked. Specifically the Indian angle."

"I am now ready to find the genetic links between several clans of the tribe and a new archaeological discovery that is six hundred to seven hundred years old. So I was wondering how I can engage your firm's services to check the genetic links between that old source of DNA and today's generations. How do we collect samples of DNA to send you?"

"Well, for living people it is simple. We take a saliva swipe. We'll send you the kits you need to take swipes. How many individuals are we talking about?"

"Seven or eight people."

"But for the DNA from an old source, we have to have a forensic archaeologist go out and extract…"

"Oh, excuse me. We've already done that. We've recovered DNA from the old bones—a fellow you recommended to me by the way—and they have already been profiled and genetically tested to find the relationship to an Indian who died thirty years ago."

"Who did the profiling?"

"Someone at a lab at the University of Colorado at Boulder. And they are sending me right now the DNA code of the older sample and the more recent sample."

"Oh, that's good. But that's a research lab not a commercial geneaological firm like ours, right?"

"Yes, that's right."

"Do you know what medium they are sending the DNA results in? A print-out? On electronic memory?"

"No, I don't. Won't know until their report gets to me here."

"Fine. Well that should save us a whole bunch of work. I think the price that I quoted you will be a lot lower for the other tests, finding the genetic relationship. So do you want to do it?"

"Yes, I do. I'll send you the DNA materials as soon as I get the testing kits from you. Along with the results that the University of Colorado sends me. Can I ask you how long all of that might take?"

"You said for five to seven people? And their relationship to the old sample? I would say minimum three weeks, but up to five weeks."

"And could you send me the estimated cost once you have all the materials?"

"Yes. I can. I think it will cost more like nine thousand, nine thousand five hundred in these circumstances. It's presumably cheaper because you have the base DNA profile. And all the others should look pretty much the same once we get going. We'll know what we're looking for also. That part of the genetic code that tells us there is a relationship between two people living at different times in history."

So they agreed. Will estimated that the survey could cost him between forty-five thousand and sixty six thousand dollars. He could afford it. So he would do it. And he would put the results in their petition for federal recognition, only if they supported the Nantiquak claim of being the indigenous peoples of the Eastern Shore, and still existing. A week later in mid-August he received a large package with the testing kits from Bradley Webb only a day or two after he had received the package from Professor Houlder with the DNA profiling results and a report of genetic ancestry. The DNA code for the "old bones" was recorded on a CD disc, so he made a copy onto another disc and put it in a package to return to The Genetic Tree.

But first he had to get samples from individuals from the individual Nantiquaks, all except the Kuskaworak Band. So he made some calls; first to Carmine who right away volunteered to give some of her saliva for the testing. She said she would call around to find a volunteer from the Makadewa-Ninda Band and from the Asksesky Band and see if she could not arrange a common time to take each of the tests. He would prefer to take the samples on a day when he was already planning to be up at Beaverton checking on the progress of the reconstruction of the interior. He himself called Albert Heyden at the Puckamee Band. He only had Heyden's cell phone number, but it did not answer. Instead he got the frustrating recorded reply, "The number you are calling is not in the coverage area." Through the rest of the day, Will called the number several more times with the same result. He wondered if Heyden was at their settlement where there was no cellular coverage, or whether he was away working in a place with no coverage. He knew that there were no land lines at the settlement, so the only way he could reach Heyden was through his cell number.

But later that afternoon, shortly before Will was getting ready to drive to his 'Warshington' home to be with Minnie, Carmine called to tell him that she arranged for two volunteers to give samples from the two Bands for the next Tuesday. And they had agreed to meet at the Association headquarters along with her. But she told him that she had had to ask several people to volunteer, because the people she had first asked did not want to do it. They were opposed to investigating DNA to find genetic relationships. They just did not want to know. Carmine suggested that they could also be afraid to find out that perhaps they did not after all have Indian ancestry or at least very much. Will put this appointment into his schedule for the next week. Then he tried once more to reach Heyden. This time he got him on the line, although it was a poor connection. Will told him the issue and asked if he would cooperate in giving a saliva sample for the DNA profiling. Heyden flatly declined.

"Why don't you ask Buckham? He's so keen for this Indian project of yours, recognition and all that. He's the weroance now for our little band of forgotten Indians. Ask him for it."

"I don't have a cell number for him."

"I can't help you with that, I'm afraid."

"Maybe you can tell him to contact me?"

"Maybe. If I see him."

Will thought of another angle.

"Maybe you see Hately from time to time? Does he have a cell phone? I could call him."

"Yeah, I have his cell number. So what do you want? That I tell Buckham to give you a call or I give you Mannuel's cell number?"

"Why don't you give me Hately's number?"

"Ok, I'll text you. Goodbye."

Will thought that Heyden was rudely uncooperative, even hostile. As if he were irritated by something that Will had said or done before. He expected that Heyden would send him the cell phone number right away, but after fifteen minutes when he still had not received it, he had to leave for home so he got in his Olds and left for "Warshington." Just as he was parking outside his house, his cell phone rang indicating the receipt of a text message. It was a cell number and one word: Mannuel. Will called the number and it was answered, again with a sullen, low pitched voice.

"Is this Mannuel Hately?"

"Yes. Who wants him?"

"This is Will Eames. Remember? I hired you a few months ago to finish the carving of the headstone for my great uncle."

"Yes, I remember you. Do you need another gravestone?"

"No. I have a favor to ask of you." And then Will told him about his ancestry project and his need for a saliva sample. "So would you agree to give a sample, if I come over to your settlement tomorrow?"

"I suppose so."

"When would be the best time for me to drop by?"

"Any time after eleven."

"Fine, then I will be there tomorrow. Say around noon. Okay?"

"Yeah." And then the line went dead. Will thought that was a strange manner of signing off, and he told Minnie about the conversation when he entered the house. She was just beginning to fix dinner of baked fish and potatoes, so she only partially paid attention to what Will was telling her.

"The stereotypical taciturn Indian." she said. "What's so unusual about that manner of talking on the phone? Does it bother you?"

"Yeah, I suppose it does. So you think he talks like that to everyone, especially over the phone? It's not just an Indian way of talking with Anglos? A tone of resentment in his voice and a reluctance to talk with me?"

"It could be. I don't know that man from Adam. Maybe he just has personal problems. Or he doesn't talk on the cell phone much."

"Heyden spoke almost the same way."

Minnie put down her spatula and turned to Will. "I wouldn't be surprised if they talked like that with everybody, Indian or Anglo. But then maybe poor Indians hold attitudes toward whites that they are the oppressive race. I don't, but I've known some of my tribesmen who do. They talk then like black former slaves spoke to whites, or poor Mexican illegal immigrants talk to white farmers here. So they all talk feeling inferior. They don't want to speak up or be revealing when they talk."

"Yeah, maybe you're right."

"Will, you better not think that if you succeed in everything you're doing for this Injun Project the Nantiquaks Indians will let you know that they are appreciative or thankful. You'll be disappointed if you think that way. There will be no gratitude. You're pushing things on them that maybe they should want and will benefit them, but they are things that they do not want just now and don't really believe will benefit them."

"As always, Minnie, you're sagely right."

"Now do you want to eat dinner with me? Or do you want to probe more into the mysteries of Indian behavior?"

"No, I want a kiss from you. And then eat dinner with you." He took her in his hands and kissed her full on the lips. "And afterwards I want to probe deeper into your mysteries."

Minnie smiled and gave him a playful whack on the arm and took up her spatula again.

After dinner, Minnie and Will took a stroll hand in hand up Connecticut Avenue and then down a small trail in a ravine park which led down to the Rock Creek. Will was surprised to see how low the water level was in the creek and it reminded him of the ongoing drought that was also affecting the Eastern Shore and his farm. After a few hundred yards, deep in the Rock Creek ravine, they walked under the arch of a high bridge, and then they turned up hill and walked up the little Klingle Valley trail in deep shade. As they walked slowly still on the sidewalk along Connecticut Avenue, Will proposed that they take a summer vacation together in September. "Around Labor Day or just after your birthday. It would be our first vacation together— as if we were truly a married couple." Minnie was surprised by this proposal, but intrigued and curious as to what he would propose.

"And I was thinking we could combine a little business with our travel pleasure. I am suggesting that we take a week-long vacation trip not to the beach, but to the mountains. And specifically to Cherokee,

North Carolina. To visit the Cherokee Indians there. And to go hiking and fishing."

"What a wonderful idea. We can study how other tribes actually work their reservation and governance and cultivate their culture."

"Yes, that was my way of thinking too. As well as to inquire about how they got their casino off the ground, and how it's working."

"Maybe you're getting a little ahead of yourself, Willeams."

"Maybe, but it wouldn't be all work and no play. I was thinking we could try some fishing too. I understand that the streams up there in the mountains are full of trout. We could both learn how to do fly fishing. I've always wanted to try that. How does that strike you?"

"I don't know. I don't know anything about fly fishing."

"Neither do I, though I understand you need to wade in the river in order to cast your line. But that's the point, we'll go with a guide who will teach us how it's done. Something new. And trout are delicious too."

"I think we'll be finishing up our case against Delaware just around that time. So I'll have to check to see if I could take a week off. You say early in September?"

"Yes, something like that. As a birthday present for you, leaving just after we celebrate it here but before Labor Day weekend. We could drive down there in my trusty Olds. And we could stay three nights in Cherokee and three nights in a mountain lodge I read about. It would be relaxing, and something very different for both of us. Shall we do it?"

"Yes, let's Nike. This is a really good idea, Will."

"Okay, you check with your bosses at the office. And as soon as you let me know it's okay, I'll start making bookings and plans."

"I've never eaten trout. Ever before. That'll be another new experience with you Willeames."

The next morning, after Will had checked in at his office, he picked up the testing equipment and mouth swabs, put them in a bag, and then got back in his car to drive out to the Puckamee settlement. It took another thirty-five minutes to drive out there from Bristol and it made Will feel tired after the two hours he had already spent driving from D.C.. He stepped out of his Olds and realized he didn't know how he would find Mannuel Hately. He didn't know which mobile house—which Heyden had snidely called wigwams—was Hately's. There seemed to be no one moving about outside. There were a few scrawny looking dogs lying about here and there, and although most of them raised their heads to look at Will, none of them started to bark. Will approached slowly hoping to be able to meet someone who could tell him where Hately lived. He had walked the full length of the lane on which the houses were lined up and no one came out to confront him. He tried calling on his cell phone, but then he noticed that there was no service coverage where he was standing. So he started slowly walking back down the lane. As he passed one of the houses a metal door slammed behind him and he spun around. A middle aged, dark skinned woman with long black hair pulled back behind her head was coming toward him. Will had the first impression that it was Hately, as the face he saw looked so much like what he remembered Hately looked like. "Mannuel? Yeah, I know where he lives. He's my brother. I'll show you."

She led him to a second small trailer that had been fixed into the ground behind her mobile house, and she banged on the door and shouted. "Manny, get up. You have a visitor."

Mannuel finally came to the door looking disheveled and maybe hung-over. His sister left without a word.

"Oh, it's you again." Hately said without offering to let Will go past him into the trailer. "Tell me again, what is this sample for?"

"To examine your genes that are expressed in the sample, in your saliva, and compare them with bones of Nantiquaks that have been found and tested to be more than six hundred years old."

"Whatever for? Sounds to me you're doing tests to find out that water is wet. You'll only find out that I am a Nantiquak Indian? I already know that."

"But bureaucrats in Warshington want to have proof of that so they can decide to officially call you a Nantiquak tribesman, and a part of a sovereign Indian tribe."

"It'd be more worthwhile to me if you delivered to them my willingness to carve them their headstones."

"I understand. This won't take but a minute. Maybe I can put these things on this table over here?"

"If you like."

Will put his bag down and took out the test tube and opened the sealed cap and stood the tube up in a small frame stand. Then he took out a paper sealed packet and tore it open to reveal a short wide white swab which looked somewhat like an ordinary cotton ear swab, only broader.

"Now, Mannuel, if you please. Open your mouth for a moment."

When he had, Will quickly put the swab into his mouth and wiped the material end against the inside of his cheek several times stirring it around as if rubbing a slimey stain off a surface, then he quickly threw the swab into the test tube and sealed it up again, just as he had seen Dr. Houlder do it.

"That's it. All done."

"Maybe you can give me ten dollars for being so cooperative?" said Hately as he seemed to be cleaning out his mouth with his tongue.

"You want me to pay you for that sample?" Will asked in disbelief.

"Yeah, of course. Why else would I do this? For the benefit of some nameless bureaucrat in Warshington as you said? No way."

Will didn't know what to think. He had only a five and a twenty dollar bill in his billfold. He didn't want to give Hately twenty dollars.

"Here. All I have is a five dollar bill. Take it."

Hately did not say anything. He frowned and reached out for the fiver and then looked at Will with an expression that mixed resignation and contempt in it. Hately put the bill in his jeans pocket and turned without a word and went back into his trailer house.

Will was thinking how difficult and distasteful all this way. After a moment's pause, he put his testing materials back in the bag and went back to his car and drove back to his office across the county.

That weekend Minnie and Will spent out at the farm. They had decided that they would call it the Hampton Farm. They had made it very much more comfortable, especially with the addition of the air conditioning. And Minnie had had curtains made and hung for the huge windows of the main bedroom where they slept so that they weren't awakened by the bright light of earliest summer dawn which was then still around five am. And she installed a new colorful shower curtain to draw closed around the bathtub. Before, showering in the large tub which stood high on four legs, was difficult. Either she had to stand up and splashed water all around the bathroom, or she had to squat which was difficult because she had to hold one wall of the tub to keep her balance, while with the other holding the shower head on the end of the hose. With the curtains pulled closed she could stand and not feel so foolish and exposed and especially not splash so much. It helped also that Will installed a hanger to fix the shower head above their heads. Minnie also added some fabric covers and new cushions to the sofa and overstuffed chairs in the living room. She had also asked Will to get some blinds installed on the downstairs windows. They had ordered them but by this weekend in mid-August they still hadn't arrived.

They met first that evening at Tony's place, the Poseidon Palace, after Minnie had driven out in her car. There they had a seafood dinner before driving on in both cars to the farm. Will took along with him a half gallon plastic bottle filled with Tony's latest craft beer. When they arrived at the farm this time, it was still light and it became starkly clear the extent of the damage the summer's drought had had on the crop. It appeared that Max and his team had completed the soy beans harvest and the fields at the front of the farm plot, where the gravel lane turned off the main road, were now bare, cracked earth that spouted up dust with even the slightest breeze or disturbance. In the distance they could see the yellow-brown stalks of the corn field. "This looks really bad," said Will. "A bad year for the harvest, for sure."

They drove up to the farmhouse and saw that Max's car was still standing out the open barn. But they couldn't see Max anywhere. So they went into the house with their bags and supplies and came back out and sat next to each on the rattan divan on the porch looking out at the waning sun and the bare earth fields. Shortly afterwards Max appeared, dusty and tired looking.

"Hey Max. How'd you like a beaker of cold beer?"

"Evening ma'am." said Max. "Yes, a beaker of beer, thad be nice just now."

"Do you want any beer, Minnie?" She shook her head no. "How about some iced tea?" And she said yes.

Max hesitantly stepped up the six stairs onto the porch but remained standing while Will went back into the house to get the beer.

"It's a disaster this year." Max said, addressing the broad outdoor sky but not speaking directly to Minnie. "Worst I've seen it since I've been farming out here."

Will came back out bearing a tray with two tall beakers of beer and a plastic tumbler with the iced tea.

"I was telling your woman here, that this is the worst I've seen in fourteen years." said Max.

"How bad is it? All from the drought?" asked Will. "Here take a seat."

Max remained standing, leaning a bit against the white post at the top of the stairs. He took a deep quaff of the beer and said "mmm" with satisfaction.

"And my woman has a name too. She's Minnie. And you can use it when you speak to or about her." said Will before taking a draft of his beer.

"I think the harvest will be down by two thirds what it usually is. For both the beans and the corn. We've finished taking up the beans. A truck will come out to pick them up tomorrow early. But I think we can only deliver one, maybe one and half truck loads this year. Most of the damage was due to the drought. But that hellacious downpour back in June damaged an awful lot of the plants. And so few recovered enough from that to survive the drought. I told you we need to install a watering system."

"You mean like the ones that stand up on wheeled trestles above the fields around here?"

"Yeah, you mean on wheeled trusses. They're called wheeled line irrigation systems."

"The ones that go around in a big circle?"

"Those are called center pivot wheeled lines. We could use one of those, but the wheel line would be enough, and it's cheaper. It drives itself across the field on the wheels."

"And how much does such a system cost?"

"You mean the wheeled line systems?"

"For instance."

"I'm not sure. They are custom made to fit the area of your fields, so we would make one to the size of the corn fields. I can ask. But the center pivot lines cost a lot more, like fifty-sixty percent more, because they use steel pipes."

"Fine, we can discuss this and make a decision in the fall after the end of the harvest."

Will thought Max looked even more haggard and depressed than usual. He seemed to take on personally the problems of the farm was having. Yet he was still only an employee. A very involved employee granted, and he obviously worked very hard to deliver the best results, as if it were his own farm. Max put his empty beaker on the balustrade and stepped off the porch and slowly and slouched over he walked to his car, looking like a defeated man. Then he drove off into the sunset.

Will turned to Minnie and said. "He looks like a defeated man."

"Yes, he does. I think farmers often are defeated by the elements and the misfortunes of bad weather. I know the farmers around our reservation have real troubles making ends meet all the time. Because of the weather."

"Maybe. But tomorrow, they forecast wonderful weather. Sunny but not too hot. Perfect for fishing for rockfish."

They remained seated close together on the porch looking on the sunset and the deepening blue sky and then purple of the western horizon until it was fully dark.

"Can you afford to run this farm, Will, even with your inheritance money?" Minnie asked. "You're spending a lot on it and you've been spending a lot on the Nantiquaks as well."

"I think so. Don't worry. As reserve, I've put half of the inheritance into a Nasdaq Index fund. It's been growing like a weed these past two months. And I expect it will continue to do very well. As for the Nantiquaks I'm only lending to the tribe. I expect once they start getting income from the casino, they will pay me back."

"But that's a risky investment. Don't you think?"

"What the Nasdaq or the Nantiquaks?

"The Nasdaq. I read where they consider it to be very speculative."

"No. It's a market that's growing based on real changes in our economy. Don't worry. Everything will come good. We'll do alright. And you will marry me and we will all live happily ever after. How could things turn out differently?"

"You're such a head in the sky optimist, Willeams."

"You bet I am. Everything is going to work out with the Nantiquaks. And we'll get our casino. Optimist is my middle name. Didn't I tell you?"

Then they went in the house.

The next day they went fishing and caught five good sized rockfish. Will felt he got too sunburned, but Minnie was covered up and had her broad sunhat on all day. In the midafternoon, they took their catch to his parents' house and after Will cleaned and scaled the fish, Mar Sue showed Minnie how to prepare them on the grill. They ate outdoors and each got one fish to eat. Mar Sue also prepared a potato salad and a kale salad with eggs. They left to return to Hampton farm only after dark.

Earlier that day, even before they went out to go fishing, barely after they had left bed, two trucks had come to the farm and loaded up with the soya beans and drove off. Max told Will later that it was really bad, the worst he had ever seen: the harvest was seventy percent off the previous year's. That was somewhat offset by a fifteen percent higher price than the year before—everyone on the Eastern Shore had suffered damage and poor soya bean harvests that year. But Max told Will that the year's results were going to be at least sixty percent lower than that of the past few years.

On Tuesday, after he had arrived at his office from D.C., Will checked his inbox and his phone messages and mail and saw that he did not have any realtor appointments that day. So he picked up his bag with the DNA testing materials and after drinking a cup of coffee from the office coffee maker he left for Beaverton. The team was already at work inside the building and the work on the first floor on first glance appeared to be mostly finished. The huge shopfront windows had been replaced with brick walls and two small windows to the left and right of the door. The doorframe had been changed to a heavier frame ready to receive a metal door lacking the full length pane of glass. The walls in the front room were ready for paint and the concrete floor was already clean and ready for the final flooring material to be installed. The washroom was finished and the water already reconnected. And the other offices were also already finished and cleaned and ready for painting. The boardroom downstairs already had its flooring put in and a new back door had been installed. Upstairs the work had not quite progressed as far and three of the workers were up there working on spackling the plasterboard walls of the three upstairs rooms. The bathroom was finished with tiles and cleaned and ready for use. And the new staircase to the roof was installed as well as the roof door. Will was impressed at how quickly the team had completed all this work. It looked to him that Nantiquak Incorporated would be able to occupy and start using this office by the middle of the next month, after Will and Minnie got back from their vacation to Cherokee territory.

After checking all the works in progress, Will asked the foreman—the contractor himself was not on site—whether there were any materials that were still needed. And he said that he needed more paint and rollers and paint solvent. Will offered to pick them up himself in Salisbury before the end of the day. And with that he left for Millville for the offices of the Association, where he would meet with Carmine. But she was late and Will sat in the front reception area to wait for her or the others to give their samples. He waited more than an hour before a man drove up. He introduced himself as John Blackmon. He was from the Asksesky Band and lived just over the Maryland border near DelMar. Will was prepared to explain to Mr. Blackmon what the DNA profiling was all about, but Blackmon was not interested. "What difference will it make? The Bureau is not going to give us federal acknowledgement. They don't do that anymore." He gave his sample and he left five minutes after arriving. He said he wasn't interested in getting the results back either. "It won't change anything in my life, to know by DNA analysis."

At that Will called Carmine's cell number. She answered after five rings. And she obviously had caller ID on her phone. "I'm coming, Will. Don't worry. I'll be there in eight or ten minutes. I'm bringing Andy Healy from the Black Face Band. He was a little delayed today." And she cut off the line. After twenty minutes she drove up in her little Toyota Corolla and she climbed out looking to Will, apologetic and embarrassed. A man—dressed in overalls-- climbed out of the passenger side of the car and followed Carmine over to where Will was standing. Carmine introduced Will to Andy Healy, who did not in the least look like an Indian, and certainly did not resemble much the Nantiquak Indians Will had met in the other Bands. He looked like an anglo; with the high forehead and long slender face that are typical of English faces. Will thought he looked more anglo than even he or his father did. "You don't look very much like an Indian." said Will after the introductions and a short explanation of what the saliva sampling was for.

"Everyone tells me that. But my parents, who both admitted to being mixed breeds, both insisted that they were mostly of Indian ancestry."

"So, the DNA profiling will tell us if you are descended from the group of Nantiquak Indians who lived around here in the region in the fifteenth century. But it might also tell you that you have a preponderance of other non-Indian ancestors."

"Will, as you requested, we checked out the family name with the Methodist Church records up in Dover," said Carmine. "The name first appeared as a convert, that is in their baptism records, in the late 1820s. And the baptism occurred at the old church that was on Injuntown Road out on Injun Branch, right by the territory that used to be reservation land. No indications then that they were mixed breed."

"Okay. In any event or outcome, we won't use the findings to disqualify you, but I want you to be prepared in case you find the results surprising or objectionable."

"I understand. I'm not afraid of the results. Let's do this."

So Will ran the swab on the inside of Andy Healy's cheek, dropped it into the test tube, sealed it, and turned to shake Healy's hand.

"What, don't I get a lollipop after that procedure?" Healy joked. "The dentist always gives me one."

Will chuckled. He had not encountered any of the Indians with such a wry sense of humor.

"No, that is actually a way to promote the use of more dental services. I'm sure I won't need to run future tests on you. And by the way we will not identify you by name in the filing we make with the Bureau. But I want to thank you for offering up your spit for the government. As they say; 'Every man's spit counts.'" Will smiled as he shook Healy's hand.

Will turned to Carmine. "We need to talk about the preparation and writing of our filing document. I'm looking to you to contribute a big part."

"But I don't write all that well," said Carmine.

"I think your writing skills are probably better than most others in your tribe. I'm confident of that. Maybe we can talk tomorrow about an outline and divide up the work between us. The research results that you have already typed up provide a good basis to start writing."

Carmine's expression showed clear signs of panic.

"Don't worry, we can consult Minnie too. She will have a lot of insights, as for several years she was evaluating tribal applications in the Department of Federal Acknowledgement in the Bureau. By conference call. Would that help you?"

"Oh, I'm sure it would. But maybe we can meet on a weekend day. Face to face would help even more."

Packed up, Will drove to Millville and stopped at a brickfront former store that had been converted to a grill restaurant where he had a late lunch of grilled fish. Then he drove on to Salisbury and went straight to the Post Office. There he bought an express mail box and carefully packed the samples he had collected as per the instructions from Bradley. He sealed up the box, marked it fragile: glass, and gave it to the agent for two day delivery. Cost only eight dollars, which he thought was a good deal, especially when he considered that he might be paying forty or fifty thousand dollars for the DNA profiling.

After he left the post office, when he got back to his office in Bristol, he decided he would give Bradley a call to tell them him his package was on its way.

"Great, when I see the materials, I'll make up an invoice for the work and send it to you. Looks like it will be five tests then, right?"

"No, I think only four. The test and results of the old bones have already been done. I sent them to you earlier."

"Oh yes. Thanks for that. We'll get right on it. I'll send you the invoice by e-mail."

The rest of the afternoon, Will was feeling triumphant. He was making real progress, moving forward the collection of materials needed for the Nantiquak application. It excited him and he began thinking about making love to Minnie that evening as he was driving all the way back to Washington. He began flirting and seducing her almost from the moment he arrived home when he found her in the bedroom changing out of her professional clothes. But she pushed away his advances just then. Minnie wanted to go out to eat just at that time because there was nothing to fix for dinner in the refrigerator. She had not had any lunch. So later that evening he pulled her to the bed and began the seductive cycle that was part of their love making. They reached their ecstatic peaks almost at the same time, an occurrence that was happening more and more often in their love making. He wanted more, but Minnie fell asleep. He watched her breasts heaving gently up and down for a long time but then he covered her up and went to the kitchen for a drink.

The remainder of that week, while Will was driving to Bristol and carrying on with both his business and the preparations for the Nantiquak, Minnie had to drive up to Baltimore where she was contributing to the testimony and arguments of the their case in hearings at the court up there. She expected that she would be there each day all day long through Friday afternoon. And on those next two evenings when she got back home, she told Will how exhausted she was. This gave Will the idea of attending an Orioles baseball game with Minnie. He hadn't seen one game all that season so far, and the Orioles were playing that evening. He could drive up to Camden Yards and meet Minnie and introduce her to the game of baseball.

Of course having come straight from hearings at the court, Minnie was overdressed for the game. She thought the stands were rather dirty and littered, and the crowds by contrast to her were shabbily dressed men, most of them pot-bellied, wearing frayed, faded jeans or shorts and worn tee shirts and baseball caps.

"Baseball, for the spectator, is mostly about sitting outdoors in the good weather," said Will as he started to explain the game, "enjoying a beer or two, hot dogs, companionship of other fans, sharing news, the general banter in the stands. Almost everything besides the actual events of the game. Each team gets nine turns at bat, when their entire team sits down and one man tries to hit a small ball out of reach of the other team which defends the field. It's a pretty static game actually and for long periods it seems like only two players are playing. That one in the center who hurls the ball at the batter, and the one with the white bat who tries desperately to hit the ball and not get hit himself."

"Do you like this game?" asked Minnie in disbelief.

"Well, I liked it a lot when I played it in high school. But I found out that it's a totally different game from the perspective of the spectator."

So they watched the game as the evening turned to twilight and then faded into night as the stadium high powered lamps came on and the swarms of flying bugs and insects appeared around the haloes of those lamps. There was noise and ruckus in the stands that did not seem to have any relationship to what was happening on the field. It was the Orioles playing the Cleveland Indians. And when Minnie looked closely at the Cleveland team mascot on their uniform she exclaimed,

"I really don't like that racist logo for the Cleveland team. It's disgusting."

"Yeah, I can understand what you mean. It's an old artifact of a different age in America. And it should no longer be used. But the depiction used to be worse. They have toned down the racist elements over recent years."

"You mean it used to be worse? A more exaggerated crooked nose, bigger teeth?"

"Yes, it was worse. And I understand that they changed the skin color of that fellow who they called Chief Wahoo, from ocher yellow to that tone of red, but that was long ago."

"It's disgusting. Insult and condescension everywhere you go."

"Yeah. But I think all the cultural associations with Indians or native Americans, is mostly fading away."

"You mean people no longer call us savages?"

"Yeah, and more important I think people no longer think of Indians as being savages they were labeled from the 17th century until early in this century. I, for example, I have never noticed anything the least bit savage about you." Will said with a sly smile.

Minnie hit Will hard in the shoulder where his scars were.

"Ow, now that hurt."

"Sorry. I shouldn't take my anger out on you."

"Maybe you'd like a beer?"

"No, not really."

"I'll get one then for myself. But I have to admit, their beer here is not nearly as good as what Tony makes."

Sometime later, in the middle game, Will asked Minnie about the progress of their case against Maryland.

"It seems to be going well. The defense cannot show any reasons or justifications for the sale of reservation land by the state of Maryland. We were scoring major points all week long. And the judge's instructions point to a favorable ruling too. Next week both legal teams are going to start negotiations on how to compensate the Nantiquaks."

"That's sounds promising."

"I think it is. But we'll see. I'm not sure if I have to participate in the negotiations. But I'll know on Monday."

The game itself was a bore, very static. In the nine innings only one run was scored and only two hits occurred. Even the players on both teams appeared bored and lethargic. When it was all over, the spectators, including Will and Minnie, slouched out of the stadium slowly and sullenly.

"I have to admit, Will. That did not seem very interesting or worth the time and effort to come up here. I can't say I understand baseball or like it much either."

"I think with that game, I have to agree with you. I've always felt it was more fun to play the game than to watch the game."

"Maybe we can go home and not to Hampton Farm tonight?"

"Yeah sure we can. Sorry about the baseball."

"It's okay, Will. You were only trying to please me. I still love you."

They drove out together to Bristol on Saturday and after lunch at the Poseidon Palace, they went on to the Hampton Farm. Everything was quiet out there, no sign of Max or any of the other farmhands. The barn was chained and locked closed. In the distance the burnt yellow stalks of corn could be seen; to Will's eye even at that distance, the corn definitely seemed stunted and shorter than in past years. Outside it was very hot and stuffy, but when they stepped in the farmhouse, it was cool and dry, very refreshing and comfortable. They agreed to go canoeing the next day.

Out on the Choptico they paddled for an hour or so upstream from the rental place on Indian Creek, then they paddled across the river to Bermuda Point where there was the sandy beach and a firm bottom. It was there that they got in the water and splashed and cooled off. But Minnie still did not swim. She really does not know how to swim thought Will. After cooling off they paddled back across the river to the same place where Will had dunked her a few months earlier. Minnie remained in her swimsuit with her broad sunhat protecting her head and neck. There they decided to have lunch in the shade of the lone oak tree. The sun was intense and the temperature had gone up just in two hours. They ate and drank and then again jumped in the water to cool off, but it wasn't as nice as on the other bank. The mud was too gooey and deep, and they sank up to their ankles. They got out, and Will pulled out a bottle of one of Tony's beers from the cooler. Minnie accepted the beer and then lay back in the shade and promptly fell asleep. Will drank more of the beer and sat admiring Minnie's figure in the black one piece swimsuit. They had not made love the night before because her period bleeding had started and she was still against sex when she was bleeding. But looking at her reclined like a Greek goddess from all the old paintings and images, he thought of slipping off her swimsuit and making love to her there and then in the open air. But after a imagining a number of fantasies about doing just that he restrained himself. He knew she would not like that at all. And she was so sexy lying there. He adored looking at her, and it was enough just to study her dozing form. After a long while, he noticed that maybe a dozen, little orange and black-winged butterflies were flying around her head. Some were landing on her hair, apparently to lap up the beads of water from her hair. Butterflies get thirsty too, he thought. One butterfly even landed on her right eyebrow. As if they were kissing her, he thought. He did not attempt to wave them away, and they did not disturb Minnie in her sleep. It left an indelible image in Will's mind's eye. Canoeing with Minnie would always thereafter be the image of the sleeping woman in a black one piece swimsuit with a crown of little butterflies.

When Minnie woke up, the butterflies dispersed as she sat up. She looked at Will in a strange way.

"I'm so hot. Let's cool off in the water again."

They carefully stepped back into the river trying to avoid the deepest muddy spots. They moved out until the water was up to their waists and then Minnie dunked herself and stayed crouched in the water which lapped at her shoulders.

"I had such a vivid, bizarre dream. In it, I was sleeping, naked. I dreamt that you were hovering over me, like flying with wings, and that you somehow picked me up and kissed me. And then you made love to me as you were hovering above me in the sky. And then you let me down in a bank of clouds. And they were hot, but comfortable.

And then you flew off, but I was suspended in the sky on the clouds. Strange. Don't you think?"

"Yes. But I can tell you that there were butterflies kissing you while you slept?"

"What? Really?"

"Yeah, real butterflies. Thirsty, kissing you with their long proboscis, wanting to share the water on your head."

"Where are they?"

"They flew away."

"You're kidding me again."

"No, I am serious. It was real, just like your dream. It occurred."

They got out of the water a bit refreshed. Minnie wrapped a towel around her and took off her bathing suit and put on her clothes under the towel, still uncomfortable to bare herself in front of Will in the open air. Will merely tore off his swim trunks and stood naked to the sky. When he pulled off his trunks, he already had a strong erection, and he pranced around Minnie, laughing and teasing her by tugging at her towel as she tried to dress.

"I am just trying to fly and carry you away." he joked.

But after a few moments he stopped his naked dance and got dressed quickly, still wet from the river. More sober, they carefully loaded up the canoe and after Minnie stepped into the bow and took up her paddle, Will pushed the canoe back out into the stream and hopped in. They slowly paddled back to the boat dock.

The next week, Will decided to go to Indian River again to meet Carmine at the Association offices to kick off the writing of the application for recognition. But before he even could call Carmine, he got a call at the office from a potential buyer looking to buy a house along the water, preferably in Bristol. He made an appointment to meet this buyer, but the latter could only come to Bristol on the weekend. So Will signed him up for a Sunday morning appointment and possible showings. And then almost before he could register that bit of extra work, he got another call from a potential client, a seller. But this time it was his least favorite type of seller, it was an old man named Joshuah Taylor who wanted to sell his sizeable farm that he could no longer work and who would leave the county in retirement. Over the previous six years that he had run his real estate brokerage agency, these were always the saddest stories. Farming was on the retreat in the county, and farmers were not leaving their farms to their offspring. The case of Hampton leaving the farm to him was the rare exception. When Will asked the man where exactly the farm was located, the man, in a very frail voice said, "Just north of Exeter on Indiantown Road. Do you know the Hammond House?"

"Yes, of course I do. It's a historical monument in the county."

"Well my farm encloses all the lands you can see around the Hammond House."

This lifted Will's heart a little. This farm was exactly adjacent to his plot of land, his neighbor in other words, and it lay smack in the middle of the lands that were once in the Nantiquak reservation for the Kuskowarok, the so called Chacogoan Indian town and tract, and these lands were the subject of their lawsuit against the state.

"You know it could take a long time to sell your farm? There hasn't been much demand for farm land in the past few years."

"I figured that might be the case."

"Like it could take a year or more to find a buyer. Have you brought in your harvest yet?"

"No, I didn't plant it this year. All the fields are fallow. I just don't have the stamina or capital to farm any more."

"I understand. This year has been a hard year also. So maybe you made the right decision. Well, I can come out to your place and we can meet and discuss the situation. Would you be able to do that?"

"Yes, thad be swell."

They set a time on Wednesday at 11:30 for them to meet and Will got off the line again. He had clearly forgotten for just a moment that the last full week before Labor Day was also the second most active time of year in his line of business. Both buyers and sellers looking to get in a transaction before Thanksgiving started their search at this time in late summer. Will thought he would just have to fit this seasonal surge in demand into his schedule for work on the Injun Project. Brokerage was still, after all, his principal source of income. After he hung up on Mr. Taylor the farmer, Will finally got around to calling Carmine. She was open to getting together on Wednesday or Thursday. So Will suggested Thursday and they agreed. And he sat down at his office desk and turned on his computer. But even before he could go to fix himself a coffee, an e-mail landed in his in-box. It was from the Genetic Tree of Life and was an invoice. Will opened it eagerly and read through the invoice. What an unexpected relief. The invoice was for a lot less money than he had expected. For the four new DNA profilings, they wanted thirty-two thousand dollars. And for the work linking and comparing those profiles with the genetic code of the old Nantiquak bones, they wanted another five thousand, three hundred. And for the genetic ancestry report they wanted one thousand four hundred dollars. Altogether their work would cost him (or the tribe) thirty eight thousand, seven hundred dollars—a lot less than he had estimated. And, he noticed, the invoice indicated that they would have all the reports ready in two weeks. He felt a rising eagerness to see the results which seemed to be so soon now. He wrote a check for the amount and put it on the pile for the letters to take to the post office. He paused a moment as he was writing it—he had never before written a check for such a large sum of his own money and it suddenly grabbed him and gave him a momentary shock.

That evening at home he told Minnie about the Taylor's interest in selling his farm and he told her how it occupied the biggest and best known Nantiquak settlement and was afterwards the heart of the first reservation.

"Have any archeological works been done on that property?" she asked.

"I surely don't know, but I'll ask Mr. Taylor on Wednesday."

"Because, you know, it seems that an important part of your application is a report from an anthropologist who has done work on your tribe. The Bureau even keeps an anthropologist on the staff of the Recognition Department. She checks to see if there have been anthropological studies done on the tribe. And that is mostly supported by archeological findings."

"Really? I'll have to ask Hank, I mean, Professor Alvey if he knows of any anthropologists who've worked on the Nantiquak." Will paused. "Come to think of it I could ask that archeologist who is working on the old bones out near Salisbury if he has an anthropologist working with him."

"I never understood the requirement myself." Minnie continued. "An anthropologist can only fill in some of the pre-history of an Indian tribe. And that means patterns on pottery, types of clothing, diet, that sort of thing. I think you're DNA findings from those bones, are much more important. We've been warned with our application that we don't have enough anthropological information, but we couldn't afford to hire a professional anthropologist. And if no studies have been done, then that's that, even though our tribe has lots of historical material going right back to 1607."

"Well the Nantiquaks don't have too much of that. Maybe you could this weekend give a professional consultation as part of your NAILS advisory work on how to best write the application. Maybe over at the Association on Indian River?"

"Yes, I think I could do that. And put it to chargeable time too."

"I think it would only be me and Carmine attending. But she needs some guidance and support."

"No, I understand. No one is ever prepared or experienced in putting together one of these application documents. Some tribes which apply hire professional consultants to do for them what you're doing. And usually those consultants are Indian lawyers who have done the work for their own tribe before."

The next day, Will remembered to call Hank Alvey. As he half expected, but feared also, the phone was answered by what sounded like Susanna's voice. But instead of giving Will bad news about Hank's decease or total incapacity, she said he'd be glad to speak to Will, just hold the line. And she brought Hank to the phone.

"Hey, Will. Long time, haven't heard from you."

"And you sound like you're feeling better."

"I certainly am. They changed my medication and it's been effective. Added two years to my life. That's a joke. So how is your Injun Project?"

"We've incorporated the greater tribe in Delaware including all the small outlying remnants in Maryland. And we have taken Maryland to court to restore the tribe's reservations which were unlawfully sold. And we're getting ready to file the application for federal recognition."

"What's that?"

"That's the only way for Indians today to become an officially recognized Indian tribe."

"Wow, you've done a lot since we last talked."

"And did you know that archeologists have uncovered a large tell quite near you there in Wicomico County and that they found the ossuary—we call them 'Old Bones'—of the Nantiquak that are almost 650 years old?"

"Really? That's amazing. No, I did not hear that. No one ever tells me anything like that these days, and that is not the type of development that gets into the news."

"And what is more, I have had them DNA tested and they showed that they are Nantiquak Indians. We'll call them the baseline DNA for the tribe."

"They can do that? That really is amazing. What science can do these days. It's amazing. Fantastic."

"Yes, it is. And I wanted to ask you if while doing your book on the Nantiquak if you ran across any professional anthropologist who had dug into the tribe's pre-history culture?"

"Yes, there was one girl, a young woman. She was not long out of graduate school then. But you understand that was even before I had finished writing my book, way back in the early seventies. I don't remember her name. I'd have to look it up. You think she can help you?"

"I don't know, frankly. But we might need the services of an anthropologist

"Well, I will search my records and see if I can still find her name. I think, if I recall correctly, she was a specialist in the tribes of the Virginia Tidewater at the time of the first English colony at Jamestown. That's right she worked at that time at the Jamestown Foundation, specializing on the Powhatan Indians."

"You mean the Powhatan Federation."

"Yes, that's it. Say, maybe you could come out here and visit me sometime. We could just talk. And I'd like to learn more about what you're doing for the Nantiquaks."

"I'd be glad to, Hank. I'm out your way about once a month. I'll call you."

"Fine. If I find the name of that girl, I'll call you first and tell you. But I suppose she wouldn't be a girl anymore. More likely a mature matron and full professor somewhere. It was a long time ago."

Afterwards Will then called Dr. Houlder and caught him up on the progress he was making on the DNA genetic ancestry links. But he wanted the contact phone number of the head archeologist who they had met out at the burial mound near Salisbury the previous month. Dr. Houlder sent Will right back the full name of the man and his cell phone number through a text message. When Will then called that name from his cell phone, a man answered and acknowledged that he was the self-same. Will told him that he was looking for any anthropologists that he might know of that had worked on the Nantiquak Indian tribe's cultural background.

"Oh yes, I know of just the man. He's Davis Thompson, and he's working with me here in this dig just as we speak. He previously worked on some Nantiquak materials from findings that were made twenty five years ago. He normally works at Jamestown. Would you like to speak to him, right now, while he's here next to me?"

"Yes, sure."

"Davis Thompson speaking."

"Mr. Thompson. My name is Will Eames of Bristol, Maryland, about thirty miles from where you are just now. I'm working on a project to get official recognition for the Nantiquak tribe of the Eastern Shore. And as part of the petition document we need to file with the Bureau of Indian Affairs, we need a statement or summary report on the anthropological and cultural background of the tribe. Would you be the man who could produce such a report for the Nantiquak?"

"No, I don't think so. I know what you mean. I have produced such a summary report for a few Virginian Indian tribes. But the right person to ask is Professor Susan Broadhead at Richmond University. She has co authored with me a number of studies about the Nantiquak's pre-history. And we have written a book together too on the anthropological foundations of the Powhatan tribal confederation. If you like, I can send you her coordinates."

Yes, thad be helpful, I think. I would like to speak with her. So can you send me or text me her details to this number? And could you send me the name of that book that you said you co-wrote with her?"

"Yes, I could do that. But not just now. My hands have too much dirt on them just at this moment. And I have her contact numbers in my cell phone."

When Will got off the line, he felt pleased that he had accomplished something important; easily. But of course all he had done was to have tracked down a reference.

He was on the road back to 'Warshington' listening to country music he didn't recognize when he got a call on his cell phone from Hank. Although he knew that it was not recommended and considered dangerous to talk on a cell phone while driving, Will took the call. It was Hank. In his reedy, weak voice, he greeted Will and told him he had found the reference to that anthropologist girl he had told him about earlier.

"Just wanted to let you know that her name is Susan Broadhead. And I think she teaches at Old Dominion University in Norfolk. And I was right when I told you she's no longer a girl. She must be in her fifties, late fifties."

"Good. Thanks, Hank, for that lead. I'll look her up. Can't talk right now. I'm almost on the Bay Bridge. But thanks for finding her name."

Now that he had Professor Broadhead's reference from two different sources, he'd have to look her up and try to talk to her about the needs of the Nantiquak Indians. He wondered if Minnie had ever heard of her, or come across her name in the applications of Virginia tribes. He would try to contact Professor Broadhead on Wednesday. But he didn't have to look far for her contact numbers. Even as he was sitting down to dinner with Minnie, his cell phone rang with the incoming text message from Davis Thompson which had the Professor's addresses, phone numbers, email address, and even had the name of the book she had written on the Tidewater Indians of the Powhatan Confederation. Will smiled his smile of triumph.

"What is it, Willeames?" asked Minnie, curious as to why Will was suddenly smiling so jollily.

"I think I have found the best qualified anthropologist for helping out on our Project. You know, you said we needed the stamp of authority of an anthropologist for our application document. I have found one."

"Oh, really. Someone who has conducted work on the Nantiquak tribe?"

"Yep. I think the only anthropologist up to now who has."

"Well, if she will contribute an article to your application, I think it will help immensely."

"What did you do for the anthropological section of the Massoponax application?"

"Nothing. There was nothing we could do. We did not have any anthropological studies done on our tribe, and we couldn't afford to hire an anthropologist to write one."

"Did you run across a Professor named Susan Broadhead while you were studying at the University of Richmond?"

"No. The name is not familiar to me. I was at the law school don't forget. I didn't have any time for anthropology."

Will later that evening, before they began necking and the ritual of caressing and petting that led to love making in the bedroom, took out his laptop computer and looked up on Amazon, that new internet book store, if there were any of Broadhead's books still in print and available. And he found just the one; it was her magnum opus on the Powhatan Confederation. He right away ordered it. It would be part of Minnie's birthday present. Maybe she could use it to supplement her tribe's application to the BIA. This sudden rush of the excitement of discovery spurred him on when Minnie approached him purring and ready for his advances.

The next day, he eagerly drove into the lane that led up to Mr. Taylor's farm. He was especially interested as the farm sat on the very heart of the original Nantiquak reservation from three hundred years ago, and also on the remains of what was the largest Indian settlement of the Eastern Shore, at least it was when Captain John Smith first visited in 1608. Mr. Taylor surprised Will. He was expecting a frail, weakly old man, but instead of a wan shrunken ninety year old, he found a man who looked in ruddy health, was short but still looked strong, and in spite of his weak reedy voice, had a joyous outlook and eyes that sparkled.

"Hi, I'm Will Eames, your local friendly realtor."

"Say, you're probably related to my old friend Hampton Eames, I suppose?"

"He was my great uncle. But he passed away."

"Oh yes, I heard that he had died. Not too long ago. Sad. A great man, and a really fine friend and fabulously successful farmer. But we all have to go sometime."

"That is true. You know that I now own the farm? Hampt left it to me for reasons that are still beyond me."

"No I didn't know."

"And I am the owner of the plot adjacent to yours directly on the river?"

"You mean the plot in the marsh that the Old Injun Pell Randell owned?"

"Yeah, so you knew Pellmell too, Mr. Taylor?"

"Yeah, he worked on my farm here for nearly forty years. But call me Josh, please. Now I need to ask you: 'Would you like some ice tea?' before we forget our social niceties altogether."

Over iced tea Josh Taylor gave Will all the details about the farm and the old house, which he built sixty years earlier. He even told him that he had made a nine hundred thousand dollar profit the previous year from corn and garden vegetables— green beans, peas, and sweet corn-- for sale to supermarkets on the Western Shore.

Josh then led him on a tour of the two story Victorian house. All the rooms looked clean but unused, both upstairs and downstairs.

"It looks like you don't live here."

"I don't. I haven't lived in this house for the past nine years, since my wife died. It's too big for me. Too many echoes. Too many stairs. I moved into a smaller, one story house in Exeter and come out here only to supervise the farm work."

"But you say you farmed this land until last season?"

"Yep, all seventeen hundred acres, young man. We farmed it all. Except for the two acres that are around the Hammond House. That's more than two and a half square miles. But it's been a lot of hard work over the years."

"Yes, I can imagine. How did you manage it by yourself?"

"For a number of years, my sons worked it with me. But they both left when they saw that there was no future in it for them. I have used a lot of Injun labor. As I said, Pell worked for me along with several of his fellow Injun tribesmen, for many years. Also I have had a good contract farmer working for me, as the main farm manager. But I won't hire any of these Hispanics who've been coming here in recent years. Why should I? They have no commitment to the area."

"It's a big farm, and it will be hard to find a buyer. Not everyone in the county with sizeable farms is making a profit you know."

"I know too well. Almost every five years, the markets change. What worked ten years ago hasn't worked for the past five years, and what has worked since then already is not working out so well now."

"Speaking of the Indians next door, you know that you're sitting on the land that was their former town and reservation?"

"Yes, and do I know it. My family goes back to a man named Taylor who in the early 1700s acted as the Injun agent in this part of the county. He knew their language, and after Maryland became one of the free American states, it was another ancestor, his grandson, who swooped in to buy these lands. And you know, almost every year over the past sixty that I've been farming here, every time it seems, when I deep plow, I turn up Injun artifacts. The Hammond House was bought by my grandfather about one hundred and twenty years ago. And it is said to be sitting right on top of the old Injun capital of Chacogoan."

"What do you do with those artefacts?"

"Nothing, I keep most of them. I have a whole shed out back full of them. Lots of arrow heads, some stone axe heads—or so I think—lots of bone tools, and wood and stone clubs. Lots of pottery pieces, some painted, some just small pieces, one or two pieces where you can tell it was a pot or something. Some hardened smoothed sticks—maybe tools. Sometimes some old fabrics, like deerhide. And sometimes we'll plow into piles of animal bones, mostly deer and piles of oyster shells. I've always assumed they were kitchen middens."

"Has any academic ever looked at them?"

"No. The stuff doesn't look all that interesting. Would you like to see the stuff?"

"Sure. We've got time."

"Follow me then."

Josh sprang up. "Come with me" he said as he grabbed a set of keys that were hanging on a board by the front door. He led Will out to the back of the farmhouse where there was a building that looked like a two car garage. Taylor opened a single door on the side and stepped inside and switched on an overhead bulb. There were four rows of low tables, all spread out with what looked like nothing more than rubbish that had been sorted and classified.

"Here, here are the best pieces. In my view anyway. Some painted pieces of pottery." Taylor pointed to the right on one of the middle tables. It was clear to Will that these fragments and shards were from pots, some had bottoms and sides, some were just side walls of pots and some had pour spouts. Most had wavy painted designs on one side.

"You know I ran across the name of an experienced anthropologist who has worked here on the Eastern Shore on things Nantiquak and she might be extremely interested in these discarded pieces. Would you mind if I told her about this small treasure trove?"

"Not at all. If she wanted to take it all, I wouldn't mind that either."

"I'll tell her then. I was planning on calling her today or tomorrow."

"That would be fine by me. But if she wants to come see these things, remember I need advance notice. You know, I have always been told that the original Hammond House was built directly over the center of Chacogoan town, and for archeologists it should be interesting to dig underneath it."

"Yeah? I'll remember that."

Will was thinking that the farm with the house could easily fetch two or two and a half million dollars. No one was investing that kind of money in the county these past few years. Certainly not in farming. But he accepted the assignment and would list the property. Maybe if the Nantiquak lawsuit against the state of Maryland went successfully, the state would buy it and present it to the Nantiquak tribe. But that would depend on so many imponderables; Will daren't mention the possibility to Mr. Taylor. He drove back to his office in Bristol and entered the property in the state listing system. If there was any interest, the potential interested buyer would have to come to him.

After lunch, Will started trying to reach Susan Broadhead by telephone. But he had no success that afternoon, and could not leave any messages either. He'd have to try again the next day. After he arrived back at his office the next morning, he again started calling Professor Broadhead. On the third try, a woman answered.

"Yes, this is she. Who is this calling?"

Will told her his name and the reason for his call. And he especially emphasized the importance of her anthropological research into the Nantiquak Indians for the application for recognition to the Bureau. She responded enthusiastically at once.

"Yes, I did some fair bit of work on those Indians twenty or thirty years ago, not long after I got out of grad school. I remember those days very fondly. You know I published a monograph on the Indians of the Eastern Shore, which means mainly the Nantiquaks?"

"No, Davis Thompson told me only about the book you co-authored with him on the Indians in the time of the Jamestown colony."

"That would be like him. So you spoke to him too?"

"Yes. He also referred me to you. He's working now on a new find of Nantiquak bones in a mound near Salisbury. He's very excited to be working on them. I even had those bones tested for their DNA profile."

"Ah, new technology. There's so much more we can pry out of digs these days than when I first started. If you can just afford to use the new technologies."

"So here's the title of my book," she continued. "It may not still be in print, but it can probably be found. If not at the university publisher, then through inter-library loan."

"I was hoping to ask if you might contribute a short report about the Nantiquaks—from the anthropological perspective—that we can put in our application."

"I'm very busy just now. I would have to go back into my writings and field reports to be able to write something now."

"Perhaps we can pay you as a contributing consultant for your article? A small honorarium, or a consulting fee for your efforts?"

"That would be helpful. But you know my research only concerned a material culture and a spiritual culture that haven't survived. They are historical and even pre-historical artefacts. I can't imagine how it would help any consideration by bureaucrats today for the tribe's eligibility for federal recognition."

"No, I can't either. But it is a requirement that they have imposed. And we have to supply them with this information."

"So by when do you need this summary report?"

"I was hoping by no later than the end of October," said Will. "I think we should make a consulting contract to get things started, where we can put in the requirements and delivery conditions. And we would put your remuneration. I might suggest a fee of four thousand dollars. Would that suit you?"

"Oh, that would be very suitable," she responded enthusiastically. "Perhaps too much. I would not be doing any new research. Just summarizing and compressing what I did earlier. But send me an email with the draft of a contract that you think is appropriate and we'll discuss this further. Let me give you my e-mail address."

"I think in our application document, we would acknowledge you as the author of this part. We would also want to cite your book, as well. That would be alright, wouldn't it?"

"Yes, I believe so. I have never done this before—writing a summary report for a tribe's application for recognition. But I would be pleased to help in this little way. By the way you said that Professor Alvey was the one who pointed you my direction. How is he doing, if he is still alive?"

"Hank, is still living, although he is very ill. He seems to feel he is terminally ill. He's weak and is looked after by a nurse-care giver in his house, but he still is quite lucid and still remembers a lot about the book he wrote. And he remembers you only as an attractive young girl straight out of college, first time getting your hands dirty."

Broadhead giggled on the line. "I'm glad to hear it. He was a spicey one when I was working there. He was always I think flirting with me, even though he seemed to me at the time an old codger."

"Well, then, he's still an old codger." said Will jokingly. "Only older now."

"He was such a nice man."

"I think so too."

"Give him my best memories and regards when you next speak with him."

"I will."

Straight off the phone line he wrote a short e-mail to Professor Broadhead giving her all his contact numbers intending by that to check that a connection was made. He got a bounce back reply that his email was delivered. And a couple hours later, he got an indication that she had opened it. But by then he had already started drafting a contract for her work. He sent the contract off to her even before he left for home again-- he was less and less referring to his commute as a drive to Warshington. He now referred to his commute as a drive coming from and going back home.

Also that afternoon, Will checked on the Amazon website again for the book Professor Broadhead called a monograph. And he was surprised to find that it was listed and it was available for sale from an antique books dealer. He was surprised that it had not shown up in the search he had undertaken the night before. It was expensive—he thought a sixty dollar book was very expensive—and delivery would take several weeks but he immediately ordered it for the promptest delivery he could get. We can use this in a citation, he thought to himself. And it should go to the Nantiquak Indian Corporation to put in the tribe's offices. Maybe someone in the tribe might even read it, after he finished reading it, of course.

The next day on his way up to the Association offices near Millville, Will stopped in to see the progress of the build-out of the Corporation headquarters in Beaverton. He was gratified to see that now nearly everything was finished and that most of the finished rooms were painted, or tiled, and cleaned and ready for furnishing and occupancy. The water was connected, the toilets flushed, the electric sockets were all live and someone had even brought a few folding chairs and a folding table. Now it was time to begin furnishing and equipping the offices. He would need to put the issue of funding such furnishing and equipping on the next extraordinary board meeting which was going to be on the Saturday before Labor Day. They would need to present a preliminary budget, but they couldn't do that until the Corporation officers had met to agree what kind of furnishings they wanted, the number of computers and printers that they needed, the telephone service they would like, the lighting fixtures and lamps, and painting the name on the front window. And someone was needed to draft a simple corporate emblem. He was one of the officers, as was Carmine, and Morley, but he needed to get them together at the same time, along with President Chief Clarke to discuss plans for the lay-out. And getting all them together before the board meeting was not going to be easy.

This issue was the first thing he spoke of with Carmine when she finally showed up, about thirty minutes late, at the Association offices. She was breathless and apologetic. She had had a hard time getting away from her regular job as a law clerk up in Centerville and then she had to speed down the ten miles to get there. Her first reaction to Will's pressing for the office furnishing was to dwell on the secondary issue.

"I think I know of one of our women who is a really good artist who could design a tribal logo for us. I'll ask her. She's done some of the art work for the advertisements for our powwow."

"That be good. But when do you think we can get all of us officers in one place to begin talking about what you all want for the Corporation offices?"

"I don't know. I will just have to call around. Would next Tuesday suit you? Near the end of the day?"

"Yes, I suppose so. But Minnie won't like it. As I probably won't be able to get back home that evening."

"You mean in Bristol?" Carmine asked with a confounded expression on her face.

Will suddenly realized that he had let slip that Minnie and he were living together.

"Yeah, Bristol." Will stammered. "She is planning on giving me a call that evening after dinner to consult on the progress they are making in preparing the next civil suit."

Carmine suspected that Will meant something different. Maybe they were going to have a date, she thought.

"So you call around and see if you can get these guys together on Tuesday. I'll get a catalogue from Staples that will give us prices for the office furniture and equipment and bring it with me. And we can then make our preliminary design of how they want the offices to look and how much it might cost to make a functioning office. I know we will need at least one computer with accounting software and a printer for the accountant. By the way has anyway advertised yet for a full time accountant or bookkeeper? We already have accounts and turnover."

"No, I don't think any advertising has been placed."

"Well, I guess that's another item for the board to discuss and take care of. Now let's sit down and see if we can't write an outline of our application document."

Will gave a yellow legal pad to Carmine and took one for himself and picked up a pen.

They spent the next hour looking at the Bureau's requirements and reviewing the materials they had already collected or the records they had surveyed. The first section would be on the history of the tribe in the two centuries after Europeans first encountered them, which could easily be summarized from the two history books that had been written, one of them by Professor Alvey. The place of honor in that section would be the full text of the Treaty and the Addenda which awarded the tribe its different reservations. This section would be followed by the anthropology report about the culture identity of the pre-historic Nantiquaks. This section would be followed by a second section on the tribe's history since the 1820s when most of the emigrations had finished and when the tribe began changing its organization and identity, a time when Nantiquaks began to convert to Methodism and when they completed the change from Alkongian family names to English family names, and finally when they began to seek official recognition, a move that led finally to the founding of the Association.

It was clear that Carmine was having trouble writing down what he was saying. She was not accustomed to outlining a paper or report.

Will continued. Then they would need to write a section about the census records of the tribe from the late nineteenth century. This section would need to identify by name the tribesmen that were cited in the census. "We can also introduce into this section the grave stone and church records we have," he said. "And in this section we can combine the oral genealogies that your group had been able to collect from each of the Bands, in our internal census." They had the census materials that they had found in the archive in Washington for this section. And of course the genealogical records that they had. Will thought that the results of the DNA profiling and the relationships that that profiling showed would go into this section. This would show the continuity of the tribe through many centuries. Then they would need a section on the tribe's current structure, it current members, which would be enough, Will thought, with just a list of the names of the current members, including their children, and its organization and governance rules. Then Will thought of something that wasn't in the Bureau's instructions.

"You know, we have up to this point looked at and tried to establish consanguinity as the basis for our claims of being a tribe, but we should also put into our document evidence of proximity. What the anthropologists trying to define a tribe call propinquity."

"Wait, Will, wait. What's consang eh ity? What's pro pin quin ?"

"Consanguinity is the closeness of blood relationship. So, for example, if your uncle Morley had a son he would be consanguine with you and generally, as a cousin would not be allowed to marry you."

"That's exactly what uncle wants, though. But not me."

"I'm one-eighth Nantiquak from the Kuskowarok Band, so I am not very consanguineous to you, but still related. Most societies would allow me to marry you because we are not too closely related."

"Oh, I'm glad. We could get married then?" she said with a twinkle in her eye trying to bait Will.

"Yes. But propinquity, is being physically close. For instance, it's very hard to get married if you and I live, as we do, sixty miles apart." Will replied to Carmine's lure. "Think about it. Propinquity is what the tribe demonstrates over four centuries. They have lived closely together, intermarried, and continue to live in propinquity, in close proximity to each other. It is a key cultural identity of the tribe. Like the saying, 'Geography is destiny.'"

"I see. Yes. You're saying we are a tribe because we are related by blood and because we continue to live close together. In proximity."

"Yes, that's the point. You look at any of the Indian tribes, and one of the key elements of their identity is that they chose to live together. Propinquity. Very much unlike the English colonizers who came to America. As we know their families would settle in one place, reproduce and then their children would all move to other locations or states. So they are not tribes, even though they remain related in blood."

"I understand. That's an interesting idea. That a key part of our identity is founded on our proximity, our geography." said Carmine, her face lighting up as if she had just had an eureka moment. "Pro pin quin ity."

"Propinquity. Yes."

"So we have our outline." Will continued. "Now we need to start filling in the words and writing the text to fill that outline. Are you up for it?"

"I'm not sure I am. I really don't write so well."

"Well, we'll give it a try. Say you start by writing the first section. Remember? Based on the two books the tribe has on its history since the coming of the English."

Carmine reluctantly agreed. "I'll give it a try."

"Maybe it would be easier for you to write in longhand first and then we can enter it in the computer Word program."

Later that evening, back at home, Will brought up with Minnie the issue that he had discovered."

"You know Minnie, you said a while back that you weren't sure about your tribal identity. But a key part of the ongoing identity of a native American tribe is their propinquity. Physical proximity. Members of your tribe remain living close together. Not only are they related by blood, but they remain in close propinquity. Living next to each other. Unlike white Americans who every generation move to other places in America looking for other or better opportunities. Those opportunities come before blood relationships and staying near parents, cousins, and all the other members of the extended family. What do you think of that?"

"I hadn't thought of that before. But it makes a lot of sense. We keep our own society." Minnie began thinking about the implications of Will's statement. Then her brows knotted together.

"You could say then, that when I decided to move to Richmond for my university education, that I already was leaving the tribe, because I chose to be far removed from my blood relatives. And when I then moved to work in D.C. I moved even farther away. That would seem to be the consequence of tribal life versus leaving to make my own career."

"Yes, I guess you could say that is one implication. Certainly it's the case with the Nantiquaks. Most of their numbers chose to emigrate in the eighteenth and nineteenth centuries. And they then ceased to exist as a tribe. They became something else."

Then Will had another thought: "And as you have already committed to moving away, and as you say losing that part of your tribal identity by giving up propinquity, then it would seem to me that one barrier to your marrying me would be removed. Unless of course you intend to move back to your reservation, soon."

Minnie looked sad for a moment. Her eyes were downcast and her brows knit, and she frowned.

"No I don't intend to." she finally said quietly. "I want to live with you and I want you to live with me. In close proximity."

"Well, yes, of course. But that doesn't mean that you have to cease being an Indian. It's just one key part of a continuing tribal identity in this modern day and age. But after all, you can have face to face chats over the internet, regardless how far away you live. And yes, I want to continue living with you, too. Close, like cheek to cheek. As my married wife. The proposal is still open."

Will took up her hands in his. Then he kissed them.

"Don't be so hard on yourself Minnie. You said your father moved to Bowling Green from the reservation because he found good work there. So you could say he already started the move away from the tribe. Yet he was the chief before you. I didn't know him, but I think he still thought of himself as an Indian."

Minnie smiled.

"Willeams, you're a very persuasive person, you know."

"Well, I hope so. I sell property as a living. Have to be persuasive and persistent. And I hope to persuade you. And now I need to persuade you to come to Bristol next Thursday so we can observe your birthday with a little party. With my parents and maybe my sister and her family too."

"I think I can be persuaded to do that. And you said we were leaving on vacation that weekend. So maybe I would take off Friday and we can then start our vacation with the birthday party in Bristol." Now she was smiling. "You really do love me, don't you?"

"With all my being, Minnie. I fell for you the second time I saw you."

The next day back in Bristol, Will had to think what else he would get for Minnie's birthday, which was now only a week away. He also called the yacht club to book a table and to reserve a birthday cake. The manager asked him if he would like to have a small band play for a couple hours if it was going to be a special party. He said he'd think about it. And he then called his mother to ask her if Kate agreed to come and if she might have some ideas for a birthday present. Mar-Sue said she was planning to get Minnie a nice jewelry box she had seen that was made of onyx and gold trim. That made Will think of a necklace, maybe and emerald pendant to match Minnie's emerald earrings but then he remembered he had already bought her one of those. So maybe an emerald ring. Her emerald collection would be complete. He really liked them on her, and he thought she did not have enough occasions to wear them. As soon as he got off the phone, he got a call from Jackson.

"Hey mate, long time no see. Have you got plans for the Labor Day weekend?"

"Yeah, actually on Sunday Minnie and I are heading out on a vacation trip. What's up?

"MariAnne and I were thinking of a beach weekend. Of going out on Saturday and spending the day at Assateague Beach and then having a dinner at Hopper's Crabhouse. And we thought we'd like you and your Indian girl—what was her name?—join us. Whaddaya think of that?"

"Well, sounds mighty nice. But my girl, her name is Minnie, doesn't think much of beaching. Or getting in the surf. So I think we'll pass. And Sunday we're leaving, early I hope, on our vacation. Driving down to the Smokey Mountains. But I have a counter proposal for you. Why don't you two come next Thursday to the birthday party I'm putting on for Minnie? At the yacht club."

"Oh, yeah. We'd like that. What time?"

"I was thinking of about seven o'clock."

"Okay then. We'll be there. You can count on it."

"I will, too."

Will decided to go out to the Mall in Salisbury. He could pick up the office furniture catalogue at Staples and he would go the jewelry store there that had a nice selection of emerald jewelry. The only problem he had would be that once he bought it he would want to give it to her immediately. He'd have to wait another six days and try to keep it secret too for the surprise. But when he got to the store, after choosing a nicely shaped emerald, he faced another immediate problem: the young attractive woman, maybe even still a high schooler, promptly asked, "What size ring does your woman wear?" Of course, Will did not know. He then realized that you cannot buy rings for someone else, without her presence to try them on. But he looked closely at the fingers of the attendant's hand and thought they looked the same size and shape as Minnie's.

"I'll go with the size that you might wear. Your fingers look just like hers. The size I mean."

"Don't worry if it doesn't exactly fit, you can always come back together and get it adjusted to her size, especially if it is too large, which is usually the case."

So he bought the emerald ring in a white gold setting. It could serve as a stand in for a wedding ring, until Minnie decided that she would agree to marry him, and it completed her emerald set of jewelry.

"Is it a gift? Would you like me to wrap it in a nice presentation box?"

"Yes. Please do." said Will. But as soon as he said it, he thought it would be nice to slip it in the jewelry box that mother planned to give her. But it was already wrapped.

When he got back to the office, he found that the book about the Powhatan Indians by Professor Broadhead that he had ordered for Minnie's birthday had arrived. He'd have to remember to wrap it in the next week, and that meant he had to buy giftwrap and scotch tape, maybe at the Walmart. To complete the coincidences of the day, he found an e-mail from Professor Broadhead with the signed consulting contract attached to it and a short note, saying she would start at once. Will gave a big sigh; things looked like they were falling together for their application. He spent the rest of the day occupied with the current flow of real estate offerings, which were still minimal. And shortly afterwards he got a call from Carmine just before he was about to leave. She said she had coerced the officers of the Nantiquak Corporation to meet on the Tuesday afternoon at four in the afternoon. "Would that suit you, alright?"

"Yes, that works well for me too. I got the catalogue and will bring it along. If we can agree on basic furnishings we can work up a budget to give to the board for their approval next Saturday at their meeting next week. Thanks for that. We also got Professor Broadhead's agreement to do the anthropological article for us. Just today. And she wrote that she would start writing it today."

"Oh, then I'd better start writing my part." said Carmine. "I have a hard time starting to write anything."

"I understand. I need to start my sections as well."

That weekend at the Hampton farm, Minnie asked if they couldn't go crabbing again. Will had already asked Phyllis to come and fix dinners on each of Friday, Saturday and Sunday evenings and fix a Sunday brunch of waffles. And she would stay over and do another cleaning of the place—a lot of dust had fallen over the dry summer, the blinds they had put on the downstairs windows collected dust especially quickly.

"If we get some crabs, maybe she can make crab cakes for us. She can freeze what we don't eat and if we catch a lot of crabs, we can have her special crab cakes for a couple months."

So on Friday evening before they headed for each other's arms and then the bed, they agreed to go crabbing on Saturday. Will called his father first thing the next day to ask for the boat the next day. Bob granted it and even told Will where there was a new spot where the crabs seemed to be quite numerous that summer. "I think someone sunk a cow carcass there. It's been feeding crabs ever since." said Bob. They prepared their clothes and Minnie packed her sun hat and they were just about ready to leave for the Bristol docks when Max came up onto the porch.

"I wanted to give this to you for the past two weeks but have missed you each weekend." said Max as he drew a check out of his shirt pocket. It was the check from the grain processing company at the silos in Delaware, for the soya beans Max had delivered earlier that month. It was in the amount of sixty eight thousand four hundred dollars and some change. The first revenue for the farm after more than three months of outlays.

"This is great, Max."

"But it's a small amount. Not what we usually turnover in the past few years. It's been a really bad year."

"What can we do? Buy a futures contract to insure our returns? Bet against the weather and the harvest?"

"No, I'm not saying that. But if we had irrigation we could have gotten through the drought with less losses. We also could use an application of fertilizer next spring, before the planting."

"I hear you."

"And with the hot dry weather, the corn harvest is going to come in sooner, and smaller than usual."

"When, then exactly?"

"The way things look, I think the corn will be ready to bring in around the second week in September."

"Fine." said Will. "We'll be back by then from our vacation."

Phyllis came to the farmhouse while they were still on the water and started cleaning and dusting, and straightening up in the kitchen to be ready to fix the crab cakes. They spent three hours out on the water, enough for Will to get sunburned and for them to catch twenty-two good sized blue crabs. Minnie was so pleased; she pulled up twelve of the crabs and was able to net them herself without the help of Will. She had mastered the art of pulling in the baited line in one hand and the net in the other. Bob had been right about the large number of crabs. Will decided to sell a dozen crabs to Tony before they headed back to the farmhouse, but still Phyllis was surprised at how many they brought her. "This should make eight crab cakes." she said. "How'd you like them tonight, fried or broiled?"

On Tuesday, Will drove over to the Association building near Millville, stopping by the new offices in Beaverton to look at the finished project and take measurements of the rooms. He had already made copies of the front door keys and aimed to distribute them to the other officers at this meeting. As usual discussions about what and how to furnish the offices took longer than he expected. Some of those in the group wanted to keep the office bare and furnished with the simplest and cheapest of furniture. Carmine wanted a more comfortable and professional looking office, with plusher chairs and full desks with drawers that would look less temporary than what was in the Association's office. Will came down more on her side, but was sensitive to the others' concerns about keeping costs in check. The compromise was that they would purchase for the moment more expensive chairs and desks for only three of the six rooms, steel folding chairs and tables especially for the board room, and only one computer and printer to start with. They would leave the guest bedroom upstairs unfurnished for the time being. And they would buy the rest of the furnishings as they could afford them. This collection of furniture still came to a bill of four thousand five hundred dollars. It took three hours discussion and arguments to agree to this amount. Before they left, Carmine announced that they had received a few replies to their advertised position for a bookkeeper-accountant. "Good, the board can decide on that this week when they meet." said Will. "None of them are of Indian ancestry, just as you said." said Carmine, "But one of them has worked for several years as the chief accountant of a non-profit organization up in Centreville." answered Carmine. "She looks like a good candidate."

Two days later, Will left home in D.C. with all the clothes he needed for their vacation packed in a new suitcase. Will had bought two at the Walmart's and he and Minnie had packed on Wednesday evening after walking back from dinner at their usual place on Connecticut Avenue. As they were packing it became clear that Minnie lacked a few critical pieces in her wardrobe that were needed for their vacation trip. Will understood by this time; Minnie did not like shopping for clothes, and so she had always had a minimum wardrobe, just a few suits for work and almost nothing else. Will liked buying new clothes for Minnie, but he recognized that she still did not have enough jeans, shorts, casual tops, or warm outdoors clothes. She agreed that on Friday she'd go with Will to Walmart's buy some more clothes and shoes for their vacation. On the day of her birthday she followed Will out to Bristol in her own car after spending half a day at the office.

Will met Minnie at his cottage late that afternoon when he presented her with a bouquet of red roses. Minnie giggled when he presented them. No one had ever given her such a big bouquet before. Will also had never had such a bouquet in his house for any occasion, and because of that they could not find a vase or suitable container for them in his house. The roses ended up in a cooking pot, standing in their original wrapping. Will gave Minnie the flowers, wishing her a happy birthday and, after setting them aside, hugged her deeply and began to sway and dance with her in his arms. After some time dancing to the unheard music he went into the kitchen and came out with a bottle of champagne. "You liked it the last time we had a party," he said. "There's even more reason to enjoy it now." And he poured out two glasses for the both of them.

"To Minitoka on her birthday. The woman and joy of my life." he offered as a toast. They drank up and then kissed again. Will thought Minnie was blushing a little. He poured out a second glass for each of them, and momentarily thought about making love to Minnie there and then. But he restrained himself. They would be late for her party if he followed his instincts right then. Will finished his second champagne, but Minnie put hers aside. They slid into each other's arms again and returned to slow dancing. At seven, they left the house and started walking slowly to the yacht club. It was a warm evening, maybe forty minutes from sunset, and clouds on the horizon gave the sky a gray, early twilight appearance. Will put his arm around Minnie's waist. His head was spinning from the champagne and he was feeling the warmth of Minnie's body pressed close to him. His feet seemed not to touch the ground, or at least the ground had suddenly seemed to go soft under his feet. He was sure that he had never felt so comfortably happy before. He wanted the sensation to last forever. But the yacht club was still only a twenty minute walk away, even ambling slowly.

His parents were waiting for them when they finally arrived. As were Jackson and MariAnne. As in May, Will poured around the leftover champagne from the half finished bottle he brought with him. Then altogether they wished Minnie a happy birthday. She smiled a smile half a mile wide, her green brown eyes sparkled. "This is so nice." she said. She even allowed Will to embrace her and gave him a big full on the mouth kiss in front of his parents. Just at that instant the clouds must have lifted off the horizon just as the sun slipped down. It threw a sudden, surprisingly golden light over them and across the river it seemed to enflame the tree tops. It was as if someone had switched on a strong yellow light overhead. Everyone was amazed by the quality of this strange golden light. "Someone is signaling you his birthday greetings too." said Bob. Dinner flashed by, it seemed to Will. He was so hungry and the food so delicious. Each ordered their own entrée dish, but all had sweet white corn on the cob. He had asked for the kitchen to prepare a baked Alaska cake for Minnie's birthday cake. And while they were waiting for dessert, the others presented Minnie with their birthday gifts. She opened the gift proffered by Mar Sue. It was a fair-sized rectangular jewelry box made of polished serpentine stone.

"Hey, it's green like Minnie's eyes." said Will in surprise.

"That's why I got it, son. It matches her eyes and the emeralds you've given her."

"Yes, I will put my emeralds in it, proudly." said Minnie.

"And from now on you're to put all of your precious and beautiful things in this box." said Mar Sue.

"And I have just the thing." said Will as he handed her the small wrapped box.

"What is it?" asked Minnie as she started to open it.

"A ring." Minnie uttered. "And emerald again." She tried it on and it fit her ring finger snugly.

"How did you know my ring size?" she asked.

"Good guess, I guess. Just think of it as an engagement ring."

Minnie lifted her hand and looked at it closely. Then she showed it around.

"You mean you two are not married yet?" asked MariAnne in a concerned voice.

"No." said Will. "I've got to convince her to marry me still. I've asked but she still hasn't accepted."

"Oh, marry this guy, Minnie ." MariAnne replied looking surprised. "There are no better than Will, available men, I mean." she said as she hit Jackson on the shoulder.

"Oh, it's so beautiful." said Mar Sue. "And it matches the emerald choker you're wearing."

"And I have matching earrings too." said Minnie. "Will also got them for me." Minnie was feeling like a little girl again with the birthday party and the suspense of opening wrapped birthday gifts.

"Are you going to live then in the Emerald City?" asked Bob. "You know the one, in the Land of Oz, where the wizard lives." And then he faintly chuckled at his own joke. No one else thought it was a joke. It seemed a strange thing to say.

"No I don't think so. I'm living here with Will and in D.C. with Will. He's no wizard, but there's something magical about him. I'll wear the emeralds though and keep them in this lovely box when I'm not wearing them."

"So you should agree to marry him." said Mar Sue. "And remain living with him. You can have a family, and you can paint your house green and put in green tinted glass in the windows."

Minnie blushed. And she looked to Will for a sign about how she might answer Mar Sue.

"And here's a second birthday gift for you." said Will handing over to her a book shaped package.

Minnie took it and slowly ripped open the wrapping paper. It was the big anthropological study of the Powhatan confederation by Susan Broadhead. She immediately opened it and starting leafing through the pages, stopping at a printed map of the Western Shore and the three peninsulas.

"Look, this even shows the towns of the Massoponax and of the Doeg correctly on the middle peninsula." said Minnie.

"I saw it, and I thought you could use it in your tribe's application to the BIA. As a supplement." said Will. "To successfully complete your own Indian Project."

"Will, you really are sweet. This is the nicest gift I've ever gotten." Minnie closed the book and reached over to kiss Will again.

"And we have a gift for you too." said MariAnne. She handed Minnie a wrapped package that was apparently a very thick book. Minnie opened it and then held it up to show the others. The title was 'Cases and Commentaries on American Indian Law.'

"I saw in the trade news that this book was just published." said Jack. "It's very authoritative and it's gotten good reviews. I thought you could find it useful in your current position. So I grabbed it right away. Boring bedtime reading for you, I think, but it will be only for nights when Will's away."

"Nights when Will is away? You mean that will happen?" said Minnie. Jack did not answer what he thought was a rhetorical question.

She thanked him. "It's like most case books." she said. "A thousand pages of text. It'll take me ten years to read it all! Thank you so much, Jack. It'll go to the center of my library at work. We don't have any such case books at my office."

"I told you she'd like it." said Jack, more to MariAnne than to Minnie. "It's brand new. Just came out. Only another lawyer, like myself, and especially a lawyer who is an Indian could appreciate how important it is to you."

"Books and jewels. I'll be damned." said Bob. "I got you a more frivolous, mundane gift. Nothing so valuable. But maybe you'll use them next week." Bob handed Minnie a plain blue box without gift wrap which was a little bigger than the ring box she had gotten from Mar-Sue. Minnie opened the box and looked inside and saw three tiny clusters of feathers and thread, but she didn't know what she was looking at. Her expression showed consternation and she looked up to Bob as if asking him what the contents were.

"I understood from Will that you're going to learn how to fly fish for trout on your vacation to the Carolina mountains. So I got you these three flies. They're very special. They're made to look like juicy select insects which trout like to eat. And they float on the water's surface." Minnie held one up to show everyone. "They are so pretty."

"Careful, they're delicate but there's still a sharp little hook in those feathers." said Bob. "If you like fly fishing, you can even learn how to tie these flies yourself. No one around here does that much."

"Thank you so much, Bob. I don't know what to expect next week, but these look very nice."

Will looked at the flies. "They're so small. My fingers are too big to tie such things."

"You have to use tweezers." said Bob. "But I bet you Minnie's fingers are delicate enough to tie the smallest of flies."

The waiter brought out the baked Alaska cake and set it on the table in front of them. There were no birthday candles on the cake. The waiter instead gently ladled a cup of rum over the meringue and carefully ignited it with a long match. The cake flared up in a soft blue flame. Will began to sing the 'Happy Birthday' song and the rest joined in. Soon other diners also joined in singing Happy Birthday. The flames burned themselves out shortly after they finished singing. And the whole restaurant gave a cheer and applause for Minnie. The flame added additional brown streaks of caramel to the brown highlights which were already on the cake.

"How old are you Minnie?" asked MariAnne with a sly look on her face.

Minnie blushed but promptly answered, "Thirty five. I'm so old."

"Oh, that can't be. You don't look any older than me, and I'm only twenty seven years old."

"Really? So old?" Jack asked MariAnne in jest.

"I'm afraid to disappoint you, but I am older than you, and older than Will too."

"Really? How do you manage to keep your figure and skin looking so young?" MariAnne asked in dismay.

"Undoubtedly, a secret Injun formula." said Bob jokingly. "And her hair remains so black too. Mine was already turning gray at that age."

"I don't think she looks old at all." said Mar Sue. "Certainly not old, not like me."

Meanwhile the waiter took a long sharp knife and carefully sliced through the meringue and ice cream and served Minnie a thick slice. He wiped the knife blade clean and cut slices for everyone. Will loved this masterful confection; the blend of ice cream, crispy chocolate, yellow cake and thick caramelized meringue which stuck to his fork seemed the most special and exquisite cake he had ever eaten. When the waiter came back to the table and asked if there would be anything else, Will asked for a cold bottle of champagne to be brought. "I propose a toast to the birthday girl." said Will. "To the sweetest girl born on this day, I wish you happiness and love." They all raised their flute glasses full of the bubbly chilled wine, and then drank up. Even Minnie drank hers. They kissed again passionately this time. Then Will pulled her from the table to join him in dancing to the music that a trio was playing in the far end of the room. Jack and MariAnne joined them in dancing. Minnie and Will danced slowly and pressed close together through four songs. Will breathed in the warm, spicy smells of Minnie's hair and skin. She was not wearing the cherry blossom perfume, but she smelled as if she were perfumed with something dark and fruity. Will remembered that he had read somewhere in one of the anthropology works that Indians lived habitually in smoky wigwams. He wondered if Minnie smelled faintly of smoke, and if it could be a scent that was inherited. They told a break, but after only one more song, Will again led Minnie to the dance floor and they remained in a close dance embrace for another half hour. By then Will could hardly wait until they got back to the cottage. His head was spinning giddily, but he was also aroused. It seemed to him that he had never been so in love with Minnie and so happy by her side then he was on that evening. They stayed that night in the broad, firm bed of the cottage, making love as soon as they got back home, and again after they woke up the next morning. Later that day they moved out to the farmhouse and spent Friday puttering around the farmhouse, affectionately giving one another their attentions.

On Saturday morning, after his run around the farm roads, they drove in their separate cars together to the Association building for the Corporation board meeting. Will especially wanted Carmine to notice that they arrived in separate cars. Minnie had also left the emerald ring back in her new jewelry box in the cottage so no one would get any ideas. Indian women in Minnie's tribe, and she had noticed in the Nantiquak tribe too, did not generally wear any jewelry in public. The board meeting started late as usual. While they were waiting Will looked at the resumes they had received for the position of chief bookkeeper/accountant. He agreed with Carmine that the one candidate, Martha Givens, looked the best on paper. After forty minutes of waiting, Minnie finally called the board meeting to order. Will again sat in the back as an observer. The first order of business was the presentation of the previous meeting's minutes. At this minute, Carmine was recording the minutes. Then Minnie presented the Corporation's bylaws which she had drawn up. No one raised any objections to the bylaws, so there was no discussion. So she then put it to them that, in accordance with those bylaws, the different bands should hold meetings where they would elect their weroance or chief, who would become representatives on the board. One of the board members raised the objection that they had already been selected by their band to represent them on the board. But Minnie patiently said that the band would still have to hold elections. And probably they would choose him again for the formal position.

Then Minnie asked Morley to report to them about the preparations by the Association for the upcoming powwow. He told the group that most preparations had been already completed and that the powwow itself would start on Thursday, the 24th of that month, and last through Sunday. That they would have guest performers coming from the Six Nations of the Iroquois and from the Ojibway of Wisconsin. This year they would have in addition to the various dances, they would also have two cooking classes which would prepare two different traditional feasts of Nantiquak foods on Friday and Saturday. They would also have an archery competition and an oyster shucking competition. And they would have courses on how to sew traditional Nantiquak costumes and moccasins from deer hide. And there would be demonstrations on making beads from bone and mussel shells. "And this year, something special, will be the first year that we be making our sassafras beer, that is root beer, from sassafras leaves, bark and roots." concluded Morley with a flourish.

"That sounds all very good. Now have you invited the other bands to attend?" asked Minnie.

"No. I guess not yet." said Morley.

"I think you need to," said Minnie assertively, "and you need to arrange transportation for the people who want to attend but who live in the distant bands, like Puckamee and Kuskowarok, for instance. I know it is an expense but we want all Nantiquak tribe members to feel that they can attend. Especially the children. The tribe has changed and the powwow needs to take that into account."

Morley tried to protest. "But this will cost more than what we have budgeted, I mean to provide the transport for the four days for the four outlying bands. This is the Association's powwow. I mean the members of the Association."

Clarke interrupted Morley. "We are no longer just the Indian River Nantiquaks. We are a larger tribe spread over a larger territory. The Association will change too. So you will arrange for this and no more objections. Or maybe you don't want to continue to be the director of the Association?"

"I understand." Morley grumbled and he sat down.

Following this report, Minnie then reported on the state of current initiatives for the tribe. She told the group that the legal firm NAILS in Washington had filed its case and claim against the state of Maryland to restore the unlawfully sold Nantiquak reservations. She told the board that she was personally involved in this case and that it was progressing well. Maybe they could expect a ruling in the coming quarter. She also reported that NAILS with her participation was preparing a second case for similar claims against the state of Delaware. And that in her assessment it now looked as if they would be ready to file the suit in the second week of October. The aim of both lawsuits was to restore the historical reservations which the king of England had granted to the Nantiquak people. And finally she reported that the application for federal recognition was being written and should be ready for submission before the end of the year. Will then offered to say that they were working on the end of October to able to submit the application.

Minnie then asked Will, as an officer of the Corporation responsible for finance, to address the tribe's financial situation at the beginning of that quarter. Will reported that the Corporation's initial capital now was fully paid up, although this had been accomplished by a loan from Will, himself. There was no income to report, and none foreseen in the coming quarter except for the proceeds from the powwow. Further he said that the Corporation had incurred $12,850 in expenses for rent and upgrade on the new headquarters offices in Beaverton. These had also been paid for out of loans. Will concluded with a proposal for a budget expenditure of $9,925 for furnishing the offices, and he was asking the board to authorize this expenditure. Finally he reported that when the Corporation appointed the accountant, they would establish the Corporation's financial statements and present them at the next board meeting. He said that he forecast expenses for the next quarter to come to about $17,000. That sum would include the salary for the accountant. But maybe they could hire the accountant on a half time basis until more reliable income could come into the Corporation. He concluded that the Corporation had opened a bank account in Beaverton at the Sussex National Bank.

When he concluded this report, Minnie thanked him and pointed out that the tribe's finances couldn't continue to rely on loans from Will Eames.

Then Minnie addressed Morley again. "Could you tell us what your expenses and forecast revenues will be for the upcoming powwow?"

Morley again stood up, a pained look on his face. "I can tell you that to date we have spent $6,200 on preparations. We now need to spend more, maybe a thousand dollars on van transport for the distant bands in Maryland to attend over the four days. We have not accepted any promotional or sponsorship money, although we were thinking of that. I think we have another one and a half to two thousand dollars in planned expenses coming up before we open."

"We earn money from the sale of concessions, drinks, wampum, souvenirs, and barbecue dinners on which we make a margin. Last year we had net margins on those sales of about four thousand five hundred dollars. And the rest we get from ticket sales. We charge sixteen dollars for four day visitor's passes. Ten dollars for single day entry, and four dollars for four day passes for our tribesmen. Children under sixteen are free. Last year we made about four thousand nine hundred dollars from ticket sales. This year we were expecting a slightly higher attendance than last year's powwow, but now after we account for the larger tribe, I guess we could make more than five and a half thousand in ticket sales. But as usual attendance depends a lot on the weather."

"So from your own estimates it looks like the powwow makes a small profit margin, or just breaks even." said Will.

"Yeah, I reckon you could say that. I haven't made the calculations myself."

"Have you spent anything on advertising?" asked Minnie.

"No, we've relied on public service advertising over the radio and public television in Delaware. But we've also sent announcements to the Wilmington, and Bawtimor and Warshington newspapers."

"That's good. But next year we will need to do better." Minnie answered.

Minnie then proposed that the board vote on agreeing a budget for the furnishing of the office headquarters. The board voted seven to two in favor, and Minnie declared that the vote authorized the President, Clarke, to spend that amount of money and to acquire the furnishings.

Finally, in the new business part of the agenda, Minnie introduced an initiative. "The Nantiquak Corporation needs to have created its own website. I don't know how that is done, probably a consultant will design one, but we have to have the materials that go in it. It will be the principal method through which we inform the world about the tribe and advertise our activities. I propose that Carmine, as the Vice President of Communications, start and direct this project. It shouldn't take long. And maybe web designers are only found in Dover, or maybe in Salisbury. But the tribe needs this. Do we all agree?" There was silence. The other board members did not really understand what this issue was all about. A few kept silent because they did not know what a website was, but were afraid to admit that. After a long silent pause, the board member from Askesky band raised his hand and stood up. "I'm sorry, but could you explain to me and the others what a website is and what purposes it serves?" Minnie asked Carmine to answer. Carmine started by explaining it was a computer program that was used on the internet and it was an important tool for communicating with the outside world. Then she went on to explain the kinds of information that could be put on a website and how interested users could use it, and how the tribe could use it. She cited examples from a few of the large consumer goods companies, and also from the University of Delaware website. When she had finished the man thanked her and said, "But you know, no one in our band has computers."

Carmine was quick to answer. "They will. It is a technology that everybody will have to have."

Will cut in now. "The computer and the internet will be the primary technology of the future for communications. More even than the telephone. Everyone will use it, and computers will become much cheaper than they are even today. I feel confident that the Nantiquak tribe will be quick to take up this technology."

"You know, our tribe was quick to take up iron tools and weapons when the English first arrived. The same will happen with computer and computer networks." added Carmine.

Minnie then concluded the discussions with a negative challenge. "So is there anyone who is opposed to setting up a tribal website?" No one answered. The same kind of response Minnie had so often encountered in her tribal council meetings with her own tribe. "Then I will take your silence to be consent, and Carmine will begin this project as a priority initiative."

"So if no one else has any business they would like to address, I call to adjourn this meeting." Minnie said. "Our next board meeting will be in the first week of December. And I suggest that we will hold it at the new offices in Beaverton. Agreed?"

There was a muttered agreement that came from the other board members. The meeting had taken more than two and a half hours. Will looked around at the board members. All of them were frowning, except for Minnie and Carmine, the recording secretary. Minnie looked relieved, while Carmine was beaming with delight. Charlie Clarke was shaking his head. Will wondered if he was doing that in disbelief or in disapproval. Once again Morley had organized a luncheon to be brought in, and this time Will and Minnie took their time eating it. Only Charlie Clarke joined them at their table. At around four thirty, they climbed into their cars and drove back to Hampton Farm.

That night, at the farmhouse, they made final preparations and packing for their vacation trip. Around nine o'clock Will stopped and asked Minnie if they shouldn't stop by and visit with Gaila on their return trip next Saturday. Minnie was surprised that Will suggested it. But he did not seem to bear any animosity toward her mother, and she appreciated it. She agreed that they should stop on the way back. It had been a long time since she had seen her mother or her sister.

Early the next morning they got in the Oldsmobile and set out. She had never before taken such a long trip away from home and she was a little anxious. Will had gotten the car serviced earlier that week, and he had bought a travel package, which included road maps and instructions, from the AAA. Although he appeared self-confident, he too had never driven so far away on any trip and he was feeling anxious about the long drive. The AAA guide said it would take ten to eleven hours to drive to Cherokee, North Carolina. Almost at once after their start, he had to stop in Bristol. He had to buy gasoline because the fuel gauge showed that the tank car was nearly empty. So they finally pulled out of Bristol at eight fifteen on that Sunday morning. Will drove three hours before he was ready to take a break at a rest stop on I-81. The road was smooth and mostly empty. So he proposed that Minnie drive the next couple of hours down to Roanoke. Minnie was a little intimidated by the suggestion—she had not driven the big Oldsmobile very much before—but she accepted. She drove slower than Will had, so they only reached Roanoke around 1:30 and by which time she was ready to stop. The car was ready to stop as well: it needed a re-fill of gasoline, and they both needed to take a lunch break. They resumed driving about forty minutes after that stop, with Will at the wheel. Minnie made a joke of it, using a mock eastern European accent she laughed, "watch out, weel is at the wheel." And he remained at the wheel until after they got to Tennessee and turned south on the new I-26 up into the mountains. They took a break at Johnson City and looked at the maps and recommendations over a cup of coffee. It was apparent that the mountains were major and the road was bad in front of them. Will decided that he should drive the stretch to Asheville. Minnie was pliant on this point. It was one thing driving on a straight wide interstate highway, and quite another thing to climb up switchbacks and down again over high mountains in failing light. It took more than an hour to reach Asheville and the drive, Will had to admit, was nerve racking. Minnie enjoyed the broad views and mountain vistas and she tried to ignore the steep fall-aways on the side of the narrow highway, especially in the switchback curves. At the top of Sam's Gap, the pass into North Carolina, she noticed that some of the trees were already turning color. But it was only seven thirty when they reached Asheville. "You can drive now the rest of the way." said Will. "I'll navigate." The rest of the way was still a little more than an hour's drive, after which Minnie turned the car and pulled into the drive at their hotel, "The Indian Princess", an hour after dark. "Whew," she said. "I'm exhausted." "Me too." Will agreed. "More than six hundred miles in one day is a lot. A real challenge." They checked in and had soup for dinner and then went straight up to their room and fell into bed almost at once and were soon in a deep slumber with dreams of endless stretches of concrete reaching out to the horizon.

Will had arranged a few appointments for the next two days. He wanted to interview people involved in the recent governance issues of the Cherokee tribe and as well their experience in getting permission to build an Indian casino and finding financing for the project. First thing that morning after breakfast Will and Minnie stepped out of the hotel and into the cool mountain air. It was dramatically different from the air in Bristol; it had a forested scent, woody and piney at the same time, with some hints of grass. On the land all around the hotel lay fields of grasses which were still green and fresh looking unlike those browned fields back in Dorset County. Single oak trees stood here and there and cast long shadows over the green fields. There was a large fast running stream babbling down the hillside next to the hotel. They had not even noticed it when they pulled in that night, but its steady gurgling music of water running and splashing over rocks was quite noticeable now in the still of the morning. Looking upstream to where it emerged from a dark forest the fields were still embraced by morning fog lifting only slowly from the ground. In all directions their view was halted by a high horizon of looming forested mountains and hills. It was no longer summer here, instead it looked and smelled like fall. The hotel clerk told them later that they were seeing the village of Cherokee at its best; after Labor Day, the hordes of tourists stopped driving through on their way to the Great Smokey Mountains National Park right next to them. Now it was quiet and peaceful with hardly any visitors and the sounds of automobile congestion. They walked around the park like area in front of the hotel, down to the stream bank

They were expecting the Cherokee tribal chief, Joseph Leatherback, to come meet them at the hotel at nine. He was late, but he drove up in a big pick-up truck driving slowly about a quarter past nine and jumped out of his truck with his arms showing an apology. "Welcome to Cherokee and to the Qualla of the Eastern Band of Cherokee Indians!" he shouted before he reached them on the porch. "It's mighty pretty weather we're having these days. Soon the autumn colors will start. You can sleep mighty well with the windows open." And as he stepped closer, "Hi, I'm Chief Joseph Leatherback. Just call me Joe." They shook hands and Will introduced himself as Will Eames of Bristol who was representing the Nantiquak Indian Tribal Corporation in its efforts to regain its reservations and to get federal recognition. And he introduced Minnie as the chief of the Massaponax-Doeg tribe of the middle Peninsula of Virginia—once part of the Powhatan confederation, as well as a lawyer working for NAILS, and the chairwoman of the board of the Nantiquak Corporation. "Very impressive. I'm pleased to meet you." Chief Leatherback addressed Minnie. "And you too Will Eames."

"He's more than a mere consultant, representative." said Minnie. "He's also part Nantiquak Indian."

"Is that so? Who are the Nantiquak Indians?"

"They are the remnants of the main tribe of Indians on the Eastern Shore of Maryland and Delaware. The inhabitants of the Chesapeake and Atlantic coasts before the English arrived."

"Ah yes, the arrival of the English speakers. Algonquin speakers I presume?"

"Originally, yes. But not now." said Will.

"And our tribe also spoke Algonquin," Minnie added, "but no longer."

"You may know that we were lucky. We had that great chief, Sequoyah—maybe the name is familiar to you? like the great trees—

who saw that our tribe, the great Cherokee nation, needed not only its spoken Iroquois language but also a written language. And he devised our syllabary and taught our peoples how to read and write in it. Thanks to him our language has survived. We teach it in our schools."

"You teach Cherokee language here in your schools?" asked Minnie in surprise.

"Yes, nearly all of our tribal members know how to speak at least a little bit, and most know how to write our language. Come with me now to my office on the Qualla and I'll show you traffic signs in our language on the way."

"Our language is unfortunately probably lost forever." said Minnie.

"I understand. But our language is still in danger of being lost, as the young people don't like to use it all that much."

They drove out of the hotel lane and down to the main street of the village. And then they drove on through the light and on up a highway up the hill out of the village and away from the stream for about a mile when Chief Joe turned off the highway, onto a small gravel road. "I came to pick you up, because no one can find our offices in the Qualla. There're no addresses and all the lanes are unnamed and unmarked too, except in our Cherokee writing." said Chief Joe with a small chuckle. "Visitors all the time get hopelessly lost in the Qualla."

"Here we are. Our offices are just behind the McDonald's just over the Soco Creek. We tell people that but visitors still can't find us. Although we can smell the aromas of their burgers and fries all the time in our office. Encourages poor eating habits." said Chief Joe, chuckling, as he parked the truck.

They settled in his office, he offered them coffee, and then brought three mugs of coffee in. The office was sparsely furnished, a folding table as a desk with a side table of drawers, a wooden book case, a rotating arm chair and three chairs in front of the table.

"I'm not the principal chief of the Cherokees, you understand." said Chief Joe as if apologizing for his rudimentary office. "Just one of several sub-chiefs. Still I am elected. I've been here in this position the longest however of any of them. And it is a paying position. Requires my full time attention. If the principal chief, our big honcho, Chief Blue Eagle, comes around, I'll introduce you."

"We've come to talk to you," started Will, "about how the Cherokees got federal recognition and also to ask about how your tribe was able to get the casino off the ground and running. Now I read that you all set up the Qualla as trustee land which you bought in 1870 or so. So you got recognition then?"

"No actually. We were once a sovereign nation until Jackson's hateful racist Indian Relocation law of 1830. But that law revoked our sovereignty and all the treaties we had had with the English and the Americans after them. The Qualla was set up in the 1870s when the Federal government allowed the band of Cherokees who stayed behind in hiding to buy lands in our traditional areas and give them over in trust to the Federal government. But the trust land of the Qualla did not legally become established until 1924. So technically it wasn't a treaty reservation, as the government did not reserve it for us, we bought the lands and it was not Federal land then, but the Qualla was set up as a protected area for our exclusive use, with the trustee forbidding white men from buying any of the lands inside the Qualla or disenfranchising Indian owners. All this was accomplished by negotiations which were long and complicated by politics at both the state and Federal level. And at that time, it seemed the Federal government's attitude to the Indians everywhere changed every decade. One decade, they did not want to recognize Indians as sovereign races, another decade they wanted to stamp out our Indian identity and insisted on full assimilation into white society, and yet another they recognized us as a colored people, and so applied Jim Crow laws to us and claimed there was no such thing any longer as an Indian. We received U.S. citizenship in 1946 and the right to vote a bit later."

"But you might ask, when did we gain Federal recognition? The short answer, the lawyers tell me, is that we never did. The Qualla was finally put in Federal trusteeship in 1924 and that came with rulings that effectively inside the Qualla, Cherokees were not subject to

North Carolina laws, rules, or taxes. So we are not a sovereign nation as many of the Federally recognized tribes are, as our Cherokees in Oklahoma are. And then the IRA came into effect in the thirties and we gained rights, almost as if we were a recognized tribe. But still the state of North Carolina could impose some of its rules and laws. And there have been lawsuits over lost tax revenues, challenging our rights, for examples our schools. And so we had to fight for our cultural and traditional rights and beliefs right on through the last decade."

"Sounds a bit like the sad history for the Nantiquaks." said Will. "We have state recognition, but we are nowhere near Federal recognition or restoration of our tribal reservations."

Minnie looked over at Will. It was the first time it seemed to her that Will had spoken collectively of the Nantiquaks, using the inclusive first person plural and the possessive. It surprised her, but she did not make any comment. She'd have to ask him later what he meant.

"And then of course they changed the rules in 1988." continued Chief Joe.

"What were those changes?" asked Will.

"The passage of the Federal Indian Gaming Law." interjected Minnie.

"Exactly."

"That law raised all kinds of possibilities and conflicts for us. And we discovered how we were not legally a sovereign nation. Many in our tribe wanted to set up a casino, although many were opposed. But the state of North Carolina was strongly opposed and they made it difficult for us. In the end we had to negotiate with the governor. And he insisted that we have a limited range of gambling games, and that we cannot serve alcohol at the casino—North Carolina is a dry state. We were able to live with that. Because at the end of the day, we wanted a casino not so much to serve the gambling hunger of our tribesmen, but rather we wanted to attract outsiders to come and gamble and spend money here in Cherokee. And it helped that there is an Indian Gaming Commission to provide regulatory oversight. And now we have a casino. Have you seen it? So we have gotten lots of outsiders to come to our casino and we live like a sovereign recognized tribe, but it has taken a huge amount of lawyerly work and lawsuits, constantly, to achieve that."

"No, we haven't been to the casino yet." said Will. "But we do want to visit. And talk to the people who were closest to getting it built."

"You mentioned that your tribe has struggled to keep its culture and traditions alive as well as to preserve its sovereignty. How have you managed to preserve your Indian identity?" asked Minnie softly but firmly.

"You know, it has always been a real struggle. It helped, of course, to have a living language. Even though there was a period when the state authorities tried to wipe out the language from schools and public transactions, early in this century. In those days, the state authorities and the Feds wanted to actively force full assimilation on us. To wipe out all elements of our Indian, Cherokee identity. Now that is past, but nowadays the problems might even be worse. The overwhelming weight of American cultural output—on TV, in films, in advertising, in pop youth culture, like music or dancing or drugs, and on the internet—simply overwhelms our efforts. Our young people are drawn to American whiteman's culture, or blackman's culture like moths to the flame. And then they are gone to us. I understand all Indians everywhere in the U.S. are facing the same challenge. The Navahos come to my mind as an example of a large, vibrant tribe crumbling under the weight of American culture. We both share massive amounts of tourists running through our lands."

"So what have you done to perpetuate your culture and identity?" asked Minnie.

"Simple things that support and promote our past traditions and way of life. You, for instance, would be encouraged to wear your hair in a braid. Or a double braid. Of course, you would stick out elsewhere in the larger American society, but not here on the Qualla."

"I've never tried to wear a braid. And in my tribe, even on the reservation, I don't think I've ever seen any of the women wear braids.

It takes a lot of time and effort to get and keep a proper braid. But it does look nice."

"We've never tried to preserve traditional dress, because, well you know it just isn't practical. I mean all the historical documents say that men and women during much of the year went around mostly naked. And then only wore deerskin capes and leggings in the coldest weather. They also wore a lot of bear fat, to help keep the biting insects off and to keep warm. I think we'd all freeze to death if we tried to carry on traditional dress like that. No one wants to dress like that these days."

"Same goes for diet. No one has tried to preserve the traditional diet. For one thing, it was a subsistence diet that relied on a lot of foraging and hunting, with some fishing. The elk were hunted to extinction in these hills even before we got our first treaty almost two hundred years ago. And deer are hard to hunt with just the old bows and arrows. And bears even harder to hunt and kill that way. And no one wants to go around foraging for acorns feeling hungry. Certainly not if he or she has a choice."

"Acorns." muttered Minnie. "I remember once eating acorns cooked into corn bread when I was a little girl. And liking it. I guess it was a tribal tradition. But I later grew up being told that you can't eat acorns."

"Well, they are edible, I can assure you, and they were an important part of the pre-Anglo diet for us Cherokees, especially where there are lots of pin oak trees. They just are not really delicious. And there were beech nuts and pine nuts too. But from here you have to go really far up in the mountains to get pine nuts. And we can no longer collect them up in the National Park."

"I suppose that your women had to collect a lot of acorns to feed the whole tribe through the winter and spring." said Will dreamily.

"Tons of them, literally tons. And every year there isn't a mast year when they are plentiful. Even though there are lots of oaks and oak groves hereabouts."

Chief Joe paused. And looked pensively out the window. "I'd rather eat a Big Mac, though, than a bowl of acorn mush. And maybe some more coffee?"

They all stepped out to get refills of coffee. He continued speaking as they were filling up. "And we never tried to preserve or reconstitute the traditional Cherokee religion. It was eradicated years ago. By deliberate efforts of the white man. That was in the 19th century when they thought that they could wipe out the Indian by eliminated his religion and assimilating him fully into white society. Missionaries converted us and the traditional priest was driven out. We preserve only small portions of our traditional spiritual identity. Dances and masks, and some rituals and ceremonies which, frankly, I don't understand. But those things do not comprise a religion. Nearly all of our band members worship in the Baptist or Evangelical Churches."

"For the Nantiquaks, the same thing happened." Will cut in. "Methodist missionaries and circuit riders converted the surviving Nantiquaks starting in the 1820s and 1830s."

"Really? said Chief Joe as they re-settled at his desk. "They did try to reach us here at about the same time. But they only got as far as Asheville. We do have a Methodist Church here just the same."

"But we are not de-tribalized," he continued, "as the anthropologists like to say. We as a tribe still live together and breed together. Members of our band live almost nowhere else, very few leave the Qualla and don't come back. And we still look like Indians after all."

"Breeding together is understood." said Will. "But not many of those specialists stress proximity—that your tribe lives in proximity and propinquity—in spite of the pressures of assimilation and economic opportunities away from the tribe."

"Propinquity?" said Chief Joe. "Yes, I suppose that is an important characteristic of our people as an Indian tribe. Just as it is for the Oklahoma Cherokee tribes who are Cherokee but do not qualify to be members of our band."

"And how do you judge Cherokee descent?" asked Minnie.

"Well, our rules of membership recognize matrilineal descent, descent through the mother's line. So if your mother is a Cherokee, for example, you are a Cherokee too. But membership is restricted to quarter blood, that is your mother has to be at least half Cherokee."

"By that system," said Will addressing Minnie, "it would mean if we had children they would be Massaponax Indians."

"Oh, you two are married? I didn't know." said Chief Joe.

"No we live together and are considering marriage." answered Will.

"No, more properly, I am resisting marriage." said Minnie.

"Whatever for? We have lots of mixed marriages here on the Qualla. It's none of my business, but the fact that Will is not an Indian shouldn't get in the way of your getting married to him."

"Yes, so I've been told." said Minnie.

"Anyway. Among other things we've done to preserve our cultural identity was to set up an artists' cooperative. Back in 1924. It has promoted and preserved traditional crafts, like basketry, or pottery, or wood carving. But if there hadn't been the National Park it probably would not have survived, because if tourists had not come and bought those items as folk art, then they would've been just of peripheral interest. We'll go over to our museum now and the curator there can show you the collection of our former material culture. Then she can take you to the arts and crafts cooperative and you'll see the results and programs that we conduct. But there's no preservation of traditional bow and arrow making, for instance. No interest in that and tourists don't buy old style bows. So such items are just dust collectors and our craftsmen don't make them. It's funny, the tourists eagerly buy toy miniature bows, made in China, to entertain their kids. I think they break after the third use."

"So let's go there now." said Will.

They got in the pick-up truck and left for the museum which stood on a sunny plot on the banks of the Oconaluftee River near the entrance to the National Park, about a mile distant from the tribe's offices and not far from their hotel. Chief Joe led them in and greeted every attendant he saw there by first name. They did not pay the five dollar entrance fee but the ticket seller did not even mention it as they passed her. It was clear to Will, just from the looks of the women, that they were all Indian women, mostly middle aged.

"Is Emma in now?" Chief Joe asked one of the attendants tending the gift shop counter.

"Yes, she is. Over in the arts studio."

Emma was a heavyset, short, older woman wearing jeans and an ordinary puffy, white cotton shirt. Her skin was not dark, but she wore her long gray hair in a single braid. She was all smiles when Chief Joe introduced them. He didn't actually introduce Will, but he stressed that Minnie was the chief of a small Virginia tribe that was once part of the Powhatan confederation and that she was leading the effort to get Federal recognition for her tribe. Will did not push to introduce himself or to add anything to Chief Joe's introduction.

"Oh yes, the Powhatan tribe is the most famous in the native American experience with the white man. I'm so glad to meet you. And I'm really glad to hear that you are trying to gain Federal recognition. I think you'll like the museum of our traditional material culture. There's so much here that probably is familiar to you."

Chief Joe excused himself. "Don't forget that you have an appointment with John Tall-owl at two o'clock over at the casino. I'll join yo'awl there at four."

"Let me show some of the museum's holdings. We're arranged by historical periods and we have a special exhibition just now on the achievement of Sequoyah."

Emma led them around display cases filled with artefacts and pieces reclaimed from archeological finds. There were stones weapons and tools, bone and antler tools, lots of pottery--mostly shards or fragments, but quite a number of entire fire burned pots-- old baskets, and fragments of deerhide moccasins and leather capes, wooden masks and flutes, and lots of white clay pipes. In the Sequoyah exhibition the emphasis was on the written syllabary. Minnie was impressed to see all the original printed documents from the early nineteenth century, all in good shape, many in glass frames hung on the walls. "There are so many." she exclaimed. "Even a newspaper."

"Yes, the first Indian newspaper published in an Indian language and using Sequoyah's invention." said Emma. "There was a real blossoming of writing in the first decades of the last century, before the Removal law. Before that hateful law, that was a time when the young U.S. government encouraged Indian civilizations."

Will thought about the small museum that the Nantiquaks had at Indian River. It was a poor collection in comparison to the rich collection of materials he saw in this museum. Even that big pile of fragments that he'd seen in farmer Taylor's shed would not begin to improve their museum to near the level of the Cherokee's. Minnie was thinking much the same thing. The Massaponax needed a museum, although she wasn't aware of any artefacts that could go into one.

"And we have an even bigger archive with Cherokee language documents in the back room." said Emma. "That's where we keep most of the historical photographs as well, although you can see here in this next room that there are a lot of old photos hanging on the wall. I especially like this one." She pointed to a photo that seemed to show a group of young Indian men on one side, all without shirts, and on the opposite side a group of well-dressed young women, either singing to each other, or receiving some sort of school lesson outdoors.

There was one display case that showed dried flowering plants with large tubers attached. The label said they were puccoon or bloodroot.

"What is puccoon?" Minnie asked Emma.

"It is a perennial flower that was one of the most important trade items amongst the Indian nations before the white man came. It is an early spring blossoming flower. And the tuber yields the most valuable dye of all, red or yellow dye. Our warriors used the red dye as facial paint, the so called war paint. But there were so many uses for the tuber root."

"Yeah, I read that puccoon was traded from the Powhatans to the Nantiquak." said Will.

"I think the word is an Algonquin word." said Emma. "These woods are full of the bloodroot flower in the spring. We traded it too. Who are the Nantiquak?"

"They are a tribe of Algonkian Indians of the Maryland and Delaware Eastern Shore of the Chesapeake. We are both working on getting them Federal recognition."

Emma showed them the last of the rooms. There were two photos, both posed portraits, hanging on the wall over one display case that really caught Minnie's attention. One was of a young Cherokee maiden said to be in 1910, and the other a young Cherokee warrior, said to be 1908. Minnie could not help noticing that both had silver earrings and ear pendants hanging from their ear lobes and from around the edges of their ears. The silver ear pendants were shaped like birch leaves. She thought that traditionally Indian women did wear jewelry of sorts, all the time. At the same time Will was wondering how such a large store of ancient materials had been collected and he finally could not help asking Emma:

"Where did all these display pieces come from? Does all of this on display come from archeological diggings?"

"That's a good question." said Emma. "Not many people ask how we got all these artefacts. The surprising thing is this: only the materials from the earliest ancient periods, before 1500 AD are exclusively from archeology. The later more recent periods comprise materials that, believe it or not, our ancestors used and kept, and only set aside when no longer used. They did not discard any of this. And they were kept until the Qualla was set up and a museum collection was begun. And then they were contributed over the past ninety years. So this bow and set of arrows, for example, was preserved from two hundred years ago and given to the museum many generations after it was no longer used. The same for the bead work cloaks you see, and the carved muskets and many of the old masks."

"Wow." said Minnie and Will almost in the same breath.

"Now, unless you have more questions, let me take you next door to our artists' cooperative. It is the conservator of many of the Cherokee's important crafts."

They walked across a small lane and over a grassy plot, maybe forty yards, to a wide low building in front of which was a large sculpture of an Indian man's head that had been carved out of a whole tree trunk standing about twelve feet high.

"We have lots of really fine sculptors in our tribe, and they are all members of this cooperative." said Emma pointing to the sculpture.

On the wall just inside the door next to the name of the cooperative which was also carved from wood, there was a big photo of a man and a woman dressed in ordinary street clothes standing on either side of a large sculpture of a standing Indian warrior. Minnie looked at the caption and read, 'Philipp Standing Eagle, Principal Chief of the Eastern Band of Cherokee and Wilma Mankiller, Principal Chief of the Cherokee Nation of Oklahoma, 1994.'

"Oh, yes. Have you ever heard of Wilma Mankiller?" said Emma, addressing Minnie. "She's the leading Cherokee woman of the past fifty years. She was for many years the chief of our cousin Cherokees in Oklahoma. You should read her life story. Inspiring for another woman chief, as yourself. She's accomplished so much for our Cherokee people. A real activist and champion of Indians rights and sovereignty."

"Yes I should learn about this woman." said Minnie. "I have not heard of her before. But I knew of a former Cherokee chief at the Bureau when I worked there. An older man. I think he was also from the Oklahoma Cherokee Nation."

"Undoubtedly. They are much more progressive then we are. We've remained here rather more conservative and unassertive by comparison. Until we got the casino, that is."

"I wouldn't recognize her as an Indian, if I met her on the street dressed like that. Her face doesn't look all that Indian." said Will.

"I think she may have looked more Indian when she was younger." said Emma scowling at him as she lead them into the facility.

The Arts and Crafts cooperative was laid out in several spacious rooms furnished with many glass display cases, like a museum. But these were all displays of art and craft wares for sale. There were many cases of jewelry made from silver and semi-precious stones. Minnie's eyes rested on the silver birch leaf ear pendants like she had seen in the photograph next door. Will looked too.

"Would you wear them if I bought you a pair?" Will asked her. "You know tourists on vacation always buy souvenirs. These can be our souvenir purchase."

"Yes, I just might, but only on my earlobes." said Minnie.

"So try them on, and we'll get them." Emma patiently waited for them as Minnie tried them on, looked at herself in the mirror, and then agreed to take them. Will paid the attendant with his credit card.

Emma pointed out across the room. "All the crafts you see in the display cases are items for sale. But they are all hand-made by our top craftsmen and artisans." She was trying to encourage them to move with her to see other display cases.

"Much of the artwork on display here comprises ceramics. But not much of it is traditional Cherokee pottery, like what you saw in the museum. Most of it is contemporary art ceramics. That's why I think I like the wood carving the most. Especially the masks. They still represent the traditional significance of the mask in old Cherokee society. These for example are the different animals that were the names of the different clans, or other effigies of Cherokee legendary creatures that represented different parts of religious ceremonies. I like this one of the screaming man. If you like you perhaps you can meet the artist. He's still living and working here in the Qualla."

Another middle aged Indian woman joined them and introduced herself as Gena, the director of the cooperative's center and store where they were. "In the summer season, there are so many tourists coming through here, it is almost impossible to see anything. We're re-stocking just now after the heavy outflow of sales. You're lucky to have Emma as a guide. She's a real specialist in Cherokee arts."

"We also have studios here where established artists teach young people their crafts." she continued. "Would you like to see the basket-weaving lessons which are going on just now?"

Minnie said she would very much like to observe, if they did not disturb the class.

In all they spent another hour in the arts and crafts cooperative. They did not buy anything else, but were repeatedly attracted by different items. Some of the art work was quite expensive, glazed ceramic bowls going for thousands of dollars. Finally they made to leave thanking Emma profusely for her efforts and attentions.

"I cannot even conceive of being able to put together such a cultural center in our little tribe." said Minnie as they stepped away. Gena answered back, "It's taken decades of hard work by many people working ceaselessly."

After lunch, Will and Minnie relaxed outside their hotel along the bank of the Oconaluftee River. They were sitting in green adirondak chairs side by side trying to hold hands across the wide arms of the chairs.

"You know, Will, today you used the inclusive 'we' when you were talking about the Nantiquaks. Do you now consider yourself to be a Nantiquak Indian?"

"No. It was just a manner of speaking. Of course I have Nantiquak blood but I don't think I could ever presume to be a Nantiquak Indian. For two very important reasons: I don't in the least look like an Indian, and I wasn't raised as a Nantiquak Indian and thus don't behave like one. I'm working for them and want only the best outcome for them. So I include myself with them only in relation to those efforts."

"I see. So born and raised an Indian, I will always be an Indian. And no amount of assimilation will change that. Is that right?"

"I've never asked you to cease being an Indian and become a white woman. Minnie, just the contrary. I love you because you are an Indian. A truly unique person. If you feel you have assimilated and have ceased to be an Indian, I think that is a mistaken impression you have."

Will paused to think where the questioning was going. "And if you believe that you will cease to be an Indian if you marry me—finally—that is also a mistaken belief. Still you have taken on white man's disciplines –the practice of law and of course using the language—but it is more credit to you. You haven't lost or thrown out your background or the way you were taught to live and behave. And I love all of that. I've never asked you to change yourself one bit. But I think if we continue together and you marry me, we will both change a lot—growing closer to each other."

"So you mean, if I wore a long braid you wouldn't be ashamed of me?"

"No, I might even volunteer to help you tie your braid. And I wouldn't be ashamed if you started to wear those silver Cherokee style earrings all the time, not even if you started wearing moccasins to work. But I might think it strange and uncomfortable for you. I'd still love you just the same."

"But let me ask you:" continued Will "If I started wearing deerskin shirts with bead work, and a loincloth, and dyed my hair black and wore feathers in my hair, wouldn't you be embarrassed by me? Wouldn't you think I was being presumptious and even foolish?"

"Yes. I would."

"Of course you would. Even our Nantiquak clients would think I was a looney and a fool, not to be dealt with any further. And my parents would probably try to have me committed as a crazy. But then again maybe I will go crazy trying to be a farmer."

"You're no farmer, Willeams." and Minnie laughed at him.

As the appointment time approached they got in Will's Oldsmobile and drove the three miles across the valley to the newly minted Harrah's Cherokee Casino. Will had read that the Harrah Corporation had come to the rescue to help the Cherokee community finance and build the casino and hotel building. The description of the casino and hotel was given as a resort and he had read that it was very large. But Will was surprised to see the place when he finally drove in. It was an active building site with several cranes and yellow backhoes standing around several unfinished large structures all surrounded by security walls. There was a small outdoors parking area which was not even half filled with cars and the entrance was more than sixty yards away and hard to see from the parking lot. A lot of hardwood trees had been cut and cleared around the parking lot and the new saplings that had been planted were still struggling to take root and grow. The first impression to Will was of a place not yet ready for business and still under extensive construction. But inside it became quickly apparent that that appearance had not deterred gamblers who were working the video game machines. They introduced themselves at the very broad, front reception desk and asked for Mr. Grey-Owl who was the head of the Cherokee Gaming Enterprise, the company which organized and ran the casino.

They waited several minutes at the counter. Traffic was light, no new players came in and none went out while they were waiting. The place had that certain 'new' smell, fresh paint, new carpeting, and no cigarette smoke masking the smells. They could hear a fountain tinkling somewhere near them by the front desk. Looking into the bright and airy main room they could see what looked like many slot machines, most occupied by gamblers, set in a high ceiling deep hall that ended with tall windows that looked out to the green forested hill behind the casino.

"Welcome to the Cherokee casino," said a man approaching them. He was dressed in a black suit with a brick red shirt without a tie. I'm Barry Barnes, or Bredlica Grey-Owl in our local naming practice." He offered his hand to Will. He was as tall as Will and his face was burnished brown and deeply wrinkled, but he was not old. Minnie thought he looked familiar to her, like a familiar, stereotypical Indian face she had seen many times.

"Let me give you a tour around our casino, and I can show you our future planned expansion as well." said Barry.

Barry led Minnie and Will around the main room. Its bright airy space was filled with rows of electronic slot machines, which were about a quarter occupied by gamers.

"Once we got permission, we were able to open this facility early, because we had first built this as a bingo hall with the idea that we would convert it to the casino."

"But there are only slot machines here. Don't you have any other kinds of games? Roulette for instance?"

"No, we are only allowed these machines. But they are video slots,--not the traditional one armed bandits that eat up quarters and spin mechanical reels-- they require some player input and skills. I'll tell you about that in the office."

Brad led them to the wide view windows. "And here you can see our future. We aim to become a casino resort. And you see there we're building a hotel tower there, and an extension for more gaming space as well as a show theatre. And over there you can see our future parking garage, because we expect most of our future users will drive here from far around and will stay for days at a time."

Barry had a large, wood paneled office on the second floor with a large window that overlooked the entire gambling floor below.

"Will, you noticed that we only have slot machines. It's a complicated story. We were held up more than four years by the Governor of North Carolina who wanted to enforce the state constitutional ban on any form of gambling. He was very adamant. And we went to court a few times to force our right to develop a casino. But the governor did not want to let us. And technically he was right, because although we have the Qualla Boundary—it is not a reservation in the true sense, and we are not recognized as a sovereign tribe in the fully legal sense. But Federal law did state that we had the right to operate a casino free from North Carolina's prohibition or regulation. So finally it was Federal court that decided the issue in our favor."

"But that ruling also required a compromise of sorts. The court required that both sides, we and the Governor, concede some things. Governor Hunt did not want criminality, and did not want the Indians to have a Vegas style casino in the state. But we did not want to be limited to just a bingo parlor, which really would have only served our own people. The compromise was that we could only have games that required a bit of skill. That ruled out the classic slot machine, and roulette wheels. There were these computer run video machines which have videos of rotating wheels like slot machines and which the player can freeze one or two digits in a re-spin. That can increase the gamer's chances of hitting a winning roll. But not really by much. And it seemed to include an element of memory and skill. That was enough for the Governor, so that is what we have for the time being. We'll get some of the key card games later—you can't argue that they don't involve skill and player talent. We'll get poker and twenty one, and baccarat after we have the hotels finished."

"Hotels?" asked Will.

"Yes, as I said the plan is a casino resort. A place for people to come, both gamers and families, for gambling and entertainment. You see, in all the states around us, there are very strict anti-gambling laws. So we will attract most of our clientele from Georgia and Tennessee and South Carolina, gamers who will come here for a week or two week-long stay, instead of, say, flying to Las Vegas. So we have building plans for two, maybe three hotels here and a convention center, as well as the full line of entertainment and sports. And we will be the entertainment hub for all the states around us. We will be building here through 2005 with an initial aim of building more than 300 rooms." Barry pointed to a large blue print layout spread out on a drawing board that showed four central buildings and two outlying larger buildings.

"These are the hotel towers, this the central gaming building, this is the convention and entertainment center, and these two outer buildings are the parking garages. As you can see there is a lot left to build."

"And Harrah's has provided the financing?" asked Will.

"Yes and no. They are our exclusive consultant, overall project manager, and they will be the operator. They manage the contracting and the building. But they will not be owners, not even part owners. Our casino enterprise corporation will be the owner. And the financing costs will be debt on the tribe, which owns this enterprise corporation."

"But you will take all the profits for the tribe, right?"

"Yes, but profits are after Harrah's gets paid a healthy operating management fee. So everyone is happy."

"And you're sure that there's enough demand, and especially repeat demand to sustain a big load of debt?"

"We have our projections on gamer demand. And so far in this past year, every month we've beaten our earlier expectations. And I think that will continue to be the case until after we've finished building the third phase, that is a second and third hotel block. And then we will begin to offer more games. More attractions."

"Such as?"

"Well, North Carolina is also a dry state. So for now we cannot serve alcohol in the casino, and outside in the Qualla there is no alcohol either. We really don't want our tribesmen and women to come here for drinking, but we hope to be able to offer drinks to our out of state visitors who come and stay at the casino's hotels. Most of the neighboring states are also dry states, you know."

"And of course, the great outdoors here, the mountains and rivers, and the National Park are pretty big attractions."

"Yeah, we've come here also to try out fly fishing." said Will.

"For instance. Or golf. Or hiking in the mountains."

"But don't you think the people attracted to gambling are not the same who participate much in outdoors sports?" continued Will.

"Probably a fair point. But we want to attract families and so they might not be exclusively motivated by life on the video reel. There'll be a gigantic outdoor pool. And we will it a smoke free environment."

"And you think you can keep away the criminal element?" asked Minnie. "That has always been one of the chief concerns in my state of Virginia.

"And in Maryland too." added Will.

"We're banking on it. We think our partner, Harrah's, helps keep the mafia out. And we do have supervision from the Indian Gaming Commission. I think we can ourselves keep out the racketeers. And the state itself will have to continue to keep the bootleggers and alcohol smugglers out. But you know it has worked out in some of the smaller casinos in the West so far. We are studying the experience of FoxFire resort up in Connecticut. But unlike us, they do not have any tribal numbers and no tribal infrastructure. We have our own police force, you know."

"Did you hire an architect to do the design and lay-out for the resort?" asked Will.

"Yes, a good one. A specialist in hotel resorts. Williams and Cansoni. They delivered a plan that looked like the very duplicate of our expressed desires. And they came here and absorbed the feel of the local environment and tried to capture it in our panoramas and multiple views. In the future hotels every room will have an unbroken view of green hills and forested mountains."

"How much did their design work cost you?"

"Less than a million. And they delivered very quickly. The construction contractor said it was very clear and buildable."

"And what do you anticipate the end of the first phase cost your tribe?"

"We're looking at one hundred and thirty five million or thereabouts. All debt financed, unfortunately. But that's the only way. With debt payments worked in it will cost us more than one hundred and eighty, last I heard."

"And Harrah's are managing the construction contractor and building works?"

"Yes, they have a top notch team working for us. Looks like they will meet all their schedules. But first phase only ends in about three and a half years from now."

Will looked over and saw that Minnie was having trouble hiding her boredom. There was so much more Will wanted to ask about, but there was more to see also.

"So your company is responsible for the development of all new Indian enterprises here in Cherokee? Or are you only the developer for this casino resort?"

"No all major enterprises fall in our view. There are a number of private Indian entrepreneurs investing in new small hotels all around and even in the Qualla. And we have planned building a championship golf course down the road a ways--about twelve miles from here-- to add to the entertainment attractions. But that will be in the next century."

"Yeah, if we ever get to where we are recognized and can hope of building our own casino that will also be in the next century. If we don't hurry, maybe even in the second decade of the next century."

"It takes a long time now to get Federal recognition through the Bureau." said Minnie.

"I understand. But in some respects our route to this point took even longer. More than a century. And still the state here lodges lawsuits to deny us sovereign rights. We spend an awful lot on lawyers and court proceedings."

"Maybe, you'd like to see the view of our future 18 story hotel?" asked Barry.

"But it's not built yet." said Minnie.

"True, but we can go up the elevator to the tenth floor on the crane. Super view."

Minnie looked scared, but Will responded enthusiastically.

"Well then come with me. There are no winds today. Perfect weather." Barry turned around and took a white hardhat off a bookshelf behind him. The front was emblazoned in the Cherokee alphabet. "That's my name in Cherokee." Barry said as he fit it on. "We'll get yours at the worksite. They left the office, and walked down to the main level and out by a rear door to a patio behind the gaming hall. Across a space of about forty yards was a gate in a plywood fence painted green. They entered there and then stepped into an elevated container that had been converted to a worksite office. Barry asked them to register as visitors and they gave them the summary safety instructions for the worksite after which they signed liability waivers. Then the duty manager gave them yellow, hard plastic hardhats. Minnie's hair would not cooperate and it kept falling out first from one side to the other, sometimes into her eyes.

"This way." said Barry leaving through a back door. Outside there was a big foundation pit that was already lined with concrete and full of jutting pillars of blocks and rebar, and from the side walls pipes both metal and plastic. It was not very noisy, just a few vehicles moving around, and a few workers directing them, and directing the dumping of construction materials. They walked around the pit to a building that was already two or three floors above the ground.

"This will be our first parking garage. It should be ready in about a year. It will have five hundred parking spaces, and room for a score of tourist buses as well." Barry shouted.

"Here. We go up the elevator to this crane."

It was a narrow crane. Minnie looked up and was blinded by the light looking at the lifting boom high above her. She had never been up a construction crane before. It looked very tiny and perilous. She wondered how it ever managed to stand straight when even a little bit of wind blew up.

"It's the equivalent of a twelve story building just now. Only two can go up at a time in the lift here. There's no one in the cabin just now. So maybe I'll go up first with Minnie and Will then you can follow."

The lift was small and narrow. Minnie had to crush in next to Barry. "Don't worry Will. I won't fondle your woman too much. I've one of my own. I'll keep her safe." They slowly ascended to the cab and then the lift cabin came equally slowly back down. Will stepped inside and looked for the button to push. A speaker box squawked, "Push the blue button." shouted the disembodied Barry. "There's only one you can push." With a jerk or two the lift began to rise and soon the foundation pit looked like a gray and orange scar below. At the top, a side door slid open and Will stepped into the driver's cab where Minnie was standing on one side of the driver's seat and Barry on the other.

"We're really lucky now. Late afternoon and the skies are really clear. You can see all the way to Clingman's Dome over there. That's the highest mountain in the state. It used to be in Cherokee territory, but logging companies wanted those forests so badly that we couldn't include it in our Qualla Boundary. It was saved by President Roosevelt. During the war, the second World War."

The view was vast and green everywhere. Minnie was still afraid to look down, but she was impressed when she looked out over the hills and mountains in every direction, all encased in green leaves which looked like velvet and moved like waves in response to wind over grassy fields.

"It does take your breath away." said Minnie shyly.

"And in that direction is Mt. Unahala. said Barry as he pointed in the opposite direction. "Very steep. A sacred place for us Cherokees. We hid there in the time of the evacuations. It's now in the National Forest. Soon there will be autumn colors all around. Are you planning to go up to Clingman's Dome?"

"Yes. Is there a road to the top?" asked Will.

"Well, almost to the very top. You have to walk the last five hundred feet up. But I think you'll be able to do that."

"Tomorrow morning we'll go up there. And visit the park."

"Go as early as you can. It's great to see the sun rising on the mountains. And you're much likelier to see bears foraging for berries in the early hours of the morning before the swarms of tourists get there."

"Thanks we'll do that."

They went back down, Will and Minnie in the lift together this time. "Isn't this beautiful country?" asked Will. He was excited. There was so much to see.

"Fabulously." said Minnie who was still trying not to look down.

"And with this crane ride, we don't have to go to an amusement park for a short little overpriced ride. We can say we've already had our adventure ride for the day."

"For the week, I think."

They waited at the bottom for the lift to go back up and fetch Barry down. They thanked him profusely as he led them back through the site office where they returned the hardhats. Barry saw them all the way to the main entry doors of the casino. There at the reception desk was a display of books. Barry went over and picked one up. It had a colorful cover and when he handed it over to Minnie, the title on the cover became clear, 'The Story of the Cherokees of North Carolina'.

"Here, take this as a gift from the casino." said Barry. "Read it and enjoy it. It is a good overview of our tribe. Maybe you'd like to come back later and enjoy some gambling on our state-of-the-art video machines?" Barry offered.

"We'll think about it. There's so much to see yet. We're going to try some fly fishing."

"Good fly fishing hereabouts. Are you going out with a guide?"

"Yes. Day after tomorrow we get our first lessons."

"Well good luck with your Indian Project in Maryland. And yours in Virginia too, Minnie. And you'll need some luck too to catch any trout. Come back any time." And Barry waved them good-bye.

That evening they both ordered broiled trout for dinner. It was the first time for Minnie that she'd eaten trout, and Will thought he had eaten trout before but couldn't remember when. Maybe in Germany. But they both thought the fish was delicious.

"I wonder if we catch some, if the kitchen can fix them for us?" asked Minnie. "It is so light and sweet."

"I doubt if they can." answered Will as he picked some small bones out of his teeth. "Besides I think trout fishing locally is only catch and release. Fishing for trout is pure sport. No rewards."

In bed Minnie began to talk about what they had learned during the day. "I've seen a lot that perhaps I can introduce to my tribe. And you've seen how difficult it is to launch a casino, especially in a non-gambling state."

"Yes, a visit here really demonstrates what Indianness means in the late twentieth century."

"Yes, it has."

"But now I want to make love to you. And maybe afterwards we can practice braiding your hair." And he rolled over closer to Minnie and began to tickle her. Later as she was coming down from the highs of their passions, Minnie suddenly thought that they had made love in Indian territory, in an Indian owned hotel. She wondered if their physical act was any different than any other Indian couples through the past centuries in this area, if her loving of Will was any more authentic or comfortable as an Indian woman in Indian lands. She wanted to think this idea out and maybe talk to Will about it, but instead she curled up against the sleeping Will and dozed off into a pleasant sleep.

The next day they drove into the National Park and up to Clingman's Dome arriving around seven in the morning. They hiked up to the viewing platform and spent an hour looking around at the panoramic views and the changing morning light. Only a short distance away from the platform they saw a mother black bear and her cubs hanging in a mountain ash tree, feasting blithely on the red berries. After eight they went back down to the parking area where there was a small shop offering hot coffee. They stepped inside to drink some coffee and to warm themselves and found the place full with other tourists needing the same warmth. The park attendants were all wearing heavy jackets and looking amused at the several tourists dressed only in shorts, tee shirts and flip-flops. They then drove slowly down to the Tennessee side and visited the historic display areas; old farmsteads and log cabins that had been left behind when the park was established. The fields around this area were planted with corn and the dried, yellow stalks looked ready for harvesting. The mid-morning was already warming up under a hazy sun.

The next morning, they checked out and drove further up into the mountains toward South Carolina. They drove an hour through thick forests passing only occasional isolated houses or small settlements until they came to a small village called High Hamilton. There Will was looking for a fishing outfitter and tour guide firm that he had found on the internet. Finally he saw their sign outside a small cabin that looked like an old gasoline filling station, or a toll booth. Inside the guide, a young man named Mac, was expecting them.

"It's the first time that you've done fly fishing for trout?" the guide reconfirmed. "You'll need a few hours of supervised training and complete outfits, waders, boots, fishing tackle, the whole package. Right?"

Will agreed.

"Fine. Let's get you set up. You'll need to rent this gear and tackle for three days. My partner, Judson, here will be on the river with you for four hours today. He'll teach and show you all about casting lines. And even how to catch the devious trout. And tomorrow we'll take you to a morning location on a different river, and in the afternoon I'll come back and move you to another river, the Feather Rock River. And then Judson will do the same on the third day, on the Okachuba and French Rivers. So you'll get the experience of five different locations."

"And you think we'll learn enough that we'll catch any trout?" asked Will.

"We've seen reports that the trout are really striking these past few days. But there's only one place where you can catch and keep trout. And you'll need to buy a license to keep your catch there. We'll tell you all about it. River levels are low just now at the end of the summer, so you can wade even in the mid-stream on all these locations. Here I'll show you on a map."

"Let's get your woman fitted first in the waders." said Mac pointing to the back of the cabin.

"I have three flies that were given to me by Will's father." asked Minnie. "Are they good for what we're going to do?"

Mac looked at them, pushing them around in the little box.

"Yes, they look like they'll do the trick. But we mostly use barbless hooks here. So maybe you'll need some red flies. A seasonal local insect that is favored by trout hereabouts. You'll need three or four more for Will's rod. Flies often go flying off by themselves. Especially near hemlocks which sometimes overhang the river. Unfortunately you have to buy the flies. We don't rent them."

Then over the next hour Mac bustled about in his shop pulling out rods and reels, waders and thermal boot liners and socks, nets and boxes. "It's not too warm today and I don't think you'll need sun block because you'll be mostly in the shade."

Mac took Will's initial payment for the rentals, the purchase of thermal socks, and flies, and the services and then they began loading the firm's truck. They drove out down the main road about two miles and then turned off onto a small one lane unmarked road that first headed up a small rise and then turned and wended down a gently forested slope. After a short while the road turned to a gravel lane and the slope became steeper until it came to a dark grove of hemlocks. There Mac stopped the truck. "Here we are. This is the best place in the county." Minnie couldn't see any signs of the river, but as soon as she alighted from the truck she could hear the gurgling and splashing of a nearby river. The air was fresh and aromatic from the hemlocks. They carried their gear through the hemlock trees, ducking under branches and stepping carefully on the spongey soil covered in the short brown hemlock needles until they came out to a rocky bed and found themselves standing at a brown water river running swiftly over a wide bed of rocks. The river bed was about forty yards wide and there were lots of washed up branches, bare bleached trunks and other tree detritus on the rocky banks on both sides above the water. Will could hear rocks clacking against each other in the force of the water and he could follow a deeper channel running roughly down midstream.

"First we'll learn about casting." said Mac, handing a rod already loaded with reel to both Minnie and Will. "The fly, or the lure if you like, is actually lighter than the line. And it is actually the weight of the line that throws the lure out. I'll show you. Like this."

And Mac unrolled a number of loops of his line and then arching his rod, threw the line out in a giant hyperbola against the sky that seemed to hang in the air for an indefinite period before the lure plopped down gently on the water's surface. It must have been forty feet from where they were standing in the very middle of the fast current. Mac reeled in the line and repeated it, this time the line dripped water as it flew out over the river. Then he put up his reel and instructed Minnie to try; holding her wrist so that the rod was in the right position, aiding her in running out the line, then stepping back and showing her again how to move her casting arm. "You try it too." he said to Will. "Step over there so you're far enough away so that you won't tangle your lines. And throw more to the upstream." Minnie gave her first try but much of the slack line just fell at her feet. Will tried his first cast and was able to throw an arching line about twenty feet. Mac showed Minnie again the wrist movement for the gentle toss of the line. And he encouraged her to draw out less slack line for her next casting. She cast out a second time, achieving a nice arching line that floated out almost twenty feet. Will's second casting was not as successful. They repeated and Mac again gave pointers and advice. After five or six castings, it appeared that Will was getting the hang of casting his line out beyond twenty five feet. Minnie continued to have problems with balancing the amount of looped slack she let out and carried in her left hand and the correct throw of the line and whip of the rod. But she patiently continued to cast out line and reel it back. After more than an hour and half she was beginning to make smooth distant castings. "Now, try to envision a spot there in the mid-stream that you are trying to land the fly in." said Mac. After that Minnie started to concentrate on aiming her line. Will was beginning to toss the line and cast more than thirty feet and he was occasionally striking his target spot. "You're trying too hard to throw it, too much arm movement, like you might use in casting out a line with weights and bait on the hook." said Mac to Will. "If you don't hit your target it spot, just reel it straight back in and start over." Will thought how ridiculous he must look to Mac, but he clearly was only barely getting the right hang of the technique. Then he thought that Mac probably encountered this all the time in new inexperienced clients. After almost three hours, Mac announced that it was time to look for trout and combine the casting technique with the hunting eye so that they could land lures over where the trout were. "Now we can put on the waders. And we'll add your caddis fly lures to your lines." Minnie looked carefully at the fly and realized how realistic it looked.

"I've seen that kind of fly before, clouds of them." she said. "They gather in clouds."

"Yes, and they are favorite food of the wily trout."

And for the next hour they stepped into the river and resuming practicing their casting, trying to land the fly gently on the flowing water surface.

"And remember, the line is heavier than the fly lure."

Mac showed them a spot where the water was blocked by a fallen log and had formed a gravel lined pool. It was also so transparent that they could even see the different color of the stones on the bottom. It was at that point that Minnie recognized her first trout hanging still in the water in this pool, like a dark shadow. Will came over and saw it too, and then he saw two more nearby. "So that is where you want to cast to, just above their heads." said Mac.

So for another hour, they practiced casting to this transparent pool in the river. Sometimes the trout scattered, other times the lures missed their mark. Just as they were getting ready to call it quits for the first session, Will got the first strike. A good sized speckled trout took the lure and ran with it. A tug from Will on the rod and the fish crested and jumped clear from the water showing off its rainbow colors before splashing back. But the jump and the splash freed the fish from the hook, and Will's line immediately went slack. He reeled it in and found that the fish had taken the fly along with him. "Well, I'll be." swore Will.

"It happens. All the time." said Mac. "But now you know you can catch those wily creatures."

After a sandwich lunch at a small café, they drove to another river, putting their waders on from the start by the truck.

"Now for the next two hours, you're going to show me how to fly fish for trout." said Mac. "Late afternoon is usually the best time. When they bite the most."

This time the sun was bright and falling over their shoulders as they cast, giving long shadows onto the river surface. This river had many pools where there were each several good sized trout. It was Minnie who caught the first trout. She was so excited at the strike that she began to squeal and giggle and nearly dropped her rod. Mac came over to her and stabilized her grip and helped her begin to reel in the fish. As she pulled it up out of the water near her, Mac netted the fish and together they walked to the river bank to inspect it. She took hold of the squirming fish while Mac extracted the hook. "This is a good sized trout, but we'll let it go." he said. "We'll keep any that are bigger than this one." Minnie smiled at Mac and then looked up triumphantly at Will who was still standing in the river but looking at them. Minnie smiled at him as if to say, 'Don't think you can you beat that.' She was so proud. "Great, you're still the champion fisherwoman!" shouted Will.

Minnie also caught the next fish, which also was too small to keep. After an hour Will caught a trout that remained hooked so that he could net it. It was a keeper, more than twelve inches long. Mac put it on ice in the cooler. "Congratulations, Will! You now have begun a lifelong hobby of fly fishing for trout."

As the sun sank below the trees on the hilltops on both sides of the river, it became harder to see where to cast the line or to see the shadows of trout in the water. Still Minnie caught another trout and it was also as Mac put it, a 'keeper'. So they had two when they walked back out of the stream. Minnie said her feet were cold and she told Will that her back was sore from the long standing and holding the rod in several fixed positions.

"It's not as active as when the striped bass are running, is it?" Will asked her.

"No. It's completely different. But the scenery is certainly much more beautiful."

"And you're not scared to death of falling out of the boat. Are you?" asked Will with a smirk on his face.

Back at the outfitter's shop, Mac took the gear, boots and the waders, and put them in the back. "We'll use the same tomorrow. As for the trout, will you want to cook and eat them tonight?"

"No, we'll be staying in the Hamilton Lodge. I think we wouldn't be able to cook them."

"That's probably right. We can offer to gut and clean them and flash freeze them and then send them by courier to your address if you like. That way you can eat them when you like. But now we'll need to take your money for a fishing license."

The next morning they returned early to the outfitter's shop where they were introduced to Judson. They bought four more red sedge flies to replace the ones they had lost. They would not be using the flies that Bob had given to Minnie as a gift. Apparently they did not reproduce the right kinds of insects to suit the local tastes of trout. "I hear Mac En Cheese, took you to a spot where the trout were striking." said

Judson. "I hope today you have as much success." Judson took them to a river that flowed into the Tennessee River valley about fifteen miles to the west. "I'll spend the morning with you here, because this spot is so far away, but this afternoon, you'll be on your own on another creek closer in."

Will was beginning to get the hang of fly casting. That morning he regularly threw out line twenty five to thirty feet away from him. Minnie was still having trouble consistently casting out line much beyond twenty feet. Still after they spotted a section of the river where boulders formed a natural weir and clear pools, they began getting regular strikes. By the time they took a break for lunch, they had caught three brown trout, two by Will and one by Minnie. "They are stocked here, every year." said Judson. "So it's rare that you catch a keeper. But three in one morning. My word!" Judson was casting also and he seemed to hook a trout on every cast. But he released all of them. "I fish for the pure sport of it. Just to stand in the stream and watch life flow by." said Judson very philosophically. That afternoon, Judson left them on their own by a rapidly running creek that again was hidden in a hemlock gorge. Before leaving them he pointed out to them a spot where there were usually trout waiting. "They like to hide in the shade of the hemlocks, so you have to be careful not to snare your lures in the branches. Good luck." In the next two hours they did indeed lose two lures in the branches but they also got five or six strikes each. Will lost two fish as he tried to net them, and he caught three others. One of them was a 'keeper', but the others he had to release. Minnie lost three fish after hooking them, one gloriously jumping out of the water and flying off the hook. She landed two that were good to keep, and a third she released. But in the late afternoon, an errant cast by Minnie caught Will in the neck. "Ow!" he shouted. "A wasp has stung me." His hand immediately reached up and felt the lure and hook buried in his skin. Minnie did not tug on the line and fortunately the hook was without a barb, so Will was able to pull it out without any damage. "You got me now, Minneoka. Hooked and reeled in. I'm your keeper. No release required!" A small bead of blood oozed out where the hook had pierced him.

"Oh, Will. I'm so sorry. I don't know how I did that." Minnie put up her rod and stepped over closer to Will. She rubbed the site with her finger and then gave Will a kiss. "Forgive me." He kissed her back.

"I think no harm done." said Will. "I think though that might make the trout jealous of me. To be caught like that by a real Indian princess."

In all they ended their day with three more good sized trout which Will also asked to be prepared for freezing and shipping to them.

In the truck on the way back to the outfitter's shop Minnie asked Judson if he knew how the Cherokees caught fish.

"With weirs and fishing spears, I've been told." said Judson.

"What's a weir?" Minnie asked.

"It's like a partial dam on the river. The Indians would move rocks and tree trunks into the current to partially block the flow. This would create the deeper pools that the trout prefer, but would not completely dam up the stream, and it also meant there was a platform that the Indian fishermen could use to see the fish and spear them. You know, I'm part Cherokee myself. But I've never seen anybody using this technique. I mean fishing from a man-made weir."

Will said that he had read that the Nantiquaks had also largely relied on weirs and fishing nets. But they had to go far upstream because of the size and depth of the coastal rivers.

The next day, their last for fly fishing, Judson took them out in the morning to another river that ran through a hardwood forest. Its waters as a consequence were coppery in color and sparkled like dark garnets when they splashed over the rocks and caught the sun's light. Judson took them to a spot he said had been especially productive only that prior weekend and then he left them for two hours. And they caught nothing. Didn't even have a single strike, although they could see trout suspended in the waters and they were aiming for them.

"Canny trout. They know not to bite our flies." said Will.

"And maybe they can see us too."

When they quit casting and took off their waders, while they were waiting for Judson to come back, Will was feeling frustrated by the lack of success. But then he suddenly recalled something related.

"When I was in high school, we had to read a short story about fly fishing by Hemingway. The teacher said it was an important piece of literary work by him. But I could not see it at the time. Nothing much happened, except casting flies into the streams. A little like today. Our two days of fly fishing have not given me any further insight into that story, or why it is considered important."

"Maybe, fly fishing is a very manly thing to do. Whether you catch trout or not. Now I think if it were early spring and you had not eaten well for a number of days like most Indians in the time before the white man, catching fish by any method was urgently important. No time to consider it as merely a sport, a pleasant outing that is meant to serve its own ends."

"You're probably right. But you still look very feminine while casting your line. Not masculine at all. I mean you have a killer figure, standing there in the river up to your shins, in hip waders. Have you liked fly fishing so far?"

"I'm not sure. It seems to me its main aim is just to spend leisurely time standing in a pretty river. A cold river. Develops more reserves of patience. I think I can do that in other ways." Minnie paused. "But I have to say I think I prefer fishing with line and bait for striped bass, even from a boat. Although it is really beautiful up here in the mountains."

"You think, then, we've had enough? We can call it a day now?"

"If it's alright with you, yes."

"Fine, no problem. We can pay up through midday and go back to the lodge for the rest of the day."

They did that, returning all the gear and tackle and making arrangements for courier delivery of the trout to their Washington address early in the next week. They drove to the lodge which was serving an open buffet lunch. The weather had gotten warmer and many diners took their plates of food out to the terrace. Will and Minnie joined them.

"I think I'll have a burger. Would you like some trout? They have poached lemon trout here."

"Why not. It's still easier to eat than to catch."

Behind the lodge there was small lake made by damming the stream that flowed down between two high hills about a mile above the lodge. The lodge offered its guests use of row boats, and tackle and bait for weighted line, baited hook fishing for the perch and crappies that were stocked in the lake.

"Would you like to go in a row boat around the lake?" asked Will after they finished lunch.

"Yeah, sure. That would be nice, especially if you do the rowing. But I don't think we need to do anymore fishing today."

"I can understand that." said Will.

Will rowed the boat out first across the lake, which was no more than two hundred yards across and then around the far banks of the lake, which were up to eight hundred yards from the lodge. The waters were still and opaque green and the banks were obviously cleared of fallen timbers and undergrowth, which lent an artificial feeling to the entire lake. They could not see any fish, but they did see turtles occasionally bobbing their heads out of the water, and then quickly disappearing as soon as they became aware of the boat. As there was no current, the boat would stop almost as soon as Will stopped rowing and the drifting from the last strokes ended.

"Now that we're in the middle of the lake far from the shores and the lodge, I feel like making love to you here right now under the sun."

"No sir, mister. You'll be lucky if you get a kiss."

"Oh well, I could settle for a long, tender kiss." And Will leaned forward toward Minnie, who bent over toward him and they kissed for a long while.

"This scene reminds me a little of that film we watched a couple of months ago. You remember, the one with Henry Fonda and Katherine Hepburn?"

"On Golden Pond, wasn't it?"

"Yes that's the one. It was so sad."

"No I don't think that's appropriate to us, just now. That was about the end of married life of two elderly married people. We don't qualify."

"No I only meant the scene, not the meaning or theme. Just the two of us alone in a row boat out in the middle of a small lake—really no more than a pond. Breathing in the stillness and green beauty all around."

"There are no loons here."

"You know what I mean."

"That film made me cry. It made me think about the last years of my father and mother together. Not so sentimental and affectionate, but…. I don't want to think about it. He died prematurely. And I think they still loved each other."

"Okay. Change the subject. It's still warm enough we could go swimming in this lake while the sun is still hot. There was a small beach there by the dock."

"Today? No I don't want to. The water's too cold."

"We could still try to " Will paused a long moment, "maybe get married. And that way in a few years we could pretend to have our own Golden Pond moment."

"I said change the subject."

"But you're enjoying our first vacation together as a couple, yes?"

"Will it has been wonderful. Everything is, well, it's just wonderful. Actually it's the first vacation trip I've ever had. And the first and only one I've ever had with a man that I love."

"The same for me. My first vacation with the love of my life and a lovely woman too. Very romantic too."

"Especially taking the hooks out of trout." said Minnie as she giggled.

"Or taking a hook out of my neck."

"But I never want this feeling of the moment—just drifting in this boat next to you --to end, the feelings I'm having just now. Too bad we need to head back tomorrow."

Not long afterwards Will took up the oars and began to row back across the length of the lake to the dock. The squeaking of the oarlocks was the only noise on the lake. Once back onshore, they walked a little up the shore to a spot Will had noticed where a brambles of wild raspberries were growing. There were still an abundance of bright red, ripe raspberries, so they began to collect them and ate as they progressed through the prickly stems.

The next morning, they packed up and got in the Olds for the trip back home. Will drove the first three hours until they were well down and out of the mountains and heading east on I-40 to the flat lands of Carolina. It was then time to take a break, have some drinks, and fill the car with gasoline. Then Minnie took over the wheel. She drove another hour and a half when it was time to stop for lunch, just before turning north toward Virginia. Traffic was heavy, with lots of heavy trucks on the road. They had stopped at a restaurant that had advertised for miles about the native Carolina barbecue, 'Best in the State'. In their booth Will checked his cell phone and was surprised to see that he had a large number of missed calls from the week when they were in the mountains without microwave signals. "So much business. So many people trying to call me?" he spoke almost to himself. Minnie took out her cell phone and looked. She had one missed call, and a text message, both from Ron Parchesi. "Call us when you're free," she read out loud. We won!" she read out loud the text message. "I wonder what that could mean."

Will looked at her for a moment over his Carolina style barbecue sandwich.

"I think there's only one thing that that could mean." he said as he began to smile. "You've won your suit in court for the Nantiquak reservations in Maryland."

Minnie frowned, put on a look of concentration, and then smiled. "I guess you're right. Yeah, that's the only thing. It must be. You're right. Willeams, we won our first case!"

"Well, I can't call today. It's Saturday and I don't have Ron's number." she said.

"Yes, you do. It's attached to his message. You can reply. But you can probably wait until Monday." said Will. And they left the matter for later.

"But I do need to call my mother to tell her to expect us. When? In three hours?"

"Yes," said Will over his barbecue sandwich. "We have at least that much driving left depending on the traffic."

So Minnie called. And as she spoke to her mother, telling her that they would drop by around five o'clock. Will could hear her mother shouting over the line, and Minnie's expression grew serious. She hung up.

"She really doesn't want to see us." she said. "She's still angry with me. And doesn't want to see you especially." It looked to Will that she was about to cry.

"We can still drop by." said Will. "I can't believe she wouldn't open the door when we come."

"It won't be pleasant. But she said my sister, Alicia, and her kids will be there. So I do have to stop to see them."

"Yes, we have to. You haven't been to see her in a long time."

"I know."

They drove on into Virginia in silence. As they were nearing Richmond, Will asked Minnie to search for some music, preferably classical music. She began turning the radio dial until she hit a piano playing with orchestra in what sounded like classical music. She left the radio dial there, saying, "I wonder what it is." "Sounds nice, whatever it is," said Will. After another fifteen minutes, the piece concluded and an excited woman announcer declaimed that that was a concerto by Robert Schumann performed by Martha Argerich.

"Did you hear that?" asked Minnie. "Martha Argerich was playing for us. A piece by Schumann. What a coincidence."

"Yeah. Especially since you look like her."

"Oh, stop it. It's not true."

"Yeah, you're right. You're prettier than she is. And you look a lot younger than she does."

"I should hope so. I am younger than she is."

Will pulled the Olds into Bowling Green at four forty-five. He asked Minnie to direct him to her mother's house, a small, indistinct house set back off a shady street just off Main Street near the center of the small town. They arrived only two minutes afterwards. It was a surprisingly small town.

Minnie led Will up to the porch and to the front door and rang the bell. Jemima did not come to the door, but Alicia, Minnie's sister did. She pushed open the aluminum screen door and spoke a little something to Minnie. Will only heard, "Mataoka" and nothing more as Alicia was practically whispering. Minnie turned to Will and said "Let's go in. We'll have coffee or something." They went inside.

Alicia led them to the small living room, and asked them to sit down and excused herself. She came back a few minutes later, with her two children aged eight and six. "Say 'Happy Birthday' to your Auntie." she prompted them. Then she dismissed them and they rushed away to the back of the house. And then she offered Minnie a small gift wrapped box. "A belated present for your birthday which was last week. We don't get to see you that much. We were wondering if we would hear from you around Labor Day."

Minnie unwrapped the box and opened it. Inside were a pair of leather winter weight gloves and a silk scarf.

"For the coming winter." said Alicia acting a little abashed. "The kids picked them out for you."

"They're really nice. Tell them, 'thank you' and that I will wear them this winter as soon as the weather gets cold. I walk about half a mile to the metro every day, and then another half mile from the final stop to my work, so I need such things. And I never think of getting such items for myself."

Jemima still did not emerge from elsewhere in the house. Alicia sat looking embarrassed by the impasse, not being able to privately talk with her sister. Will could see that Alicia looked a lot like her older sister. The same pretty face and eyes. But she no longer had Minnie's lithe figure. In fact Will concluded that Alicia looked more like she was the older sister and Minnie aged only twenty nine.

"Is mother in?" asked Minnie. "Is she feeling alright?"

"Oh yes, quite alright. Until you two showed up. She was playing with the kids."

"Well maybe we need to go. We are returning from a vacation trip we took to Cherokee, North Carolina. It was like a dream."

"Bob's never taken me or the kids on a vacation. It's simple: we can't afford it. Anytime."

"I understand. Is he still working at the garage and towing business?"

"Yes. But there's not a lot of work. We've moved back to the reservation, and so he has to drive a ways to his work, and work night shifts to make enough." Alicia lowered her head and was rubbing her hands together. "But maybe you'd like some coffee?"

"Yes, that would be nice." said Minnie. "Maybe I can leave you some money for the groceries or clothes?"

Alicia did not answer. Instead she stood up and went into the kitchen. Minnie stood up, and motioned to Will. "I'll be just a moment." And she followed Alicia into the kitchen.

Will could hear the low voices of Minnie and Alicia, but he could not tell what they were saying. They spoke for five minutes or so, when Will became aware of a third much louder, angry voice: it was their mother, Jemima. Minnie did not raise her voice in answer and so Will still did not understand. A moment or so later, Minnie, followed by Alicia, brought a tray with three mugs of coffee on it, a creamer and a sugar bowl, and a plate of Oreo cookies. Minnie distributed the mugs and then sat down on the sofa next to Alicia. Will sat on a large plush chair in the opposite corner just across the low table, quite close in this small living room.

"I'm sorry. Mom says she won't visit with us." said Minnie sadly. "She's really angry with me for not visiting her these past four months. Understandable I guess."

The three drank their coffee slowly and without a word. After a short while, the door to the kitchen opened and Jemima slipped through. She did not greet Will or even look at him.

"My daughter actually lives with you still?" she said in accusatory voice looking at a spot on the wall next to Will.

"Yes, we have a house together in D.C. and a weekend house on the Eastern Shore of Maryland."

"So you're not a simple farmer."

"Mama, I told you." interrupted Minnie. "He works in real estate, and he owns and manages a farm."

"I make a good living if that is what you're concerned about. I can support your daughter. And want to have a family with her too."

"Yes, and why aren't you married yet?" It was unclear who Jemima was addressing.

"Mama, he's asked me to marry him. I have been reluctant to accept so far."

"So you live with him like some common mistress?" said Jemima returning to accusatory tone of voice.

"No, we live together like husband and wife. We share expenses, as well as chores, and we do everything together. As fate would have it we are working together on the same project for an Indian tribe in Delaware and Maryland. But I've told you about that before, you know."

"And you'll of course convert her away from being an Indian, completely."

"No, I don't think I can or will do that, Mrs. Warrens. As you may know she resigned as chief of the Massaponax, but now she is the chairman of the Nantiquak tribe. Like the top chief."

"No she didn't tell me."

"It's the tribe we're both working on to get Federal recognition and to return its reservations." said Minnie.

"Why, she'll never live on a reservation again. Not her own tribe's anyway."

"Why is that important?"

"It's important, because without living close with her own kind on their own reservation she will cease being an Indian."

"And you?" said Will. "Have you ceased being an Indian? I understand that your reservation is more than forty five miles away from here. Why haven't you gone back there? To live near Alicia and her family?"

"I would if I could, but I don't have a house there."

"I will build you a house, then," said Will. "Or will have it built for you. Two bedrooms, long house. A wigwam if you like."

All three women looked up directly at Will with surprise on their faces.

"You don't believe me? Maybe nine hundred square feet, one story. Should take four months to build. Are any of the Indians living on the reservation capable as builders?"

"Will, you don't have to." said Minnie softly.

"What do you mean? She says that she can only remain an Indian—and you too-- if she lives on the reservation with the rest of the tribe, but that she cannot afford to buy a house there. I can afford it and want to help her. You've always said you were afraid that being with me you would cease being an Indian altogether. Well, here's an opportunity for her to remain an Indian in her own tribe. What do you say, Mrs. Warrens? Would you like that? Maybe it could be ready for you to move in by March next year."

Jemima did not say anything but she was shaking her head slightly from side to side, as if answering in the negative.

"I can't." she said without looking at anyone. "I mean I can't accept this kind of charity."

"Why. Can't your daughter give you a gift? And I am your daughter's civil husband. This could help you—you'll live next to your grandchildren—and you will enjoy life more in your own true community."

"Mama, you have to accept this generous offer." said Alicia, and then the same was repeated by Minnie. "You've always said after papa died that you wanted to go back. That you don't like Bowling Green. And now we live so far away from you."

"Mama, you can say what you like." said Minnie. "But I think you cannot say, truthfully, that you don't want your own house in the reservation. Am I right?"

"Mrs. Warrens, you don't have to answer right away. But when you're ready and do agree to accept my offer, we can start straight away. Just have to find a suitable building site and I suppose get permission from the tribe."

Jemima made a wry little smile. She was thinking about a house of her own next door to Bob and Alicia, and stepping out on the stoop and watching her grandkids running around on the grassy fields around both houses.

"You're like your daughter. She wants desperately to agree to marry me, but something, unspoken, is keeping her from accepting and becoming Mrs. Eames. I will wait for your acceptance. The offer will remain open until you're ready to accept it. Just like my offer to Minnie to marry me."

There was a long pause. And as if she only slowly realized what it was Will had said, Jemima finally said in dismay:

"Minnie, Will proposed marriage to you and you did not accept? Why are you still living with him then?"

"I haven't turned him down, either, Mom. But something keeps me from accepting just yet."

"Are you a fool? What could keep you from accepting? You have already given away your sex. He's made you his consort, live-in mistress. He has no obligations to you. You have no guarantees and no rights in your present state. And he doesn't have any family relations to us."

"That's a little unfair, Mrs. Warrens." interrupted Will. "She has her reasons, and they seem to be important ones. But I have pledged myself to her and I love her. And she loves me. She's just not ready to call our relationship a marriage. But my offer to you still stands. Think about it and let me know if you want it."

"Will, I think we need to go." said Minnie standing up from the couch. Jemima, still standing, moved away from the others. Will stood and reached for Minnie's hand and they moved to the entry.

"Tell the kids that I really liked their birthday gifts—even though we both know that you bought them, Alicia. We'll visit again soon. Good-bye, Mama."

They left the house and as they stepped down the path, they both could hear Alicia shouting at her mother, although the words were not clear. It was still late afternoon and they were earlier than they had expected, so they decided to drive the rest of the way home to their place in Cleveland Park instead of staying at a motel on the way. After they got back on I-95 Minnie turned her head to Will.

"You are so generous, Will. I love you so much. But you did not have to offer to build Mom a house."

"Offer was rejected. There's not much generosity in making a repudiated offer."

"No, you're wrong. She accepted. She wants that house from you. She just doesn't know how to say it."

"Strange way of showing it, then. I don't think I can hire a builder just yet. As least with you, you only seem to have rejected my offer for the time being and our relationship continues to grow."

"Will, I love you so much. There're not enough ways I can show you that and prove to you how much."

"Yes there are. Let's get married."

Minnie paused for a long time as if reconsidering her position. Her face looked sad. "I'm still not ready. But I'm almost there."

Then they fell silent. Will at first was feeling irritated with Minnie and her mother. The gift that is not accepted is the most galling and upsetting kind. And it seemed both Minnie and her mother were pushing back on him, refusing to accept the generosity of his heart. Perhaps it was for fear of being taken over by a white man. That could be Jemima's reasoning. But Minnie, why was she still resisting fully committing to him? She seemed ready. He didn't understand what was blocking Minnie. They remained quiet for the next hour and a half until they were descending into the valley of the Potomac, nearly home.

"And this coming weekend," said Will. "Don't forget we are going to attend both Saturday and Sunday the Nantiquak's powwow.

"I kind of forgot that it's this next weekend. I was too absorbed in fly casting to think about the dates."

"And we have to try braiding your hair."

"Right. That will be a challenge."

"I think this week I won't commute to Bristol. I've got to write the application, and I can do that at home with my laptop as easily as I can in Bristol."

They got to their house after eight in the evening, just about the time of sunset. Both were exhausted from the day at the wheel.

"Let's walk down to our favorite little restaurant and have something light for supper." Will suggested.

"I don't feel much like cooking or eating, so I think that's a good idea. We also could use the walk to stretch out a bit."

Later that evening, before going to bed, Will wrote an e-mail invitation to Professor Broadhead to come to the Nantiquak powwow in the coming weekend.

The next day, after he had taken his run around the neighborhood and Minnie had left for work, Will started writing the application document. He organized it in the seven sections that were required by the instructions set out by the Bureau. He started writing on the section on the ancestry of the current Nantiquaks who were listed in the incorporation documents. This section was intended to demonstrate the continuity of the tribal community. It would include what little information they had from the census records. He wrote fast and furiously all day.

Around ten that morning, Minnie called.

"Will, that strange message was just what we thought. We've won our case for the Nantiquaks. It's a great triumph! The state court has ruled that Maryland has to retore the reservation lands! This is fantastic for us. Ron Parchesi told me all the details and he was very congratulatory for my efforts. There's so much detail. I'll tell you all about it all this evening."

"Minnie, this is a real credit to you. I'm sure your boss—what's his name again? —will give you lots of credit and praise. Maybe even a bonus."

"Yeah, maybe. But there's always the prospect of an appeal going against us. We can't tell the Nantiquaks just yet until we know how the decision will be enforced or whether Maryland will appeal. We'll talk this evening."

After Will's excitement faded, he decided to call Carmine to ask how she was coming with her sections.

"I've written some of the history section, but it needs to be looked at, Will. And I've started writing some of the fourth section. But this week looks bad for writing. I'm helping in the last minute preparations for the powwow."

"Okay. I've started too. I'll see you on Saturday if not sooner. I've invited Professor Broadhead to come."

"Oh, that would be good. There are some people here who remember her when she did her field work here twenty five years ago or so."

"She hasn't answered yet. But I would hope she comes."

"Oh, I needed to tell you that last week we hired that woman-- whose resume we looked at--to be our new chief accountant. She's already started."

"Oh, then I need to see her. Maybe I'll see her later this week. We need to put together the starting account statements for the Corporation. It's time I need to apply for the Corporation's tax-free status with the IRS and the Delaware revenue department. Is she working at the Laurelton office?"

"Yes, on a three day basis just now. Wednesday through Friday."

"What's her name?"

"Jennifer Robinson."

"Okay, I'll call her on Wednesday. Bye for now."

Later that afternoon, there was a knock on the door. When Will opened it he saw a black man in the brown uniform of a courier service. "You need to sign for this." he said as he handed Will a large cardboard parcel. It was their trout from the previous week. Will unpacked the box and removed the styrofoam wrapping and put the frozen fish in their freezer. He thought that they would take them out to Bristol and maybe share them with his parents.

On Wednesday, he got an email answer from Professor Broadhead. She wrote that she would be very happy to visit the powwow of the Nantiquaks on Indian River on the Saturday date at the end of that week. Then she also wrote she had finished with her contribution and she was attaching it as a file with the email. She asked if he would review it to see if it met their needs and was helpful. Will eagerly opened the file document and began to read the report she had written. It summarized much that was in her book on the Nantiquaks, and Will approved of it as a scientific reconstruction of the evolution of the tribe from the early 17th century to the end of the 19th century. But then at the end of the paper, Will was unpleasantly struck by a conclusion that he found very objectionable. Professor Broadhead wrote that by the beginning of the 19th century the Nantiquaks had become de-tribalized.

"There's no way we can submit this conclusion to the Bureau." Will thought to himself. "It is like an admission that the tribe ceased to exist. We'll have to get the professor to change this." He thought he would have to have a long talk with her at the powwow.

In the meantime he sent a message back to her expressing his desire to meet her in person on Saturday at the powwow. And writing, "We have to talk about a number of things."

Then he called Jennifer Robinson in Laurelton.

"Hello, Miz Robinson. This is Will Eames. The others may have told you about me. I am a consultant and the finance director for the tribal corporation. There was no one to answer the phone?"

"No, the receptionist I think has stepped away and forwarded all calls to me. But yours is the first call of the morning."

"Well, I wanted to introduce myself, and find out if you've gotten clear instructions of what needs to be done with the accounts first."

"I've gotten some minimum instructions, but I could use some help in getting started."

"Fine. I was also calling to say I would come up there on this Friday morning and we can go over your duties and our immediate needs. Would you be working on that morning?"

"Yes. That would be a help for me. There's nobody that I've met who seems to know what's needed exactly."

"Fine. Then I will meet you on Friday at say around 9:30."

That evening after dinner, Will showed Minnie Professor Broadhead's printed-out article. He patiently waited at the kitchen table, his head in his hand, as she read the article. He had not told her about the contents of the paper but wanted to test her reaction. Just as Will had earlier that day, she reacted to the de-tribalized line, unfavorably. "That line cannot go into your application, I have to say."

"Yeah, I suspect that there is something going on in the anthropology profession about what comprises a tribe. But I agree with you, we don't want that intruding into our application. We should tell her to omit it, don't you think?"

"Definitely." said Minnie looking at Will with wide eyes. "Why would she feel she needs to write such things? She obviously doesn't know her audience."

"Well, she confirmed that she will be coming to the powwow this Saturday. We'll have to get her to change this part."

"That's for certain." said Minnie. "But you know, I worked six years in the Bureau and got to know their consulting anthropologist. An older woman named Susan Danielle. She broke her teeth on studies of Indian tribes in New England. We got along well. I can ask her what she thinks of this term, de-tribalized. And I'll relay to you her reaction to see what it might mean in the anthropology profession."

"Could you? That would be great. We need all the insider help we can get."

Then Minnie related to Will all the details about the trial and the court's decision. It was all very complicated. But from what Minnie understood, it seemed that the state of Maryland was charged with buying back all the reservation areas that it had sold in the 19ᵗʰ century and granting them back to the Nantiquak Corporation.

That next evening at the dinner table again, Minnie shared with Will what she had heard from Susan Danielle. Apparently the term de-tribalized had become a contentious subject among anthropologists and it had reached the Bureau as well. And for an Indian tribe to be considered de-tribalized was the kiss of death for Federal recognition. It was tantamount to saying that the group was no longer a tribe at all. At the root of the term was the rejection of the term tribe by many anthropologists. They no longer felt it was an accurate or justified social identifier, that other classifications were needed, especially for Native Americans. It was aimed squarely at tribal groups that had no reservations and lived mixed in with the majority white community. Minnie had asked her if the Eastern Band of Cherokees would be considered to be de-tribalized. She had answered that she didn't think so. But she would consider the Massoponax to be de-tribalized even though they had a reservation and a large part of the tribe lived together on it. Minnie said that she had asked Susan about proximity and consanguinity as sufficient qualifications for a people to be considered a tribe. She said she had quibbled over that. But she agreed that they were important characteristics of being tribal. In some regards Susan told Minnie, the term de-tribalized represented the complete assimilation of a former group of American Indians into white society and the loss of coherence and all Indian identity. But also it was a term that meant that a group related by blood and close association had lost all of its characteristic ways of living and surviving from their Stone Age period prior to 1600. Will and Minnie agreed they would have to get Professor Broadhead to drop the term from their application document.

On Friday morning when Will let himself into the Nantiquak office in Laurelton, he was surprised to see that there was still no receptionist. He started looking for the new accountant, Jennifer Robinson. He saw her sitting in the second room back from the entry. She was a short slight woman, at most twenty-eight years old, slender in the hips and waist, with hardly any bust, and with short bobbed brown hair. He also noticed that she seemed to be braless. She stood up and shook Will's hand as he introduced himself.

After introductions, Jennifer confirmed that she had locked the door just as Will had instructed her because the receptionist hadn't come again that day. She led him to her office, which was the second from the front of the building. She had already set up her work station, and the computer screen was on, although it was solid green in sleep mode.

Jennifer showed him what she had accomplished so far. She was still setting up the accounts reports and was just then working on the opening balance sheet. On her desk in one pile were the receipts for construction materials for the refurbishment of the office building as well as receipts for the furniture. In another stack there was the opening bank statement for the account they had opened in the First Delaware National Bank just three doors down the street on the corner with Main Street. There were also the statements he had written to account for the loans he had made to the Nantiquak Corporation for the refurbishment expenses and for the initial capitalization account. Will sat down next to Jennifer at the desk and she began to explain to him what she was doing. After only a few minutes, Will realized he was beginning to feel aroused sitting so close to this young woman, feeling her warmth exude through her blouse, seeing her nipples stand erect through her blouse, and noticing the outline of her crotch and vagina in her stretch pants, seeing her very white small hands and slender fingers, and smelling the cigarette residue from her mouth. He felt ashamed of himself and moved his seat a bit further away from her. Jennifer was doing everything correctly as far as he could see. The most important and urgent document that he needed was the opening balance statement. The only issue he could see was the assessment of the value of the assets of the Corporation. They were few enough: the building that served as the offices of the Association, and the building of the old historic schoolhouse which served as a museum. He wondered how he could get a proper assessment of their value. They were not marketable properties. Jennifer had not included them, because as she said she had not been informed about them.

Will offered Jennifer a guess for the values of these assets-- pitching them on a low side-- and reminded himself that he would have to ask Morley if there were any records for the expenses of acquiring and building the Association's building. She was left with the challenge of balancing the assets to the liabilities of the Corporation. She said she would think of something.

"Good, and could you have this done by end of day next Wednesday?" Will asked as he stood up and moved yet a bit farther away from Jennifer. It was only then that he noticed that she was wearing a gold wedding band on the middle finger of her left hand. He wondered if that meant she was married or divorced. He wasn't sure what a wedding band on the middle finger meant, if anything at all.

"Yes, I think so. But could I call you if I have any more questions on important issues?"

Will agreed and gave her his cell phone number.

"Looks to me like you're doing a good job. Keep up the good work. And if you will, could you keep track of when the receptionist appears or is absent. Even if he comes and leaves for long periods during the day. He's a paid employee and we shouldn't pay him for non-attendance. The other officers are not salaried just yet so their full time attendance here is not so important."

She agreed.

"And early next week, you should start getting the earnings that the tribe has gotten for the powwow. First income for the Corporation. And by the way, do you plan to attend the powwow?"

"No, where is it exactly?"

Will told her and invited her to come either on Saturday or Sunday.

"Oh, sounds like it could be fun. I'll bring my son, probably on Sunday."

"Okay, then I'll probably see you there." Will felt relieved. She probably had been married and now was divorced with a young son. And at just that moment Jennifer looked directly full in the face at

Will, and their eyes locked together for a sustained moment. Her pupils were quite dilated. She seemed to be telling Will that she wanted him or found him attractive. And he seemed to feel that she was a very strong personality and had a strong sexual craving. They broke eye contact, and Will turned for the door. He felt flustered. Jennifer stood up and followed him out of her office and to the front door, where Will turned back and again gave her encouragement in the work she was doing and then said good-bye. He could hear Jennifer locking the front door behind him as he stepped away toward his car.

Once in the car, Will began to feel disgust, shame, and arousal all at the same time. He wanted to have Minnie in his arms right then and there and he wanted to undress her and make love to her unabashedly there in the car. If only she was next to him at that moment. He craved being inside her and bringing her passion to a climax right then, as if they had not made love together in weeks, even though they had coupled only the night before last. He felt dirty about lusting over Jennifer, but he also felt stronger than before that Minnie was the sole passion and desire in his life, and she wasn't there by his side when he was distracted by this strange young woman. On the drive back to Bristol all he could visualize was being on top of a naked Minnie and bringing her to a screaming heaving climax. Could he wait four or more hours for her? As soon as he got to his desk in his realty office, he called her.

"Minnie, I love you." he said as soon as she answered.

"Will, what's the matter? Why are you calling and speaking like that?" she immediately detected his distress.

"You're still coming this evening in a few hours, aren't you?"

"Yes, of course. What's happened?"

"Nothing. It's just that I suddenly I got a strong craving for you. A panic sense of missing your physical presence like I never have before. And I just can't wait until I have you in my arms this evening and fill you with my love."

"I'll be there as soon as I can be. And I want to hold you close, too. But it still takes two hours to get to you there in Bristol."

"I'll count the minutes until you get here. Meet you at the cottage house. And remember, I love you more than all the world."

"Don't do anything rash, Willeams. I'll be there. I love you too." And Minnie hung up.

Will felt a little better. He held in his mind's eye a vision of Minnie smiling at him with her faint smile, and her green-brown eyes boring into his. And when she finally did arrive near seven o'clock, he led her straight to the bedroom and began laying on her bouquets of kisses and adulations of caressing hands all over her. They made passionate love in waves over the next three hours, until complete exhaustion forced both of them to collapse into a light dozing sleep perfumed by their sweat and intimate juices. When they recovered and it was already dark and too late to go out to eat, so they had tea and the almond cookies which Minnie had brought with her, eating in the kitchen in their bathrobes, seated close together. Will's hands kept stroking her thighs. And Minnie was humming a tune that Will did not recognize.

Early the next morning as they arose, Minnie was surprised to see that she was naked in the bed, that she had not put on her nightgown. She looked for it while trying to keep herself covered by the sheet, and finally she found it under the bed on the floor. Will was still lightly snoozing and did not take notice of her as she slipped on her nightgown, the green satiny one he had bought for her when they started their love. He barely noticed when she stepped out of bed and went into the bathroom. She came back before she had taken a shower.

"Will, Will, get up. Don't you want to go on your run? Remember you promised to tie a braid for me."

And then she went back into the bathroom and began to run the shower. Will got up and had to go to the other toilet because she had locked the door behind her. But he heard her now lightly singing in the shower. Maybe in was the same tune she had been humming the night before. Will got into his running gear and knocked on the bathroom door. "I'll go running now. Will be back in thirty or forty minutes."

When he got back, Minnie was already dressed. She was wearing dark gray slacks and a light brown tunic. And embroidered onto the tunic was the elaborate, colorful beadwork that she had bought in Cherokee. And she was wearing the silver birch leaf earrings, two on each ear.

"Do you like it?" she asked him looking at him with girlish delight.

"Beautiful."

"Now we need to see if you can do a braid."

"A single braid right?"

As it turned out, Will did not know how to weave a braid of hair, even with Minnie's instructions, even as they stood in front of a mirror and she could give him instructions, step by step. It took more than forty minutes to complete the task with Minnie frequently taking over the pleating and folding. Finally it was finished and Minnie draped it over her right shoulder behind her silver earrings. Her hair was not so long that it reached even as far as her bosom, it barely draped over her shoulder. But it looked so right for Minnie and it enhanced her dusky Indian skin color. She also wore the emerald pendant on a silver chain that was visible beneath the tunic when Will stood close to her.

"You're so beautiful, Minnie. I adore the way you look."

"Good. So let's have some breakfast. I'm going to fix pancakes. I brought all the ingredients, in case we've run out here. I'm going to try to make cornmeal pancakes."

"That would be most appropriate. And I think if they are like cornbread, also most tasty."

They drove up to Indian River in Will's Oldsmobile. Will thought that arriving amongst a crowd there would be no one who recognized them or understood the significance of their arriving in the same car. And Will felt that maybe there was nothing really to hide any longer, not even from Carmine, or Chief Clarke. Minnie didn't object. She was also ready to admit her closeness to Will and their ongoing relationship.

The powwow was just getting started for the day when they arrived at a plot of land of sandy open fields covered in crabgrass mixed with stands of pine woods. They parked in a field that had been cordoned off into three areas, and there were already maybe sixty cars parked and at one end of the field were five yellow-orange school buses parked. People were walking from the sandy parking lot toward a copse of pines. They all looked outwardly like Indians, but they were uniformly dressed in western wear: blue jeans, cowboy boots, wind breakers and flannel shirts, and many of the men wore baseball caps. Minnie was pleased to see that many of the women also wore braids, although many of the older women, those with grey or silver white hair, wore long twin braids. In her tunic she looked dressed for the occasion. But she noticed many of the women wore moccasins with beadwork. Minnie felt strangely comfortable being among these people she did not know. She felt as if she were one of them. And at the same time she felt it was a little odd strolling among these Indians with Will, clearly an Anglo in dress and physiognomy, at her side. She took his hand and walked on, feeling for the first time that she was proud to be seen with this man, Will Eames.

They paid the entry fee of ten dollars per person and wandered into a broad area of pine trees and sandy lots. These areas were surrounded by concession stands offering soft drinks, water, beer, and in some of them sandwiches, boiled corn on the cob, and french fries. In the middle area on a big open sandy patch there was a ceremonial fireplace set up with a tall stack of firewood waiting to be ignited. There was a wide apron of tamped down earth around the fireplace where dances obviously took place. People, mostly Indians, were strolling around this area going from concession stand to benches, or to one of the five or six crafts displays. These were set up in large tents with a long table across one side where the crafts were on display for sale. Some had demonstrations such as bead working, or stitching beaded strings to deer hide shirts, or flaking stone points for arrow and spear heads, or basket weaving from cane or making mats from cattails. There was a tent with several wood carvers showing their craft, and selling wooden bird whistles. And in another tent there were several women making beads from the nacre of oyster or clam shells. On some of the trees were posted paper announcements of the scheduled events for the day. On a far side of the powwow park, there was a large tent set up in front of which were picnic tables with benches. The announcement had indicated that at 12:30 there would be a barbeque lunch on offer. There were already several men engaged with tending cook fires in half oil barrels set up to waist height. The smell of marinated pork filled the air around most of the park. They stopped by to watch an archery demonstration. There several young men were taking turns drawing their bowstrings back and releasing their reed arrows at a target of a buck deer that was pulled along a track slowly about 12 yards in front of them. They showed that they were very capable of hitting the target every time.

One commented: "Shooting the deer at this distance with these arrows and this kind of bow was not very difficult. The arrow badly wounds the animal and then you can chase it down until it dies. The hardest part of the hunt was being able to creep up on a deer or its family to within fifteen yards without scaring them off. Often this took hours of careful movement."

One of the young men missed the target and the arrowed whizzed by and lodged into the wall of haybales that was erected beyond the target rail. "And the next hardest part, was if you missed on your shot, you had to find and retrieve your arrows from the thick bracken or ironweed creepers. Of course it was also not easy if you hit your target, you then had to haul your kill usually many miles back to your settlement."

They did not see anyone they knew or recognized until it was time to go to the tent for lunch. And there standing in line they saw several of the men from the tribal council or the corporate board as they now were, and Will also saw several tribesmen and their families from the Kuskowarok band and from the Puckamee band that he had met earlier in the year. After getting and paying for barbecue sandwiches, beans and drinks they sat down at a picnic table under a pine tree which from the pine cone litter piled up next to the trunk had clearly been a favorite eating spot for squirrels not too long before. When they sat down and looked back over the park they became aware that there were several hundred people in attendance, many more than they thought they had seen. Not too long after they had started eating Chief Clarke came over to them and greeted them.

"Hey, valued tribal elders and honorary Nantiquaks." he said in a hearty and friendly voice, not his usual tone of speaking. "I'm so glad to see you two here. I presume this is your first visit to our annual powwow?"

Will stood up and shook Clarke's hand. "We're enjoying what we've seen so far."

"Make sure that you attend the demonstration of the Moon Dance by the Shawnee Indians, our special guests this year. It will be at two o'clock by the main fire pit. Oh and by the way. I saw a certain Professor Broadhead here. She said she was looking for you, Will. Keep an eye out for her. It's been maybe twenty years since I last saw her. I think this is her first visit to our powwow also."

And then Chief Clarke wandered off, greeting others at the tables.

"That's the most I've heard him speak at one time, ever." said Will. "He must be really excited by the doings here."

"Undoubtedly." said Minnie. "He's the main host and so many people are in attendance. I wonder if yesterday and Thursday were as well attended."

Near two o'clock they strolled back to the main fire pit where a crowd of viewers was already gathered to see the half dozen big men standing under some pines. They were all dressed in deerhide leggings, had painted bared torsos which were quite brown, faces painted in reds and yellow, and they were all wearing hair pieces with feathers and porcupine quills mixed in with long braids. In spite of the large gathered crowd the air was still and quiet. A couple of men dressed entirely in deerhides and moccasins but without the body paint started beating at large skin drums and the six dancers began their moon dance without any prologue or explanation. They danced frantically with howls and whoops and jerky movements of their arms for almost thirty minutes without a pause, until they were dripping in sweat. They did not carry any weapons. Finally the drummers stopped and the dancers filed off back to the shade of the pines. One of the drummers stood up and addressed the spectators.

"We are Shawnee Indians from Oklahoma. Our sub tribe is called the Absentee Shawnees. Like you we were speakers of an Algonkian language. We are distantly related to you Nantiquaks and to the Lenape Indian and our legends tell us we originally came from areas hereabouts perhaps four hundred years ago when several of our clans moved to western parts of what is now Virginia. We lived for many decades in Ohio. We resisted European settlement in a wide area. And our last contact with you Nantiquaks came in the 1740s when we sent envoys to you to a place near here inviting you to join us and many of our confederates in Ohio, Kentucky and western Virginia and Pennsylvania in a revolt against the colonies. Our tribe was beaten however and driven from Ohio and Kentucky on to what became Missouri and Kansas. After the Civil War we found our last haven in Oklahoma. We are honored to be invited here by our distant cousins."

"The moon dance is not a war dance in spite of its appearances. We have tried to re-create it from our ancestors' instructions. It is a harvest dance, a celebration of our harvest held under the moon in the autumn. We bring it to you to show you that we actively strive to preserve our Shawnee Indian legacies. Just as you try to preserve your legacy through the holding of this powwow. We will now perform a short dance, called the wounded deer dance. It was a dance seeking to gain success in our annual hunts. We hope you enjoy it."

He and his partner resumed beating on their drums with a slightly modified beat and rhythm. And the six dancers came back out and danced a less frenetic dance that entailed dancing in files that curled back on themselves and incorporated a sort of limping step. It lasted about fifteen minutes.

Shortly after that dance ended and dancers and spectators began moving away from the fireplace, Minnie saw Carmine approaching them through the mingling crowds.

"Will! Minnie!" Carmine called out as she drew closer. "I'm so glad to see you've come. I have a guest who's been looking for you."

Trailing along behind Carmine they now saw an elderly, heavy-set woman dressed in tan and blue clothes that were loosely draped off her shoulders and hips. She was walking with a limping gait. Carmine rushed up to Will and made to embrace him and planted a kiss on his cheek. She then turned to Minnie and embraced her. Minnie was taken aback: Carmine had never before been so physically attentive to them or acted so jaunty publicly. Minnie felt a pang of jealously again seeing her kiss her man.

"Will, this is Professor Broadhead whom you invited to supply us with the anthropological statement."

Professor Broadhead heaved forward and offered her hand as Carmine completed the introductions.

"I'm glad you could come, Professor." said Will turning on his usual realtor's tone and manner of speaking. "I hope you found this place with no difficulty."

"Oh no. It was not difficult to find. But I had forgotten how far away this place is from Richmond. Took me more than four hours this morning to drive here."

"It is far away." said Minnie. "I myself commuted here a couple times from Bowling Green. Once it took me six hours to get here."

"Have you had time to see anything around the powwow?" asked Will. "I think you missed the Shawnee dances. They were impressive."

"Yes, I missed the dances and I've seen only a couple displays on my way in."

"Have you had lunch already, Professor?" asked Will. "If not let's go get you some."

"You can call me Susan. And yes, lunch would be nice." said the Professor.

They went back to the dining area. On the way Susan, who walked slowly with her old woman's gait, turned to Minnie and said, "You look like you're an Indian, Minnie. Are you a Nantiquak?"

"No. I am an Indian indeed, but I come from the Massaponax-Doeg tribe of the middle peninsula of Virginia."

"Oh, I know something about them. They were a tribe of the Powhatan confederation."

"Yes, that's right."

"But your bead work that you are wearing are not either Nantiquak or Massaponax, if I might offer an observation. They're very pretty nevertheless."

Minnie was surprised and acted a little embarrassed. "Yes, you're right again. We bought them in Cherokee, North Carolina just last week."

"I don't know anything about Cherokee beadwork. But they look authentic enough. Unlike a lot of things around here."

Will offered to buy the Professor her lunch. She protested weakly.

"But you're our guest, and you could consider this a work trip. After all we've hired your expert insights and you're here doing additional field work."

Susan chuckled and accepted Will's offer to buy her lunch. Will brought her a tray laden with bowl of bean soup—really more like a stew-- corn bread, a salad of dandelion greens, and sassafras tea.

"Now this seems appropriately authentic Nantiquak fare." said Susan as tucked into her food. "Thank you for treating me."

After Susan had eaten a bit—she ate slowly and carefully—Will raised the issue of the draft paper she had written for their submission for Federal recognition. He was very complementary at first, full of praise for how well written and comprehensive the paper was as a summary statement, and he said how much he appreciated all the important points she had made. Minnie could see that the Professor was susceptible to complements and she even saw her faintly blush at some of the nicer language that Will used. He even brought into his evaluation of Professor Broadhead's article, mention of a discussion he had had with Professor Alvey, when the latter had poured praise on the young Susan Broadhead as a young scholar, her intelligence, her thoroughness, her major contributions, and her understanding of the ancient Indians' way of life. But with that as a prelude, Will let the Professor preen in his praise for a while, and then he shifted quickly to his real aim.

"But I am more than a little troubled by your concluding statement at the end of your paper, Susan." Will continued.

"What would that be?" she asked as she took a last bite of the corn bread.

"I am bothered by you're saying that the Nantiquaks were de-tribalized by the beginning of the nineteenth century. Frankly, this is unacceptable and counter-productive for our aims to get Federal recognition. I do not understand why you feel that you need to say this, and why it is important for your article. After all, we are applying to the Bureau of Indian Affairs to gain Federal acknowledgement that we are a bona fida, living, tribe. But you say that the Nantiquaks are de-tribalized. That they ceased being a tribe almost two hundred years ago. That can't be good for our assertion that the tribe still exists and deserves recognition as a sovereign Indian nation."

"Oh that." said Susan smiling. "That is a bit of an insider technical term. I don't think it is as serious as you make out."

"Something related to the dispute over anthropologists' definition of what a tribe is?"

"Yes. You are indeed well informed. It rather means that the political structures of the tribal people had ceased to function and their independence was lost to the European Americans who had overrun this region."

"Well, then it will be better for everyone for you to take the term out and state what you really mean to say. Because although many clans of the greater Nantiquak tribe had left the Eastern Shore and had migrated to the far west or to the north, several bands or clans remained in isolated pockets in what became Maryland and Delaware. Their population was not great throughout the nineteenth century, but they slowly grew in numbers. And we are organizing them to re-unify and reassert themselves as one large tribe."

"You don't need to go on. I will take that term out. Without a problem. I should've remembered who my audience was when I was writing this paper. I don't need that point at all. I'll take it out."

"Oh," said Will a little surprised. "Just like that?"

"Yes, it's not a problem. I'm glad you pointed it out to me. We want to help your efforts, not hurt them."

Will had been getting ready to spout a number of arguments, consanguinity, proximity, the genetic relationships shown in the DNA tests, the long history the bands living in one location together. But all those arguments could be shelved now. He looked at Susan and then smiled.

"Well then. You can make the needed amendments and we'll put it into our submission document. And more important, we'll put a check in the mail for you."

"That would be very nice." said Susan. "Now I think I better have a look around to see the various displays. I have to leave I think, no later than four thirty to get back to Richmond at a decent hour."

Will and Minnie looked at each other.

"You can't do that. You won't see anything." said Will. "And you'll miss the evening dance program. You drove up all this way just for lunch? Come with us tonight and stay with us for the night and we'll come back to see tomorrow's programs. We live only about an hour from here."

"Oh, that's a very kind invitation. But I couldn't impose."

"No, really. Come stay with us after tonight's program ends." said Minnie. "We have a big farmhouse. It has lots of space and you'll be very comfortable. And you know the house used to belong to the son of a Nantiquak Indian. You really must. We can even drive you there with us and back here to spare you the extra stress of driving."

Professor Broadhead seemed to consider the offer. But was struggling over whether or not to accept.

"We insist, Susan." said Minnie again.

"That would be very nice of you. If I wouldn't be too much of a bother…"

"No, no. Not at all." said Will. And besides you haven't met anybody here. There's so much to see and learn. Things have changed a lot since you last did your field work here. Minnie can fix us a nice breakfast and we can leisurely get back here when the gates open at eleven, refreshed. Then at the end of the afternoon you can head back toward Richmond."

"Thank you, Will. I accept. And I'll stay to watch the Nantiquak fire dance this evening."

The three of them spent the afternoon together slowly moving around the grounds and visiting the craft displays. They spent a lot of time watching several women making beads from the nacreous insides of mussel and clam shells. It was a tedious and time-consuming task. Minnie was fascinated by the tools the women used. They were made entirely from wood, bone, or leather. And the simple drill was most impressive as it used a bone drill bit that still was hard enough to drill a clean hole though the tiny beads. The women used a spindle drill, using a leather thong to spin the drill stick rapidly.

"Bead making goes way back into furthest antiquity." said Susan in a lecturing tone. "The basics had to be re-discovered by every ancient people in different parts of the globe. This drill is similar to ones used from pre-historic times found in the Middle East and North Africa. This is a very authentic Nantiquak craft and it seems that it was also women that made beads and strung beadwork. Some linguists tell us that the very name Nantiquak means 'bead maker'. Their beads were traded amongst Indians all over the eastern United States up to the 18th century. Their beads were used not only for decorative purposes—usually for the families of the chiefs—but also as wampum, the universal Indian trade money. It is fascinating, isn't it?"

After they had stood watching more than fifteen minutes, one of the craftswomen stood up and brought a chair over for Susan.

"Oh, thank you. I guess you figured I cannot stand for very long."

The display booth had a small selection of beaded goods for sale. Minnie realized at once that the beadwork she had seen in Cherokee, even the ones she had bought, used modern glass beads and were not handmade, certainly not hand-made by the techniques she was watching.

They wandered eventually off to other craft displays. Minnie was most interested in the women who were stitching together deerhide moccasins. Will was excited to see a group of Nantiquaks using fire and coals to hollow out a cypress log for a dugout canoe. They had already gouged out an indentation about twelve inches deep into the log and said that this process had to be repeated many times until a usable canoe was fashioned. They expected to continue through the end of day on Sunday to finish this canoe.

"Of course it would a lot easier to use saws." said one of the younger craftsmen. "We cheated a bit by using an electric saw to get the shape and dimensions of this log so we could work it using these traditional means. The log is very heavy, and even hollowed out it is a very sturdy craft, but hard to manage, especially in rough waters."

At the end of the afternoon, they went back to the food tent and had some dinner. The offering was venison stew with hominy. "I really like this," said Minnie. "I should fix it for you, now and then, Will."

"You know," Susan started again in lecture mode, "the ancient Indians of Mexico discovered that soaking dry corn in water mixed with wood ashes made the hominy more palatable. And this secret method had spread already to the Chesapeake apparently long before the English arrived here. Your people, Minnie, the tribes in the Powhatan group made hominy this way."

"We both like the resulting food." said Will.

After dinner and shortly after it became dark the central fire was lit, a big fire that sent wild shadows roaring through the pine trees around the fire site. The dance display lasted about an hour and then the crowds began to disperse and go home. Minnie and Will walked slowly back to the Oldsmobile with Professor Susan. On the way she asked, "So are you two a married couple?" Will answered at once, "Yes" while Minnie answered at the same moment, "No."

"Minnie is my common law wife." said Will. "But technically we don't have a marriage license."

Minnie was pleased that he did not explain her reluctance to have a wedding and get such a license.

"Oh, I see." said Susan. "But you both look like the happily married couple."

"And we both live together in a happy, big house." said Will trying to quote the words of nursery rhyme he suddenly seemed to remember. "You'll see the big house today. We come to the Eastern Shore to live on weekends. I'm from Bristol, Maryland, originally."

"And we live together in a house in D.C. on weekdays." said Minnie.

"Mixed race marriages are the end of native American tribes, as the Indian spouse invariably leaves his or her tribe."

"Perhaps." said Will. But I am the product of a mixed race marriage. I am part Nantiquak."

"Oh, I see. I would not have guessed that."

"Yes. No one does. My great grandmother was pure Nantiquak. And Minnie is not as she seems either. She was until quite recently the weroance of the Massaponax tribe, the chief, a position she inherited from her father."

"Oh. I know the term weroance. You're the first woman with that title I have ever met, Minnie."

My family name, Warrens, is a adaptation from the word weroance." said Minnie.

"One moment," said Susan, "I need to get a sweater from my car and my overnight bag. It's getting rather cool outside now. I packed an overnight bag in case I decided to stay at a hotel here overnight. Little did I know that it would take me such long time to drive here." She dropped the topic of their marriage status.

They took exactly an hour to reach the farmhouse. The last gleams of twilight had just disappeared from the sky and the vast night chorus of crickets, cicadas and other insects sounds had started. The house was completely dark.

"That's strange." said Will. "Usually Phyllis leaves the front porch light on after she comes here."

As they stepped in, the house inside was fresh and had obviously been thoroughly cleaned.

"What a nice classic old house. And this is your weekend house?" asked the Professor.

"Yep. I inherited it from my great uncle only a few months ago. He was half Nantiquak, one of the three sons of my great grandmother, I was telling you about. This is a pretty large farm. And just these past several days we're bringing in the corn harvest."

"Very impressive."

Minnie asked which room to put the Professor in. Will said the downstairs room, so she wouldn't have to contend with the stairs. "Let me show you the way. Do you think you will need the heating for tonight?"

The next morning, early, just as Will was first getting out of bed, there was stomping sound out front followed by a loud pounding on the front entry door. Will quickly pulled on his trousers and a tee shirt and rushed down the stairs to the door. Through the glass he could see it was Armand Driggers. Even before he answered the door to him, Will began to feel agitated that against his instructions, Armand had come to house and was banging on the door. But when he answered the door, Armand looked distressed.

"Will. Come quickly. I think Max is trying to kill himself."

Will reached for his cell phone. He had it already in his pocket. He slipped on some galoshes by the door and he ran out and down the porch steps following behind Armand. "This way, sir." Armand said as he waved his arm. He ran around the house and over to the barn. Will ran up right behind Armand and when he entered the barn he saw Max's car running. The door of the car was open, and Max's head was slumped on the steering wheel. Will glanced quickly at the exhaust pipe. It was blocked. He promptly reached in pushing Max's upper body back into the seatback and switched the car off.

"Give me a hand here, Armand. I think you're right. He's tried to poison himself."

The two started to lever Max's upper torso out from behind the steering wheel, and then they dragged him under his shoulders out of the car and out of the barn to the open yard and there they laid him on his back. Max made a kind of groaning sound as they succeeded in pulling his legs out of the car. Will got his cell phone out and made a call to emergency services. "Yes, I think he's got carbon monoxide poisoning." Armand heard him say. "No I don't have any bottled oxygen here or nearby." Then Will was giving instructions over his phone for how the ambulance would reach them there at this farm. All the while Armand was standing over Max and looking very upset, and seemingly not knowing what was happening or what to do.

"Come on, Armand. Help me raise him. He's passed out but he's not dead yet." And Will tried to raise Max up to a sitting position, but he was limp and seemed heavy and unresponsive. Max moaned again like someone in a deep sleep having bad dreams. "We have to treat him as if he is drowning victim." said Will. "We've got to get some good air into his lungs and press out the bad." Armand did not move. Will put his arms around Max at the mid torso, where he estimated his diaphragm was, and then he gave a mighty squeeze. "Come on,

Armand help me. You haven't seen a person in next of rescue before? This is a suicide, can't you tell?"

"Actually I have seen suicides before. But I never could help."

"Well, hold him up like this. By the shoulders. The ambulance won't be here for another half an hour. And we have to give him artificial resuscitation." Will took hold of Max by the lower jaw and forced open his mouth, grabbing his tongue with his thumb. Then he made as if to kiss Max on the open mouth, but instead he blew hard into Max's mouth. He waited a moment. "Now hold Max, like this from behind and try and squeeze him just as I did." Armand moved around behind Max and took his limp body up in his arms and hugged him tightly. Then Will repeated the breath of life technique, blowing again hard into Max's mouth. "We have to do this a few times until Max starts breathing normally himself."

They did this four or five times until they were both so exhausted they had to lay Max back flat on the ground. Max still was not breathing himself. He groaned a little, but his eyes were still closed and he had not moved any of his limbs. After a few moments to catch his breath, Will got down on his knees next to Max's head and began to breathe in in lifeguard style. "Here Armand, after I breath in, you push up from his stomach." Another five minutes went by like this. When they stopped Max was breathing shallowly but still seemed to be unconscious. Will stopped again to rest and recover his own breath. It was then that he noticed Minnie, fully dressed, walking around the side of the farmhouse. When she saw Max's body lying prone and lifeless on the ground, her hand came to her mouth and she turned away so she would not see any more. Will stood up and walked over to her and took her by the shoulders. "Look, it's Max. He's had carbon monoxide poisoning. An ambulance is on its way. Should be here in ten or fifteen minutes. Could you wait out front and direct it back here when it comes?" Minnie nodded and walked back to the front of the house. Will went back to Max and he and Armand resumed the resuscitation routines.

In about ten minutes the ambulance appeared. The medics rushed out, one carrying an oxygen bottle with a respirator the rubber strap of which he wrapped around Max's head, the mouthpiece tight over his mouth. The other broke out the stretcher and put it down along Max's body. They checked his pulse and listened to his heart rate. "You think it's carbon monoxide?" said one to Will. "I'm almost certain of it. Look I dragged him out of a running car." They lifted him onto the stretcher and then transformed it into a gurney, raising it up to the level of the back lip of the ambulance rear door. They then pushed the gurney with Max easily into the rear of the ambulance. "We'll take him to the Salisbury emergency center. They've got a hypobaric center there and that should fix him up. Are you his family?"

"No, I'm his employer."

"Do you know how to reach his family?"

Will reached up and put his hand in Max's trousers pocket. He pulled out a cell phone. "I think I can find it now."

"So what's his last name?"

"It's Turner. He's Maxwell Turner. Lives over the river in Wicomico County. I'll call his wife and tell her that there's been an accident."

"Okay, we have to dash. Time is of the essence for this guy." And with that the medics jumped back up into the front seats and drove off, the ambulance's tires spitting up gravel from the lane as it went.

Will looked over at Armand, who was standing next to the barn door as if in a state of shock.

"There was nothing I could have done to save him."

"Armand. He's not dead yet. And someone had to open the car door. Presumably that was you."

"Yes I did."

"Well that could have made a big difference, in just the three or four minutes that you were gone to fetch me."

"But I didn't turn off the engine."

"No. But we'll see."

"You think it is suicide?"

"As I told the medics. I'm almost certain of it. But I can't imagine why."

"He was really, seriously depressed, the past few days."

"Ya'll were bringing in the corn harvest?"

"Yeah we were supposed to finish it off today. We're expecting two trucks to carry off the corn in a few hours' time."

"Where's the combine harvester?"

"It's parked out in the field."

"Do you know how to run it?"

"Can't say that I ever have. Max always did that."

"So how much is left to harvest in the field?"

"There's about eight acres left. No much really. We've got all the rest."

"You know how to load the trucks when they come?"

"Yeah. It's a cinch. And there's another Injun from my band working with me. He's out at the combine now."

"Well, let's do that today and leave the combine for the last eight acres for later."

"As you say."

Will went back to the front of the farmhouse where Minnie was waiting sitting on the front stairs. She looked as if she had been crying.

"I think he'll be alright. I'll call and check later today. No more we can do today for Max. Let's have breakfast."

"It was suicide, wasn't it?" asked Minnie.

"I'm pretty sure it was. But I have no idea why."

When they stepped in the house, Susan was waiting at the bottom of the stairs.

"I saw an ambulance drive away. Has anything serious happened?"

"Yes, my farm manager has fallen sick and they came to take him to the emergency room."

"Oh my. I hope it's nothing serious."

"I'm afraid it is."

Will led them to the kitchen where they sat at the kitchen table against the back wall. Minnie fixed a breakfast of eggs and sausage and served coffee before sitting down herself.

"I suppose this gets in the way in our plans for today." said Susan.

"Yes, probably so. I think I won't be able to go to the powwow today. I have to look after the end of harvest here."

"Oh so you own this house as part of a working farm?"

"Yes, it's like that. A big farm with a big old farmhouse. I own it all. Or should I say, it owns me? I've never done a lick of farm work before this year. But I'm determined to make this an ongoing farm. Minnie I think you will have to drive the Professor back to the powwow without me. Do you think you can manage that?"

"You mean in the Olds?"

"Yes. I'll give you the driving instructions on how to get there. It's not difficult at all."

"So by leaving my car up there, I've greatly inconvenienced you. Haven't I?" asked Susan, seeming a little distressed.

"No, not at all." said Minnie. "No change in our plans, except that Will can't go today."

"I'll put my things together and will be ready to go in no time."

"No need to rush. It's not even nine o'clock yet." answered Will. "You don't need to leave here for another hour, because the powwow doesn't open until eleven. We can show you the whole house and the family photos before you have to go."

While she was cleaning up, Minnie was acting distressed.

"Don't worry about driving. It really is simple. I'll give you the instructions. It's almost a straight shot there. And Susan can act as your navigator."

"Okay. But I've never driven your car without you in it to direct me."

"Susan will be able to act as a navigator. I'll start writing the instructions now. But first I need to call Max's wife."

"And he tried to kill himself here, under our noses."

"As I said, I don't understand the reasons why."

He opened Max's cell phone and quickly found his home telephone number. He called it and after several rings a woman answered on the line.

"Hello, are you Max Turner's wife?" Will asked. "I'm Will Eames calling from the farm where Max works."

"Yes, why what has happened? Is Max alright?"

"Well, there has been an accident. And he's probably already now at Salisbury Community Hospital."

"Are you sure? He's been in such bad shape for a long while."

"I didn't know that. But he's getting treatment now. Does he have medical insurance?"

"No. We get by with my family medical insurance from the school where I work."

"Do you have a way to get to the hospital?"

"No he has the car."

"Okay, his car is still here. Maybe I can drive it over and pick you up and take you to the hospital."

"Thad be nice but I think a neighbor can take me."

"I'll try to visit him early this evening." He didn't say what he was thinking: 'If he recovers.'

Before they left, Minnie turned to Will and said she would drop Susan off at the powwow and come right back.

"You don't have to do that, Minnie."

"Will, I'm needed more here than at the powwow. And Professor Broadhead can get herself home whenever she wishes. So I'll come back. Expect me here around lunchtime."

"Okay, I'll be pleased to see you whatever you decide to do, whenever you come back. By the time you get back we should be loading corn in the trucks. So to speak I will be practicing my third career." Will smiled at her weakly and kissed her when she was ready to get in the car.

"I can't thank you enough for your warm hospitality." said Susan, before getting in the front seat of the car. "And for inviting me to the powwow. Everything these two days has been like a return to my earliest years working out here. Will, Minnie you are wonderful people and your project for the Nantiquak people is really noble."

Minnie drove off slowly and carefully, the way she always drove. Will watched the car go all the way down the lane and onto the farm road before it disappeared behind a cluster of roadside trees six hundred yards or so away. As the car disappeared he felt a pang of fear. He felt as if Minnie was leaving, and she might never return, he might never see her again. He feared momentarily as if she had been torn out of his heart. But then he thought that was nonsense. It was an impression he had had many times: departures of familiar people or family ever since he had first left for the Marines. And especially when he went to war, where often the departures were final. He shook off the sensation, and whispered to himself that of course she was coming back.

Will skipped back up the stairs to the front door and locked it. Then he went back to the barn. Armand was standing like a statue by Max's dark blue Ford. The car door was still open. Will bent down and pulled out the rags from the exhaust pipe. He then leaned into the car and took the key out of the ignition. He looked momentarily at the dashboard. Ironically the gas tank meter showed that it was nearly empty. Perhaps that was deliberate, or just an oversight of Max's. He then closed the door.

"Hey, Armand. Where you're gone to? Wake up! You have no reason to blame yourself for anything here."

"No, the Injun hired hand is always to blame. Maybe this time I was too late. I got here too late to prevent this."

"Whaddaya mean, 'too late'?"

"I tried to get here at six fifteen like Max had told me to. But I got here only at about seven. Maybe for him that was the last straw. I always let him down."

"How did you get here?"

"Talleck dropped me and Bobbie off on his way to work up the road."

"Who's Talleck, have I met him?"

"He's the new chief of our band at Kuskowarok. We elected him last month as your madame, the chairman or chairwoman, suggested we ought to. He should be on the tribal council now up there at your Delaware tribe."

"Well, then Talleck was responsible for dropping you late. Not you. Let's go get this guy Bobbie."

And they walked out to the far end of the corn field where Bobbie was sitting leaning against one of the large tires of the combine. He looked to be about twenty five or thirty years old. Armand introduced them.

"Oh so this is our big landlord, you were telling me about?" asked Bobbie his eyes focusing on Will.

"Yeah, and he owns this farm too, and he's got an Injun woman as his wife, and he's even my distant cousin, believe it or not."

Bobbie shook his head, mostly in awe and disbelief. Will surveyed the remaining stand of corn. Eight acres seemed like a lot when Armand had first said it, but when he looked at the stalks rustling in a morning breeze when compared to the other one hundred and seventy acres—he had been told to visualize an acre as equivalent to a football field—it didn't like so much to him. But then again he was only able to visualize the size of three football fields together, just as he had seen at the playing fields of his university. "And you said that it would take the rest of the day to harvest what remains here?" "No, no." said Armand. "Maybe three hours. Not more." And you Bobbie, you don't know how to operate this combine/harvester?" "No sir, not me. Max wouldn't let me touch this thing. Didn't trust any of us." They all went back to the barn and began to wait for the trucks to arrive, which they did as arranged at shortly past eleven. Will watched as Armand and Bobbie directed the drivers to under the conveyor belt from the storage bins and they began loading the first truck and were just finishing the second when Minnie drove back.

"You were right. It's not at all difficult to find from here." said Minnie walking up to Will. "Even without Susan's help, I got back here alright in less than an hour."

"I'm glad to hear it. Especially happy to get you back safely. We're just about ready to send off most of our corn harvest."

"So how much does it come to?" asked Minnie.

"According to Armand, it looks like more than six truckloads here. He says in the past few years the usual crop comes to more like sixteen to twenty truckloads. We're harvesting almost three weeks earlier than usual because of the long hot, dry summer which followed that gutter flusher rain storm, you remember."

She did. "We've lost a lot. That could have caused Max a great deal of grief."

The trucks came back from Laurelton about an hour and a half later and filled up again on corn and came back again after three. Just as Armand had said it came to six and a quarter truckloads. When they came back the last time, one of the drivers gave Will the receipt and the spot price that he would receive for the harvest. "The bad news is that we've produced much less than on average over the past many years. The good news is that we're getting a much higher price at the grain elevator because supply everywhere in the Eastern Shore is down so much."

As the afternoon was ending, Will came to the house to get something to eat. "You know it seems to me that we need to take into account the trade-off between selling spot at harvest and holding in storage to sell at a later month when prices are higher. We need to look into the futures price as well. I wonder why Hampt didn't do this? And why Max didn't advise him on this?"

"Will, one day working and you're already sounding like a modern farmer," quipped Minnie. "I think you might give up on all your other jobs."

"I think we need to take Max's car to his home and then go and see, if he's in recovery room, just how he's doing. You'll get to drive the Olds again today without me. You'll just have to follow me."

"Okay. Do we leave now?"

"Yep, we can close up the house here now and we'll be back in Bristol in a few hours. We can have dinner there."

They drove off, Minnie in the Olds, and Will driving Max's Ford, heading for Burris Springs in Wicomico County. They found the Turner house without a problem and spoke briefly to Max's wife, named Jenny, who was just back from the hospital.

"He's out of the oxygen chamber and the emergency room, and out of his coma, but he is still not very communicative." Jenny told them. Her eyes were red, obviously from crying. "The doctor says he might need a day or two to get over the effects of the poisoning. With lots of oxygen doses, but that after that he should be fully recovered and I can bring him home."

"Will we be able to see him? Or talk to the doctor?"

"I think so, but the doctor treating him might not still be there. Max is very groggy, barely conscious. He doesn't say much. And you know the doctor said something very revealing. He told me that suicide is highest among farmers than any other social group in America. And in this farming region they see lots of suicides and treat lots of suicide attempts. I think I've known that for a long time."

They decided not to go to Salisbury, but instead they went straight back to Bristol and had dinner at the Poseidon Palace. Will told Minnie he needed to stay through Monday night, because he had to arrange for the last of the harvest and send the combine back to the rental center. So he had to find an operator. She decided right there that she wanted to be close to him through the night, and so she would go to work early on Monday morning. Will was pleased to hear that. "Yeah, I can take you in my arms and keep you all night pressed against me." "Yes, exactly what I want."

Tony came out and came to their table as they were eating.

"So how's your Injun project coming, Will?"

Minnie jumped in speaking as if with a mock Indian accent usually portrayed in old movies: "Injun project on hold. White man Will a corn farmer, today. He sold entire harvest."

"Wow!" Tony chuckled. "You never cease to amaze me Will. Maybe you'd like another glass of our new brew?"

"I would actually. It was a stressful day."

"I should say so." said Minnie cryptically in her normal voice.

After an intimate night together, they both got up early and prepared Minnie for her commute to work. She left at six, just after sunrise so she would have time to go to their house before heading to the office.

"I'll come tonight. I think I can take care of the last bits of the harvest and return the harvester today." said Will as he saw her off.

On Monday he called the county extension service and asked if they had any combine operators looking for work. He felt certain that they would have a number of applicants, and sure enough they did because of the drop in the harvest, there was a drop in the work for operators. He picked the man up at nine o'clock and drove him out to Hampton Farm. Armand was there waiting. "I thought maybe you'd run away with your Pocahontas to across the Bay." he said snidely. Will got them working on the last eight acres. In four hours they had put away the last of the corn in the bins and closed up the barn. The operator began the drive to Rosedale and got there in about forty minutes. Will met him there, paid him sixty dollars for his day's work and then drove him back to Bristol. Unfortunately this man did not have a cell phone, so Will took his home phone number in case in the future he needed his services. Then, for the fifth time that day, he tried calling Minnie on her cell phone. She had been too busy all day to take his call but now, near five o'clock, she picked up.

"I'm finished. I just wanted to tell you that I'm coming home tonight. Maybe get there at around eight o'clock."

"Good. I'm finished today too. And really I'm finished. I think we've finished the case for our suit against Delaware. We're putting finishing touches and arguments on to it maybe tomorrow. I'll fix you a nice dinner of sea bass when you get home. Okay?"

Will agreed and when he got home in DC he gave her a big hug. The rest of the week he stayed at home in Cleveland Park working on his text for the application to the Bureau. He made a lot of progress. And then on Thursday evening, after Minnie came home, he announced that he had made enough progress that he could go the next day to Laurelton to look after the opening balance sheet that Jennifer claimed she had finished. "And I have an announcement too," Minnie said. "We're ready to file our case in Delaware against the unlawful pre-emption of the three reservations granted by the English King through his deputies in Maryland to the Nantiquak nation." We're planning to serve the court in Dover, on Tuesday next week."

"Oh that's wonderful news! Does your boss—Carl, Cal, what's his name?—plan to present the case to the tribal council or the board in advance, like he did back in June?"

"It's Cal." answered Minnie. "But no, he's assigned Ron the task of informing the tribal council. It's kind of funny. He's going to find that I'm the chairman of the board, and head of the council, so to speak. So he's trying to convince Chief Clarke of the need for another presentation. They want Saturday to present. But I think this will fall to sometime next week."

"So progress all around. Maybe more than our tribe can handle at one time."

"Maybe."

"Because, at the rate I'm going, with Carmine's section finished, and Professor Broadhead's finished, I think I'll have the document ready to submit before October."

"That's only next week."

"That's what I mean—at the same time as you file your suit."

"So maybe you need to present to the board, a summary of your application. When by the way will you be able to share it with me to review?"

"Monday evening. Tuesday at the latest."

"Okay, so we're on a race delivering actions to the tribe. We will overwhelm them." said Minnie and she laughed.

"Next week let's say we have to drink to our coinciding presentations and actions."

"Okay."

"All our harvests are coming in at the same time."

"I would say, actually, we are sowing rather than harvesting. We still have a long way to go before we can expect to harvest results of our work up to now."

"Okay. But you know what I mean." They both began to giggle.

"The Injun Project is moving into inauguration mode." said Will and he kissed Minnie. "Ready to launch. Thanks so much to you"

The next day in Laurelton he was mildly surprised to see that Jennifer had composed an opening balance sheet which was a marvel of the accounting art. It was just what he needed to apply for the tax exempt status for the Nantiquak Corporation. "I dated this the first of September, so it doesn't show the net seven thousand three hundred dollars which the powwow deposited earlier this week." she said. That afternoon he set about getting the application forms from the IRS and the Delaware state bureau of taxation off the internet. He worked on these over the weekend at the farmhouse and they were ready to be filed on Monday morning. He mailed them from Washington, D.C.

Meanwhile Ron was unable to persuade Chief Clarke to muster a quorum of the Nantiquak Corporation to hear their outlines for the suit against Delaware much before the first day of October, which was the next Thursday. His boss, Cal, was furious with Ron, and then furious with the Indians. "Always dithering. Never able to make decisions, or to conduct business in a reasonable or timely manner." he vented. Chief Clarke called Minnie at her office to tell her the decision and the proposal that her colleagues had made for a presentation.

"Yes, I know about it. I'm drafting a lot of this suit and this presentation." said Minnie. "We thought it was only proper that we discuss it with you before we file it. And you understand, I will have to sit with the other lawyers and not in the chairman's seat."

"Sure, I understand. So we'll do it, we'll listen politely to what you all have to say, and you will go and do it whatever we might think of it. Right?"

"Right. But understand we are really seeking to restore reservation lands to the tribe in the state of Delaware. And we think we have a good chance of getting them."

"I suppose that is good. But the historic reservations were not located where most of our tribe now lives. I don't quite know what purpose they might serve."

"That's a different problem, and another step, on the way to winning Federal recognition."

"Fine. We'll follow your lead."

So the meeting took place on Thursday the first, in the newly furnished conference and board room of the new Nantiquak Corporation offices in Laurelton, at eleven in the morning. Minnie arrived in her car separate from Cal and Ron who came in a Mercedes.

Will decided it was better not to attend, and Minnie could not persuade him to come. Even when she tried to convince him that he knew the story about the properties, acreage and the sales of those properties better than anyone. He had collected all the details about the transactions, after all. Just as Chief Clarke said, they were preached to for about an hour and a half. There were no questions put to the lawyers. Cal was again impatient to leave. But Ron had prepared much better maps and displays showing the lands at issue, some nine thousand acres in three unequal parcels, the main one being on Brant Creek quite near Laurelton. And after he had spoken about them, the board members came up and studied the maps.

After Ron had finished and the Indians had studied his maps Minnie made a suggestion.

"I think we can look at the possibility of putting the land holdings of your members who live on the Indian River into a federal trust, just like the Qualla is for the Cherokees. It is a virtual reservation. And this can be done once you get Federal recognition."

This idea was new and caused a good deal of positive reaction from the board members. It was new to Cal as well, and he was both surprised and annoyed that she put this idea out as a target without consulting him first. When Cal and Ron had nothing more to say, just as they had the last time, they rushed off, heading back for D.C. Cal made a mental note to remember to reprimand Minnie for inserting her idea into the meeting before first consulting with him. The next day they began to investigate with the clerk of the court when they could file their suit in Federal District court in Dover, Delaware. They came up with the date of the next Wednesday, the 7th of October. Judicial calendars move slowly just out of procedural ensnarements. Cal told Minnie that he and she would file the case and make first representations. He expected it would take less than fifteen minutes, not counting the waiting time outside the clerk's office. So she should prepare for going up to Dover and spending the night before up there to be able to be at the courthouse by nine thirty. Even though she could not see that there were any conflicts of interest thrown up by her close relationship to Will, she did not want to tell him that she could stay with Will either at the Hampton Farm or in Bristol. She still did not want to reveal to him or Ron or anyone else in the office her "conjugal state" with Will.

The date was the same that Will decided was the proper time to submit the official application for Federal recognition for the Nantiquak Tribe of Delaware and Maryland. He had already given it to the lawyers at NAILS to review and approve of. And of course that meant that Minnie reviewed it again and approved. Just as her colleague Gail Halstead did. He had invited Carmine and Morley and Ron Woodson to come to D.C. and they would all go to the Bureau's offices together to submit the application document. And they had a sizeable document full of data, historical records, support documents such as the copies of the archived treaties and letters of endorsement from two congressmen and one senator, reports on the anthropological background of the tribe, copies of baptism records in both Delaware and Maryland along with birth and death records, and the document from 1870 which granted the tribe state recognition as an Indian tribe by the state of Delaware. In all a report of nearly three hundred pages, covered with the six page official application form filled in by typewritten text. Will already knew from Minnie that it was more than most tribes managed to submit, and that it contained much more concrete, historical documentation than most tribes submitted, even those tribes that had already obtained Federal recognition through the Bureau. He felt he had done a good job with this document which covered all the bases, addressed all the issues, answered all the concerns the Bureau had, and even posed a challenge: this is an application that demands your consent and acceptance. Minnie concurred, and some of her former colleagues in the Bureau whom she consulted also concurred. They also told her that they were in a period when they were not reviewing any pending applications. Everything was in amendment and corrections mode, which meant the Bureau's analysts were waiting on further data and information from earlier applications made by other tribes, including Minnie's. So while Minnie was idling in the corridor outside the court clerk's office, and Cal was sitting on a hard wooden bench opposite her, Will and his team were being led through the corridors of the Bureau of Indian Affairs back to where he had started eleven months earlier, to the office of Nighthorse Ward, acting Assistant Deputy Secretary of the Department of the Interior, Bureau of Indian Affairs.

When their turn came to be invited into Mr. Ward's inner office, Will strode proudly in at the front of his team, introduced them one by one to Mr. Ward, and then presented the bureaucrat, who looked like he dressed like a plains Indian from the far West, in other words, more Indian than the Nantiquak Indian petitioners in front of him, with their application. In fact, an original and two copies of the full document with the cover of the official application forms. Mr. Ward babbled some bureaucratic mumbo jumbo about what a great milestone the Nantiquak tribe was aspiring to, how thankful he was that they had taken so many efforts to prepare the document, and how hopeful he was of a favorable outcome, to add another tribe of Native Americans, one from the Eastern states of the great United States of America, to the growing list of Federally recognized tribes. They were finished with the meeting in twenty three minutes. Morley was uncharacteristically smiling, as was Carmine. But in Morley's case his smile was misleading.

"What of load of horseshit that Nighthorseshit Ward is! What a pompous arrogant ass he is. He's no more an Indian or a proponent of Indian rights than that fire hydrant there, which all the dogs piss on." And then Morley laughed. "I expect, he'll make all kinds of excuses of why he cannot grant us Federal recognition."

"I reckon you're right, Morly." said Will. "He has blocked up the process over the past two years in consideration of the political winds blowing from the White House. Winds that do not support giving any more rights to Indians. But if those winds were to change directions again, so he would shift his views again."

"Cannot like such a scoundrel. I wonder if he could be bribed?" Morley continued, and then fell into daydreams thinking of ways that that might be achieved.

Standing outside on the pavement in front of the Bureau's offices Will thought at once of Minnie. He saw her in his mind's eye as Pocahontas, slender, young looking, in deerhide tunic with colorful beadwork on her bosom, her black hair in a single braid. He took out his cell phone and sent her a text message. "Mission accomplished. Document delivered. Will." In a couple moments he got back a text message answer from her. "Not yet gotten into the office of the clerk of the court. Mataoka."

"Let's go to lunch folks. I think you all deserve that at least."

Minnie and Cal were finally invited in the Court Clerk's office where they filled in a filing document. And handed over a case summary statement. They were in and out in twelve minutes. The clerk's deputy who handled this transaction said merely, "We'll get back to you in a few days after we review it and deem whether it is suitable for review by the court to be taken up for a hearing." They stepped back outside.

Cal wanted to take Minnie to lunch. He was feeling lustful and she had been all morning sitting opposite him as attractive and juicy in his eyes as any young woman he had seen in the previous month. At almost the same moment, his cell phone rang and hers beeped. She took hers out of her purse and looked at it. Cal did the same with his phone. Both had a text message from Ron. All it said was: "We won. Further details coming later this week. Hurray!"

Chapter 4

Washington D.C., November 5, 1999

Earlier that morning Minnie had driven down early to Fredericksburg to see her gynecologist for a routine check-up. The doctor looked at her, reviewed her medical history, and finally asked if she was still having pain or dryness during intercourse. Both of those complaints had disappeared more than a year earlier following her treatment and they had not returned. The doctor asked if she had regular sex, and this struck Minnie as funny, and she answered facetiously, "A lot of regular sex, but only with one man." The doctor smiled at her response; she was pleased to hear it. But Minnie had other questions on her mind.

"Do you think I can have children?"

"I don't see anything wrong with your works, no problems with your uterus. Of course you can have children. What makes you think that you can't? Have you been trying, without success?"

"No. It's just that I am so old. And I have never had children before."

"What do you mean? You're not too old to have children, even a first child."

"But I read that the older a woman becomes, the less likely she is to conceive her first."

"Well yes, that's true in general. The probability of conception does go down as a woman ages, beyond the age of thirty five. But you no doubt still have eggs in your ovary. Do you still have a normal menstruation?"

"Yes."

"Are you still taking contraceptives?"

"Yes. The ones you prescribed." Minnie could still not confess her deep fear even privately to her doctor. She still feared that after she had been raped, she could not conceive. It was a strange notion, but she thought it was true. After all, both those men had ejaculated inside her—she had remembered that even in the violence of the moment-- and she had not conceived then. After all, her sister, Alicia, had conceived after she had been raped the first time. And she had had an abortion afterwards. And she was still able to have children.

"Then, if you and your partner are ready," said the doctor, "and want to try having a child, stop taking them. That's a doctor's recommendation. Or we could try a whole range of tests over the next month to see if your system is releasing all the right hormones at the right time for ovulation to occur. But I suggest we leave those tests until after you find you are having difficulty conceiving. Say in about six or more months. In the meantime, for the next several months, you should try to be especially sexually active starting two weeks after your menstrual period starts. Try to keep close awareness of your monthly cycle and be sure to count and record the number of days. And I will prescribe for you this special mix of vitamins and hormones which promote fertility health. And a prescription for folic acid. You should start taking these every day, from today." said the doctor as she wrote out a prescription and a list of supplements for Minnie.

Minnie went away feeling only a little relieved. She was not sure about the mechanism or the hormones involved. And she did not know the details about ovulation and how everything came together to allow for her eggs to be ready to be fertilized. She had never had sex education classes in school, and her mother had not told her anything about sex, or even anything about menstruation. On the boring drive back to D.C. she wondered if she should ask Will if she could start having sex with him without protection. He had only said once or twice in the past year that they should have a family, if only she would consent to marrying him. Only a few times had he said that he wanted kids. As she was crossing the Potomac, she finally decided that she would stop taking the pills and hope for the best. She was nearly ready to accept his proposal for marriage. If she could show that she could have children, then that was one more obstacle thrown off in the way to her consent.

She got back to her office by eleven o'clock. Cal and Ron were not in the office, and that day there was not much she needed to do. NAILS needed a new client, maybe two. There was now very little work left for the Nantiquaks, and without new clients to advise, there were probably going to be some dismissals by year end when they saw how much the firm would be paid by the public law service agency. Last year, she had been well paid, more than promised when she had been hired. And she had gotten a sizeable bonus, twenty-five thousand dollars. But in the current political climate apparently, money-raising for public service legal assistance was low, especially for work on Indian rights. The case against the Bureau was in its final consideration in front of the judge and they were waiting any day now on the court's decision. She called Will, who was working from home that Friday, just to tell him that she had gotten back from the doctor's safely, and that everything was alright. "I would expect as much." said Will brightly. "You're an excellent specimen of woman." "But we need to talk this evening about what the doctor told me." Will always said things that made her feel better. He was always offering her encouragement and praise. She turned off her cell phone and punched in the number 16 on her desk phone and when Alia answered Minnie asked if she would go to lunch with her. Over the past year and a half Minnie had grown to like Alia more and more. They were the two foreigners in the office-- in spite of Irine's supposed Indian ancestry which at no time in Minnie's presence had displayed itself—and as Alia's English got better she had become more forthcoming on sharing her background in Somalia, her move to America, and her interests in life. And they often talked about the racism they encountered around town. Their experiences with mildly racist attitudes and expressions were surprisingly similar.

After lunch Minnie returned to the office and saw that Cal and Ron had returned. Their office doors were closed. She began reading some case histories of lawsuits and filings made by small tribes in California over the previous twenty-five years. Around two o'clock, Cal burst out of his office and knocked on the door of first Ron and then Minnie. "Come on, Judge Canning's JA just called to say that Canning's ready to read out his decision on our case. Get your notebook and put your coat on. We'll get a taxi down to the courthouse."

At the courthouse, the three of them walked quickly up the stairs, passed through security screening and almost jogged to the courtroom on the third floor. The Bureau's attorneys were already sitting at their table. Cal led the way to beyond the bar where they took off their coats and sat at a table. At three o'clock the court bailiff announced the court to be in session and the entry of Judge Canning. Everyone stood up, and waited for the Judge to sit before they sat down again.

Judge Canning was an experienced judge in deciding constitutional issues. He was a lean, white haired man in his late fifties and he had a long track record of interpreting the Constitution in a strictly literal manner, as he believed its drafters had wanted it to work. He did not like legislation by the judiciary or legal decisions by regulatory bodies. Cal and Turino thought that they had gotten the most favourable judge on the circuit to judge their case against the Bureau. And on this afternoon, they found out that he was strongly opposed to administrative rules or regulations which should not take precedence over the laws and workings of treaties as laid out in the Constitution. He began reading out first the summary of the case and the grounds for the complaint—namely that the Nantiquak Indian Tribal Corporation had been denied Federal acknowledgement because they had not fully complied with the rules and requirements for such, according to the Bureau. Then he read out the issue regarding the overriding authority of the treaty with Indian tribes on the North American continent. He summarized the history of the treaty between King Charles of England who was the sovereign on the one part, and the tallecks and weroances of the Nantiquak people in 1682, who were sovereign on the other part. Then he made the statement that when the sovereignty changed from the King of England to the United States of America, the treaty continued to be valid and was protected by the U.S. Constitution and its rules about treaty making. And then the key to his ruling,

"Although the U.S. government has made nearly 500 treaties with native American Indian tribes, and although it inherited another three score treaties made earlier than its establishment, the U.S. government, its military, and many of its states have uniformly and repeatedly violated and transgressed the terms of all of these treaties, including the one with the Nantiquaks, that at no point did either the King of England or the United States afterwards move to terminate this treaty or to replace it with a new one. That the defendants in this case could not show that this treaty at any time has been voided or terminated, or revoked for cause or arbitrarily, it is my decision that the treaty is still valid and the governing document of the relationship between the U.S. government and the Nantiquak Indian tribe. And that furthermore this validity of the treaty takes precedence over the rules and regulations of the Bureau of Indian Affairs which were drawn up out of the general conditions set forth in the Indian Self-Determination Act of 1975 until such time as the parties both declare the original treaty to be null and void."

This was the heart of Judge Canning's ruling. He read on his ruling further. He said that the Bureau was incorrect to decline the application of the Nantiquak Indian tribe. That the tribe had been able to demonstrate its continued existence and the continued validity and power of their original treaty. And since the Bureau was unable to demonstrate that the tribe had ceased to exist or that the treaty had been terminated there was no other course for the Bureau other than to grant the tribe recognized status in the eyes of the United States government.

And he briefly read out instructions for remediation of the situation. Namely, that the Bureau was to rescind its decision to decline the application of the Nantiquak Indian Tribal Corporation and it was to enter its name in the list of acknowledged and recognized native American Indian tribes in front of the U.S. government, recognizing its sovereign self-governing status, and recognizing the reservation lands awarded to the Nantiquak Tribe both under the terms of the treaty and then re-established by the suits brought against the states of Maryland and Delaware. That the Bureau will grant recognition at once and without any delays or additional requirements, or claims laid against the tribe. And that the Nantiquak Tribe will be able with immediate effect to receive the rights and benefits that the United States government has established for recognized tribes without any circumscription. The Bureau will at the soonest opportunity inform the Nantiquak Indian Tribal Corporation of the decision of this court and the registration of the tribe into the list of Federally recognized Indian tribes.

"That is the decision of this court in the matter between the Nantiquak Indian Tribal Corporation and the Bureau of Indian Affairs of the Department of the Interior."

Minnie, Cal and Ron looked at each other all smiles and back patting, and let out small whoops of joy. It was a moment that was probably the happiest day in Minnie's professional life. Not even their successes in the courts in Baltimore and Dover were as definitive and satisfying as this triumph. Tom Turino had been right in his advice to sue the Bureau over the issue on constitutional grounds. But it was especially satisfying for Minnie because it was a stern rebuke to Nighthorse Ward and his highhanded arrogance. And it would open the door to other small and poor tribes holding treaties—and there were a few of them—to also go after the Bureau in the court.

"Let's go back to the office," said Cal. "This deserves a small celebration. This is a milestone decision. And will set a precedent for many more cases, ruling for ignored and violated treaties. Students will read about us in the case books in the future."

Once they were out of the courtroom, as she was putting on her long coat, Minnie took out her cell phone and called Will.

"Will, drop whatever you're doing and come down to our offices now. We've won against the Bureau. The Nantiquaks are now a federally recognized tribe! We have to drink to our success."

"Hurray! That's the best news of the year. I'll bring a couple bottles of champagne and be right there. I'll call Chief Clarke and Carmine, and Talleck right now."

Back at the office, it was just after normal quitting time, but most of the staff were still there. Cal told the secretary to tell everyone to gather in the big conference room. Then he told Alia to set out glasses, soft drinks and ice and the reserves of pate, sardines, and water crackers that they usually kept for client meetings. He threw off his coat in his office and his suit jacket and brought out a bottle of Hennessey cognac and an unopened bottle of a rare Strathspey whiskey which he took to the conference room. Minnie hung her coat in her office and left her case bag there. She then also went to the conference room and almost immediately had to put up with a rather too intimate hug from Ron. She was able to shake him off easily without any more physical contact by Alia's offering her a Coke and ice. Alia also asked Ron in a commanding voice, "And do you want a whiskey?" Minnie looked at Alia and understood that Alia had deliberately broken them up.

Only several minutes later Will arrived at the NAILS offices, bearing a sack with four bottles of chilled champagne. He took off and hung his coat at the front cloak room and came to the conference room. He stood at the door and surveyed the lawyerly joy. But he was the client and he and the tribe were the real winners. He put the bottles on the table and went first to Cal to congratulate him. Cal put down his whiskey glass and gave Will a very hearty handshake. "We have done it!" Cal shouted, a big smile on his face. "We have beaten the government! The bureaucrats put down—in their place! The Constitution triumphs. Ron, come shake our client's hand. Minnie, here is our client sharing in our triumph."

Ron and Minnie both came over to Cal and Will and the all shared the excitement. More patting on the back.

"And you can't imagine how important Minnie's contribution was." said Cal. "She took Tom Turino's advice and made it into an iron-clad case."

Alia asked Will what he would drink. "I think I'll have a whiskey." Minnie then asked her to bring her a glass of champagne.

"Everyone." said Cal. "Today marks the rebirth of an ancient American Indian tribe. This has been accomplished by the efforts of our firm. All of you. Those who did the footwork of research, long hours of searching the case books. Irena and Gail you both did a splendid job. Those of you who drafted the arguments and checked the facts and history. You all contributed. But you all must know that the real success lay in the efforts of Ron and Minnie. I want to raise a glass in a toast to the massive success of Ron and Minnie."

They all drank up. Minnie had her champagne and Will had a champagne as a chaser to his whiskey. Minnie noticed that Alia, who was Muslim, was not drinking. But Minnie went over and toasted to her, clinking her champagne with Alia's Coke in a small glass.

"I want to raise a toast to the project team of Project Oyster." said Ron, already on a third whiskey. "Our oysters have borne real pearls. In my view, you're all really gems! Our third triumph in two years."

"I've called a few of the top chiefs of the tribe," said Will to Cal but also so Minnie could hear it. "We'll get together tomorrow and celebrate this accomplishment out at Indian River."

Minnie had a second glass of champagne. She wanted to give Will a big hug, and even a full kiss, but still she did not want to show too much of their love in the office. Only Alia knew that she and Will were a couple. But she could not finish the second glass of champagne as she already was feeling heady from the alcohol. She had a glass of water and a bite of pate on cracker. Irina came over to her and congratulated her, and then Jared Levy did as well and Gail Halstead came to her to express her happiness at Minnie's success. But it was only Will who knew that a large part of Minnie's feelings of success came from the clear sense that she had triumphed over Nighthorse Ward. She had gotten back at him. She had rebuked him for taking what was mainly a political decision in turning down the Nantiquaks' application.

After about an hour, the people in the room were ready to slip away. Cal had already stepped out of the room a few times to call other people, presumably to boast, and to inform Tom Turino. Minnie was feeling distinctly drunk and Will was giggling a lot. Ron was telling stories about incidents that had occurred during the hearings, the strange things that the defence lawyers proposed and said, and he was laughing at the awkwardness and lack of preparation those lawyers had displayed. Will looked across the table to Minnie and winked and cocked his head toward the door. She was certainly ready to leave. They both slipped away, Minnie to her office for her coat, and Will to the entry foyer. He got his coat and waited outside the main entry for Minnie to join him. They left the building and walked to the Metro station, but they did not walk arm in arm until they got out of the station at Cleveland Park and began walking up the hill to their house.

"You know, Miniaka, not only do I adore you, but I am also extremely proud of you. You can't believe how proud I am."

"Yeah, even when I'm so drunk?"

"I'm pretty soused too. It's a pretty safe bet to say that we won't go to the farm tonight."

"No way, mister."

"I guess that probably means we won't be able to go rockfish fishing tomorrow. But we can try to go out on Sunday."

The next day they drove out in both of their cars to Bristol and from there in the Oldsmobile together on to Indian River and the old Association building. There was a group from the Indian River band and the Black Face band waiting for them. From the other bands, only John Talleck from the Kuskowarok band was there. Earlier in the year the adult members of that band, at the urging of Hank Sockum, held an election for who would be the next weroance for the band. Sockum no longer wanted to perform those duties and he did not want to be required to travel to Laurelton for meetings of the board of the Tribal Corporation. Sockum wanted to live out his life sitting in his dilapidated mobile home with a blanket over his shoulders as the wise old, fat *midew* whom his neighbors would consult, just like the medicine man he had seen in his favorite movie, *Dances with Wolves*. John Talleck was about forty years old, vigorous and handsome, and had had a varied career working and living away from the settlement. When he was elected he had only recently returned in early 1998. He had money and experience in how the world outside really works. He looked like a stereotypical Indian; he was tall, strong, and lean, with dark, ruddy skin and he wore his hair long. But most importantly he owned a new model pick-up truck so he could attend meetings in Laurelton without difficulty. After his participation at his first board meeting, it became clear to Minnie that he also was a natural leader. And he supported the development of the tribe and getting Federal recognition. She found him quite attractive and was glad he was on the board. His positive outlook offset the conservatism and negativity of guys like Morley Norwood. Unlike earlier meetings when everyone was morose and reticent, today Will noticed the group were speaking amongst themselves animatedly, and Talleck was the most animated of them all. He was talking about opportunities, projects to develop the tribe, and the benefits in money and support they could now start receiving.

After a short while, Chief Clarke started pushing the men—Carmine was not there—to take seats and listen to what Minnie had to say to them. He led Minnie up to the raised platform and insisted she sit at the table there. "Now tell us what has happened and what it means to us." he instructed her.

"I come to you today in my capacity as one of the team of lawyers at NAILS to tell you of the successful law suit we broad against the Bureau of Indian Affairs. As you remember last year at about this time we submitted for you an application to the Bureau seeking their approval to become an American Indian tribe recognized as a sovereign nation by American law. Will Eames and Carmine Norwood prepared the application document, along with a supporting report by Professor Susan Broadhead and assistance and advice from NAILS.

We at NAILS thought it was a very strong application, and as you may recall it included new genealogical evidence and data which are up to now not part of the requirements for recognition. This included DNA genetic data that show historic relationships and continuity within the tribe and all its bands much more definitively and scientifically than any of the traditional measures that have been used in the past—the so called racial relationship rules, "one drop of Indian blood makes a man an Indian or a black man'—those kinds of rules. Or the explicitly racist U.S. census rules, which you may know considered that the tribe had ceased to exist after the 1830s and until the second decade of this century."

"As I said, it was my view—and I myself have once before prepared such a document of application for my own tribe, and I have while working at the Bureau been party to evaluating many other applications—and the view of my colleagues that it was a very strong application which fulfilled all of their requirements. So it came as a surprise to us when the Bureau rejected your application flat in early April of this year. They gave not very specific reasons for their rejection, but said that we had not included key required data and probably could not find or submit this data. They seemed to mean the census data. That the Nantiquak Indians were not recognized as being of the Indian race for more than half a century, but were counted as either being of the white race or the black race, but in most of their countings your ancestors were not counted and included in the census figures at all.

"We decided to contest this ruling in the courts, as mistaken and failing to acknowledge oral genealogies we submitted, as well as new local church records we submitted from the early nineteenth century. We consulted with the father of modern Indian law, and the most successful practitioner of this minor branch of American law, one Mr. Thomas Turino who had sued the state of Connecticut for the Pequoddy Indians and won Federal recognition for them. He advised us that we needed to take a complaint to court against the Bureau based on Constitutional law. He said our earlier court rulings showed that our having a treaty established our claims to recover the reservations which were wrongfully taken from us. And that under the Constitution there are rules and laws provided for dealing with treaty relations that supersede regulatory laws, even if those are derived from statutory laws.

"We followed Turino's advice and we brought suit against the Bureau claiming that the Treaty the Nantiquak leaders signed at the end of the seventeenth century was still valid and should be in force and should be protected by the Federal government. And that this Treaty was proof that the tribe should be a recognized entity even without the decision of the Bureau in response to our application. The Bureau's lawyers were not prepared to argue such as case. In two hundred years of experience the U.S. government has broken nearly all treaties with Indians without any consequences and this was a first in U.S. history where the courts declared that the Nantiquaks are a surviving recognized tribe.

"And the judge in our case saw this and ruled that the Treaty indeed established beyond any question that the people claiming to be direct descendants of those original Nantiquak leaders remain a sovereign Indian nation that the U.S. government has to deal with, as it does with all the other tribes that they have entered into the list of Federally acknowledged Indian tribes.

"This judge instructed the Bureau to at once inscribe the Nantiquak Indian Tribal Corporation into the books. And begin to provide the services, benefits, and support to the tribe that all others enjoy.

"So we expect in the next several weeks the Bureau will do this. They have really no recourse to appeal, as we have already established that within the Constitution the laws dealing with treaties are superior to regulatory laws. And their only avenue for appeal would be to the Supreme Court. I am sure they will be advised that that would be a waste of taxpayers' money and the Court's time and would go nowhere.

"So now this ruling has stated that you are now a fully-fledged sovereign American Indian tribe with treaty established reservation lands and the rights to move forward. As I said we should expect to get formal recognition, which will be delivered in a letter and a large certificate —which looks like a treaty—by the end of this year."

Minnie fell silent. The room was silent. And then one of the men in the back, Will thought it was Morley, began to clap. And soon all of them stood up and began clapping, not really knowing what the most appropriate response was in such rare circumstances."

John Talleck, in the front of the room, stood up and shouted for all to hear, "Well done, Madame Chairwoman. Well done, Minnie Warrens. Without your guidance and efforts we would still be invisible people, divided, and without our ancestral lands—what little was left to us."

Chief Clarke came up to the podium and standing next to Minnie he turned to Will and said, "And let's acknowledge the success of the man who has made all this possible. The driving force, who first proposed that we go after this, and who has pushed us every step of the way, who brought us together with this law firm and with Minnie, and who has supported us and even financed us when we needed help, when no one else would. Selflessly, I might add. And of course we all know I am talking about Will Eames. Will, we owe you a tremendous debt of undying gratitude for all that you have done for us. We would never have done this on our own. But you showed us it was possible, and that we should pursue these targets. And every Nantiquak Indian must know; they owe their continued existence and prosperity to the efforts of Will Eames."

The room erupted in 'hurrahs' and 'yeahs' and some clapping.

"And we have to hold a celebration as a result of this outcome. Morley, do you think you could organize another powwow? A day long celebration of thanksgiving, with a feast and one of our autumn dances around the camp fire? We have to do it in the next two weeks--at the powwow site—before the weather gets too cold. Can you swing it?"

Morley spoke out from behind a few others. "We'll do it. For a Sunday, maybe two weeks from tomorrow."

"And arrange the transport for everyone from the other bands to come along. And of course our guests of honor will be Will and Minnie. And we should invite the other two lawyers from your firm, what's their names, Cal and Rod?"

"Ron, Ron Parchesi" added Minnie in a soft voice.

"Yes them."

"And Professor Alvey." said Morley. "He was the one who wrote the book on our history. He deserves a lot of credit for launching us back on the path of recognition."

Will did not want to contradict Morley out loud. But he would tell Morley separately, discreetly, that Hank Alvey had since died over the past summer. "You could invite Professor Broadhead." said Will, directing his comments at Morley. "She might come. She contributed too and she likewise did a lot of research on the life of the tribe a long time ago." As Will looked around among the dozen or so Indian men that it was the first that he ever noticed that this usually dour crowd was entirely in smiles, looking brightly and happily at one another. 'Maybe they do show their appreciation.' Will thought to himself.

They drove back to Bristol in the Oldsmobile. They were no longer hiding the fact that they were a couple in front of the Nantiquaks. Carmine had surmised that months earlier, and she had spread the word to a few people, mostly on the board. Driggers had over the summer told Talleck that Minnie and Will were living together, but in his usual manner he told him in a snide, condemnatory voice. No one on the Nantiquak board thought their acting like a married couple was a problem or worthy of questioning, or cause for a conflict of interest. Only Carmine felt some little bit of jealousy. For most of the others, it raised their opinion of Will. He was not such an alien white man, after all, whose motives were to be distrusted. Minnie and Will decided not to go to the farmhouse, and as there was no food in the Bristol cottage, they decided to go to the Cedar Island Bar and Restaurant for an early supper. They sat in what had become their usual table in the far corner of the restaurant room far away from the bar which was around the far wall, at a table in the so-called 'family' section in the brightly lit part of the restaurant out of sight of the low-lifes and barflies who would lean on the bar even in the early hours of the evening. They ordered and began eating.

After a short while, Minnie saw a tall, brown-haired, voluptuous white woman in tight fitting lavender stretch pants and a white long sleeve knit shirt which emphasized her breasts leave the bar area and stagger toward the 'family section'. It was clear to Minnie at once that she was headed their way. Will did not notice her at once because his back was to the bar area. The woman, who was not bad looking and of indeterminate age, came right up to their table, looking all the while at Minnie, who was trying to avoid her gaze.

"So you must be the newest sex toy of Will Eames, the playboy of the Eastern Shore. Has he been fucking you good, missy? He did to me for a while. That was for sure."

Will turned around and looked in horror at the woman.

"Go away, Karen. Leave us alone." he shouted.

"I won't go away," said Karen who was clearly drunk. "Until I've had my say. It's a free country after all. Missy, this Will fucks 'em and leaves 'em. Remember that. He did me. He's a very shallow man, who looks at women only as sex toys. But, say, you're a lot older than I thought you'd be. And you're clearly an Injun princess. Nice dark skin, almost like a nigger, but black straight hair. I suppose that he bought you that emerald pendant that you're wearing?"

"Shut up Karen. You're making an ass of yourself."

"Oh and you like groping asses, don't you? She don't have no ass worth groping. How's her pussy? All dried up?"

Will stood up and tried to grab Karen's arms and push her away from the table. He shouted for the waiter to evict this drunk.

"That's right. I'm a drunk. A lush. But you always liked playing with my breasts, and bouncing them in the bed with me on top of ya. Does he do that to you, honey? No, I don't suppose so, your breasts are not big enough for that." The other diners, which did include some families with children, were shocked and began to shout at Karen too.

"Shut up, Karen!" shouted Will. "Get out of here. Leave us alone."

A bouncer from the bar section finally came over and picked up Karen from around her waist and carried her to the outer door of the bar and took her outside. She screamed on the way. "Take your hands offa me. You goon!" And then from outside she continued shouting in a harsh voice. "My coat is in there. Gimme my coat. And my purse!" The barkeeper collected her coat and purse from a stall that was hidden from view of the restaurant and he took them to the door. He didn't shout, but everyone could clearly hear him telling Karen that she was too drunk to stay, and she needed to go home and sleep it off.

The barkeeper came over to Will. "I'm so sorry, Will. I should've sent her packing a couple of drinks ago. And should've when I saw you come in with your missus. I'm really, really sorry. Don't hold it against us. She's been looking for a scrap with you for some time. I should've sent her home and told her to come back later."

Will dismissed him. "It happens. I didn't see her, or maybe we woudun've come in." He then sat down and addressed Minnie. "I'm so sorry that Karen tried to humiliate you. She was really trying to insult me."

"I think she more than tried."

"Minnie, please believe me. I had no idea that Karen would be in here at this time of evening. We would've gone to another place."

"Yeah, that would have been better. Let's go. I want to leave this place."

"She was too drunk to realize what she was saying."

"I'm not so sure. Maybe drunk enough to say just what she really feels and thinks."

They got up and Will brought Minnie her coat and then turned to pay the floor manager. They left and drove over to the cottage. Minnie did not say anything until they were settled inside, she with a cup of coffee, he with a cup of tea and a short glass of whiskey. She was in shock. He was burning with shame and embarrassment.

"I don't know how I can make it up to you for that, Minnie." he said.

"Don't talk. I don't want to talk, just now."

After more than an hour sitting quietly together, Minnie softly said: "So she was your girlfriend and sex toy for a number of years before me? When did you stop seeing her?"

"Well, our final break-up must've been in the summer of '97. But we had really stopped being a couple some months before that."

"Have you had sex with lots of girls? I mean regular partners?"

"No, I can't really say lots. Since I went to university, maybe I had two other girlfriends where we made love together more than once or twice. And I don't keep track, but maybe four or five more times, casual sex, one-night stands, but that was when I was a boy. In the marines. You're the first woman that I ever, really have fallen in love with Minnie. Believe me."

"Not this Karen?"

"No, not Karen. She was as she said a sex toy. She did not love me, and I didn't really love her. Over six years. Believe it or not. At first we really liked it. Sex I mean. But after a while we were just having sex for amusement. And we realized we really didn't care that much for each other."

"We don't have sex just for amusement, do we?"

"No, I have never been with a woman like you, before. Making love with you is the most wonderful act, the most beautiful thing. And I would like to make a family with you. As soon as you relent, when you're ready."

Minnie felt a pang, but she did not say anything. Gradually over the past few months more and more she had been having feelings that she wanted to have children, his children. She first felt these longings, faintly, the previous Thanksgiving at the parents' house, when Kate brought her kids, including their already six-month-old infant girl. Kate paid almost exclusive attention to those kids and she appeared to be loving it. And later that summer, first MaryAnne, Jake's wife, delivered a baby boy and she and Will had gone to visit them about six weeks after that. He was so cute, it tugged at her heart. And then late that summer she had invited her sister's family to come for a weekend at Hampton Farm. During that visit, Minnie spent most of the time playing with her nephew and niece. She didn't talk much to Alicia then because she was looking at the farmhouse with such covetous eyes, Minnie couldn't get her attention. At each of these occasions Minnie had a stronger visceral feeling that she too wanted to become a mother, she wanted a baby. But just then, she couldn't tell Will what she felt just yet about having their baby. She couldn't tell him about her meeting with the doctor just the morning before.

"Maybe you'd like to take a walk?" asked Will.

Minnie shook her head. She continued to mope, and remained quiet until she was ready to go to bed. She laid down in her green nightgown but did not sleep. When he came to bed and began to caress her, she said simply, "I don't want to tonight. Just hold me." She could feel his erection against her lower belly, but they remained still. She was filled with a jumble of mixed emotions. She felt she wanted him, but she also had to tell him the last secrets that were holding her back. She wanted to share her shame, she wanted him to tell her he loved her in spite of that. Long after his erection had waned, and after Will began to breathe calmly as if he had fallen asleep, she asked quietly:

"You know when we first made love, that it was the first time a man had ever loved me? And remember I was afraid? Afraid of pain?"

Will was not sleeping. "Yes, I remember that night, crystal clear in my mind."

"Well, I may have seemed it, but I was not a virgin."

"You don't have to tell me, anything that you don't want to."

"No, I have to get rid of this shame. Because, you were the first man I ever loved and made love to, but I had had sex before. I had been raped before."

"Oh, I know that. I was there. I saved you remember?"

"No, not that time. That was not really rape. He did not penetrate me. No earlier when I was much younger. I was raped. And not once, but twice. I've never told anyone. I was so ashamed, so disgraced. Can you really love a woman who has been raped twice? I mean truly love me? Knowing that I am soiled goods?"

"You are not soiled goods, Minnie. You are the love of my life. Really. And you don't need to feel shame. The disgrace and shame belong only to the rapists. You were a victim, not a perpetrator."

"The first time, I was at a party at a dorm room at university. I was drinking. And I began dancing with this sophomore. I was a freshman and he was older, maybe even a junior. Not bad looking, with red hair and freckles. He seemed at first to be so attractive and he dressed as if he were rich. And we danced and he caressed me through my dress, even caressing my private parts. I didn't push him away. And when we finished at the party he walked me back to my room. Almost as soon as he closed the door behind me, he started to kiss me, open mouth. I didn't push him away then either or protest. And then he was pulling off my panties even under my skirt. And then he pushed me on the bed, jumped on top of me and penetrated me. All in a flash. I didn't resist. But it hurt. It hurt so bad. That was the first time the pain occurred, a tearing pain. I think I screamed a little. But from pain not pleasure. He came inside me and I seem to remember he jumped back up almost at once, put his erect penis back in his pants and left. I remember all this vividly still, like a bad nightmare." Minnie was speaking low, slow and with long pauses between sentences. Perhaps it helped that the room was dark and she could not see Will's face. They had never had pillow talk like they had on this night. Except that she could feel his arms, it was as if she was talking to the inky darkness or to herself in a bad dream. "I felt like I was to blame. That I led him on."

"Sounds like date rape." whispered Will. "You were not to blame for anything. He was out that night just looking to score. He was a scumbag."

"But didn't I lead him on? Didn't I encourage him?"

"No. In what way? He grabbed you. He forced you. You didn't invite him to take you. Sounds like you didn't even invite him back to your room. He just came with you."

"For the longest time before that I believed that that was how Indian girls were supposed to behave with white boys. Be submissive. Let them take you. No love or passion in the act, just let the boy have his pleasure with you."

"I can't imagine where you got those ideas, Minnie. Not from your mother for sure. At school maybe."

"Well he got what he wanted. And he never came back, thank god. I cried a lot that night after he left. The pain was awful. And after that I was immensely fearful of any white boy who even so much as glimpsed at me. And equally afraid of black men, because you know in Richmond the city is full of black men strutting around the streets, and the papers are full of accounts of black men raping mostly black women. I kept away from all men. I felt like everyone could see my shame and was blaming me for being a slut and a whore."

"I'm sure no one has ever thought of you as a slut and a whore."

"Except for the man who raped me about five years later. That time it was much worse. Much more violent. I had driven up from Richmond, really late at night to pick up by sister, Alicia. She was working afternoons and evenings at that time—I haven't told you—as a prostitute, and I had gone to pick her up on Highway One after she had finished twelve hours work. I had done that often. This time I stopped at a McDonalds and went in to have a coffee while I waited. This time I wasn't being especially careful or cautious. And when I went to my car, he grabbed me from behind and hit me hard on the side of my head. I was not really fully conscious then. But the next thing I know, he had pulled down my pants, I was in the back of his pick-up truck. He was white, maybe a soldier, and then the same awful, cutting pain came back. Just like the first time. I really fully came too with that pain. He was inside of me and banging me hard. He had torn up my clothes a bit. But I was still mostly dressed. He was banging me hard against the bare metal of the truck bed. I remember the metal was hard and cold and it smelled like fertilizer. And I was silent, but he was cussing and cursing, and he hit me one or two times more. He tried to bite my breast. And after a while I felt him come. And he then pulled me out of the back of the truck, and dumped me in the dirt on the side of the road like I was a sack of onions or something. I don't think I looked at him even. He was a white boy, probably one of the soldier recruits. And he spat on me after he threw me on the ground. And said something like, "you nigger slut!" and he drove off. I cried a lot. But I didn't tell Alicia when I picked her up and took her home. She didn't say anything either. I was in complete shock and a daze. I didn't know how I got home that night."

"I didn't tell anyone about either of these attacks. I have never been able to talk about them before. I felt like damaged goods. You know the pain? I thought they had torn something and that I could never work properly again. I feared that if I had sex again, the pain would be intolerable. That I'd bleed, like a knife cut."

"You told me to be gentle on our first night together. Remember you told me about the pain. Did I hurt you then?"

"Yes, it still hurt then."

"I felt so much that being raped by white guys was the destiny of Indian girls who tried to join white society. I have had this strong feeling that I was to blame for the times I was raped. Something I signalled to men, or carelessness."

"Oh come on. Two of those guys could not have seen or realized that you were an Indian woman. Both of those times it was dark and they couldn't tell what race you were. Except maybe they thought you were a black girl. The university student, well I doubt that he could have known that you were an Indian. Probably he thought you were some swarthy skinned girl from Central America or India."

"Maybe you're right there. But the red-headed kid, he knew."

"I seem to remember," said Will. "I seduced you, didn't I? You didn't think I was going to rape you? You don't think now it was rape?"

"No, because I wanted you so badly then. I wanted you to love me. And you were so gentle and careful with me. I still do want you to love me. And you have always tried to please me, so much, all the time. It was hard for me to hear this evening that you once had a sexual relationship with someone other than me. That I wasn't the one and only and exclusive love of your life."

"Minnie, you are in no way to blame for the violent assaults of three beastly men. They all had to use force and violence, or deceit, and if you had resisted them, well… we might not be talking together right now."

"But, Minnie, you know to be entirely truthful, you are and you have been: my one and only, true love. Now hug me and tell me you love me."

She moved over tight against him again and hugged him. And then she took up his penis and began to stroke it. "And do I please you, Willeams?"

"Yes, Minnie."

"And you can still love me now that you know that I have been raped several times before I ever knew you? I have not told you any of this before because I was so afraid that you'd no longer want me. And the shame was so powerful."

"Of course I can love you. I do love you Minnie and want you all the time, near me, by my side like now. All those other times, earlier, were against your will. I don't want you any less knowing now that those horrible things happened to you. You were a victim. And you should not feel any shame for being made a victim. And I didn't want you because I thought or knew that you were a victim. I was attracted to you, because you are so beautiful. Radiant. I want you to be my wife—don't you remember?-- to love me forever, to make our little Indian tribe. I want to please you, always."

And then Minnie began to cry and sob and she hugged him yet firmer. She must have cried for ten minutes before she stopped. Then she got up out of the bed and slipped over to the toilet. It sounded as if she were sick in the toilet and she was a long time before coming back to bed.

"Hold me tonight Will. We can pass on the sex. Just hold me close. And keep telling me you love me."

"I will, Minnie. I do love you, and will keep telling you that." With one hand he began to rub her head, the other was wrapped around her waist. Both of her arms were folded up between them on Will's chest

She fell asleep like that after about twenty minutes not saying a word more. Not long after Will could hear the patter of rain on the roof above their heads.

Will woke her up by giving her little nips and kisses all over her body which was exposed now by the hitching up of her nightgown. She giggled and then she moved sharply and pulled the gown back down over her hips.

"I decided after last night's talk," he said, "that I would just eat you up, just like a guppy would. In small bites. And I've enjoyed the view along the way."

After they got up and got dressed, Will took her to the window.

"Look at that storm outside. With that kind of wind, there's no way we're going to go out fishing today. Sad to say. Not in a boat, and I think with that lashing rain, not on the fishing pier either."

"Yes, it does look awful."

"And I checked the forecast. It's expected to last all day. So maybe we can go have a fish dinner at my parents' house tonight. You know, I bet you they still have frozen the rockfish we gave them last time. Shall we ask them?"

"Yes, that would be nice to have dinner with them again. But we won't talk anything about last night, right?"

"Absolutely not. But Mom might as usual ask you if you're not ready to marry me yet."

"I think maybe, I can handle that tonight. But I still cannot tell my mother or sister about what I told you last night. I still feel ashamed of what happened, and I don't want to see the horror they will have if I told them. Will you keep all of that confidential?"

"Yes, I will?"

"And you believe me, don't you?"

"Yes, I do. Completely.

"You can still love me?"

"Yes, Minnie. I still love you. And understand you even more than before."

Minnie turned to him and gave him a hug. "Hold me close to you, always."

"I will. Any time and every time you need it."

MarSue still had the rockfish in the freezer and she told them that she would put them out and love to see both of them at dinner that evening. She'd make a special dessert too. A pumpkin pie—to practice getting ready for Thanksgiving.

"Well, we're set for this evening. Now what shall we do for the rest of the day?"

"I would like to take you back to the bed, and make love to you, until we both collapse with exhaustion."

"I could like that." said Will, smiling. He took her hand and they walked back into the bedroom.

That evening they arrived at Will's parents' house all refreshed, cleaned and perfumed or soap scented, virtually shining. But Bob did not notice. The aroma of the frying fish throughout the house overpowered their scents. "Come in, come in, get out of that awful rain. It's been a miserable day, eh?" said Bob. He kissed Minnie on the cheek and gave Will a pat on the shoulder even before they could take off their coats.

"Not especially miserable," said Will.

"Excuse me if I go to the kitchen." Minnie said, "I want to watch what Mar Sue is cooking up."

At the dinner table, Mar Sue served up fried rockfish filets with a corn pudding and sautéed brussels sprouts. They were large filets, because once more Minnie had early in October caught five very large fish, to Will's one. And they were only a few bites into this meal when Bob spoke up:

"So, any more positive news about your Injun Project, Will?"

"Yes, actually. Great news." said Will. "But I'll let Minnie tell you."

"Well, Minnie. Did you win another court case?"

"Yes, but not like the one against Maryland. On Friday the Constitutional Court in D.C. ruled that the Nantiquak Tribe should be a recognized Indian tribe according to their treaty. This reverses the ruling of the Bureau of Indian Affairs. And is a major, precedent setting victory for all Indians."

"Congratulations. I suppose the credit goes to you and your efforts?"

"No, it wasn't just me. Our whole firm worked a lot on this case. It really is a breakthrough case, suing the Bureau on behalf of an Indian tribe. And winning."

"And what was this treaty you say all this was based on?" asked Mar Sue.

"It was the peace treaty between the Nantiquak nation and the King of England, signed in 1682." answered Minnie calmly.

"Really?" asked Bob in disbelief. "Such an old treaty, with the King of England, can still be valid?"

"Sure can." answered Will enthusiastically.

"Yes, that was the essential point of the lawsuit. That the Nantiquaks were recognized by the King of England and given reservation lands in a proper treaty. And our Constitution shows that that treaty is still valid and must be in force, in spite of all the violations that the states and the U.S. government have committed against it over the centuries. As the treaty is still in force, the tribe must be recognized by the Federal government."

"So that's great. You beat Maryland and the state returned or bought a huge amount of land—twelve thousand acres—to the tribe."

"No closer to seven thousand acres," corrected Will.

"And then you went and beat the state of Delaware into returning a huge amount of land as reservation," Bob continued.

"Well, pa, if you consider two thousand five hundred acres to be a huge amount of land." interrupted Will again.

"Actually, I do consider that to be a huge amount of land. And Delaware is a tiny state, so relative to Delaware it was a huge amount. I remember when the final settlement was made that the newspapers reported that Delaware gave the Nantiquaks four square miles of reservation land. For me that's a lot."

"Yes, those were big victories for the Nantiquaks," said Minnie. "And for Indians everywhere in the U.S., especially here in the East. Only once before has a lawsuit won back former reservation land for an Indian tribe in the Eastern states. And it was only eight hundred acres. If only my tribe could win so much land in a lawsuit."

"Well, why not?"

"We don't have a treaty. Sad to say. And suing the state or the Federal government would be very difficult for us. Believe me, I have looked into it."

"So now your third big triumph." said Bob. "It's wonderful news. You're a mighty fine lawyer, Minnie."

"I told you at once," said Mar Sue to Bob, "that she'd be a good lawyer."

"Just very humble." said Bob, who then turned to Will. "And have you benefited at all from this Injun Project, Will?"

"Yes, tremendously. Because if I hadn't started on it, I would never have met Minnie or been introduced to her, more accurately." Will said as he glanced at Minnie.

"And after that, I have benefited in ways I could not have foreseen. The state of Maryland, as part of its settlement, bought from me that parcel of land I bought on the Nanticoke River, you know 'Mosquito Acres'. They paid me what I had paid for it, so it wasn't a profit. But I got my money back. And the Nantiquaks got the land. And even more, I was the sales side agent for the sale of Taylor's farm to the state to be given to the Indians near Exeter. That was one of the biggest commissions I have ever gotten from any transaction. Lucy got a bonus for the first time since she started working with me. Both of these parcels were given to establish the Chicocoan reservation for the band of Nantiquaks that live in our county, along with several other pieces of land."

"Well done, son. "So now what with the Injun Project? Is it finished? Or is the next step to develop an Indian casino?"

"I'm going to try to develop a casino in the Chicocoan reservation. But first we need to get the tribe to agree on it and commit to that part of the project."

"So still want to build a casino?" asked Bob.

"Yes. I think it now can be done, but it will take time. If the tribe agreed tomorrow, I think it would still take more than three years to build and complete it. And that's of course without any outside legal challenges. And financing remains a major problem, regardless."

"Well, this is interesting." said Mar Sue. "Didn't the Chesapeake Resort here on the Choptiko River want to build a casino when they first started? They were blocked by the legislature in Annapolis."

"Yes, that's right, because the current laws ban gambling in the state. But this casino would be outside the state and the state's authority. In principle."

"Is that right, Minnie?" Mar Sue asked.

"That's right. The courts will not be able to block such a development."

"We are really targeting the Ocean City weekenders as the main audience for the casino." said Will. "We think a large number of them will stop to gamble. More maybe even then actually use the beach and swim in the ocean."

"Well, I think we need to drink a toast to your success and to your future success." said Bob. "Do we have any wine, Mar Sue?"

"I'm driving tonight back to D.C. with Minnie. So I think I'll pass on wine, thanks. But maybe Minnie will raise a glass of wine to your toast."

After Mar Sue poured out three glasses of white wine and one of juice they toasted and Bob cheered. "Hurrah."

"But there's more success this year. I should tell you about. This year the farm made a super profit, twenty times what it earned last year. I invested in fertilizer, and the weather this year was perfect for a bumper crop of both corn and soy beans. And of course we didn't have that tornado in the early growing season which whacked the young crops last year. Everything went so well that I'm going to be able to invest in an irrigation system next year. I'm really pleased."

"That's great news, son. You seem to have the midas touch." said Bob.

"No, I think I was just lucky. And Max, my farm manager, is really pretty good, especially when conditions are favorable. This year yields were off the charts—record breaking. We'll see if my 'midas touch', as you say, can carry over to our first Nantiquak businesses, which are farms we have already set up in the Maryland reservations along the Nanticoke River. Next year will be the first time that Nantiquak Indians return to corn farming in this state in almost two centuries. But this time, it will be large scale industrialized farming, intended to make large surpluses. Not subsistence farming."

"That sounds interesting." said Bob. "You think new farming ventures can work profitably?"

"Yes. The farms we're going to work have lain idle for some time, because the farmers grew too old to work them, or they lacked the investment monies to run them properly and scientifically, or they were unable to apply new methods or to innovate. I think our Indian friends will do much better."

"I feel certain," he continued, "it will stimulate the economy in the entire County, and in Wicomico County too."

"It does seem to me that you have had the golden touch on everything that you've promoted this past year or so." said Bob.

"No. Not everything. The Orioles had a miserable season and ended at the bottom of the League, after doing so well last year. And I don't see them returning any time soon. Maybe not in my lifetime."

"Do you take Minnie to any Orioles game?" Bob asked.

"No, I don't really care for baseball." said Minnie. "To me it's all rather boring and slow."

Mar Sue cut in: "And to me too. Bob and I have only gone once to a baseball game, I mean the Orioles. And it was boring, as you say. I did however go to Will's games when he was in high school. Will, I can only hope you're right; that those farms can stimulate the county. But right now I think Minnie could help me serve the pumpkin pie to everybody. Anyone for coffee?"

"But my main goal now is to get the Nantiquak tribe to build a casino. That could change the whole region, and for the good."

Over coffee, Mar Sue invited them for Thanksgiving dinner later that month. They agreed to come and have a long weekend on the Eastern Shore.

On the way back to D.C. later that evening Minnie suddenly asked him: "Do you think, Will, you could do much the same thing for my tribe the Massoponax, that you've done for the Nantiquak?"

Will did not answer at once. He was thinking. "That's a hard question for me to answer Minnie. I don't have any connections to your tribe, neither the Massoponax side nor the Doeg side, I don't know the lay of the land there in Virginia, certainly not like I do here. And I don't know very much about the conditions of your tribe."

"You have a connection through me." Minnie cooed. "And although she wouldn't admit it, my mother really appreciates the house you built for her so she could move back to the reservation. It was very much the family sort of thing to do. And Alicia and her family really appreciated that as well. Did I ever tell you that Alicia is very jealous of everything I have by being with you? She can't understand why I don't marry you right away. She thinks you're rich enough and capable enough that you could improve all their lives at the Massaponax. And the other residents of the reservation, they know what you made happen there and that it has improved their lives, and the lives of my family. Mom's house—which you had built-- is the finest house on the reservation. And now they know that they can get the same, and maybe even afford it."

"But still it is a distant connection. I know even less about them than I knew about the Nantiquaks before I started the Project. Here the Nantiquaks were not only my neighbors, but they also lived on land I'd bought. Lived as squatters, poor squatters. And some of them worked on the farm that I later inherited. And of course some of them are related to me by blood. And not so distantly related either, cousins. That gave me some connection with them—a relationship that I could work. Those connections made me feel I had a responsibility. Admittedly I did not have any connections up with the Delaware tribe. But still, you'd have to lead me into the situation with your tribe, Minnie. I'm not saying that I couldn't do something, but you would have to lead, not me."

"So Massoponax are not cousins with you, but in-laws, you could say."

"Not yet, not until you marry me. That is what in law means, after all."

"We could do it together then, no? And don't misunderstand me, I don't think our little tribe needs a casino. But it does need to get

Federal recognition. And I think I've already demonstrated that I am not the one who can drive them to that end."

"My love, I won't say no, and I won't say it can't be done, but, I cannot just now see that I bring anything more to that situation with your tribe, than what you were able to. And for the next two or so years I have to see the casino project through to its completion. And maybe it will take longer. And then maybe we can seriously look at Injun Project Two, and I can take a role."

"I suppose that is enough," sighed Minnie. It was the first time she had ever asked Will for anything and he did not consent to get it or do it for her. They got home late in the evening. Minnie was feeling tired and a little fuzzy. As they unlocked the front door to their house and stepped in she was feeling that not only was she still passionately attracted to this dynamic man, she was also extremely proud of all that he had achieved since she had first met him. He was a super decent and generous man. He was a model man of the Eastern Shore.

The next day at the office she got a call on her cell phone. The caller ID did not recognize who was calling. So she reluctantly picked up the hand set.

"Hello, Minnie?" said a familiar sweet voice. "This is Carmine Norwood. Calling from Laurelton. Don't be surprised. First, I want to ask, how are you after your big triumph?"

"Oh Carmine, I am fine. We celebrated all through the weekend."

"Yeah, sorry I could not be there with you on Saturday. But now in my capacity as Communications vice president for the Nantiquak Corporation I'm calling you to tell you that there will be a special meeting of the board of directors in two weeks' time, on Sunday, the twenty-first, at twelve o'clock. Do you think you could make it?"

"Yes, I can be there. What's the business of the day? Aren't we supposed to have a regular board meeting early next month?"

"Yes. But there are just a few items to discuss before the December meeting. And following that meeting the board will adjourn and proceed to the powwow ground in Indian River where we'll hold our celebration of thanksgiving for winning recognition as a sovereign tribe. There will be a feast, culminating in a performance of our traditional fall harvest dance. You'll be the guest of honor."

"I wouldn't miss it for anything. And Will will come with me too?"

"Of course. He's also going to be honored. The event will be outside for several hours, so be sure to come dressed warmly, very warmly."

"But you said thanksgiving celebration. I thought you don't observe the Thanksgiving holiday."

"We don't, not the one on the 25th of November, anyway, with all the associations of intolerant English pilgrims. And we aren't going to observe it this year either. But we are giving thanks for our promotion to being a recognized, independent tribe. And we have only rare opportunities to give thanks to the mysterious powers that govern all people and that have blessed us this year."

"Okay, I'll be there."

"You could come dressed as you did at the last powwow. I mean, with your hair in a braid, and the silver jewelry, that would be super."

"Okay, I will."

"I really look forward to seeing both of you in about two weeks. Okay?"

"Yes, that would be very nice. Thanks for the notice. Bye then."

"That's my duty now. Communications. Bye, bye, Minnie."

Minnie called Will who was at their Cleveland Park home. He had been called by Carmine also, just before she had called Minnie. But he had been unable to call her, because her cell phone was not answering. So they both already knew the news; they did not need to share the information.

"But what if it rains in the afternoon?" asked Minnie.

"It won't. That is not at all usual in late November. Yesterday's rain storm was the remnants of a nor'easter off the Atlantic. We only get them in rare years. Ordinarily late November is dry. But it can be frosty. So don't worry about rain. I'll bring our two big golf umbrellas just in case to keep your head dry in any weather. Especially your lovely braid."

"Frosty and rainy. That wouldn't be nice at all."

"No. But you'll have to dance very hard to keep yourself dry, and very near the fire to keep yourself warm. I'll hold the umbrellas over you while you dance."

"You're so nice and thoughtful of me." said Minnie sarcastically. Won't you dance with me?"

"I don't know how." said Will.

They drove up to the Tribal office in Laurelton, and already there were a number of cars parked all along the streets near the building where normally there would be no cars parked at all on a Sunday. The weather was dry and chilly, the sun shone weakly through a high thin white cloud, but there was no frost on the roads or ground around Laurelton. And it looked certain that there would not be rain. Minnie and Will entered the office and were greeted by name by a young man, whose name escaped Will. He took their coats and put them in the cloakroom and then led them to the back of the building to the board room, where six other Indian board members were already gathered. Will went around and shook everyone's hand, and Minnie followed him doing the same, repeating the names of each as there were some unfamiliar faces. As they were doing that Charlie Clarke walked into the room with Morley Norwood right behind him. Charlie Clarke-- people had stopped calling him Chief Clarke, he was just plain Charlie now—and he smiled at Minnie. "I like your braid, Minnie. You're very pretty, you know when you wear it."

Minnie blushed. She had let her hair grow longer, and now the braid fell well down her back, but she was so comfortable with it, that she had forgotten that she had knotted that morning. Before she could say anything to Charlie, in walked John Talleck and with him Jack Buckham.

"Sorry we're late," Talleck said loudly to the room in general. "Do we have a quorum yet?"

Charlie looked around the room, counting heads to himself. "We have a quorum, but let's wait a short while to see if we can get the two who are missing still from the Makadewa-Ninda. And one more from my band."

All three of these board members came and Charlie said they could start. He invited Minnie to take the chairwoman's seat in the middle of the long table on the raised platform. Charlie sat on one side of her and Jack Buckham sat on her other side. Everyone was there. The six members from the Indian River band, the three from the Makadewa-Ninda, the single representatives from Kuskowaroak, Puckamee, and Asksesky bands. Morley was now a board member from Indian River. And Ronald Woodson was there as the meeting secretary, writing the minutes. And Carmine was there in her role as Communications vice president, and in effect, spokesperson for the tribe. She was also taking notes. She smiled at Minnie when their eyes met. Minnie had not noticed when Carmine has slipped into the room.

"So I call to order this extraordinary meeting of the board of the Nantiquak Indian Corporation of Delaware and Maryland. First, Ron, could you read out the minutes of the last meeting?"

Ron read them out quickly. And Minnie called for a vote to approve them, which was carried unanimously.

"Now, I do not know what special business was needed to be discussed in an extraordinary board meeting," continued Minnie, "but I would like to report officially in our Corporate records that the Tribe won its suit against the Bureau of Indian Affairs earlier this month. And the tribe has now been entered into the register of officially recognized Indian tribes by the Bureau. And I understand that we have received the official document—I could say charter—along with notification of this recognition. Could we see this charter?"

"I think they call this document a diploma." said Carmine as she stood up in the back of the room. "We got it in the mail, just four days ago." Carmine then unfurled a tube and brought up a large, quarto sized sheet of paper and gave it to Minnie. Minnie looked at it and it was an official grant document with the heading "diploma" and the full official name of the Bureau, and large lettering saying the Nantiquak Tribe had been entered in the register of Federally recognized American Indian tribes. It was signed by the Secretary of the Department of the Interior, and the Assistant Secretary and head of the Bureau of Indian Affairs--both with real flourish—and had a golden seal attached at the bottom along with a red ribbon. Minnie unrolled it completely and held it up for all to see. The board members clapped.

"We'll have to have this framed and then it needs to be hung on the front wall of the entry reception area of this building. And we need to make a number of color copies of this as well." said Minnie.

"So with this business completed, I think before we discuss any future actions or initiatives of the tribe that are the consequence of this decision, we need to compile the list of all enrolled members of the tribe. And another list of the children of these members who are not yet in their majority. And once we have that list, which I think shouldn't take long at all, we should begin issuing tribal IDs to all members in both Maryland and Delaware."

"Do these need to have photos?" asked one the representative from Asksesky, whose name Minnie did not remember. She asked him if he could tell the group his name. He said Kevin Brownleaf.

"No I don't think we need to have photos on these IDs just yet. But maybe they should be credit card size and laminated, so that they last a while and people can use them for identification purposes for a long time. Carmine, I think your office should start this process. Okay?"

"So, is there anymore extraordinary business that we must do today?"

Morley raised his hand and stood up. "I wanted to get the board's approval for the expenditure of four thousand, eight hundred dollars for the special thanksgiving ceremony, which we have organized for later today. We've spent all of this so far, and we may have additional costs, for food and drink, and for bus transport so the outlying tribal bands could attend. Could I get this approval?"

Minnie asked for a vote. And it carried unanimously.

"All right, that's done." Minnie quietly said. "I think we do not need to make a financial report for this meeting. That can wait for next month's meeting. Now what else needs to be addressed today?"

Talleck stood up. "In my capacity as a Corporate officer in charge of tribal development projects, but also as a board member, I would like to schedule for the next board meeting, which is only three weeks from now, a presentation and proposal from Will Eames on the subject of the tribe's building and operating a tribal casino." Talleck then sat back down.

"So new business for next month? From the minutes, do we have a full agenda already, Ron?"

"No, just usual business. Nothing scheduled for new business."

"Then we can add it to the agenda, John. Unless anyone objects." There were no objections, only Morley was scowling. Minnie continued: "Now I want to add an item; an announcement for today's meeting."

"I was appointed as chairwoman as a kind of show of gratitude and as an honor for helping set up the Corporation. I have served you for the past 14 months through six board meetings. I want to announce that I will resign this position at the end of this year. In other words, the next board meeting will be my last. So in next month's meeting we will need to discuss and select my successor for the year 2000 and after."

There were audible groans and mutterings of objection.

"And now is there anything else for today's meeting? I seem to suspect that there is."

Now Charlie stood up. "One of the items that were especially put up for this meeting, is the motion I want to make now, especially as today we celebrate all that has happened in the past two years, and as we are preparing to hand out tribal IDs. I move that Will Eames, sitting there," and he pointed to Will, "our friend, as a sign of our gratitude to him, be enrolled as a full member of the tribe. I don't think anyone will raise objections. We would like him to be involved with our tribe for many years yet to come."

Will stood up abruptly and raised an objection. "Well, that is a surprise. And I'd like to thank Chief Clarke. But I thought that membership in this tribe requires no less than one-quarter Nantiquak blood relationship. And I don't have that, as some of you may know."

Now Morley stood up. "Yes those are our rules. We made them, but if the board wanted to select the President of the United States to be a full member of the tribe, it would be put to a vote and we could do it. We make the rules and we can bend the rules. And unlike the President of the United States, you, Will, have genuinely helped us. And after all, as some of us might also know, you have one-eighth blood relationship. And that is good enough for us, in your case. Besides, it would be best to have a tribal member occupying the position you now have in the Corporation, as vice president for finance."

Minnie chuckled. She thought, 'And I told him they would never show him any gratitude. How wrong I was.'

"Well, then, if there are no real objections," she continued. "I suggest we put this motion to a vote. But his membership will not require him to live on any of the reservations." said Minnie.

The board voted unanimously in favour. "So it is agreed, and now Will Eames you can count yourself a Nantiquak tribesman." said Minnie smiling broadly. "A Federally recognized Indian. Congratulations."

The whole room stood up and began to clap. Carmine gave Will a kiss on the cheek, and then the board members who were not on the dais, went over to him and shook his hand, and patted his shoulder.

Will looked at Minnie, an expression mixed with surprise and maybe shock on his face.

"Carmine will enrol you, Will Eames. Which Band should she put you in?"

Will shouted above the fray around him. "Kuskowaroak, no other."

"Done. So our next meeting on Saturday, the fourth of December, here at eleven. And now I propose that we adjourn this meeting and proceed to our celebration and have lots of good food and fun."

Will and Minnie drove together in the Oldsmobile and when, after thirty minutes, they arrived at the grounds set aside for parking were already over-packed, and there were people with light batons directing cars to other grounds about half a mile further down the road. There were yellow school buses parked at the second grounds. They had brought people from the "outer" Bands in Maryland and were now shuttling visitors from the distance parking areas to the powwow site. "Wow." whistled Will. "They must've gotten all eight hundred tribal members here today!"

It took them another forty minutes to park and get back to the powwow grounds. Most of the crowds were standing in lines inside the food tent. Morley and his crew had set up a very large tent so that most of the tables could be brought inside. Still with the lines of people patiently waiting to get their serving of barbecued chicken, corn on the cob, and baked beans and biscuits and the other diners sitting at eight to a table the tent was very crowded. Once inside the tent it was very snug and warm. Minnie and Will did not have to wait long to get their food and drink—hot mulled cider—as the attendants on the buffet lines rapidly filled paper plates and there were no cashiers to cause any delays. They found a table that was only half occupied by a family with two children. Minnie thought that they did not look at all like Indians and her suspicion was confirmed when the man introduced himself. "Hi, I'm Bob Johnson. This is my family. We're from the Black Face Band."

"And I'm Will Eames from Bristol. And this is my wife, Minnie Warrens from the Massaponax tribe from across the Chesapeake. I'm from the Kuskowaroak Band."

"Glad to meet you, Will. This is my wife, Roberta, and our two kids, Johnny and Cindy. Weren't you the fellow who came here and took some DNA samples for a genealogical survey?"

"The self-same."

"There's always been a dispute in our tribe about our ancestry, and whether we have negro blood. Did you find out anything about that?"

"Actually, yes and no. We sampled two people from your Band. One man and one woman. And we found both of them had the genetic signature that was the same for nearly all the Nantiquaks throughout the Eastern Shore. All closely related, and descended from a common set of Nantiquak ancestors. In the man there was some contribution of African genes. I was told that this was probably about two hundred years ago. But in the woman there was none."

"See there Roberta. I told you that would be the case. Maybe only one or two Indians married a black person. I have had a theory that the name for our Band, the Black Face, comes from older times. And has to do with black face paint that our warriors traditional wore. Not anything to do with negro ancestry."

"Hard for me to say," Will answered as he gnawed on a chicken leg. "But one of the more interesting connections that we found was that your Band and only your Band, both of the individuals we sampled showed that there was a genetic signature of people from Northwest Europe. Maybe Dutch, or Frisian or northern Englishmen."

"You know we have a legend that our tribe took in some lost white people, mainly women and children, and we adopted them and wed them. Hey, there's Hank, our self-appointed historian. He might know something and he might be interested in what you just told me. Hank, come over here."

A mid-sized man who looked like he could be an elderly Irish farmer came over to the table. He introduced himself. Bob said again that Hank was the Band's historian.

"Just a hobby of mine, actually. I collect bits and snatches of what has been lying around the county." said Hank.

"Tell Hank, whacha just told me about the genetic signature from northwest Europe."

Will did and Hank intensely listened.

"Interesting indeed. You see there was a historical incident that may be related to that genetic line in our blood. It's well documented that in the late 1620's the Dutch set up a stockade and colony of a few dozen Dutchmen at a place which is now called Lewes, several miles from here on the coast of Delaware Bay. That was before the charter for the colony of Maryland was given, and long before there was any white settlement on the Eastern Shore. It was soon destroyed by hostile Indians, said to be Nantiquak, but I doubt that. More likely they were Lenapi Indians, from the north. They killed all thirty colonists, who were all farmers, and not just fur traders."

"The Dutch West Indies Company still wanted to maintain their hold on the Delaware Bay, both in what is now Cape May and the Eastern Shore. So they put out invitations for a new colony. And in the late 1650s a group of Dutch Mennonites, wanting to leave the warfare that was still shaking Europe, volunteered to set up and run a new settlement there at Lewes. The Company sent them, three dozen men, about a dozen or more women, and even some children and they picked a site right next to the burned out ruins of the first colony. They called it Whore's Kill."

"By that time the English had laid claim to the Eastern Shore, and the colony of Maryland claimed those lands which were originally claimed by the Swedes and then the Dutch. The told their concessionaire, the Lord Baltimore, in England, about the new Dutch colony and he decided to do something about it. At that time England and Holland were nearly always at war. So it was easy for Lord Baltimore to convince the government to send a naval cruiser.

And it sailed here, not to displace the Dutch Mennonites, who were pacifists, by the way and would not fight, but to kill them all and to lay to waste their stockade and their homes."

"So the naval warship went there, bombed the settlement, and landed a force of marines who killed everyone they could catch, all the men, some thirty or so, and some of the women and even children. They burned and destroyed the town and everything in it. They said that they did not leave even a nail behind them. And then they sailed away."

"It seems about ten women and a few children during the attack ran into the dense forests, where our ancestors were hunting. Probably the loud shooting and big booms from the cannon attracted the attention of our ancestors. So they watched the massacre and when the women fled to where they were hidden they protected them from the English and took them inland, back to their villages, and adopted them. And then in time, they married all the women and the children too, that survived, and had more children with them. The Dutch language disappeared as well as the Mennonite faith. But in our group of Black Face, every now and then there is a child born who is exceptionally tall and has a high square and broad forehead and light colored hair. So it must be the Dutch genes still exist. And your DNA test seems to bear this out."

"So this is historically established?" asked Minnie.

"Only on the Dutch and English side of the story." said Hank. "The Indian side is more a traditional legend in our Band. That we adopted this group of white women escaping the guns of the English. I'm inclined to believe it was true. At that time, in the seventeenth century, the Nantiquak lived over by the Brant Creek, but their hunting parties ranged all the way to the Atlantic, in the forests of what is now Delaware and especially along the Indian River."

"Interesting." pondered Will. "I wonder if it could be even more confirmed by wider tests. If there are Mennonite families surviving in Holland who have the same genetic signals, as your people seem to. And if we can test more of the Band and get a better picture of the genetic signatures which are from Holland. It costs a lot to do the tests."

"And frankly, I don't think we need any more detailed accuracy. Not now that we are a recognized tribe. And besides your DNA samples did show that we are fundamentally Nantiquak. We are more closely related to other Algonquian tribes then we are to either Dutch or African peoples."

The weather that afternoon had been dry but it was very chilly, and as they were eating Minnie was beginning to feel cold. She wanted another hot drink, the mulled cider and went into the food tent to get some. It was warm, even stuffy inside the tent and she stood there for a while trying to warm herself up. She then returned with two large cups of the hot cider. She was thinking that her tribe, unlike the Nantiquaks, did not have any oral memories or carriers of the tribal legends. It was a shame, she thought.

As they were finishing their dinner Will saw John Talleck walking by. Will called him over.

"This Morley knows how to put on a nice party," asked Will. "Doesn't he?"

"Yeah, he ferried all of our people out of Wicomico this morning in one of the school buses."

"Did you see Armand Dreggers?"

"No, he won't be coming. He's having a hard time dealing with the death of his stepson."

"Oh. I met him once. What happened?"

"It seems his stepson was having troubles and it was worse with drugs. He killed himself on Friday. There in their home."

"That's really bad. I'll have to go over and give him my consolations."

"Yeah. Strange as he is, Armand might like that. Especially coming from you."

"He's my cousin, you know?" Will said.

"Really? Can that be possible? You two are as unlike as snow and sand."

"Yeah, really. My great grandmother was a Driggers."

"I'll be damned. We have to talk about the idea." And Talleck walked off.

Almost at once Carmine passed by their table.

"Oh, I was looking for you, Minnie. Hi Will. I wanted to ask you Minnie, did Cal or Ron come with you?"

"I don't believe so. Not with me. And I don't think they were planning to come."

"That's too bad. We invited them, since this is thanksgiving and we certainly have a lot to thank them for in addition to your efforts."

"Sorry, I didn't know anything of their plans." said Minnie.

"And Will, congratulations on being made a full member of the tribe."

"Thank you, Carmine." said Will. Does my full membership make Minnie a member as well?"

"Interesting question. But you should ask Minnie herself. She mostly made the tribal rules. Well I have to scamper before the dancing begins. I hope you'll stay for it." And Carmine continued to move through the crowds of diners.

Before they left the powwow grounds that evening as the dancers left the fireside, Will decided to call Armand. To his surprise, Armand answered.

"Yeah, who's this?" said Armand in an agitated voice.

"Armand, this is Will Eames. I heard about your sad news."

There was no answer from the other side of the line.

"Armand, I thought you said that at Wicomico you couldn't get a signal?"

"So if I said that, why did you bother to call? I'm in Exeter, getting some things. We're going to hold a wake tomorrow."

"I wanted to tell you how sad I am for you."

Again there was a long silence.

"Is there anything I can do to help you?" Will continued. "Maybe I can help you pay for the funeral?"

"Why would you want to help me? Don't you remember; I already know how to dig graves."

"I could buy you a gravestone for your son."

"My stepson."

"For your stepson. Or maybe there were some medical expenses he left behind."

"More likely debts to some drugs dealer here in Exeter."

"Would you care if I came to the wake? What was your stepson's name."

"Isaac. I'd rather that you didn't."

"So, you didn't say, if you'd like me to get a gravestone for Isaac's grave."

"So what would you put on it? 'Isaac Driggers, born a bastard, Suicide, November 1999. Aged 20."

"If that's what you'd like."

"Yeah, what would I like? His mother would really despise such a memorial."

"Well, let me know if you want a headstone. I'll have one carved for you."

"Maybe that's a good idea. Why don't you make a gravestone for me, Armand Driggers. Goodbye, Will Eames."

The line went dead. Minnie saw Will look into his handset with an annoyed expression on his face. She had not listened to the conversation with Armand, and did not know who Will was talking to. But she decided not to ask, as she assumed it was Armand after what Talleck had told them earlier.

"Will, let's go now. We can spend the night at the cottage. I'm chilled through. We can drive to D.C. in the morning. It won't matter if I get to work late."

"How about if I work tonight warming you up under the covers?" asked Will. "You can make love for the first time to an Indian." he said with a smile. Minnie chuckled.

"Oh, Will. You've changed so much." Minnie said sarcastically.

"But not my love for you, Miniaka. And my hair color is still not black."

They walked over to the shuttle bus which took them to distant parking lot. There were few people they recognized and no one recognized them in the dark.

They decided that Minnie would leave work early on Wednesday, right after lunch, so they could get to Bristol before dark. They went in one car: Will would drive the Oldsmobile. It appeared that much of the Washington work force had decided also to leave work early for the long holiday weekend and the traffic to the Eastern Shore was heavy, like normal rush hour traffic. Will had already bought some groceries for the cottage and he had asked his father to go over to the cottage and turn up the heating in the house so it would already be warm when they arrived. The day was frosty and the air was humid. They planned to stay through Friday at the cottage before going further to the farmhouse for the rest of the weekend. Minnie was excited this year because MarSue had invited her to come early on Thanksgiving day to help her prepare the feast. Minnie would get to learn how to properly prepare the huge feast with MarSue's guidance. All day Wednesday the excitement of preparing a Thanksgiving feast was mounting. It would be different from the previous year, when Minnie was just an observer during the last hour of finishing touches. That time she had to try and prise "kitchen time" from Kate who was experienced at fixing all that went into the turkey feast. But Minnie hadn't succeeded in prising Kate away from Mar Sue's kitchen. This year would be different. Mar Sue had already told her that Kate and her kids and her husband could not come until only an hour before Mar Sue planned to serve the meal. So Minnie this year would take Kate's place in the kitchen. But Minnie was also excited, if not a little nervous, because she thought that the time had come, that she was ready to announce that she would agree to marry Will. And she was thinking how she could announce her decision publicly at the dinner table. As she was helping with the dinner she was thinking how exactly to announce her decision. She wanted to make the announcement a surprise and a happy occasion, but she did not want to elaborate all the reasons that had held her back for more than a year.

At the table, after Bob had carved and served the turkey and Mar Sue had passed around the mashed sweet potatoes and vegetables Minnie began to especially take notice of Kate's daughters. The oldest, named Suzy, was a little more than two years old and was beginning to speak. She sat at the table on a booster chair between Minnie and her father, Ben, who was supervising her eating. She called Minnie "Anty" and she could not understand how Anty was related to Minnie Mouse. The other infant, Jenny, was about a year old and sat in a high chair next to Kate on the other side of the table. Minnie adored them both. They were so cute and communicative. She kept thinking about how badly she wanted children of her own. After serving everyone, Bob gave the prayer of thanksgiving in which he recited the achievements of the prior year for which the family gave thanks. He included thanks for the arrival of Jenny, for the bumper crop Will had had at Hampton Farm, and the success of Minnie in the courts getting recognition for the Nantiquak Indian tribe, and thanks for Kate's success as a mother of two daughters. The thanksgiving prayer was not a tradition that Minnie was familiar with, but it seemed to her to be comforting and genuine and part of what comprised the fibre of the Eames' family. She also noticed how Bob did not mention the 'Injun Project' in his prayer. So maybe, she thought, he was beginning to understand that it was not proper to use the old appellation of Injun in Minnie's presence. Minnie felt so securely a part of this family now after nearly a year and a half of loving Will, of sharing the community of family meals, of the peculiar character of Eastern Shore life that reflected in their behaviour.

As the chatter of the eating and talking swirled around the table, Minnie seemed to miss how it was the conversation swung over to her and Will. But she recognized it when Mar Sue said something like, " only too bad that you and Will don't get married." Minnie understood at once that this was just the cue she needed to be able to make the open declaration she had been thinking about for almost two weeks. Under the table, Minnie took Will's right hand in hers and squeezed it gently.

"But I also think it's too bad. And the time has come for me to accept Will's proposal of marriage."

Minnie had said this gently and her usual calm, quiet voice, so that the others at the table scarcely noticed the portent of her words and they were slow to realize what she had said and what it meant. Will immediately squeezed her hand, but the others fell into a momentary hush. And then the meaning became clear.

"Oh ho!" said Bob garrulously, "That's the best news of the year."

Mar-Sue still didn't quite grasp the meaning of Minnie's statement.

"What's that? You're agreeing to become officially my son's wife? My first daughter-in-law?"

"Yes." said Minnie. And Bob interrupted her, before she could say anything more.

"Now, this requires that we raise a glass to the future bride and groom." said Bob as he stood up and began pouring refreshers of wine in the glasses around the table.

Suzy was saying in confusion, "What's wrong?" or something that sounded like that. Mar Sue started repeatedly saying, "That's just so wonderful." And Bob continued.

"And here we wish all the happiness and love to the future bride and her future husband." as he raised his wine glass and then took a draft of the wine.

"And now the future bride can kiss the future husband." commanded Bob. Will promptly leaned over and gave a big full on the mouth kiss to Minnie, his right arm around her shoulders pulling her closer to him. Minnie felt a warm rush of emotions. She had now committed, and this was the man of her life kissing her affectionately. She wanted nothing so much at that moment.

"Have you set a date?" asked Mar Sue almost simultaneously as Kate was saying, "Now, finally I will get a sister. I'm so happy that you're going to join the family."

"So you and Will have finally agreed to get married?" continued Mar Sue.

"No," said Will. "This came as news to me. And this is one of the nicest surprises of my life."

"I think," said Minnie, "we just have to set a date and we can have a wedding here in Bristol."

Bob continued: "Yes in our church."

"Or maybe better," said Will, "in the church in Rosedale where great grandma Mena and great grandpa Will got married."

Minnie now started to chuckle slightly in happiness and some tears formed in her eyes. Will hugged her. No one was eating any longer. Mar Sue and Kate began talking about the preparations they would have to make. Bob and Kate's husband were talking about a possible date. Will was trying to kiss Minnie on the lips but missed and kissed her on the cheeks and ears. The enthusiasm and happiness was palpable around the table. Even little Suzy was trying to get Minnie's attention. "Anty happy? Why Anty crying?"

After the dinner dishes were cleared away, Mar Sue suggested that they put on one of the Argerich recordings she had.

"After all, Will fell in love with you Minnie here, over the likeness you bear to Martha Argerich, which he first saw here."

Neither Will nor Minnie corrected Mar Sue, but the music was still pretty and attractive, although the record was a little scratchy.

Over dessert, Will said, mostly aimed at Minnie, "I guess we need to take an unplanned trip to the mall in Salisbury tomorrow, so I can get you a proper ring."

Minnie just smiled. A proper ring probably meant a diamond ring, which Will had long wanted to buy for her.

Later that evening in the cottage as they began kissing and caressing each other, Minnie whispered:

"Will, I love you so much. From the very beginning, I wanted to say that I would marry you. You know now why I couldn't accept right away. You have been so patient with me."

"Minnie, I would wait for you to the end of my time. Just so long as you always stayed with me, and always admitted the possibility that we could be married."

As they began to make love in bed, Minnie thought momentarily about her efforts to conceive a child with Will. This was not an appropriate night for conception—by the calendar-- but she thought it was one of the nicest nights of passion she could remember with Will. They coupled four times by the time they got out of bed the next morning, each time she reached a delightful climax. She even agreed to shower with Will that morning and quickly felt aroused as he applied soap to her breasts and belly. She wanted him again.

Over breakfast Minnie confessed to him for the first time how she had recently stopped taking the pill and how she was trying to conceive, at the suggestion of her doctor.

"Nothing yet." said Minnie. "But my doctor said, if we don't succeed by May, I should get some tests done."

"I don't think there'll be any problems. Not because of your age anyway."

"But maybe by then they will need to test you too, old man, because of some misfunction due to your age."

"Let's face it, Minnie. You're not too old. You're just too attractive to be too old. And I for one would like a child by you, too. The sooner the better—so long as it is a boy."

Minnie threw a toss pillow at him. "No it will have to be a girl, with curly hair."

"Well, I guess we'll just have to have more sex. Especially when you're ovulating. Then I will make sure to be in rut."

"What's that?"

"Kind of the equivalent to the female ovulation but in males, when a lot of testosterone is released. You know, it's that hormone that makes me seem like Superman. Haven't you noticed?"

Minnie giggled. After they got dressed, they left the house for Salisbury mall. At the jeweler's it was clear that Will had a diamond ring in mind. He wanted white gold, and he kept picking out large carat stones.

"Oh no that's too expensive." Minnie protested at one ring, that cost more than four thousand dollars, for two and half carats. "That's way too showy."

"But that's the point of a diamond wedding ring." said Will showing false offense. "Showiness is everything."

"Don't you want to get another emerald?"

"Sure. It can be our color."

The sales assistant, a white haired man, jumped into their discussion. "You know, Miss, excuse me for overhearing, but a lot of our customers ask the same. And a real emerald can be a whole lot more expensive than a diamond. So much so that we don't carry emerald wedding rings, I mean made from real emeralds. We carry mainly manufactured or synthetic emeralds. That's why you see their prices are so low compared to diamonds. But we can order a real emerald for you if you prefer."

"Well, then. What is the precious gemstone for my birth month?"

"I don't know. What month were you born in?"

"September." said Minnie.

"By tradition that would be a sapphire, then."

Will didn't like any of the sapphires on sale. And they were all synthetic. He kept going back to an oval-shaped two carat diamond which flashed with fire against the white gold.

"Try this on."

"But Will. It costs more than three thousand six hundred dollars."

"He'll have to give me a discount. And besides as the De Beers company also advertises, 'a diamond is forever.' So it's a bargain."

Minnie tried it on her left ring finger. It fit nicely and snuggly. "Try the right ring finger too. You can wear it there after you get your wedding band."

"So good. It's settled then." Will addressed the sales assistant. "I'll buy it for three thousand and twenty dollars."

"My word, that's a steep discount." said the sales assistant.

"Not at all. It's you, who have a steep sales mark-up."

"Miss, you know you're marrying a very canny man."

"No. A very generous man." said Minnie.

"And we want to try on matching wedding bands, with yellow gold." said Will. You don't need to wrap the diamond ring. She'll wear it out." Will got his discount, plus another three percent on the gold wedding bands. "These are for the wedding day itself." Minnie kissed him on the cheek. "This is so nice. You're always giving me the most precious things." she said.

On the way back to Hampton Farm, they began to discuss a wedding date. Minnie said she had only begun to think about an actual wedding date a few days ago, after she had finally resolved to accept Will's marriage proposal.

"I thought that Loving Day would be ideal for our wedding." said Minnie. "But that's not until June. That's too long from now."

"I agree. But what is Loving Day?"

"It is the day that the Lovings won their court case in the Supreme Court which affirmed their right to be legally married, even though she was black and he was white. Virginia had convicted them of the breaking the miscegenation and anti-mixed race marriage laws in Virginia. The husband was named Loving—appropriate don't you think? Ours will be a mixed race marriage, also."

"So did the Lovings live in Virginia after the Supreme Court ruled in their favour and struck down the Virginia laws?"

"Yes they did. And Loving Day has become a rather informal holiday for mixed race couples ever since."

"I don't think that Maryland has any laws now against mixed marriage, although it did when great-grandmother Mena got married. But I agree that we can't wait until June. So we can have a wedding at the New Year's."

"No, I think that's too soon. I don't want a big wedding blow out. But still there are lots of preparations to make."

"Then how about Valentine's Day in February?"

"Willeems, you certainly are a sentimentalist." said Minnie. "We'll have to check the date when we get to the farm. But I think the wedding day needs to be on a Saturday, so we can get all our guests out to this remote area. Maybe February is still too early. Mid-winter."

"Well then, maybe the first weekend in March." Will answered. Minnie said that would suit her, she was thinking that there were lots of preparations and that the weather should be a little warmer.

Just as she said this they were driving through Rosedale. In just a moment they would drive past the small Methodist Church in the village, where they had agreed they would like the wedding to take place.

"Ah yes, there it is." said Will. "Quiet and abandoned, and locked up as usual."

Minnie looked at the church, a small white building with red doors, neatly painted, built on a small rise above the level of the road and the surrounding farm land. It looked much nicer than the small Baptist church she had attended as a girl with her family. But it was the same thing—a small, historic country church, standing mostly unused through the week, with a graveyard behind it and surrounded by grass and mature oak trees all around.

"On this coming Sunday," continued Will, "we can come back here and ask the pastor—I forget his name just now-- to reserve a date for us in early March."

"We can check the date for the first Saturday in March." said Minnie. "When we get to the farm, I have to call and tell momma about my decision. And of course, invite her. And Alicia and her family, and even Tanner. But maybe he wouldn't want to come."

"Why not?"

"He's so hostile to mixed marriages, and to you, especially."

"I didn't see that when I met him while we were building your mom's house."

So they agreed; they would set the date for the first Saturday in March. They both eagerly wanted to check calendars as soon as they got to the farm. And then they would start making arrangements, and invitations. The date turned out to be the 4th of March. They could not find any special significance of that date. "The significance of the date will be that it'll be the date of our wedding." said Minnie. "Simple enough. We'll always mark it."

"Yeah, more important than Jack and Marianne's anniversary of first sex." said Will with a big smile on his face. "But come to think of it, that would be about the time for our second anniversary for our first love."

As they entered the farmhouse, they noticed it was quite chilly inside. Will checked the radiators and they were cold. He then went down into the basement to check the furnace. And he came back up the stairs with a scowl on his face. Minnie kept her coat on and was keen to know what had happened.

"The furnace turned itself off. Seems that the fuel tank is empty. I better see if I can get an emergency fuel delivery out here."

"Do we have any electric heaters here?"

"Yeah, one or two. I'll have to look for them."

First he looked in the kitchen for the telephone number of the local heating and cooling technician who maintained the house. He called the number and got a recorded answer, but it left him with another number to call for out-of-hours emergencies. "It is an emergency, but it's still working hours." It was not quite three o'clock in the afternoon. Will called the emergency number and got a live answer. He explained the problem; that he needed a partial delivery of heating fuel, and a check to understand what happened. Will, still in his coat, also began foraging around the house to find the space heaters. "They forecast a strong frost tonight, so we have to get the heat going. It's already thirty-three degrees right now outside."

"And we'll need some extra blankets." said Minnie. "If we decide to stay the night here."

"Maybe. The thermometer in the main room shows it is only thirty eight degrees. It'll take a long time to heat the place."

Will found one heater and set it up in the main room. When he first turned it on, the suction on the electricity was so great that it momentarily dimmed the lights. Minnie went upstairs to look for the extra blankets, but there were none, nor any extra sweaters or other warm clothing in the house.

"Fine, after the heating man gets the furnace going again, we'll go back to Salisbury mall, and buy some sweaters, sweat pants, wool caps and socks, and some more blankets. It's Black Friday after all, we'll get the biggest discounts of the year and the stores will be open late tonight."

"That's rather grim. Why call Friday after Thanksgiving, Black Friday? It's as if someone died."

"Oh nothing like that, it's just the first day of the entire calendar year that retails begin to run in the black, instead of operating in the red."

"Oh. I never knew."

At five, just as it was beginning to get dark outside, a red and white tank truck with the words McGuinn's Heating and Cooling Service painted on the side drove up their gravel lane and stopped at the front door. A young man in a brown uniform jumped out and came bounding up the stairs and knocked at the main door. Will opened it to him. He had not seen this young man before. The man said that he had come there a couple times before and he had been the one who had performed the last maintenance check-up in the spring. He went first to the thermostat and checked it. He muttered, "That's not right." And without explaining he went down into the basement to check the equipment. Will joined him. The technician checked the fuel tank. "There's some fuel left in the tank. It's not low enough for the automatic switch off to kick in. But we'll give you some fuel now." He checked the furnace and the boiler. "I'll try to light it." After a few minutes tinkering here and there and then turning on the controls and a few clicks of the lighter, the furnace roared to life and began burning high.

"Well then. It seems to me that you had an electrical outage. The thermostat was blinking. That's a sure sign. And then the automatic switch kicked in and turned off the furnace. It'll heat the house now in a couple hours. Now I'll put the diesel in the tank. And you're all set."

The heating emergency cost Will almost $250; $50 alone for the small amount of diesel heating oil which would insure that he could keep the place warm until a full tank load could be delivered in the next week. Will had to pay the man with a check. And then he drove off with a spray of gravel strewing from his rear tires.

"Has this kind of heating emergency happened before here?" Minnie asked. "I mean a power outage."

"I don't know, Minnie. I'll have to ask Phyllis if it has happened before in recent years. But for sure we can't stay here for the next several hours. So we might as well go to the mall now." All further discussion about the wedding, a wedding date, or invitations was put off to the next day.

At the mall, Will's cell phone rang. It was Armand. He gave the slightest of greetings and asked straight up, if Will would pay for a headstone for his stepson's grave.

"I said I would. You remember Hately? The Nantiquak from near Shapp's Landing who did the headstone for Hampton's grave? Would it be alright with you to have him do the stone?"

"Yes."

"Then I will hire him. Do you already know what you'd like on the stone?"

"No."

"Well, his full name? Birth date and death date? Anything else?"

"His full name was Olle Talleck. Spelled o-l-l-e, I'll have to find out what his exact birth date was. August 1979. I know that. And he died on 19 November."

"And what kind of stone would you like? Black, dark grey, light grey? And when do you need it?"

"You talk so much, Will. There's no hurry. He's already maundering in the grave."

"Maundering? What's that mean?"

"Rotting. I heard it in a church hymn. Grey, the stone should be grey."

"Okay, I'll take care of it. Anything else I can take care of for you?"

"Yeah. Why do you want to help me with the costs?"

"We're family, you know. And you're in need. And it's a decent thing to do when you're in distress, no?"

"Yeah. So you keep telling me. Okay. I buried him in the little church near here on Indiantown Road."

"Okay, I'll take care of it."

Armand hung up the line with no further acknowledgement.

"Who was that?" asked Minnie.

"Armand Driggers. Remember the same who insulted you and who digs graves?"

"How can I forget? I don't like that man."

"I don't much like him either. How can I explain it?" said Will. "We're both Driggers. You don't much like your brother Tanner, but you will invite him to our wedding, no?"

They spent a few hours at the mall, the second time that day buying things on discount. Will enjoyed buying clothes for Minnie and in the end she got three new sweaters, a heavy one in dark green, a sky blue cashmere sweater that she could wear to work, and a thick sweater suited for outdoors, as well as winter wear, including a knit cap, and heavy socks. Minnie was still amazed at how Will could, without consulting her, manage to pick out just what she liked most. She thought again how much he did to try and please her. She rolled the new diamond ring on her finger, thinking that she was finally ready to marry him and be his wife. In addition to the sweaters and warm clothes, Will bought spare double blankets for each of their three homes: two for the farm, and one for Bristol and one for Cleveland Park. And he bought two more electric space heaters for the farmhouse. On their way back to the farmhouse, he told her that on the next day they would go looking for Mannuel Hately near Shapp's Landing.

That evening at the farmhouse the house had warmed up, so Will turned off the spot heater in the main room when they came in. After a light supper of baked beans and hot dogs, they sat around the kitchen table and Minnie started writing out the names of people she would like to invite. She wanted to invite all her family, including her brother, but she worried that none of them might come just because of the distance and difficulty of making traveling arrangements for all of them. She definitely wanted her mother to come. That might be a hard sell. And she also badly wanted her nephew and niece to attend along with Alicia and her husband. Other than family, she didn't know who else she'd want to invite. But after then listing Will's family, she had a flash of inspiration.

"I know who I would like to invite: Carmine Norwood."

"Fine, I think she might attend." said Will. Minnie noticed that he did not display any pleasure in that idea, so she concluded that indeed he was not at all attracted to Carmine, as she so often had felt.

"We can make it easier on your family," said Will. "if they spend the night, after the wedding party, here at the farmhouse before driving back home. We can spend the night at the cottage in Bristol. For the night before we leave on our honeymoon. I will be somewhat drunk anyway."

"Honeymoon? You haven't said anything about a honeymoon. But that's not a bad idea. That would make it easier on them. I think they might accept."

"And add to my list, I would like to invite Jack and Marianne, and Tony, and Lucy and Marilyn from my office. Jack might be in Annapolis at that time, but they might still come. It's a weekend after all. You don't want to invite any of your colleagues from your office?"

"No, I can't say that I do." said Minnie, but just as she said it, she thought momentarily about whether she would like Alia to come. But she also thought it would be entirely too unfamiliar and foreign for Alia, who was a Somali immigrant. So she let the thought pass.

Then suddenly, Minnie almost jumped up from the table. "Oh my gosh! I forgot to tell momma. Will, I have to call her now to tell her that I accepted your marriage proposal. I have to do it now."

She called her mother on her cell phone. She was standing in front of Will who was paying close attention to what was said. "Hi mom, this is Minnie. I have some news for you."

"I wanted to let you know that I have overcome all my objections and I accepted to marry Will, Will Eames. We're going to have a wedding in early March. The first weekend in March."

"No, I'm very happy."

"But you know, the Nantiquaks made him a full member of their tribe. Not just an honorary member. So he's an Indian, not only a white man."

"No, mamma, you should be happy. We'll make a family."

"He's not a mere farmer. He's actually very rich and he will do everything for me. Especially he will make me happy. And he wants children too."

"No mamma. We haven't discussed it yet, but I imagine we'll continue to live in D.C. I really like my job there. I just got a big bonus for this year's successes. We'll carry on as we have this past year. Probably, we'll continue to live in D.C. and come out here, I mean to the farm on the Eastern Shore."

"If you agree to come, we'll make sure you get transport here and back, and we'll put you up for Saturday night after a wedding party."

"You don't have to if you don't want to."

"Yes, we will be inviting them too. Everyone."

"Tanner of course can do as he likes. If he doesn't want to come, he won't. Too bad for him and for us." Minnie looked over at Will an expression of anxiety carved into her face.

"He does a lot of things. But above all he's involved in real estate. So don't worry about income, I'm still working too, remember."

"Momma I would be happiest if you agree to come."

"No, he's a better man than papa was. Sad to say."

"No, he's not an alcoholic. Where'd you get that idea?"

"We'll send you an invitation with the exact date and times in the mail. And as I said, we'll take care of your transport. I think you could come with Alicia and her family, if her man decides to come with them. The kids are getting bigger but I think there'd still be room for you in their car."

"Very happy. He's the most important person in my life. Yes. No. I'm serious. I really want you to come."

"If you like, maybe we can come over to your place at Christmas. Would that please you?"

"Don't worry about a place to stay. We'll find a hotel."

"Okay, I love you too, mamma. Bye."

Minnie looked at Will. "I think she's warming a little to you. And she's trying to pretend that she won't come. You know, my pa and mama didn't have a church wedding or wedding party. And neither did Alicia and her man. Frankly she just doesn't know what she would do at a wedding or worse still at a wedding party."

"Isn't it enough for her," asked Will. "just to be a witness to your happiness?"

"Should be, I guess. But she doesn't think that way."

Later as they were changing their clothes to get into bed, Minnie returned to the idea of a honeymoon.

"So Will, have you already decided on where to go for a honeymoon?"

In the bed, he turned to her and slipped his hand under her nightgown and began to gently stroke her belly and breasts.

"I have begun to think. You know, it seems to me honeymoons have become mostly a week or two for young newlyweds to go someplace to make love repeatedly to each other lots of times, day and night, and to spend the other times when not having sex, lying on the sand of a sunny hot beach in some tropical paradise, recovering from all the sex. But I don't think we need even more sex—I mean not after I get finished with you right now—and you don't particularly like the beach or sunbathing. And you wouldn't like a cruise for sure—thousands of people crushed onto a huge ship which would still feel the sway of the seas. In short, I am not sure where we might go for a honeymoon. A place where we could still make passionate love every night, that is warm and sunny, but not too hot, and where we could explore. Maybe Florida. Maybe a place where we can learn to play golf?"

"What? Golf?" exclaimed Minnie in surprise.

"Yeah, right now. I could use some practice with my putter." His wandering hand went to her vagina and began to caress her clitoris, while at the same time he leaned over her and began kissing her with deep French kisses. She was already thoroughly aroused and ready to return his passion. She so loved this man.

The next morning the house was very warm. After a small breakfast, which Minnie fixed while wearing her new warm robe, they dressed and drove out to Puckamee settlement across the Nanticoke. Will thought he remembered Hately's trailer house, but he did not as he knocked on the wrong doors a few times before he found the taciturn man. Hately acted surprised to see Will again, but he did not invite him beyond the threshold of his house. He was even more surprised to see such a beautiful Indian woman with Will, and he kept his eyes fixed on Minnie for some time, as Will was trying to tell him about an assignment. Finally Will stopped himself and said, "What's the matter, Mannuel? Haven't seen a pretty woman in a while? This is my fiancée, Minnie Warrens. She's also the chairwoman of your tribal corporation." Minnie noticed this change in Will's introduction. It was the first time, he had publicly spoken of her as his fiancée. And she liked it. Again she secretly touched her diamond ring and rolled it a little on her finger.

Hately turned his attention to Will. Still he had not said anything. Will repeated what he wanted from him. Finally Hately said softly: "When do you want it? I'm a little busy just now."

"How long will it take you to carve such a stone?"

"Three, maybe four days. But I can only start in about a week. So with my other work I can have it for you in three weeks."

"How much will it cost?"

"Oh, I think between two and three hundred dollars. You say it is for one of our tribesmen? I'll give you a discount.

"Fine. So do it." said Will and he offered Mannuel his hand to shake on the deal. He suddenly had a thought that stone carving could be one of the Indian-owned businesses which having a reservation would protect from taxes and competition. He would propose it to Talleck.

Later that day Will called Reverend Francis and asked about setting a wedding date for the first Saturday in March. The Reverend asked them to come to the church at about one o'clock just after his service the next day and they would record a reservation in the books, as he wasn't at that time in the church office. They agreed, and on Sunday they dressed up smartly and went to the church at noon and sang the hymns together, listening to the sermon, and went through the ritual of the Methodist service. Minnie really liked the interior of the church. It was not grand; its walls were painted in white and there were rows of yellow wooden pews for perhaps as many as eighty worshipers. The windows were tall with many panes and they let it lots of sunlight. The only word that came to Minnie's mind was that the place was 'charming' in its simplicity. After the service, Reverend Francis stood at the front door and shook hands and said a few words to each congregant as they left. He remembered Will from their earlier meeting a year before and as he shook Will's hand, he said: "And is this the lovely bride to be for this coming wedding?" "Yes, my fiancée, Minnie Warrens of Washington, D.C." "And can I surmise, she is a Nantiquak Indian woman?" "No, but she is an Indian, from Virginia." "Well I'm so glad to meet you, Ms. Warrens. And happy to learn that you will be marrying Will Eames at this humble church. The Eames family have long been associated with this church and this county. We're so happy to welcome both of you back to this church, and especially Ms. Warrens to welcome you into the Eames family." Reverend Francis invited them to wait for him until all the congregants had departed. Then he invited them to the back of the church where a side door led them to a small office. He took up a ledger book and looked through its mostly empty pages.

"So, you said Saturday, the 4th of March? It looks free." said Reverend Francis. "Shall I put you down for a wedding at noon on that day?" They agreed and Reverend Francis wrote into the book 'wedding for Eames and Warrens' in a florid blue ink from a thick fountain pen he drew from his chest pocket. "Then it's done. The church will be open from eleven if you need to make any decorations of set out flowers. Will you want music?"

Minnie had not thought about music. Nor had Will. In fact, she had not thought much about how she wanted the wedding to look. Or what she would wear, or whether there would be music or flowers, or any other decorations. She had never attended anyone's wedding before and she did not have any ideas about how a wedding proceeded. She had not preconceived imagines of how a church wedding should look or proceed.

"I think we will want music." said Will. "But I don't know what it would be."

"Well, that is alright. I can put you in touch with the organist and you can at a later date decide with her what you might like played. And will you want me to deliver a homily too?" Will answered that he did.

They left Reverend Francis and drove back to the farmhouse. Minnie was feeling for the first time that their marriage was becoming more concrete, that it was really going to happen and she felt elated. Out the car window she saw the flat fallow fields with the pipes and cables of the irrigation systems standing unused, the black skeletal tracery of the trees which lined the fields, and the desolate winter look of the landscape. This was the land that was going to be her new home, 'welcome to the county' he had said. It looked a lot different from the poor empty forests and small rivers around the place of her own childhood home.

Back at her office in NAILS later that week, the news of their court triumph finally hit the *Washington Post* on the front page of the National News section which usually covered gossip about congressmen or movements in obscure court cases or other local stories from outside the Beltway. And from there it was picked up by a large number of regional newspapers and disseminated widely. Cal Reiner saw this and again crowed about their triumph and what it meant for their business. He called Minnie and told her about the news item over the office telephone line. "Again, it really is thanks to you that we got that business with the Nantiquaks and that we won that precedent-setting case, Ms. Warrens. I think we'll get a generous payment this year, including bonuses. You will get a nice bonus, Minnie, I think I can say, which will more than compensate for the low salary."

"But Cal, the main idea was Tureen's, you know." answered Minnie.

"Oh you don't need to be diffident and certainly not falsely humble in this case. You'll only get ahead in life if you trumpet your achievements." said Cal who hung up abruptly.

As if on schedule, a week later a letter landed on Minnie's desk—addressed to her and showing that it was from the Wamponetcong Tribal Association. This was not a familiar name to her so she curiously opened the letter and began to read it. The letter was from a man claiming to represent the Wamponetcong Lenapi tribe of New Jersey and Pennsylvani in their efforts to gain Federal recognition. He wrote that he was himself an Indian from a Western tribe and he held a role as a consultant and advisor to the tribe, guiding on their way to achieve those ends. He had read the news of the NAILS court triumph in a Philadelphia newspaper story which had mentioned her name. And he was writing to her to see if NAILS might provide them with legal and litigation services, particularly given that they were a tribe with no money or income and that NAILS was a public service legal aid firm. Minnie made a photocopy of the letter and then took it to Cal who quickly read it and then bashed in down on his desk.

"So you see, Minnie, you're already bringing in new business. Just as I told you. This is great. Set up a meeting with this man, 'Mr. Johnstone Redcloud', before Christmas break in our offices." said Cal in his usual rapid fire style of speaking. "Good work, once again. Oh and tell Ron and Gail about all this, okay?"

And as Minnie stood up to leave, Cal continued without actually looking at her, "Oh and is that a new diamond ring on your finger, I spy? Getting married? Got married, recently?"

"Eh, yes." said Minnie.

"Well, congratulations."

Minnie made another copy of the letter and dropped it on Ron's desk—Ron was out of office just then. Then she called Alia and asked if she could go with her to lunch. "Maybe yes, at one thirty, if that's okay." At lunch Alia also asked about any change of Minnie's status as she had started wearing a pretty diamond ring on the left ring finger, which as she understood in America, was reserved as the symbolic location for a wedding ring. Minnie confessed to Alia that she was engaged to marry, but she did not reveal that her engagement was to Will Eames.

After lunch, Minnie called the telephone number for Mr. Redcloud and spoke briefly to him about his needs and what he wanted for the tribe he was representing. He told her a little about the Wamponetcong-Lenapi tribe, that they had more than five hundred members, no reservations, or treaties, but that they still existed and needed help to re-establish their former status as a recognized tribe. They then haggled over a date when he might be able to come to their offices in Washington until finally they agreed that he could come with the chief of the tribe on Thursday, the 16th of December in the mid-morning. She told Cal and he said simply, "Good, it's on my calendar. And tell Gail to attend also." "And not Ron?" she asked. "No, not for this meeting."

The meeting came and went. Mr. Redcloud was a promoter who had advised other small tribes on the West Coast on getting Federal recognition. How he had found the remnants of the Wamponetcong was never made clear, but it was clear that he was involved with them for the money he could make. Minnie would have to check a little on his background. The tribe needed legal advice and services, so

Cal agreed to represent them starting in the new millennium. But he needed some sort of legally binding engagement letter from some legally established entity. The tribe apparently did not have any such formal entity. So Mr. Redcloud and the Chief agreed to get back to them with an engagement letter. The title that had been on the letter he had sent her was just a fiction that Mr. Redcloud had made up. "We don't have to worry too much about these characters." said Cal after they had left the office. "If they show up again, we'll see what we can do for them."

And then the next week, just a few days before Christmas, Cal called Minnie into his office. Cal was sitting with the chief accountant. "Minnie, we got paid a big package for this year's work. And you are most deserving of this bonus. Merry Christmas."

The chief accountant handed Minnie a check for one hundred and forty-four thousand dollars. It was twice her yearly pay! This bonus alone was more than she had ever earned in a year in the previous ten years.

"I know it's not what you might earn in a high-class law firm," continued Cal, "but Minnie, you deserve this very much as compensation for the great work you've done these past almost two years. And, I think, that you can take off the rest of the year, find somehow to spend it, or at least don't come back here until the third of January. Nothing going on here, so enjoy your holiday someplace else."

"Oh thank you Cal. I'm speechless. Thank you so ever much." Minnie gave Cal a discreet kiss on the cheek and rushed to her office. She called Will over her cell phone. And she told him about the bonus.

"You know, Cal was right. It's only what you deserved, Minnie. For a job well done. For being successful, while still being lovely as a lily, and a top professional too. We'll have to drink to this tonight after I get home from here."

Will was sitting in an office with John Talleck in the Nantiquak Corporation offices in Laurelton at the time when he got Minnie's call. They were discussing details about the Nantiquak casino, and how it should look, and the basics they needed to complete in order to get the project off the ground. Everything was a challenge. They had argued over the past ten days about where it should be situated. They could only build it on reservation land of the tribe. That ruled out any place in the territory of Indian River Bands because they had not gotten any reservation grant from the state of Delaware. And the other reservation grants in Delaware were not suitable. Neither the Aksesky reservation, which was not large enough, nor the Brant Creek reservation which was not inhabited by Nantiquak Indians yet, and which was inconveniently located relative to Highway 50, the main artery of the Ocean City weekender traffic. That left the reservation lands in Maryland, Kuskowaroak reservation, or the Puckamee reservation, or the small parcel which was given to the Aksesky Band on the Mason-Dixon line, the state boundary between the south of Delaware and Maryland. The latter was probably too small and too swampy, and couldn't support the one to two hundred acres, both men agreed were the very minimum area needed for the casino and its buildings. That left only the possibility of building on the Kuskowaroak or Puckamee reservations, which were the largest. Will wanted to build on the land granted in Dorset County, near the parcel that he had bought two years earlier, as in his original conception of the Injun Project. But Talleck was adamantly against.

"We can't build a large compound with a hotel and parking garage and extensive outside parking in that area," said Talleck, "because the ground is too swampy or too soft. And if we move it to the other side of Indiantown Road we will be taking away good farmland from our farming project, based on the Taylor farm. And anywhere near Indiantown Road gets into the archeological sites of the former Chicocoan Indian town. We need to dig these areas up to uncover our history."

"And besides," he continued, "I've polled the members of the Kuskowaroak Band who live there, and they are all, uniformly against a casino in their backyard. They feel it would be trampling on their ancestors' bones. And I think I have to agree with them. They are convinced that a casino right next to their homes and ancestral center will only bring traffic, crime, and filth right onto their doorsteps."

These were some of the arguments that had been raised when they discussed the casino project at the board meeting on that Saturday almost two weeks earlier. At that discussion, it was Talleck who was arguing forcefully for the casino against Morley's opposition. Morley had especially argued that the casino could only bring crime, prostitution, and debt into their community. And that it would also open the floodgates for alcoholism among the tribe's younger people. In that discussion, Talleck was the fervent supporter and he dismissed Morley's concerns about crime and alcoholism, saying that that could be controlled. They would not be recreating another Las Vegas with cabaret shows, and prostitutes run by criminals. They would not repeat the glitz and glamor that the Pequoddy Indians had built up in Connecticut. They would be more sober, more like what Will had told him about how the Cherokees had developed their casino, although not the same size. Morley and three other board members from the Indian River Bands remained opposed and had voted against developing a casino, not least because of the huge debt they would have to incur to build it. But the proposal carried as eight other board members supported the idea. Minnie didn't have to cast the tie-breaking vote, as the chairwoman, and had been very relieved that that was the outcome. Despite his defeat over the casino issue, later in that same meeting, Morley—still an opponent of the casino-- was elected to succeed Minnie in the new year as chairman of the Corporation, beating Talleck in the final tally of votes, seven to three.

"So that really only leaves the Puckamee reservation on the Nanticoke River as the place for a casino." said Will. It saddened him to have to concede: the casino project, the very justification of his original Injun Project, would not be in Dorset County, but in Wicomico County. "Do you have any suggestions, as to where?"

"Yes actually, there is more than enough land inside the reservation boundaries near the small town of Marble Springs. There's an irony in that place, as it was a village built around those springs that tried in the nineteenth century to develop itself into a tourist destination—for the baths—based also on through traffic of travellers. It made a name for itself until the rail line was built farther east to Salisbury and diverted all the travellers away. Anyway, there is a large cleared plot on the banks of the Sulphur Springs Creek. It would make a scenic place for a casino. And it is not even three miles off Highway 50. On the other side of the highway from Puckamee, I might add, which makes the people in our settlement there more comfortable."

"And there is enough cleared, firm land there, to build a casino and hotel on it?"

"Yes, this place is on land that the state bought from small farmers, most of it was untended and fallow. And it has woods surrounding it, like a curtain. So it won't be visible from the Highway."

"Well, that sounds quite appropriate then. Maybe we should have surveyors go out there and lay out a plot. And maybe we could go out there and visit the terrain after we're finished here."

"That'd be fine with me. It's just around the corner from Exeter where I'm living now."

"In my proposal I envisioned a casino with slots and board card games like blackjack, a roulette wheel, baccarat. And maybe poker tables in separate rooms."

"I know your concept is that the gambling will mostly be for the tourists and day trippers or weekenders heading for Ocean City, but I think we have to strictly keep our tribesmen out of the poker rooms."

"That's reasonable." said Will. "I think we'll make it that the house will not be able to advance any money to Nantiquaks who want to gamble. We have to recognize that none of us want heavily indebted Indians living on our reservations. Right? I mean, they are poor enough to start with."

"I agree. And we'll have to find a way to control the consumption of alcohol by our tribesmen and women, too.

"Only open drinks sales with limits. So let's agree on the size of this casino so we can go to the developers with a desired, unified vision. I suggested a hotel with no more than eighty rooms, and six suites. I've looked at how much such hotels cost to build—the costs for a similar Hampton Inn with the same number of rooms are available on-line. Looks like we can build something similar—with the suites--for about eight to ten million dollars. Furnishing and interior finish might cost another four to five million—we don't have to make this a first class resort destination."

"The hotel should have an indoor swimming pool and spa, and not a tiny pool but a good-sized pool. And come to think of it, there should be an outdoors swimming pool, very large. And there should be room for a couple restaurants and breakfast rooms. Thad'll add to your estimates."

"Yes. And then the gambling hall, I'm thinking of a one story hall of about forty-six thousand square feet that would connect to the hotel. If we give it an extra high ceiling, say about fifteen feet, maybe eighteen feet, that will add to the building cost. The engineering and construction costs that I could find for such a building were really oriented to building a warehouse, not a building with building blocks and glass walls. But I think that it could cost in the range of two to two and half million dollars."

"Are you sure you're not under-estimating both the needed area and the costs?"

"Maybe. But I looked at the Harrah's Cherokee Resort casino and there's no doubt that what I envision is much smaller. They built theirs with the demand outlook that serves people both who come there as an end destination, and the three million people that pass-by on their way to the National Park next door. I'm assuming that we are primarily aiming at the passers-by traffic. And these number about three million people a year in recent years. Not many chose to stay here or buy vacation homes here in the Eastern Shore. It just isn't a real attraction, too swampy and farm-tilled to be scenic. Maybe on the ocean side, the bays and offshore islands, people go there and invest as tourist destinations but not here, on the bayside. Do you agree?

"I don't have much insight into the demand side." said Talleck. "Or how much capacity you need to build to handle a given number of gamers per day."

"Fine. I think we pretty much agree on the scale." said Will. "It looks to me like we are looking at a project that will cost twelve to twenty million dollars to put together and build. The size and location. And I've have already collected the data on the through traffic here. So let's put this together and we can fire off some invitations to submit proposals to potential developers and financiers."

"Right."

"We should definitely invite the Harrah's corporation. They did the Cherokee casino, and it's quite impressive. And we need to find out more about the Mohegan Indian tribe of Connecticut. They opened their casino on new reservation land in only two years after they got recognition. That was not even four years ago. So I think they can help us with some insights on costs and timing, and the tricks that developers throw in."

'You know, I think," said Talleck very presciently, "that any developer we find who is interested in building a casino will inevitably design a much bigger facility. Especially if we are the ones that will have to carry the debt. I think most will want to develop our little casino into a big resort."

"We'll see. I wonder if gambling demand goes down, when the general economy falls into recession. The past several years has seen only continuous boom. You know the Hyatt near us in Bristol. They way over-built their resort, and I think they wanted to include a casino in it. But demand has not met their expectations.

"Are you expecting a recession? We've been in really poor economic condition here on the Eastern Shore for some years already."

"No, just the end of the boom. Or if you will a stock market bubble. All that cash sloshing around that might go onto gaming tables will evaporate."

"Okay, so next we need to survey the developers of Indian casinos and find one that might help us to build something suitable to our situation."

"You're right, John."

"Everyone wants to cash in on the Indian casino. Quick money, quick returns. And developers and investors will take their share first leaving the poor Indian fleeced once more."

"I'm afraid you're right again."

"I learned this from hard experience working for the white man."

Will made ready to leave when Talleck asked him a question: "It was you who ordered and paid for my son's gravestone, wasn't it?"

"Yes. It was I. So he was your son?"

"Yes. When he was born I was away from the settlement a lot, working for money. Army Corps of Engineers. And my wife apparently got lonely and became attracted to Driggers. When I got back they were already a pair, and she was pregnant. So I abandoned them, and Armand raised my son as his. Olle was not yet five when I left. But as you may have seen Armand has a serious attitude problem. And it rubbed off on my son. He couldn't cope with the world outside Wicomico, not without drugs."

"I'm sorry."

"Yeah, so am I. I thought I could save him, but I came back too late. Anyway, I want to thank you for taking care of that."

"No need to thank me. I think Armand is sad too. Maybe he just won't admit it, because it is another of his failures in life."

"Yeah."

Just at that moment Carmine poked her head into the door of the little office. "I just got a call from Indian River. My uncle Morley has just died. Heart attack or something. I'm going over there. Can you lock up the offices when you leave?"

"Yeah sure, this is awful news, Carmine."

"And unexpected. I've got to dash."

Will drove back to Bristol and before the end of the work day he completed a search of the literature, primarily his subscription to Real Estate Finance, about the recent building of Indian casinos. He was looking for commentary on how the projects got off the ground and perhaps even more important how they got funded. He finally found a recent article about the finances of the Mohegan Sun casino and was surprised to learn that the chief financial backer was a hotel developer from South Africa. And the Pequoddy casino had been financed by a real estate developer from Macau. He was amazed. But he recognized also that these developers had pushed the tribes into massive resort centers, at astronomical costs, literally hundreds of millions of dollars. Such investors might have the funding, but would not be very much interested in a small scale casino. This particular article also had an extensive interview with the Mohegan Indian who was most instrumental in working on the project from the start to opening. Will took his name down and said to himself that he would start looking for how he could get in touch with him. The man was Jim White Elk Johnson of Connecticut. He didn't seem to have a finance or business background, at least from the way he answered the interviewer.

Back at home, over dinner he told Minnie the news about Morley's unexpected death following a heart attack.

"That's awful." Minnie said as she looked up at him with alarm. "How old was he?"

"I think forty-five, fifty. But I don't know for sure."

"And his family? Does he have kids?"

"I heard that he had two kids, who are adults now. But I never met his family, or his wife."

"And what did he do for a living?"

"He was a farmer. Grew garden vegetables for markets in Delaware. That is when he wasn't working on tribal affairs and activities. His baby was the Association and the yearly powwow."

"And he was just voted the new chairman. Such a shame. Like my papa. He died prematurely from a heart attack that no one saw coming."

the conflict between the rights of tribal sovereignty and the rights of states to impose their laws on all citizens living in the state. And it means a serious negotiation will be required by you. It's best to have that negotiation concluded and a compact signed instead of trying to resolve the conflicting interests through the courts. The Cherokees didn't do that and they've had lawsuits ever since against the state. Very costly and time consuming."

What Will saw was that to reach a compact agreement, the casino would have to agree to sharing some of the revenues of the casino with the state. Not a tax so much, as a kind of royalty share. And he also understood that it was essential that the tribe would have to draft and adopt its own gambling ordinance. In effect, a rule book for how the gambling would be conducted, and how the tribe would control and regulate the gambling activity. Schollenkopf said such an ordinance would have to be approved by their office. Will wondered if Minnie or NAILS could help them with drafting a Nantiquak gaming ordinance. He also saw the need to call the Deputy Chief Grey-Owl of the Cherokees whom he and Minnie had consulted the year before to ask him what went into and how they reached a compact agreement with the Governor of North Carolina.

After the morning session, which was basically a guide to how the 1988 law was put into practice and implemented among the different tribes having casinos, Will definitely thought they were going to need a lot of legal advice. And he also concluded that he would have to consult Jack to find out how all this could be done, and whom to negotiate with. He thought he'd try and reach him by phone, over lunch. Maybe Jack would still be in Annapolis. But more likely the General Assembly had already adjourned for the Christmas and year-end holidays. Which would mean that Jack was back in Bristol. He'd call Jack, but felt certain that he probably could not visit with him until that weekend.

Will was taking notes all along during the presentations from the officials of the IGC. Schollenkopf noticed, and interrupted himself, "You know, Mr. Eames, up to now most of these negotiations and discussions were conducted by lawyers appointed by the tribes. You'll probably have to refer to lawyers as well. Almost everyone in this office is a lawyer by training."

"I was thinking that too." said Will.

"For those tribes that afford their services, the most experienced law firm for issues and litigation related to the Indian gaming act is one located right here in D.C., Halwerd and Rath. They specialize in cases about Indian casinos. The law underpinning Indian gambling, you understand is both complicated and ambiguous. We all struggle with it."

Will remembered that Mr. Grey-Owl and Chief Leatherback had both said much the same thing. It only made sense when hundreds of millions of dollars annually were at stake. They had said that it was years of continuous legal action and negotiations.

Before they broke for lunch, Will had a question to Schollenkopf. "You said that the IGC is involved in all these negotiations, that they have to approve the tribal ordinances, and the formation of the compacts. We spoke with the Chiefs of the Eastern Cherokee and they confirmed that they have had more than ten years of continuous legal conflict over their gambling activities. Primarily because of the opposition of the governor of North Carolina. Yet the two Indian casinos in Connecticut, where the governor was also opposed to Indian gambling in casinos, were able to get agreements up and running in two years. Does the IGC have the respective compacts of all of these recent operating Indian casinos? And if you do, could we consult them? And I would ask the same about the tribal gambling ordinances you said that the law mandated, and whose approval had to come from your office. Can we see those documents also?"

"My first reaction would be no. But I think as an interested party, you would get them if you filed a Freedom of Information request. You're the first to ever ask that here. But it would make sense to consult what has been done, and the agreements that have been concluded between public parties."

"But you know one of our main activities here is advising tribes and states on how to reach a compact agreement. It's primarily a business agreement, but one that is heavily dependent on politics. I think we can share with you the basic outlines of compacts."

Will hurriedly wrote a note to himself. They would in the new year, file a request to see all the compacts and tribal gambling ordinances in the possession of the IGC, especially the ones where the state had laws banning gambling.

"So maybe we first need to know how we can file a request for these documents, under the Freedom of Information Act."

"We have a public information officer; he'd be the one to tell you how."

"Well, fine. We can see him today, at close of business, no?"

"I don't see why not."

Talleck was getting impatient. They were gaining information, but he thought they were getting lost in all kinds of bureaucratic and legal muddle. They could spend years just consulting with Mr. Schollenkopf without getting anything done.

"And what if we were to build and open a casino without all these preparatory steps?" John asked with an agitated tone.

"You could do that, but I think you'd run into legal challenges right away. States have demonstrated over and over again that they will not tolerate Indian gaming establishments, except on their terms. And sorry to say the 1988 law did not make that hostility and opposition to Indian casinos any less intense or less implacable."

Over lunch, Will chided John. "You know, all of this story about Indians running their own sovereign affairs and independent economic life, goes way back. Freedom from taxation and the exemption from being counted in the census, those were even put in the Constitution. And until the 1988 law, Indian tribes were mostly losing their disputes when they protested that their rights were being denied. So we have to follow the rules that have been laid down for us. Otherwise, we will not be able to attract investors or financing for our casino. Take it from me, a real estate specialist, investors will take lots of risk—for high returns—but only if they understand the rules. And we are going to need investors if we are going to open a casino."

Talleck apologized. And then he asked Will about Morley's funeral. Will could not tell him much other than a few fleeting impressions.

"But it was much more than a family affair." said Will. "I realized afterwards that it was an important political affairs—I mean for the tribe's politics. Only a shame that you weren't there as the weroance of the Kuskowaroak Band."

"Yeah, I should've gone."

"There other outlying bands weren't represented either."

"Well there will have to be a special election to pick our next head chief. I mean chairman."

"Yes, but Minnie won't do it again."

"By rights it should be me. My family name means supreme chief, or emperor, if you like, of the Nantiquaks."

"The other bands will never accept that. You have to recognize that the politics of this tribe will always be dominated by the Indian River bands. They're the biggest and the richest of the bands."

"I suppose you're right."

"I hope then we can pick," said John, "someone who will support and even help lead the development of the casino."

"Me too. So has anyone proposed an extraordinary board meeting?"

"Yes, I was called late last week with a request for a meeting just after Christmas."

"Oh, thad mean that Minnie will still have to preside over the meeting. She's chairwoman until the end of the year. She won't like that."

"Yeah. I guess that's too bad for her. It can only show the messiness of our new enlarged tribe, raw politics."

In the afternoon consultation with Schollenkopf, Will and John learned a lot more about the experiences of recently opened casinos. Will was surprised to learn that several of the key investors were foreign resort property developers. But as he heard more, he realized that these brave investors were just very canny businessmen who had in their home countries overcome the same kinds of political risks and recognized in the possibility of huge riches available in Indian gambling, despite the risks. They were real estate developers. He thought he would have to look for the real estate developers who might be willing to take a chance on an Indian casino. His regular reading of the Real Estate Finance Journal had introduced him to numbers of such developers. He knew one of those developers right away in the form of the founder of the company that developed the Hyatt Marina and Golf Resort just outside Bristol. He had met him several times over the past five or six years. But he went away from the session convinced that the key to the success of an Indian casino was not the legal considerations as Schollenkopf seemed to suggest, but the business structures and deal terms. A compact after all was not really so much a political deal, as it was a business deal where the two parties—tribe and state government-- were trying to assert and preserve their overriding rights to the business and cash a casino generated.

At the end of the day, Schollenkopf took them to the public information officer who readily gave them the instructions and forms needed to request confidential documents held by the IGC. "But you know," said the officer, "you can probably get those compacts you seek straight off the Federal Register where they a recorded for the official record. The others you can request by the forms I just outlined."

"Could we submit these tomorrow?" asked Will.

"Sure, why not? But just now it's time for me to knock off and close up shop. Do you need help finding your way out?"

On the sidewalk on K Street Will took out his cell phone and called Jackson's office in Annapolis. His secretary answered and confirmed that the General Assembly had adjourned for the year.

"But Mr. Parker will be in the office tomorrow, if you can come to Annapolis. Would you like an appointment with him?" To Will it sounded like the same officious, snotty secretary he had first encountered two years ago.

"Yes, this is Will Eames of Bristol. When can I have time to see him?"

"I'll have to call you back, Mr. Eames. Does he know you? Could you tell me what business you want to talk about?"

"Yes, he knows me. I want to talk to him about the Injun Project and the Bawlimore Orioles."

"Okay. I'll ask him to call you back. His schedule for appointments right now looks pretty free."

Will and John separated there on the sidewalk. Talleck said he would have to face the commuter traffic, but he wanted to get back home that evening. They agreed that they would meet later in the week in the Laurelton offices. It was mild and dry, but already dark, so instead of walking home, Will decided to call Minnie and see if she wouldn't walk with him over to the noisy restaurant in Georgetown— Claude's-- which they had liked so much since their first "date" in D.C. She agreed and they met outside her office and slowly traipsed up K St and over the deep chasm of Rock Creek Park. And finally up M Street to central Georgetown. He told her about the day's meetings and the clear need that the tribe would have for further legal services. She suggested that Will should come to the NAILS offices and talk with Cal about the firm's capabilities and advisory help they might be able to offer. Just as they were approaching their target eating place, Minnie stopped and said: "And Will no alcohol here, now. Do you remember, we have homework, tonight?" "No, but I think I could use the reinforcement of some cold, salty oysters." And then as Will reached to open the door to Claude's, Will's cell phone rang. It was Jackson.

"Are you nearby?" asked Jack.

"You mean, not on the Eastern Shore or in Delaware?"

"Yes. Maybe you could come join me for lunch at the Golden Bull tomorrow at twelve? Remember it?"

"Yes. You mean the place where that pretty Ukrainian girl worked?"

"Yes, that's the place. Okay. See you tomorrow then."

"Who's that 'pretty Ukrainian girl?' you met with Jack?" asked Minnie, denying Will's way in through the door.

"She was a pretty young thing who worked at a restaurant in Annapolis near Jack's office, who Jack flirted with all through the summer of '97."

"So I hope you're not going to go there to flirt with her, too."

"Not on your life, Minnie. Besides she's no longer there. She was temporary staff."

After a nice dinner, including oysters and steak in that noisy restaurant, Will and Minnie returned home and resumed their 'homework' of trying to make a baby. Will had more energy this evening, and he awoke in the morning while it was still dark outside, ready to start again. His caresses woke Minnie not long afterwards. On this morning it was Minnie who was worn out and tired of so much love making, but she consented to go farther. Later they shared kisses at the front door, and Minnie walked off to the metro, while Will went back upstairs for a shower and a shave before heading off to Annapolis. He arrived at the Golden Bull shortly before their appointed time. Looking around the restaurant, there was no sign of the Ukrainian Natasha, and in fact it seemed there were hardly any servers on the floor. Pre-Christmas staffing, thought Will. And in a moment he thought that it might be difficult to get adequate staffing for the future Indian casino and its restaurants there near the Nanticoke River. There certainly weren't many people living near the location they had selected, not in Briny Springs, nor in Exeter, nor in the reservations, nor in Spatt's Landing. It could be a problem. They would have to bus in staff from Salisbury, or Bristol, or even farther afield. But he gave up that line of reasoning as he thought he first had to get the casino approved and built. And that was what he had come to Annapolis to speak to Jack about.

Jack showed up in the restaurant only a few minutes after noon. They comprised almost the entire clientel of the restaurant at that time. Clearly pre-Christmas on a work day when the state government had already effectively shut down for the holidays, was a bad business day. But it meant that the waitresses when they finally appeared only had them to pay attention to.

"Hey there, Will. Creator of the Nantiquak Nation! You're doing so well, why ever would you come here where you can only find muddle, corruption, and backbiting?"

"I don't know. I thought I was coming to see you to get some advice. I didn't know you were engaged in all those other important duties."

Jack hung up his coat on a coat stand next to their table—he looked even stockier than the last time Will had seen him at the beginning of the summer at a party at Jack's house in Bristol. They shook hands robustly and as Jack was sitting down, he said: "We got your wedding invitation just the other day. Congratulations man. You finally hooked and landed your prize catch."

"Well, thanks. There were a lot of moments when I thought she might slip off the hook altogether. But she has finally agreed. And she certainly is a prize catch. So we'll see you at our wedding?"

"Wouldn't miss it for anything. MariAnne is worried about what she'll wear. She's pregnant you know with our first. By then she should be very plump with child."

"Oh, so congrats to you two also."

After they had ordered a lunch of crab cakes and fries, Will opened with the reason for his visit.

"As you know we are now embarked on the casino part of my Injun Project."

"That's where you started so many months ago, wasn't it?"

"And the hurdles we face now is the Maryland law that bans all sorts of gaming and especially casino gambling in the state, with only a few exceptions, like horse racing."

"Yes exactly. Exceptions. You know since you started, the support for that law is crumbling fast. I predict it might even get repealed in the coming year. There's lots of lobbying money and some heavyweight business interests—not all of them straight and clean—putting pressure on us to modify the law or junk it altogether. A lot of slush money is being handed out through the back corridors of the General Assembly, and sometimes threats too. The law, I predict won't last another four years. And you know that it turns out that Governor Connolly is not opposed to gambling at all. Quite the contrary. He supports the building of a casino in Maryland and he's made it clear that he wants the laws changed to make that happen."

"Well that's good news. Because I have to get the state's approval— and I'm not sure who that would be exactly—in order to sign a consent agreement, a compact, that would allow us to have casino type gambling on the reservation. And unfortunately maybe for you, we have agreed amongst ourselves, I mean the Indians that the casino will be in Wicomico County, not in Dorset County."

"That doesn't matter. My district includes almost all of Wicomico County too."

"So you're an interested party. Because a casino on the Eastern Shore will definitely contribute to a healthier economy for that part of the state, excepting Ocean City, which usually doesn't get anything from the government here. And you probably know all too well, how little the Eastern Shore gets."

"Yes, sadly. It doesn't help that our population is small. But Baltimore and the D.C. suburbs together get ninety percent of what's doled out in benefits from our august debating society here. Political favors pay out here. So what would you like me to do for you?"

"Well you've figured out now how the anti-gambling law works in the state. Everything is banned except where exceptions to the law are made, like the exception for the criminal racket around the Pimlico Racetrack."

"Yes that's how the law works."

"And it was politics that built in the amendment that made those exceptions to allow gambling on the horses there. They so to speak ring-fenced that enterprise from the gambling laws that apply everyplace else in the state. That is what I am seeking as a solution for our Injun casino —a ring-fenced exemption to the law so that casino style gambling would remain illegal and banned except in the case of a casino operating within the boundaries of the Puckamee reservation. Wouldn't it be easier to amend the law that way, than trying to repeal the law altogether?"

"You know, that's brilliant. Of course you're right, Will."

"And the state, or the governor could say, what is only right, that this conforms to the legal status of the Indian tribe—namely that their reservation is in effect outside the state of Maryland, and the Indians living on it have their sovereign rights. And we can then agree in our compact with the state that a certain amount of the take would go to the state to compensate the other citizens of Maryland for their sacrifice of that territory."

"So we need you, Jack, to start a movement inside the General Assembly to introduce and hopefully pass such an amendment. Obviously that's more than you can promise by yourself. You'll have to build a consensus."

"I think my fellow delegates are well disposed that way already. As I said there's been a lot of lobbying, lots of money fertilizing the fallow fields here concerning this very issue. It's become very clear that the citizens of the state support a casino, and the governor supports one too, because he sees that casinos are opening around us, in New Jersey, in West Virginia near Cumberland, in Pennsylvania. And that means money is leaving the state to go to those places to gamble. Your casino would keep the money in the state."

"So that is what I came to you to ask for. And we need to reach an agreement with someone. Who would we first approach? "

Their lunch came and they began to eat as they continued the discussion. As the waitress was about to leave the table, Jack asked for another beer.

"I would think you should approach the governor's office first, and then he would probably direct you to the state's attorney general. He is by the way also one is supporting a change to the current gambling law. But he is also the one who runs the criminal prosecution of those he finds guilty of violating it."

"Of course," said Jack as he took an oversized bite of the crabcake into his mouth, "all this is going to cost you money."

"You mean, to get our compact with the state we should expect to pay a stream of our earnings to the state or some state program like education?" said Will.

"Yes, that. But maybe if the tribe could contribute a small amount to my re-election fund."

"Oh yes. I had clear forgotten those concrete realities."

"No I'm serious because as I said a certain unnamed organized criminal structure from out of state has been lining the pockets of some of the more senior delegates-- and even the governor it is rumored-- trying to get support for their casino proposal for of all places, Baltimore.

"You're not telling me that this happens in Maryland?"

"Sadly, it is the juice which allows laws and acts to get made. Maybe it is worse in the Western Shore, but it's a reality we have to cope with. And I am up for re-election this next fall. Everyone interested in this will be checking on that and reminding me for the next several months. That is, if they don't actually threaten me."

"And we're also now beginning to look for developers who could help us get financing and build the casino we have in mind. Nothing fancy—not a Las Vegas style resort, sin city, and all that. Just a poker palace with slot machines. We want to divert and entertain large numbers of all those people who cross our homeland for the pleasure pots of Ocean City and separate them of some of their money as they rush across our counties. You know."

"Oh, only too well. During session, I am always surprised by the traffic heading for the Bay Bridge on their way there on Friday after lunch, even from sleepy little Annapolis."

"But you've given me an idea. There's a big, well connected developer in Bawlimore you ought to invite. He builds hotels, shopping malls, and entertainment centers. He's filthy wealthy, and he's a bigger political and financial supporter of Governor Connolly. His lobbying for your case—if he were the developer of course—would carry a lot more weight and import than my little reedy voice in the general roar of the General Assembly. Connolly is a Democrat who comes from Bawlimore, so he knows when to listen and when power talks."

"So who are they that I might send them an invitation?"

"Don't get me wrong. They are an established Maryland family, and they think also what's good for the entire state not just Bawlimore. It's Leonard Cornish and his companies. You should invite them. They might be interested."

"Oh yeah, I've read about some of their developments. They make the news, and they make big money."

"Yeah, you remember that MariAnne is related to the spice family of Bawlimore? Well, they are blue bloods, old money. But Mr. Cornish, even though he third generation, he is BIG money. And not conservative in the least. And it helps your cause that your group are after all still Maryland Injuns."

"Okay. I'll do that before New Year's. Even though I just now about the only one working on this project within the tribe, I can get out a good real estate proposal by then."

"Oh and beware of the Weinstein group from Las Vegas, especially. They are as I said a dangerous bunch. They have been threatening around here in the past couple months, and throwing out discrete sums. They want to build a casino in Ocean City. They may view your Injun Project as unwanted competition—both economic and political—and they don't like or tolerate competition."

"I'll remember not to invite them."

"Yeah, and remember to duck when they come calling."

"Okay, I hadn't thought of that. But I will."

Will continued, "And if you don't get re-elected as a Republican in a Democratic state, have you considered working in Indian law? There's going to be need for that expertise in the near future."

They had coffee and wrapped up their meeting with handshakes, and sad head shaking about the plight of the Orioles. When Will got in his car to head back to D.C. it was just beginning to snow lightly. But strangely enough when he looked over the waters of the Severn River, the fast setting sun was still glinting off the waves. At home Will worked on some of the details that would need to be overcome in order to negotiate a compact with the state of Maryland. Then he looked up possible locations in Florida for a two week honeymoon and decided that Sarasota on the Florida Gulf Coast had the best offerings, including both gentle bathing on the beach, golf, and opera in the evenings, so he made bookings for a beach side cottage in a resort hotel. Toward the end of the afternoon, he went down to the metro and got off in the business district, and walked over to the office building where NAILS was headquartered. He went into the office and asked to see Cal Reiner, introducing himself as a representative of the Nantiquak tribe. The receptionist acted as if she recognized him, but wasn't quite sure. Cal came out of his office and greeted Will.

"Why didn't you call ahead?" asked Cal as he took Will's coat and offered it to the receptionist to hang up. He then pulled Will toward his office. "Come on in. There's always something to talk about."

Once seated in a leather chair across the big desk from Cal Will told him about the next steps they were going to take on opening a casino.

"Yeah I saw the news release in the Post last week." said Cal. "I was expecting to hear from the tribe about any such further assistance." Will thought that Carmine was doing a top job as communications director. She so quickly got those news releases out to all the regional newspapers. He hoped lawmakers in Baltimore and Annapolis had noticed the news release as well. Will told Cal that they had already consulted the Indian Gaming Commission and would look to them for lots of advice. They needed to negotiate a compact with the state of Maryland and they needed to formulate an ordinance laying out the rules for the conduct of gambling in their casino, all in accordance with the Indian Gaming law of 1988. And it was clear from all that they had learned that they would need legal advice and assistance. He asked if NAILS would be able to provide those services?

"Let me say, first of all, Will, that our firm has not up to now assisted in any litigation relating to the Indian Gaming law. And we do not have any experience in advising client tribes on issues related to setting up and running casino operations. But we are capable of assisting your tribe in implementing the terms of the law, and we can also help you in formulating the kinds of regulatory rules that you will need in order to run a casino. So in short, we can help you, and provide pro bono legal services to your tribe. And I don't think we need to have a new appointment. But if you like, we can set one up." In his usual way, Cal delivered this short answer at a lightning fast clip.

"I have downloaded three of the types of compacts that I think would be pertinent to our case in Maryland. They are compacts with states where gambling was banned or strictly controlled or outlawed by state law. I guess they could serve as templates for our negotiations."

"Certainly. We'll have to look at the Maryland laws on gaming and we'll also consult the IGC."

"So, my question would then be: 'When can we start?'" asked Will.

"Oh, I think we can start tomorrow." said Cal. "But you have to understand that from next week most government offices will be closed until after New Year's. I'll assign Gail Halstead, you may remember her, to work on the negotiations assistance. And I'll assign

Minnie Warrens, who did such fine work for you before, to assist the tribe in formulating a regulatory system that would go into the ordinance. How does that suit you?" Cal jotted down some notes on a yellow legal pad he had lying on his desk. "Come to think of it, I think we will to do a new appointment agreement. For legal services and advice on issues related to the setting up and operation of a casino without charges to the tribe, until such time as the casino is making a certain amount of turnover."

"Okay, agreed." Will stood up and the two men shook hands.

"You can send an appointment agreement to us electronically at our Laurelton offices. And if it's acceptable, I'll come back here, along with our Main Chief, the President of the Corporation, and we can sign it."

Will was very eager to tell Minnie about all that he had accomplished that day. But he still did not want to show anyone in the office their personal relationship, so after he put on his coat in the front reception he called her cell phone. She answered and said she was just getting ready to leave for the day.

"Fine, I'll wait for you downstairs in the entry foyer of your building. And I'll wait here so we can go home together."

"Oh, that's nice. How's the weather outside?"

"Cool, dark, overcast, and dry. And the streets are sparkling with Christmas lights."

"More than the other night when we walked to Claude's?"

"Seems to me more. But I might be just so elated at how things are going that I took more notice this afternoon. I was paying too much attention to you the other night to notice how bright the Christmas lights were."

The next morning, a chilly overcast Thursday, Will drove out to the Eastern Shore. He stopped in at his office in Bristol to check on any developments and to pick up the latest copy of Real Estate Finance. And then he drove further to Laurelton, to the Nantiquak offices. When he stepped in he was surprised to find that there was a neatly dressed young man sitting at the reception desk facing the front door. He was also surprised to see large blow ups of photos of the Nanticoke River, of the Nantiquak Museum with a dug-out canoe set in front of it, and of a group of Indians dancing at what looked like the annual powwow. These were new. There were also padded chairs set out for visitors. Will introduced himself to the receptionist, who responded with recognition. "Oh yes, your office is on the second floor."

"And what is your name?"

"Mark Red Knife Harmon." Will thought he must be the son of John Harmon who was a board member from the Indian River Band.

"Is Carmine in?" Will asked.

"Yes, she's in her office, number three from the front, before the stairs."

Will ducked his head in Carmine's office. "Carmine, your press release got noticed. Good job."

"Will, I'm so glad to see you. Is Minnie with you?"

"No. Is Talleck here? Is your printer working all right? Are you busy?"

"Yes, yes and no."

"I wanted to tell you that you're doing a really good job as communications director. But I would like to ask if you have thought about your future. I mean to say wouldn't you like to go to law school and get a law degree?"

"Yeah, I've thought about it in the past couple years. But I can't afford it."

"I think the tribe probably would pay for your law school studies if you decided to do it." said Will.

"Oh, that would change things. Do you think I could get into law school?"

"Why not? There's a LSAT, right? You can study and practice for that test. And you finished an undergraduate degree, didn't you? Good grades?"

"Not the best, but maybe good enough."

"Exactly. That's enough to get admittance, especially if you can write an essay outlining your desires and ambitions."

"I'd like to be the tribe's lawyer, even if we use outside law firms for our future needs."

"Well said. I think the board will be discussing this at the next regular meeting in the new year."

"That would be great. But it probably means I'd have to be away from the tribe for two and a half, three years. That's such a long time."

"You shouldn't worry about that. Just think about what you could do. And maybe you can talk to Minnie about advice on where to study."

Carmine was smiling with happiness. She was already thinking about what and where she would study in the coming year.

"I'll be down shortly to print off some letters we need to send on your printer.

"Okay, no problem."

Then Will went upstairs to the office he shared with Talleck. He was expecting Talleck at any time. But first he opened the computer and composed a letter to Governor Connolly of Maryland. It was a letter outlining the tribe's desire to open a casino on the tribe's reservation land in Wicomico County, Maryland. He put down the plans the tribe had for a casino and the gambling market he thought they would serve. He also briefly stated that the tribe sought this opinion as the most lucrative business that the tribe could develop in the short term. He referred to his awareness of the rules for casinos that were set up by the Indian Gaming Commission. And finally, he requested that the governor's office enter into discussions and negotiations to draft a mutual agreement and compact that would be a governing document for the casino. He put as signatory of the letter, Charles Clarke, Deputy Chief and President of the Nantiquak Indian Corporation of Delaware and Maryland and co-signed it as William Eames, Vice President, Finance, for the Corporation. Talleck still had not come by the time he was finished with the letter. He saved the file on the computer hard drive and on a compact disc and went back downstairs to Carmine's office, which was the first after the reception area."

When he entered her office, John Talleck was sitting on her desk talking softly with Carmine.

"Oh, sorry to interrupt. I just wanted to print off a copy of this letter."

"It's nothing we were just talking about the future." said John.

"Is Chief Clarke coming in today?" asked Will.

"Yes, I'm expecting him at one or two o'clock." said Carmine.

"Good, this letter will need his signature before I can send it. I'll leave you a copy for your records of tribal communications. John, let's talk some upstairs."

"Sure, Will." and John stood up off of Carmine's desk and followed Will upstairs.

Upstairs Will spoke to Talleck: "We need to send out invitation letters to developers and companies that might be willing to fund, finance, and supervise the construction of our casino. I have a couple names that are big developers in resorts and hotels and whom we should address. And we probably should invite the companies that have developed the Indian casinos that have been done so far. I think we can write the same letter to each group."

"But Will, why do we need a developer? Why can't we build our casino ourselves?"

"Because I am certain that the tribe does not have the skills or resources to build a casino with a hotel. And it certainly does not have the means to finance such construction. I'm surprised you even suggest that."

"But we need to participate. We should get building jobs out of the project."

"We can stipulate that the construction firm hire members from our tribe who have the necessary building experience, or finishing experience. Do you know of any who work as either carpenters, plumbers, electricians, or painters?"

"No, not really. I haven't met yet all that many tribesmen from the Delaware Bands."

"Fine. The important thing that we need to convey to the developers that we are not aiming to build a comprehensive multi-purpose resort destination like the ones up in Delaware. We do not want to put our small tribe into hundreds of millions of dollars in debt. So do you know of any developers whom we should invite?"

"No. Other than the developer of the Hyatt Marina Resort up near Bristol."

"I'm not sure if Hyatt was the developer or whether it was another construction group that got Hyatt to be the operator. But we can send them an invitation. I'm pretty sure they won't be interested because they are a long way from getting their investment back."

"So, Will, you'll draft the letters?"

"But they will be in your name, John."

"Fine by me."

Will sat back at his computer and drafted an invitation letter. He had already made up a list of six developers that he had found and had recorded them with their addresses in another file. He had left out the big Las Vegas casino companies, like MGM and Weinburg enterprises, and also the Trump organization. But he included the Harrah's company because they had done such a good job on the Cherokee casino. It was very expensive granted, but it was done quickly and expertly built. After almost two hours he had finished invitation letters for the six developers, and he went downstairs to Carmine's office to print them out. He walked in to her office and caught Carmine in the middle of a kiss with John whose hand was also on her breast. They pulled apart quickly like two school kids caught in the act by their parents. Carmine straightened her bra under her blouse and was obviously blushing. John stood up and tried to face down Will.

"Excuse me, you two." said Will who was a little surprised as he had long thought of Carmine as rather sexless. "Didn't mean to interrupt important business. I just need to print out these letters."

Carmine moved aside in her chair and turned her computer to the word program.

"Chief Clarke called to say he will be here any time now." said Carmine.

"Good, first thing we'll get him to sign the letter to the governor. Do we have an account with Fedex here?"

"No. We haven't needed it yet." answered Carmine. "And they don't have a pickup office here in Laurelton, or anywhere near here, other than Centretown. We can always use the U.S. Postal Service for two day delivery. The post office is open here for another two hours or so."

It was at that moment that Will's cell phone rang.

"I'm in Carmine's office in Laurelton. Printing out letters."

Will stepped out of Carmine's office and headed to the back of the building. Minnie was calling to tell him the news about her bonus.

"That's great news! And what a bonus too. Entirely deserved, Minnioka."

"No, I'll be home tonight. What if I bring some champagne to drink to your windfall?"

"I'm just about finished here for the day, so I can probably leave soon."

"No, really. It's only what you should get paid. Maybe now Cal will give you a raise in the new year."

"I love you too, Minnioka. I can't wait until we fall into our arms together again. Maybe in three hours. Oh, you're going home now? Then earlier. I'll drive safely. I always do. Bye."

As Will turned around he saw Chief Clarke with his coat already open coming in the corridor. They shook hands and Will told him about the letter to sign.

"As there's no next day courier service here in Laurelton, I was thinking I will take this letter myself and deliver it to the governor's office in person tomorrow."

"Thad be great, Will. I doubt if we would get any answer before January. But if this is what we need to do we need to do it as soon as possible."

"So, you're all for it, the casino and all?" asked Will.

"Yeah. Always was. I just didn't express too strongly my support as long a Morley was around. He was so hostile to the project, you know."

"Yeah, I knew."

"Well, may his soul rest in peace in the great on beyond."

Chief Clarke signed the letters in three copies and walked off to his office.

Will and John said their farewells for the day.

"Maybe this will start the ball rolling," said Will.

"Maybe. I'll make a report on what we've done so far at the upcoming extraordinary board meeting."

"Oh, right. Remind me: when will it be?"

"The Sunday after Christmas, the 26th."

"I'll make sure Minnie is there. So long for now."

That evening at home in D.C. Will told Minnie all about the insights he had gained about starting the casino project. Minnie listened intently. "Sounds like lots of poltical work as well as legal work."

"Yes, lots of work in Baltimore and Anapolis."

"Well, let's drink to the coming new year and millenium, Will Eames. Two big projects launched next year. Our wedding and starting our family. And launching the Indian Casino."

"I'll drink to both of those projects." Said Will, who then planted a kiss on Minnie's lips. "We're already underway. Here's to our joint Injun project in the year 2000."